THE FIELDS
OF
BANNOCKBURN

A NOVEL OF CHRISTIAN SCOTLAND FROM ITS ORIGINS TO INDEPENDENCE

DONNA FLETCHER CROW

AUTHOR OF *GLASTONBURY*

MOODY PRESS

CHICAGO

PERMISSIONS

My warmest gratitude to those who granted permission for me to use their words:

Major Alasdair Hutton for the use of some of his narration from the 1993 Edinburgh Military Tattoo, pages 687–88.

Mr. Ronnie Browne of The Corries Music, Ltd., for permission to quote "The Flower of Scotland" on pages 475 and 695.

Kerr's Music to quote "Scotland the Brave," written by Cliff Hanley, pages 16 and 692.

Jim McLean for allowing me to base Princess Maia's telling of the massacre of the Picts (page 176) on the original song "The Ballad of Glencoe," words and music by Jim McLean, copyright Duart Music, London.

ISBN: 0-8024-7736-4

1 3 5 7 9 10 8 6 4 2

Printed in the United States of America

for Ian,
who shared the adventure
Philippians 1:3–9

A NOVEL OF CHRISTIAN SCOTLAND FROM
ITS ORIGINS TO INDEPENDENCE

THE FIELDS
OF
BANNOCKBURN

Donna Fletcher Crow

Ps. 145:12

DONNA FLETCHER CROW

ACKNOWLEDGMENTS

My very special appreciation to Dr. David Munro of Edinburgh University, who served as tour guide, resource person, and friend.

I am also indebted to Nigel Tranter, who was so generous in his correspondence and has brought so much of Scotland alive in his novels, especially *Columba, Kenneth, Margaret the Queen, The Wallace,* and *The Bruce Trilogy.* His books deserve a much wider distribution in the United States.

And finally, my love to my friends at Sharpe Memorial Church in Glasgow for their enthusiastic support and prayers.

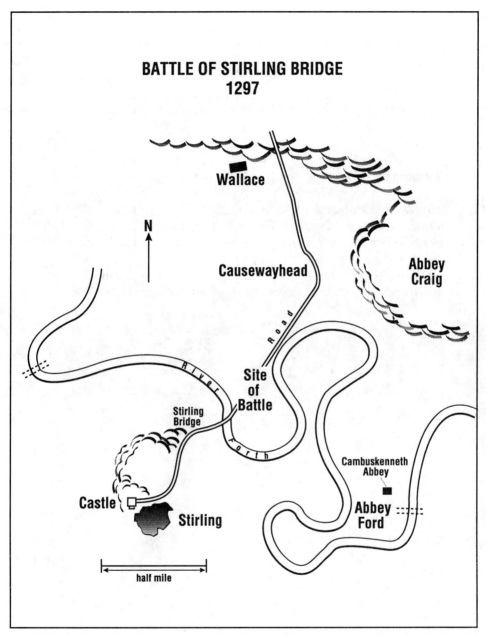

BATTLE OF STIRLING BRIDGE
1297

Wallace

N

Abbey
Craig

Causewayhead

Road

River

Site
of
Battle

Stirling
Bridge

Forth

Cambuskenneth
Abbey

Castle

Stirling

Abbey
Ford

half mile

Based on map in James Fergusson, *William Wallace Guardian of Scotland* (London: Alexander Maclehose & Co., 1938).

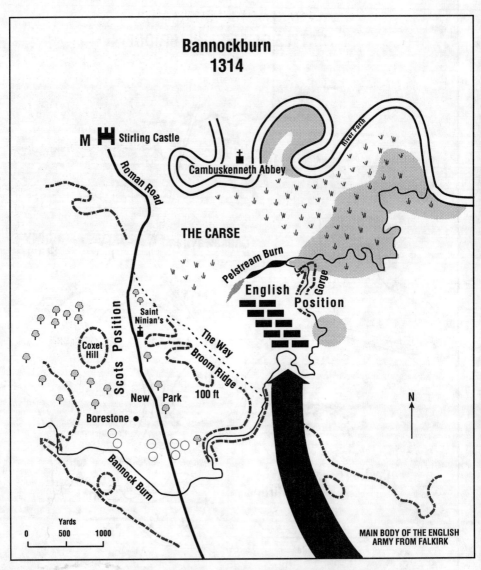

Based on data made available by the Bannockburn Heritage Centre.

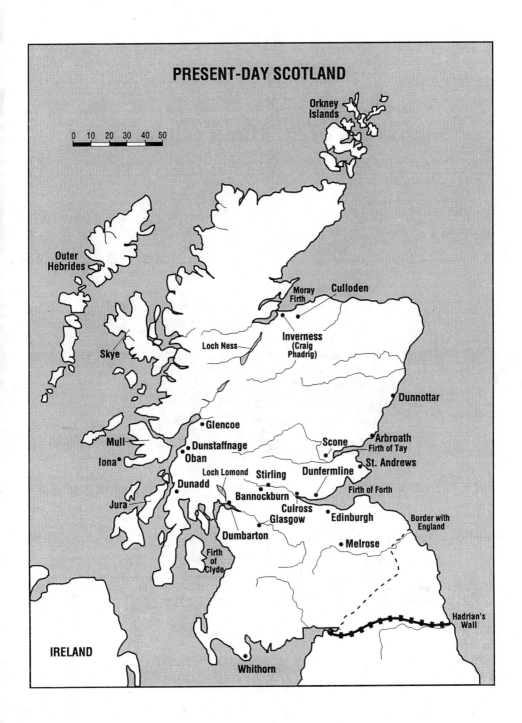

PRESENT-DAY SCOTLAND

0 10 20 30 40 50

Orkney Islands

Outer Hebrides

Moray Firth   Culloden

Inverness
(Craig Phadrig)

Loch Ness

Skye

Dunnottar

Glencoe

Mull   Dunstaffnage   Scone   Arbroath
                                  Firth of Tay
Iona   Oban   St. Andrews

Loch Lomond   Stirling   Dunfermline

Dunadd

Bannockburn   Firth of Forth

Jura   Culross
        Glasgow   Edinburgh   Border with
                                England
Dumbarton

Firth
of
Clyde   Melrose

Hadrian's
Wall

IRELAND

Whithorn

Monarchs of Scotland (simplified)

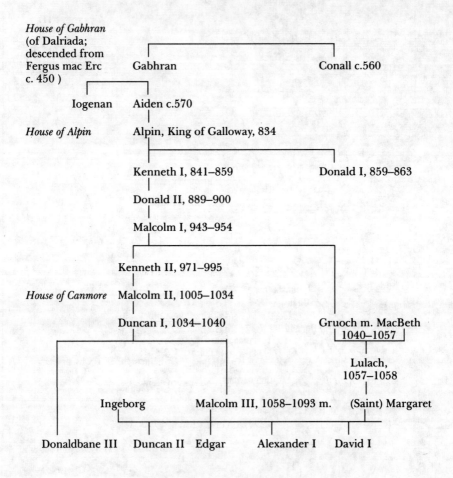

House of Gabhran
(of Dalriada;
descended from
Fergus mac Erc
c. 450)

Gabhran

Conall c.560

Iogenan   Aiden c.570

House of Alpin   Alpin, King of Galloway, 834

Kenneth I, 841–859   Donald I, 859–863

Donald II, 889–900

Malcolm I, 943–954

Kenneth II, 971–995

House of Canmore   Malcolm II, 1005–1034

Duncan I, 1034–1040   Gruoch m. MacBeth
1040–1057

Lulach,
1057–1058

Ingeborg   Malcolm III, 1058–1093 m.   (Saint) Margaret

Donaldbane III   Duncan II   Edgar   Alexander I   David I

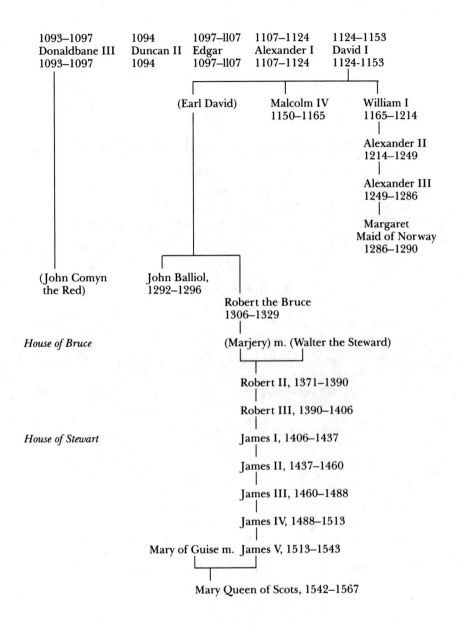

1093–1097   1094   1097–ll07   1107–1124   1124–1153
Donaldbane III   Duncan II   Edgar   Alexander I   David I
1093–1097   1094   1097–ll07   1107–1124   1124-1153

(Earl David)   Malcolm IV   William I
1150–1165   1165–1214

Alexander II
1214–1249

Alexander III
1249–1286

Margaret
Maid of Norway
1286–1290

(John Comyn   John Balliol,
the Red)   1292–1296

Robert the Bruce
1306–1329

House of Bruce

(Marjery) m. (Walter the Steward)

Robert II, 1371–1390

Robert III, 1390–1406

House of Stewart   James I, 1406–1437

James II, 1437–1460

James III, 1460–1488

James IV, 1488–1513

Mary of Guise m. James V, 1513–1543

Mary Queen of Scots, 1542–1567

BOOK 1
Of Saints and Chieftains
Sixth Century

397 St. Ninian founds Candida Casa at Whithorn
550 St. Kentigern (Mungo) is ordained bishop at Glasgow
563 St. Columba comes to Iona

BOOK 2
Of Kings and Kingdoms
Ninth Century

831 Vikings come to Dublin
839 Major Viking victory over Picts
840 Kenneth mac Alpin crowned king of Dalriada at DunAdd
847 Kenneth mac Alpin unites Scots and Picts and
establishes capital at Scone

BOOK 3
Of Queens and Clerics
Eleventh Century

1066 William of Normandy defeats Saxon king of England at
Hastings
1068 Margaret, fleeing William the Conqueror, lands at
Dunfermline and marries Malcolm III
1124 David I becomes king; establishes border abbeys

BOOK 4
Of Priests and Patriots
Fourteenth Century

1296 Edward I defeats John Balliol and sends Stone of Destiny
to England
1297 Wallace defeats English at Battle of Stirling Bridge
1298 Wallace defeated by English at Falkirk
1305 Wallace executed in Tower of London
1306 Robert the Bruce crowned king at Scone
1314 King Robert defeats English at Bannockburn
1320 Declaration of Arbroath

WORD LIST

Aethling—Saxon crown prince or princess
Alba—area of modern Scotland inhabited by Picts from above Forth-
    Clyde to Orkneys, west to Scotia
Ap—son of, Welsh
Aurochs—ox
Baldric—strap over shoulder bearing sword sheath
Barded—armed, caparisoned
Bonders—peasants
Branduth—a chesslike game
Brecbennoch—small box used in worship
Broch—round, tapered stone tower built as defense or refuge
Brychan—blanket
Cairn—burial chamber, usually dug out and lined with stone
Caledonia—Roman word for modern Scotland
Caparison—long cloth covering for horse, as defensive armor and
    ornament
Carse—same as haugh
Cashel—Celtic church monastery
Ceilidh (kay-lee)—Celtic party
Checky—divided into equilateral rectangles of alternate colors, as in
    heraldry
Clachan—small grouping of huts, informal village
Clarasch—Celtic harp
Coppice—small trees, shoots, or root suckers
Coraigh—marshland
Crannogs—artificial islands
Culdee—"Friend of God" monks of Celtic church
Curragh—small boat, usually of hides
Daub—clay smoothed over wattle as plaster
Deer grass—deer-hair; a small, moorland clump grass
Desart—hermitage
Drengs—freemen, landowners
Dun—fortress

Fash—annoy, upset
Gallus—bold, tough, or wild
Garron—short-legged hill pony
Garth—field
Hauberk—knee-length coat of chain mail
Haugh—low-lying meadows beside a river
Hundredweight—about 112 US pounds
Inch—island
Jarl—Norse earl
Kist—chest
Kenspeckled—conspicuous
Lia Fail—stone of Irish legend
Linn—waterfall
Mac—son of
Mormaors—Scottish earls
Mortuath—area ruled by mormaor, earldom
Moss—marshy land
Nae—Scots for not
Nic—daughter of
Ogham—ancient system of writing used by early Celts; a series of
    lines and slashes, indecipherable today
Pulse—legumes, pea-like vegetables
Rath—chief's enclosed residence, usually circular
Righ—high king
Rood—cross
Sark—shirt
Scop—Saxon bard
Scotia—area of modern Scotland inhabited by Scots; western high-
    lands and Hebrides
Sennachie—storyteller
Sett—pattern, as colors in tartan
Skald—Norse storyteller
Southern—one from south of England
Squire—shield-bearer or page
Sumpter—horse, pack horse
Targe—small round shield, made of wood, covered with hide
Thanes—noblemen, below mormaors
Theows—thralls, slaves
Truath—tribe
Vallum—wall, usually earthen
Wattle—woven reeds, as to form fence or wall
Wean (wee'un)—infant

BOOK ONE

Of Saints and Chieftains

Saint Columba Comes to Iona, 563

1

The storyteller was absolutely authentic. Candles flickered golden around the walls of the old meeting house. The tweed-clad man sitting by the fireplace strummed a Celtic harp, making it sing an accompaniment to Hamish MacBain's tales.

"And another fine tale I have for ye tonight. For didna Scotland's two most precious possessions come into our land by the hand of one man? And that man was our beloved Saint Columba.

"Columba it was who sailed to Caledonia over a wild and misty sea, sailed to our shores before even men had named this land Scotland. And he came bearing the Stone of Destiny and the gospel of Christ. . . ."

The harp lilted like the waves of the Hebridean Sea, and Mary leaned back in her chair with a smile. She would like to close her eyes and concentrate on the storyteller's mesmerizing voice, but Hamish MacBain was a man who commanded the attention of all one's senses.

At least six feet tall, broadly built, with flowing red hair and full beard, he chose not to wear an ordinary modern kilt but the older, more authentic Highland dress—the plaid, a great length of tartan wool pleated and belted at the waist with the extra fabric looped in billows at each side and fastened over one shoulder. All this with a homespun shirt, leather jerkin, and argyle socks.

And always there was his voice. More musical even than the harp, the melodious Gaelic voice brought every word of the story alive.

"For Columcille was a prince in Ireland, born a Scot in Donegal, a member of the royal family of O'Neill, descendants of the High King Niall of the Nine Hostages, who ruled in Tara. And Columba, a fine man and tall, bard-taught and sword-skilled, could have chosen to rule in Ireland, to sit on the throne of his ancestors. But he made dwelling place within himself for the Holy One, and the pleasures of kingly courts held no attractions for him."

Even spellbound as she was, Mary blinked. It had been a long day, and she was still more than a little travel wearied.

Only three hours earlier the London train had pulled into Edinburgh's Waverly Station. And Mary had never felt more elated in all her twenty-two years. Her cousin, Brad, even taller and blonder than she remembered him from when she last saw him at their family reunion in Boston two years ago, had been there to meet her with a welcoming smile and a strong arm for her luggage.

And then the thrill of hearing her first bagpipes in Scotland as they left the station and walked toward Princes Street. She smiled now as she remembered standing stock-still in the middle of the busy sidewalk, listening to "Scotland the Brave" while her eyes prickled. "Hark when the night is falling . . ."

At Brad's gentle urging they had walked on under the flags fluttering all along Princes Street Gardens—"Hear, hear the pipes are calling . . ."—while she admired the wonderful Victorian gothic excess of the Scot Monument. "Land of the high endeavor . . ." She looked across the vast green ravine to the castle high on its majestic crags, unable to believe it was real in the middle of a modern city. And still the pipes played in the background—"Land of my heart for ever, Scotland the brave."

Then a lumbering, maroon Lothian bus took them the length of Princes Street—shops on one side, gardens and castle on the other, and turned south toward Old Town, while Brad pointed out the sights as they approached the Meadows where he had his flat in the University area.

But now the storyteller called her back. "So a monk he was, a holy brother vowed, Columba the Dove—the Dove of the Church. But not always a dove of peace. For there was war in Ireland. And Columba prayed. Fiercely and mightily Columba prayed. For the slaying of his enemies Columba prayed. And mighty and fervent were his prayers, and mighty and fervent was the slaying. Until at the end of the day three thousand lay slain. Three thousand men that had lived and breathed with the rising of the sun that morning now bled and died in the field at the sun's setting.

"And Columba was filled with remorse. He went to his king to plead succor for his soul. For Columba knew there could be no peace for him in Ireland. He must perform the penance of exile. He must leave all that he loved best in this world. He must leave Ireland.

"'With your leave, Your Majesty,' spoke Columcille, 'I would take twelve men strong and bold against evil, twelve men who have taken vows of holiness, twelve men who would help me bear the light to the darkness beyond. And I would do penance with the wearing of a hair shirt and sleeping on a pillow of stone.'

16

"So the king gave Columba leave. 'Take your twelve men. Choose you them well. And take you a boat well equipped with all you will need. And because you are our well-loved kinsman and you go to strive valiantly against evil, take you one thing more.'

"And he led Columba to the forecourt of the High Hall of Tara, to the black standing stone by which all the High Kings of Tara were crowned. For the stone would cry out at the touch of the true king, and none would be crowned if the stone did not speak. The Lia Fail this was, the magic seeing stone, the Stone of Destiny, which long and long ago had been Jacob's pillow. The stone upon which he who was Israel dreamed a dream and saw a vision of angels and encountered the living God."

Hamish MacBain held out his left hand as if to caress a stone pillar, waist high. Then he stooped lower, as if placing his right hand on a smaller stone. "'Even the heavens grieved over the battle for which you do penance, my Colum,' the High King said. 'For as the armies raged, so did the elements. And there was fire in heaven, and God sent a great bolt of lightning to strike the Stone of Destiny. And this piece was riven from the rest. Take you it for your pillow. And God attend you.'"

In spite of her enchantment with the story, Mary's mind wandered again. As the storyteller recounted Columba's leave-taking of Ireland and his journey to the land that was to become Scotland, she recalled her own journey: saying good-bye to her parents, who had given her this trip as a graduation present, kissing Michael . . .

Yes, there it was. As she had asked herself several times a day for the past two months, what about Michael? She could still feel her heart leap when he had dazzled her with a band of diamonds that must have totaled two or three carats—all flawless, knowing Michael. Now she twisted the ring on her finger and knit her heavy dark brows that contrasted so startlingly with her fair hair and blue eyes.

She still couldn't understand why she had asked for the summer before setting their wedding date. Strange that she had asked, impulsive as she was. And stranger yet that Michael had agreed, impatient as he was. But Michael had insisted that she wear his ring—even if she had asked for the summer to think about it. And they both knew what her answer would be in the end, didn't they?

After all, no one had ever made Michael Warden wait for anything—certainly not Harvard Business School, where he had graduated with honors; certainly not Comptran, the biggest Wall Street company he had interviewed with; and certainly not Mary Hamilton, who had had the pleasure of his very pleasurable company for the past two years.

17

Still—she ran her fingers through her long, smooth hair in a subconscious gesture—five days of her month away were already gone, and she had no clearer concept of what she wanted for the future. Certainly her whirlwind tour of London, seeing three plays in three nights and hitting all the tourist sights, had left no time for reflection. But now, in the slower pace she hoped to find in Scotland, maybe here she would be able to see things more clearly.

"And so it was that it fell to Columba to enthrone the new king of his new country, and he brought out the Stone of Destiny. . . ." The musician in the background turned from his harp to a small pipe and drum for music evoking a royal procession. "And God blessed the king and his people in the land that would become Scotland, for all who heard the Word of God through the preaching of Columba turned to Him and received His blessings."

In the break while the storyteller refreshed himself before beginning his last tale, Mary turned to Brad. "I've heard of the Edinburgh Festival all my life. I can't believe I'm really here. Thank you so much for getting the tickets."

"Thank Gareth—he got them." Brad indicated his friend, sitting on Mary's left.

She turned to the young man with dark hair and the most sparkling black eyes she'd ever seen.

"You're verra welcome." He paused to grin at her. "I was afraid this was maybe a wee bit throwing you in at the deep end. Maybe the Tattoo would have been better."

Mary smiled at his delightful Glaswegian accent, wishing he'd say more. But he didn't, so she hurried to reassure him. "No, no. It's wonderful."

Hamish returned to tell the story of Saint Mungo, founder of Glasgow, and an hour later, sitting in a booth at The Argyll, Brad's favorite pub, Mary was still proclaiming how perfect her first evening in Edinburgh had been. "And that storyteller—what's the Gaelic word—*sennachie?*" She stumbled over the shawna-kee pronunciation. "Anyway, he was wonderful. He really lives like that, doesn't he? This isn't just an act for the tourists. He really collects his stories himself and wears the plaid for real?"

"Aye, lassie. But when I'm in a wee bit hurry I just wear the kilt. It's a complicated business—the putting on of the plaid."

Mary jumped at the voice behind her, then smiled into the laughing golden brown eyes of Hamish MacBain.

"Sit you down, man." Brad pointed to an empty chair next to Mary. "Share a plate of chips with us." He made the introductions. "Bradley Hamilton"—he offered his hand—"my cousin Mary Hamilton from Boston—the one in the States—and my friend Gareth Lindsay. He's from Glasgow, as you'll know as soon as he opens his mouth."

"So ye liked my wee bit stories, did ye now, lassie?" Hamish doused a chip in malt vinegar before eating it.

"They were wonderful!" She smiled, crinkling her eyes. No matter how she tried, she couldn't repress her American enthusiasm. "And you told them so well. But I wondered . . ." Her voice trailed off, and she took refuge in a deep drink from her mug.

"Aye, and what would ye be wondering?" Hamish gave the chips another vigorous dash of vinegar.

"Well, I mean, they're great stories—the adventures of those old saints—but how true are they?"

"Och, that's what you're wondering, is it now? Well and that's an easy answer. They're all absolutely true."

Brad laughed. "Sure they are. Columba really fought the Loch Ness monster, Ninian really turned people into oxen for their sins, and Mungo really found the queen's ring in a fish's mouth."

Hamish shrugged. "Who's to be saying, laddie? Their biographers write as if they believed them actual happenings. Was it a monster or a bad case of cramps that attacked Columba's companion as he swam? Did Ninian really turn men into oxen, or did the monks in his monastery just work as hard as an ox? Did Mungo find the dishonored woman's ring supernaturally, or did he force it from the one who had stolen it? They're far better tales to be telling if we allow for a power beyond the human, but the truth lies in the lives of the men and the meaning of the tales."

Mary nodded. "Oh, I couldn't agree with you more. Fiction is often stronger than fact because it gets at the truth behind the actual happenings. I was a lit and drama major, so I've just spent four years defending that position as if my life—or at least my grades—depended on it. But what I was thinking while you were telling those stories was—it's almost too bad that people don't believe anymore."

Gareth's head came up, and Mary was aware of his bright, dark eyes on her.

But it was Hamish who spoke. "And what are you meaning, lassie, that no one believes?"

"Hardly anyone, I mean. In God and all that stuff that the early saints lived for. Oh, I know science has proved much of it was nonsense, and we don't need that sort of faith now—but those saints really did accomplish a lot because they believed so single-mindedly."

"Yeah, fighting off the Loch Ness monster and turning people into oxen, for example."

19

"Brad, don't scoff." Mary wrinkled her tip-tilted nose at her cousin. "Just because you can name every layer of the earth from crust to core and tell us how it got there. There's more to life for some than science." She flipped her shining hair over her shoulder. "I'm not saying this well. What I mean is, I know there are still churches—and some people still go regularly—but really, we've gone beyond all that now. And I suppose it's good—more freeing and all that—but when I was listening to your stories I had a feeling that we'd lost something too. I don't know—innocence? Security?" She ended with a shrug.

Gareth's eyes were lowered again, focused on his hands resting on the table.

Hamish shook his massive head slowly. "Aye, there's truth in what ye speak. And a sad day for Scotland it is. For Scotland and all mankind."

At the table next to them a group of students began to sing "Flower of Scotland."

Brad leaned forward in order to be heard. "It was the part about the stone that interested me. I'd never heard it quite like that before—about the Lia Fail breaking off and all that."

Mary laughed. "And you're from the branch of the family that didn't emigrate. I knew about it."

"You did? I'm impressed."

"Well, I'll have to admit I haven't known for very long. Of course I knew about the Stone of Scone in the coronation chair in Westminster—it was one of the 'must see' items on my whirlwind tour of London. There was this American tourist in line in front of me though—the loud sort that gives us all a bad name—and she said, very loudly, 'Is that a *rock* in that chair?' And the guard very politely told her the whole story: about it supposedly being Jacob's pillow carried off to Egypt by his sons, then some king taking it to Spain, and a son of the Spanish king . . ." She groped for the name.

"Simon Brech," Hamish supplied.

"Yes, thank you. He invaded Ireland, taking the stone with him."

Hamish nodded. "Aye, that's it—or when he eloped with the king of Egypt's daughter is the version I favor. Although, truth to tell, the Westminster Stane weighs some four hundredweight, so it seems a strange object to be lugging along on either an elopement or an invasion. Although trading vessels did carry stones for ballast, so it's not impossible."

"Wait a minute!" Brad set his mug down with a clatter. "I thought you were the one believing all this stuff about the Stone of Destiny."

"Oh, aye, I believe it true that Columba possessed a very special stone, and very possibly it was being a piece of the Lia Fail. But I'm not believing that's the stane in Edward's oaken chair in Westminster."

Brad's scoffing tone returned. "You mean when those Scottish students stole the Stone in the fifties? I've heard my dad talk about that. You think they pulled a switch?"

Hamish stroked his beard. "That, I'm thinking, is most unlikely. Most unlikely. Although there's some as believe it. But, lassie, what was your guard in Westminster telling you about the coming of the Stane to England?"

"He said Edward I seized it and took it to Westminster Abbey, where he had a chair specially made to enclose it. I think that's what he said. Was it Edward I?"

When Hamish nodded, it was like an autumn bush blowing in the breeze. "Oh, aye, that was him all right—'The Hammer of the Scots.' He was so proud of that title he had it put on his tomb. And sure it is his men carried a stone all the way from Scone to London— but what would Edward be knowing about one old stone from another —that's what I'm asking you? What would he know?"

Mary's eyes lit up. "Oh, you think the Scots pulled a switch on Edward? Wow!"

"Well now, I wouldn't be the first to be pointing out that the Scots are a verra canny people, would I? And they had warning aplenty that Edward was coming, so . . . " He spread his broad hands in a gesture that invited imaginations to roam. "The fact is, I'm about to set out on a wee journey of my own, collecting tales of the Stane. Maybe it is that I'll find an answer and have a grand tale to tell at next year's festival." He picked up the mug he had brought with him and moved on to another table.

Brad seemed lost in another dimension, so Mary and Gareth turned to each other. He asked her about her family, and she told him briefly about Mark, her older, married brother who was in law practice with their father, and her fifteen-year-old twin sisters, "Becca and Julie—wrapped up in school, boys, the usual things. They're the athletes in the family—soccer champions."

"Ah." His eyes suddenly got even brighter. "Football, we call it. Now there's a game. Of course, I can't play right now, but there's a Ranger's game Saturday."

"Rangers?"

"Aye, they're the best—"

"Enough of that." Brad returned from wherever he had been mentally. "Don't get him started—mad on the subject, he is. Here now, I've sort of got an idea. What that old Highland character said got me to thinking."

"What?"

"Well, I'm not sure, but as a geologist I approach the question of the origin of a stone differently from the way a collector of folklore would. And the fact is, I've been looking for some way to supplement my grant—even thought of doing a bit of tour-guiding or something. But what I'd really like to do is write. Of course I'd thought of academic or scientific journals—something to give me a bit of name recognition when I finish my doctorate, but maybe something for the more popular press wouldn't be so bad."

Mary reached across the table and grabbed her cousin's arm. "Brad! You mean write an article on whether or not the Westminster Stone is authentic? That's great!"

"Not so fast, impetuous American. That's been done—lots of times. There was nothing much really new in what Hamish said, except the idea of the Lia Fail breaking off. But if I could say something new by approaching the whole question from a different angle . . ."

"'A Geologist Looks at the Stone of Scone.'" Mary framed the headline with her hands. "Yes! Do it, Brad!"

"Well, it'll take some background digging." He thought for several moments. "Could be interesting, though. What do you think? Any plans for the next couple of weeks?" His question included both Mary and Gareth. "How about it? Iona, DunAdd, Scone—wherever the clues lead. Like to see more of Scotland?"

Mary laughed. "What do you think I came for? But what about you? Can you just take off like that?"

"University doesn't start until October. Sharon's in France with her parents." He grinned at Mary. "I'll tell you more about her later —I'm hoping you'll have a new cousin-in-law about this time next year. Anyway, I'm supposed to be spending this time researching and writing—which is just what I have in mind." He looked at Gareth. "How about you?"

"See my doctor in the morning. You sure you wouldn't be minding taking a wee bit cripple on your holiday?"

"Good Highland air is just what you're needing to fix you up. Besides, you can keep Mary out of my hair when I need to be reading."

Gareth flashed her a quick grin, then turned to Brad. "We can take my car. How often does the ferry sail to Iona?"

While the men plotted travel logistics, Mary sat quietly, wondering. According to Hamish's story, Columba had found peace and fulfillment on Iona. What would she find?

2

A few miles beyond Loch Lomond, where Gareth recounted childhood memories of camping with his parents and two younger brothers every summer (and always getting rained on—no matter how watertight the tents were guaranteed to be), the road narrowed, and the rugged green hillsides populated only with sheep told Mary she was entering the Highlands. And the billows of rain being blown across the fields before them told her that Scottish weather was living up to its reputation. Every few minutes, however, the sun broke through tiny patches of blue.

Clumps of lacy yews with red berries lined the road, and jagged, rocky peaks thrust above the more distant stands of pine. Brad, in the backseat, looked up from his book long enough to survey the landscape. "Fascinating about the vegetation in the Highlands. These vast barren expanses were once covered with trees. They were cleared by glaciers. Then for the next two and a half thousand years the forests grew back, just to be fired by Mesolithic man to make hunting easier, cleared by medieval man to make room for grazing and the expansion of population, and finally clear-cut by seventeenth- and eighteenth-century man for farming and charcoal burning. It wasn't till the end of the eighteenth century that they began planting again. Which means that the trees you're looking at are relatively young."

Mary laughed and wrinkled her nose. "Thank you, professor. Will we be tested on that?"

"Don't be smart, young lady, or you just might be." With that he returned to his reading.

And Mary returned to gazing out the window. Their way wound around and down to a cozy, green-ringed harbor on the Firth of Lorn, then over a rise and down to more banks of dark, wet green foliage surrounding a wee loch. She smiled as she realized she was thinking the way Gareth talked.

Yet another of the sheep grazing on the lush grass beside the road strayed onto the pavement, and Gareth braked.

"Shouldn't you let Brad drive?" she asked.

"Doctor said the leg needs more exercise. Unless I make you nervous."

"Goodness, no. You're an excellent driver." From the very first she had noticed how steady he was. Her father was fanatical about driving with steady hands and feet, so she always noticed that. Especially when Michael pumped the gas pedal or brake as he drove.

From the back, Brad muttered without looking up from his books, letting them know he had no desire to drive Gareth's car.

Mary laughed again and stuck a tape of bagpipe music in the player. "No one minds if I do the tourist thing, I hope?"

Brad didn't even mutter.

"If you really want to do the tourist thing," Gareth said, "the tradition is to stick a clump of heather in your grill when you're touring the Highlands."

"Oh, yes!" Mary clapped her hands. "Let's!"

A few miles later they rounded a curve and came upon a hillside gloriously purple with heather.

"Oh, here. This is perfect!"

Gareth pulled into a lay-by, and Mary was out of the car and up the hill in a flash. In a few minutes she returned with both hands full of purple blossoms. Gareth helped her attach them—sticking them behind the number plate for a firmer hold than the grill offered.

Back in the car, she realized Brad probably hadn't looked up the whole time they were stopped. They drove off laughing, while the bagpipes shrieked and droned.

It was a few miles on down the road when Mary exclaimed, "That cow has long hair!"

Gareth grinned at her. "And have you never seen a wee little Highland cow before?"

"'Wee' is the last word I'd use to describe that monster!" Now she saw a whole field of the massive red animals, hair almost as long as her own, flowing over their eyes between curving horns.

They were still laughing with general lightheartedness later that afternoon when they boarded the ferry at Oban. The bell clanged as they made their way to the top deck. Gareth was slow on the stairs, and he took the first seat, but Mary and Brad stood at the rail. The ferry pulled smoothly into the sheltered harbor, away from the curve of gray stone buildings and the thickly greened hillside, topped with a curious, apparently unfinished, tower folly and surprising Roman coliseum structure, which Brad explained was an abandoned attempt to build a spa.

Mary tossed her hair to blow in the sea air. She felt her cheeks glow pink in the tangy spray. For once Brad didn't have his head in a book, so she asked, "Tell me about my future cousin-in-law."

His slow grin lit up his blue eyes and showed off his white teeth. Mary thought that grin was one of her cousin's most attractive features. That and his strong cheekbones.

"Oh, you'll like Sharon. She's a music teacher—composes some too. And a gourmet cook. Red hair. She's a little shorter than you. A real lady."

"And you seriously think that paragon will marry you?"

His reply was light but not joking. "As I hope for heaven."

Mary frowned. Somehow the reference disturbed her. She turned to take a seat beside Gareth in the front row of bright red molded chairs. He held up a hand for her to wait while he took out a handkerchief and wiped the chair dry.

Oblivious to the dampness, Brad sat on the other side.

"OK, your turn. Tell me about this Michael. As one with an academic interest in rocks, I have to admire the magnitude of that assemblage on your finger."

Mary slipped her hand into her pocket. Then she closed her eyes and felt the gentle rocking of the boat. "Well, I met him two years ago when my friend Jenny and I went down to the Harvard/ Dartmouth football game." She turned and grinned at Gareth. "*Real* football that is, not your brand of misnamed soccer. Anyway, Michael was a friend of Jenny's brother—both at Harvard Business School. So we all went out afterwards."

She sighed at the memory. "He really swept me off my feet. I'd dated a lot, but no one that I ever really cared about before. Michael sent me roses, came up to Hanover on weekends and took me to great little inns for dinner. I went down to Cambridge, and we'd go to the theater in Boston.

"He graduated with all sorts of honors last year and went to work for a big corporation in New York. He even has an apartment in Manhattan, and they're almost impossible to find. His folks have this great big white house out on Long Island." She paused to follow the flight of a gull swooping over the deck. "I mean, there's no doubt he'll have made his first million by the time he's thirty-five."

"He sounds perfect. Every family should have a millionaire in it somewhere."

"Brad, you're awful. It's not the money. He's great. Really, he is." Mary wondered why she felt compelled to be so insistent.

"So when's the big event? I'll have to start saving now for my ticket if I'm to do the family thing and come throw rice at you."

"They use birdseed now—more environmentally friendly. But . . . I don't know . . ." She lowered her lashes to hide the confusion in her eyes.

"Don't know what?" he prodded.

"That's what I keep asking myself. Crazy, huh? Just jitters, I suppose. I haven't been able to name the date yet. I'm sure I will as soon as I get home. Just wanted to get away and think first. I mean, I wanted to be sure. I guess I'm quite the raging liberal on some things—we all were at Dartmouth—but I'm not one of those who believe you just try out marriage."

Mary was aware of movement on her left. Gareth got up and moved to the rail. She hoped his doctor had been right about exercise being good for him. It looked to her as if he was limping more.

She walked to the rail beside him. "Are you OK?"

"Yes. No." There was a cloud behind the dark eyes that met hers. He shrugged. "I just get sae frustrated. It's been so long now, and I hate being such a drag on everything."

Mary couldn't suppress a gurgle of amazed laughter. "I've never known anyone who was less of a drag. But you said everything would eventually be fine."

"Oh, aye. That's what they say. Impatience is not the least of my sins."

She laughed again. "Wait a minute. I'm supposed to be the impatient one."

But Gareth didn't laugh with her. Somehow she felt there was more troubling him than a broken leg.

The next morning, after a night in a cozy bed-and-breakfast on the island of Mull, they caught the first ferry to Iona. One couldn't sail directly from the mainland to the holy island—rather a nice thing, Mary thought. It somehow helped to preserve the isolation the island must have had in Columba's day.

She stood at the very front of the deck, looking across the Sound of Iona. The sun shone from a blue sky with white clouds, sparking the water that was sometimes blue, sometimes green, sometimes purple in its depths. But when she turned back toward the harbor they were leaving, she caught her breath and grabbed Brad's arm. "Look at that rock! The whole harbor is full of pink rock. If the Westminster Stone is the one Columba had, the old saint certainly could have picked it up anywhere around here."

Brad surveyed the pink stone formations tumbling down to the water.

Mary, standing beside him at the rail, felt sudden disappointment. She hadn't realized until now, but she didn't want it to be that easy. She now knew that she had hoped to find evidence that the stone in London wasn't the original. And here it was, a whole harborful of candidates on their second day out.

But Brad shook his head. "Good try, amateur. That's why this project needs a trained geologist. Right color. Wrong rock. Westminster Stone is sandstone—Old Devonian Red Sandstone, to be exact. This is pink granite."

Mary grinned, and her spirits rose.

She found Gareth leaning on the forward rail, the breeze ruffling his dark hair. After a few minutes of quiet she took the plunge. After all, people expected Americans to be pushy. She might as well live up to their reputation. "Your turn today."

"Hmm?" He turned to her with a little crooked smile and a raised eyebrow.

"I told you about Michael. What about you?"

"Oh, lots of girls." He grinned very broadly this time. "I like girls. There's Sarah, a really nice girl who works in the bank with my mum. I still go out with her some. And Beth at church. Sometimes we sing together. She's really cute. But not as cute as Katy. Chances are I probably would have married Katy if it hadn't been for the accident . . ." He paused. "Now I look at things a wee bit different."

"What about the accident? Brad said it was mountaineering—you fell?"

"Yep." He nodded. "Early last spring it was. Brad, Alex, and me, hiking in the Cullins. Ever heard of them—on the Isle of Skye?"

She shook her head.

"Magnificent. Amazingly rugged. Can't even get to them by car. So we were rock climbing on this crag. It was steep, but not all that bad. We'd all done harder courses lots of times. Then it started to rain. That was probably what caused it—made the rock slick. Anyway, Alex fell first." He shook his head. "It shouldn't have happened. He was the best climber of us all, the most experienced. He was right above me."

"Knocked you off?"

"No. Not really. I more just lost my balance with the horror of it all." He paused for a long time. His voice was tight when he continued. "I was lucky—hit a clump of gorse. Knew immediately my leg was broken, wrist sprained, few cuts and scrapes . . ."

"And Alex?"

Gareth looked into the depths of the water at the side of the ferry. "He never regained consciousness. I sat with him all night while Brad went for help. At first I thought I'd go crazy sitting there while my best friend's breathing got weaker and weaker. But then . . . I don't know . . . it was strange . . ."

"What? Don't stop now." Mary shook her head to clear it. For a moment it had been as if she had been sitting on that deserted hillside beside the dying man.

Gareth looked at her levelly. "I found the truth."

Mary wondered why she felt so let down. It was obvious Gareth didn't think his answer was an anticlimax. "Oh, that's nice." Then she realized how insipid her reply sounded. "I mean, that's great—everyone has to decide what's true for them. I guess I'm a little envious. I haven't decided yet."

Gareth's forehead furrowed. "Is that all truth is to you, Mary? Something you choose like a brand of toothpaste or a flavor of crisps?"

She tossed her hair. "Well, I am very fond of salt and malt vinegar."

But her companion didn't laugh. It was so hard to avoid his eyes.

She shrugged. "After all, everything's relative."

But he wouldn't let it go at that, as she had thought he would. "You're not looking for truth. What you're talking about is the wish fulfillment Freud accused religion of being. Choosing what's true for you is not at all the same thing as seeking the absolute Truth."

Mary felt distinctly uncomfortable under the direct gaze of his brilliant eyes. He sounded so certain. Could he be right? Maybe she owed it to him—no, to herself—to consider the possibility. It was really rather exciting to think that there could be an absolute in the universe. Something one could really anchor to.

She doubted that it existed any more than Jacob's Pillow or the Lia Fail did. But if Gareth were right, one should know. She tipped her head in that thinking attitude she had assumed through so many lectures—both interesting and dull—in the past four years. This quest she was setting out on could prove very interesting indeed. And more than a little scary. Just what had she agreed to search for?

But she lost her scholarly pose as her eyes turned back to Gareth's penetrating gaze. She quickly dropped her eyes and focused on Michael's ring glinting on her finger.

A familiar voice with a sonorous lilt made her turn. "Aye, there it is now. The jewel of the Hebrides they call it."

It took her a moment to realize the speaker referred to the island ahead, not to her ring. "Hamish, I didn't see you get on the ferry." She was glad enough to turn from Gareth's disturbing topic.

28

"The jewel of the Hebrides? Is that what they call Iona? It sounds wonderful!"

"Aye. It is. Shall I be telling you a wee story about Columba's time?"

"Yes, please!"

"This is only a story now, mind you, but I like to be thinking not only of the lives of the great ones that get written about in the chronicles but also about the wee, ordinary people. I'll tell you about a shepherd boy who could have lived on Iona at the time of Columba. A wee laddie named Corban and his dog Righ . . ."

They sailed on toward the green, softly mounded island with its little village clustered around the harbor. As the ferry slowly drew closer, Mary was thoroughly taken with the beauty of the curving white beach, the sun sparkling on the water, the outcroppings of gleaming white stone on the green hill running the length of the island.

All was quiet on deck except for Hamish's enthralling voice as the ferry glided forward. Streaks of cloud-filtered light went before them as Mary looked toward the intense greenness of the turf-carpeted rocks. Then the sun broke through, making a glistening pool on the water ahead. They sailed into the brilliant, shimmering rings. Momentarily blinded, she closed her eyes. She was dimly aware of a flock of seabirds taking wing with raucous calls.

* * *

It was the squawking birds, winging dark against the white clouds, that made Corban, standing on the highest point of the island, open his eyes and look out to sea. At first all he saw was the brightness of the sun making glittering circles on the waves. The blue and green striped sail just looked like part of the sky and seascape. But the shape drew closer, and Corban knew he was seeing something he had never seen before—people from a far land. He had heard tales around the night fires, tales of Hebridean raiders long ago in his grandfather's grandfather's day—they had often carried off shepherd boys just like himself to herd sheep in Eire. Corban's head told him to run. But something held him—a strange fascination, a desire to see these unknown new people.

It was the same gripping attraction he always felt when he heard tales of places beyond his own small island. Corban knew that a double chain of islands dotted the waters of the sea west of the mainland, and that his Iona was one of the smallest. And he knew that there was a great, solid land mass beyond the Island of Mull to the east. Some said the land was so vast that there were places from which one couldn't even see the ocean. And some said there were lands beyond that land. But one couldn't be believing everything one heard.

And the old desire stirred within him, the longing he had known ever since he could remember, that someday he would see for himself. Someday he would visit those lands; he would see new people.

But now, such people were coming to him.

He called his dog, Righ, to his side, not so much to protect himself but that he might send Righ to protect the sheep, should those aboard the fast-approaching vessel threaten to carry them off. His fingers touched the hilt of the knife he wore tucked in his belt. He used it only for eating and for whittling the pipes he played for his own amusement and the calming of the sheep. Never had he needed his knife for protection; there were no enemies on Iona. But now?

Corban had spent all his twelve years living among Iona's twenty families in a scattered assemblage of round, turf or wattle huts with thatched roofs above the white cockleshell beach. For every day for as long as he could remember, he had looked after the sheep with Righ or had amused himself when it was his friend Ibar's turn to watch, while his father, Garfinn, went to the top of the island with the other men to tend their crops or out in their hide-covered curraghs to fish. Or sometimes they went to one of the sheltered bays to hunt seal, but Corban didn't like to think of that because, for all that he enjoyed eating seal-meat stew, he loved more watching the seals at play and hated to think of their being disturbed by the hunter's spear.

His six-year-old brother, Dag, was looked after, neither grudgingly nor fondly, by Merca, who lived in the hut nearest theirs. For Corban's fair-haired mother was long dead, her body in the Reilig Odhrain and her spirit gone to dwell among the faerie folk on the Shin. Merca, whose man had been lost in a storm while fishing long and long ago, before her face became wrinkled like last winter's apples, made medicines for all the clachan but most of all for small Dag, he of the pale skin and blue eyes too big for his face, for Corban's little brother was often sick.

The wind ruffled Corban's shock of sea-foam-pale hair that spoke of his mother's Norse ancestry. Then his hand moved from his knife to rub his left elbow. He was small for his age but sturdy and well-formed—except for his arm, which ever hung at an awkward angle. And as always when he thought of it, his ashen blue eyes clouded dark with hatred.

But now the black look cleared quickly to be replaced with open-faced curiosity. For the boat, long and timber-built, was pulling into the bay, and Corban could see that it was filled with a number of brown-robed men, all with shining bare foreheads. What did it mean? Was all his life as it had been for twelve years about to change?

Three of the men pulled up their long robes, jumped over the side of the hull into knee-deep water, and pulled the boat up on the fine, gleaming shore of ground shells so that their fellows might alight dry-shod. Several still in the boat were struggling to lower the sail against the whipping wind that wrapped Corban's homespun tunic and cloak around his legs. They hadn't spotted him yet.

He stood as still as one of the many rocky outcroppings and shadowed ridges on the green hill, wondering what to do. Should he slip around to the far side of the rocky spine that divided the island and run to warn the others? Or should he offer to help the newcomers? The sensible thing would be to run. Or would his father just box him about the ears and accuse him of daydreaming, as he so often did? But even if Garfinn beat him, Corban would soon be proved right. That would be very satisfying. He turned.

Righ, however, had other ideas. With two sharp barks, the long-haired, brindled hound bounded toward the men on the shore. Corban barely stopped himself from shouting and dashing after his dog. Instead, he squatted behind a boulder and watched.

The nearest man spoke and held out his hand to the animal. Corban wasn't close enough to see if the man smiled, but he felt he did. Righ jumped up, placing his front paws at the man's waist. The man patted him and pushed him gently down. So. This was a man who loved dogs—as Corban did. He had nothing to fear.

By the time the boy had made his way to the bay, the men had the sail lowered and were all ashore. The tall man that Righ had singled out seemed to be in charge. His hair was thick behind his shining bald forehead, brown with red lights and streaked with gray. His eyes were a dark, shining brown under heavy eyebrows, and his jaw a strong square. Everything about the man seemed strong, forceful, authoritative, for all that he must be very old to have gray in his hair. But not as old as Echu, of course. Echu was the oldest man on Iona, and his hair was gray as the ashes around the fire where he sat all day to warm his ancient bones.

No, this was not a man who would sit by the fire. He turned and regarded Corban with a level look, then nodded and smiled. "Is this your dog? He is a fine animal."

Corban blinked. He understood the words enough to nod his answer, but the sounding was strange, almost more as if the man sang rather than spoke them.

"I am Columba. These men are my brothers."

31

Corban nodded again as he sorted out the strange speaking. Columba. The dove. That was a good name. Brothers? The dove was from a large family indeed. But he must have it right that they were true brothers—for their hair all grew in that funny way that left the front of their heads shining bare. And they all wore the same rough-woven brown robes. Their mother must spend long hours at the loom if she wove for all of them.

Then he realized the dove was waiting for him to speak. It would be impolite not to offer his own name in repayment for the stranger giving his.

"Corban."

"Ah, Corban, well-spoken. And well-named. Gift. The one who named you was glad of your coming."

Corban stared. He must have misunderstood the unfamiliar accent to the man's speech. No one had ever been glad of him.

"And your dog?" the newcomer persisted.

"Righ."

"Righ." Columba smiled. "Ruler. That is who I would see. Corban, will you take me to your ruler—to the high man of your island?"

Corban considered. Ruler? He had heard the men talk of a king who lived somewhere to the east in a place they called DunAdd, but that could not be what the dove asked for. Old Echu was considered very wise for the weight of his years and the long thoughts he dreamed, sitting by the fire. Echu would know what to do. Corban nodded.

Columba signaled two of the others to join them. "These are Baithene and Diormit. They will come too."

Again Corban bobbed his head, then stopped. The sheep. He could not leave them unattended. "Righ, stay with the sheep."

"And Laisran too." Columba signaled another of the brown-robed men. "Laisran, tend the sheep while we are away."

"There are many new lambs. They are very stupid," Corban warned Laisran.

It was a long walk across the most rugged part of the island, past the side of the mountain where great slabs of gleaming white rock with green veining stuck up through the soft grass. But Columba had no difficulty keeping up. It was the younger Baithene and Diormit who lagged at times.

Echu sat cross-legged on his sheepskin mat before the fire, where oatcakes baked on a circle of flat rocks.

Full of importance, Corban explained the coming of the strangely robed men with the funny hair and presented them to the old man. "And the dove one was kind to Righ, and one of his brothers is watching the sheep."

Echu nodded. "That is good. Now be you quiet, cubbling." He rose to greet the visitors.

"As you have heard, I am Columba. I come from Eire with twelve brothers. We will establish a monastery and teach all who will listen about the holy God of Father, Son, and Spirit. My kinsman Conall, son of Comgall, king of Dalriada—" Columba gestured toward the mainland to the east "—has granted us leave for this undertaking and land to build on this island, but I would have your welcome too, if you will give it."

Echu motioned that they should sit on a bench beside his hut. He sat long with a faraway look in his pale eyes. At last he put a gnarled hand over his heart. "Yes, I know of the holy One and His Son Jesus the Christ, but there are few here who remember. Long it has been since I heard the holy name spoken." Again he sat in quiet, while the sun shone on his wrinkled face. "My father came to this land with Fergus Mor mac Erc from Dalriada in Eire. It is in my mind that many were true worshipers then. But there was much to do, and we had no teachers . . . many married with the Pictikind and took their gods. . . ."

Corban inched closer. He loved tales of the old days, but never had he heard Echu speak so of the gods.

At last Echu stood and drew his plaid cloak around him, his gold ring brooch shining in the sun. "Yes, Columcille, it is good. Our sons' sons know not the God of our fathers. They should hear. Make you welcome on Iona. We have a holy ground of burial places." He looked around at Corban. "The cubbling will show you the way to the Reilig Odhrain."

Corban couldn't have been happier for an excuse to ramble across the island. The turf lay green and soft underfoot, and clumps of spring bluebells and yellow iris nodded them on their way. To the right, the waters of the narrow Sound of Iona lapped the shores of their own island and the neighboring Mull beyond, while fishermen bobbed in small curraghs, bringing in nets of wriggling silver fish.

Echu had said to show the holy men Reilig Odhrain, but Corban did not want to darken this bright day with a visit to the place where his mother lay buried, so instead he hurried on to the little hill he loved best because it made such a fine place to sit and look out across the water and think.

"Tor an Aba," he announced to Columba, pointing.

"Yes." Digging his walking stick into the ground with each step, Columba climbed the hillock, followed by Baithene and Diormit.

Corban, uncertain of what was expected of him, stopped halfway up.

Columba went on to the top. "My brothers," the dove said, "the place we are standing on is holy ground. We have gone out seeking the place the Lord God would show us, and this is the place, this Iona. From here shall we carry the Word of the Lord to all this land."

Baithene and Diormit knelt while Columba stood between them, his hands outspread.

Not knowing what to do, Corban knelt too.

And Columba's voice rang out from the top of Tor an Aba. "It is written, 'Without vision the people perish.' This is a land that has lost its vision. But by the grace of God we shall enkindle a fresh vision in all of Dalriada and the land beyond.

"For the Lord's promise unto Jacob is unto us His servants as well: 'I will deliver unto you every place where you set your foot. I will be with you. Take possession of the land which the Lord your God is giving you.'"

Corban did not fully understand the words, but there was no mistaking the ring of confidence in Columba's voice or the shine of glory on his face.

When Corban tried to explain it all to his father that night, however, there was no making Garfinn understand.

"They are holy men, Father, come to tell us of the great God. Echu sent me to guide them. And I did not leave the sheep unattended. Righ and one of the—"

It was no good. Corban fell silent and gave all his energy to stifling his sobs as the blows fell about his head and shoulders.

"It was not Echu's lamb that was lost, was it? Nor was it the holy man's. I will not have these men on our island. They have no right to take our land. My sheep that was lost today was but the beginning. They will take the best land for their farm place, kill the fattest seals for their cook pots, catch the first fish. This is but a small island. It is not big enough for the likes of them. They must go."

"No, Father." Corban put up his good arm, not so much to fend off Garfinn's fists as his words. "They have come to help us. The High King gave them leave, I heard Columba say so."

At last the blows stopped, and Corban lay on his pallet by the central fire between Righ and little Dag, who sobbed himself to sleep.

"They will go. I will see to it." Garfinn went out into the night, letting the leather apron fall against the lintel with a harsh slapping sound.

Corban closed his eyes, adding to his heart another stone of the hatred he bore his father.

34

The next morning there was no sign that Garfinn had slept on his pile of sheepskins on the far side of the fire, so Corban gave Dag a cup of milk from the tall clay jug to go with his oatcake and told him to see that he minded Merca well. Then, with Righ at his heels, he went out to unfold the sheep. On the way he noticed that his father's curragh was not leaning against its usual black rock by the bay.

That evening, however, when Corban had the sheep folded for the night and returned himself to the hut, Garfinn was there, somewhat mollified by the fact that Brother Laisran, feeling responsible for the lamb that had fallen from a rock and broken its leg, had brought a sack of meal and a box of salt from their own precious stores as repayment.

"But still they must go," Garfinn said and would hear no more on the subject.

Two days later it was the turn of Ibar, the boy two years Corban's senior who lived three huts down along the beach, to watch the sheep. And Corban, who would usually have spent the day watching for seals at the Bay of the Back of the Ocean or exploring Spouting Cave on the wild, west side of the island, chose to go instead toward Tor an Aba.

Already the brothers had made great progress in building the circle of little round huts that would be their homes. Corban was fascinated, for instead of building the walls with wattle or turf and then putting on a separate roof of thatch, as all the houses of the clachan were, these men wove from ground to ceiling, forming a cone-shaped dwelling in a single process. They wove the walls double and filled the space between with heather, moss, and straw—insulation, they called it, to make their little beehives warm and watertight. Each simple structure had only a low doorway and a single opening in the top for smoke from the central, peat-burning fire to escape, and room enough for a stool, a small kist, and a pallet against the far wall. Could their needs really be so modest?

Those who had finished their own little cells, however, were now engaged in a far more elaborate undertaking. The structure they had begun to build on the smooth green land just up from the bay would be larger than all their cone huts together. Columba, who directed the work, had planted stakes deep in the turf, forming a rectangular room large enough to accommodate all the people of Iona at one time.

"Ah, Corban, my friend, see the fine building materials brother Ernan brought over from Mull." Columba approached him with his arms full of sturdy reeds. "In time we will have good strong timbers

35

sent from the mainland, but for now God will not object to being worshiped from a church of wattle. Will you be helping us build?"

Corban reddened, his cheeks turning as bright as the dusting of freckles across his nose. "I'm not much use . . ." His eyes went to his twisted left arm.

Columba dropped his sticks and strode to Corban. His fingers felt strong and warm on the firm flesh of the boy's arm as he examined the crooked elbow. "Aye. It is weak, but not withered. Can you do this?" He held his own arm out from his body.

Corban tried. The arm moved only an inch or two.

Columba nodded. "How long has it been thus?"

"Six years. My father . . ." Corban bit the words back and stuffed them down with his own bitterness.

Columba shook his head. "Six years is a long time. Still, we will try what massage and exercise will do. Massage and exercise and prayer. Come to me every evening after the sheep are folded. Can you do that?"

Unsure of what he was getting into, Corban nodded.

"And for the present, one strong arm will be sufficient for steadying the uprights as we weave."

So Corban worked through the day with the brothers. And as they worked, the monks explained to Corban what a church was and about the God who so loved mankind that He gave His own true Son to die for them that they might know Him.

Corban listened and felt the sun warm on his head. This was perhaps more interesting than watching seals.

At midday Corban shared their pot of fish stew—but not until he had washed his hands at Columba's direction and joined the brothers in a prayer that fell strangely, but not unpleasantly, on his ears:

> "The blessing of God be on you,
> The blessing of Christ be on you,
> The blessing of Spirit be on you.
> O giver of the sweet honey,
> O giver of the sour cheese,
> O giver of the Bread of Life and Living Water,
> Be with us by day,
> Be with us by night,
> Be with us for Thy service."

At the day's end the walls of Columba's church were knee-high to Corban. He regarded it with satisfaction.

"The Church of the Dove," he said.

36

"What?" Columba placed his hand on Corban's shoulder.

"Echu said Columcille means 'dove of the church.' This is your church, so it is the Church of the Dove."

The tall monk threw back his head and laughed. "And did you know, my young friend, that the dove is the symbol of the Holy Spirit, the part of God who lives within us and guides us? You have named our church well indeed. Come now."

Columba led the way to his own beehive hut and held the door flap for Corban to enter. "Sit you on the stool."

Corban sat on a rough, three-legged stool, and Columba knelt beside him. He began by running his hands the length of the boy's arm from shoulder to fingertips. Then he stopped and looked deep into him with his warm brown eyes. Corban felt himself draw back under the fierce gaze. "You cannot help?" he whispered.

"We shall see. But I am thinking that the stiffness is not so much in your arm as in your soul, young Corban. Cannot you tell me what squeezes your heart so that you cannot move your arm?"

Corban squared his shoulders and glared at the large man. "You are wrong."

Columba shook his head. "I do not think so."

Corban held a strong silence.

Columba sighed. "Very well. If you will have it so, we will see what can be done here. But I do not believe I am wrong."

Corban felt guilty for his lie as Father Columba began kneading the muscles of his stiff, useless arm in the way he had often watched Merca kneading the dough for bread. But guilty or no, he would not speak of what was in his heart. To speak it would be to live it again. And that would be too painful. He would go through life with his arm stiff rather than live that night again.

At first the large, powerful hands were gentle, but then the strength of their grip increased. Just when Corban thought he would cry out with pain, Columba stopped.

"Now, lift it again."

Corban tried. Tried with all the strength he could gather. But it would not lift even the inch or so that it had earlier.

Columba put his hand on his shoulder. "No. You are tired now from the massage. But when you are rested, try again. Ten times, with all your might, lift as far as you can. Three times every day. Will you do that?"

"I will."

"So. It is good. And our Lord who was once Himself a boy like you will help you." Then before Corban could absorb that amazing fact, Columba crossed himself, and, kneeling beside Corban, he prayed, "God's blessing be yours, and well may it befall you."

Then he held the door flap for Corban to leave. "Now do not forget. It is important that you come every day."

Just then, streaks of the setting sun fell on the rough gray stone at the head of Columba's pallet.

"What is that?" Corban ran his fingers over the coarse, hard surface.

"It is my pillow."

Corban, thinking of the softness of the flaxen bag stuffed with shorn wool on which he lay his head every night, was horrified. "Pillow? For your head? But it is so hard, so rough. Surely you do not sleep on that. And it is so large. It would bend your neck."

Columba smiled, a rather sad smile. "You are very observant. Truth to tell, I more sleep with my head against it than on it. But you see, this stone pillow is very important to me because it reminds me of two things. It reminds me of my sins, which are so grievous that they can be covered only by the blood of Jesus Christ, and it reminds me of my homeland of Eire, which I love greatly but will never see again. And in remembering that, I am reminded that my true homeland is heaven and that someday I will live there forever."

Corban considered. He understood little of what this strange man had said, but one thing seemed perfectly clear. "If you must be sleeping on a pillow of stone, it is seeming to me that it would be better to have one of our fine white Iona marble. It would not be so rough."

Columba clapped him on the back. "A fine thought indeed, my friend. But the harshness of this stone from Eire ever reminds me of the harshness of my sins, for which I do penance."

And Corban felt that he saw a great sadness inside his friend.

Later, when he tried to answer his father's questions as to where he had been and what he had been doing that day, Corban saw nothing but anger. It seemed that his father had a hardness in him more stony than Columba's pillow.

"They need not bother to build. They will not be here that long. They have chosen the wrong island." Garfinn would say no more.

Corban lay long on his sheepskin that night, worrying. Was his father right? Would Columba and the brothers leave? Would any chance that Columba might be able to help his arm be taken from him? What did the glint in Garfinn's eyes mean? What did his father intend to do?

3

Columba wakened the next morning to the howl of the wind lashing rain against his cell and driving in waves on the shore. His first sleep-fogged thought was that he was hearing the waves dashing against the rockbound coast of his beloved Ireland. But even as his mouth curved in a smile, the pain of memory cramped his heart. No, not Ireland. Not the sweet green homeland where his mother and brothers and all he knew and loved still dwelt, but a harsh new country to which God had led him in penance.

Columba had come hither because he truly wanted God's will more than life. But even then it had been a struggle to leave his homeland—such a painful struggle he had thought it might cost his life. Only in God's strength could he have made it so far. And only in God's strength could he endure to keep his vow never to look on Ireland again.

The wind raged so at the walls of his tiny hut that Columba thought it might be torn from over his head. As he addressed his Creator, who knew his heart better than he did, Columba tried to keep the fear out of his voice.

"My God, help me to endure. Help me to triumph. Help me to love. Help me to endure the ache of loss. Help me to triumph over the temptation of self-pity. Help me to love this land to which I've been sent. In Your strength, Lord, for I have none of my own." And then he repeated the heart of the matter. "Help me to love."

Again the wind lashed his cell. Even in the time between spring and summer, the climate could be wild and harsh on this island, it seemed.

He repeated his prayer. Then, as he lay there, it was not the image of a storm-battered, wind-whipped island that filled his mind but rather of an Iona bathed in sunlight and peace, lambs gamboling on its hillsides, flowers blooming through its turf, blue and turquoise waters lapping its white beaches, the bays defined by curves of black rock. And over all, the benediction of God as soothing as an angel's wing.

And then it seemed not an angel over Iona but an angel inside his very hut spoke to him—and yet spoke not in words but in pictures, as if the sides of his hut fell away and he saw the monastery that he would build for this time and for the years upon years to come—a monastery not of wattle and thatch but a great abbey of stone that would stand against all the winds of time. And a scriptorium where books would be copied and illuminated with leaves edged in gold and letters glowing with all the colors of precious stones. And then Columba heard a sweet singing as of heavenly voices. And for a moment he felt as John the Evangelist must have felt when he was lifted to the highest heaven.

And Columba knew he could face this new day in a new land. The pain was no less. He loved Ireland no less. He missed his family no less. But now he could believe that God would give him a new love, a love that would exist alongside the pain, and each could be endured because of the other.

Columba clutched his breast. "Please, God, soon. Let the love come soon. Before the pain overwhelms me."

For a moment, memory of the soft green beauty of Ireland threatened to engulf him. But Columba pushed it aside. No. He would not give in to that. He had his work. He could keep the pain at bay with his work—God's work—and with the faith that, when the time was right, God would send the love.

Now as the vision faded, he knew it was not heavenly voices he heard, but rather his own band of brothers, and it was time to lead them in prayers for the morning. For no matter how the elements raged, no matter how water-soaked the tents of the brothers whose huts were not yet built, all would give thanks to God, for the day was glorious in their hearts whatever the conditions outside.

Their robes whipping about their legs, the rain dripping from their cowls, the brothers gathered on the sheltered side of Tor an Aba while Columba prayed. And because God had met Columba in his cell, he could pray for the brotherhood with fervor:

> "My voice shall Thou hear in the morning, O God,
> My song shall Thou hear in the morning, O Christ,
> My heart cry shall Thou hear in the morning, O Spirit.
> In the morning will I direct my prayer unto Thee,
> And I will look up to You."

And they broke their fast with the blessed celebration of His Table.

"My brothers, let us put all our energies into the building of our church that we may soon celebrate the blessed Eucharist in the blessing of a dry place. For the Lord in His mercy revealed to me this morning that there is a mighty work to do here, and many shall come to us."

Although the rain continued, the wind lessened, with the happy result that the dampened rushes were easier to weave and the portion of yesterday's weaving that had blown away was quickly repaired. And the wall rose.

And with the calming of the water it seemed that Columba's prophecy of visitors was to see fulfillment, for three small curraghs, coming from the north, bobbed into the bay at the foot of the village. Columba left his work and signaled Diormit to follow him. If these newcomers sought him rather than a villager, he would offer them welcome.

He had covered only half the ground to the bay, however, before Corban ran up the path, panting with news. "They are holy men who come from Coll to have words with you."

Columba could now see his visitors, white-robed, with tonsured foreheads, a tall, ruddy-complexioned one to the front, wearing a large silver cross on his breast.

Columba approached them. "Greetings in the name of the Lord."

"Greetings to our brother in the faith. I am Aclu, leader of the faithful, come to have speech with you."

"All who come in the name of the Lord are welcome indeed. I have no shelter to offer you. But we may sit by my cell, and I will hear you." He turned to Corban. "Run to Brother Laisran and tell him to prepare cups of wine for our visitors."

Aclu held up his hand. "We thank you, but there is no need. Our message is a short one. I regret that we could not come sooner to save you the wasted work of building." Holding his staff for support, Aclu bowed deeply from the waist.

The two behind him followed his example, the short, fat one having considerable difficulty executing his bow.

Columba's eyes narrowed. He observed the newly shaved appearance of the visitors' half-moon tonsures. "What mean you? Speak clearly."

Aclu's face broke into a wide smile. "Why, we have come with the best of news. Apparently you have not the knowing that your work is unnecessary here. We have already the faith."

"Indeed? And what faith is that?"

"Why, the faith in the one true High God-Creator."

"And in His Son the Christos," the young one in the back added quickly.

41

Again Aclu smiled and puffed out his red cheeks. "So you see that you are not needed here. You have the wrong island. I am sure that in the outer Western Isles there would be need of your work. There are many who have not heard, so I know you would not be choosing to waste your time here. It is indeed a pity, but the rebuilding may be quickly done."

Columba considered. Was it possible? When Fergus Mor mac Erc founded Scottish Dalriada sixty years ago, surely he would have brought a priest from Ireland in his company. Echu told him there had been no teaching on Iona, but it was a small, remote island. Perhaps the larger of the inner islands and the mainland still knew the faith. Could he have misunderstood? Could he do more elsewhere?

But then he remembered his vision. God had come to him this very morning. On this island. He smiled. "I am indeed grateful that you have come to me. And I am delighted to know of the strength of the faith in our Lord Jesus Christ in this land. You must join us in prayers before you go." His smile broadened. "You must lead our prayers, Father Aclu."

Aclu's smooth smile faded. "Ah, I regret that pressing needs elsewhere . . ." He took a step backward.

And Columba knew his sensitivity to the Spirit had not failed him. "No. Hear me." He advanced. "Our enemy the devil often goes in sheep's clothing to deceive the unwary. But Satan is a defeated adversary, for our Lord Jesus Christ overcame all the powers of hell when He rose from the dead. It is the power of the resurrected Christ that we bring to these islands and to the land beyond, Aclu of the sheep's clothing. This is a power that you and your false druids cannot stand against."

With each sentence Columba had taken a step forward, the imposters a step backward.

Now they turned and fled.

But they fled not to the boats but toward the village, demanding of a bystander to know the whereabouts of the hut of Garfinn.

"No!" Corban cried when his father's name reached his hearing. He darted forward, but Columba restrained him.

"Let me go. I knew my father was plotting something. He was gone long the night you came. Now I know. He went to the druids on Coll. They are very powerful. They will do you much harm. Perhaps you should go—" He bit his lip, and the brown specks in his blue eyes darkened.

"Fear you not, small friend. Hitherto hath the Lord led us. We will not be dissuaded. Come, let us build strong walls that they may stand against all the winds of the devil."

But Corban resisted Columba's hand on his shoulder. "You do not know their power."

"That is true, I do not. But I know a higher power. That is enough."

Later they watched as the three white-robed figures returned to the bay, Aclu carrying a lamb under one arm.

"They demanded a sacrifice of my father," Corban said. "They will be back."

The coming days, however, were quiet. The brothers finished building their huts and the church. Then they went to the machair, the low-lying, grassy land next to the sea on the western side of the island, and set out fields of oats, barley, turnips, and cabbages, fertilizing them well at Brother Ernan's direction with the rich seaweed that grew in profusion just offshore.

And as the days grew warmer, and the seeds sprouted in the field, and the lambs grew in the pasture, and the fish swam silver in the sea, and God provided for all with His abundance, the brothers turned once more to building. This time it was a long, narrow refectory where all could eat together and hear the reading of the lessons at the lengthy plank table that Brother Laisran fashioned from the wood he bought on Mull. And next to the refectory was the scriptorium for the work so dear to the heart of Columba, who loved books above all things.

So it was that while some of the brothers were still engaged in constructing a high turf vallum to encircle all the monastery buildings, Columba and brothers Diormit, Cainnech, and Virgno began their work of copying books for the library they would build.

It was a day Corban was free of his sheep tending, and so, as he almost always did, he came to Columba.

"Well come, Corban, my friend. We are much in need of your help in gathering supplies for our work. Will you aid us?" Columba knew he had no need to ask, for the lad was ever as willing a worker as he was a willing listener to the stories of the Lord.

"Good," he replied to Corban's ready nod. "Take a basket and go with Brother Virgno. Find the best holly bushes on the island, so we may crush their leaves for ink. And gather the brightest flowers. I fear the yellow iris are past their prime, but I believe there are buttercups aplenty."

"Oh, yes, I know the very place."

"Good. And then look you for the brightest of your gemstones. Garnets and aquamarines, are there not? And others? We will crush them for the most jewel-like of illuminations."

It was one of the happiest days Columba had known since he left his beloved homeland under the weight of a heavy penance. Was it a great burden or a great gift, this charge to bring Christ to the land of the Scots?

He had thought the burden unspeakable when first he heard the pronouncement. They had won the war. His clan, the High Nialls, whom he had called into battle to fight for a righteous cause, had won over those who would keep from them a most prized copy of the Word of God. No man should deny that to another, and he had so proven in battle. But the battle of Coldrevny was a bloody, dearly won battle, a thing that no man of God should countenance, leading brother to fight brother in a dispute over the faith. And so the council had sent him forth—to win as many to live for God as had been lost in battle.

His mother, Eithne, had given only one sharp, brokenhearted outcry at the pronouncement. And then she had shown the strength of a daughter of the High Nialls as she set about baking bread, repairing a tear in his cloak, and preparing all else her son would need for his journey.

"I shall be with you every day, my son. My prayers will never leave you. Send me a letter when you've opportunity. But I shall never be farther than a prayer away."

Already Eithne's prayers were being answered, for he had made progress on his charge. Many from the village came daily now to be taught and to pray. And with each that came, Columba's joy increased, and his vision increased, and he thanked God for his mother's prayers. Three thousand had been lost in battle. But he would not stop with the winning of three thousand, or with three thousand times three thousand. The whole of Dalriada and their children's children unto the third and fourth generation and down through the years of time—this land should be truly Christian, a land that would flourish in the grace and benediction of God. Surely this was what God had planned, for did He not create this land with a special beauty, a special richness? It was only right that its people should then have the ultimate blessing of God in their hearts.

And not only Dalriada but the land beyond as well—Alba, the dark land of the Picti, who had no knowing of the truth, and Strathcluta beyond the Clyde, which long and long ago had known the hand of the Romans. A bright showing filled Columba's mind, a vision of a land of shining greenness, of rugged mountains piercing the blueness of the sky, a place of tumbling waterfalls and trout-filled rivers, a land of freedom and beauty at peace with its Creator.

The vision faded with the sound of pounding feet and sharply drawn breath.

"Father. Father Columba," Corban panted. He dropped a basket of holly leaves at Columba's feet. "Father, they have come again. They say they have won. The druids say you will leave."

4

Columba strode to the church and took the finely wrought silver cross from the altar. It was of delicate openwork, an interweaving of loops and knots all formed in a continuous line as a symbol that God's world was without end. Holding the cross aloft, he went forth to confront the druids.

The red-haired Aclu was backed, as before, by his two companions. Their false tonsures were grown in, to show the beginnings of druidical forelocks. But it was not these in their soiled white robes that took Columba's attention.

The leader this time was clearly a vibrant dark man in a multi-colored robe. The druid was as tall as Columba himself but more lightly built, with long thin bones, long fingers, and a long thin nose. His heavy black forelock fell over an olive-skinned forehead to yellowish, almond-shaped eyes that narrowed to long slits when he frowned. A torque of twisted silver encircled his neck, ending in two animal heads glaring at each other with bared teeth.

So did the druid bare his teeth at Columba. "I, Broichan, am archdruid of Brude, High King of Alba of the Picts. I come from his high seat at the royal dun of Craig Phadrig, bearing a message." The manner in which this was spoken told clearly, however, that Broichan was no mere messenger boy.

"I will hear the message of King Brude. But hear you me first, Broichan." Columba held the cross before him as he spoke. "In this land of Dalriada I bear allegiance to Conall, High King of the Scots. He has given me leave to teach the Word of God in this kingdom. But above all, I bear allegiance to Jesus Christ, High King of heaven and earth. And His Word will not be silenced."

"Ah, fine words, bravely spoken, prophet of foreign ways." The Pict spoke in a heavier, less lilting accent than the Scots, and some of his words were unfamiliar to Columba. "But hear you this and make no mistaking: the mighty Brude allows Conall his puny lands for that Brude has no need of them at present. But the Picti outnumber the

46

Scoti as the stars of the sky outnumber these isles. Brude can and shall make his will known when it pleases him."

"Then King Brude has no need to fear my work." Columba's voice was mild, with just the slightest hint of humor.

"Brude the mighty, Brude the powerful fears no one!" Now Broichan was shouting.

"In that case, I am sure he will be pleased to receive me. I would explain my mission to him."

"It shall not be. You shall not sully his ears with tales of your god. You will not weaken our people with foreign gods. Brude will not see you!" The yellow eyes glowed as live coals; the dark skin was suffused with red.

The other druids backed away from the force of Broichan's anger.

But Columba stood firm. "It is in my mind that we should let the High King make that decision for himself." Again holding out the cross, Columba advanced. "I shall go forward in the name of the Lord Jesus Christ, most holy, most mighty Lord of heaven and earth, in whom all dominion and power reside forever and ever, world without end."

Before he reached the end of his litany, the druids had fled.

Now Columba was besieged by the brothers, who had watched, open-mouthed, from a short distance away.

"Father, you do not mean to go into the enemy's country?"

"Surely you will be killed."

"No, no, Father Columba, do not go."

Columba held the cross over his own flock and looked each one in the eye. "It is not one druid we are fighting. We are fighting for the soul of this land. I go in two days' time. Who will go with me?"

The twelve monks looked at each other, consternation on their faces. A low murmuring went through the group.

"I will go! Take me, Father."

All turned to the voice at the back of the group. Corban stood at the full height of his small stature. Beside him, Righ wagged his tail.

Diormit shook his head and shrugged. "Let us go also that we may die with him."

Thus did all the brothers volunteer for the mission to King Brude of the Picti.

But Columba held up his hand. "I will take three."

"Three?"

"You will march into the jaw of the lion with only three companions?"

47

Columba smiled. "It is in my mind that such is the number Daniel had with him on a like occasion. If Brude chooses to slay us, he could kill twelve as easily as three. And three may travel more easily, leaving the rest to carry on the work here —and to send word back to Ireland should our mission fail. I will choose two of you. In addition, I will call at the court of King Conall and beg the assistance of one to serve as guide and interpreter. That will be sufficient."

Twelve tonsured heads bowed before their spiritual father in acceptance of his decree. That was as it should be, for was not obedience one of their vows? As Columba was obedient to Christ, they were obedient to him.

Columba considered. Which should he take? Diormit, his most faithful attendant, careful in all things? Virgno, or Cainnech, both skilled scribes who had begun labor in the scriptorium with such joy? Baithene the tenderhearted, who cared for the animals? Or Ernan, whose greatest service of love was to the tender shoots of crops growing on the machair? It seemed that they were all needed here.

Laisran, who ever reminded them of our Lord's earthly life as he plied his skills as a carpenter? Lugbe, skilled with boats? He looked on around the circle. The danger they spoke of was real. Who should be called on to prove his obedience unto death?

"Diormit, you have been ever faithful, the first of all I chose for my mission to the Scots. Come you now on our mission to the Picts."

Diormit stepped forward. "I will."

"It will be a long sailing, first to DunAdd, then northward to this mighty fastness of the Picti. We will have need of your boat skill, Brother Lugbe."

"It is yours, Father."

"So. That is good. Step you forward to receive my blessing."

But before they could obey, a small figure in a dark green tunic with a shock of silver hair falling in his eyes pushed his way to the front. "No, please, Father, I would go too! I can gather berries and catch fish for you to eat. I can help carry things, for my arm truly is stronger—"

"Corban, my stalwart friend, the danger is too great. And your father would not be permitting it."

"He has gone seal hunting on Tiree. I am in Merca's care. She will be glad of one mouth less to feed."

"Nevertheless, your enthusiasm must learn obedience."

Corban's blue brown eyes looked wet, but no tears fell. "You said I must not miss my arm-rubbings." It was obviously his final argument.

Columba smiled. "And so you shall not. Brother Baithene, I appoint you to the carrying on of all my duties while I am gone. See to this one as you would one of your sheep."

And so it was that on the morning of the third day Columba bade all those from the village who would acknowledge their belief to gather with the brotherhood on the shining white shore of the bay below the church, for he would not leave new babes in Christ unbaptized.

Corban stood between Merca and old Echu. His friend Ibar stood behind him, while Brother Baithene watched the sheep so that both herd boys could be away at once. And many others filled the beach behind, for large had been the response to Columba's teaching.

Columba had told them they were to come in clean clothes, although, if this was a washing ceremony, it struck Corban as wasted effort to do the washing beforehand as well. Nevertheless, Merca had scrubbed his least-tattered tunic and spread it on the rocks to dry yesterday. The trouble was, it had rained most of the day, so the undyed woolen garment hung damp and itchy on his back. He tried not to wriggle.

Echu was first to be led into the water by Columba to evidence the washing away of his sins and the new birth in his heart. Then the ceremony moved slowly through all those who had come to profess their faith in the God that Columba had brought to them.

Corban, as the youngest—in truth, he had just seen the coming of his twelfth summer—was the last. As he waited he tried not to be resentful of the man who had done so much for him and for all the people on his island. And yet, for as long as he could remember, he had dreamed of seeing the world beyond this small piece of land. And now those three were setting out on a journey beyond his imagining, a journey that he could be going on as well, had Columba but said the word.

He looked from the circle of the villagers' curraghs beached helter-skelter on the shore to the smooth waters of the sound beyond. He could sail as well as any. Almost as well, for he was adept at paddling with one hand. He could say he was going fishing and follow the brothers. Once they were beyond sight of Iona, they would not send him back. He considered. It could be done . . .

"Corban mac Garfinn, come you forward."

He stepped into the stinging cold water.

Columba took his hand and led him till he was waist deep. Three times Corban felt the water close over his head as Columba laid him back into it, then raised him, dripping, to a fresh touch of the sun.

> "In the name of the Father, who washes you clean
>   from sin,
> In the name of the Son, who is the Living Water,
> In the name of the Spirit, who moves upon all. . . ."

And as Corban stood, smiling and blinking, the brothers on the beach began a lilting, half-singing, half-chanting of the hymn they called St. Patrick's Breastplate:

> "I arise today
> Through the strength of Christ's birth with His
>   baptism,
> Through the strength of His crucifixion with His
>   burial,
> Through the strength of His resurrection with His
>   ascension.
> I arise today
> Through a mighty strength—the invocation of the
>   Trinity."

Columba led him to dry ground. "Go you now in His purpose and blessing, Corban mac Garfinn, in the strong name of the Trinity."

Corban hung his head, for his heart told him that lying and rebellion could have no place in his life now. He must abandon his bold plan to go on this longed-for journey. It might be that he would never leave these shores for more than a fishing trip or seal hunt. But if it were to be so, he must obey.

He raised his eyes to Columba.

"Corban, my friend, there is one thing more I would ask of you. Since the day my penance was laid on me by the high council of Tara, I have had no pillow but my Eirean stone. I would take it now, but it is not suiting a voyage in so light a vessel as a curragh. Corban, I would make you keeper of the stone. See to it that my hut is cared for and nothing happens to the stone while I am sleeping on rocks hewn from foreign soils."

"I will."

Then Corban turned with the others to the higher ground above the bay and watched while the brothers loaded their three sturdiest curraghs with sheepskins, food, water, and other supplies, for they were too few to sail the heavy wooden longship they had arrived in.

Then Columba, in a dry robe, placed in his boat his small, portable altar and a bag with the sacred elements for the saying of mass.

Corban could not let them go like this. Something of him must accompany Columba.

With a rushed, jerky gesture, Corban dug under his cloak still lying on the turf. He brought out his favorite pipe and thrust it at Brother Diormit. "Play you it for him, since I cannot."

Diormit blew into the lovingly carved white tube, his agile fingers moving up and down the scale. He had not played since he left Ireland, he said, but his fingers easily found the holes. He thrust the pipe under the rope belt holding his brown robe and nodded at Corban with a single flash of a smile.

Now Columba called for the attention of all and held out his arms to encompass the little flock. "The Lord watch between me and thee while we are absent one from another:

"God's blessing be on you,
Christ's blessing be on you,
Spirit's blessing be on you,
My blessing be on you."

And then he pushed out into the sound.

Corban watched as the three round dots bobbed southeastward. He stood still until they were out of sight. His heart was heavy, but it was not hard.

Those remaining on shore left to be about their work, but Corban, grateful for the dry cloak Merca put around his shoulders before returning to her hut, stared into the distance. Then he blinked. What? Were they coming back?

Had they changed their minds? Were they coming back for him? He knew the unlikelihood, and yet his heart leaped. He ran forward, waving, as the small vessels dipped and nodded in the choppy water and drew ever closer.

The boats were almost to shore when he froze. This was not Columba and the brothers but his father and the seal hunters.

"Carry you my seal, boy." Garfinn did not bother to greet him.

They were halfway down the path to their hut, Corban humping the heavy seal on his back and dragging its tail, his father carrying his hunting spear and holding bag, when Garfinn asked, "Why is your tunic wet?"

Corban turned to face him. "I went into the bay with Father Columba. He calls it baptism. It is a sign—"

The first blow knocked the seal from his grip. The second knocked him from the path.

51

"All the island knows I do not approve. You have made me a laughingstock. You will spend no more time with the foreign monks. You hear me?"

Corban hardly felt the third blow.

"Do you hear me?"

Corban nodded. Now his heart was hard.

5

It had been only a week, but Columba felt he had lost count of the days—lost track of all time and space and motion. There was only the rocking of the boat and the rhythm of his paddling. Conall had received him graciously, and in spite of his skepticism regarding a mission to King Brude—or any other undertaking having to do with the heathen Picts—he sent Hynish, his best guide and interpreter, with them.

It was unlikely they would need more than a few words translated here and there—mostly the names of places and unfamiliar objects— once they got used to the somewhat different inflections of Albannach speech. Indeed, the languages were very similar—only unalike in matters of custom and usage, with the differences that always grew up when people lived separate from one another.

But already Columba was glad of their new companion, for Hynish, with red gold hair that told of his Scoti father's people and swirling blue tattoos on his arms that told of his Picti mother's, had sailed near to every loch in the land, undertaking the life of a sometimes trader between the tribes and sometimes spy. Conall told Columba he might doubt the man's loyalties at times but never his ability to navigate or communicate. Columba was satisfied.

It now began to rain, as it had for four of the seven days of their journey. Columba pulled his cowl farther over his bare forehead and huddled deeper in his cloak.

Hynish told them they would paddle to the top of this water he called Loch Lochy, then they would camp for the night before carrying their curraghs overland to the next loch. Such was the process all the way to the top of the land, just as they had sailed the length of Loch Linnhe and portaged their boats overland to Loch Lochy the day before.

The lochs of this land were strange things to Columba. Long and straight, they bore more resemblance to wide rivers than to the rounder, pool-like loughs that he had so loved in his native land. But Hynish had assured them that tomorrow's loch would be the last, for

Loch Ness was the longest of all and would take them to their final walk to Brude's fortress.

The assurance that they approached the final phase of their journey was good news. The fact that they could find no dry ground to camp on was not. This was the month of high summer, and the heather was in bloom. The great hillsides of glowing purple fascinated Columba, and at night it was usually a good thing to raise one's tent over a cushiony patch of the low-growing plants, for topped with sheepskin they made an acceptable pallet.

But tonight Columba sought the firmness of a rock for his sleeping place. It would provide a footing the moisture would not seep through, and it would remind him of his stone pillow and all he had left behind on Iona. Waking in the night as he always did, he could pray the better for those he had ministered to on Iona and those he would minister to on Craig Phadrig—if he was allowed to.

And so it was that in the wee hours of the night Columba awoke with the weight of his call heavy on his chest—the burden of the souls of the people of this land who knew not the Lord God. And he conversed with God and reminded Him of the promise He had placed in his heart: *"All the land you tread upon I shall give you. As I was with Moses I shall be with you. Be strong and of good courage that you shall have good success wherever you shall go. Have not I, the Lord your God commanded you?"*

"Let it be so, Lord. I claim this land and the souls of its people for you."

This journey had brought a great new awakening to Columba's heart. Many months ago now it was that he had gone out from his homeland in blind obedience to the council and to what he believed to be the will of God. And from the first, in spite of his homesickness, he had been aware of God's anointing on this new work. He had been aware of God's presence with him and His promise for the future. And so both presence and promise had flowered in his love for the people of Iona and in the success of his work—although it was but a beginning.

Then, once more, he had left those he loved, a work he loved, a place of great beauty, and set out in obedience on a journey he dreaded but in no way could refuse. And again, as always, God was with him. As he had sailed the lochs and tramped the heather-covered land, he had seen people everywhere—women at their cook pots and grinding mills, children romping with sheep and dogs and tumbling around the doorways of their small huts, hunters with bows and arrows and spears, fishermen with nets, gatherers with their baskets, silversmiths at their delicate work, carvers of the great stone slabs that decorated their village places and marked their journey paths, defining the boundaries of their tribes and telling of the great feats of their people.

Columba knew that even for all the beauty of their surroundings and for the peace of their way of life, these were people who lived in darkness. They were people who spent their days doing and getting—consumed by the needs of the moment and fears of the future—with no vision of their own worth or of the God who wanted them to love and worship Him. Truly, without vision the people were perishing.

But Columba had vision—vision of this land populated by people who knew and loved and served the Lord. A country where the beauty of the people's minds and hearts were a match for the beauty of the land God had given them.

> "Father, be glorified,
> Christ, be glorified,
> Spirit, be glorified.
> Be glorified in this land.
> Glorify Your name."

And as he prayed, Columba was filled with a love for these people that he had not known was possible to feel for those not kindred-born. Even the feather and bone ornaments in the often-matted, long black hair; even the unwashed bodies under rough, animalskin clothing; even the heathen tattoos on their blue-painted skin—the higher the caste the more tattoos, it seemed—even such repugnant practices could not dim his love.

Their souls meant more to him than those he had left in his homeland. This land meant more to him. Suddenly a great wave of joy washed his heart. He realized God had indeed heard his prayers. Now he would not go back to Ireland even if the penance were lifted. This was truly his home until he should reach his truer, final, home of heaven. And he cried out to God for the souls of the people.

The next morning it seemed that God had heard Columba's cry and smiled on him. The sun shone golden on the purple heather, and the long blue waters of Loch Ness beckoned to them from between its green banks—smooth and welcoming on the right, steep and rocky to the left.

After the morning blessing, Columba said mass and served their small company that they might take unto themselves the grace of Christ through His body and blood. And then they were on their way.

It was late in the afternoon, after hours of pleasant sailing on the sun-sparkled blue waters of the loch and birds singing them on their way from the trees on the far bank, that Columba noticed a small group of people at the foot of the western slope. That side of the loch was a high—almost sheer—drop to the water with jagged black boulders sticking out from the green embankment and lying tumbled along the lapping edge. It was a strange place for people to gather.

At first Columba thought the sharp, sudden sound that rent the air was a gull, then he realized he was hearing the cry of a woman among the four or five people there. He paddled closer, and the agony of the woman sounded clearer. Then he could see the horror and pain on the faces of the others. He signaled Hynish to head for shore.

And then he saw the body.

It lay broken on a boulder at the water's edge. The loch lapped red at the jagged cuts on arm and leg. A garish line of red ran through the intricacies of the blue and brown tattoo covering the man's chest. This had been an important man to have been so adorned.

A mourner stood uphill of the group, a short, stocky man with black hair tied in a leather thong and his single tattoo, that of a fantastic animal, showing on his chest in the opening of his ocher cloak. He was the first to see the little group of curraghs approach. He barked a few guttural sounds that turned the attention of all toward the loch.

The other men drew back. The woman threw herself against the boulder where the body lay and clutched one lifeless, bloodied arm.

At a signal from Columba, Hynish called to them, "Have no fear. We are friends, come in peace. Run not from us."

The three men who had begun backing up the hill stood still. The woman did not look up.

Columba stepped from his little boat to the smoothest spot he could see amid the fallen rocks. "What has happened here?"

Hynish repeated his question.

The man who first saw them spoke.

Hynish listened carefully, nodding. "Monster?" He interrupted the man's narrative, then switched his query to Picti words.

The man spoke more and gestured toward Loch Ness.

At last Hynish nodded, made a brief reply in a reassuring tone of voice, and turned to Columba. "The monster they speak of is the chief druid. They seem to be hating him even more than they are fearing him, for they call him a name which roughly translates Monster of the Loch. Anyway, they say he is engaged in summoning all the spirits of the mountains and the lochs for a great battle at the Festival of Badb. Each spirit is summoned with a human sacrifice."

Columba shook his head in heavy sadness for the darkness these people endured. "That is monstrous indeed. So this man was sacrificed to the spirit of the loch?"

"No. He was Norr, headman of the fishing village across the loch." Hynish gestured toward a cluster of huts on the other side of the water. "The druid took his daughter, Rom-Aln. She is of great beauty, just come on her womanhood—such as the spirits most favor. She will be sacrificed with the others at the full of the moon in two nights. She will be slain by the silver sickle in the sacred grove on Craig Phadrig, her blood caught in a basin and returned to the loch so that the spirit will empower the archdruid."

"And this druid—his name?" Columba knew before he asked.

"Broichan."

Columba nodded. Was his coming the battle for which the druid prepared? Had his coming precipitated this loss of life—the loss of a life he had come to save?

"But how came her father to so violent a death?"

"Norr was away fishing up the loch when Broichan came. He returned just after they left with Rom-Aln. He leaped into his curragh to follow. He would try to dissuade Broichan—offer himself as sacrifice. At the least he would bid his daughter farewell. But Broichan would not be followed or questioned. No one was allowed speech with Rom-Aln. He ordered the two subdruids who accompanied him to attack Norr. These others had followed in their boats—they held back but observed it all."

The speaker for the Picts, his services not required at the moment, turned to the woman keening by the body. He attempted to raise her.

"She is Durno, wife of Norr, mother of Rom-Aln. She has lost husband and daughter in the same hour," Hynish explained.

"Tell her we go to King Brude. Tell her not all is lost. Her daughter is not sacrificed yet. We will try what may be done," Columba said.

But the relaying of the message caused wilder wailings yet.

The man spoke.

Hynish repeated. "He says do not go. You will be killed and worse. Beyond that, if you speak for Rom-Aln there will be retribution on the village. Broichan will not be opposed. His powers are great. The spirits serve him."

Columba stood silent for a moment, his thoughts punctuated by the rise and fall of the woman's wailing. "I would have more speech with these people. But not here. Can we not go back to the village where other women will help Durno prepare the body for burial?"

Hynish conversed with the villager, then turned again to Columba. "They wish to return, but it is so far to walk around the loch, and they fear sailing, for already the spirit has been roused. He has tasted Norr's blood. He will want more and more until he is appeased with Rom-Aln."

"Point out that we have sailed on the loch all day in the smoothest of journeying, that even now Lugbe and Diormit sit undisturbed in their curraghs."

After the exchange of a few rapid sentences punctuated with unfamiliar words, Hynish said, "Even if they were willing to sail across the loch, they could not, for Norr's curragh is gone, carried back to the other shore by the current, and their boats are too small for more than one."

Columba considered, then nodded with a smile. "It is time for a demonstration of the power of God over all demons of fear." He turned toward the water where the two brothers sat, rocking gently in their small curraghs. "Lugbe, you are the strongest swimmer amongst us—it must be you. Go you to the other shore and bring back that curragh you see caught in the reeds there."

Lugbe looked. "Certainly, Father. But why must I swim when I could be paddling in my nice, dry boat?"

"I am sorry for the inconvenience, my son, but these people need a strong showing of the power of God. It is our calling to defeat the kingdom of evil in all its forms."

Without further discussion, Lugbe stripped off his robe and dived into the water. He struck out for the opposite shore with the strong, sure strokes of one who had lived all his life by the water and swam before he walked.

A great, horrified cry rose from the Picts behind them.

"Tell them I will call on our God. Lugbe will be safe," Columba directed Hynish. Then he took footing on the largest boulder he could find at the loch's edge, spread his arms wide over the water, and prayed, "O mighty God and Creator of all, O You most high who made the great and wide sea wherein are things creeping innumerable, both small and great beasts, You who made even that great leviathan who plays in the sea, grant Your strength and protection to our brother Lugbe who goes forth in the confidence of Your power."

Columba paused to look. Lugbe was a third of the way across the loch. "O Christ, who made all things and without whom nothing was made, O You who breakest the head of leviathan in pieces and givest him to be meat to the people inhabiting the wilderness, these people to whom You have sent me cannot draw out leviathan with a hook nor his tongue with a cord. You only, O Christ, can command all of Your creation. So show Your power now."

Lugbe's head was only a dark spot in the blue waters when the woman Durno shrieked in alarm. She saw what Columba, focusing on the One to whom he prayed, had not seen until now.

The water behind Lugbe churned white. A sharp, black fin broke the blue surface, surrounded by foam.

"The spirit! The spirit will have blood!" Her keening rose, making Columba chill.

Had he been foolhardy to send Lugbe? Did an evil spirit indeed possess this loch? If so, all the more important it be confronted. And defeated. He prayed with renewed vigor, his words driving back Durno's shrieking.

"Holy Spirit, You who directed to be written in Your Word that 'in the day of the Lord He, with His sore and great and strong sword, shall punish leviathan the piercing serpent, even leviathan that crooked serpent, and He shall slay the dragon that is in the sea,' O Spirit of all might and power, defeat this monster of evil and bring forth Your good."

The waters churned in a great splashing. Columba could not see the battle. But he saw by faith the One who directed the outcome of all battles. "O Lord, God of might and power. Defeat this evil one."

When Columba opened his eyes, the waters were still. Lugbe was in the curragh, already paddling toward them.

An hour later, with the sun lowering gold and orange to the west, Columba and his companions sat by the fire in the center of the circled huts of the fisher village. In the hut behind them, the slightly larger home of the headman, Durno and the other women lamented softly as they prepared Norr for the journey to his ancestors. Columba, aided by Hynish, answered the men's questions about the God he served, who was so powerful He could defeat the monster of the loch.

"Our God rules all. It is His to do because He created all. I will tell you a story."

Heads nodded around the fire, and Columba saw on many faces the first smiles since he had come. He nodded to Diormit, who drew out Corban's pipe. Diormit played a simple tune that evoked the rise and fall of waters, the play of light on a blue surface, and silver fish swimming beneath.

59

"Jesus the Christ who was God and yet the Son of God, who was man and yet very God, lived on this earth long and long ago before even your grandfather's grandfathers knew this land. And Jesus Christ lived in a land far away, and yet not so very different from this land in that He lived much by the shores of a loch."

Columba paused for every man to form his own picture in his mind while Diormit played his peaceful, watery-sounding music.

"And Jesus the God-Man had many friends who were men like you. Indeed, it is in my mind that they were just like you, for many of them were fishermen."

The men around the fire looked at one another and nodded.

"And it is in my mind that His loch was much like your loch, for it could be a water of great beauty and great calm, giving up heavy netsful of silver fish."

Again the men nodded.

"And at other times it could be a water of great danger and great fury, for the winds would howl and the waves toss mightily, as if many monsters fought in the deep."

Heads nodded a third time.

"And one night Jesus got into a boat. Not a curragh but a long-boat built of wood, for many of His friends sailed with him. And Jesus was tired, for He had worked hard that day helping many people and telling them of the great Father God who loved them. So Jesus laid His head on His folded cloak in the back of the boat and went to sleep. And the sailing was long, and there arose a fierce storm in the loch."

Now the pipe, which had played music of soft waters and gentle sleep, rose in swirling, jagged sounds calling up images of howling winds and lashing waves. "And the waves rose, and the ship was covered with the waves. But Jesus slept."

The men looked at each other in amazement when Hynish translated this.

"But Jesus' friends did not sleep. They were afraid."

Faces broke in understanding smiles.

"So they came to Jesus in the boat and shook Him awake and cried to him, 'Lord, save us; we perish.'

"And rubbing his eyes, for He was heavy with sleep, Jesus looked at them. 'Why are you allowing such fear in your hearts?' He asked them. 'You are not having enough faith.'

"Then Jesus stood in the tossing boat and held up His arms." And Columba did just that, to aid the picturing in their minds and to recall their own seeing that day when God had calmed the winds of fear on Loch Ness. "'Peace! Be still!' Jesus the Christ called to the winds."

The pipe music rose in rebuke of the storm.

"And the wind was still. The waters calmed."

The pipe was silent.

The men of the village sat long around the fire that night talking of this mighty God whose power they had seen demonstrated on their own loch. They would, indeed, worship Him—if King Brude would permit.

The next morning Columba turned his face toward Craig Phadrig. By nightfall he would face King Brude and Archdruid Broichan.

6

"What do you know of this Broichan?" Columba asked Hynish as the boatman rhythmically dipped his paddle in the blue water, skimming them toward the top of the loch.

"He is a man of great power—next to the king the greatest in the land. His family has long held such power. But that is the heart of the matter, for it is said Broichan is not happy to be second power. He would be first."

"You mean Broichan wants to be king?"

Hynish shrugged. "Not now, perhaps. Not realistically, at least. What he can best hope for now is to control King Brude, I think. But I have heard tales around many a fireside—stories from old men who were mighty warriors when Brude's father was chosen king—chosen over Broichan's father."

"Was his right to rule as great?" Columba asked.

"Some say greater. Indeed, there was little doubt of the royal descent of either man. But it is the Albannach way that the royal woman has choice. Her husband becomes king and war leader. Queen Thara chose Brude's father, Maelchu."

"If the throne is not handed father to son, how did Brude become king?"

"Maelchu was killed in battle. Queen Thara did not desire another man, so she chose her son. But when it is time for a new king-choosing, the choice will be that of Brude's sister, Thetargus.

"That also is a bitter pill for Broichan. Brude's sister will become royal woman of Alba while his own sister—of whom it is said he was very fond—was made sacrifice."

Columba was so shocked he could not speak for a moment. "You mean Broichan's sister was sacrificed as he is preparing to sacrifice Rom-Aln?"

Hynish shrugged. "So it must be—for the gods are more fearsome than king or archdruid."

Columba started to remonstrate with his guide. It seemed this

62

man had not yet truly put the ways of his mother's people behind him.

But they were now at the top of Loch Ness, and they must hide their curraghs in heavy underbrush and continue on foot, and it was many miles yet to Brude's fortress.

All the way, Columba knew he should be calling out to God for aid and protection, for mighty armor for the contest he was to face— a contest he realized was even more deadly than he had supposed, now that he knew more of the people involved.

But even as disciplined as Columba's mind was, it would not be so contained on that day. For always he had loved beauty: the beauty of nature, the beauty of a richly illuminated book, the beauty of the touch of God on all life. And today his mind was filled with nothing but beauty. There was, indeed, the green and rugged beauty of the land they walked through, but that was not what most Columba saw. Always there was before him the vision of the shining land this Alba could become when the hearts of its people were turned to God. It was a place of natural beauty now. But with God as the King of its people, there was no greatness it could not reach.

For much of the afternoon they marched beneath tall firs with clumps of rust, gray, and brown toadstools growing at their feet and a carpet of fallen needles covering the path. At last they came to a river, and here the trees stopped. A smooth clearing lay beyond, and a high fortified hill rose at the back. Other hills rose around them, darkly green with their thick covering of pine. But Brude's stronghold stood apart, forbidding and impregnable in its isolation. Waiting, it seemed, for them.

Surely this was a place of large population, of hunters and animal herders, of farmers and fishers, of warriors and women and children. But none were visible. The smoke of fires rose from behind the heavy timbers of the oval palisade around the hilltop, indicating cooking and smithwork progressing, but no one was to be seen.

That also meant there was no one to hinder their progress. Whatever Broichan had planned to stop Columba, nothing was in evidence now, so he would proceed.

He led their small party up the steep, sharply winding path toward the sentry post. Was it only his imagination that made him feel that carefully scrutinizing eyes followed them? Had watchers signaled a silent message for warriors to wait in ambush? Was it watching eyes that raised the warm spots on the back of his neck?

Columba told himself it was merely the sun shining as warmly on him as on the heather and on the little brown birds that scrabbled in the bushes like bright-eyed field mice, then flitted away. But he could not escape the feeling that at any moment small, brown-skinned warriors could spring forward with bared knives and lances.

God's warning to Ezekiel came to him: *"Hard of face and obstinate of heart are they to whom I am sending you. But you shall say to them: Thus says the Lord God. And whether they heed or resist—for they are a rebellious house—they shall know that a prophet has been among them."*

The words brought comfort, and yet the prickling at the back of Columba's neck continued. The soft grasses beside the path, the broom, gorse, fern, and shamrocks growing between purple patches of heather, all gave just enough cover for Brude's men to hide and watch but not enough for an enemy to sneak up on the fort.

At the top of the hill Columba halted. The massive wooden gate, hung on heavy iron hinges, was closed. Closed and barred. There was no sign of a guard. It was late afternoon, several hours before the time to shut the gate against wild animals and enemies and enfold the people and cattle of the dun for the night. But if the fortress were closed against an impending attack, where were the guards?

"Hynish, call out," Columba directed.

A long, singsong request in the Pictish tongue rose to any who might be lurking on the other side of the heavily timbered wall.

The only reply was the song of birds in the pines.

Columba pushed on the gate. It did not respond even when he shoved with all his weight. The heavy planks resisted as if he were not there. He looked up to the top of the barrier, more than twice his own height. There could be no scaling it. He looked at their poor tools—walking staffs, knives for eating, a small hatchet for cutting firewood. A forced assault was unthinkable. And Columba had learned in Eire that the way of force was not to be his way.

"My sons, I will pray." But before even the first words could be spoken, with the closing of his eyes and the lifting of his head, the words came to him: *"Seek and you shall find, ask and it shall be given you, knock and it shall be opened unto you."*

"Brothers, knock on the door as Christ would knock on the hearts of these people. And let us pray that their hearts shall prove no harder than this gate."

Diormit knocked.

Nothing happened.

Lugbe knocked.

There was no reply.

Columba raised his staff to knock with it, then he had another idea. "Brother Diormit, play for us on your pipe that my knocking may not fall hollow."

The pipe trilled a gentle air, and Columba knocked. Almost immediately a dark mustachioed face appeared over the rail of the guard platform beside the gate.

"We have traveled from far. We would speak with King Brude. We claim hospitality," Hynish replied to the Pict's query.

"He wants to know if we have music for the feast," Hynish relayed to Columba.

"By all means. Music, song, stories—we'll provide all they want." Columba flung his arms wide.

It was a few minutes only until the sound of wood grating on wood reached them and the bar holding the gate was lifted, followed by the rasping screech of iron on iron as it swung open.

Columba stepped forward, then stopped so suddenly that he could feel Brother Diormit's breath on his neck.

Standing before them was a circle of dark-haired, olive-skinned warriors, naked to the waist save for wide silver bands circling necks and arms and thongs with bunches of bright feathers around their necks, accenting the blue of their animal tattoos.

The shortest of the group, the one who had spoken from the platform, came forward. A red-dyed leather skirt ended just at his knees; a sword hung at his waist in a silver-embellished scabbard.

Hynish held brief conversation with him, then explained. "He is Divach, chief guard. The gates are shut because this is the yearly tribute day of Gorsen, a subking of the Orkneys. It seems that many lesser kings of the area pay tribute to Brude. Brude considers it good policy to be giving them a fine show while they're here, so all the people of Craig Phadrig are assembled."

As they crossed the fortified enclosure behind the guard, Columba could well see why no one had been tilling the fields below the hill or practicing in the warrior field. All had apparently answered the call to King Brude's feast. The space between the mud-plastered buildings was filled with people wearing bright cloaks and tunics, their arms, necks, and hair adorned with intricately engraved silver ornaments. After only a few days in this country Columba had already developed great admiration for the delicate artistry of their engraving and carving skill, especially in silver, which the Picti seemed to prefer to gold for ornamentation.

"The coming of King Gorsen has fallen on the feast day of the god Badb, the victory giver," Hynish explained after a few sentences from Divach. "It is therefore a double feast we are bidden to. He seems to think we are a troupe of traveling bards. I haven't persuaded him otherwise."

Columba nodded. It would be his job to make explanations enough to King Brude.

The rectangular thatched hall was lined with elongated wooden tables set on stone supports. Long benches were filled with men and women as colorfully adorned as those Columba had seen outside. An ox carcass roasted over a central fire, from which slaves were cutting large chunks to serve on wooden trenchers.

But above all, it was the decoration of the hall that took Columba's attention, for once again, the Picts' love of skillfully executed pictures was evidenced on every flat surface. The heavy support timbers, the planked walls, the backs of the long benches, all were covered with elaborate, brightly painted carvings of animals, both recognizable and fantastic, of crescents, rods, and circles that perhaps told some story, all woven together with trailing vine scrolls inhabited by birds, fish, and more animals. The light from pine-knot torches danced on the rich colors and dazzled Columba's imagination, which ever sought for new motifs with which to illumine the manuscripts he so loved. True, many were pagan images, but the celebration of creation evidenced in the work and the skill of the designs could most certainly be applied to the glory of God.

Brude, a man perhaps in his mid-thirties, black hair, beard, and mustache oiled to a high gloss, sat at the front of the hall on a chair with arms and legs carved in the shapes of animals. A massive carved boar's head topped the high back of the seat.

Beside him, on a slightly smaller chair, sat a tall man whose flowing white-blond hair and mustache identified him as King Gorsen.

Brude listened to Divach's explanation of the presence of the newcomers, then dismissed the guard. He spoke to Columba in the same oddly accented Gaelic that Broichan had used. "Divach says you will pipe for our feast. That is good. A feast may never have too many pipers, as a forest can never have too many birds. But I think you have not traveled so far merely for thus?"

Columba considered. Should he postpone his answer, awaiting a more propitious moment? Or should he run straight at the thing?

Brude waited, a deep scowl creasing his forehead.

Again, God's word to Ezekiel came to Columba: *"Neither fear their words, nor be dismayed at their looks, but speak My words to them whether they heed or resist."*

Columba drew breath. "I have come from my kinsman King Conall of Dalriada, whom you know. I seek permission to tell your people of our God and to send others to live among your lands and teach."

66

And when he saw that Gorsen was listening as well, he added, "And to make known His ways in the Orkney kingdoms as well."

Brude shrugged. "We have many gods. We need no more. But perhaps one more will be no harm—as with birds in the forest and pipers at a feast."

Columba smiled at what appeared to be the king's favorite analogy.

Firelight danced on the broad, silver plates circling the king's neck and covering the front of his striped tunic. Each plate bore an expertly incised boar, echoing the boar's head finials of his silver torque. There was little doubt as to the identity of the sacred animal of the Picti.

The king shrugged once more. "Matters of the gods are for the druids. My archdruid Broichan prepares now for the Festival of Badb. He will hear of your god later. Join you the feast now, and let your piper play." With a vague wave to the far end of the hall, Brude turned back to the visiting kinglet.

Columba, Lugbe, and Hynish found seats at a table in a far corner. Diormit stood behind them and filled the area around them with the sound of bird calls to match the decorations on posts and benches.

Columba looked about the room. Many graceful dark-haired women, lavishly adorned with wrought-silver jewelry, passed along the tables filling drinking horns from long-necked pottery pitchers painted with colorful, complex patterns of intertwined beasts and flowers. But only one woman sat at the high table—Queen Thara, he was told. Brude's mother. Royal woman of the Picti. Her black hair was so heavily interlaced with slim silver bands that it was impossible to see the gray that must be plentiful on the head of a woman old enough to be the mother of this man. But Queen Thara sat erect, her olive skin gleaming in the firelight.

Columba was certain he had never encountered a more fiercely proud people. Could such ever be brought to see their need to kneel before the God of heaven?

Hynish's next words added little comfort to such a thought. "Brude maqq Maelchu is a mighty man," the guide explained between bites of roast ox, sheep, and fish. "He is the first ever to rule both the north and south Picti. It is a vast kingdom from Forth to Moray and much divided by rivers and mountains. Many client kings pay him tribute such as you see Gorsen do. If Brude will allow your preaching and the establishment of monasteries in his lands, you will have area enough to occupy you and your monks for nine lifetimes."

Columba nodded. He had been thinking much the same thing.

Then Hynish added, "But of course, if your request fails, if Brude refuses, the door-slamming will be doubled and redoubled beyond nine times ninety."

Again Columba nodded. He had thought of that also.

He also watched the deepening of the shadows outside the open door of the hall. He had not forgotten that Rom-Aln was to be sacrificed tonight to appease the spirit of Loch Ness. Surely that was the arrangement to which Brude said Broichan attended. The time drew short. And Columba had formed no plan for saving her. He had thought Broichan would be attending Brude. He had counted on speech with the druid before the ceremony. Now it seemed that such was not to be.

Columba turned to dip a handful of plump red and black berries from the bowl a slave offered him. But he was not allowed to finish their juicy sweetness before he felt a hand fall heavy on his shoulder.

There was no need to have Divach's tone and gestures translated. King Brude summoned him.

Columba was less than a third of the way up the crowded hall when he saw the reason for his summons. Broichan stood beside the king. He appeared taller and more gaunt than before, his wraithlike figure seeming to bend in the dance of torchlight surrounding the hall. His black forelock glistened as did the writhing figures engraved on his jewelry.

Brude scowled at Columba. "My archdruid tells me he has already had speech with you. He says that he has heard of your god and that our people have no need of him for he is but a feeble, minor deity." Brude's glare darkened. "Furthermore, Broichan tells me he has already instructed you not to come into my land."

"Fear neither them nor their words when they contradict and reject you," God had told Ezekiel. Columba nodded at the memory. "And I told him I would have speech with you that the decision could be of your making once you had heard of the power of the one true God I would proclaim unto you."

Brude raised his carved drinking horn to his lips, tipping it far upward so that the boar's head on the end seemed to look down on him. At length he lowered the vessel and wiped the heather ale from his lips with the back of his hand. He said something aside to King Gorsen.

The Orkney ruler laughed.

Brude folded his arms across his chest and leaned back in his ornate chair. "It is our custom to be entertained by tales after our feasting. Let you entertain us, Columba."

Columba glanced toward the dark doorway. Stars shone now in the blackness beyond. He could not have much time before the sacrifice. But he must do his best. He signaled Diormit.

A high-pitched trill focused all on the storyteller.

"Long and long ago our God had a holy man much like myself who would do challenge with the druids of false gods." He leveled a long look at Broichan.

"And Elijah was this man's name. And at Elijah's bidding, the druids of the false god Baal built an altar and placed a sacrifice on it. But Elijah said, 'Let you not strike flint or in anywise enkindle your fire. Ask your Baal to do that.' And so the druids of Baal called unto their god from morning until noontime, saying, 'O Baal, hear us. O Baal, hear us.'"

And the pipe fluted in tones of desperation.

"But there was no answer. And so the druids leaped upon the altar, and cut themselves with knives and lancets until the blood gushed out. But Baal was silent."

The silence of the pipe underscored the hush in the hall.

"Then Elijah built an altar of twelve stones and made a trench around it. And he placed wood for burning and bullock meat for sacrificing on the altar." Columba paused. "Then did Elijah give instructions that four barrels of water be poured on the sacrifice and on the wood."

A surprised murmur went through the hall, accompanied by a pipe tune singing of suspense.

"And a second time did Elijah so instruct."

The pipe accompanied the imagined pouring of the water.

"And a third time yet again. And the water ran around the altar and filled the trench."

Columba raised his arms as he prayed with Elijah, "'Let it be known this day that Thou art God, and that I am Thy servant, and that I have done all these things at Thy word.'"

Columba lowered his hands, and all waited.

"And the fire of the Lord fell and consumed the sacrifice and the wood and the stones and the dust and licked up the water that was in the trench."

Then Columba's voice rose above Diormit's pipe and Broichan's outcry. "And when all the people saw it, they fell on their faces, and they said, 'The Lord, He is the God. The Lord, He is the God. The Lord, He is the God.'"

And from the back of the room Lugbe joined the chant, and Hynish pounded the table before him in rhythm with the words he translated, "The Lord, He is the God. The Lord, He is the God . . ."

69

And around the hall many took up the table banging, but none repeated the words, for the king sat silent.

Then Columba silenced them with a sweep of his arm and turned directly to Broichan. "Such is the power of our God. But such is no longer His way. For God was not pleased with the sacrifices made by men, and He would have an end to them. So He sent His Son to earth to live as man and give Himself as sacrifice. And Jesus Christ was the last sacrifice that was to be made on earth."

Broichan gave a contemptuous snort.

Columba stepped closer to the sneering druid. "God has forbidden further sacrifice. He loves all people. His way is to live in their hearts and give them joy and beauty. Our God calls men to be living sacrifices by living their lives for Him."

Columba took one more stride forward. "Further, to make sacrifice of blood is to deny the sacrifice of Jesus Christ. This above all things God abhors—the rejection of the blood of His Son. He will punish any who do so." He held Broichan in his stare for the space of three heartbeats.

Then Brude rose. "So, Columba, you bring us fine stories. But they are only words." The king struck his breast with his fist, and his silver bands jangled. "They are powerful words. But they are words. We would have action."

Columba turned his back on the druid to face the king. His time to save Rom-Aln was short. "King Brude, you must stop Broichan's sacrifice. A sacrifice made to spirits can only be a sacrifice to the evil one. I tell you true—the devil is a being of power, but he is a second-rate power, a defeated power. King Brude should not serve a weak power as his druid would have him do."

King Brude's fist slammed down on the table, making the drinking horns bounce and the wooden bowls clatter. "There is no weakness about Brude maqq Maelchu. I will have only the greatest power. Show you the power of your god."

With a final sneer Broichan turned to lead the king and all those at the high table from the room.

Columba followed, his head up, his stride strong. He must show no faltering. But his mind raced. He had said all the words that God had given him. Now what was he to do? How did he show the power of love? These people understood only strength—the right of the mighty. What could he do that would not be interpreted as mere weakness?

And now Columba understood the problem more fully. This was not a simple matter of the druid's rejecting the true God in favor of false deities. This was Broichan's whole life structure. His life that was built on a bid for power—the power of the throne of Alba. To control the power if he couldn't be the power.

It was also a matter of validating the death of the sister Broichan cared much for. If he were now to reject the old ways, declare human sacrifice unneedful, he would be declaring his sister's death a needless waste. Instead, he would condemn more of his people to such.

Broichan led the way down the narrow pathway Columba had come up a few hours earlier to a field beyond the dun. Well before they arrived, Columba heard the beat of drums and the hollow thrumming of a tune played on bulls' horns. Then he saw the glow of a ring of fire.

Only when they were fully at the sacred spot did Columba see that a fire illuminated each monolith in a circle of age-weathered standing stones. The fires cast long, wavering shadows, making the entire circle appear to dance. Each stone was carved with a deeply incised symbol that he guessed represented the spirit that stone honored. And before each stone stood a bound victim—the sacrifices to the spirits.

As Columba surveyed the circle, certain of the intended offerings took his attention: a man grayed with age, his bared skin covered in swirling blue designs that proclaimed his importance; a muscular young man with a curving black mustache, silver armbands and neckbands accenting his warrior's tattoos; a woman whose pregnant belly proclaimed that the spirit to which she was forfeit would receive double.

By the stone nearest Columba stood a girl about Corban's age, black hair like a waterfall to her waist, her round dark eyes turned to him. It was the look of hollow despair that smote him.

Such was the condition of all without the Savior. This hopelessness, this going off into an unknown void for which there was no help. Such was all life without God in it.

"Rom-Aln?"

The widening of her eyes at her whispered name told Columba that, indeed, this was the one he had promised to rescue.

And he knew now what he must do, though it seemed the greatest folly possible. It spelled the end of all.

And yet he knew. This was his call. To deny it was to deny all.

He turned to Broichan. "Let this maiden go. I will be sacrifice for her."

Hynish's mouth fell open. He looked from Columba to Broichan in confusion.

"You heard rightly," Columba said. "Translate it so."

71

When the words were spoken there was a great gasp of indrawn breath from all assembled.

Broichan sneered. "You hold your life so cheaply? Is it that you know you fail and so will be slain anyway? You do not even ask for the release of them all, but only for this one small maiden?"

"You mistake much, Broichan. I do not hold my life cheaply. Life is the thing of greatest value on earth—it is that for which Jesus Christ died in order that my soul might dwell with Him in heaven. It is not that I know I fail. It is that I know I cannot fail. For it is not I, but Christ who lives in me.

"It is not that I sell cheaply but that I can ask no higher price. For although Christ's sacrifice atoned for all the world, had there been only one soul to save, had there been only mine—or yours, Broichan—Christ's sacrifice would have been the same for that one. So will I be sacrifice for one."

All around the circle was silent. It was as if the very standing stones themselves held breath. All looked at Broichan.

A faint smirk curled the druid's lip. "But of course. I had not thought it would be so easy. So do the gods deliver you to me by your own will." He turned to Brude. "You see what weakness this Christian way is?" Broichan signaled his subdruids to bind Columba's hands with leather thongs.

"There is no need of binding. I go freely." Columba stepped into the ring of standing stones.

Broichan slashed the thongs holding Rom-Aln and flung her from the circle.

Columba, eyes shining with a distant light, took his place before the carved slab.

"So it shall be. We begin." Broichan strode to the flat stone altar in the center of the ring and poured a heavily spiced oil over it. He grasped a silver sickle in his right hand and held it over his head, waving it in rhythm to a strange, mesmerizing chant.

The other druids joined in the intonation. They wove a strange, undulating pattern around the altar, and the shadows of the stones bent among them as if the stones danced as well.

Then the white-robed druids took packets from the altar and moved to the outside of the ring. Dancing and swaying sunwise around the circle, they threw strange-smelling powders on the fires. The flames sizzled and sent out showers of sparks, filling the night air with a sweet odor.

When all the fires had been fed, one of the assistants grasped a stone basin and followed behind the archdruid in a procession, this time inside the circle, as drums beat and horns sounded. The firelight flashed off the intricate carvings on the silver sickle of sacrifice.

The circle complete, Broichan stopped before Columba. The druid raised his sickle and began a new, more frenzied chant in a piercing voice. He whirled the sickle round and round in a slicing motion, coming ever closer and closer. Suddenly a shout commanded, "No!"

Together Diormit and Lugbe rushed into the circle and thrust themselves between Broichan and Columba. "No! Not Father Columba. We will stand in his place. Our people need him. The monster can have our blood."

Broichan, half drugged from his own ritual, looked confused. He staggered backward a step, his sickle faltering.

It was King Brude who stepped into the circle in full command. He had removed his tunic for the ceremony and his tattooed body shone in the firelight with the gloss of bear grease rubbed on his torso. The weirdly curving, interlaced animals on his arms and across his chest danced with the rippling of his muscles. The rich otterskins of his skirt and cape glowed as did his own flowing hair.

"There shall be no sacrifice."

Brude's black eyes blazed, commanding the attention of his druids and subjects. "I have seen the truth of it. Columba did the right thing. But it was his place to do such. It is the duty of the leader to die for his people. I was impressed but not moved. I would have done the same."

Now he turned slowly, regarding his warriors and subjects gathered in the shadows beyond the circle of stones. "But it is not the duty of the people to die for the leader. None of you would do so for me. Yet this man's people would do so for him. My people serve me out of fear. His people serve him out of love. There is a power here I do not understand. Let the prisoners go. There will be no more sacrifices until I learn further of this new god."

"No! The spirits have been promised a sacrifice!" Broichan brandished his sickle toward the moon, which was just approaching its apex where it would shine directly upon the circle of stones. "There must be shedding of blood before the moon wanes! The gods will be avenged. The spirits will not be mocked."

He leaped upon the altar, his arms raised to the moon. There he began a shrieking chant, his body writhing in rhythm to it, his feet stamping a harsh tempo, faster and faster, louder and louder. And just as the prophets of Baal who had leaped upon their own altar and cut themselves with their sacrificial instruments, so did Broichan cut himself.

Perhaps it was the oil he had spread there earlier, perhaps it was the frenzy of his own drugged vengeance, perhaps it was the spirits of his demon gods seeking retribution, but any who heard Broichan's agonized howl as he fell on the silver sickle knew this was no act of human reason. Broichan's soul had looked on the face of the pit to which it descended.

The druid lay as if dead, his blood streaking the altar on which he would have sacrificed his victims.

"Bear him to his hut. I will bind his wounds with herbs," Columba instructed Broichan's assistants.

But the archdruid revived at the touch of his men. "Do not let him touch me." Then he turned eyes glowing with yellow malevolence on Columba. "I will win yet. You will see. I will win."

7

Corban was on the hillside tending the sheep, just as he had been on that day at bud-bursting time when he had been the first to see Columba's boat arrive. And so was he the first now at barley harvest time. The little skin-covered boats skimmed the sound as fast as the gleam of the sun could follow them across the water, for each vessel had its small sail billowing before the west-blowing wind, and each occupant paddled with the glee of homecoming.

Corban's feet barely touched stones or turf as he raced toward them. But this time it was not a solitary welcome, for all from the monastery—save those farming on the far side of the island—and many from the village came running to greet their beloved Father who had returned safely from the kingdom of the Picts.

Corban would have been the first to the bay had not Merca stopped him as he sped by the open door of her hut.

"Corban, have you left the sheep?"

His smile disappeared in a gape. Not the stupid sheep again. It wasn't fair. Father Columba would want to see him almost as much as he wanted to see Columba. And he wouldn't be long. "I told Righ to stay." He made to move forward.

Merca shook her head. "We have our jobs, you and I. For I do not leave Dag."

Corban stopped. His little brother of whom he had always been fond in an offhand way now lay whimpering and sweat-soaked on a pallet of reeds in Merca's hut. So it had been for three days and nights now. Garfinn, as usual, was off on a hunt, this time for the red deer that lived on Jura. But he could have been of little help. For indeed, even the best herbs of Brother Baithene had not broken Dag's fever.

No, Merca could not leave Dag, and Corban could not leave the sheep. He turned back with dragging step.

So it was later, long after the crowd had left the beach—and Corban knew he had missed the excitement—that a shadow fell across his lap, and he looked up. "Father Columba! You have come."

"I have come. It is in my mind to give you a special hearing of the events of our mission."

Corban jumped to his feet. "Did the king see you? Did you defeat the druid? Did the king grant you leave to preach? Oh, tell me what happened!"

Columba laughed. "That I would do if my small friend would grant me the hearing."

"Was it good?" Then Corban grinned and was quiet.

"It was very good. We are granted freedom to teach and start monasteries in all of Pictland, and King Gorsen of the Orkneys guarantees the safety of any who would come with the Christian message to his isles. Now there is much and much to do. Brothers Lugbe and Diormit will sail to Eire, before the autumn storms make the passage difficult, to seek many more brothers who will come for the work.

"Iona will become a training center. Hynish, whose services King Conall lent us, will teach the Pictish dialect to those who will go to Alba. We must build guest houses and study rooms, for when those who come have gone out, others will come to learn for themselves and to take the Word to their homes. So will the Word of the Lord spread to all the islands and across the land."

"And Broichan. How did you defeat the evil one?"

Columba's strong jaw and piercing eyes took on the set look of a stone carving that would not be moved. He told his young friend of the events at the stone circle but silenced Corban when he would have clapped his hands. "Not so, rash one. Not so easily is evil defeated. The archdruid is much reduced in strength and status just now. So will his revenge be the harsher. Our adversary the devil goeth about like a roaring lion seeking whom he may devour. It is I he would devour. Always we must watch and pray."

Columba closed his eyes briefly while Corban sorted out which tumbling question he wanted to ask next.

But before he could form one, the sound of a silvery laugh made him turn. The sight was the most alarming he had ever seen. A girl near to his own age but barely a scrap of his size, with the blackest hair and eyes imaginable, stood on the hill beside him surveying the beauty of his island and laughing with a joy he had never known.

"This is Rom-Aln. We saved her from Broichan. It is the way of their people that when you save a life it is your own. I explained to her mother and the people of her village that such is not our way— that she is as free as any of God's creatures. But she said that if she was free to choose she would choose to follow us."

For a moment the monk looked embarrassed. "I think had we not all been holy men sworn and Hynish already supplied with a wife, one of us should have been obliged to marry her. As it stands now, perhaps Lugbe may return with holy sisters to start a nunnery here, and we can give her to it. For now it is enough that she stays with Ibar's family—his mother will keep her as one of her daughters while she learns our language and the Word of God. Then we shall see what God will be making of it all."

Corban tucked his crippled arm under his cloak as he regarded the girl with a frown. "She is noisy. She will be scaring the sheep." But his words carried little weight, for the girl's hand rested on the head of a young ewe.

The next day Corban was still frowning about Rom-Aln's bringing disruption to their lives. He sat on the back side of the high ridge that divided the island where he had taken the sheep for grazing that day. In the normal course of things this would not be his day, but Ibar had asked him for a trade-off, and Ibar was ever a friend to be granted a favor when one could.

And truth to tell, Corban had little else of importance to do. He had fetched fresh reeds for Dag's bed place and fresh water for Merca to wash his fevered body. Then she had sent Corban away so that he would not get underfoot.

If Ibar had not asked him to tend the sheep, Corban would most likely have gone to the monastery in spite of his father's forbidding friendship with Columba. It was a dangerous thing to disobey Garfinn, but Corban could not live forever without his friend. Besides, there was the matter of the stone.

Corban pulled his new-carved pipe from under his tunic and put it to his lips. But before he could take his first breath to blow, the air was filled with sweet melody. He blinked and held the pipe at arm's length. Still the melody continued. Now he recognized it as human. A girl with a high, light voice was singing.

Corban looked in the direction of the Spouting Cave. At this moment the tide was up, and the incoming waves flung white foam and silver spray high, high into the air with each inrush of water, only to fall back and a moment later crash forward again. It was a sight Corban never tired of watching.

And walking along the glistening white beach toward the rocky promontory of the cave must be the source of the melody that floated up to him. Fand, Ibar's sister, wearing a green tunic, the sun shining on her red gold hair, stooped to pick up a pretty pebble.

Corban raised his arm to wave and shout a greeting to his favorite of Ibar's three sisters. But he stopped when he saw the actual singer.

Rom-Aln, still singing, stepped from around a rock-sheltered curve to see the bauble Fand held out to her.

Corban frowned. Why did that one take him like sand in his shoe? Then his frown deepened as Ibar came running and laughing down the beach, a rope of dripping, black green seaweed in his hand. He held it toward Rom-Aln. She lowered her head to it, smelled, then pushed him away with a sputter and ran toward the rocks where the surf still spouted. Fand and Ibar chased after her.

Corban stuck his pipe back in his tunic in disgust. If he had known Ibar would be wasting his day so, he would not have agreed to shepherd for him.

With Righ's expert help Corban drove the sheep to the communal wattle-fenced fold as early as possible that evening. Sheep herding was silly, useless work anyway. Certainly an occasional dumb animal would wander off a steep hill, or catch his leg in a cleft rock, or get caught in the tide, and then he or Righ must rescue the creature, but this was no work for one nearly a man.

Perhaps in the old days when it was said she-bears from Mull would swim across the sound for their calving, or when perhaps there were poisonous snakes on Iona as Brother Baithene had told him there were in Eire before the coming of the blessed Patrick, then such constant guarding would have been necessary.

But now there were no wild beasts on Iona. And no matter how often one of the brothers would try to inspire him with stories of the shepherd boy David who grew to be a great king, Corban found no inspiration in the work. Perhaps soon Dag would be well and could be trained to take his place. Corban had tended sheep when he was his brother's age and younger.

But for now there was nothing for it. Garfinn had ordered him to sheep tend, so he must obey. Once again the dream of seeing far places filled his mind. Someday. With one of the brothers or without. With his father's permission or without, he would go. The brothers forever preached obedience, but that was a thing he had no liking for.

Nor would he obey his father's injunction against seeing Columba. He fastened the leather thong holding the wicker gate that enclosed the sheep and hurried down the path toward the outcropping of great white rocks at the southern tip of the island.

Now, with the sheep safely folded for the night and Righ standing guard, he was at last free. It was the usual hour when Merca would ladle the contents of her black iron stew pot into his wooden bowl and give him a fresh-baked oatcake, warning him as she always did not to burn his fingers. But tonight, as for the three past, Merca's

78

attention would be taken up with Dag, so Corban would not be missed.

At a gray green broom bush growing as tall as his head by the edge of the cliff, Corban knelt and rolled out the object he had worked long on—a round stone the size of a curled-up baby lamb, fashioned of white Ionian marble. Its fine green veining was polished to satiny smoothness, and a cross was incised on the top.

Corban ran his hand over its cool surface, then with a smile rolled it into the crook of his right arm. His smile was for the pleasure in what he was doing and also for the fact that he was able to help the maneuver somewhat with his left arm. Not much could he do but some, and it was a joy.

As he walked back up the path, the weight of the stone increased, for indeed it was a heavy object, but his heart was light, for this had been a labor of love for Father Columba.

The monk, however, was not in his cell, so Corban must carry the stone farther. But not too far. He knew where to seek the holy father. For always Columba loved to meditate atop Tor an Aba. Corban climbed the little hill.

Columba indeed sat on top, as still and silent as if he were sleeping, even though his eyes were open, gazing out over the sound where the long last glow of evening color rode the water.

Corban sat quietly until Columba returned from within himself. "I have something for you, Father—a sleeping stone for your head."

Columba ran his hand over the stone's smooth surface. "It is a beautiful thing, Corban. Made beautiful by your love. I shall cherish it for the gift it is. But I may not sleep on it for its very smoothness."

"But why, Father? Is it not a rock as fine as that from Ireland?"

Columba ruffled Corban's thick cockleshell-white hair. "That is the trouble of it—it is too fine. Too fine for doing penance for my sins."

"But surely you had a great triumph with King Brude and Broichan. Everyone talks of it. Surely now—"

"Now to the weight of my sins I must add an additional guard against pride. For that would be the worst sin of all—to take credit for the Lord's victory." Columba sighed. "I fear our Lord has sent warning to me already."

"What do you mean?" Corban sat on the stone that was too smooth to be a penance pillow.

"Brother Ernan, our chief crop tender, has brought me report of our fields so carefully tended on the machair. I fear I chose wrongly in laying out that land for our crops. It was smooth and green, fine-looking land. The seaweed for fertilizer grew on that side

79

of the island. Yet I chose in rashness and followed human wisdom without seeking our Lord's guidance in the matter. Now I fear the whole community must pay the price for my folly."

"But I do not understand. The fields are green, the plants grow. I have seen."

"Yes, the stalks and leaves grow, but they make no corn. It is too cold and wet, too battered by the winds on that side of the island, exposed to the great ocean. The turnips rot. The oats and barley will not make maturity before the end of the growing season. And if Brother Lugbe is successful in bringing more workers to us before winter, the harm will have been doubled. I fear there will be many empty bellies for which I shall bear blame. I have sworn to abandon my sheepskin pallet and sleep on a stone mattress as well as pillow. So may my sin of rashness be forgiven. But the harm will remain—as is always the way of it when we step out of the will of God."

Corban's protest was stopped by an angry voice calling his name.

"Father has returned from the deer hunt." Corban's voice was tight. He more slid than ran down the hill. He would have fallen at the bottom had not Garfinn grabbed him with a strong grip on his shoulders.

"Is this the way you are obeying me?" Garfinn shook him but more for emphasis than for the head-rattling punishment the boy had often known. "I told you no son of mine is to go to Columba. I return home and find Dag ill and you where I have forbidden."

At the mention of his brother's name all other thoughts left Corban. "Dag—is he—

"Merca says he is unchanged, that he has remained thus since shortly after I left."

"I am sorry, Garfinn." Columba spoke from his hillock perch. "I did not know. I will pray for your son."

Garfinn shook his fist toward the top of the tor. "Leave him alone, Columba! Leave all my family alone." He strode off, pulling Corban after him.

That night Corban sat by the pallet of his small brother. In the dim light of the banked fire he bathed Dag's pale skin with a sponge dipped in heather water and placed a few drops of dandelion and honey elixir on his tongue.

"Thank you, Cor." Dag gave him a small, sweet smile.

Corban tried to smile back but felt choked. Dag, who had known little but sickness for all of his seven years, was ever so gentle and uncomplaining. But Corban did not feel uncomplaining. Why did

God, who—the brothers said—could even raise the dead, not make Dag better? Why must this little one suffer so?

He tossed a handful of vervain leaves on the peat embers, filling the hut with their astringent aroma. Dag's labored breathing seemed eased.

Corban closed his eyes. He would not sleep, just rest his heavy eyelids for a moment. The smoke swirled upward toward the roof hole, and the round walls glowed with an unusual bright goldenness from the fire.

And Corban saw it all again, as he had in innumerable dreams both waking and sleeping since that night when he had wakened to the sound of his infant brother's sharp cry. Now Dag's hoarse breath rasped in his ears. Yet it seemed not Dag that breathed so, but rather their mother. The beautiful golden-haired Anu, who had lain for two days with the breathing sickness and now struggled for the slightest gasp of air that could sustain her life.

Even in his half-sleeping state, Corban put his hands over his ears to shut out the horror of the sound. And then Anu began choking.

That was when it happened. Garfinn had sprung across the fire and began beating her on the back. Now Corban shifted his hands from his ears to his eyes, but the images would not go away. When his mother was so sick, Garfinn hit her and hit her.

Then her breathing stopped. But still Garfinn would give her no peace. He shook her . . . slapped her . . .

A rasping breath jerked him awake. It was not his mother's breathing he heard, but his brother's.

As if replaying the dream, Corban saw his father pull Dag from his pallet. The child hung in Garfinn's arms like a wet cloak drawn from the water with no body in it.

And Garfinn shook him and hit him on the back. "Breathe, you! Breathe!"

Corban sprang at his father. "No!" He grabbed his father's hand. "You killed our mother so—you will not kill Dag!"

And again, just as in that nightmare more than six years ago, Garfinn flung him away.

Only this time Corban did not land in a crumpled heap with his arm twisted under him. This time Corban landed on his feet, and he darted out the door. He didn't care what Garfinn forbade or threatened. He must get Columba. He must keep his father from killing Dag as he had killed their mother.

He ran down the path toward the monastery.

But it was not the large, comforting figure of the monk that Corban encountered on the narrow track. Instead he ran full bore into the diminutive Rom-Aln.

"I could not sleep. I heard cries. What is it?" the girl asked in her halting, heavily accented cross of their two languages.

"My brother!" Corban pointed toward their hut. "He chokes." And he ran on to the monastery.

Although darkness had fallen on the island, Columba was still on the tor. He appeared almost before Corban's first call of his name. "My friend, you have been forbidden. 'Children obey your parents.' It is written."

"I'm not caring. I won't obey him. I won't. He killed my mother. He's killing Dag. I hate him!"

Columba kilted his robe above his knees that he might stride the faster.

Corban ran ahead. But he did not reach his hut before he met Rom-Aln coming out. "Dag?" Corban sobbed, out of breath.

"Your brother breathes. He will mend now. My little brother was once so. I know the way of it." Her hand was so light and gentle on Corban's arm that she was gone into the night before he was aware of its warmth.

He turned as Columba joined him. "You heard? She said Dag will be well."

Columba nodded, but he did not smile. "Yes, I heard. That is good. It is much to praise the good God for. But my friend, I am fearing more for you."

"For me?"

"Yes, for the hatred in your heart. For love and hatred cannot abide together—one must squeeze out the other. Let your love for God squeeze out the hatred for your father before it is the other way around and the hatred takes control."

Corban shook his head. "Love my father? I cannot."

"You speak truth. You cannot. But you can make room for God to love him. And you can forgive him."

"Forgive him? Forgive him for killing my mother? For almost killing my brother? For crippling me?"

Columba shook his head. "I do not know the way of it, but that is not what is concerning me most. The fear in my heart is for what he is doing to you now."

"To my arm, you mean? The beatings?"

"No. The harshness to your body is a bad thing indeed. But the hardness you allow to your soul is a far worse thing. You must forgive, Corban."

"I cannot."

"Again you speak truth. You cannot. But let me ask you this—are you willing that God should forgive him?"

Corban was silent for a long time. A slash of orange light fell across the path from the half-open door flap of their hut. Corban bowed his head and muttered. "I suppose so."

Columba gave a single nod. "That is a start. Let us go to him."

Corban held back. "He will be angry."

"Perhaps so, but we must not hide. You are needing to learn obedience, Corban—I told you that once already, and still it is true. Hiding your disobedience is not the path to obedience, any more than hiding your arm is a path to healing. Come."

Corban turned and with reluctant step led the way into the hut. He stopped with a gasp. On the far side of the fire sat Garfinn with the sleeping Dag on his lap. The look of tenderness on his usually harsh face made Corban blink. Was it possible that his father cared for Dag? Truly cared?

The startling idea drew forth a gentle approach from Corban. "Father, I disobeyed. I feared for Dag. I ran to Columba. I-I-I must ask you to forgive." They were the hardest words Corban had ever spoken. And they were barely audible.

Yet Garfinn showed that he heard. "You sent Rom-Aln. It is good. She pulled the ball of choking from Dag's throat. It was like your mother. If I had known what to do—if I had had Rom-Aln's skill—perhaps . . . But all I knew to do was to try to shake it from her."

"You mean you were trying to *save* her? But when I woke in the night and saw you hitting her—I thought—"

Garfinn nodded slowly. "Yes. And then I pushed you too hard, and you were hurt too, but I could not come to you, for the gods took Anu from me." He paused for the space of several heartbeats, and he looked up with hollow eyes and sunken cheeks. "And I cared for nothing. I should have done better for my cubbling sons. But I cared only for the hardness I felt. If I could feel the hardness, I did not feel the pain of her loss.

"But then Dag, who had never been strong, had the breathing sickness just like her, and all the pain returned." The distant look in his eyes cleared somewhat, and he regarded Corban. "My son, I pushed you again. Are you—"

"I am fine, Father. See?" And Corban raised his arm almost halfway to his head. "Father Columba has made it better. He prayed —as he prayed for Dag to be well."

Garfinn shook his head. "I do not know. I have hated all the gods. I have blamed them all for Anu's death. But now I am wondering. Can it be that Columba's god is different?"

Columba came then into the small circle of light around the fire. "Our God is not a different god. He is the only God."

"What does he want of me?" Garfinn clutched his sleeping child closer as if in fear that this god would require a life.

"He wants to love you. And He wants your love in return. He wants to forgive you."

Garfinn's brow wrinkled, and his eyes darkened. "I want no forgiveness." The hardness returned to his voice. "I do not need it."

Columba shook his head. "We all need forgiveness."

Garfinn made a scoffing noise. "You talk! What do you know?"

"I most of all. I am the chief of sinners. I caused the death of thousands."

"And have you been forgiven?"

"I have. Though I carry the weight of regret for my misdeed. So must you, Garfinn, ask God's forgiveness for your sins. And so will you yet regret—perhaps even the sharper when it is contrasted with His love. But He will give you strength to bear both the regret and the love. For both can be heavy."

It was silent in the hut. And then Corban saw a thing he had thought never to see. His father's eyes were wet.

"Anu was the best of women. I never meant to hurt her. I thought to help. But truth to tell, I had overmuch of the barley beer. I meant to help, but you are right, my son, I did wrong. Her life is on my hands. And you, Corban my son. I meant you no harm. It was the fierceness of the barley beer. And yet it was my action. Forgive me."

Corban moved around the fire to sit by his father's side. Wordlessly he reached out to him as far as he could with his left arm. And it was not until much later that he realized that the arm had fully encircled Garfinn's shoulder.

8

It was the coming of the trader a few days later that first gave rise to the idea—two ideas, really. This time Corban, entertaining Dag with a game of branduth in a sheltered, sunny corner of the high earth-and-stone vallum that enclosed the monastery, was not the first to see. But neither was he the last, for when Fand and Rom-Aln came running to tell the monks of the arrival of a wooden boat with a green and yellow sail, he bundled Dag onto his back and outran all from the enclosure.

Already a tall man with a mustache even more golden than his flowing hair and wearing a fine nut-brown cloak with a large, enameled ring brooch was approaching the cluster of huts, carrying a heavy wicker kist by its two bronze handles.

This was the first trader to come to Iona in all of Corban's days—until the coming of the brothers, their community had been too small to bother with. It was a distinction of great honor to be so visited by one from far shores.

Telieu introduced himself and bade all gather around to see his wares.

Corban left Dag with Righ on a patch of soft grass and drew closer. The women stared with amazement and longing at the man's assortment of fine clay pottery, much of it bright glazed red adorned with black swirls. Merca ran her work-roughened fingertips over the rim of one such bowl, and Corban knew she was thinking of the wooden bowls and trenchers all on the island used.

The men, however, were far more interested in the iron spear tips, axes, and hunting knives—especially those with finely carved handles of bone or engraved bronze.

Columba and several brothers came from the monastery to inquire the price of wine from a place the trader called Gaul and to ask if he carried among his wares a certain mollusk for the making of purple ink—or gold that could be beaten into fine leaves for the beautifying of their manuscripts.

It was while the trader was busy with the brothers and several of the men had slipped away to check their store of sealskins for barter that Corban noticed Rom-Aln fingering a comb. It was finely carved of bone with a high, ornate back in an openwork design of circles and curves. As one with some experience in carving, Corban could only admire the skill that had made that comb. He could imagine Rom-Aln sitting on the white cockleshell beach, the sun shining on her glossy black hair while she sang to herself and combed her hair with just such a thing of beauty.

Rom-Aln cupped it in her hand as if it were a baby bird she would protect. It should be hers, Corban decided. There was a rightness about it. He was thrilled with his inspiration. He would buy it for her.

But how? What did he have of value to trade? What did he have at all? Until this moment he had never thought it important to own anything. The only things he owned were his clothes and the pipe he had made himself.

Then he knew. That was it. This pipe was special. He had worked on it all summer, carefully crafting it so that it appeared that the sound of the music came from the open beak of a bird. He pulled the pipe from his tunic, slipped the leather thong over his head, and approached Telieu.

"And what is it you would have me be doing with this, my friend?" Telieu regarded the carved tube Corban held out.

As answer Corban raised it to his lips and blew a trill.

"Ah, very pretty. Very pretty indeed!" Telieu slapped him on the back. "Unfortunately I lack the skill."

"But take it for trading to one who has the skill. In exchange for the comb." He pointed to where Rom-Aln stood, still caressing the pretty object.

Telieu hesitated. "The comb is of Pictish workmanship. It is of good value."

"Too much value for such as this, surely." Ibar approached the circle with a swagger and dismissed Corban's pipe with a wave of his hand. "I'll give you this for the comb and two bowls." He placed an iridescent round pearl in Telieu's palm. "I found it just two days ago in Loch Staoineig"—he referred to Iona's single loch. "I'm thinking you'll not see a finer in many days."

Corban gritted his teeth. "You left the sheep," he accused, but Ibar ignored him.

Corban had heard Ibar bragging of his good fortune of late. Finding such a pearl was fortunate indeed.

Telieu struck a bargain.

Corban stuck his pipe back in his tunic and turned away, but not before he saw Ibar making a present of the comb to Rom-Aln. Although it was no longer so twisted and awkward, Corban hid his arm under the shelter of his cloak.

He was well past the outer circle of bystanders when Columba caught up with him. "My friend, it is as well you weren't trading your pipe, for your playing will give much pleasure to us tonight, if you will."

Corban stopped his pebble kicking and looked at Columba.

"We will offer hospitality to our visitor. We would have you and your bird pipe to be joining us."

Corban gave a half grin and nodded, then turned back to collect Dag, whom he had forgotten and now must be taken home for a rest as his strength was far from full yet.

There had never been greater attendance at evening prayers on Iona than there was a few hours later. And although Columba acknowledged that he knew it to be owing more to the presence of the newcomer than to a sudden increase of devotion, he welcomed all with gladness. And then the brothers chanted the response to his prayer:

"May the Light of lights come to our hearts tonight;
May the Lord's peace come to our hearts tonight;
May the Spirit's wisdom come to our hearts tonight.
Be the love of the Son ours this night.
Be the love of the Father ours this night.
Be the love of the Spirit ours this night.
And onward for each morning and evening of our lives."

Seal oil lamps lit the long room of the refectory, and a fire burned on an open hearth at one end. Columba sat on a stool at the head of the table, Telieu on his right, honored guests from the village on his left, old Echu first and then Garfinn, newest friend of the brothers.

The company ate roasted meats, flat wheaten bread, and small tart apples brought from Jura on Garfinn's last fishing trip, while Corban sat on a low stool behind Columba and played light, birdlike tunes. But when the talk turned to places beyond the islands, Corban's interest became so rapt he could play no more.

"Oh, aye, I've sailed most all the waters of this land. But to my thinking there's none finer than the Clyde. To my mind there's no water better sailing or brighter shining than that great, wide estuary taken at full tide—and then on upwards, past the green banks of the river and the vast crags of the Rock of the Clyde where King Rodercus rules from DunBarton . . ."

Never had Corban's imagination been more alight, never had the longing to journey and see such sights for himself burned brighter. But for all his yearning he forced his pipe back to his lips. No matter how he longed to travel abroad, he had a job to do here.

Then Telieu began talking of the holy Mungo, who did a great work over all their land from his monastery at Glasgu. And Corban was drawn once more into the tale, for traders were as good as bards—often as welcome and more so for their tales as for the goods they brought. And a wise trader knew this and made the most of it.

"And Tannoc, daughter of the royal house of Gododdin was a gentle girl and innocent but set upon and deceived in her innocence by a member of the king's household. And she was beautiful to behold with white skin and golden hair. But when her father, the king, found her to be with child and unwed, he invoked the harshest of their laws and had her set in a cart and cast from his dun atop Traprain Law.

"But God's hand was on Tannoc, and the angels guarded over her with gentlest of wings, and she landed at the bottom of the mountain bruised and shaken but unbroken. And the babe was safe within her. And with the guidance of the angels, Tannoc found in her way a curragh by the waters of the Forth. Small it was but watertight and sound, and the princess of the Gododdin curled in sleepfulness in the boat with her head on her cloak. And the angels gave her cover of their wings and guided her little vessel down the waters of the Forth.

"And when the sun was breaking in the morning and the birds singing the world golden—" Telieu paused for a trill from Corban's bird pipe "—the little boat washed ashore, and Princess Tannoc opened her eyes that were blue and gentle and looked into the face of the blessed Servanus, who, like the daughter of Pharaoh, had come to the water to wash and fetched forth the woven vessel.

"And when the babe was born, the sainted Servanus christened him Kentigern, which is meaning 'the worthy lord.' It was a good name, and Kentigern bore it worthily for the many years of his growing up. It was when he came to manhood and began his blessed work, turning all in Strathclyde and Lothian back to the ways of the Christ from which they had strayed—having first received the preaching of the Word from the sainted Ninian in the time of the Romans—then the people of Glasgu did name Kentigern 'Mungo, the beloved,' for they do love him so. And so his work flourishes on the banks of the Clyde on the very spot where Ninian once preached."

At length all was silent in the brother's refectory.

And Corban felt that his heart would break for the swelling of the longing within it. And so it might have but that he raised his pipe to his lips once more and put into his song all the longing he felt in his heart to sail those blue waters, to look on those distant green banks and rugged crags, to visit the beloved Mungo. It was a tune of great beauty and great sadness.

And the longing spoke to Columba's heart. And the bud of an idea was born. For he was feeling much the same as Corban. For so can the heart of a youth and the heart of an aged man know the same longings. And something else Columba's heart knew. In all the land of the Scots and the Picts to whom he had come there was none to be his counselor, his confessor, his guide on the journey to the kingdom of God. But now, in this neighboring land of the northern Britons that the sainted Ninian long and long ago had claimed for Christ, even before blessed Patrick had carried the word to Ireland, now there was this Mungo.

The thought made his heart swell with the plaintive tone of Corban's pipes. Not since he had left Eire and the beloved counsel of his dear Cruithnechan, the holy guide who had opened to him the ways of the Lord and set his foot on the sacred pathway, had Columba known the joy of a spiritual counselor, for always it was his place to give counsel and to lead. And the idea flowered.

"I shall go to this Mungo." He spoke from the fullness of his heart, before giving thought to his words. In the silence of the hall— for his words had silenced Corban's pipes as well as the conversations around the table—he thought the better. What had he done?

Already the monastery was short of food. Lugbe and Diormit might yet return with new recruits from Ireland before the winter storms arose in the western sea. He had recently returned from a journey, and there was much he longed to do here, especially in the scriptorium. Yet the desire burned.

"Father Columba, that is wonderful!" The quiet Cainnech, who labored ever over the copybooks, was the first to speak. "May it be that I could go too? I have heard of this Mungo. It is said he has visited the blessed David in Wales and made many journeys even to his holiness in Rome. Surely such a one must possess many books. Perhaps even it is not too much to hope he might make us the loaning of one to be copied."

Columba smiled. Cainnech knew his weakest point.

But before he could answer, Laisran of the wood skills spoke. "Father, I would go too. You would be much missing Lugbe's gift of knowing the way of boats. My ability is small indeed, but it is for your using."

And then Ernan and Virgno added their voices.

"Brother Baithene, what have you to say to this?" Columba turned to his assistant.

"I say that you must go, Father. If Diormit and the new ones return, they may better make use of your cells while building their own. And forgive me, Father, when my mind should be on spiritual considerations, but our poor stores would then stretch the farther."

Columba nodded. Such practical advice was indeed what he needed. And then, to his surprise, Echu spoke, his eyes shining bright as if seeing a far shore. "Once in my youth I sailed south past Jura and Islay and around the Mull of Kintyre. It is a fine journeying for those of young bones. Never did I go such a distance as this far traveler speaks of, but I would do so were I a young man. I am thinking, Father Columba, that there are those from our village who would join your journeying."

But it was Garfinn who spoke most to the purpose of Columba's concerns. "Is it food you're needing, Father? You have done much for my family. Happy I would be to make repayment with fish and seal meat. Your oatcakes, indeed, might be in need of pounding thinner unless we can trade with the crop growers of Mull or Coll, but of fish and seal there should be no shortage."

Then Columba felt a tug at the sleeve of his robe. Corban stood there, his blue brown eyes shining round, his cheeks pink. He opened his mouth to speak, but the words stuck in his throat.

"Yes, my small friend," Columba said. "I think it is time. If your father will permit."

Columba turned to Garfinn. "And may your son accompany us? Brother Diormit, who is still in Ireland, is our only other with pipe skill, and we have seen how helpful it can be to have a piper on a journey."

Garfinn placed a hand on Corban's shoulder. "He may go."

"Take you good care of Dag, Father. He can be tending the sheep soon. He *likes* the silly creatures."

And father and son smiled at each other.

And so Columba appointed Baithene to take charge once more in his absence. He knew well that the community was in good hands with Baithene's care, but Columcille had one concern that never quite left him.

Broichan. What if the archdruid chose to wreak his threatened vengeance while Columba was away? What might he do to the brothers who stayed behind and to the gentle islanders who had taken the Lord Jesus to their hearts?

"Watch you carefully, Baithene. My prayers will be ever with you. The evil one does not surrender so easily. The archdruid has been defeated and humiliated before the king he sought to dominate. The personal power he cares more about than the gods he worships has been undermined. Nothing will stop his pursuit of revenge."

This time they would not journey in curraghs but with a large party in the wooden longboat in which they had first come to this land. Besides Corban, enough villagers would go to fill the seats of the boat.

And when more desired to go on the pilgrimage than even Columba's vessel could hold, Telieu offered to take many aboard his, for he had had good trading among all the western isles and was ready to set sail homeward to Glasgu. And glad Columba was for Telieu's striped sail to lead the way.

As he had warned, it was indeed a long sailing, but one of great beauty, as Telieu had said. It was on the tenth day of sailing—the whole time blessed with fair winds and little rain—that they sailed beneath King Rodercus's great fortress-topped crag of DunBarton and up the waters of Telieu's Clyde.

Then it was that the first worry struck Columba. He had been so anxious to meet Mungo that he had given no thought to what the coming of so large a number might mean even to such a well-established monastery as Mungo's apparently was. In spite of his own impatience to meet the holy father, he knew it must be put off for one more night.

Columba went to the front of his vessel and waved the red flag, which meant that he would have speech with Telieu. In a few minutes the boats were rocking gently by the northern bank of the river, and Columba explained his concern.

"Sa," Telieu said. "The holy brothers are well-known for their hospitality, but we indeed are making a large number. Ahead is a protected area where we may dock for the night. I will go to Father Mungo with word of your coming if you are wishing."

And the preparation time was good, for Columba and all his party were much in need of washing and praying, and although they had made port each day for the saying of mass and for resting, they were very weary.

Columba called Corban to him and asked him to play a restful pipe tune. When the melody was ended, he asked the boy, "So, what think you now of traveling the world?"

Corban grinned. "Oh, it's fine, indeed. But the world is a very big place, is it not? I had not quite understood that God had made it so large."

"And would you see more of it, my young friend?"

Corban considered. "I would be glad of the seeing. But always I would return home after. It is in my mind that Iona is none so bad a place."

Columba nodded. He had been thinking much the same thing. He knew that the work that was yet to be done for this land would require much journeying. But always he would be glad of returning to Iona. And he hoped that this time he might return with a lighter heart to apply to his work.

Besides his concerns for the evil Broichan might attempt, he hoped that his meeting with the beloved Mungo would somehow untie the knot of sadness, lighten the weight of the stone that he carried within him. At first he had thought it the longing for his homeland. And sometimes he wasn't certain whether the longing was for his native Ireland or his truer homeland, heaven.

These two journeys had taught him that in finding Iona he had found his earthly home. And yet the weight of his sin remained. And it seemed that no amount of sleeping on a stone pillow could remove the stone inside him. For did not the Holy Scripture say that it was better to have a millstone tied around the neck and be flung into the sea rather than to offend one of God's creatures? And he had offended so many.

But in the morning it was not a matter of millstones and sins to be thinking of but rather of rejoicing and praising God. For Telieu returned with a wide-armed welcome from Mungo. "Already he assembles his brothers. They all come to greet you by the river. I will show you the way."

Columba put his best white stole around his neck and took up his staff with the silver cross on top and signaled the rest of his party to follow him, brothers first, then villagers. They walked under trees of sunburst gold and bright rust, and squirrels scurried along the branches overhead as birds sang them on their way and brown leaves crunched underfoot.

At a little stream tumbling toward the Clyde, Columba stopped, for he heard Mungo's party approaching. It was the sound of a chanted psalm that reached him first:

"Praise, glory, and honor be to the Lord most high.
 Evening, and morning and at noon will I pray
   and glorify Him. . . ."

At first the brothers' brown robes just seemed a part of the autumn woods. But as they came closer, Columba saw that this was a young group, many still untonsured novitiates.

Corban, at his side, asked, "Is he among them—the blessed father?"

Columba considered the group carefully, then shook his head.

The first company reached the stream and stood facing the newcomers. Behind them the voices of another group joined the chant:

> "Ever will I go singing of Your power;
> Yes, I will sing aloud of the Lord's mercy in the
>   morning. . . ."

The second group advanced with measured step. These were all cowled and tonsured, and many wore carved wooden crosses on their breasts.

"Is he there?" Corban asked, standing on one foot in his impatience.

Again Columba considered, then shook his head.

When the second group had taken its place behind the first, a third came through the woods. These, some grayed, some bowed with age, some leaning on sticks, added their mature voices to the chant:

> "It is ever a good thing to give thanks unto the Lord,
> And to sing praises unto the Lord, most high God,
> To show forth lovingkindness in the morning,
> And to sing of His faithfulness every night."

"Now? Is he there now?" Corban hopped on his other foot.

And Columba looked. And there, in the midst of the last group was a short, rather plump monk, his tonsured hair just beginning to gray. This holy brother shone with a radiance of countenance. He was under a tree, and yet he glowed as if the sun shone on him. Such was the face of one who had looked upon the Lord.

"He is there."

Now in a special salute the monks of Glasgu greeted the monks of Iona:

> "In the ways of the Lord how great is the glory of the
>   Lord;
> The way of the just is made straight, and the path of
>   the saints prepared."

And the Ionian brothers responded:

"The saints shall go from strength to strength
   Until the God of gods appeareth to everyone in Sion."

And from both sides of the stream the two groups blended their voices in the morning air with a great "Alleluia!"

Both of the holy fathers started forward.

Mungo reached the stream first and leaped across. And the two embraced in the love of God and greeted each other with the kiss of Christian brotherhood. Then Mungo turned and led the way back through the woods toward the monastery.

Columba, anxious to hear of Mungo's work and not willing to waste a moment of time in the company of this holy man, began asking him about his converts among these British people to whom he ministered.

"I have been given a most blessed patch indeed." Mungo walked with a bounce to his step as his short legs kept pace with the much taller Columba. "For I plant and harvest on ground that was tilled by another. Though long and long ago it was when the Ninian of blessed memory was husbandman here, and much of the soil had become stony once again, and the thorns had grown up thick and choked the good plants, still there was the memory of truth among the people."

Columba bent a little to his host to make the hearing easier above the sound of crunching leaves. "It had been in my mind that Ninian had worked to the south of here."

Mungo bobbed his head. Never had Columba seen on a man of mature years skin that glowed so pink and white, fairer than that of a young maiden.

"In Galloway it was, yes. In the time of the Romans, Ninian built his *Candida Casa*—his 'white house.'" Mungo paused and sighed. "And a fine sight it must have been. I have seen stone churches in Rome, and a joy they are to behold, but such a one in this land and so long ago 'twould be a wonder indeed."

"And Ninian sent missionaries from his stone church to these lands of the northern Britons?"

"And came himself. He planted the faith with his own hands. But there was great apostasy in the land when first the Lord brought me here. It was my task to root out the thorns by overcoming their false worship with the truth of the gospel."

Now the procession emerged from the woods extending upward from the Clyde and began the ascent of a sharp incline. On either side clustered thatched wattle homes with dogs, children, and geese tumbling together around the doors, interspersed with storehouses and workshops of every description. Columba could see cattle garths and tilled fields stretching beyond the buildings far on either hand.

The monastery on the top of the hill, though to Mungo's obvious regret not structured of stone, was as large as any Columba had seen in Ireland, save Patrick's own Armagh. In the center stood a fine timber church and beside it a wooden refectory. Clay-daubed wattle cells for the many brothers and all manner of work buildings and cattle sheds clustered to the edges of the earthwork enclosure while the brothers' fields stretched beyond.

But to Columba's mind the most appealing site in the whole enclosure was the cemetery on the far side of the church. Tall stone crosses and incised slabs that appeared to be of great antiquity marked the graves in peaceful repose beneath dense overshadowing trees that now blanketed them in leaves of falling gold.

Mungo led the way into the church.

A wooden altar of fine interlaced carving stood before row upon row of wooden benches. A large bronze cross studded with amber beads and blue and red gemstones held the center of Columba's attention until he looked at the walls. There, wooden planks had been plastered with pale clay and painted with the exquisite care he would lavish on one of his beloved manuscripts. A trail of vine leaves encircled the room at the top of the walls and framed each of the small, high windows. The walls to north and south depicted the parable Mungo had just alluded to: the sower spreading his seed; that which had fallen on the wayside being eaten by birds—bright, fat birds of yellow and red; and those seeds on the stony soil sprouting, then withering in the heat of the sun; while others were shown choked by thorns; but that growing in the good soil was pictured lush and verdant, flourishing even above the heads of the reapers who worked joyfully in the field.

Mungo smiled at Columba as he observed the story. "Aye, it is a fine thing to labor in God's good soil."

Columba nodded. "The faith prospers here under your husbandmanship."

Mungo extended his hand toward the illuminated Scripture that lay open on the reading table. "Glasgu shall flourish by the praising of His name and the preaching of His Word."

Then they turned to the front of the church, where the finest painting of all adorned the eastern wall—Christ, positioned so that the morning sun shone like an aureole from the window above, stood smiling as the apostle Peter brought Him the tribute money miraculously found in the mouth of a fish. And there was no mistaking this fish—a fine, still-wriggling, silver salmon drawn from the local waters the artist would know best.

"And it is a fine thing to be a fisher of men," Columba replied.

Then Mungo, after washing and placing a fresh, white alb over his cowled, goatskin robe, led his much-enlarged congregation in the mass. "May we experience the salvation Christ won for us and the peace of His kingdom."

When the mass was ended, they repaired to the refectory. This, near to double the size of the one on Iona, was also painted with scenes on its long side walls: Christ feeding the five thousand on the left, Christ partaking of the Last Supper with His disciples on the right.

Because the monastery would honor their guests, tangy, dark-gold goat cheese was added to the morning menu of porridge and wheaten loaves. Columba broke a piece from his loaf and smiled as he chewed its crispy goodness, then turned to his host. "And was there a monastery in this place before you came?"

Mungo nodded his round head. "Long and long ago—of the blessed Ninian's establishing. When I left my dearly beloved Servanus, who had been father, teacher, and priest to me, I went out looking for the place our Lord would have me minister. I came upon an aged holy man who lived alone in an isolated hermitage. The godly man was near to death, and he begged that I might place him in his oxcart and walk beside him to whatever place the oxen should choose for his burial."

Mungo paused for a drink from his ale mug. "And in truth, the bulls, in no way being restive, without any tripping or falling, came by straightway, in spite of there being no path, and halted here at the very cemetery which you have seen beyond our church. I reconsecrated the ground once blessed by Ninian himself and buried the holy man in it—the first Christian burial in Glasgu for more, I am thinking, than a hundred years. And so I gathered a brotherhood here and built the monastery." He finished with another drink.

"But you did not always abide within this enclosure?"

"That is true. And strange is the way of it. For I had gone into Wales and was blessed with the privilege of serving at the holy David's very monastery. And I thought never to leave it, save for journeying to Rome. But then I was returned from my journey and secure once more in the monastery, contented never to set forth again. But King Rodercus of Strathclyde, seeing that the flame of faith was waxing dim in his kingdom, sent messengers to recall me once again to my first work.

"And on receiving the king's message I was silent, nor did I that day return a definite answer, for I had prepared to end my days in that distant monastery which I much loved.

"But in the wee hours of the night, while I was consulting God on the matter, a heavenly messenger stood before me and said, 'Go back to Glasgu, to thy church, and there thou shalt truly acquire unto the Lord thy God a holy nation, an innumerable people to be won unto the Lord thy God.'

"And I replied, 'My heart is ready, O God! My heart is ready for whatsoever may please Thee.'" He spread his hands and smiled shyly. "What other answer could I be giving?"

And Columba agreed that Mungo could have given no other. And he hoped that the holy man would have as clear an answer for him when the others around the table were dismissed to their work and he could consult the father alone on the matter of his own heaviness of soul.

And so it was that, when the others were departed, Columba turned to Mungo and poured out the story of the battle of Coldrevny, of his leading forth in his own selfish prayer for revenge, of the great slaughter, and of the guilty burden he bore.

Mungo listened carefully, a gentleness shining from his blue eyes, at times a tiny nod of understanding encouraging Columba's words. Already Columba was feeling better for the telling—the burden not gone but somewhat lightened. He waited long for Mungo to reply as the holy father seemed to search his soul for an answer that would be beyond his own human understanding.

At last he drew breath to speak, and Columba leaned forward.

"My son, my brother in the faith—" but Mungo got no further, for the heavy wooden door at the far end of the hall swung open with a great clatter, and there was a thudding of boots on the clay floor as a messenger clad in heavy leather tunic bearing the stag's head crest of King Rodercus's household strode forward.

"Holy Father—" the messenger dipped his bared head to Mungo "—Queen Languoreth is much in need of help. She bids you come at once."

9

The journey to DunBarton, riding the monastery's finest horses along the green banks and through the thick woods beside the Clyde, took the better part of the day. Long shadows were falling across the path, and the evening wood thrush was singing its plaintive song when the wooden rampart encircling King Rodercus's strongplace atop its great rock came into view. The bronze fittings on their leather harness jangled, and the horses' hooves hammered on the packed earth. And Corban pulled his pipe from his tunic and played a bright tune to cheer the wood thrush. For his heart was singing at being off yet again on an adventure.

Father Mungo had chosen one of his brothers to accompany him, and—wonder of wonders—Father Columba had chosen his own small self. Corban was uncertain what service he could supply, but he was determined to do his best. For the moment, playing his pipe seemed to be all he could do.

The gates of the dun of the rock stood open, and leather-tunicked guards holding spears attended on each side. Inside, the palisade was thronged with people and animals rushing between the numerous buildings. The court of King Rodercus was not a languid one.

Nor was it a happy one. The travelers had no more than dismounted and handed the reins of their horses to a stable lad of about Corban's age than a serving girl with tear-streaked face ran from the hall house, which stood tall above all the other buildings like a mother hen with chicks gathered around her.

The girl threw herself at Mungo's feet. "Oh, holy Father, you have come! You must help my lady. She is in grave danger."

Mungo raised the girl to her feet, and after a hiccup of a sob she continued. "Come, I will take you to her."

Queen Languoreth sat on a chair piled with bearskins in her chamber at the side of the hall. Unlike her serving girl, the queen was not dissolved in tears. But the tense whiteness of her face and the hollow stare of her gold brown eyes were far worse to behold. Her

98

hands gripped the carved and painted arms of her chair as if she would surely fall should she let go.

The single window of the room stood unshuttered, allowing the evening light to illuminate the gold braid that trimmed sleeves, neck, and hem of her green tunic.

Mungo spoke first. "Would you have private counsel, my queen?"

Queen Languoreth shook her head of long golden hair. And it was more of a shiver than a mere nay-saying. "There is no need of privacy. All the dun knows. My lord Rodercus was very angry. He accused me before all the court." Her shiver was now so violent that she could speak no more.

At last she drew breath and began again. "The king has gone hunting. He will return tomorrow at sundown. Then I will know the fullness of his wrath."

In bits and broken pieces, with careful prodding by Mungo, the story emerged. Five summers ago and beyond, in the first flush of King Rodercus's love for the lovely Languoreth, he had given her a finely wrought ring of many golden wires entwined together and looped on one side into the figure of a delicate, winged bird. Because of the fineness of the wires and for her fear of their breaking, Languoreth did not wear the ring every day but kept it only for high occasions.

She had worn it for the feasting a month and more past when there came to Rodercus's court an emissary from the Pictish court of King Miathi of Perth. Elifer he was. A young man, tall and black-haired with gleaming brown skin over his powerful muscles. It was said he brought peace talk from King Miathi, who ever squabbled with Rodercus over the cattle Rodercus's men would raid from Miathi or Miathi's men would raid from Rodercus.

Languoreth dropped her head so that none could see her face. "But he spent more time playing the harp and singing tales of valor and love in the place of the women than he did talking of battles and cattle on the men's side. And Elifer of the Pictikind was splendid to look upon and his songs wonderful to hear . . ."

Her voice was so low that Corban had to strain forward to hear.

"And I was foolish and weak. And King Rodercus much preoccupied with his affairs . . ." Her pause was long. "Later Elifer admired the ring I had worn for his welcoming. So I gave it to him."

The room was silent, but Mungo did not reproach the queen.

At length she continued. "Yesterday when the king and his fellows returned from the stag hunt, I hurried forth as usual and greeted him with a glad welcoming. But instead of returning my greeting, there proceeded from his mouth the harshness of threats, contempt, and reproach. With flashing eyes and menacing countenance my lord demanded where was the ring of his special gift-making to me."

Again her voice dropped to barely above a whisper. "Holy Father, forgive me, for my sins are many. And again I sinned against God and my marriage lord and the truth. For I was frightened and knew not what to do, and I lied. I told my lord Rodercus that the ring was laid up in a casket in my chamber."

Corban inched forward as Queen Languoreth paused and shook her head at her own folly. "The king demanded that I bring the ring to him in all haste. I fled to my chamber and called Clodha—" she indicated the serving girl huddled beside her chair "—her I sent to Elifer to require of him the ring. Imagine my dismay when Clodha returned with the word that Elifer had lost the ring while hunting and had not realized it was gone until that moment."

Languoreth raised her head, and her eyes were clear. In full possession of herself she rose from her chair and knelt at Mungo's feet, her hands crossed over her breast. "Holy Father, forgive me. I have sinned. Pray our Father in heaven that He may forgive me also. And beg of my lord Rodercus that he might find mercy in his heart to forgive me as well." She took a deep breath. "Father Mungo, do not spurn me in my sin. Do not cast me out unforgiven." Languoreth bowed her head.

Mungo placed one hand on her head. "The blessed Servanus did in no wise cast out my mother when her curragh washed up to his hermitage, but he showed her loving-kindness and the way of salvation. Nor did our Lord spurn the woman taken in adultery but rather turned her from her sins. My child, seek the Lord and His salvation with all your heart, and sin no more."

The room was long silent as the queen prayed. At last she looked up with shining face. "Praise be to God for His mercy and kindness."

"Alleluia!" With that single word Mungo helped the queen to her feet. "Now we shall see what may be done to soften Rodercus's heart. Pray that he may show earthly forgiveness as a reflection of our Father's heavenly forgiveness."

The travelers sat at table that night with others of the court, but the queen did not join them, for she would keep to her chambers until the king bade her leave them—whether in restoration or in disgrace.

"It is in my mind that it would be helpful to have speech with this Elifer," Columba suggested to Mungo.

Mungo agreed, so Columba turned to Corban. "Inquire you of the servants to find this man. See if he would come to us."

Corban nodded and jumped to his feet immediately, without murmur or backward glance at the fresh platter of honeycakes a slave had just brought to table. But in spite of his alacrity, none of the hall servants could point out the Pict.

"I'm thinking he was not in hall at all tonight. The court is much reduced with the king a-hunting and the queen in disfavor—but perhaps you, being new come, have not heard . . ."

Corban nodded and backed away from the talkative servant. The Brythonic tongue of these northern Britons was closely akin to the Scotic Gaelic, but none so alike that he could converse without effort, and Corban had no time for gossip. If Elifer had not come to eat, he would seek information in the horse yard. He hoped the man had not gone hunting with the king again today, but that seemed unlikely for one who had been accused of committing adultery with the queen.

And indeed Elifer had not gone hunting that day, for the stable lad who had first taken their horses gave Corban two very alarming pieces of information. "Not around here, he isn't. And not likely to see him again, that's what I say. Gone back home to his foreign Picti-kind. That's what he's done. Gone like a frightened hare with his ears flopping."

This time Corban listened to the tale telling, in hopes he might learn something that would be of use to help the beautiful Languoreth.

"There's many of us that think he did it on purpose—made trouble over the queen, that is. Most like he threw the ring away or stole it. Just like a Pict that would be. Make trouble at court so they can sneak in and steal more cattle."

Corban had about decided that was all that could be learned, when Clodha, her blue cloak billowing around her, ran into the byre. "Oh, Wemis, I have just heard. . . ." She stopped at the sight of Corban, but Wemis was not inhibited from putting his arm around her.

"And what is it you're hearing, my pretty? Are the girls of the cookplace teasing you then for my fondness?"

Clodha tossed her head. "I have no caring for their jealousy."

She pulled away from Wemis's arm, but Corban thought that the doing took some effort of will.

"We must not think of ourselves now," she said. "It is my lady the queen. I was just hearing from Bantha, wife to Elu who cares for the hunt dogs, that he saw King Rodercus remove the ring from Elifer's finger when the hunt rested in the glade."

"But why then did the king demand the ring of Queen Languoreth?" Wemis frowned.

"Do you not see?" Clodha sounded impatient. "To shame her before the court—to punish her for her unfaithfulness."

"So the king had the ring all the time?"

Clodha shook her head. "Bantha said Elu saw him take the ring while the others slept. Then Elu followed the king through the woods, for he was curious what the king would do."

"Well, what did he do?" Now it was Wemis who sounded impatient.

"He threw it into the Clyde."

Corban found the answer stunning. "But why would he do that?"

Clodha shrugged. "Mayhap in his rage he thought only to shame the queen and so remove the ring from anyone's possibly finding it and restoring her good name." Then she turned back to Wemis. "But you must be telling me what to do. I do not know what is best. Should I tell my lady? Will she not feel even greater despair if she knows the ring lost beyond all recovery?"

She had asked Wemis, but Corban answered. "You must come now with me and tell Father Mungo. He will know best what to do."

In a few minutes Corban and Clodha stood before Mungo and Columba in a nearly empty hall. Clodha repeated her story and her question.

Mungo shook his head. "It makes no difference whether or not you tell the queen. Her hopes are fixed now on heavenly help." He paused. "And yet there is no harm in attempting earthly means with one's hands while one's heart is fixed on heaven. Corban, come you to me at first light in the morning."

It was actually a few minutes before the first streaks of red broke the clouds over the high dun of the rock when Corban slipped from his straw pallet, smoothed his pale rumpled hair, and ran to Mungo.

But he did not arrive before the holy father was awake. Indeed, it appeared to him that Father Mungo had slept little, if at all, for the settled kneeling position Corban found him in and the rapt look on his face gave the impression of one who had spent many hours in prayer.

But he turned to Corban immediately. "Ah, well come. Father Columba assured me you would be energetic."

Mungo picked up a small satchel and led the way from the guest lodge, across the dun, down the long path that scaled the steep crag, and never slowed his pace until they reached the Clyde. The sky was streaking golden and all the birds of the woods singing as if the rising of the sun depended solely upon their effort.

Mungo opened his satchel and handed Corban a coiled line with a hook on the end. "I will remain here in prayer. Go you down the river to the spot where the bank widens green and smooth and many moss-covered rocks tumble into the water. Wait until the tide is full spate. Then cast your line. Make sure it is before the turning of the tide. Bring me the first fish you catch."

Corban nodded. He would obey, but he couldn't have been more disappointed. Fishing? The holy Mungo had brought him fishing when they should be making preparation to save the queen from dishonor? The blessed father had seemed to give so little thought for clothing, drink, or food, Corban could not believe he would place such importance on having fish for breakfast.

It was, however, a beautiful morning, and Corban did think that a bite of well-grilled fish would be a fine tasting thing. He turned in the direction Mungo had indicated.

He had gone only a few yards when the sound of splashing turned him around. He could not believe his eyes. It was a beautiful morning but cold. The water would be like new-melted ice. And yet Mungo had removed the goatskin robe he habitually wore and plunged into the frigid waters.

As Corban watched, the holy man, standing in water that flowed above his waist, raised his hands and chanted:

"In the morning will I lift my hands to heaven,
In the morning will I lift my voice to heaven,
In the morning will I lift my heart to heaven,
In the morning and all day long will I lift
    praise to my God."

Corban walked some distance until he came to the spot Mungo had described. He knew it immediately. Beside the tumble of mossy rocks the father had described lay a smooth white stick, as if it had been prepared for his coming. Corban tied one end of the line to it. Then, observing the fish at their morning feeding jumping for flying insects farther out in the river, he caught a fine, fat bug to place on the hook. His father and most of the men of Iona preferred to fish with nets—indeed, that was Corban's only experience—but fishing with a line was not unknown, and he could imitate what he had observed.

Keeping careful footing, he clambered over the rocks to one that put him farthest into the water, right above a deep-looking place that surely could be home to a large hungry fish. Judging by the watermark on the rock nearest him, the tide would be full in soon. He must hurry before it turned.

His first cast tangled and fell limp at his feet. He longed for a lissome, well-weighted net as he smoothed the knots from the line and recoiled it. This time he tried flipping the pole over his back, then flinging it forward. But for the gorse bush behind him, the maneuver might have been a success. In disgust he scratched his fingers on the thorny branches as he disengaged his line. The bait was now lost from his hook, so he must catch another insect.

The tide was now full. Before it turned, the father had said. Finally positioned again, he merely dropped his line into the water.

The hook barely broke the surface. His pole jerked with such force it almost leaped from his grasp. Gripping the stick with both hands, and thankful not for the first time that he now could work with both hands, Corban let out more line, hoping the fish might tire itself before he pulled it ashore.

The waiting was hard. The flashes of silver breaking through the churning white water excited his every instinct with a desire to pull in the beauty and run with it to Father Mungo. But good sense prevailed. Corban worked slowly and steadily to master his prize.

At last it was ashore, the largest salmon he had ever seen. As fine as the one St. Peter brought to the Lord in the wall painting in Mungo's monastery. What a fine breakfast this would make.

He ran all the way back to the place where Mungo, just emerged from the water, was putting on a bristly hair shirt.

In a moment the garment of self-mortification was covered with his robe, and he turned, pink and glowing, to Corban. "Ah, a fine fish indeed. Fine."

"It will be making a good breakfast, will it not?" Corban hoped he would be invited to share it.

"We shall see," Mungo replied. "We shall see."

Once they were back in the dun, however, Mungo took the fish not to the cookplace behind the hall but rather to the smaller building beside it marked with a cross beside the door.

Corban could not believe his eyes when the holy father strode forward and placed the fish on the altar. Mungo then took a small knife out of the satchel. At the sight of the leather bag, Corban remembered he had left the father's hook and line by the river.

But Mungo seemed unconcerned. He elevated the silver salmon in consecration, then returned it to the altar, slit it open, and began gutting it.

Corban thought of the picture over the altar in the monastery in Glasgu. Was perhaps Mungo planning to represent the miracle of our Lord's taking tribute money from the mouth of the fish for his morning homily?

And then Mungo pulled an object from the stomach of the fish—a finely wrought ring of golden wires with a tiny-winged bird on one side. "Take you this to Queen Languoreth and tell her all will be well."

Corban held back. "But won't you take it, Father?"

Mungo shook his head. "I will remain here and pray for her that she may have success before King Rodercus as Queen Esther had in pleading before Ahasuerus."

At the door Corban turned back once. Already the monk was looking to heaven with an expression that told him he was not seeing things of this world.

As he approached the hall house, Corban saw that their errand was finished not one minute too soon, for King Rodercus was even now handing the reins of his horse to Wemis.

Corban ran to the back of the hall to enter by way of the cook-place and bake ovens and crossed to the queen's chamber as the king entered the front of the hall. The long tables were near to filled with those of the court who would break their fast, but none sat at the high place.

Corban slipped into Languoreth's room.

She sat much as she had the day before, still in her chair, her gown and hair showing careful preparation. But this time there was a difference, for the stiff fear was gone.

"The king has come," Corban blurted out.

"I pray he has had good hunting. I pray all good things for my lord."

"*We* have had good hunting." He held out the ring. "Fishing, really it was. Father Mungo told me where to drop the line. I think he knew somehow."

The queen rose with quiet grace, not the excitement Corban had expected. Then he realized that she had won her battle yesterday before the Lord of heaven. Now she could face her marriage lord with calm. She took the ring from Corban's fingers and walked into the hall.

King Rodercus had just reached the top of the hall when he saw her. He turned and stood, tall and fair in his red and gold checky cloak over a leather tunic. His face was stone hard as his queen approached.

When she was two paces from him she fell to her knees and held out the ring in her cupped hand. "My lord king, I am not worthy to beg your forgiveness, but that God has forgiven me. As emblem of the absolution of my sins, He has granted the return of your ring."

Rodercus took the ring from her and looked at it long, while all in the hall held silence. At last he fell to his knees before her, took her hand, and slipped the ring on her finger. "If God has forgiven you, I could do no other. And truly, it gladdens my heart." He raised Languoreth to her feet before all the court. "We will go now to our Brother Mungo for the saying of mass."

Corban started to follow those from the court who went with the king and queen to the church, but then he saw that Columba, who had been sitting at the far end of the hall, did not join the company.

"Father?" Corban asked when he reached the monk's side.

Columba shook his head. "I cannot partake of the blessed body and blood this morning. My sins are too heavy on my heart."

Corban blinked. It was unthinkable that Father Columba should bear such a weight. Especially when Corban's own heart was so light. Had they not just witnessed a miracle?

"Go you to the service. Say a prayer for me," Columba said.

Corban nodded and went out with a smile. Golden autumn sun shone on the path and on his head. He quickened his steps toward the church. It was only when he saw Wemis and Clodha walking hand in hand ahead of him that his pace slackened. What was there about that sight that made him want to be back on Iona?

Columba, too, was thinking of Iona as he sought Mungo later. Would he ever be worthy to return to the work there? How could he lead others when his own need was so great?

He found Mungo still in the now-empty church, glowing with the radiance that seemed never to leave him.

"Ah, my brother, we have been much interrupted since I had the sharing of your heart."

Columba nodded and sat on the front bench before the altar. Indeed it had been only two days ago when they had talked in Glasgu, and yet it could have been that many weeks or months. For each hour the weight had grown. And he knew before even Mungo spoke that there could be no answer for it. A sin as great as his could only be carried until it weighted one into the grave. Death would be his only release.

Mungo smiled, and yet his words were not cheering. "My brother, there is so little to say."

Columba nodded. It was as he thought.

"There is nothing I can tell you that you do not already know about the love and goodness and forgiveness and grace of our Lord. Nothing I can say that you have not said to many souls in your care, times beyond counting. And yet I can see that you need to have it said to you.

"The grace of God covers all sin and guilt. All. You have only to give it to Him. You have given Him the sin for forgiving."

Columba nodded.

"But I think you have not given Him the guilt for carrying."

Columba thought.

"It is to my thinking that by your continuing to do penance you are refusing to surrender all to God's grace. You must put all behind you and go forth in the freedom of His love."

It was silent in the little church. Could it truly be so simple? And yet was not simplicity the very heart of the gospel? Slowly he nodded. And with the motion a tiny lightness crept into his heart. A mere speck of dust was removed from the stone he carried. And yet speck followed speck until pebbles were falling away and then whole rocks.

Mungo's smile brightened, his radiance increased. "It is all love. Love is all. We are ministers to a dark and pagan world. It is only love we can show them. Let it start in your own heart."

And Columba knew he was free at last. He needn't sleep on his stone pillow any longer. He would find a new use for his stone. For the penance was gone. Only the glory remained—the glory of God's presence and of God's dealing with his heart and the glory of the vision of what his adopted homeland would become with God in its people's hearts.

That was the key—glory in the people's hearts, shedding light on all around them. Each monastery a center of holy fire with the love and glory in the people's hearts reaching out to form a great shining to encompass the land.

10

Seven times the season of new-lambing came and went on Iona. And in spite of the continued worry that Broichan would put action to his threatened revenge, they were peaceful, fruitful years.

Numerous monasteries were established throughout the western isles. All Dalriada was brought to the knowledge of Christ and the ancient places of pagan worship consecrated Christian. And, in spite of Broichan's best efforts to hinder their work, Columba's monks made inroads carrying the light into Pictish Alba.

But it near to broke his heart to consider how much more could have been accomplished in that vast and beautiful land to the east had it not been for the archdruid's opposition. Missionary brothers struggled to plant monasteries in the Alban lands, and many responded to their teaching. But there was no flourishing of the faith as there was in Dalriada.

The darkness remained over the land held in the powerful grip of one determined to battle the light. Long Columba prayed. Strong he clasped his faith that God had given him a vision for the redemption of that land—and God would not promise what He would not fulfill. But still the land waited.

On Iona, the work of copying the Holy Scriptures and the works of the church Fathers continued. And the brothers spread the Good News far afield through those who came to the holy center to study and then went out to preach. And all the brothers rejoiced.

Yet every morning Columba climbed Tor an Aba with a heart heavier than the marble pillow Corban had carved for him. And there he prayed for Alba. "'I come to gather nations of every language. They shall come to see My glory,' You have promised, Lord. Let it be true through the work of Your servant Columba, as You have promised. Let the Albannach proclaim Your glory among the nations. Let brethren from all the nations be brought as an offering to the Lord."

Daily Columba prayed. And still nothing happened. Still word came to them of monasteries wrecked, of missionaries beaten, of the people held in darkness.

And as Father Columba's lead-streaked hair grew fully gray, Corban grew to full manhood and took his place in the hunting and fishing expeditions and so visited most of the islands of the western sea. But this venturing out, which should have served to fulfill his wanderlust, only further enticed it. Even though he was glad to return again to his island with the glow of a successful hunt upon him, he ever hungered to venture farther on bolder errands.

All on Iona was peace and beauty and joy—save for the one thing that rankled as he was sure Father Mungo's hair shirt must. The thing was that Ibar, too, was of flourishing manhood, and Rom-Aln of lovely womanhood.

Although it was the friendship between Rom-Aln and Fand and Ibar's two other sisters that was much the excuse, it was to Corban's thinking that the black-haired girl spent too much time in the company of the brother of the family. And not since her first coming to Iona had Father Columba made further suggestion of sending her to a house of holy sisters—even though a small flock of Eirean nuns had for six years now ministered in their own establishment beyond Columba's monastery.

And so it was the sight of Ibar and Rom-Aln walking on the beach, even more than the brightness of the late spring day, the call of the seabirds, and the flighting of the white clouds, that brought Corban's venturesome spirit upon him full force when a messenger arrived from King Conall of Dalriada.

Corban sped to the monastery to hear the news. King Brude, at the urging of his ever-power-hungry druid, had turned his eyes toward Conall's land. Brude would break treaty with Conall and take the land of the west for his own and its people as his subjects. Would Columba come to the aid of his king and kinsman?

The Scotic people needed a man of prayer as well as a man of arms to lead them in battle. Conall had sent to his royal nephews Aiden at DunStaffness and Iogenan at Inverary for more troops, but he could turn only to Columba for prayers. They must be strong prayers, indeed, to defeat the evil one whom Broichan served.

The holy man's brow furrowed, and his shoulders slumped. He turned away from the messenger and the cluster of brothers awaiting his answer. He walked almost directly into Corban.

"Father, I have heard. May I go with you?"

"And I too."

Now it was Corban who turned, with a frown. He had not realized Ibar had followed as well.

"My spear throw is the straightest in the hunting run. If you are to go into a place of battle you will need such skill as mine."

Corban could resent the handsome Ibar's bragging, but he could not disagree with the statement. Ibar's skill was the best.

Columba looked at them both for the space of several breaths. "I shall seek God's will in the matter." And he walked away.

But Corban would not wait for the father's word. He would make his own preparations now.

First he sought Dag, watching the sheep on the western side of the island. Hard to believe it was that small Dag was now older than Corban himself had been that long ago day when he saw the blue and green sail of the brothers bearing them to Iona. And Dag was fine-grown now, for seldom—only in the coldest weather—did he have the breathing trouble. And—a never-ceasing wonder to Corban—he never tired of the sheep but watched over them with the care that Merca had once lavished on the small sick boy.

"Little brother, King Conall has sent word that Dalriada hosts for war against Alba. If Father Columba answers his call, I will go as well."

Dag's smile had not outgrown its sweetness. "I will miss you. So will our father."

Corban nodded. Garfinn seldom hunted far afield now and spent more and more time telling tales by the fire. In time perhaps he would take the place of old Echu, who these four years since had slept on Reilig Odhrain.

Corban laughed. "Well, at least the sheep won't miss me any more than I'll miss them. There is only one thing you could be adding to your care for them." He fished inside his tunic and pulled out the pipe he had carved for Dag, this one with two tiny lambs gamboling on the sides.

Dag blew a few wavering notes, then grinned. "I'll try to have a tune mastered by the time you return. If I don't scare all the sheep off in the learning. And shall I tend Righ for you?"

Corban shook his head curtly. "Na. He's too old for the sheep. I'll leave him with another." He jumped to his feet and called the old dog, whose brindled coat showed far more ash than charcoal now.

As he walked back through the clachan, he noted Father Columba's brown-robed figure kneeling atop the tor. Apparently the matter wasn't settled yet. Still, he would make his farewells.

He found Rom-Aln tending a small cabbage patch. He told her shortly of the news that had come from Conall. He wished he could

110

talk to her without the stiffness he always felt around her. Why couldn't he joke and tease with Rom-Aln as he did with Fand and the other girls? Why had he come at all? His message delivered, he started to back off.

"So, you will leave Iona?" Her dark eyes looked wide with concern. Then the thick black lashes covered them.

"If Father Columba says so." There seemed to be no more to say.

"You will take care, Corban?" Her voice was warm and musical.

He nodded. Why could he think of nothing to say? Righ moved forward to lick Rom-Aln's hand.

She laughed and scratched behind his ears. "Poor old thing. Righ would comfort me for your going."

Then Corban remembered. That was what he had come for. "Will you see to Righ when I'm gone? His teeth are dull—he needs his meat cut small in broth."

"Yes, of course I will."

Now there was truly nothing more to be said. Corban turned away.

"Corban."

He stopped.

"Godspeed."

Atop Tor an Aba, Columba knelt. Once again the horror of the battle of Coldrevny overcame him. Since he had been guided by Mungo into accepting the freedom of God's grace for his sins of blood lust, Columcille had had nothing to do with war. He had truly earned his name Dove of the Church. But now was he to go once again into the fray?

Conall mac Comgaill was a Christian. Although Brude had given permission for the Christian faith to be taught, Brude himself remained aloof—and in the grip of his evil druid. And Brude's strongest companion would most likely be that subking Maithi, whose noble had caused such near disaster at the court of Rodercus. Did not that make the difference?

Besides, the Albannach were breaking treaty—they were the ones attacking Conall. Conall was not starting the trouble—at least as far as it had been told Columba. Often and often enough God had led His people to fight against heathen idolaters in the Promised Land. Had not this land been promised to Columba when first he came here? "I will deliver to you every place where you set foot."

And was not the entire history of the conquest of the Promised Land a prophecy of spiritual conquest in the world through the church under the leadership of Jesus Christ? So could Columba refuse this request, no matter how he recoiled at the thought of going into war?

And then it was not the words spoken to Joshua that came to mind but the words of God to Ezekiel. As God had quickened them to him long ago when he visited King Brude and first did battle with Broichan, so now they rang afresh in Columba's heart.

"Son of man, stand up. I wish to speak to you."

Columba stood.

"Son of man, I am sending you forth. Hard of face and obstinate of heart are they to whom I am sending you. But you shall say to them: Thus says the Lord God. And whether they heed or resist—for they are a rebellious house—they shall know that a prophet has been among them. Speak my words to them, whether they heed or resist."

Conall and his troops had already left when Columba and his little party arrived at DunAdd. As was usual, Brother Baithene remained behind in charge of Iona. Brothers Laisran and Diormit accompanied Columba, although he sorely missed the faithful Lugbe, who was now prior of his own monastery. Many others had gone to establish houses of God throughout the western islands, into the Orkneys and across Dalriada.

But they were not now going into peaceful lands. Therefore Columba had accepted the young men's pleas. Corban and Ibar served as bodyguards, both sporting gleaming bronze armbands to match the shining of their spears.

Conall had left behind a man to show Columba the way to his hosting, and Columba was much pleased when he saw that it was none other than Hynish, who had long ago escorted him to King Brude at Craig Phadrig.

The armies met at the top of Loch Lomond. The campfires of Conall's men spread far up the green countryside along the river flowing into the loch. And on the other side Columba saw a seeming equal number of flickering lights piercing the grayness of the May gloaming.

Hynish took him to King Conall's tent.

"My kinsman!" The king greeted Columba with a kiss on each cheek. "You have come as I was sure you would. Now with the strength of your prayers and the strength of my warriors we cannot fail. Our success shall be as sure as that of the High Niall at Coldrevny."

At the king's gesture, Columba sat on a small stool. "It is that which I have come to speak to you of, my kingly cousin."

"So speak."

"I will pray mightily for this battle."

At Columba's words Conall smiled smugly.

Until Columba continued. "I will pray for God's will to be done, and for His protection, and for His peace to be upon the land."

"And for our total victory over the heathen, surely!" Conall rose to his feet again.

Columba shook his head. "God is not the enemy of your enemy."

Conall gaped at him. "What did you say?"

"You heard aright. God is not the enemy of your enemy."

"But . . . but . . . surely . . ." Conall began to sputter.

"God is the Creator of all. All—Picti, Scoti, Briton. He would be loved and served by all. Such I have come to this land to proclaim. So I proclaim to King Brude as well."

"But Brude is a heathen! He worships the sun in rings of standing stones. His druids read the entrails of animals rather than the Word of God. Such practices are disgusting!"

"And so they wound our Lord, who would have all know the truth."

"And what do you propose to do? March into Brude's camp and tell him this? Did you not do such once many years ago? See what good it has done. Now sword must answer sword."

Columba was adamant. "They must hear the Word of God first. Will you make loan of curraghs for the crossing of the river?"

"No!"

Columba bowed his head. "So be it. Then I will swim."

"Oh, go ahead." Conall slammed his fist against the table so hard the ale sloshed from his tankard. "Take anything you need. But when you are sacrificed to their heathen gods, see you that you pray for us before Broichan slits your gizzard with his silver sickle."

Conall strode from the room, his leather armor creaking.

Columba sat. There was truth in what the king said. Columba knew what he must do, yet the possibility was real of his being made a sacrifice. It had so nearly happened once. Would he be spared again? Or this time would God ask of him the ultimate sacrifice for the soul of this land?

And then God's words came to him once more: *"Neither fear their words nor be dismayed at their looks, for they are a rebellious house. But speak My words to them, whether they heed or resist."*

Columba rose. He could do no more. His orders were to speak. The results were in God's hands.

He sought his small company to tell them his wishes. Diormit, his closest companion, would take charge of his followers here.

"Father, I would go too!"

Columba smiled at the eager voice. Diormit might be his closest companion, but Corban was ever his most enthusiastic.

He shook his head. "I go as a man of peace. A spear-bearing warrior has no place on this mission. Guard you well these brothers I leave behind, for, if I have no success, I fear the battle will be fierce indeed, and even the holy brothers may be in need of protection."

Then Columba turned to Diormit and Laisran. "If I do not return before the battle, stand you on yon hill—" he pointed to the dark shape looming behind them "—and pray for God's will to be done in this land. I will join you there."

Soon the dipping of Columba's curragh oars in the river was all Corban could hear.

Columba did not return that night. Nor did he return when Conall's war horns sounded through the camp at first light the next morning.

Corban's heart was heavy for the fate of the man who had stood larger in his life than even his own father. And his own darkness was increased by Ibar's excitement over the battle preparations taking place all around them.

"We are to go with the brothers," Corban growled at Ibar and stalked off, little caring whether or not Ibar followed.

Ibar did not follow.

Halfway up the slope Corban turned and shouted, "Come you! Father Columba said. He will return soon and find you missing."

"Go on then. Go to the holy brothers and pray with them," Ibar shouted back. "I will join the men."

When Corban was atop the little green hill, standing sentinel beside Diormit and Laisran, who were already at prayer, he looked long to find his friend among the milling war host. If Ibar had worn a leather or bronze helm like most of the others, he would never have been able to pick him out.

But then he saw the shining blond head approach a burly soldier. The warrior pointed to the far side of the field where the sun glinted off a forest of spears. Ibar took his place among the battle-ready men.

And Corban was not sure whether it was the beating of the war drums or of his own heart that boomed louder in his ears. The leader of the spearmen, a man with a flowing orange mustache that reached the bronze collar above his leather breastplate, sat on a shaggy brown garron, shouting orders loud enough that the sense of them reached

Corban on the hill. It was clear that the cavalry would go first, led by Conall himself.

It was the king's strategy to be first over the river with his men—the easier then to drive the Picts back into their land. Archers from the other side of the field would go next, that their flight of arrows might do what damage possible to Brude's rear troops. Then the footmen with spears and swords.

Corban noted that most of the foot soldiers were armed with iron swords as well as with spears. Perhaps Ibar would seize one from a fallen comrade, but he had had little enough practice with such a weapon. Swords were of no use in the hunting runs, and that was all Ibar knew of weapons skill.

Across the shallow river Corban could see the Pictish host rallying under Brude's black boar banner. The sun glinted off the bronze bosses of their small round shields and their fierce battle-axes.

And then, before he could wonder which army was larger or better weaponed, Conall gave signal for the horn blast, and the Scoti cavalry charged forward behind Conall's streaming blue banner with the white wolf.

And so the thudding of horses' hooves was added to the thudding of the drums and the thudding of Corban's heart. And Corban felt his own blood rise with that of the warriors. A jubilant cry broke from him as Conall and his men, with water spraying white and high beneath their horses' feet, charged across the river well before the Picti, who seemed to have been caught in disorder.

But then Brude's horsemen thundered forward. And the black boar and the white wolf clashed. And the ring of iron on iron and the shouts of men and cries of horses reached to Corban. Behind him the gentle murmur of prayers continued unbroken, but before him the white-foamed river ran red, for the Picti more than made up for the lateness of their charge by the ferocity of it.

Another trumpeted signal called forth Conall's archers, and for the space of several minutes the sky was shadowed with the dark flighting of arrows. And here the Scoti had superiority, for the Picti-kind did not care overmuch for fighting with bow and arrow. But when the Scoti archers had moved forward only a few yards they were within range of Alba's spearmen, and so the rushing twang in the air was now from the iron-clad spear tips of the Picti. And many a Scoti bow was stilled. Now was time for the men of Dalriada to show their spear skill.

Corban's eyes never left Ibar as the company moved forward. Then, after only a few minutes of forward thrust, the whole force of the battle moved backward. It was several minutes before Corban could make sense of what was happening. Then he saw. A contingent of horsemen under Maithi's red banner had gained Conall's side of the river.

The fierce little Picti garrons charged among the foot warriors, their riders slashing right and left with wide iron blades that ever returned red for the next slash.

Where was Ibar? Corban searched far afield toward the place he had last seen the spear troop. But nowhere could he see the shining yellow hair of the young man who had been his friend and competitor since childhood. Had Ibar fallen? Corban's heart lurched.

Then he realized he had been looking too far afield. Driven backward, the tail of Conall's band struggled at the foot of the very hill where Corban stood. Corban readied his spear, for, as Columba had foreseen, it well could be that the monks praying behind him would need protection.

And there just below him was Ibar with red on his spear tip. He had apparently armed himself from a fallen warrior, for he fended off the blows of a Picti battle-ax with a bronze-studded targe.

Then Corban saw what Ibar, engaged in combat, could not see. A Picti horseman, victorious in his clash with a Scot, now bore down upon the foot warriors. His sword felled the first of Conall's men he reached. Ibar would be next.

As instinctively as if facing a stag in a hunt, Corban let fly his spear.

At the same moment the Pict swung his sword at Ibar. The spear reached its target first. The Pict fell from his horse. But not before his blade slashed Ibar's back.

Corban darted down the hill before another could finish the Pict's work. With one hand he retrieved his spear from the chest of the fallen horseman, with the other he gripped Ibar's arm and dragged him from the fray.

He had gained more than half the hill when he paused to consider what he had done. He had saved Ibar for Rom-Aln. It was an unworthy thought, but there it was. If Ibar had fallen, the competition would have been eliminated. But then, it was no competition anyway, was it? Ibar held the field, just as Brude and Maithi held in the clash of armies below.

Corban looked again across the swirling throng. He felt the chill up his spine before he realized what was wrong. In truth, Picti troops pushed farther and farther into Conall's territory, but no farther than Conall had first pushed into theirs. And did not a battle often surge back and forth? No—that was not what set off the alarm signal.

Then he understood what was wrong. The blue wolf banner was not in the field. Conall was captured or fallen. Soon the Dalriadan men would notice, and there would be chaos.

Unaware of the disaster for the moment, the Scoti warriors fought on but seemed to be losing momentum. And then the realization of a yet greater disaster came to Corban. Why had he not thought sooner? Columba had not returned as he had promised. Columba too was dead or prisoner. And they were losing the battle. So if Columba was now a prisoner, he would soon be dead. Broichan would have made good his threat of revenge.

With a final exertion Corban dragged Ibar the last six spear lengths up the hill. "Laisran, get you the ointment against wound fever. Ibar has need of it. And say a prayer for him." Then Corban was off.

He slipped around to the far side of the hill and made his way downstream beyond the clash of battle to where the rocky riverbed could be easily crossed. Then, keeping to covering bushes, he worked his way back toward Brude's camp. He was within sight of Brude's deerskin tents and the scent of burned-out campfires when a stronger, more acrid, smell reached him.

Corban stopped, peering in the direction the charred odor seemed to come from. A thin line of black smoke led him to a thicket of saplings behind the Picti camp. Crouching low, he inched forward. Was he too late? Had the unthinkable sacrifice already been made?

At first he saw the blackened remains of a small animal on a stone at the side of the grove. He crept onward, eyes darting every direction to spot the druid priests. Broichan would be here somewhere. Had he already claimed his evil victory?

So intent was Corban on looking for the tall gaunt druid with a silvery black forelock that he almost stepped on another sacrifice, lying on the ground before him. This one was unburned. A raccoon lay on its back in a pool of blood, its entrails exposed to whatever deity it was meant to invoke.

And then he raised his eyes to the center of the thicket. He barely suppressed the cry that almost tore from him. Columba lay motionless on a flat stone.

An anguished sob broke from Corban. He was too late. He ran forward and flung himself beside the body—then jumped in terror as the body turned.

"My Corban, you look so fearful. Am I such a terrifying sight after a night of prayer?"

"Father Columba! I thought . . . I thought . . ." He shook his head. "Why did you not return?"

"Oh." Columba looked at the position of the sun nearing midday. "It is so late. I had no idea. I have been deep in prayer. Transported. I would not have stayed away so long, but it is of little consequence. Surely my prayers are as effective here in this ancient holy place as they would be with our own people."

"Holy place?"

"Oh, a place of mistaken worship, to be sure—a place where the sun was worshiped as God by those who knew not the Son. Now we must cleanse this druid ring as symbol of the cleansing of the land that we pray for. Will you help me?"

Corban drew back. The place stank of demon worship. "But Father, the war—"

"Because war is raging, we must win the spiritual battle."

Corban stood firm. What could the abbot be thinking of? "This is no place for a Christian."

Columba smiled. "You speak true, my friend. Broichan's worship was an abomination. He well knows the power he serves. His is no ill-informed groping toward truth. But long before him there was, not Christian worship, but an honest reaching toward God. We must honor that cry of the untaught heart yearning for God as all hearts do, even when they know it not."

Corban sighed. "Then why bother cleansing the place if there was some truth here, as you say?"

Columba talked as he turned to bury the remains of the sacrificed animals. "'Some truth' is the devil's greatest lie. He will use a storehouse of truth to hide three kernels of lies. But the lies will rot all the rest. We honor the sincerity of those who were here before us—but we to whom the truth has been entrusted must cleanse away the lies. Satan is the father of lies. Our weapon is truth."

Corban nodded. He had heard it all many times before. At first there was much controversy among the brothers who thought Columba should tear down the ancient places of worship. But Columba insisted—all things were to be made new in Christ. Not destroyed but given a new birth in the truth.

While Corban thought, he peeled two white rods and bound them in the form of the cross he knew Father Columba would want to raise in the center of the circle.

And Columba continued to talk as he worked, scraping blood and ashes from the altar. "Christ was the perfect sacrifice, the complete sacrifice, that no more blood need be shed on stone altars such as these. But just as the Hebrew altars of the Old Covenant were a

118

foreshadowing of the coming of Christ, so were these pagan altars a foreshadowing—however dim and mistaken."

Columba set to washing the altar.

"But where is Broichan?" Corban looked over his shoulder nervously.

"Gone to the battle. I tried to talk to him, but he was drug-frenzied after his ritual sacrifices. There was nothing I could do. So I did the most powerful thing of all and prayed." His smile was sweet, in sharp contrast to the harsh battle cries that now rang from beyond the hill.

"Oh, the battle!" How could he have forgotten? Thinking Columba dead had put all else out of Corban's mind. "Father, that is what I came searching to tell you. Conall is fallen. All is lost. Leave this. We must flee!"

Columba picked up the cross Corban had fashioned and set it firmly in the ground at the head of the altar. "When we've more time we must incise crosses on these stones."

Corban tugged impatiently at Columba's sleeve. "Did you not hear me? Brude triumphs. Come! Broichan will be here any minute."

"Then it is all the more important that we make good of our work while we may." Columba fell to his knees before the newly cleansed altar.

Corban was opening his mouth to argue when, to the sound of yelling and crashing, two panicking warriors broke through the brush to his right. Picti warriors, weaponless, their tattooed bodies bloodied, running for their lives. They were followed by more and more of their fellows. Those who could do so ran, others limped or crawled.

Corban turned back to the altar. "Father." He approached, shamefaced. "Forgive me. I was wrong. Weak of faith. Your prayers have triumphed."

Corban and Columba returned to the hilltop where Diormit and Laisran still prayed. And their prayers left even less doubt of the outcome than had the sight of fleeing Picts:

> "O shout unto the Lord a mighty song,
>   For He has done marvelous things.
>   His right hand and His holy arm have gotten Him
>   the victory.
>   The Lord has made known His salvation.
>   His righteousness He has openly shown in the
>   sight of the heathen.

Make a joyful noise unto the Lord, all earth;
Make a loud noise, and rejoice, and sing praise."

Ibar, his wounds expertly salved and bound by Brother Laisran, rested on the hillside at the monk's express orders. He was careful to explain such, lest the newcomers think him cowardly, before he launched into a detailed account of the shifts of fortune in the battle.

But all was not victorious rejoicing. "Indeed, Conall is slain. I saw his body thanes bear him from the field. We thought all lost."

Another wounded Scot, likewise medicined by Brother Laisran, sat just beyond Ibar, nursing an arm wrapped in bandages newly soaked through with blood. "Aye, it was a dark day. But then Prince Aiden arrived with his warrior troop from DunStaffness. Did you not hear the sounding of his battle horns and the pounding of his horses' hooves?"

Corban and Columba both shook their heads.

"It was a fine thing. A pity it is you missed it. A fierce man the princeling is—cousin to Conall mac Comgaill—and to my thinking the man to be our next king. But they say the king naming is in the choosing of some holy father from a western island. Although what he would be knowing more than the king's own warrior troops, I'd not know." The man stopped suddenly and considered to whom he was speaking. "Oh . . . er . . . ye be brothers from a holy isle. Mayhap ye be knowing this Columba, as I've heard him named. If so, I meant no offense."

Columba smiled. "I know him well and can speak for him. He would take no offense. And what say you to Iogenan mac Gabhran, brother to this Aiden you rate so highly? Would he not make a fine king also? I've heard he's a far better scholar and more regular in his prayers."

The Scoti warrior snorted. "Aye, and where was he today? There'd be no Dalriada for such as him to rule over if all stayed home at their books. That's what we have monks for." Again he seemed to realize he had been too bold, for he stopped suddenly.

Then, as the sun lowered toward the west and the last of the Picti war band retreated across the river and beyond, the final work of the battlefield began—stripping and burning the fallen enemy, tending the wounded, and burying their own dead. The Ionian brothers were busy with the satchels of herbs and salves they had brought with them, applying some themselves and directing others in the use of many more.

The work was well under way—for speedy were the victorious warriors at gathering the gold and silver armbands and necklaces from the painted bodies of their fierce enemies—when the sound of horses and the whipping of a green lion banner announced the arrival of a new contingent.

Aiden, who had taken over for his fallen cousin and was directing the work in the field, strode toward the newcomer. The late arrival stopped not far from where Corban was digging a grave for a soldier no older than himself, who still had a Picti ax buried deep in his shoulder.

"And about time you arrive, brother. Think your men to gather a share in the booty they had no part in winning?" It was more a challenge than a greeting.

"We came as soon as we received word, and well you know it, Aiden."

"And is it so much farther from Inverary than from DunStaffness, Iogenan? For surely our cousin Conall sent messengers to both at the same time."

"And where is the king?" Iogenan asked.

"Fallen. His body rests in his tent. I have given orders that he is to be buried on Iona."

"You have given orders, brother? And is it then that you have appointed yourself our cousin's successor?"

"I was the only one of the blood royal here. Now that you have chosen to join us, Iogenan, perhaps you will be willing to bloody your hands with the labor that remains." He turned sharply to his own work.

Corban, reminding himself of the many graves remaining to be dug, turned over two more shovelfuls, then paused again to observe Prince Iogenan.

In spite of the uselessness Aiden had implied, Iogenan appeared to have come well prepared with much-needed bandages and ointments, and Corban had heard Brother Laisran lament the shortage of his supplies. Iogenan directed his men to join the work, and Corban was glad of help, for already red spots that would soon be blisters were beginning to wear on his hands. He was more concerned, however, for the apparent signs of blisters between the princely brothers.

Nevertheless, now he could turn to the king's tent to offer help to Columba in his sad task of laying out the body of his fallen kinsman and king.

Columba had finished washing the grievous gash that ran the length of the king's left side when there was a disturbance outside the tent. The royal brothers fighting again—and their cousin's body not yet cold?

121

But a startling sight met Corban's eyes when Columba lifted the tent flap. It had been many years, and the false tonsure had grown back with an amazing fall of red hair over the man's forehead, yet Corban was sure. He had never thought to see Aclu again.

The druid struggled against the guard who would send him away. "No, I would have speech with the priest of the white Christiani. I must. The archdruid sends me."

Columba held up his hand in a sign of peace. "Let him speak. Why have you come?"

"Broichan sent me. You must come. It is his only hope. He says your prayers are the only thing strong enough. He will die if you refuse him."

"Broichan asks for me? For my prayers?" It was apparent such was too much for even Father Columba's faith.

"What's happened?" Corban asked. "Was he wounded in battle?"

Aclu shook his head of flaming hair. "Not by a sword. He stood on the hillside to invoke the gods for his king . . . as is his task . . ." Aclu looked around uneasily.

"Go on." Columba nodded.

"He was struck down with a fever. Before even the triumph of your army. He has no use of his limbs. He can speak. That is all. He says only your god can help. Come." The druid gestured back down the hill.

Columba made no answer. Instead he walked slowly across the field, his eyes on the ground. At last he stooped, picked something up, and came back. Corban saw that the abbot held a smooth, white stone. Columba drew the knife he wore at his belt and carefully incised a cross on the stone.

"Let him who has ears heed the Spirit's word. 'To him that overcometh I will give a white stone, and on the stone a new name written, to be known by him who receives.'

"Take this to Broichan. The white stone was ever a symbol of victory. And on it, the cross of Christ. Tell him to meditate on it day and night. It has healing for all the world. And he must pray to the living Christ who died on the cross for his sins. Pray and meditate and believe. Therein is all healing."

Columba placed the stone in Aclu's hand and returned to the tent.

11

What would happen in Alba, Columba did not know. Would Broichan accept the cross? Or would he reject it and launch his final, dying power in a desperate attempt against the truth? And what of Brude—defeated but unbowed? Had winning the armed war meant they would lose the spiritual? Would Brude now close Alba to all missionary effort?

But Columba could not think on that now. He had a more pressing matter before him. For the wounded warrior had the truth of the matter. As abbot of Iona, highest ecclesiastic in the land and highest representative of the house of the High Niall in Dalriada as well, the choice of king to follow Conall mac Comgaill was indeed Columba's. And he must get it right. Next to their faith in God, nothing else was so important to the well-being of a people as their king. The prosperity of Dalriada rested with Columba. He must be certain they had the best earthly king, even as he taught them of the heavenly King.

He walked to the far side of the encampment, where he had left the satchel of supplies he carried when he arrived at Conall's camp just twenty-four hours earlier. He reached deep in the leather pouch, and he smiled as his hands closed on the precious object.

Ever he carried his book of the beloved Scriptures with him when he traveled. Once even, it had fallen from his grasp and landed with a sickening splash in a river he and his party were crossing. And the Lord had granted a miracle that day, for the holy volume was recovered undamaged, floating in its leather case far downstream. So now it was doubly valued by him as the Word of God twice given.

Columba walked some distance along the evening-blue waters of the loch to the solitary green slopes of Ben Vorlich. He would be alone to hear the will of God for his people, just as Moses had gone alone up Sinai to hear God's direction for his people. The night thrush sang, and the last red streaks faded from the western sky as Columba found a sheltered spot where he would seek the face of God.

He sat long, listing in his mind the abilities of the two men.

Aiden was the older, although that provided no absolute directive for succession. He was also the bolder, quicker, more forceful, although Columba was not convinced that would always be to the advantage of Dalriada as it had proven to be today. Aiden was rough, sharp-spoken, and not overly devout.

Iogenan, on the other hand, was as devout as any who would be a prince of the church, let alone an earthly prince. And he was learned. Columba suppressed a selfish thought of the books that might flow to Iona from the largesse of such a king. And Iogenan was ever the kinder, more thoughtful prince.

Columba could not deny that his own job would be the easier with Iogenan as king of Dalriada. With the king providing spiritual leadership, the abbot might then keep to his own monastery and spend more time in his scriptorium—ever Columba's greatest love.

Iogenan was the one Columba would choose for his own son. But the choice could not be a personal one alone. If it could be, it would be an easy matter.

With a sigh Columba turned to strike flint to the candle he dug from his satchel. He would seek God's Word. He turned to the account of the prophet Samuel seeking a ruler for his people: "And Kish had a son whose name was Saul, a choice young man, and a goodly. And there was not among the children of Israel a goodlier person than he. From his shoulders and upward he was higher than any of the people. . . .

"And when Samuel saw Saul, the Lord said unto him, 'Behold the man of whom I spoke to you! This same shall reign over my people. . . .'

"Then Samuel took a vial of oil, and poured it upon Saul's head, and kissed him, and said, 'The Lord has anointed you to be captain over His inheritance.'"

As Columba read, he could see Iogenan in every line, the finest young man of the truath, head and shoulders above all the others, and he was sure Saul must have had gleaming red gold hair like Iogenan's. And so the choice was made.

Columba returned the Holy Book to its leather satchel, blew out his candle, and drew his cloak around him. He sat thinking of all the good that could be accomplished for Dalriada with Iogenan anointed king. At last, with the Book still cradled in his arms and his mind filled with bright images of the future, Columba fell asleep with his head pillowed on a slab of gray green slate.

And the sky filled with a bright radiance, not of a blinding light like fire but as the glowing of a pearl. And shimmering streams descended from the sky to the earth like a ladder. The sky opened, and Columba saw bright angelic beings going up and down the ladder with a gentle humming that was music and yet not music—more like unto the glowing harmony of all things.

And one of the angels turned to Columba. "Choose not Iogenan. Aiden is God's man."

And Columba, knowing that often God tests the determination of those who would serve Him, said, "I have chosen. It is Iogenan."

Then he turned over, his head still on the hard stone, and slept more deeply. And the vision came to him again. Again the ladder with angels ascending and descending, again the harmony of the spheres, again the angel who said, "Choose not Iogenan."

And again Columba said, "I have chosen." And this time he noticed sadness on the angelic countenance before the being departed.

This time Columba lay on his back, then on his left side, then on his right, but now the stone, which had before seemed softest goosedown, was hard and cold. And the damp of the earth made his joints ache. He could not sleep. A cold wind blew at his cloak and tore at the sacred volume in his arms.

And Columba's thoughts returned to Saul, whose anointing had provided such a sure sign that he should so anoint Iogenan: Saul, tall, handsome, and humble, beginning his reign with a brilliant victory; Saul, whose humility rapidly gave way to pride; Saul, deliberately disobeying God. And God saying to Saul, "Because you have rejected God, God has rejected you."

Columba sat up, chilled to the bone. Would such be the end of it all if he persisted in his choice? Disaster for Iogenan and disaster for Dalriada? Was not Saul's first mistake when he himself offered the sacrifice that was to be the exclusive function of the priest? Was not God telling Columba that a nation needed both—a leader for earthly matters and a leader for spiritual? The people needed Aiden's strength of leadership. Columba must provide the strength of devotion Aiden lacked. Columba's own job would be the harder for this choice, but it would be the right choice.

With that assurance he lay down again and slept. And a third time the heavenly vision appeared. And the pearlescent sky glowed brighter, and the harmony of the anthem sounded sweeter. This time the heavenly being that appeared to Columba held a book in his outstretched hands, a book of shining crystal. A book with one word written on it: Aiden.

And Columba said, "It is so."

With that he slept peacefully until the gold of the morning sky and the melody of bird song wakened him to a new day.

He rose filled with a sense of joy and well-being, not as one who had spent the night on a cold hillside sleeping on a slate pillow and wrestling with angels but as one who had slept while all creation smiled. And Columba smiled.

And set to work. He thought to dig up all of his Jacob's pillow—or at least to break off a large chunk, but when he began digging and chipping with the only tools at his disposal—a sharp stick and another rock—a small piece of the greenish slate broke off in his hand, something the size of a loaf of unleavened bread such as the Lord might have eaten at the Last Supper.

When the digging, which was really a breaking, was done, Columba drew from his pouch his own small oatcake and flask of ale—poor elements for Eucharist but all he had. So, using the stone for an altar, he offered up thanksgiving to God for His faithfulness.

Then, bearing his chunk of slate in his arm like a replica of the stone tablet Moses carried down from Sinai, he strode back to camp with shining countenance.

Corban saw him and came running. "Father Columba, let me help you carry that." Then he blinked. "Another stone? What can you be wanting it for? Not yet another pillow, surely?"

Columba threw back his head and laughed. "My young friend, always you are perceptive. But this is not a pillow of penance, to be sure. Rather, a marker of promise. As Jacob at Bethel upended the stone on which he had a vision of angels and then anointed it as a witness to the faithfulness of God, so will I mark this stone that the people of Dalriada might never forget that it is God who is their true leader."

Corban looked at the stone Columba placed in his hand, then up at the abbot. "Once, many years ago, you asked me to be keeper of your Eirean stone. Would you have me so care for this one?"

"Yes, that is a fine idea. And when we are come to DunAdd, there is one more service I will ask. You who are so clever with your wood carving and who so deftly incised my marble pillow, I would now have you also inscribe this stone of Dalriada."

Corban nodded. "Would you have a cross on this one also, Father?"

Columba considered. "I am thinking that this one I will have lettered. Young warriors have not much time to practice the writing skills the brothers would be teaching them. Do you remember your letters, Corban mac Garfinn?"

"Yes, Father. What would you have me write?"

126

"This is to be a stone of remembrance, a stone always to recall our Scotic people to God. So let it bear His name: IN NOMINE DEI—'in the name of God.' And let you work with the best stone-carver tools in DunAdd and take advice from the most skilled workmen there, for this stone is to speak to the ages."

12

So returned the court to DunAdd, bearing with them the sad body of the king who was and the proud personage of the king who was to be. It was a journey of three days and into the fourth, for traveling was slow, all matching their pace as they must to that of King Conall's garron pulling the cart with his body on it. For most of the way Aiden walked on one side of the fallen king, Iogenan on the other. Columba and the two brothers from Iona followed behind. Following them came the war leaders of the truath, then their men.

Near the very end of the winding procession walked Corban, keeping as much devotion to his task as Aiden and Iogenan did as honor guard to the king's body, for Corban carried the stone piece that had pillowed Columba when he argued with the angels over who should occupy the throne of Dalriada, the stone that he would now inscribe with the name of God as a reminder to the people of this land that they might not forget His hand upon them.

Each night they stopped at the dun of the overlord of the region through which they passed. Each was a strong man who ruled under the king of Dalriada; each had contributed warriors to the hosting against Brude. And in each dun the warriors from the nearby steadings returned to their hearths, but the overlords made ready to join the journey to DunAdd, careful to take with them a small bag of soil from their own dun.

By noon of the fourth day the procession passed through the fine green farmsteadings of the valley of the River Add. And finally, before them was the great lion-shaped rocky outcrop towering above the Crinan Moss that held the High Seat of Dalriada. For near to one hundred years since Lorn, Angus, and Fergus, the sons of Erc, came to this land from Eirean Dalriata, the Scots had held their king-making here, and so ruled here.

Corban looked up the rugged hillside. Its various levels and terraces edged by wooden walls made five enclosures, forming the strong-place at the top of which stood the stone-walled fort. The procession must now go single file through the natural cleft in the rock that formed the entranceway. And Corban chafed at the seeming stand-still pace. For he had his commission to perform. As soon as he was through the gate of the dun, he slipped from the cortege to seek out the chief stonecutter of DunAdd and set to work with his tools.

Early the next day those of the fort and all the overlords from the various duns of Dalriada who had received word assembled on the flat area outside the main enclosure, a ways below the summit. The assemblage of monks, warriors, and rulers stood around a flat outcropping of the living rock of the mountain. The smooth-worn, rectangular granite slab, seven or eight feet long, was carved with the print of a foot and a deep, cup-sized basin.

When all were assembled, Columba, carrying the cross-topped staff of his abbacy, led Aiden down the path. Columba wore a simple white stole over his customary homespun woolen habit, but Aiden, looking a different man without his war leader's armor, was clad in a white tunic, symbolic of his integrity of heart—a pledge that he would be a light to his people and maintain the true religion.

Aiden strode firmly to the inaugural stone and took his place upon it, standing a full stride behind the carved footprint. Brother Diormit stepped forward and handed Columba a smooth white birch rod. Columba presented it to Aiden. "Aiden, chosen king of Dalriada, take this rod of ruling and keep it ever before you as a reminder that you, indeed, have been invested with the power to rule. But ever you must rule with justice—not with tyranny and partiality but with discretion and sincerity."

Aiden bowed his head in acknowledgment and took the rod in his left hand.

Brother Laisran then stepped up to give King Conall's sword to Columba. "King Aiden of Dalriada, I give you this sword of your kinsman, signifying that it is your duty to protect and defend your people from all incursions of their enemies in war and in peace."

Aiden took the sword with his right hand, then stood firm while his armor bearer flung his best, gold-embroidered cape over his shoulders, a signal that it was time for the fealty swearing.

Each in turn, the overlords of Dalriada came forward. Each knelt to pledge his obedience and sprinkled a few grains of the soil of his own dun in the incised footprint. In the background the monks chanted:

> "The Lord liveth.
> Blessed be my rock,
> and let the God of my salvation be exalted."

Iogenan knelt first before his brother, then the others came, the sun gleaming on the gold of torques, brooches, and armbands as the chant continued:

"I will give thanks unto the Lord,
Among the heathen will I sing praises unto His name."

The footprint was full and overflowing with all the soil of Dalriada as the last of the overlords made obeisance.

Columba stepped forward, holding a small silver box with a gabled lid. He took out the precious spices the Benbrennoch held and sprinkled the pungent scents over the oil in the basin behind the footprint. Then he dipped a yew branch in the chrism and sprinkled the soil of Dalriada with a shower of golden droplets while the scent of spice filled the air.

"Great deliverance You have shown to this king and to this land. Bless now this chosen one and his seed and this land forevermore, O God." Columba made the sign of the cross in blessing on the king, on the people, and on the land.

Then, with a salute of trumpets from the ramparts of the fort ringing out over the broad moorland, Aiden placed his foot on the soil filling the print, symbolizing that he reigned over all the land.

Columba scooped up another handful of the sacred oil. With this he anointed the head of the king. "Great deliverance God gives to His king. He shows forth mercy to His anointed."

Then the abbot, majestic as the breeze blew the white hair behind his tonsure and the white stole gleaming over his robe, turned to the leaders of Dalriada and to all the people assembled. "Hear the word of the Lord. If you will fear the Lord and serve Him and obey His voice and not rebel against the commandment of the Lord, then shall both you and also the king that reigns over you continue in prosperity. Only fear the Lord and serve him in truth with all your hearts; for consider what great things He has done for you."

Columba paused to survey all the people covering the hillside, and his voice rang with the strength of a much younger man. "But hear me. If you forget the Lord your God and turn to your own selfish ways and follow the path of evil, ill will come upon the land and sorrow and despair. Do not forget the Lord your God and the goodness He has done unto you."

And Aiden responded, as he had been schooled to do by Columba, "Therefore will I proclaim You, O Lord, among the nations. And I will sing praise to Your name, You who gave great victories to Your king and showed kindness to Your anointed, to David and his posterity forever."

And with the cheering of the people so ended the inauguration of King Aiden of Dalriada.

Columba had made quick work of the king-making because, Corban knew, this was but the first stage of the ceremonies that were yet to be. And Conall's body must not be kept waiting too long—even though his soul was already with its Creator.

He held out his hand, and Corban placed the newly polished roundel in it. Corban bit his lip. Would it do? Was it as the abbot had instructed? He had worked most carefully to get it right. Was it good enough?

Columba smiled, and relief flooded the boy.

Columba bent and scooped a third handful of the anointing oil. Holding the inscribed stone toward the people, he poured the chrism over it. "As Jacob anointed the stone which pillowed him in Bethel as a remembrance for the people of his land, so I anoint this stone for the people of this land. Let it serve you twofold, as a memorial to your excellent King Conall mac Comgaill, and as an ever reminder of Him whom you serve even above your present king, Aiden."

Columba held the stone so that at least those standing closest could see the inscription as he read: "IN NOMINE DEI—'in the name of God,' who has blessed you and whom you serve."

"Oh, praise God . . ." The chant began.

The brothers faltered on the final Te Deum, being interrupted by the pounding of running feet and the shouting of the guards.

Columba gazed in the direction they ran. Across the Crinan Moss the sun shone on an alarming sight. Picti warriors—a strong band, only a few days ago defeated in battle—and now, so soon, helmed and armed for war again? The black boar banner on a silver field flapped over their heads.

Columba's heart sank. This then was Broichan's revenge. The druid had taken offense at the cross he had sent him. Even paralyzed, he had power to summon an army. Now that sacrifice for which Columba had offered himself those years ago on Craig Phadrig would be required.

A guard sounded the horn for those in the fort to make battle ready. But Columba shook his head. He knew what was needed. Dalriada's war band had dispersed after their victory. DunAdd held only the new-crowned king's bodyguard. The priests and nobles gathered for the crowning could not be thrust into unprepared battle. This was a personal struggle between Broichan and himself.

"Secure the gates behind me," Columba ordered.

All in the court seemed too shocked to protest.

Columba walked out. His soft leather boots felt the rocks on the descending path, but his mind was filled with images of the past years, the few short years God had given him in this land of his penance, which he had come to love above all next to heaven.

He would not choose to leave it so soon, for there was much left to do. His vision was so little fulfilled. And yet he was thankful that it had been given to him to make a start. And someday God would send one worthier than himself to complete the work. Always God's ways could be trusted, no matter how hopeless matters seemed to man.

At the foot of the hill he stood. The armed band approached with fluttering banners. He would not flinch. God helping him, he would stand strong.

"Columba!"

He looked up as one horseman pulled ahead of the others. For a moment the sun glinting off the man's silver ornaments dazzled Columba's eyes. He blinked and looked again.

"Greetings," the man said. And there was no mistaking. It was Broichan. Fully recovered.

The druid dismounted and clasped Columba's arms. "It is true —all that you said. I have seen the strength of the cross. Brude sends his best men and asks that you teach them. When you have time to journey to him, he will be baptized as you said he must."

And so the crowning day of King Aiden mac Gabhran of Dalriada was a crowning of another sort for Alba as well. And all rejoiced.

All but Corban.

The brothers stayed at DunAdd to begin the instructing of Brude's men, but Columba went back to Iona to give burial to King Conall. And Corban went with him—Corban and Ibar, now well recovered from his battle wounds.

And all the way, Corban's mind whirled. He looked into the distance across the shining water. There were the green hills of Jura. Beyond that, Iona. And Rom-Aln.

He had thought of her so much of late, seemingly more than he had when sharing space on that small island with her. And the more he thought, he had come to know with breathtaking intensity that no matter how far he traveled or how many adventures he might encounter, there could be nothing better than living on Iona with Rom-Aln.

The wind caught the sail, and the boat sped. There rose the monastery from its green footings. There the sparkle-white beach. And then there was Rom-Aln herself. Her dark hair streamed behind her buttercup yellow tunic as she ran toward him.

And past him. Into Ibar's arms.

So that was the way of it. He had long feared so. Yet he had continued to hope. Now hope was gone. And only the pain in his heart remained.

Corban turned away. He was more than halfway up the beach when Righ came barking to him. He was glad someone was happy to see him. He stopped to scratch the grizzled ears. Then he heard her calling his name. He turned without smiling.

"Corban mac Garfinn, are you not going to greet your old friend?"

He was surprised that she had noticed him. Even more surprised that her voice sounded disappointed. He waved a brief greeting, then turned again to Righ but did not continue walking.

The beauty around him startled him anew, as it did at every homecoming, whether from a mere two-day's fishing trip or a return from bloody battle. Even with such an unwelcome scene as Rom-Aln in Ibar's embrace filling his mind, he was still glad to be home. Home, that was the only word for it. A sense of rightness filled him at returning to Iona.

Ahead on the path he saw Dag waving excitedly and Merca, ancient and stooped but with a basket of fresh oatcakes in her arm.

At last his wanderlust was satisfied. After all his years of wanting to get away, he *had* gotten away. He had seen the wider world in peace and in war. And now he was satisfied. He would choose nothing but to stay on Iona. Yet not to watch Rom-Aln become the wife of another. Now when he would choose to stay, he must go.

He would pledge his services to Aiden, and from now on his home would be wherever the court of Dalriada had need of his poor spear skill.

He turned at a light touch on his arm. "So, Ibar tells me of your saving his life."

Corban nodded. He was not wanting to regret his action toward his friend, and yet he realized how different all might be were Ibar not here.

"I will always be grateful that he who has replaced the brother I left behind in Alba has been returned to me. Even if it is that he chooses to go again to Aiden's war band."

She waited, but Corban could only blink stupidly.

"And what of you, Corban mac Garfinn? Will you be off again as well? Will all those dearest to my heart leave yet again—even he who is dearest?"

Corban stood in the middle of the sun-warmed path gaping at Rom-Aln, before him now in truth as she had so often been in his

133

dreams. "Do I hear right? Are you caring whether I go or stay? I thought . . . I thought . . ." He looked from one to the other, from Rom-Aln to Ibar, who stood a little way behind them, and back again. "I thought you two . . ."

"Then you thought wrong, Corban mac Garfinn."

A very slow, very bright smile spread slowly over his face and moved upward to light his eyes. "What say you? Shall we go to Father Columba and tell him he has yet another ceremony to perform?"

Rom-Aln put her hand into the one Corban held outstretched to her, and they walked toward the enclosure.

13

Gareth held out his hand, and Mary grasped it as he led the way. "Come on, we've just half an hour until the last ferry. We don't want to miss the museum."

"But I wanted to climb Tor Abb." Mary sighed. Their time on Iona had been all too short. They had come over by the first ferry from Mull that morning and were waiting until the last one to return. Still she felt she could spend days here. If her clothes and her toothbrush weren't back on Mull, she would try to talk Brad into changing his reservations. But as it was, she could only give in to Gareth's insistent pull.

His hurrying up the narrow, uneven path on his weak leg resulted in a little hopping sort of gait that made her smile again. It was amazing how agile and surefooted he was even while lame. She could easily imagine how good he must be at the football he loved to play.

"And have ye seen Columba's pillow yet?"

They both turned to the voice as they entered the abbey precinct—the spot where Columba had built his monastery. All just as it had been in Hamish's tale. Mary smiled at the giant of a man with his flaming bush of a beard and well-worn kilt blowing in the wind. "Columba's pillow? Really? The stone he slept on?"

"So they say. Shall we go have a wee peek at it?"

The Abbey Museum had probably once been the monks' infirmary. Now rows of early Christian gravestones filled the small building. When the structure had been restored thirty years earlier, the stones were moved there from all parts of the island, especially from Reilig Odhrain, the ancient burial ground that once held the bodies of kings from all over Scotland, Ireland, and Norway.

Mary wandered for some time, gazing up at the great slabs of slate and granite bearing the effigies of knights, warriors, abbots, and bishops. Suddenly she stopped before a small, rectangular stone engraved with a cross formed of multi-intertwined lines. "Oh, here it is! I have a friend who's into Celtic jewelry. She has a necklace of this. She said it was the Iona cross. I'd forgotten all about it."

"Aye," Hamish said. "And it's reproduced on the gold plates at the abbey altar. Or perhaps you noticed? They were using them for Communion."

Mary shook her head. "No. We didn't go to the service."

"Ah, now that's a pity. Verra fine service it was, verra fine. It strikes me as a verra fine thing that, right to fourteen hundred years since Columba's bringing of the faith to this very spot, it's still alive and flourishing. Do ye not think that's a fine thing?"

"Mmm, yes. It's nice," Mary responded.

"Aye, it's champion," Gareth put more energy into his response.

And yet Mary was puzzled. How could it be that he seemed so . . . If it hadn't sounded so silly, she would have thought so . . . distressed. Surely he was just deep in thought. She shook her head as she followed the men toward the museum. What a strange man her cousin's friend was. What was his problem? How could he seem so carefree—as if he had the world by the tail—one minute, and so troubled the next?

Inside the building they found Brad on his knees, measuring a smooth gray stone. He took time to jot a few notes before he looked up. "Ah, Hamish. Hello, again. Have you found your new stories?"

"Naething for clearly certain yet. But these things mustna be rushed. They've been here for hundreds of years—they'll not likely come at the snap of the fingers. But is not this wee island a grand place?"

This time Mary's agreement was more enthusiastic.

"And here's what we came to see, is it not?" Hamish, too, knelt by the stone Brad was examining. "Columba's pillow."

Mary giggled, then wished she hadn't. "You mean he really slept on that? It's not possible, is it? The chiropractic complications alone are unthinkable."

Hamish shook his head. "Who's to know for certain? Who's to know? And yet these stanes have been carefully authenticated."

"Yes, the best our poor science can do," Brad agreed. "Of course, the most careful evaluations still leave room for error. But I'd say the carving on this stone appears to be of the right general time."

When they emerged from the museum, Mary was met with the unwelcome sight of the ferry nearing the Iona dock. It was time to go, and she wasn't ready to leave. So much she still wanted to do. So many questions she still wanted answered. So much yet to be experienced on Iona. The captain gave two short, sharp blasts of the boat's horn, and she turn her steps obediently toward the harbor.

She took a seat in the front row of chairs facing the island. At least she would look at Iona as long as possible. Hamish sat on one

136

side of her, Gareth on the other. Brad, his nose already in a book, was on the end.

"You're sad to be leaving, lassie." Hamish didn't even make it a question. "So always, I think, must be the feelings of the true pilgrim."

"Oh, but I'm not . . ." Mary stopped, unsure of what she was denying. Confused, she turned to smile at Gareth, who seemed to be thinking deeply. "Sometimes you're worse than Brad. Where were you off to in your thoughts?"

She loved his little lopsided grin.

"Back in the pub, actually."

His reply startled her, but he went on. "Thinking of all that happened on Iona reminded me of something you asked Hamish that night after the storytelling—about the saints achieving so much because they were able to believe."

"Mmm. Yeah, I remember. So?"

"Well, I was thinking that Columba couldn't have done all that because of just some sort of positive thinking. He accomplished it because of the power in the object of his belief."

"Hmm?" Mary supposed he had said something profound, but all she could think was that first night in Edinburgh. Had the time gone that quickly? It had all gone so fast, and yet she felt she'd been here for months. Had she been in Scotland only a little less than a week? Had she known Gareth such a short time? Been away from Michael such a short time? She twisted the ring on her finger.

She had come to Scotland to sort things out. And already she felt more confused than when she left home.

The ferry had been docked at Fionphort for several minutes, and other passengers were disembarking, before Mary returned to an awareness of her surroundings. She was silent all the way down to the dock. Finally she turned to Hamish. "Will we see you again?"

"I would hope so, lassie, but who's to say? I go where my stories take me."

In the parking lot she started around to the right side of their little red car.

"Thinking of driving, were you?" Gareth grinned at her.

The reality of being in a strange land where they couldn't even put their cars together properly jerked Mary out of the dream world Iona and Hamish's story had created. "Oh," she said and turned to the left-side door Gareth was holding open for her. She did not meet his sparkling eyes.

On their drive up the Ross of Mull she half turned to address

Brad. "So. I guess none of us spotted outcroppings of red sandstone on Iona. What does that prove, Dr. Hamilton?"

"It proves very little. There's always the possibility of an incidental stone showing up anywhere—moved by a glacier, carried by a trading ship—who knows? But as to what's likely . . ." He scrabbled among the papers beside him on the seat. "Ah, here." He pulled out a colorful pamphlet titled *The Geological Map: An Anatomy of the Landscape*.

Mary laughed. Who but Brad would have such a document at his fingertips?

He pointed to Mull and Iona on the map, then held the booklet closer so that Mary could see. "Dull purple, see? That's the code color for shales, mudstones, graywackes, some limestones."

"Which means no Old Red Sandstone natural to the area?"

Brad nodded and moved his pencil tip. "The rusty brown strip you see here, like a belt above the 'waist' of Scotland, and these bits in the eastern Highlands—those are Devonian sandstone."

"Ah!" Mary found the information very satisfying.

Until Gareth asked, "But what about the theory of the Stone of Scone coming from the Lia Fail? What does Ireland look like on that map of yours?"

The pencil tip moved. "Old Devonian—sandstones, shales, conglomerates, slates, and limestones—here in southern Ireland around this cluster of lochs and on up here."

"But not necessarily Old Red?" Mary couldn't understand why it seemed to matter so much to her that the Westminster Stone not be the original.

Brad shook his head. "Can't tell from this map."

"And what about the legends of the stone being the original Jacob's pillow?" Gareth asked. "Aside from the complications of how it got here, of course."

Brad riffled through some more papers. Then he turned to the ledge behind the backseat, and at his first touch the papers stacked there fell down on him. It was several minutes before he emerged triumphant from his muddle.

"Yes. Knew I had it somewhere. Had a harder time getting a good geological map of the Holy Land."

"And keeping hold of it," Mary said not quite under her breath.

Gareth grinned, but Brad was oblivious as he adjusted the glasses he wore for close study.

His voice took on a decided classroom tone. "Now here—" he pointed to a spot just a few miles north of Jerusalem "—is Bethel. As far as I can make out that is where Jacob wrestled with the angel in

138

the desert and anointed his stone pillow as a memorial. See how that whole area is keyed with close dots? That indicates Cretaceous and Jurassic structure."

"Er . . . yeah, right." Mary grinned. "Thanks for sharing that, Brad."

"That translates mainly chalk, clays, limestones, and sands."

"So, no red sandstone?"

He pushed his glasses up on his nose. "I haven't spotted any yet. Judging from photographs, I'd say there appears to be a lot of sandstone in the area, but it's all yellow."

Mary's nod had a smug, satisfied air to it. "Right. So whatever Edward put in that coronation chair, it certainly wasn't Jacob's pillow."

"I've read theories that Jacob's pillow was a meteorite," Gareth said.

Brad nodded. "You're getting closer to Hamish's territory than mine, but it's certainly true that the ancients considered such stones —which they called thunderstones—to be very special. Just the sort of thing Jacob might have chosen, supposing he happened to have one at hand, of course. Some claim the original Stone of Destiny was black basalt, which is an igneous rock and so more in step with that theory. I haven't been able to find much academic basis for such statements, however." And with that dismissal Brad returned to his work.

Mary slipped a tape in the player. The selection offered by Gareth's glove box was eclectic: popular, light rock, and classical—mostly baroque—which he already had there, plus the Scottish ballads, bagpipes, and medieval music she had picked up at gift shops along the way. This time she chose popular—a Scottish group she had never heard of but rather liked.

Gareth soon began keeping time to the music with a light drumming of his thumbs on the steering wheel—an unconscious extension of his sense of timing and rhythm Mary had noted before. He was so much fun to be with. And yet there were times she would glance at him unawares when he looked—well, haunted, although she knew that made no sense.

She shrugged it off. Probably his leg was hurting him.

The winding, single-lane road dropped over a small rise, and there, for at least the tenth time since leaving the village, was an approaching car. The turnouts were never far apart. Gareth swung into one and waved a salute to the other driver, which was returned as he drove by. Always so patient, so courteous, Mary thought. Whether the thought was for Scottish drivers in general or for their particular driver, she didn't bother to sort out.

By the time the tape had finished its second side, she had gathered her thoughts to focus on the object of their quest again. "So, judging by what we saw and from Hamish's account, there seem to be several candidates for the stone that could have become Scotland's Stone of Destiny. Do we know what became of any of them? Besides Columba's pillow, of course, which seems to be in safe enough keeping in the Abbey Museum."

Brad looked up and blinked as if to make sure he was being addressed, then removed his glasses and rubbed his eyes. "Yes. And the way Hamish tells it, Columba seems to have had more than one pillow—just to add interest, or confusion, to the case. I rather like the idea of the original Stone being of Ionian marble myself."

"Why, you romantic soul," Mary teased. "I always suspected something like that under all that academic dust."

He grinned. "You can ask Sharon about that sometime. But let's see—the *In Nomine* roundel is in the National Museum of Scotland; it was excavated in an archeological dig at DunAdd at the first of this century. I'll take you to see it when we get back to Edinburgh.

"Now, the Lia Fail, no one knows for sure what happened to it." Again he paused to search for a book. "Yes, here a writer says, 'We know that the Irish Lia Fail remained at Tara till 1798, when it was removed to mark the burial place of some rebels—the Croppers.' Unfortunately, the writer fails to explain how we know this or to tell who the rebel Croppers were."

"And even if that writer's correct, that doesn't discount the idea of a piece of the Lia Fail coming to Scotland with Columba or someone else." Brad nodded in agreement as Mary continued. "But what about the coronation stone at DunAdd? Is it still there?"

"It's very much there—and what's more amazing, it's there in unspoiled glory. Matter of fact, I suggest that for our next venture."

"Great!" Mary clapped her hands.

Gareth dipped his dark head in easy assent.

Later that evening they sat around the glowing coals of a low fire in the snug guest parlor after a satisfying supper cooked by the hostess of their farmhouse B & B. Mary was just thinking how lucky they were to be in such a cozy, warm place when Brad put down his book and took off his glasses. "Anyone for a walk?"

A gust of wind rattled the shutters, and Mary frowned. But Gareth jumped to his feet—a little too quickly, because he had to grab a chair back for a moment's support. "That's a grand suggestion. We can go to that stone bridge up the road and play Poohsticks."

Mary gave a quick thought to the character who suggested sending the mad-seeming Hamlet to England because no one would notice—"They're all mad there." And they were even madder in Scotland. But Poohsticks did sound irresistible. She reached for her coat. She'd soon be as mad as the rest of them.

Their hostess supplied them with torches, and they stepped out into the chill, black night.

"Ah, isn't that grand, now?" Gareth took a deep breath. "Crisp, fresh, Highland air."

Crisp? It felt below zero. How could it possibly be this cold in August? She thought of the sun-warmed New Jersey shore where her family was vacationing right now. No wonder even the cows grew long hair here.

They turned down the dirt lane leading to the narrow road, and Mary huddled deeper inside the two sweaters under her coat. She put her hands in her pockets, then took them out again to protect her cheeks from the stinging wind. Why hadn't she brought gloves? "This is the most insane weather I've ever seen in my life!"

"Ah, yes, it's a wee bit chilly. But have you noticed? The wind has cleared the clouds." Gareth pointed to the glorious clear sky overhead. "Have you ever seen such stars?"

She started to reply that she had seen them frequently—back home, where the appearance of sun, moon, and stars was a daily event. But then she stopped. It was incredible. It wasn't just the absence of clouds. The air was so clear. That was it—an absence of smoke, dust, pollution. This was the clearest night she'd ever seen.

They walked on without turning on the torches, their faces skyward.

"Ah, wouldn't it be grand to see a falling star? On a night like this you really might see one." Gareth's enthusiasm was so unaffected that Mary refrained from dampening it by pointing out that of course they probably would—after all, one usually did on a clear night.

At the gently arching stone bridge they switched on the torches to search for sticks. Mary chose one forked on the end—for easier identification when it sailed under the bridge first. Brad chose a larger branch—to catch more of the current. Gareth's was slim and smooth. When he had peeled off the bark, it reminded her of the white birch rod Hamish said King Aiden had carried at his inauguration.

"All right, on three." Even Brad seemed like a little boy as they leaned together holding their sticks over the side of the bridge in the light of the torch.

"One, two, three."

They waited to see the sticks fall and the current take them, then hurried to the other side to lean even farther over the rail this time.

It seemed it took a long time for three little branches to float under the bridge. It would be disappointing if they had swirled to the side and stuck there.

"Ah, there's one!" Gareth caught it in the light of his torch.

"Hurrah!" Mary clapped her hands. "It's mine!"

"No, it isn't, impetuous one," Brad quelled her. "No forked end. See, it's Gareth's."

"Oh, you're right. Good for you, Gareth. But look, mine's right behind it."

Brad's was slower coming.

"That's what you get for being a geologist and not a physicist."

"Right. Only very small rocks float."

Then Mary realized Gareth wasn't joining their banter.

His eyes were fixed on the sky again. "I just wish we'd see a falling star."

And then he did.

Mary wasn't looking up at the moment, so she missed it.

"Did you see that?"

She turned at his shout, just in time to see him leap into the air with arms spread wide.

He gave another shout, and Mary hurried toward him, afraid he had hurt his leg. Then she saw that with his superb balance he had landed on his sound leg, and the little hopping movement that followed was a dance of joy.

It took several moments of this ecstatic craziness for the truth to hit her. "You mean you really had never seen a falling star before? That was your first?"

"Yes, of course. I thought it was something really rare—something that only happened once in a lifetime."

Now she understood, and his excitement welled up in her too.

"Of course I'd only just seen the sun for the first time a few months ago," he added as they both wiped their eyes.

It was just the typical Scots humor about their weather, wasn't it? And then she glanced up and saw three shooting stars at once. And they were laughing, shouting, and jumping again.

"Impressive, huh?" Brad strolled over to them from wherever he had been in the dark.

"Incredible!" They both answered at once.

"Too bad we're only getting in on the end of it." Brad craned his neck backward.

"End of what?" Mary asked.

"Don't you read the papers?"

"Not while I'm traveling."

142

"Well, if you had, you'd have known that a meteor shower has been predicted for months. This has been going on all week. Of course, this is the first time we've had a clear night to see it."

Just then another bright light fell from high in the heavens. And another after it. And not even Brad's most logical scientific explanation could dim the magic.

Mary's neck was getting tired, and it was hard to keep her balance while looking up. So, bundling their coats closer about them, they sat on the bridge and leaned companionably against its stone side, out of the chill wind that kept the sky clear for the starry display overhead.

For several moments the scene held with thousands of stars blinking at them from the deep black. And Mary realized she was holding her breath.

A comet with a fiery tail streaked from one side of her vision to the other, blazing a wide path through the sky. And then it was gone.

This was beyond shouting and laughing. It took her breath away. It was truly a once-in-a-lifetime experience.

A little later Brad got to his feet, saying something about not staying out all night, and headed toward the farmhouse, but Mary barely noticed.

The sky remained brilliant, and they never took their eyes off the shining heavens, but with that grand finale the display seemed ended.

"Wow. It gives a whole new meaning to Psalm eight," Gareth said.

And because Mary didn't know how to respond but felt some reply was called for, she said, "Mmm. Brad tells me you're studying to be what we'd call a lawyer."

Gareth was so slow to respond that she thought he was lost in the stars, and she started to repeat herself.

Then he spoke. "An advocate, we call it. Guess I'm a wee bit a slow starter. I began university right after high school. Studied maths. I suppose I thought I'd be a teacher, but it just wasn't right, so I quit and spent three years working for an insurance firm. I saw a lot of the legal profession there and was really intrigued. I decided that was for me, so I went back to uni last year."

"So one of these days you'll be running around with one of those funny little wigs perched on top of your head." She turned her gaze from the sky to regard him in the dim light. "I think it'll suit you—rather rakish."

But instead of returning her banter, he shook his head. "Well, we'll never know. I told you everything changed after that accident last spring."

"What? But your leg can't be that bad." She reached out but did not touch him.

"Ah, no, no. It'll be right as rain soon." He paused. "No, it was Alex dying like that and my sitting there so helpless and alone. And then I realized I wasn't alone. Of course, I'd always believed in God—in the sense of believing that He existed—I just never did anything about it. I guess I figured in a vague sort of way that I would sometime. And suddenly it was time to make the truth personal, not just leave it an abstraction out there somewhere that didn't affect me."

"And?"

"And then things like maths and insurance and law didn't seem very important. Making money certainly wasn't important enough to live my life for. So I switched to divinity."

"*Divinity?* You mean you want to be a *preacher?*"

"Yep. That's it."

"But that's impossible!" She sounded scornful, incredulous.

He nodded. "You're probably right. I want to sae much. But—yes, probably impossible when I—" He shrugged. "I don't know."

She was so stunned she just sat there. She was sure she couldn't have heard him right. She looked back up at the sky just in time to see a thick cloud cover roll across the firmament as if a giant hand had pulled a curtain.

"Well, it's a relief to hear you're normal. I don't see how anyone can be sure enough to preach to others. How can you preach about a good, all-powerful God when there's so much evil all around us?" She pushed back against the bridge and felt the sharpness of the stones against her head.

He was quiet for a while, then his voice came softly. "People often say they can't believe in God because there is evil in the world. That's a verra weak argument. It makes just as much sense—more, I think—to say they do believe in God because there is goodness in the world. Especially when you look at events in the light of history—all the way from Columba to Hitler—and see that good is stronger."

"So why does God"—she held back from saying, "this God of yours"; she really didn't want to sound snide—"allow evil? You may be right that good is stronger—I certainly hope you are—but that makes the presence of evil all the more abhorrent if we agree that God could eliminate it and doesn't."

He was quiet for so long she thought she had won. She almost gasped when he reached out to take her hand. Then, feeling foolish, she realized he wasn't trying to hold her hand—he was pointing to the diamond on her ring finger.

"And how much value would there be in your love for Michael if you had no choice in the matter—if you were forced to take him or no, without looking at anyone else or no matter how you felt?"

Now she was the one who couldn't answer. She merely covered her left hand with her right and clasped them very tightly. The wind had dropped, but she felt more chilled than ever. Had she been wrong to come? Why in the world had she thought coming to Scotland would help her think more clearly? Three weeks yet till her return flight. It seemed like an eternity.

She got to her feet, and they walked silently back to the bed and breakfast.

Then, when trying to wash up, she froze one hand under the right faucet and scalded the other under the left. She turned toward bed without even drying her hands, longing to be back in the land of central heating and mixer faucets.

Tomorrow she would send Michael the prettiest postcard she could find—and write a very romantic note on it to let him know how she felt. Snuggling deep in her thick down douvet, she smiled. Maybe she'd send the funniest card—one of those silly, shaggy Highland cows. But she would certainly tell him how much she missed him.

BOOK 2

Of Kings and Kingdoms

Kenneth mac Alpin Unites Picts and Scots, 847

14

It wasn't so much that she forgot the next morning as it was just that they didn't stop in Oban, and there really was nowhere else to shop—even for a postcard. They drove back down the single-lane, twisting, dipping road, along firth and sea loch, beside hills purple with heather and dotted with sheep.

And as always, every few miles they met an oncoming car and performed the ritual of each car turning aside, one driver or the other pulling ahead, and the drivers saluting each other. Or sometimes both drivers started forward, and then the pattern must be begun again like a stately dance.

After one unusually busy stretch, Gareth switched arms to wave with. "That one's getting tired," he said. And they joked about devising a mechanical arm to raise by pulling a cord.

They stopped at a small grocery in Kilmartin and bought pre-packaged sandwiches—cheese and tomato, curried chicken, tuna and cucumber—and a bottle of lemonade for lunch. Mary could have bought a postcard too. But she didn't think about that until later. Besides, she was out of stamps.

Just out of Kilmarten they found another farmhouse bed and breakfast right across the road from where a ring of upright stones stood in the middle of a pasture.

Mary gaped. "I can't believe it. A miniature Stonehenge—prehistoric stones just standing there with a herd of cows eating daisies at their feet and scratching their backs on them."

"What do you expect them to do—dance?" Brad teased.

"You know what I mean. Standing stones are something magical—from another world—and yet they're just here."

"Yes." Brad nodded. "They are from another world. Archeologists figure the oldest surviving monuments are Neolithic and early Bronze Age—that's around five thousand years ago. The burial cairns on up the valley are a bit newer—about four thousand years old or so. Want a closer look?"

"Yes! But can we? Isn't that private property?"

"It is. But we're allowed access to the stones—just so long as we don't chase the cows."

Mary didn't even ask for time to unpack.

In a few minutes Gareth was holding a gap in the barbed wire fence for her while she ducked through. The grassy ground underfoot was softly damp, but she didn't actually sink in mud as she made her way to where seven weathered and broken stones stood in an incomplete circle that must have been about one hundred fifty feet across. She could only imagine what the place would have looked like in its glory five thousand years ago. Even now it evoked awe as she stood gazing up at the tallest of the stones rising well above her head. Was it at a place such as this that Columba confronted the druid Broichan?

"Look, isn't this ogham writing?" Gareth ran his finger slantwise along a series of marks cut into the back of the stone.

Brad nodded. "Sure is. That would have been added much later. Ogham writing is comparatively new—since the time of Saint Patrick."

"You mean it's Christian?" Mary asked.

"No. Not necessarily. Only the crosses—which were often incised on the backs of pagan stones—are identifiably Christian. Nobody has ever been able to decode the ogham."

"Oh, I wish they could," she cried.

"Well, who knows, maybe someday some farmer's plough will turn up the Rosetta Stone of Ogham writing. It would be a great breakthrough, so little is known about the pre-Christian era."

Mary's brow furrowed. "I don't understand about the Scoti. Wasn't Columba about the same time as King Arthur? In stories I've read the Scoti were fierce heathen. Yet Hamish said Fergus mac Erc came from Ireland, which had been Christianized and civilized long before Arthur—or am I confused?"

"No more than most of the rest of us, because no one really knows for sure." Brad led on across the pasture toward a small, tree-lined road running up the green glen.

The sun that had been playing chase with the clouds all morning broke through a patch of blue, warming the field. Mary took off her coat and folded it across her arm. A few paces further she felt it being lifted gently.

"I'll just carry that for you a wee while."

She smiled at Gareth.

Brad strode ahead, still lecturing. "In the broadest terms the Picts and Scots were the same people—all part of the great westward migration of tribes from somewhere in Asia that spread across Europe in waves for about two thousand years before Christ. The Picts

—or Caledones—settled in what is now central Scotland, driving into the hills the little dark people who had lived there apparently since the beginning of time. The Scots went on westward to what is now Ireland, then gradually returned to settle the Western Islands and coastal districts of Scotland—naming the region after Dalriata in Ireland from which many of them came."

Now Mary was sinking in the mud from which grew the tall, reedy grass covering the land between them and the road.

Brad looked back over his shoulder. "Carry on. We'll just bash our way through here. Once over the fence we'll have clear going up to the burial sites. He waved the small map he had extracted from a pocket of his well-worn Barbour.

Mary lost a few lines of his narrative as she concentrated on not losing her shoes in the muck.

At the fence Brad placed one hand on a pole and was over in a leap. Gareth steadied Mary while she climbed the wires. "I think we'll hold out for a stile next time," he said.

She returned his grin, then hurried forward to catch Brad's words.

"The traditional founder of the Dalriadan is the Irish Prince Cairbre Riada. He was driven from his home by a famine in Munster and led his kinsmen to the Western Islands around A.D. 258. But there are traces of Irish settlements on the West Coast as early as 200 or even 300 B.C.

"Of course, you're quite right about Patrick. He was Christianizing Ireland around A.D 450. Which is a hundred years before Arthur —or whoever the Romano-Celtic war leader was who held the Saxons out of western Britain. And some believe he ruled in Scotland as well. Which brings us to your question about Fergus son of Erc, the founder of the Dalriadan in this area.

"He and his two brothers arrived just before the year 500—in other words, between Patrick and Columba, so he well might have had some acquaintance with Christianity. But there's no evidence for widespread Christianity beyond the work of Ninian among the northern British in Galloway. Certainly all the Picts and most of the Scoti would have been pagan when Columba arrived."

Mary was now breathing hard with the work of keeping up with her long-legged cousin. "Thanks, Brad. I think I got most of that."

"Good, because here we are at Nether Logie." He led them up a small path to their right, and this time the fence did have a stile. "This is one of the best cairns in all Scotland because you can actually go down into it."

They climbed the massive pile of loose stones forming the cairn, then, following Brad, Mary ducked down into the narrow chamber where men had been buried hundreds of years before Christ. Stooping low, Brad took them into the second chamber, dimly lighted from an overhead opening.

She ran her hands over the piled thin flagstones lining the walls. Pebbles crunched under her feet.

"The chambers were probably used for cremation by Stone Age people, then for uncremated burials by their Bronze Age successors," Brad said over his shoulder. A few more crunchings of pebbles and they were out again into the uncertain sunshine.

Brad swept the broad green valley with his arm. "This whole valley is filled with ritual and burial monuments. We don't have time to see nearly all of them, but there's a particularly good cup and ring stone in the corner of the next field. We might just hack our way around there and take a peek before we get on."

Mary nodded. She felt dizzy with the closeness of history, overwhelmed by time and space and her desire to make sense of it all.

The cup and ring stone was a broad, flat slab of granite such as those that had been upended to form the circle of standing stones they examined earlier. But this had been left resting flat on the earth and was engraved with repeated patterns of multiple rings. The largest was a circle of nine rings radiating out from a central circle, like ripples from a stone thrown into a pond. Many were simply one or two circles around a central indentation. And some were cups—engraved hollows forming small basins.

"What does it mean?" she asked.

Brad shook his head. "No one knows. But there are hundreds of stones like this all over Scotland."

Gareth grinned. "Bet I know."

They looked at him.

"It's a game board. See, they tossed pebbles at the circles for points. Probably piled their counting stones in the cups."

Brad laughed. "Why not? It's as good an explanation as any I've heard."

Kilmartin Glen stretched green and inviting with open fields and tree-lined paths that led to dozens of mysterious ancient sites. All were well marked with signs explaining what was known or could be reasonably surmised about the people who had lived there thousands of years ago. Lived, perhaps fought, certainly worshiped in this ritual valley. And, a fitting conclusion, at the top of the valley was a small church. Its foundations dated back to medieval times, and its churchyard housed an excellent collection of Christian tombstones and Celtic crosses. So Brad and his guidebook assured them.

But the object of their quest lay at the other end of the valley—the ancient hill fort of DunAdd. There Columba had proclaimed Aiden mac Gabhran king of Dalriada on the ritual stone where each ruler of that land, stretching far back into the mists of time, had placed his foot as a symbol that he stood in the footsteps of those who had gone before.

Early the next morning, a winding dirt track took them to the foot of the hill fort, which rose from the flat surrounding land that had in earlier days provided protective marshes to keep would-be attackers at bay.

The wind blew her long fair hair as Mary gazed up at the great slabs of moss-covered granite thrusting above the green turf. Banks of ferns, dandelions, and bright buttercups grew in every sheltered cranny. But the truly captivating sight was the luxuriant purple heather covering the lower slopes.

Mary's feet easily found the ancient entrance path through the natural cleft in the rocks and began the ascent to the accompaniment of bird song and the baaing of distant sheep. She paused at the first of the level terraces.

"There are five of these terraces—probably courts of the ancient fort." Brad referred only briefly to the book in his hand—he seemed to know most of his history by heart. "They were each surrounded by stone walls—or most likely turf and timber first. Most of the courts contained buildings." He pointed upward to the flattened top of the dun. "The summit fort was enclosed by an oval wall, which defined the inner citadel."

Mary nodded, and Brad continued.

"The archeological finds here have been rich, indicating that it was a place of high status—ornamental metalwork, imported pottery, weapons, artifacts, tools, jewelry of glass, enamel, gold, and semi-precious stones."

She nodded again. It was nice that science corroborated what she could sense about the place anyway.

It was so quiet that the wind brought only the sound of a tractor from a faraway field and the whistling of a farm worker somewhere out of sight. The ancient hill fort stood nearly deserted—another carload of sightseers was leaving as Mary ascended the path. But it was not difficult to picture this as once a place of bustling activity, a place where kings were made and from which armies marched forth.

She climbed first to the very top—to what Brad had called the inner citadel—where she could see traces of the fortifying rock wall amid the turf, heather, and buttercups. And then she looked out across the flat green sweep of the narrow valley that had once been marsh, where the silver blue ribbon of the River Add wound to the hills beyond.

Glad that the men were exploring on their own, she then retraced her steps to the terrace just below the summit. This was what they had most come to see. Feeling herself on the edge of the world, she sat on one side of the long, slightly rounded rock face. It was deeply seamed and cracked so that at first she had to look carefully for the famous carvings. Then she saw them.

With one finger she gently traced the pattern of a realistically carved boar delicately incised in the stone. Strange that Hamish had not mentioned that in his story about Columba. She moved on to shake her head over the locked mysteries of the Ogham writing carved just beyond the boar, then turned to the other end of the great gray slab. She was surprised at the depth of the cup carved there. She had expected it to be no deeper than the gentle depressions in the cup and ring stones she'd seen earlier, but this was a small bowl. What had it held in pre-Christian times? Sacrificial blood? Meal offerings to some god?

She had saved the best for last. She stood on the rock as fresh Highland air blew around her and white clouds billowed above the lush greenness stretching in every direction. Here was the birthplace of the Scottish nation. With a sense of history welling up in her and an awareness of her own strong ties to this land of her heritage, she could imagine the sound of drums and horns, the chanting of monks. She placed her foot in the deeply carved footprint of kings.

* * *

Kenneth son of Alpin placed his foot in the deep footplace of the rock. A tumultuous blast of horns and the triumphant beat of drums rent the monks' sonorous chanting. The new-made king spread his arms wide, the white rod of ruling in one hand, his father's sword in the other, as if to encompass all his people—the mormaors of the Scots of Dalriada, who supported his rule, the warriors so needful to keep his people free, the workers and craftsmen from farmstead and clachan, the monks, priests, and princes of the church. He would ever seek to be a good and just ruler as he had vowed. But he knew the work had only begun.

For Kenneth was inaugurated king of a small nation beset on every side by fierce neighbors who looked greedily at the land around them, neighbors who were divided in their own loyalties and who were only nominally faithful, if at all, to the faith that had been so long established in Dalriada and Alba by the much-revered Columba three hundred years before. Even Ireland, that great cradle of the faith since the days of Saint Patrick, was much beset by heathen Danes, and some areas were ruled by half-pagan Norse.

But Kenneth was determined. He would keep the faith alight. He would strengthen the House of Gabhran, descended from that first Dalriadan king, Fergus mac Erc. He would not let freedom and justice die in this land.

And in pledge of this he had added something new to this enthroning ceremony that he had repeated from his father, Alpin, just as Alpin had repeated from his father, Eochaid, and he from his father, and on back as far as anyone knew.

Or perhaps this that he now did was not so new, but was rather a renewal, for many said that so had Columba anointed Kenneth's ancestor, Aiden mac Gabhran, seated on the stone that had been Jacob's pillow and which Saint Columba himself had brought from Ireland for his own pillow.

But Kenneth would not have the sacred chrism poured on his head almost as an afterthought to the ancient king-making ceremony of placing his foot in the print of his ancestors. The sacred anointing, as far as anyone knew, had been begun by Columba in imitation of the anointing of King Saul by the prophet Samuel. It was to serve as a reminder that the role of the king was to be the spiritual as well as temporal leader of his people. So Kenneth would have Abbot Dairmait perform this religious rite as a separate ceremony.

Kenneth had thought even of having it performed on Iona for the great love he bore the holy island both for its sacredness and its beauty—as well as for the fact that he had been born there. But his mormaors had persuaded him of the folly of undertaking to move all the court to so vulnerable a spot at a time of such danger. Far better to bring the holy brothers and their stone to DunAdd.

And so now, as the clash of cymbals rang out over the flat green Moss stretching on all sides of DunAdd, the new-made king of the Scots and the abbot of Iona led the procession from the third courtyard of the royal fortress upward to the stone-walled inner citadel, where a small stone church stood beside the king's timbered hall house. The company arranged itself: monks before the church; mormaors, thanes, and warriors to the outside of the court. At the sound of the trumpets Abbot Dairmait led four of his youngest, strongest brothers from the church bearing the sacred stone.

When first the abbot had shown him the stone, Kenneth had been worried about the ceremony. The stone was too small and oddly shaped for a dignified ceremonial seating. Surely this was the one often referred to by the bards as the Stone of Destiny. The carefully incised cross on it spoke to its sacredness, and other carvings to its antiquity. But had he misunderstood the tradition that Columba seated his ancestor on this? Perhaps it had been used in another manner.

Then Brother Corbanac, the sacristan who cared for all the sacred relics on Iona, suggested a solution. Could not the stone be encased in a seat—one carved and painted with great beauty?

Kenneth had immediately called his most skilled carpenters and woodcarvers and set them to work. He ordered a carved seat intertwining sacred images with the flowers and animals so beloved of his people—and with openwork on the sides so all could see the stone encased within. The image that had immediately grasped Kenneth's mind had been that of the ark of the Covenant, which had contained the stone tablets bearing the Ten Commandments given by God to Moses on Mount Sinai. The analogy was imperfect. Certainly no ruler of Israel ever sat on the ark—or even touched it—but the image persisted in Kenneth's mind, even to his wondering whether perhaps some other object should be encased in the chest with the stone; the ark had held a pot of manna and Aaron's rod as well. Few objects seemed of equal value, however. The Viking raids on Iona over the last fifty years had left them so few of their sacred relics.

Then he thought of Columba's Brecbennoch, the little house-shaped casket containing a vial of sacred chrism, which Columba was said to have worn around his neck. Although the metal-covered wooden box was adorned with intricately carved, red-enameled metal disks and bars, no Viking had thought it worth carrying off. Certainly no Viking could have understood the great value Kenneth placed on it. So Brother Corbanac had been dispatched to Iona to collect the Brecbennoch, and now it lay in the casket with the stone.

Also somewhat as a shadow of the sacred Ark, the holy brothers who bore the seat behind their abbot carried it on their shoulders by means of long poles passed through iron rings in each corner. With a final clash of cymbals they placed the seat between king and abbot.

Kenneth bowed his head and sat. If the stone were really from the Lia Fail as some said, and if there were any truth to the saying that the Stone of Destiny should cry out when the true ruler of the land sat on it, none could tell whether this had been fulfilled, for the seating of the king was accompanied by a flourish of trumpets.

Then all was silent on the crest of DunAdd.

Dairmait, the sun shining on his tonsured forehead and white robes, poured the vial of holy chrism over the head of Kenneth mac

Alpin, symbolizing that he had been chosen by God for a special purpose.

And the monks chanted.

"May the Lord our God grant you what is in your heart.
May He fulfill your every plan.
May we shout for joy at your victory, our king,
And raise the standards in the name of our God.
The Lord grant all our requests."

King Kenneth's thick brown hair was made more shiny than usual by the sacred oil, and the sun gleamed from the great gold brooch that held his saffron and scarlet plaid cloak. He stood and replied:

"Now I know that the Lord will give victory to His
    anointed,
That He has heard and will answer His servant from
    His holy heaven with the strength of His victorious
    right hand."

And the people responded:

"Some are strong in chariots; some in horses;
But we are strong in the name of the Lord our God.
Lord, grant victory to the king."

The ceremony ended with a ringing shout, and Kenneth led the way to the royal hall house for a great feast. That is, as many followed as would fit into the hall house. The others were to be served at trestle tables in the courtyard, which even now servants were scurrying to set up. And in the lower courtyards, opened to all from Dalriada who cared to make the journey, great platters of roast venison and boar and oxen, and trenchers of wheaten bannocks and oatcakes, and horns of ale and barley beer would be passed among the people to honor this new day for the nation of Dalriada when Kenneth son of Alpin began his reign among them.

15

It was barely a week later, when the monks had returned to Iona, the farmers to their garths, and the mormaors to their duns and raths, that Kenneth's new-given authority met its first challenge. And his sister Cathira meant to see that he lost.

The golden disks on the ends of the embroidered cord belting her green and purple plaid tunic clanged in rhythm to her determined step as she strode the length of the hall house from the women's place to the seat of King Kenneth. She would answer her kingly brother's summons. But she would not take his orders.

Their brother Donald sat beside him on the dais, taller but more slightly built than Kenneth, with lighter brown hair. And quieter. Donald was ever a good general for Kenneth during the five years he had ruled as subking in Galloway, the southwesternmost region of Dalriada. And then Alpin of Dalriada was killed fighting against the Picts—killed and beheaded—and his elder son was chosen high king of the Scots. Donald, the second son, never seemed to mind being second in command; he was good at taking orders.

Cathira, their younger sister, was not.

She glared at her brothers from her emerald green eyes and spared no smiles for the captains seated on the other side of Kenneth. Not a smile for Barr the bald, nor for Dungal of the gray-streaked beard, and today not even for Talorgen mac Cetul, he of the black hair and eyes, who always wore a sleek leopardskin pelt over his plaid. For surely Talorgen had acquiesced in this plan of the king's. But Cathira did not acquiesce. Did not and would not.

She tossed her cloud of red hair and raised her chin as she mounted the dais. It was a signal to Kenneth that she was as determined as ever to have her own way. And as always she knew what that way was. For always Cathira had known her own mind—since her first bite of oatmeal porridge, when she decided she did not like the slimy, bland stuff and blew a mouthful of it all over the servant who had been sent to feed her. The girl had wiped the porridge off herself and the infant Cathira and began again. Only to be met with a tightly clamped pair of lips.

"Leave her be. She will open wide enough when hunger is upon her," the infant's brother Kenneth had advised.

But she never did, even in times of hard winters that emptied the hills and cook pots of game. Cathira would eat oatcakes or barley bannocks but not porridge. She knew her mind.

And now, eighteen years later, she still knew it. She would not marry Nechtan, brother to the king of Alba, no matter how fervently her kingly brother wished for an alliance with the most powerful mormaor of the Picts. She would marry no one of her brother's choosing. On second thought, she smiled at Talorgen.

"Sit you down, sister." Kenneth indicated a stool to her right, draped with thick-furred bearskin.

"I will stand."

"As you will." His slight half smile enraged her. But she knew better than to show it. It was far too early in the contest to lose her temper.

"My counselors and I have been considering heavy matters of state. As you know—as indeed all the people of Dalriada know—I seek peace for our land. But our neighbors will not live peaceably, so other means must be used."

She made no reply.

"Even now our cousin Eoganan prepares to journey to Fortriu as my emissary to seek an alliance with Drust, high king of the Picts. Our countries must work together in this matter of defending against the Vikings." Kenneth indicated the seat beyond Donald recently vacated by Eoganan.

Cathira gave a scornful laugh. "Drust will spit on your envoy, brother. He will see such an alliance as a sign of weakness—as fear that you cannot defend your own land and as an insult that you think he cannot defend his."

"It is because I foresee just such an outcome that I send Eoganan with an overlarge, well-armed guard. Drust will see no weakness in Dalriada."

"Still, Drust will spit." *As I would,* she could have added.

"No doubt you are right, but I would not have war with a people so long and so closely associated with our own. I seek a peaceful alliance."

"I will *not* marry Nechtan mac Ferat." There. She had made her announcement before Kenneth made his.

To her surprise, he threw back his head and gave a shout of

laughter that momentarily rang from one end of the hall to the other. "Indeed and I am glad of that, my sister."

Then he turned serious again. "The Albannach are not our only worry. Indeed they would be little worry did not the Vikings so harry our shores. It is as an alliance against the Vikings that we need the Picti and they need the Scoti. It is on the matter of defense against the Danish that I would speak to you."

Cathira's wide, white brow wrinkled in a frown. She did not understand.

"Barr, who returned from Ireland just before my enthroning" —Kenneth's stout captain dipped his head, and the light of the seal-oil lamps shone on his bald pate—"brings news that Olaf the White, king of Dublin, has put away his wife, Aud the Deep-minded. She has been sent back to her father, Ketil Flatnose, Jarl of the Western Isles. It is said she has some scheme of her own for making a settlement in Iceland. But be that as it may, the fact remains, Olaf is without a wife."

"What—" But Cathira had no need to finish her question as the full implication of this struck her. Now she wished she had accepted the seat she had spurned. She needed something to hold onto.

"Olaf? Olaf the White, king of Dublin? You would marry me to a heathen Viking?"

"No, my sister, I would marry you to a Norseman. And he is Christian, at least in name."

She glared at him in defiant, stony silence.

"Cathira, your mother was Norse." He said it gently.

"And yours was Pictish. So that means you can tell me what to do?"

"I tell you what to do because I am your elder brother—"

"Half brother."

He ignored the interruption. "Your brother, standing in place of our father. Also because I am your king, and because it is for the good of all our people, Pictish and Norse—and above all, Scoti."

"The Picts would not thank you for making an alliance with their enemies."

"You speak truth. But all know that as king of Galloway I sought heartily to make treaty peace with Pictland and with all our neighbors. So am I trying again as king of Dalriada. So will I continue to seek."

"And they will not because they will not be ruled over by a Scot." *Nor will I be ruled by a brother.*

"I speak of alliance, not of kingship, but it has been done before. Our father's cousins Constantine and Oengus were none so bad rulers for Pictland for all their Scots blood."

"And would still be ruling had they not been slain by the Vikings to whom you would now send your sister as treaty pawn."

Kenneth ran his hands through his hair and began pacing the dais. "No. I would send you to the Norse. But what you say of the Danish Vikings is true and all too true. For so is the royal house of Alba cut down until the inexperienced Drust rules in Forteviot. Drust, whose father, Ferat, was the weakest mormaor ever known in Fortriu. And mark my words—as king, Drust will not last the year unless he will stand with Dalriada to resist the Danes. And yet I have little hope for Eoganan's mission."

Kenneth whirled abruptly with one of those quick motions that was so characteristic of him. He grasped both Cathira's hands. "Sister, let us put away this conflict between us—there is enough of that in the world. Cannot we talk reason before my council?"

Indeed she had forgotten the presence of the others—even of Talorgen, toward whom she glanced now as Kenneth continued, still holding her hands.

"Dalriada is pressed on all sides. Danes maraud and pillage on the west. To the south the Angles and Saxons are content for the moment with making war on Strathclyde, but King Roderick cannot hold forever. And Alba to the north and east in the hands of a weak leader is worse than no neighbor at all. I will apply to Drust first—for all my lack of confidence in him—because of our linked bloodlines and the old ties of our nations. Olaf is of the old enemy, it is true, but he is a fine man. A strong man."

"And you will make marriage treaty with those who sacked your beloved Iona?"

The shadow that crossed Kenneth's face showed how sorely her thrust had gone home, how truly the desecration of the holy place of Dalriada pained him. But he held to his theme. "It was done by Vikings, not by the king of Dublin. The Norse and Danes hold none so close a friendship."

"And so you would send me as missionary/wife to make a monk of Olaf the White?"

"You overstate, my sister, yet you are not so wide of the mark. For such will be part of your task—the harder part. The matters of state you take on for the Scots. The matters of faith you undertake for all Christians. Olaf is Christian in name. But he understands little."

And what do I undertake for myself, brother?

"Will you take this on, Cathira? If not for me, then for our Lord?"

"Are you *asking* then, Kenneth mac Alpin? And not telling?" For the first time, Cathira softened the slightest bit in her determination.

At that moment a servant entered the hall house to inform the council that Eoganan and the envoy of guards were ready to depart under Kenneth's white wolf banner.

The men went out to see them off, but Cathira turned toward her bower. She had much to think on.

She walked more slowly now. In spite of her fiery, headstrong ways, which she knew all around her saw as simply stubborn willfulness—and she bothered little to correct that impression—her outbursts weren't just for the sake of getting her own way. Or even for the sake of making life difficult for those around her. At least they weren't when she had taken time for cool consideration. Her demands and holdouts were truly because she wanted things to be done right. The slipshod, the rather close, the almost right would not do for her beloved Dalriada—or for a princess thereof.

And so, when things were not right—right as she saw right to be—she was given to lashing out at those nearest her.

"My lady."

She turned at the voice of Garbh, her most trusted servant, he who had served her own mother before she died of the milk fever shortly after Cathira's birth.

"The goldsmith has finished the brooch you requested." Garbh held out a small wooden tray covered with sealskin.

Cathira lifted the soft covering layer and scrutinized the circular gold ornament engraved in an intricate, interlaced design and adorned with garnets. The sun sparkled on it. From its warm sealskin bed it appeared a lovely thing. But as she looked closer she saw the truth of the matter. The engraving was uneven, as if begun by a master and finished by a student. Two of the garnets were fine, glowing with deep, blood-red warmth. The third was off-color and flawed.

Her temper flared. That such inferior workmanship should be produced at the place in all the land most noted for its fine metalwork was unthinkable. Did the goldsmiths of King Kenneth believe they could get by with the shoddy, because the king was occupied with pressing matters of state? Or that his sister would not know the difference? She dashed the tray to the courtyard stones with a single word.

"Unacceptable!"

She whirled and strode into the women's place.

And this idea of her kingly brother's to give her in marriage to Olaf was likewise unacceptable—as Kenneth's idea to seek an alliance of peace with the Picts was unacceptable.

By the time she reached her bower, a room separated from the hall of the women by a wall hung with rich furs and colorful weavings, an idea was forming in her mind.

Drust was weak. Kenneth had said so. To make treaty with a weak king would weaken Dalriada. To swear an alliance for mutual protection with a weak neighbor would simply draw Dalriada into wars to protect Alba, to Dalriada's harm. Could not Kenneth see that? His plan must be stopped for the sake of Dalriada.

She put from her mind the fact that if all failed to go smoothly with Eoganan's embassy to Drust, Kenneth would be too preoccupied to see to her forced marriage and she would have more time to work on Talorgen. She would do what she did for the good of Dalriada. Her own matters she could manage easily enough.

But what could she do?

Sinech, her serving girl, began a soft strumming on her harp but stopped abruptly at an impatient wave of Cathira's hand. The only sound in the room then was the measured tread of Cathira's pacing on the rushes of the floor and the soft clanking of the golden disks of her belt.

At last, when the savory odors from the cookplace were heavy enough to penetrate even Cathira's intense concentration, she turned to Sinech. "Get you to your table, girl. I will not eat until this matter is settled, but you need not go hungry." The girl rose. "And send you Garbh to me when he has eaten. I shall have all prepared by then."

Alone in her room, she sat at a small, richly carved table by the western window where enough light still fell to make burning a lantern unnecessary. Cathira disliked the stink of seal oil and hated the black smoke it produced. She drew out a sheet of the finest vellum and dipped a newly sharpened heron quill in her inkpot. The congealed ink fell from the quill tip in a blob.

She grasped the pot and threw it across the room, unmindful of where it landed. Her orders were clear. Her writing materials were to be kept ready at all times.

"*Sinech!*"

The second inkpot followed the first just as the girl reentered the room. The flying jar narrowly missed the servant's pale head.

"Fresh ink!"

"Yes, my lady." The little blonde mouse scurried out.

A pot of freshly mixed ink was on Cathira's table in half the time it would have taken a less well-trained servant to cross the courtyard to the royal clerk's chamber. Now the room held only the soft scratching sounds of Cathira's pen moving swiftly across the vellum.

At length she stopped, put down the quill, and read. A smile played around the corners of her full, red lips. She picked up the pen again and signed with a flourish. Now the smile was full-blown. This was not the first time she had put to use the careful imitation of her brother's signature that she had learned when the children of Alpin were taught their letters by Brother Grillan from Iona. That had been one advantage of having Alpin's first wife come from the Picti. They were a matrilineal society, and the life of the tribes as well as the succession to the seats of power came through the women—therefore the daughters were educated with the sons. And the court followed the ways of its first queen in that matter long after her death.

She sprinkled the ink with sand, then blew it off, rolled the vellum, sealed it with a blob of wax, and stamped the seal. The triumph of her smile reached her eyes. Kenneth had not even thought to ask the whereabouts of their father's second seal.

She recognized Garbh's slightly shuffling footstep before he had time to request entrance.

"Enter, Garbh."

She rehooked the thick bearskin that gave extra protection against cold draughts around her door—and extra muffling to any words spoken in her bower—then began without preamble. "My kingly brother has charged me to carry out a most delicate mission for him. We shall ride forth at the first light. You and I only. Tell no one—only that I have taken it into my head to hunt the roe deer in the forest beyond the Moss. With luck we should be back by sundown tomorrow, but bring supplies for an added day's journey if necessary."

"Yes, my lady." He withdrew.

And it was that simple. Garbh's loyalty could be counted on to the last breath. And his obedience and efficiency. The perfect servant. There was now an air of triumph to Cathira's stride as she paced, holding the rolled vellum before her in both hands. She gave careful thought to every aspect of her plan. Yes, Eoganan traveled with a large guard. Two mounted on swift horses could easily catch them in time. Perhaps she would even shoot a roe deer on return.

If not, it was little matter. Who would connect an innocent hunting foray by the king's sister with the disaster that was to befall King Drust? But all Albana would blame King Kenneth. And then he would be forced to take the action he should now be preparing for did he not harbor this ridiculous vision of Dalriada and Alba living as

164

peaceful neighbors under the laws of man and God. Kenneth must seize the crown, and that was the end of the matter.

If anything, she had underrated the success of her plan—of the first stage of it at least. She caught up with Eoganan well before he had reached Inverary the next day. He ordered his guard to ride ahead and take refreshment on the shore of Loch Fyne while he pulled aside to confer with her in a sheltering thicket of birch and alder.

Cathira toyed coyly with her amber necklace, then smiled when he looked up from his reading of the vellum document, knowing well the full effect her favorite green and red gold hunting tartan served when she was flushed and her hair blown from a spirited ride.

A response to her powers flickered in Eoganan's eyes, then he returned quickly to business. He shook his head in disbelief. "Drust will invite us to a banquet in seeming goodwill but means to murder us? All? Is it possible?"

"And have you never heard the tale of the Saxon lord who long ago invited his Celtic neighbors to a great feast, and when their bodies were made slow with rich food and their minds fuddled with wine gave the signal for his men to draw the daggers hidden in their tunics and slay their guests?"

It was clear from his blank look that Eoganan had not heard, but Cathira's careful instruction by Brother Grillan had not fallen on deaf ears.

"And so we are to strike first?"

"First and swiftly, with careful aim."

"But how would Kenneth know of this? Does Drust even know of our approach?"

Cathira tossed her red hair and took time to see that the effect was not lost. "Eoganan, do you question my brother the king—or his sister?"

"No. No, forgive me. Yet I wondered."

"And know you not that in these evil days there are spies at every court? That is why my brother would have this carried by no hand but my own. And were you not aware of the arrival of a trader with his pack mules even as you were leaving DunAdd? I should have thought you would have passed him on the Great Moss if not at the very entranceway of DunAdd . . ." It hung in the air. The suggestion was safe enough. There was enough coming and going at the strongplace of Dalriada. Who was to say?

"But to rise up and strike those who are giving us hospitality . . ."

Cathira threw her hands into the air, and her gold bands jingled on her white arms. "Fine. Let them strike first. Then you may fight back with honor—any of you who have lifeblood left with which to fight."

Eoganan half turned from her and looked again at the carefully written document. "A trap under the tables into which our benches are to fall—it seems so unlikely . . ."

She shrugged. "And have you never heard of hunting boar or bear thus?"

And Eoganan had to admit that he had once caught a very fine boar by the trick of luring the animal to run over a thinly covered pit. He shuddered at the thought of meeting such an end. "Tell Kenneth we will strike."

"That is good." Cathira held out her hand for the vellum. "My brother bids me return his document. It must not fall into the wrong hands."

Cathira returned to DunAdd in double triumph, for she had also taken a fine roe deer with a single arrow in the neck.

It was many days of waiting until news of the disaster at the high palace of Alba at Forteviot reached DunAdd. Cathira was in the lower courtyard practicing with bow and arrow—a pastime her ladies had little taste for but Cathira could spend hours at—when she heard the clatter of a lone horse's hooves making rapid ascent up the entranceway to the fort. She thrust her weapons at Sinech, gathered the skirt of her gown, and managed to stroll in a side door of the hall house at the same time the messenger flung himself breathless before Kenneth.

"They are all slain, my lord." He would go on, but he choked on his next words.

The king signaled a servant for a cup of heather beer.

The man drained the cup at a single gulp and wiped his mouth with the back of his hand.

"Who are slain? Eoganan's men? My envoy?"

The messenger shook his head, and his heavy leather jerkin creaked. "Drust and his court. Two Albannach thanes, many warriors . . . the number is uncertain."

"And our men? "

"A few slain. Several wounded. Eoganan killed by Drust's bodyguard after he gave the fatal thrust to the Picti king."

Cathira hid her smile. So. Her luck had held. Her plan worked to perfection. That had been her one worry—that Drust's guard

166

might fail to avenge his king's death. Then she would have had to think of some way to deal with Eoganan. But now all was done.

Kenneth stood and pulled his plaid from his shoulder in the motion of an Old Testament king rending his garments. "But how could such be? They were on a *peace* mission. They sought an alliance of friendship." He shook his fist in rage.

The messenger fell back as the king's fist slashed near his own shoulder. "My lord, they say it was your order. Eoganan told his men you had discovered treachery at Drust's court—that they must strike first or be stricken."

"Who says so?"

The messenger retreated another pace. "I was told so by Fechnon mac Eoganan. He holds the high place now while the Picti mormaors gather."

Kenneth groaned and with both hands to his head flung himself into his seat. "And so all Alba blames me for this treachery. I, who would unite the people in friendship, am accused of dividing them by treason." He looked up. "There is nothing for it but that I must go to Fortriu."

"Yes, my brother, spoken like a true king." Cathira strode forward from the shadows below the dais and grabbed his shoulders. "Now is your moment. No mere alliance but the kingship! Did you not always long to unite our people? March into Forteviot with your army at your heels and be enthroned at Scone. What a triumph! That your dreams should be fulfilled so quickly. Alba has fallen like a ripe plum into your lap."

He jerked her hands from his shoulders with a wide-flung gesture. "Are you mad, sister? Think you I want to be made king by means of treachery? I will be lawful king or none."

"King is king. And once you hold power you may make all the laws you want."

"And think you I will have time for lawmaking when the mormaors of all the seven regions of Pictland march against me? Need I remind you that even divided as they are and weakened by Viking raids, the Albannach are a far more numerous people than ours? And what think you the Vikings and Angles will do when they see Dalriada and Alba at war? Will they sit on their hands and give me time to make order and give laws? This treachery could easily spell the very end of both Alba *and* Dalriada—and the Christianity we have stood for these three hundred years."

Kenneth sat quietly for several long moments, his head covered with his broad, strong hands. When he looked up he was calm, determined. He spoke to a waiting servant. "I will take only my personal bodyguard. Tell Donald he is to hold here as my general. And tell Father Ernan I will hear mass."

"Yes, my brother. See that you are well-shriven." Cathira raised her chin. "For if you insist on going in weakness, it is certain you go to your death."

16

In the end it was two days before Kenneth could set out, for there was much to see to, and he would not leave Dalriada uncared for. Donald was ever a good second-in-command; he would carry out Kenneth's instructions to the letter. But the instructions must be given, for Donald was not a creative leader. And Kenneth must carefully choose those he would take with him—the strongest, most loyal of his household, and yet not strip DunAdd of those best able to support Donald. Kenneth was not unaware that there were those, even in the high place of Dalriada, who had somewhat different views on how best their nation should be ruled—not the least being his strong-willed sister.

Of his captains he would take the bald, stout Barr, whose baldness seemed a symbol of the strong mind his shining crown encased and whose stout body exemplified the sturdiness of his heart. And he must have the gray-bearded Dungal mac Machar with him, for Dungal's father had been captain to Kenneth's father, and Dungal had been Kenneth's closest adviser when Alpin succeeded to the high throne of Dalriada and Kenneth was chosen by the council of thanes and mormaors to rule the subkingdom of Galloway.

Kenneth considered Talorgen, he of the black hair and shining eyes and quick wit. Talorgen's quick wit could indeed be useful at Forteviot Palace, but it was also a quality Donald might have need of relying on. And what of Cathira's liking for this bold warrior of the Dalriadan? A liking of which she made no secret, especially when Kenneth would discuss the matter of Olaf the White with her. Kenneth did not doubt his sister's loyalty to Dalriada, but her loyalty to her brother she might interpret as another matter.

He gave swift thought to the further entanglement of Brocessa nic Dungal, who had been hand-fasted with Talorgen two years ago, although there had been little talk of marriage of late as far as Kenneth knew. But the high king of Dalriada had no time for the gossip of the women's place. Donald needed Talorgen, so Talorgen would stay.

In the bright shining of an August morning, when early-blooming bell heather was faded and the dark purple ling heather blanketed the lower slopes of DunAdd, Kenneth mac Alpin rode forth to the sound of trumpet and cymbals with twenty of his best warriors.

They crossed the Crinan Moss with his red banners bearing the white wolf of the Scoti flying proudly for all his people to see. They went on to the northeast along the blue waters of Loch Fyne, where they spent the night at the stronghold of the mormaor of Inverary. The next day the going was less swift, for they crossed a land dotted with lochs and steep hills and crossed the southern end of the mountains most often referred to as the spine of the land.

And now they went with banners furled. For they were in Pictland, the region of Fortriu, central of the seven regions of Alba. It was from this region that the high king of Alba had ruled since fierce attacks by the Viking raiders many years ago had forced the Pictish kings southward from their northern fastness at Craig Phadrig.

The mormaors of Findach, however, still held sway at Craig Phadrig, descendants of that Brude whom Columba converted. And Kenneth knew it would take a similar miracle to bring the present mormaor of Findach to treat with Dalriada, for Bruide mac Feredethus was known for being fierce as a boar, hard as granite, and cruel as any Dane. Kenneth's father had slain Bruide's father in battle. Kenneth would not look to Bruide mac Feredethus for support in the court of Alba.

He struggled to form a strategy for the chaotic situation he was certain to encounter at Forteviot. First he must look to his own men. His general, Eoganan, was slain, the messenger said, so Kenneth could only hope his captain Aed was keeping the Dalriadan men in control. The worst thing that could happen would be for them to view themselves as a conquering army and begin claiming the spoils of war. Kenneth himself was ever firm—stripping fallen enemies of their weapons and gold was no more than the warrior's due as victory prize, but he would not have the countryside pillaged or the women raped.

Of what the slain Eoganan's son Fechnon was doing he also had concern. Holding power while the mormaors gathered, the messenger had said—did that mean the ambitious Fechnon thought to hold the throne of Alba? Kenneth shook his head. Bad enough to have to worry about the imponderables of the Alban rulers without the matters of his own people to tangle it further. And all complicated by the belief on both sides that Kenneth mac Alpin had ordered treachery.

He scanned the map of Pictland in his mind as he assessed the situation. Fortriu, across which they traveled, would now likely pass to Nechtan mac Ferat, half brother to the slain Drust and therefore some exceedingly distant cousin to Kenneth himself through his mother. Nechtan he knew to be an able and reasonable mormaor, one likely to support Kenneth's idea of alliance if there remained any hope of reaching him after the seeming treachery.

Cruithne mac Boanta mac Ferat, mormaor of Atholl, the region just northwest of Fortriu and of all Pictland the region sharing the longest border with Dalriada, had ever been a good neighbor. Kenneth smiled as he pictured the bandy-legged, kilted Cruithne with his black, jutting beard, looking exactly like the model for Picti warriors carved on so many of their memorial stones. Cruithne had ruled Atholl long and well and had kept the cattle raids between their two countries to a reasonable level. He could be expected to support Kenneth's proposal but that he was grandson to Ferat, father of the slain Drust. Kenneth slammed a fist against the high shoulders of his saddle. If he ever got to the bottom of this matter of the killing of Drust and his court . . .

But for the moment he must concentrate on matters as they were. Above Atholl, running from the Isle of Skye in the west to the River Spey in the east, the length of Loch Lochy and Loch Ness, was Bruide's Findach. He could look for no support there.

In the forested lands of Cait running to the north of Findach, from Moray Firth to the Orkney Islands, however, Kenneth could hope for a friend. Reuther mac Galan was an old, wise head, respected among his people in spite of the weight of years that bent his shoulders and weakened his sword arm. And Reuther of Cait knew better than most the threat of the Viking, pressed as he ever was from the Norse-ruled Orkneys.

Kenneth's mind moved back to the mouth of the Moray and eastward along the great jutting of land into the Norse Sea between the rivers Spey and Dee. He had heard that the region of Ce was held now by Derile mac Riogan, whom he had met once and remembered for his eyes, blue like the sea that surrounded his land. It was a sea that ever opened them to Viking attack, such as the one in which his father had been killed less than a year ago. A good man, Derile, but barely a man. Could he even be bearded yet?

And this was much of the problem—or opportunity—depending on how it fell out. For Euan mac Crinus, mormaor of Circinn, just below the region of Ce, was likewise young and untried and was known as a hothead. And Fergus son of Eochaid of Fife, just east of Fortriu, couldn't be above fifteen years. So were the houses of Alba decimated by constant Viking attack that they must now be ruled by unbearded boys—boys that Kenneth could only hope and pray could be made to see the sense of forming strong alliances and not going off in their own youthful, willful way.

It was late on the fourth day when they reached the palace of Forteviot, sitting in its fine position on a high rock above the River Earn and rich fields of barley, oats, and spelt. Garths dotted with red cows and black-faced white sheep spread in every direction. This Alba was a rich and beautiful land. Little wonder that the Vikings—pressed as ever they were by the need to feed their people in a land with shallow soil and short, cool summers—should look with avarice on such a region.

And sadder still that, rich with land producing such crops, hunting runs full of deer, rivers that ran silver with trout and salmon, as well as oysters and pearls, and mines ribboned with silver providing the favorite ornamentation of these artistic people, the Picti had become weak. They were weak in war, failing to defend as was needful against the strong threats of the Viking; and weak in faith, falling away from the strong beliefs planted here by Columba.

The forms were all here. Kenneth had noted again and again, as they traveled this main route through the land, the numerous memorial stones standing monument to great battles and leaders, so that it seemed almost that they traveled a ceremonial path. And always, no matter how fierce the battle depicted, or how wild the incised animals, or how enigmatic the engraved symbols telling their stories dear to hearts of the Albannach, always—on the stones carved since the time of Columba—the rock bore a cross on one side or the other, testifying to the fact that this was a Christian country. And even many of the older stones that had been left plain on the back by the original artist had had crosses added by a later, devout hand. And also were there many freestanding crosses with the great wheel of the sun circling them. But how many still prayed devoutly there, save in a few pockets of faith such as Abernethy, DunKeld, or Kilrimont?

That, too, Kenneth would restore to these people by sending abbots and monks from the monasteries of Dalriada. But all must come in time. First there must be peace.

And there was little enough of peace in Forteviot.

Barr looked at him doubtfully and tipped his head toward the furled flag the captain carried at his side. For the three days of riding through Alba, Kenneth had ordered the banner lowered. There was no need to disturb the rural population, had word of the slaughter at Forteviot reached them. But this was a different matter. Should they alert whoever held power inside the Albannach palace that Kenneth of Dalriada had arrived? Would it only give them time to take arms against him?

"Unfurl the flag. Sound the horns," Kenneth ordered. "They will know soon enough who we are if they don't already. The high king of the Scots approaches no one as a sneak thief, no matter what tales may be told of him."

And so Kenneth rode in state up the entranceway to the palace and through the great gate of the palisade surrounding it. But once inside, he saw that it made little difference. Confusion reigned throughout all the courtyards as the servants of newly arrived mormaors argued with those of rulers who had arrived sooner and taken the best stabling for their horses. Palace slaves scurried between storehouses, wells, cookplaces, and bake houses to supply the tables at the king's tall hall house, which stood on the highest ground in the center of all the upheaval.

One mormaor was determined that no mere servant would oust his right to pride of place. The harsh voice of Bruide mac Feredethus rang through the stable yard as three lesser animals were moved to make way for his black stallion. The engraved silver trappings of his harness and sword sheath shone against black leather. His heavy boots sounded on the stones of the yard.

He stopped a pace beyond Kenneth's roan mount. "So. Kenneth son of Alpin. You dare to show your face in Alba. Good. It will save me the trouble of hunting you down when I am proclaimed high king." He spun on his heels and strode to the hall.

Kenneth left his horse in the care of Dubtach, his armor bearer. He would not miss the scene that was sure to follow in the hall.

This was the hall that only a few days before had been the site of such brutal slaughter. But now King Drust lay in the royal cairn. The blood had been washed from the benches where others now sat to eat, and fresh rushes covered the floor. Only the memory of the deed hung in the air—and in the looks of the Albannach.

No action would be taken against the Dalriadans. Fechnon mac Eoganan, temporarily sitting in the high seat, had told his story first—that they struck to prevent treachery. And none could disprove him. But the looks of doubt remained.

At the moment, however, attention focused on Bruide as he strode to the high table. All places were full. Only the aged Reuther mac Galan of Cait, the region farthest from Fortriu, was yet to arrive. The seats were occupied by the other five mormaors and two Dalriadans. Apparently the messenger had had the right of it, for Fechnon mac Eoganan as peacekeeper sat in the center seat, the place of power, although not on the carved king's chair, which had been pushed to the back of the dais.

Kenneth was thankful for that bit of tact on the part of his man. Beside him sat Aed. Kenneth was even more thankful that Eoganan's captain had apparently assumed the control of the Dalriadan warriors he had hoped for.

The loud talking and laughter, barking of dogs, and clatter of serving vessels gradually hushed as more and more became aware of Bruide mac Feredethus striding toward the dais.

The hall was holding its breath by the time Bruide reached the high table. He stopped and glared, stone-hard, at Fechnon mac Eoganan.

Fechnon returned his gaze, not as a stare, but more with a look of interest.

Bruide drew his silver-hilted dagger and slammed it into the table before Fechnon. "Move, Dalriadan. I will have the seat of the high king of Alba."

Fechnon nodded. "As you will, Bruide mac Feredethus." He waved an expansive arm toward the highly carved, boarskin-draped seat left empty by King Drust, now pushed to the back of the dais. "Although you may find it a less convenient place to eat." With his other hand Fechnon signaled a servant to kneel before the king's chair with a large horn of strong barley beer, ready for Bruide's refreshment.

Bruide removed his dagger from the table with a jerk and strode to the seat he had demanded. None at the high table betrayed the least flicker of amusement at Bruide's besting. Not, that is, until his dagger was resheathed and he was sitting where he could not see their smiles.

Now it was Kenneth's turn. He nodded to Barr and Dungal, who had joined him in time to witness the last of the scene. Barr unfurled the Scoti banner, and Dungal blew a flourish on the trumpet. Every eye in the room was riveted on this scene of yet more unplanned drama.

But by the time Kenneth reached the dais, Aed had dumped the scraps from his silver platter to the dogs waiting under the table and wiped it clean with half a barley bannock, ready for a king's dining.

Kenneth took the place offered him at table. Barr stood behind him, holding the Scoti banner, while Dungal saw to the serving.

Round one to the Scots.

But Kenneth knew round two would not be so easily won. At least, however, the lines were drawn. Between servings of roast meats and boiled vegetables he greeted the others at the high table and tried to assess their reactions. Which side of the line would these choose?

Cruithne of Atholl wiped the beer foam from his jutting black beard and replied to Kenneth's inquiry that he had, assuredly, journeyed well from his mountain-fast land. That was hopeful. Euan of Circinn and Fergus of Fife, indeed with only the softest of fuzz on his boyish chin, regarded Kenneth with a suspicion that was far from welcoming. Derile of Ce was little older than his fellow new-made mormaors, and his manners showed more seasoning. Nechtan of Fortriu, of the family of the slain king, had perhaps the best reason to be unwelcoming but spoke the most warmly. And so the meal progressed, each sizing up the other, each keeping one eye on his own men while weighing the coming events for tomorrow's council.

When all at the high table had eaten their fill, Kenneth turned to Nechtan. "Nechtan mac Ferat, did you bring no harper with you from Doune?"

"I brought a harper." Nechtan nodded to the end of a long table in front of them. "The most skilled in Fortriu, however, had no need of bringing, for my half sister, Maia nic Ferat, is of this palace."

Maia—beautiful princess; *nic Ferat*—daughter of Ferat. Kenneth felt certain there was little chance that the sister of the slain Drust would sing for him. Yet Nechtan waited for his answer. It would be impolite to refuse the offer of the house of Ferat. Or was it not an offer but rather a challenge?

"I would gladly hear the lady. Picti women are well-known for their bard skills. I well remember my own Albannach mother's singing."

Nechtan snapped his fingers at a servant. Kenneth toyed with his half-full drinking horn while he waited. The women's table was to the side of the hall nearest their bower, so Kenneth could not observe the progress of the servant.

It was only a matter of minutes, however, until the princess stood before him, a woman seemingly as tall as himself and broad of shoulder, yet slim beneath a blue tunic richly embroidered with silver thread. Her thick black hair she wore in a single braid that fell to below her waist. The light of torches burning in brackets on the carved, painted support posts of the hall caught the glimmer of silver wires and pearls entwined in the braid. Pearls strung on knotted silver wires hung around her neck and from her wrists.

Her hand rested on the frame of a polished white birch harp. Unlike the smaller instruments that the bards of the Scoti carried with them everywhere in leather bags, Maia's triangular-shaped instrument rose from the floor to her shoulder.

"You are well-named, Princess Maia," Kenneth said.

"I will sing." Her face was without expression.

A servant brought a small stool with a low curving back and set it before the harp. The stool's corner posts ended in the shape of warbling birds. Maia sat in a space between the dais and the lower serving tables in a pool of torchlight that should have been warm, yet somehow chilled Kenneth.

The song began as simply as the sun rising over the Ochil Hills to the singing of a lark. A lone white flower opened beside a flowing stream.

Then a single plucked string introduced the refrain:

> "But cruel was the day that the riders came,
>> and brutal the hands that struck their blow,
>> and murdered the house of Albana.
>
> "They came from the west,
>> this host of Dalriadans.
> They drank from our horns,
> They ate of our meat.
> They came from the west,
> Men on murder intent
>> and butchered the house of Albana.
>
> "And cruel was the day
>> that they murdered the house of Albana.
>
> "Some died in their seats,
> Some died in the hall,
> Some died in the night.
> But some lived to accuse him that slaughtered
>> the house of Albana."

The song ended with a single plucked note. The sound hung on the air. Maia rose, still expressionless. She looked long at Kenneth, then walked from the hall.

Round two to the Picts.

17

Later, in his room, Kenneth called Fechnon mac Eoganan to him.

The young captain entered with his long stride and did not even wait for his king to speak first. "Why have you brought so few men? Will you not seize power now? I have held all for Dalriada, as my father would have done had he lived. But even with the success of his coup, you will need more troops. Their mormaors gather."

Kenneth struck the side of his chair and came to his feet with a force that made Fechnon step backward. "Of course they gather. They must now select a new king. And will most likely present Dalriada with a poorer ally than ever Drust would have been. Nechtan would be the best choice, but he is of the royal house through the father only. The mormaors will look to the female line. Cruithne of Atholl was of the royal grandmother's line. Bruide of Findach from farther back yet, but he does have matrilineal claims. God send that they not choose Bruide king. There is little chance he of Craig Phadrig will make treaty."

Fechnon's mouth gaped in open confusion. "But you are to be king. Is that not why we marched to Alba? Why we unsheathed our daggers?"

Kenneth grabbed his warrior by the shoulders and shoved him to a seat on a fur-covered bench. "Cannot you understand? I wish alliance, confederacy, perhaps even union. I do not wish war—not with these people whose support we need against a far stronger enemy."

"Then you will not take the throne of Alba?" Fechnon shook his head to clear it. "You will let their council meet?"

"Of course I will. And then I will meet with the new king. And let no man among your troops mistake my order that he is to behave himself as a lawful guest in this land. We are Christians, not barbarians."

The next morning, his own words still fresh in his ears, Kenneth looked but saw no sign of priest, abbot, or bishop at Forteviot save for those two who had come expressly for the council meeting and would be occupied with affairs of state. So Kenneth directed Father Ernan, who had come with him from DunAdd, to take the lead and serve mass in the apparently little-used chapel near the hall house. He had small hope that any of the Albannach mormaors would choose to attend, but perhaps his prayers could attend on them, for the decision of their council was as vital to Dalriada as to Alba.

In keeping with those instructions, the father appeared in the entrance of the small stone building and struck several bright notes on his brass handbell with a small wooden mallet. Kenneth was just leaving his guest place when he saw Princess Maia emerge from the women's hall. Her pale yellow gown glowed as subtly as the sun behind a thin mountain mist.

"Princess. Our Father Ernan rings his bell for mass." Kenneth approached her. "Would you join us?"

Her face had yet to show any expression. "And would you, Kenneth mac Alpin, stab me even at the Lord's Table as your embassy stabbed my brother at his high table?"

"Maia, will you not believe that I had nothing to do with that killing, that I am as sickened by the treachery as you are, that I have come to make peace between our people?"

Again, her level, expressionless gaze. "And why should I so believe, Kenneth mac Alpin?"

Indeed, he could think of no reason.

Kenneth had a hard time keeping his mind on the mass, knowing the importance of the decision that might, even at that moment, be in the making in the council chamber. Nechtan mac Ferat was the obvious choice for king of Alba, but he would meet strong opposition from Bruide. And perhaps there were others of the matrilineal descent whom Kenneth did not know. Or perhaps the council would depart from their ancient tradition. *Let it be anyone but Bruide,* Kenneth thought, *anyone but Bruide.* Then let them get on about their choosing so that he could have his treaty talk with the chosen king.

It was late afternoon before the sound of ox horns announced that Alba would have a new king to rule under the black boar banner.

Don't let it be Bruide, Kenneth thought again as, flanked by Fechnon and Aed, he walked to the courtyard where still the horns sounded.

He was halfway across the yard when Bruide strode red-faced from the hall, his escort at his heels. They clattered toward the stables. So. It was not Bruide. Had Kenneth then won round three? Had the council chosen a king he could work with?

The other mormaors emerged from the dark hall and faced the rapidly filling courtyard in front of the still-bleating horns. Kenneth scrutinized their faces. He was pleased to see that his old friend Reuther of Cait had arrived in time for the council. There was little chance of Reuther's being chosen king, for he was too old to lead in war, but the council would have needed his sage advice. Young Derile of Ce looked even younger, standing by the gray-haired man. Kenneth looked at Cruithne mac Boanta of Atholl. His black beard jutted even farther forward than usual. Cruithne would be none so bad a choice for king. Perhaps it was to be he. Yes, Cruithne would listen to sense. With Cruithne as king of Albana, Kenneth might well get his treaty.

The youngsters Euan and Fergus erupted from the hall, the hotheaded Euan several paces ahead of Fergus. Kenneth suspected they had supported the losing contender. Bruide might be just such a leader as these two would choose.

Last of all came Nechtan mac Ferat. Beside him was a large handsome man with thick black hair, his gleaming, V-shaped beard a model in a nation that highly favored that fashion.

Kenneth turned to Dungal with a questioning glance. Did any know who this was?

"Bran mac Ferat," Dungal said.

Bran? "Is there yet another son of Ferat? Brother or half brother to Drust, Nechtan, and Maia?" Then Kenneth answered his own question. "Oh, yes, the brother who is abbot of Kilrimont. But surely his name was not Bran."

"No, that is another. Finguine is holy man avowed."

And at that moment, indeed, two figures emerged from the hall in clerical robes—the abbots of Abernethy and Kilrimont from their seats at the council. Now the ox horns were silent.

Abbot Finguine of Kilrimont stepped forward. "The council has chosen. In one week a new king of Alba will be inaugurated at Scone. Bran mac Ferat."

The horns sounded again, seemingly as much to cover the surprised gasps of the assembly as in salute. Bran came forward, obedient to a shove from Nechtan.

And then Kenneth remembered. He had heard of Bran. Ferat's third son was simpleminded. So, not being able to come to an agreement on one of their own members, the council had chosen a dark horse whom each mormaor undoubtedly thought he could manipu-

179

late for his own ends. Round three had been lost by both Dalriada and Alba.

The next day the sons of Ferat led a hunting party in the wooded, deer-rich lands along the Earn Water. Reuther of Cait had been glad enough to pull back with Kenneth when the king of Scots indicated he would have private speech with him. Reuther, as Kenneth had foreseen, was sympathetic.

"Yes, Kenneth, son of my old friend, long our people have been allied in spirit. It would be none so bad a thing to have a formal treaty uniting us more closely. But I can tell you there are those who would not thank me for saying so."

Reuther shook his gray head. "Those who have had less experience of Viking attack in their regions or are too young to know their own limitations will hear nothing of treaty talk, I am thinking."

Kenneth nodded, thinking of Euan and Fergus. To be successful, a treaty would need the full support of their unbridled energy and all the troops they could supply. "And yet, Reuther mac Galan of Cait, would you support this matter of alliance before King Bran?"

Reuther adjusted the blue and gold plaid cloaking his stooped shoulders and shook his gray beard slowly in a gesture of dismay, not refusal. "King Bran. He will be needing all the help he can get. We all will—God help us." He paused, and the birds chirping overhead and twigs snapping beneath the hooves of their horses filled in the space. "Certainly I will speak for the cause of a strong defense against the Vikings. But how much good my words will do I am not overly optimistic."

"And if the high king of Alba will not agree, will you make treaty for Cait? I would far rather have this a matter of the whole nation, but what cannot be accomplished in a leap must perhaps be done by steps."

A banding together of high kings would send a far stronger warning to the Vikings that they meant to defend their lands and would not tolerate theft and barbarism on their shores. But if such was not possible, Kenneth would begin with as many subkings as he could gather. He turned in the saddle to look straight into Reuther's gray blue eyes.

"I will think on it, Kenneth mac Alpin. But I would not wish to be seen as leading revolt in our land or—" He paused and shifted in his saddle.

"Or as conspiring with one who committed treachery?" Kenneth finished for him.

Reuther sighed. "It is talked of. Many would accuse you openly. It was your men who struck the first blow under the cover of friendship."

"And what of the claim of my captain that they had discovered a plot by Drust to so strike them first?"

Reuther nodded. "It is in my mind that the possibility of truth in such a charge, coupled with the chaos among our own princes and mormaors, is the only reason you and Fechnon mac Eoganan, who held power here for you, have not met armed resistance. Although you would be best advised to look to your back whenever Euan of Circinn or Fergus of Fife are nearby."

"And what of you, Reuther? Will you not believe my vow that I knew nothing of the treason my general planned and would have done all in my power to stop such a thing?'

Reuther looked at him long. The trail they followed here was a wide one, allowing for riding side by side. "I believe it because it was a stupid, senseless deed that left Dalriada weakened as well as Alba. And I believe it because I know you are no butcher. But many—I would even say most—do not know so."

Kenneth nodded. "Most believe as Princess Maia."

He turned his horse and rode back to Forteviot. If the hunt went well, Bran would hold council this afternoon, and Kenneth could speak of his treaty matter. If not, then it must be tomorrow morning.

The matter must be settled before the court moved to Scone for the enthroning, for Kenneth, himself so newly made king, had much to see to in his own lands. And the fact that high summer was ever the time of fiercest Viking raids left him worried for his own shores. Soon the harvest would be gathered in the northland, leaving the Norsemen nothing to do but pillage and plunder the richer lands to the south until winter storms should close the seaways even to the intrepid Viking seamen with their dragon-headed longboats.

The sun was a little to the west of the tall roof of the royal hall house when the sound of ox horn and the clatter of horses' hooves on the cobbles of the courtyard told Kenneth that the new-chosen King Bran had returned successful from the hunt. Which discreet attendant had sent an arrow to fell the deer so that the king could return flushed with glee? he wondered. Whoever it was, Kenneth sent him silent thanks, for it would be no bad thing to have Bran in a good humor for the council meeting.

Servants scurried to bring extra chairs to the high table where kings, subkings, and abbots refreshed themselves from horns of heather ale. Bran sat in the center, while his body servant held the black boar banner of the Picts on a standard banded and capped with ornately engraved silver. Nechtan mac Ferat sat to his left; to his right, Kenneth, backed by his red and white wolf banner held by the faithful Dubtach.

At a nudge from Nechtan, Bran spoke. There was no ceremony to the opening of the meeting. Significantly, to Kenneth's mind, there was no prayer, although two abbots—those from the most important monasteries in Alba—sat at table with them.

"We will hear you, Kenneth mac Alpin of Dalriada." Bran spoke well, if just a shade slowly, his enunciation clear, as if he might have been rehearsed. But certainly no one who had not heard tales of the lad's being slow would suspect on a first meeting. If the council were looking for a figurehead, they had chosen well.

"Bran mac Ferat of Alba, we greet you." Kenneth looked the length of the table. "As we greet all seated here. I come in friendship." That was as close as he would come to speaking of the killing of Drust and his warrior guards. A high king did not apologize. "I come for the mutual benefit of our peoples, proposing a treaty that we unite for common protection against the Danes that ravage both our shores. Each year they gain strength. Each year they take over more permanent land for their people to settle. Each year they push further inland. It is time they are stopped."

Reuther slammed his fist against the table in a gesture of agreement. Kenneth heard one other fist so salute his remarks, that of Cruithne mac Boanta of Atholl, he thought. If so, that would be significant, for Cruithne with the jutting black beard was also of the house of Ferat.

But the next fist that slammed the table was not in applause. Euan of Circinn, his dark eyes blazing hotter than the sun that warmed the thatched roof of the hall and streaked through the high windows, jumped to his feet. "So. If you come in friendship, Dalriadan wolf, why is the blood of our brothers barely dry from the benches of this hall? Do you offer a treaty that you will strike only Vikings in the back hereafter?"

Kenneth did not choose to talk of the past or to be put in the position of defending himself, but before he could make reply, an answer came from a surprising place.

Finguine mac Ferat, abbot of Kilrimont and youngest member of the royal house, fingered the silver cross that hung on the front of his robe and leaned his tonsured forehead toward a mote-filled beam of light falling on the table. "My brothers, this is not a council for placing blame. There are accusations and counteraccusations enough on both sides. None may ever know the truth of the matter—"

He was interrupted by Fergus, jumping to his feet. "We know the truth well enough! The Dalriadans say they were warned of trap-doors beneath the tables where their bodies were to be dumped. See you any such doors beneath your own benches? Does Kenneth mac Alpin think that if such a weapon were available to us now, he would be sitting here in comfort and not roasting in a trap hole?"

The strength of Fergus's argument was vitiated by the servants who, at that moment, uncovered just such a pit at the far end of the hall and lifted the carcass of a succulently roasted boar from its depths. True enough, the roasting pits were not under the tables, nor placed there in secret, but it took great force of will on Kenneth's part not to look for such a one beneath his table.

"The past must bury the past," the abbot continued. "Someday all will be known before a Judge far wiser than we. And then each will make answer for his own sins. Let us hear what the son of Alpin would say, so that we can judge if it might be of benefit to Alba's future."

The silence that fell on the table was far heavier than the boom-ing of drums—and harder to talk over. Yet Kenneth persisted. All gathered there needed little reminder of recent Viking attacks on their lands or their neighbors'. Nor did they need reminder of the enormous size of fleet required to patrol even a portion of the coast-line of mainland Dalriada and Alba. Securing the inner Western Isles, those not already under Norse control, would be impossible, riddled as they were with coves and sea lochs where the invaders could hide their ships, then strike and run.

But if a combined naval force could be readied on both sides of the seacoast, plus a host mounted on horses—for the Danes, al-though fierce land fighters, were at a disadvantage once out of their ships—if both of these forces could be battle-ready and well-informed by a clear system of spies to warn of the most likely places of the next Viking attacks . . .

Kenneth laid his careful plans before the council—how many ships he calculated would be needed, how many warriors.

Young Derile of the sea-exposed Ce shook his head. "It is a fine-sounding thing to be talking of. But there are far more Danes than all the Picts and Scots together. For every two we kill, five will take their places."

"So would you just surrender, my friend?" Kenneth held Der-ile's sea-blue eyes in a level challenge.

"None has ever accused Derile or any son of Riogan of surren-dering in cowardice. I merely state facts."

Kenneth nodded. "It is so. We cannot obliterate the enemy. But we can make it costly enough to attack our shores that they will sail their serpent-headed longships farther on."

Euan, caught in the midst of quaffing from his drinking horn when Kenneth gave that answer, lowered his drink and sprayed his neighbors with heather ale in a shout of mirth. "Yes! So be it! I'll agree to any treaty giving Ireland to the Danes!"

Fergus struck his hand against Euan's shoulder. "And Fife will agree too. Ireland and England we'll give to the Danes!"

Kenneth glared at them. "And let the Vikings use Ireland and England as bases from which to attack us as they now use the Orkneys and their own northlands?"

That restored quiet to the table.

Nechtan spoke. "You would make treaty with Ireland and England as well?"

"I will make treaty with all who will stand by me to protect our people."

"You'll get no help from the British. Roderick of Strathclyde has his hands full and more with harrying from Ecgfrith of the Angles. And a good thing it is, to my mind." Nechtan, whose region of Fortriu bordered Strathclyde across the waters of the Clyde, speared a slab of roast boar from the trencher that was now being handed around the table.

"And think you—any of you—" Kenneth looked at each one "—think any of you that we will forever remain free of British and English pressure from the south? And that any of us will be the stronger for standing alone? Cannot you see that we must unite against all enemies?"

Now the quick-tempered Euan came near to exploding. He slammed his fist against his drinking horn, spreading its pale gold contents across the carved surface of the dark oak table. "Unite. That is the word, is it not? Wolf-in-sheep's-clothing Scot. You talk of alliance, but really you want union. Dalriada is too small for your appetite. You are greedy for the throne of Alba. It is not the Viking we have to fear, but you. It is little wonder you sent your men to strike Drust and his warriors."

"If I chose to take the throne of Alba by force, Euan of the hothead, I would be sitting there now." Kenneth pointed to the high seat where Bran chewed contentedly on a thick slab of crisp roast boar.

But he could see that it was hopeless. He might get some of them—Cruithne and Derile, perhaps even Nechtan—to listen to him if they were alone. But this unruly council was impossible. And as well try to negotiate with one of their carved memorial stones as with their puppet king. Once again, both nations had lost.

Kenneth rose and inclined his head with dignity. "I thank you for your courtesy in listening to me." The irony was lost on the mormaors, now snarling and growling around the table with far more heat than the hounds under the table to whom King Bran had just tossed a bone.

His banner following him in a red streak, Kenneth strode from the room.

For a moment the sun, hanging bright and low on the horizon, dazzled his eyes. The woman who stood in the aureole appeared insubstantial as a dream—or perhaps an angel. Then his sight cleared.

"Princess." He bowed.

"Is it true? All that you said in there?"

"God's truth. As I see matters."

She inclined her head and walked on a bit—slowly, as if inviting him to join her. He did so.

"You were listening then? You heard all?"

"I heard. I am the Royal Daughter. Through me passes the royal blood. From me will the royal house of Alba descend. But I will not be merely a brood horse. I will use my mind for Alba as well. There is much to think on here in these dangerous times." She turned her steps to a wooded path that led to the River Earn.

Kenneth would have liked to ask her opinion of what she heard —ask if she believed his testimony. But he had too great respect for her deep concentration and for the great silence surrounding her thoughts to pry. Besides, he feared her answer should he push her too far. Better to wait for what she chose to give.

Their steps disturbed a lark from among the dark, shiny leaves of a holly bush. It took flight to the branches of an alder nearer the river.

This slight interruption of nature seemed to break Maia's concentration. She turned to Kenneth. "You really believe the Vikings are so serious a menace? Serious enough to threaten our very existence as a nation?"

"I do. It did not seem so, I am told, when the raids began in our grandfather's grandfather's time. Oh, serious enough, to be sure, for those attacked and dragged by the heels through live coals after watching their women being raped. But there would be a few such raids a year by groups of two or three dragonships, then all quiet until again the scourge from the north fell upon another farmstead the next year.

"But now such pirates as Turgus the Savage and Ragnar Ladbrok come with fleets of twenty—fifty—ships or more. They are an invading army. They do not rape and burn and leave with women and cattle from the farmstead and gold from the church. They hold the land for their own. Look you to the Orkneys—they are Viking, not Albannach. Or to many of the Hebridean islands that are ruled by Jarl Ketil Flatnose. Or to Ireland where Dublin has a Norse king. True, the Norse are not Dane, and such leaders as Olaf the White have turned from plunder to the plow, so that they make good neighbors. But they were savage enough when first they invaded. And Dalriada and Alba can give only so much land even to the most peaceful of farmer-kings and remain Dalriada and Alba."

Now her silence was longer than before, suited to the long shadows of evening that fell across the Earn Water. Silver trout feeding on the clouds of midges hanging above the river rippled the surface in concentric circles like the cup and ring marks Maia's Picti ancestors had left on stones across the land.

"So what is it, Kenneth mac Alpin, that makes a nation? Are we no longer Alba or Dalriada if we allow new people to settle on our land?"

Kenneth blinked at the woman beside him. Never before had he encountered such a mind. Often he had been laughed at for thinking deeply when the job of king was to be a war leader. But this one asked questions even he had not thought of—nor any priest or abbot that he knew. He was delighted when she indicated that they should sit on a fallen log by the riverbank. And the settling of themselves gave him some time to gather his thoughts.

"Princess, new people with new farming methods, new arts, new ideas can strengthen our own peoples as new strains of cattle can strengthen our own. Or they can weaken them as a defective bull can do to a dairy herd. It depends on what they bring. Fine metal-working patterns and stirring new hero tales we welcome. False gods and lawbreakers we do not welcome."

She was quiet, so he continued. "But if we are to continue as a nation we cannot allow so many of even the welcome ones that our own traditions, laws, and faith are smothered. Look to the south of us. The Angles and the Saxons pushed our Celtic cousins far to the west of England. I think we would not choose to be so pushed by the Vikings."

"And only armed resistance will prevent this pushing of our people into the sea?"

"Strength in our own hearts and armed resistance when required." Kenneth nodded.

"What if a Viking becomes a Christian?"

"Then he is our brother." For that Kenneth did not have to seek an answer. "That is the best solution—the only true solution. Let the Viking become our brother in Christ. But first he must hear. And to hear he must listen. And to listen he must cease pillaging and burning. By force of arms we must halt the heathen rage. When he is quiet, then we shall see if he would be our brother."

Maia traced the interlaced looped and knotted animals engraved on the silver brooch she wore, and Kenneth thought her mind followed a similar pattern. "So that is what makes a nation—that all be Christian?"

Kenneth smiled his first relaxed smile in the presence of Princess Maia. And it felt good. "Is that how you see the sum of all I said? Perhaps it will be so in heaven, but I doubt if even Saint Columba himself could have answered you that. He was famous for preserving ancient places of worship because they once were centers of honest searches for God—however misguided they might have been.

"To be truly Dalriadan or Albannach means to be 'Christian,' for such have our nations been these three hundred years and more. All our laws, traditions, understandings, and hopes for the future are built on this faith. None can truly share these without at least understanding the gospel. But to say all nations must have that basis in order to be nations would be to say that there are very few nations on the face of the earth."

"So then—"

"You push me to define what makes a nation, Princess?"

"I push myself. I would hear your answer and think on it because, in spite of my earlier dislike, I have come to respect you as one who thinks."

Kenneth bowed his head in acknowledgment of her accolade. It was a humbling moment. It was perhaps the highest compliment that had ever been paid him. Now he must give more care than ever to his answer.

"You must forgive me. I have not defined these thoughts even for myself previously, much less put them into words for another." He began slowly. "There are the obvious aspects of nationhood— shared land, commonality of race, the same language, shared traditions, shared experiences . . ."

"So all must be alike to form a nation?"

Her probing disturbed him. His answer couldn't be right—at least not in whole. There were too many exceptions to that definition in his own nation—in his own intermarried family. "No, I named merely some of the externals that help people come together."

He groped to define his own goals for Dalriada, his own vision of his role as king. "It is perhaps harder for people with different backgrounds, different traditions to forge a nation, but the important thing is their values, their goals, and ideas for the future. There will be disagreement on how the goals are to be reached, but there cannot be a nation unless her people would work for the same things. United under a strong king, of course. For in final sum, the nation is the king. But the king's task is the easier if his mormaors are in agreement."

With the final setting of the sun, a gray chill rose from the water. Soon a mist would likely rise too. Kenneth stood and offered his hand to help Maia to her feet. She accepted it lightly, but when he would have unfastened his plaid cloak and placed it over her light tunic she stopped him with the briefest shake of her head.

She did not speak another word all the way back to the palace, and Kenneth did not see her at the women's place in the hall that night.

He could only hope he had not offended her in anything he had said. He also wished he could remember all he had said. It had made sense at the moment—all those fine words about faith and goals and nationhood—and yet what did it all come to in the end but the need to do battle against the Vikings?

In the morning they would return to DunAdd, for if he could find no treaty help here, he must lead Dalriada to stand alone until he could find other allies. And the mormaors of Alba must do what they could with their handsome, simple figurehead of a king.

18

The next morning Kenneth moved briskly among his men as if he had given orders to prepare for battle. His captains Barr and Dungal, who had accompanied him from DunAdd, he ordered to have his personal guard ready to travel in one hour with full trumpet sounding and banners unfurled. None would say that Kenneth, king of Scots, folded his tents and slipped away in the night. He would depart through the gates of Forteviot palace as if he, not Bran, were the reigning monarch—or at least as one who had made full treaty with the ruling monarch.

Fechnon mac Eoganan and his captain Aed would lead their troop out with equal order but less fanfare. Those who had stabbed Drust and his palace guard were not to be given a hero's farewell, no matter what the right or wrong of the treachery charges.

Dubtach was ready to lead Kenneth's horse from the stable when Finguine mac Ferat approached across the cobbled courtyard.

Kenneth greeted the abbot of Kilrimont. "Farewell, my lord Abbot. It is hoped we will meet again in less strifeful times."

"God's grace on you, Kenneth mac Alpin. And must you ride toward Dalriada today?"

"Your brother Nechtan promises us hospitality at Doune for the night, although he will, of course, be making for Scone himself."

Abbot Finguine nodded. "As must I myself and all the court, but as I must make the lengthy detour to Kilrimont for the vestments and vessels needed for the enthroning, I had thought to enquire whether you would care to accompany me to the chief holy site of Alba."

Kenneth frowned, not in dislike of the idea but in surprise. Surely something was behind this suggestion. Perhaps a power play between Finguine and Abbot Constans of Abernethy? Although why it should matter to either of them which the king of Scots should think of higher import was a mystery.

If asked, Kenneth would have supposed DunKeld to have been more important than either, established as it was by both Saint Co-

189

lumba and Saint Mungo. Certainly Kenneth knew more of DunKeld, since it had given a home a generation ago to monks fleeing Viking raids on Iona. But perhaps that was all the more why he should learn of Kilrimont.

And yet time pressed him. "Thank you for your offer, Abbot, I—"

"Perhaps King Kenneth would like to know that the idea was put to me by Princess Maia. She said that you have an interest in the traditions both sacred and secular of nations. Since Kilrimont houses the most sacred relics of Alba, it occurred to me that you might make pilgrimage."

Kenneth considered. "Does Princess Maia make pilgrimage also?"

"The princess prepares herself and the women of the court to go to Scone for the king-making."

"Yes, of course." Kenneth felt more confused than ever. The suggestion was kindly made. He had not found many who offered him kind invitations in Alba. If the suggestion had come from the princess, he might offend doubly by refusing. And yet he sorely needed to return to Dalriada. The failure of his treaty attempt made it all the more important that he see to his own defenses.

Dungal approached with a metallic clink of spurs on the cobbles. "The guard is ready."

"Fine." Kenneth knew what he would do. "We will ride forth as planned. Abbot Finguine will give us escort. When we are beyond the palace, I will have you, Dungal, and Dubtach accompany me on a brief side trip. Barr will lead the rest to Doune under my banner. We will ride no more than a day and a half behind them." He looked sideways for confirmation of this, for he was not certain of the distances.

Finguine nodded.

"We will catch up to them before they cross the spine of Alba."

And so, an hour later, Kenneth found himself riding eastward rather than the due west he had planned.

Except for his feeling that he needed to be with his men, needed to be making haste for DunAdd, the ride to Kilrimont couldn't have been more pleasant. They wound through rolling green hills covered with fertile farm strips. Every few miles they passed another clachan of clustered thatched houses. Children, chickens, and dogs played around the doors while women and older siblings saw to the geese, pigs, and cows in outlying garths. Sheep dotted the uncultivated, heather-covered hillsides, now a blaze of bright purple.

Although they had something more than twenty miles to cover, they made good time because this region of Fife was not broken by incessant lochs, mountains, and rivers as was so much of Dalriada. Kenneth found himself hoping fervently that the boy Fergus would prove to be a worthy mormaor for these friendly people who waved to them from field and doorway as they passed.

Many recognized the abbot, or more likely the robes of his office, and ran to him for a blessing, which he never failed to give.

"I am surprised to see such signs of devotion among your people, Abbot," Kenneth said after a grandmother and three children had thanked Finguine profusely for the brief prayer he said with his hands on their heads.

"The faith is much weakened in Albana, but there are many who hold true in more than mere form. It is true that we could do far more if we had more monasteries, more workers—but such is always the case, is it not? We must pray the Lord of the harvest for workers, for the fields are ripe."

It was a particularly apt metaphor for this time of year when the spelt was golden and the barley nearing silver white.

"It is more at the court than in the clachan that people want Christ as their Savior but not as their Lord—if they want Him at all. The great ones are ever tempted to want to rule their own lives and their own lands, believing they can do so better than He who created all." Finguine sighed. "But so it has ever been, I am thinking—although these times seem particularly trying."

Kenneth nodded. Finguine was a man of great wisdom. Kenneth himself would need to think more on the distinction the abbot had made.

The approach to the small village of Kilrimont, which surrounded the monastery, was particularly pleasing. Three streets, more or less defined by the placement of thatched homes, workshops, and barns, converged at the foot of a small hill. The rocky knoll was topped by a sturdy wattled church, encircled by smaller, round cells that housed the Culdee brethren. Beyond the sharply angled promontory spread the sea, the color of a gentle sky, its sun-silvered ripples reminding Kenneth of Princess Maia's blue tunic, adorned with silver threads.

The abbot spread his arm toward the open ocean to the north. "It is not always so peaceful as you see it today. In the winter the storms lash the waves against this rocky coastline. But our fair harbor"—he turned eastward to indicate a sheltered cove where fishing coracles rocked peacefully—"remains gentled. So would it have welcomed Saint Rule."

Kenneth made no reply.

"Ah, perhaps you are not knowing the story of our first abbot?"

191

Kenneth agreed that he did not know, so as they rode the short distance to the turf wall ringing the monastery, Finguine enlightened him while the ever-present dogs, chickens, and children scurried from the horses' path.

"Near to five hundred years ago it was that the blessed Rule, a monk of special devotion in Patras in Greece, served as guardian of the relics of Saint Andrew—he deserving of special veneration because he was the first apostle to be called by our Lord."

When they reached the enclosure, Finguine dismounted.

Kenneth followed his example and signaled Dubtach to take his horse, as the abbot's servant took his. Dungal stayed behind as well while king and abbot walked toward the church, and Finguine continued his narrative. Kenneth listened attentively but did not fail to take in the special beauty of this mount and its king's church.

"The apostle Andrew was crucified in Patras, and there they say his relics had remained undisturbed for four hundred years, always watched over by a servant of our Lord such as Rule. But Rule was to have a special task. Just as Joseph, the earthly father of our Lord, was warned in a dream that he should take Mary and the Holy Child into Egypt for safety, so did an angel, it is said, come to Rule while he slept to warn him that the sacred relics of Saint Andrew were to be made pawns in the power struggle between Rome and Constantinople. The Lord was not pleased that the relics of His servant should be used for political purposes—even for politics within the church."

Kenneth smiled. Were not politics within the church often the worst kind? He warmed toward this Rule for his understanding.

A dark-robed brother emerged from a nearby cell. His smoothly tonsured forehead was bowed in devotion until he looked up at the sound of their footsteps. He raised two fingers in greeting. "Peace, Father Finguine. Peace, my friend."

Finguine responded with the sign of the cross. "Peace, Brother Ekeld. I have brought Kenneth of Dalriada to see our shrine."

"May God's light ever shine on your path, Kenneth of Dalriada." The monk walked on, apparently on his way to join several of his brethren hoeing a pulse field just beyond the wall.

"Now, where was I?" Finguine asked.

"Politics in the church."

"Ah, yes, the Council of Constantinople in 381 had declared Constantinople to be the new Rome, taking precedence over old Rome. A measure highly resented in Rome, as you may well imagine."

Kenneth smiled again. He could imagine.

"So, obedient to the angel's warning, Rule took his precious relics—smuggling them in a bale of hemp, some say—and boarded a trading vessel for the west. The ship was caught in a sudden violent storm such as can blow up in the channel waters to the south of us, especially in the autumn. When the ship found safe anchorage in our harbor, Rule led all aboard in a service of thanksgiving. Then, knowing with a certainty that hitherto had the Lord led him, he put ashore in a coracle with his sacred charge."

Finguine led him not to the church, as Kenneth had expected, but to a small wicket gate in the turf wall on the seaward side of the enclosure, where a steep path led down the rock face toward a pebbled beach. Just before they reached the level ground, Finguine indicated a small, damp-looking cave to their left.

"Saint Rule's cave, where he first placed the relics of Saint Andrew until he could build his church."

The cave stood empty now, save for the flicker of a single rushlight, which Finguine said Brother Ekeld always kept lighted. It was Brother Ekeld's duty to see to the precious relics of Saint Andrew at Kilrimont as it had been the duty of Saint Rule at Patras, and so would there always be one of their Culdee brotherhood to care so for their holy charge.

Now Finguine turned his steps back up the path. "Saint Rule ministered here for thirty years and established the greatness of Kilrimont." The abbot looked at the crumbled wall of the enclosure, at the monks' cells in need of repair. "Well, the work has fallen on bad days, but it was great—and it can be again. Kilrimont, the Church of the Royal Mount, can become a center of holy fire to shine out across all Alba and call men back to the true faith."

He turned toward the church. It, at least, had not been allowed to fall into disrepair. It stood a sturdy rectangle of pale amber, claydaubed wattle and had a well-trimmed, thickly thatched roof above the small monks' cells, just as a king's hall house would stand above the other buildings at a royal dun.

Inside the small sanctuary, dust motes danced in the bright beam from the high window and fell on the simple altar, adorned only with silver cross, chalice, and monstrance. But there was nothing simple about the carved stone casket that held the most elevated position in the room against the eastern wall.

Kenneth admired the sarcophagus from every side. The end panels were ornately engraved sun crosses with angels kneeling over the top and intricate boss patterns adorning the spaces on either side of each cross as if studded with jewels. The long front panel was framed at each end with interwoven elongated animal bodies. In the center was a richly carved tapestry portraying scenes from the life of King David.

193

He was stunned. Even in a nation renowned for its rock carving, such workmanship seemed near to miraculous. "Never have I seen animals portrayed so realistically. Look—the wool on the sheep, the muscles of the lion, the delicacy of the dog's legs . . ." He rested his hand on the hip roof that gave the casket the appearance of a small church. "Surely such workmanship is not of Rule's time?"

"No, no. It is of this century. Ordered by King Unuist, he who was wed to the sister of our own Queen Mother." He crossed himself in reverent memory of the departed lady, and Kenneth mentally shook his head over the tangle of understanding matriarchal descent.

"King Unuist it was who also ordered this abbatical seal struck." Finguine picked up a bronze seal from a small table and handed it to Kenneth. The seal showed Saint Andrew looking up to heaven, standing behind the tall, thin X of a saltire cross formed by two timbers lashed together in the center.

"It was on such a cross as this that Saint Andrew died, for such was the style of crucifixion in Greece. And so the blessed apostle hung, his wrists lashed to the upper beams, his feet to the lower. And he ceased not from preaching and praying aloud for two days and two nights until death at last released him from the great agony of his ordeal."

Kenneth looked long at the seal in his hand, thinking of the great wonder that such sacred objects as the bones of Saint Andrew should be brought to these shores by the very hand of God. Surely a very great miracle indeed.

He thought of the journey the trading vessel would have made across the Mediterranean Sea from Greece, around the jutting land mass of Spain into the open waters of the Atlantic Ocean, then up the narrow channel between England and the Empire of the Franks —he had heard many traders entertain his court late into the night with tales of the dangers of such sailing. At what point, he wondered, did the storm capture Saint Rule's vessel? Certainly none could doubt that such a journey was guided by the hand of God.

He started to speak but was interrupted by a clatter at the back of the church.

"My lord." Dubtach hurried forward. "A messenger has galloped all the way from Barr, who directed him to us. Already the news is three days coming from DunAdd."

"Yes. What?" Foreboding gripped Kenneth.

"The Vikings have struck Iona again."

19

Kenneth was in the saddle pushing westward almost before Dubtach had time to finish his sentence. It was unlikely he could have prevented this disaster even had he been at DunAdd, yet he felt guilty for the extra hours he had lingered here. He should have departed immediately after the council meeting, not staying for dialogue with Princess Maia or making pilgrimage to Kilrimont.

At Falkland, a fortified residence of the mormaor of Fife, Kenneth secured fresh horses and the services of two men who knew the land well to guide them—all night if need be—to reach the Dalriadans at Doune.

As it was, they reached the fortress two hours before dawn. Kenneth was for pressing on then, but Barr, roused from his bed by a sleepy guard, persuaded him of the wisdom of sending a messenger ahead with his orders and allowing himself two hours of sleep.

Kenneth would not be satisfied to send a mere messenger. Barr himself must go. Scouts were to be sent out immediately to track the path of the Vikings. Most likely they would be working out from a base hidden in one of the island harbors. By now they may have struck again, increasing their chances of being located. Kenneth must know where they were and how many there were.

And his own navy was to be readied. No less than six longboats—ten would be better—fully manned and equipped by the time he arrived. Tell Donald to send to King Huel of Man and King Merfyn Vrych of Gwynedd. If the raiders were active, it was likely these nearest kingdoms would have felt the thrust of their cold steel and the heat of their fires.

It was unlikely an attack on Iona would be an isolated strike-and-flee assault, for there was little enough left on Iona to pillage. Since the first attack on Columba's monastery in 795, when sixty-eight monks were brutally slaughtered on the white cockleshell sand of the now-named Martyr's Bay, there had been repeated attacks, including one in the time of Kenneth's father when the monastery had been burned to the ground. It could only be sheer pagan hatred of a Christian holy place that spurred further attacks, for surely these barbarians knew nothing of value was there. Nothing they valued. Such men knew only the value of gold and silver and other material objects.

For that, Kenneth could give thanks. Although many valuable books—that of greatest value next to the lives of the monks themselves—had been burned and stolen, and the ancient carved stones and crosses marking the graves of kings and saints smashed and broken, that other great treasure—the relics of Saint Columba himself—had been left untouched. So far. God send that it still be so.

Perhaps seeing the repository of the relics at Kilrimont had helped Kenneth realize he could no longer leave that of such great value in so exposed a place. God forgive him for doing so for so long. He prayed that it would not be too late to make amends. He would remove the relics to a safer place.

And he would strike a blow to the ravagers that they would not soon forget. But first he must find them. And before that he must get back to DunAdd. He spurred his horse forward.

Riding from Fortriu to DunAdd in just under three days required near to superhuman effort and many changes of horses, but Kenneth arrived full of energy, determined to press ahead. Only Barr and Dubtach had kept up with him. Dungal would have, but Kenneth ordered him to remain with the warriors and bring them on at a steady pace. He needed them to arrive battle-ready, not swaying on their feet.

Kenneth swept Donald before him into the hall house and called loudly for ale and meat. Ever the good second-in-command, Donald reported that nine ships now stood in Crinan harbor ready to sail. At least three more should join them from Galloway in a day or two. He had not yet heard from Merfyn or Huel—indeed his messengers had barely had time to reach those kings.

And Iona? What of the damage? Kenneth washed down a heavy bite of barleycake with a gulp of ale, scarcely knowing what he ate.

All the monks had escaped with their lives. Most of the buildings were burned. What little there was of value—a few silver plates, a cross set with semiprecious stones—had been taken. Abbot Dairmait had set sail for Kells the next day, taking all the brothers with him.

Kenneth nodded. It was good news that the holy men were alive. And yet he could feel only sorrow that this cradle of Christianity, this place of great holiness that had stood for the faith for three hundred years, should be abdicated. "So. The heathen have won. All gone? All abandoned?"

Donald nodded. "All but one. Brother Corbanac. My men found him still in his cell. He claims it has been always in his family that one should be keeper of the stone—whatever that means. Anyway, he said that as long as Columba's bones remained on Iona, so would he. I did persuade him, however, to come here to report to you. I knew you would want an eyewitness account."

"And so I do. Send in this Corbanac."

The small towheaded monk with tonsured forehead and brown robe was before Kenneth in a matter of minutes. The king recognized him as the monk who had taken such care over the memorial stone he sat on at his anointing. "Brother Corbanac, all Dalriada owes you a debt."

"I only stood by my duty. As any would have done."

Kenneth smiled grimly. Dairmait and the others were now snug in Kells. But he would not speak that thought. "Let us hope so. Many will have to stand so before this matter of the Vikings is settled. Now. Did you see how many men? How many ships?"

"Three dragon ships. Perhaps sixty men to a ship. Or do I exaggerate? It seemed like hundreds."

Kenneth shook his head. "I fear you underestimate, rather."

He considered. If only three dragonships struck Iona, this must have been merely a small raiding party from a larger fleet. These scourges from the sea came in great fleets—twenty, fifty, sixty, more —to show their invincibility; to take all they wanted. But this time they would be stopped.

It would take time, perhaps years, to rid the land permanently of such threats. And in the meantime there would still be much loss of life and property. Kenneth must take temporary measures to prevent as much loss as he could.

"Brother Corbanac, I would entrust a very special task to you. I would prefer to do it myself, but I must be about the battle preparations here. You have shown your loyalty and courage in battle; now you must show it in stealth."

"I am the Lord's servant and yours, my king."

"I am told that, as before, the raiders left Columba's relics and the sacred carved stones of Iona free from harm."

"Praise God, it is so."

"Yes, I do praise God. But I am thinking that we must not always rely on Him to do for us what we can do for ourselves with a little application of common sense. I believe it is time and past that these most precious objects be removed to safer keeping until this time of danger is past. I would have you see to this for me, Brother Corbanac."

"It is a great honor to be chosen for this task."

"I hope it is an honor. It will also entail considerable labor, and I hope not too much danger. Tomorrow at first light I would have you and Father Ernan and the four armed men I will send with you to do the rowing and heavy labor take the Dalriadan Stone of Destiny with you from DunAdd. Return to Iona for Saint Columba's relics. Sail with them back up the Firth of Lorn to the mouth of Loch Etive to DunStaffness. I would like it better if that dun were less exposed to seaways, but I have thought long on this, and Staffness is the strongest natural fortress in the land. It is atop a great outcropping of rock and could only be taken by prolonged siege, which the Vikings will not undertake—especially as there are so many easier pickings around."

Kenneth rose and began pacing the dais. He was impatient for action, and yet action for its own sake would not do. The plans must be carefully laid. "I will send word to my steward there to give you every aid. Find the most secure hiding place the fortress offers for these treasures. And bide you with them, Brother Corbanac. Will you do that? Leave the beauty of Iona to live atop an enclosed mountain of rock until I can come for you?"

"I will do it gladly, my king."

"Good. Get you to Father Ernan and tell him I bid him prepare for another journey, barely returned though he is from the last. He will know what sacred chrism he might need to perform the rite of translation of the relics."

Corbanac was halfway down the hall when Kenneth called after him, "God go with you. May you and He guard your charges well for all Scots."

Kenneth returned to his seat and pressed his hands to his temples. He could only wish his next task would go so smoothly.

Cathira refused to admit her nervousness as she prepared to answer her brother's summons. Her conscience was clear. She had done what she thought was best. Perhaps it would still prove to be for the best. But in the meantime she must not let Kenneth guess where the order to strike King Drust had come from.

Her hand paused with her beautifully carved, bejeweled comb halfway to her hair. What if he already knew? Could Eoganan have told someone of her secret visit? Of course she could simply deny the charge. She let her dark-fringed lids droop as she gazed into the gold-framed mirror. It mattered little that her brother was high king of Dalriada. She could handle him.

She gave a final flip to her hair, made certain her rich red and gold tunic hung to its best advantage, and walked to the hall house.

"The king my brother would have speech with me?" She did not really kneel, but there was just a hint of the bended knee as she looked up at him from under her thick lashes.

Kenneth gave a shout of laughter that made all in the hall look to the dais. "When were you ever so submissive, sister? What mischief did you commit while I was gone that you now think to make it up with innocent looks?"

"I am sorry that you had ill luck with your treaty making, brother."

Now Kenneth did not laugh. "No, you aren't. You are smug because you told me it would fail. And you were right." He ran his broad hands through his unruly crop of hair that was much in need of cutting. "And yet none could have foreseen the act that caused it all to go awry. But do not gloat behind those green eyes, Cathira. For you will suffer with all Dalriada if the Vikings triumph over us."

"Is that what you think? Truly, Kenneth? I do not wish for a Viking victory. I do what I do for the good of Dalriada." And she spoke truth.

"Do you? And do you judge it best for Dalriada to refuse me in this matter of treaty with our neighbors to the west? Is that why you refuse to marry King Olaf—for the good of Dalriada?" Once again he came to his feet and began his long-legged pacing around the dais. "Cannot you now see that we need Norse help against the Danes? Now. With the Danes attacking—perhaps even at this very moment somewhere close to our shores."

Afterward even Cathira, she who always so carefully calculated all that she did, wondered why she responded as she did to Kenneth's challenge. Perhaps she felt some guilt over what she had done in Alba—no matter how often she reminded herself that she meant it for the best. Yes, perhaps it was a sort of penance. And a sort of shield so that Kenneth would not doubt her loyalty. And perhaps—just perhaps—she was a bit curious to see what this Olaf the White looked like.

She placed a hand on his arm, and the light glowed on the garnets and amber inset in her gold jewelry. "Kenneth, have you sent to Olaf for help?"

He shook his head. "Even great as the need is, I cannot take time to go now. And I cannot send a deputy to a king I have never met. Huel and Merfyn are a different matter—we have long known each other."

"You could so send if it were a deputy highborn enough."

"Yes. That is true. But I cannot spare Donald."

"And is Donald the only other of the royal household on Dun-Add?" She tossed her hair just enough to add subtle emphasis to her question.

Kenneth stared. "My sister, I cannot send a woman into such treacherous waters."

"In the waters of treaty talk a woman may possess skills a man lacks, my brother."

"That may be so. But I meant the physical dangers of Viking-infested sea."

"I know you did. So I would take a secure guard. Although I could as well argue that many of our Scoti women who stayed secure in their beds have met a Viking fate as sharp as if they had not so bided." She held up a hand to prevent his protest, and the gold of her bracelets made a soft jangling. "I will need only a few men, but bold warriors. And do not tell me you cannot spare a ship. I do not require one of your heavy longboats. I shall do much better with a lightweight vessel that can outrun and out-hide a dragonship. You will not be needing such for your war preparations." She paused to consider but then spoke before Kenneth could interrupt. "Six to row beneath the sail. And Talorgen for escort. That will do very well."

Perhaps it was a testament to the weight of the pressures on Kenneth that he agreed.

So the next morning two small vessels sailed from the peaceful cove of Loch Crinan on missions of importance for Dalriada.

In the first was Corbanac and Father Ernan, with a final warning from Kenneth's boatman, Struan, to be certain they sailed north of Scarba and avoided the maelstrom waters of the Gulf of Corrievreckan. The monk and priest crossed themselves and set sail, chanting a prayer of thanksgiving for the wind that billowed their canvas, for the sun that sparkled their waters, and for the seabirds that sang them a good voyage.

Cathira and Talorgen smiled at their own prospects of fair sailing, although Cathira interrupted her smile to turn with an extra flounce at the sight of his overlong leave-taking of Brocessa nic Dungal.

Truth to tell, Cathira was rather bored of flirting with Talorgen. She probably wouldn't bother if it weren't for the fact that he was hand-fasted to Brocessa and therefore a challenge—a challenge that was safe because unlikely to get out of hand.

She stood in the V-shaped prow and watched him spring lightly aboard with one hand on the boat's side. Yes, if he weren't hand-fasted *and* so exceptionally handsome. The sun shone on his wealth of black curls, and his black eyes snapped as he gave orders to the men on shore to push them off.

The sailing to Dublin was as calm as if there were no Vikings within a hundred miles, never had been, and never would be. And it was easy enough to believe that to be the case as they glided southward past the green slopes of the Mull of Kintyre on their left while the vague shape of Ireland grew ever clearer, larger, and greener before them.

At the tip of Kintyre, Talorgen gave order that the sail be adjusted to catch the wind at more of an angle and reset the long handle of the rudder from where he stood at the side of the boat. They slipped smoothly down the North Channel, Ireland on their right, Galloway on their left, the Isle of Man straight ahead.

They were now sailing along the coast of the Dalriata region of Ireland. Cathira scanned the green, rocky land with great interest. So this was the place from which their ancestors had come—those who hundreds of years ago had sailed the reverse of the voyage she was undertaking and established their own Dalriada. On around a particularly jagged coastline where fishing boats bobbed as thick as the rocks that broke the shore behind them, she noted a narrow inlet flocked with gannets, kittiwakes, and fulmars, following the many fishing vessels in swirling patterns, sometimes swooping so thickly to feed on the surface that they appeared as white foam on the waves.

"What is that river?" she asked Talorgen, who, his rudder set, had joined Cathira at her favorite position in the prow.

He shook his head. "Not a river. Lough Strangford. A sea loch near to twenty miles long, and no more than five even at the widest. One of the snuggest harbors in all the western waters. Perhaps the snuggest."

Then to their left the water was silvered with a shoal of herring just below the surface, and the air filled with the raucous cry of gulls swooping in for a feeding.

Shortly after passing the protected entrance to Strangford Lough, Talorgen ordered another reset of the sail, and they angled more sharply to the west across the Irish Sea. Man was now behind them, Dublin lay ahead.

Cathira could scarcely remember ever feeling more exhilarated. The breeze tossed her hair, sea spray stung her cheeks, sun sparkled her eyes.

And then they were lowering the sail and slipping into busy Dublin Bay, filled with long, square-sailed, dragon-prowed ships of all sizes. They sailed up the River Liffey and docked at a wooden quay on the south side. Several large cargo vessels were being loaded and unloaded. Stacks of baskets, barrels, and bales held trading goods of walrus ivory, silk, wool, wine, pottery, and furs.

Leaving all but two of the men with the boat, for there was no need for their envoy to attempt a show of strength, Cathira bade Talorgen find the most reputable inn in town and bespeak a private room where she could prepare to meet Olaf.

Talorgen also sent a messenger ahead to Olaf's rath—it was easy enough to spot the great stone-encircled strongplace atop the highest land around. "Inform the king that envoys from the court of Dalriada have arrived and the Princess Cathira would have speech with him."

The messenger departed, and Cathira and Talorgen made their way more slowly up the path that crossed the marshy land surrounding the river. A few warehouses, shops, and wine taverns stood on high patches of ground and straggled up the hill toward Olaf's fort.

Clasping the handle of her rush basket firmly, Cathira raised her chin and surveyed the inn Talorgen led her to. "This is the best in Dublin?"

"So they tell me."

Loud noises and louder smells emerged from beyond the blackness of the doorway.

"It will not do. I had better prepare in the street for my meeting with Olaf. I would have better chance of arriving without that putrid odor clinging to me."

Luckily, Talorgen had been to Dublin before. Although it was many years since, he had no difficulty remembering the way to the monastery on the back side of Coraigh Hill. And the brothers had no difficulty providing the royal lady with a guest room where she could refresh herself. A boy was sent scurrying for water so the lady could wash, and the brother hospitallier brought mugs of ale and slabs of sharp, herb-flavored cheese for their guests.

The room was small and bare but clean, so Cathira judged that it would do very well, especially since she would not be expected to spend the night here. Olaf's rath had looked as though it would offer a most acceptable royal guest room. In the meantime, since she had taken forethought to bring everything she needed, including her silver mirror, lemon-grass soap, and best linen towels, the monks' room would serve very well.

The evening light from the window was not sufficient, however, so she struck a flint and lit the small lantern on the bare wooden table. Now she could consider the matter of her hair. Should she bind it around her head in a regal coronet of braids with gold wires?

She fingered the delicate golden wires as she lifted them from her case. Or should she catch it back in a net of woven gold with just a few tendrils curling around her cheeks? In the end she decided to leave it loose, flowing over her shoulders like a copper cataract with just the dangle of looped golden earrings to give emphasis to her gestures when she chose.

She slipped on her ivory wool tunic, richly embroidered with gold at neck, sleeves, and hem, wrapped her small waist with golden cords so as best to show off the curves above and below, and completed the effect with a necklace of green beads that exactly matched her eyes. She smiled in her mirror, considered, then turned back once more to her case. Yes, just a touch of crushed berry paste on her lips. A man whose wife had been named Aud the Deep-minded would be sure to appreciate a woman who looked nothing monkish.

Cathira had no intention of arriving at King Olaf's court on foot, so Talorgen borrowed the finest horses the monastery had to offer—which, truth to tell, were none so fine. Even sitting atop her red-coated pony, Cathira still found it necessary to take care that no mud splashed on the hem of her tunic as they made their way through the busy, winding streets of the port city that until the coming of the Norse had been merely Baile atha Claith—'the town at the ford.'

The heavy, iron-hinged, wooden gate in the stone wall of the royal rath stood open, guarded on each side by two burly, iron-helmed men. Both guards had straw-colored mustaches sweeping almost to their leather jerkins.

"I am Talorgen mac Cetul, escort to the Princess Cathira nic Alpin of Dalriada. We come in the name of her brother Kenneth mac Alpin, seeking King Olaf the White of Dublin."

The guards looked at each other in some confusion.

Talorgen tried again, repeating each word more slowly and considerably louder and adding, "I sent a messenger announcing our arrival. You have been informed of our coming?"

The guard on the right replied in a heavily Norse-accented voice that told Cathira he was not accustomed to the Gaelic. "Ja. We have been told. You may enter. King Olaf, he is not here."

"What do you mean not here? Where is he?" Cathira took his absence as a personal affront.

A less guttural voice than that of the guard answered her, still in the clipped tones of the Northman but as one well in command of Gaelic. "The king of Dublin would be much distressed at missing your arrival, Princess. It is hoped that he will meet speedy success in

Lewis of the Western Isles and return perhaps even tomorrow. In his absence may I offer you the bounty of our table?"

Cathira's chin rose a fraction. "And you are?"

"Bersi Thordson, house carl to King Olaf. Will you dismount, lady?"

Her chin a fraction higher yet, Cathira stepped from her horse, ignoring the hand Bersi held to assist her—until she found it convenient to deposit her reins in his hand.

A number of stable theows, most wearing the iron ring of slavery around their necks, led the horses away. The newcomers followed Bersi, Cathira holding her skirt high.

King Olaf's hall stood to the back of the rath, a stone building with smoke floating upward from the hole in the center of its turf-covered roof. Inside, smoke stung Cathira's eyes and made her cough. The room was strangely arranged; platforms ran the length of the hall on both sides of the fire, and the high table was not at the far end but rather to the right of the fire. The place at the table to which the house carl led her, however, appeared to be clean enough, so she consented to sit.

But not to smile. Displeasure smoldered in her green eyes. Her red lips pouted.

She did eat. A day of sailing with only cold provisions from a basket had left her with a sharp appetite indeed. These Norse seemed to be inordinately fond of fish. Three kinds of fish, all white-meated and accompanied by white potatoes, were followed by a great steaming bowl of seal stew. Seal stew she disliked only slightly less than porridge. But the whitefish, while boring, was not distasteful. Perhaps it would have been less boring if she had consented to eat it, as the others did, with the sauce made of strange, sour berries and fennel herb. As it was, however, she felt the horn of frothy, sour mead added quite enough sharpness to the meal.

Cathira observed these strange North people. In the light of the flaring torches attached to the support poles circling the room, their hair appeared barley white. The men wore it long, at least to their shoulders, and their mustaches drooped well below their mouths, giving them a very fierce appearance in the flickering light.

The women wore their hair in thick braids hanging below the white linen headrails that surrounded their faces. More than one woman stared at Cathira in open-mouthed amazement. Guessing it was the color and style of her unbound hair they found so shocking, Cathira gave an extra flip to her head as she turned to talk to Talorgen beside her.

204

The Norse, men and women alike, wore tunics woven of a single color—green, blue, dark brown, or dull red. Nowhere did Cathira see the plaid so favored by the Scots. The men wore their long-sleeved tunics belted over trousers, while the women's were merely two long rectangles joined at the top by straps over the shoulders. They were brightly embroidered and belted over long, plain shifts.

Her hosts' favorite ornamentation seemed to be glass beads and semiprecious stones. There was some metalworking evident, especially in the twisted neckbands the men wore and the massive brooches all used to fasten their cloaks. But all around the room it was the gleam of topaz, lapis, and amber that most caught the fire-light.

The women—even those who appeared to be highborn—passed among the tables, filling and refilling silver-banded drinking horns with mead from large, red clay beakers. And then the women sat at table with the men. Of course, it was right that, as a princess, Cathira should sit at the high table. But she could not imagine how uncomfortable that arrangement must be for the other women—the lack of privacy—the exposure to coarse manners. At home her women would have been granted the sanctuary of their own table.

When the eating had ended and the more serious drinking began, a silver-haired skald took his place before the central fire below the high table. He had a small harp slung over his shoulder, which he snuggled into the crook of his arm, and began to strum almost absentmindedly until a strong, resonating chord called the attention of even the least sober guests.

"*Krakumal.*"

The announcement of the title of the tale he would recount was greeted with great cheering and pounding of the table.

Bersi Thordson, on Cathira's left, leaned forward to translate for her in his strange, flat Gaelic. "A popular choice, as you see. Hallur has chosen to recount the story of the coming of our people to Dublin from Norway fifty years ago."

Cathira inclined her head in a gesture of granting royal permission to proceed.

Without regard to her gracious consent, Hallur told in his song-speaking voice how the kings of Vestvold in southern Norway searched for better farmland for their people and richer trade routes.

"They looked to their south. And to the west. To the islands of the Hebridean Sea. And they sent their people forth, valiant and high of heart.

"King Herthiofur of the royal house of Vestvold made fine set-

205

tlement of his people in the Western Isles and led on to settle a war camp and trading station they called Dublin."

The skald named, to cheers, several bold kings of their history.

"Until, as the years passed, the crops grew, and the people flourished. And the ships sped over smooth seas carrying grain and cattle to Oslofjord and bringing slaves and mead in return."

Then the harp vibrated in a threatening sound.

"Until came Ragnar Ladbrok and his son Ivar the Boneless. Their dragon-prowed warships breathed red dragon-breath fire upon the Norsemen. And the Danes would be lords of Dublin."

A great howl went up. Some of those deepest in their drink brandished their eating knives as if they would charge forth to do battle that very moment.

A chord strike of the skald's harp brought them back to the poet's words.

"Then Olafr the White, king of Vestvold, sailed forth."

A great cheer rose.

"And never were there men of such high deeds. Olaf the brave, Dane-destroyer; Olaf the good, Peace-securer; Olaf Finehair, Wealth-bringer; King Olaf, Valiant-sword."

Cathira scowled. She had had enough and more of praising this barbarian and his rough court.

But the skald continued. "And Olafr of Vestvold punished those Dane-born Vikings who harried his lands. And Olafr established the peace." There followed more cheering and pounding until the drinking horns rocked and the serving vessels clattered.

No matter how heartily tired Cathira was of hearing about the valorous ventures of Dublin's Olaf, however, she was heartened by the tales of his conflicts with the Danes. And however overblown the skald's praise may well have been, she was thankful for whatever part of it was true. Olaf should make a fierce and willing ally for Dalriada—if he returned from his foray in the outer isles in time to help Kenneth.

But she had had quite enough for tonight. She turned to Talorgen on her right, placing a hand lightly on his leopardskin cloak. "You may escort me to my chamber."

She did not follow the ensuing exchange between Talorgen and Bersi Thordson, but no excuse or apology Olaf's house carl might have made could have lessened her outrage at the information that the high rath of Dublin did not include a guest chamber suitable for a royal lady. Of course, the Dalriadan men could stay right here on the sleeping platforms as soon as the trestle tables were moved against the wall—an event that would come too late for the comfort

of many Norsemen who already slept sprawled across the tables—
and Cathira would be most welcome in the women's lodge, where
those servants who had not followed Aud the Deep-minded back to
her father would wait on the Dalriadan princess. But there was no
separate accommodation.

Cathira did not even deign to reply. She exited the room with
her chin so high she almost tripped over a brindled Irish wolfhound
sleeping in the space between two tables.

20

Following his princess's exit, Talorgen did his best to thank Bersi, organize torchbearers to see them back down the hill, and keep up with Cathira in a dignified manner. It had rained while they were inside, making Coraigh Hill seem even more appropriately named "Marshland." The horses slithered and slid down the steep parts of the path, then, when the descent became more gradual, raised their heavy feet with a sucking sound.

It took repeated knocking on the barred door of Saint Patrick's monastery wall accompanied by night-rending shouts to rouse the sleepy brother hospitallier. At last, however, the iron hinges creaked, and Cathira rode through.

Her room, when she reached it, did nothing to soften her spirits. It was smaller, colder, and more barren than it had seemed earlier that day. The only saving graces were the deep sheepskin covering the slabbed wood cot, which was then piled with thick woolen rugs, and the fact that Cathira was so bone weary after the long day now spreading into tomorrow that she could have slept standing up.

She slept well into midmorning, then flung open the door of her small cell to find a young acolyte sweeping the walkway beyond.

"I require hot water and breakfast," she informed him.

He dropped his broom and scurried toward the kitchen in a far corner of the enclosure.

The dry roll, sour beer, and hard cheese he brought on a wooden tray made something of a penance of breakfast, yet no doubt was more generous than the monks had allowed themselves several hours earlier following morning mass.

Cathira had no desire to appear again at Olaf's rath as an over-anxious suppliant. So she sent Talorgen in the afternoon to inquire whether the king had returned. It was as well that she hadn't gone, for Olaf had neither returned nor sent word of his pending arrival.

Idleness was not Cathira's favorite state. As soon as she was dressed she set out on an inspection of the enclosure.

Two monks, their brown robes kilted to the knees, were hoeing in the herb garden along the eastern wall. She observed their labor for several minutes before she spoke. "You would do better to weed your herbs on your knees. You rout out far too many good plants with your hoes."

The monks stopped their hoeing and regarded her with open-mouthed amazement.

"Do you understand me? Do you have the Gaelic?" she asked.

They nodded that they understood.

"Then do not gape as if you were simpleminded. I never allow my gardeners to hoe the plants at this stage. And this end of the garden needs to be better drained." She pointed to the southwest corner, where water pooled around pale green thyme plants. "See how some of the leaves yellow? Root rot will follow if these plants are not drained."

She turned away. If they would not take her advice, it was their loss. But she did know what she was speaking about. Princess Cathira's herb garden at DunAdd supplied all for miles around the Great Moss with fine herbs for both medicining and cooking.

She found little to complain of at the fish pond. It was well-maintained, with sufficient water grasses growing in it to provide food and shelter for the trout living there without the water's becoming fouled with too much moss. She was gratified to see several large black snails cleaning their way along the rock-lined bottom. And the small, thatched duck houses on the tiny crannogs in the pond seemed equally well cared for. The abbot should be generously supplied with duck eggs. She would ask for one, well-boiled and flavored with mustard seed for her breakfast tomorrow. She made a face at the memory of the dry bread dipped in sour beer she had been forced to eat that morning.

"Young man, what do you think you're doing?"

An acolyte at the top of a ladder, its sturdy oak poles well lashed with leather thongs, pushed back the floppy-brimmed straw hat he wore to protect his tonsured forehead from the afternoon sun. "I am pruning this cherry tree, my lady."

"Well, at least you can speak. What is your name?"

"Finn, ma'am."

"Finn, do you not know that this is no time to be pruning?"

"Forgive me, ma'am. But the tree has ceased bearing. And a fine crop of sour red cherries it was producing too."

"Well, I'm gratified to hear that, Finn. But it will not be giving you so fine a crop next year if you prune it now. Put your shears away until October. When the first frost sends the lifeblood of the trees downward to sleep in the roots, then you may prune."

A bright smile broke Finn's face. He had fine white teeth. "And thanking you I am for telling me that. I'm ever fond of stewed cherries. And I'd not be wanting to harm a tree of our Lord's own making."

"You are quite right, Finn. Quite right. I see you're a ready learner. You'll do well."

Finn smiled again, then apparently remembered that humility was one of the virtues he was supposed to be learning, for he quickly ducked his head. "I thank you, ma'am. Praise our Father, who gives all good gifts."

Cathira left him standing in the middle of the beaten dirt path as she continued her inspection. There was a great deal in this Dublin that needed improving. Much could benefit by the firm grip of a hand such as hers. What had the horse-faced Aud done? she wondered—for so she mentally pictured the woman. Sit in the women's lodge and read books? If so, it's little wonder she went beetling back to her father in the outer Hebrides. Now, Cathira thought, if *she* were queen of Dublin, some changes would be made. Not that she had any intention of becoming such, of course.

The clanging of a mallet on an iron handbell, calling worshipers to evening prayers, recalled Cathira to the present. Shadows from the monks' cells fell late-afternoon long across her path. She had wasted a whole day waiting for this Olaf. Cathira did not like wasting time. She did not like waiting. But for the moment she had as well attend prayers. At least that could not be a waste. There were several matters she wished to lay before the Lord.

From all across the enclosure black-robed figures turned their steps toward the chapel that stood just inside the western wall where it was easily accessible to those from the haphazard, cluttered clutch of circular huts that straggled between monastery and Coraigh Hill. The monks approached with bowed, tonsured heads, prompting Cathira to toss her red mane and raise her chin as she walked to the plain, gray stone building.

"Let us serve the Lord in holiness, and He will save us from our enemies."

The canticle pronounced by the priest in front of the altar seemed particularly appropriate.

"Let your holy people rejoice, O Lord, as they enter Your dwelling place," the monks responded.

During the reading of the psalm, Cathira let her mind wander to the improvements Olaf needed to make to this Dublin, but returned again to the service for the psalm-prayer. Perhaps the harshness of the cold stones she knelt on had something to do with focusing her thoughts.

"You are our King, Lord God. Help us to find a place for You in our hearts. Let all who enter here for prayer take You as Savior of their souls, the forgiver of sins through the blood of Your Son Jesus Christ."

"Christ, we take You as Savior of our souls. We take You as Forgiver of our sins. Blessed be the name of the Lord."

Everyone in the room responded and crossed themselves.

The priest continued. "And Lord God Almighty, let us take You not only as Savior but also as Lord. Be You the Lord of every heart here. To reign in absolute authority over every life, with every heart surrendered completely to You, every will seeking to do only what You will."

"Lord, we take You as our Lord. Reign in absolute authority in our lives. We surrender our hearts to You. We will to do only what You will."

Cathira responded with less enthusiasm to each sentence. At last she crossed herself in silence.

"We ask this through our Lord Jesus Christ, Your Son, who lives and reigns with You and the Holy Spirit, one God, for ever and ever."

The little flock looked toward the altar to receive the evening blessing.

The priest extended his hands as if over the head of each one. "Depart you now and go forth in peace with God and man, remembering that everyone who exalts himself shall be humbled, and whoever humbles himself shall be exalted. Alleluia."

Cathira did not raise her chin, but her eyes smoldered a black green. A fine mess the world would be in if all were as spineless as this priest's theology.

And so she waited for two more days and yet a third. She was sitting on a small wooden bench by the fish pond when she heard the sounding of aurochs horns and the beating of wolfskin drums that told all Dublin that King Olaf had returned to his rath.

It was not until the next morning, however, that Cathira sent word to Talorgen that they would approach the king. And then let it be late in the day. Olaf had surely been informed of her presence in Dublin. It was now his turn to wait for her.

And she was determined that she should be worth waiting for. She dressed in her finest tunic, the color of a copper beech tree ornamented with amber. And she wore her most royal torque: the wide one that emphasized the length of her white neck, the one that met with green-eyed wolf heads facing each other.

Her orders to Talorgen had included a thorough grooming of the monastery horses they were to ride. She would arrive mounted on a steed whose hair shone as brightly as her own.

It was unfortunate that Olaf missed the fine spectacle of the princess of Dalriada and her entourage riding into the rath of Dublin just as the westering sun hung brightest above the wall, turning all Cathira's careful preparations to a blaze of copper and gold. He must have been deep in council indeed, or else very deaf, for she rode the full length of the ascent of Coraigh Hill with trumpets blowing beneath the unfurled red and white banner of Dalriada.

When only Bersi Thordson came to meet them, Cathira considered refusing to dismount or then refusing to enter Olaf's hall without the king's personal escort. But she realized she would only look defeated or ridiculous if she retreated now. So instead she tossed her hair, raised her chin, and allowed Bersi to escort her.

She paused at the back of the hall and observed the scene. Olaf and his men were standing about an object spread on the center table. Perhaps ten men leaned on the table or walked around for a better view, talking and gesturing. And there was no need for Olaf the White to be pointed out. He stood half a head taller than any other. His shoulder-length hair was silver white, bound back by a silver cord. Over his tunic of unbleached wool he wore a cloak of some northern animal, the color of the snow it must hide in. The boots that rose to the knees of his breeks were of this same pale fur. And yet for all this, there was nothing pale about Olaf the White. His skin was tanned a rich nut brown, emphasized by the twisted silver rings he wore around his neck and fingers.

Bersi urged their party forward.

Olaf looked up, and Cathira saw that his eyes were the deepest cobalt, a color so rare and so prized by the monks that it was reserved only for dressing the Virgin Mary and our Lord.

"*Ja*. The Dalriadan princess. I was told you wished to see me. You may approach."

Without waiting to see whether or not she accepted this gracious invitation, Olaf returned to what Cathira could now see was a map.

When Bersi, Talorgen, and Cathira reached the high table, Olaf turned to them again. "Cathira nic Alpin, sister of Kenneth son of Alpin, king of Dalriada. Long I would have speech with your brother, but these Danes will give us no peace. It is good that you are here. You may speak."

Cathira was the more outraged by the fact that he gave her no means of expressing her outrage than by his manner itself. Had he offered her a seat she could have refused. Had he offered her a drink she could have refused. Had he offered her pleasant conversation she could have refused. He offered to listen to her speak. And that was what she had come to do.

But to speak the words of diplomacy and treaty making, not to give this Norwegian king a much-needed lesson in manners. And her pride demanded that she show Kenneth she could succeed in the matter of treaty making. So the lesson must wait.

"My brother the king sends greetings. He would have come himself, but, as you say, the Danes are vigorous in their harassment. They have recently attacked Iona in the inner Hebridean Isles. My brother believes this was but a small raiding party, part of a large navy which he would repel that all our shores may be free of burning and pillage."

She stopped for breath—and to see if now Olaf would choose to make gallant comment on Kenneth's choice of ambassador.

Olaf, however, showed merely by the incline of his head, which was little more than a dropping of his startling blue eyes, that he was listening.

Cathira raised her chin and continued. "King Kenneth seeks treaty help from King Huel of Man and Merfyn Vrych ap Erthil of Gwynedd. He would also have alliance with Olaf of Dublin to form a fleet strong enough to defeat the present raiders and send them home with a message that in future they may not so easily invade our waters. He would also keep a fleet patrolling at all times, ready to respond to news of attack. The Danes may think it less ready sport if they have to pay dearly for their spoils."

She would go no further. Certainly she would not speak of numbers of men or ships or of more specific strategy until Olaf should tell her his view of the matter. She flipped her hair and waited. She was fully prepared to wait quite as long and as silently as he.

"Come." He led her to the map on the table and indicated that his men should make way.

She recognized the area represented, although she had never before seen such a detailed drawing of Ireland. Her own Dalriada was shown in bright ocher, Alba to the east in green, its seven regions undifferentiated, which might mean that Olaf didn't know much about Picti government or simply that he didn't care. To the south, Lothian was a hazy gray, and an inaccurately drawn Strathclyde to the southwest a slightly bluer shade of gray. The inner Hebrides were green as the rest of Alba, the center isles purple, as was the Dublin area of Ireland.

"This land is Norse." Olaf pointed to the purple regions. "This—" he tapped the island of Lewis "—is ruled by Ketil Flatnose, jarl of the Hebrides. I have just returned from helping him repulse a Danish attack—perhaps some of those very Vikings who attacked your Iona."

"Let us hope so." She would show him that Olaf the White was not the only one who could be cool. And she well remembered who this Ketil Flatnose was—the father of Olaf's former wife, who had returned to said father and was even now snug on her island of Lewis —with Olaf still dancing attendance on her?

From just above Dublin to the northern border of Ireland, including the coastland Cathira had sailed along just a few days ago, was a region shaded in brown.

"This is Oriel, ruled by King Godfrith. He of the Irish mother and Norse father is double ready to defend against the Danes."

Cathira leaned closer. There was Lough Strangford, whose narrow inlet had made it seem from the ocean to be a river. Now she could see the impressive size of the so thoroughly protected sea loch.

Olaf's lean, tanned finger moved westward across the top of Ireland. "King Ferdach of Ulster would be glad enough of help against the invader Thorguser, who calls himself king of Donegal. But Ferdach could give little help in return. All his time is spent guarding his borders against this nearest foe."

He moved down to the center of the map. "Maelsechlaind, high king of Tara, will not treat. He sees himself too high and too strong for such alliance. Even if it is the work of the others of us that provide him such luxury." He pointed farther down, to the southwest corner of the island. "King Cerball of Ossory will be ready enough to show himself thanks-giver for the sword skill we lent him when Targes the Savage invaded his lands and his heathen wife danced on the high altar of the church at Clonmacnoise."

Cathira nodded. The skald had sung of the drowning of Targes the Savage—and of all the glory heaped on this man next to her as a result of the victory. She glanced upward from the map she was supposed to be studying to observe him from under her lashes—Olaf the Bold, Olaf the Good, greatest warrior-king of the western sea . . .

"*Ja.*"

She jumped as Olaf's fist slammed the table with decision. "It could well be a thing of might making. You may tell Kenneth of Dalriada, Olaf of Dublin will think on the matter of joining him as sword brother. Godfrith, Cerball, and Ketil perhaps as well."

For the first time Olaf seemed to remember the council he had shooed away from the map. "Herthiofur, my general, what think you of this bold plan?"

A burly Northman with tangled yellow brown hair and full beard gave a lengthy reply accompanied by wide gestures, but Cathira could not understand the words he spoke.

Then Olaf turned to the youngest member of the group. "Thorstein, my son, think you we shall be rid of the Dane peril?"

Son? This Thorstein with the carrot red hair was Olaf's son? A boy not yet able to produce the flowing mustache so in fashion at this Norse court and yet near enough to man to be admitted to battle council and no doubt ready in his sword skill.

In response to a snap of Olaf's fingers, a slave wearing an iron neck ring brought an enormous drinking horn frothing at the brim with pale mead. Olaf seized the horn and held it high. "We drink."

He quaffed a goodly portion and handed it to Cathira. The horn, she knew, would then be passed to Herthiofur and Talorgen, then to the rest of Olaf's men. She had no desire to drink with the son of Aud of the Deep Mind.

Then she recalled: she was there as Kenneth's alliance emissary. This had nothing to do with the matter of her betrothal. She flipped her hair and tossed back a gulp of the sour drink to match the one taken by Olaf.

When the horn had gone round to all present, Olaf returned it to the slave. Then for a long moment he regarded Cathira with the full gaze of his cobalt blue eyes as if seeing her for the first time.

She met him levelly with the full power of her emerald green stare.

"*Ja.* It is good, Cathira of Dalriada. Kenneth your brother will have my answer before spring hosting time." With a curt nod, Olaf the White, king of Dublin, returned to his council.

Cathira departed with her gold and amber bracelets jangling and her hair flouncing. It would be a hot day in the north country, indeed, before she gave another thought to Olaf the White. One of such singleness of purpose and imperviousness to distraction might well make a fine battle ally for her brother, but he would not be husband for Cathira of Dalriada.

21

Kenneth was restless. Winter had settled uncommonly early on the westerlands. The Scots had been successful enough in their one foray against the Danes, but now as winter storms lashed the islands and coastlands, sometimes with as great a fury as that of attacking Northmen, he could do little more than plan, prepare, and hope.

While the golden days of autumn held, Kenneth, Donald, and Eochaid, subking of Galloway, himself a cousin to the house of Alpin, had sailed forth with their gathering of twenty longships. Following reports that raiding activity was centered on the Isle of Skye, they located the full fleet based in Loch Snizort. If this was part of the same party defeated earlier by Olaf and Ketil, as seemed likely, it was a serious invading force indeed, not intended merely to harry, raid cattle, and carry off what women and treasures they found handy. Their goal was likely to penetrate far inland and take over land permanently.

In the dark hours of night—while most of the Danes drank and wenched on the shores of Snizort—Kenneth, Barr, and Dungal, each leading a small party, boarded the largest of the dragon ships under cover of darkness, overcame the sleepy guards, and set the vessels ablaze. The surviving navy, which still more than doubled Kenneth's fleet, gave little more than a token fight and allowed themselves to be chased northward. Kenneth realized that such easy success owed far more to the fact that the Vikings considered it time to be returning to their own hearths for winter than to any battle skill of the Scots. Yet he was glad enough of the victory.

And now, with autumn turned to winter, his restlessness expressed itself in an almost compulsive desire to visit Donald at Loch Crinan, where the king's brother was overseeing the repair and building of the Dalriadan navy, then to go farther south to Galloway, where Eochaid likewise superintended the shipbuilding for his mortuath at Loch Ryan. But such trips could do little more than work off excess energy, which did little to relieve Kenneth's mind. He sent the hosting call to the mormaor of every region of Dalriada. Every war-

216

rior that could be raised was to be ready as soon as the seed corn lay fertile in the ground.

He could only trust that Huel of Man and Merfyn Vrych were following their promises as readily. Certainly they had been glad enough for Kenneth's pledge of protection. He could only trust that they would be as glad to stand by him in battle.

And Kenneth was restless about Alba. Would those divided and largely inexperienced mormaors under their weakling king be able to withstand the assault that was sure to come upon them, whether soon or late? And if not, would Dalriada then be bordered by lands ruled by barbarian 'black foreigners,' as the Picti were fond of calling the Danes? And what would become of his friends among the Albannach?

How might it all have gone differently if it had not been for that act of treachery committed by his own general. Thoughts of that haunted Kenneth when idleness allowed his mind to roam. Again he called Fechnon mac Eoganan and Aed to him, as he had so many times before, to question them carefully regarding the matter. It seemed no one would ever know the truth of it, and yet there must be truth to be known. One side or the other had struck first. One side or the other had believed itself in peril or had behaved with barbaric dishonor.

And as always, Fechnon's report was inconclusive. Just before they went in to the banquet set for them by King Drust . . .

"And how many were in attendance?" Kenneth asked again.

"Our company numbered near to fifty. Warriors and captains only. Our servants and armor bearers were still seeing to our horses and gear." Fechnon barely bothered to suppress a sigh of boredom for the many times he had told the story.

"And the Albannach?"

"A similar number. Only the king's highest warriors, those of equal rank to ours."

"And the women were not in attendance?"

"Perhaps they were to have come later. If Drust were planning to strike, it seems unlikely he would have wanted women in attendance."

Whatever the reason, Kenneth gave hearty thanks for it. "And weapons?"

"Both companies bore only their eating knives—as customary. But ours were newly sharpened—by my father's orders."

"And you sat each by other, Scot and Alban?"

"That is much the way of it. We sat according to rank. With my father next to the king, as your representative."

"Yes, yes." Kenneth rose from his high seat and ran his fingers through his thick brown hair. "That is what I cannot get past. Eoganan was my representative—and yet he struck the first blow."

He began to pace.

Fechnon shrugged and repeated his story, letter perfect. "Before we went to the king's hall—just before—Eoganan called myself and Aed to him. We were to tell every man individually ourselves. My father had received word by private messenger, personally from you—a messenger who had come secretly under the cover of night, but one who could not be doubted. Eoganan said your spies had discovered a plot at the Picti court. A trap had been laid for us. When the Albannach first raised their drinking horns we were to strike them before they could spring their trap—"

"Spies? What spies?" Kenneth leaned close to Fechnon and yelled. "I have no spies at the Picti court. The Picts are our friends—*were* our friends until this terrible thing happened."

Fechnon shrugged. "My father believed you had spies."

Kenneth resumed his pacing, thinking aloud. "Who could have done it? Who taken such a message? It could have been no one from this court. What did your father mean—a messenger who could not be doubted? Did he carry a special seal? Did your father recognize him?"

Fechnon shook his head helplessly. "Eoganan, my father, did not say."

Kenneth pounded a fist into the palm of the other hand. "It must have been a plot of one of the mormaors of Alba to seize power. A plot to kill Drust and discredit Dalriada. Who could it have been? Bruide? He wanted the high kingship enough to kill for it and bears Dalriada no love." Again the fist pounding. "Or Euan of Circinn. He seems too young for plotting such treachery, but he's hotheaded enough to so strike anyone he saw as his enemy. I cannot believe it could have been Nechtan or any of the household of Ferat, and yet they would not be the first to commit fratricide." He continued pacing.

Cathira, who had sat at a shadowed end of the high table throughout, now spoke. "Why do you not leave it, brother? You work yourself into a distraction to no avail. In the end, matters did not fall out so badly for you. You have your alliance to the west, and Alba is weak enough not to attack from the east. Dalriada is safe enough."

Kenneth whirled to face her with such violence that she drew back into her seat. "I would not have Alba weak. I would have them a strong friend. More than friend—I would have them . . ." What? He

218

had been about to say "family." Why did he choose *that* word? And why did Maia's image come to him more and more often in unguarded moments—accusing him, questioning him. And he had no answers for Maia or for himself.

And further yet, Kenneth was restless about the state of the church in Dalriada. He had been appalled at the shallowness of faith in Alba, where even the form of worship was often abandoned, surely indicating that true heart faith had been long dead among a majority of the people.

And yet, how much better did matters stand in Dalriada? This last attack on Iona had borne far more shattering results than he had at first realized. Abbot Dairmait had not just fled to Kells for the safety of his monks and the few precious books they had managed to take with them. He had permanently abandoned the island. Kenneth had sent to him repeated requests that they return, if not to Iona then to some more secure place—one of the many monasteries that Columba had founded throughout their land.

But Dairmait was adamant. The Lord had led them to safety. They would rest in the Lord.

And it seemed that with the abandoning of the cradle of Christianity in their land—the holy island from which workers had carried the torch of faith to every area for three hundred years—with this abandoned, all the torches had dimmed. Father Ernan still labored valiantly in his chapel at DunAdd, but the Columban church was ever monastic. The monasteries were the centers of learning, the beacons of faith. People came to them to learn and to worship; people went out from them to teach and to work. The greatest monastery in the land was gone. So were all weakened.

Kenneth sought guidance as to what he could do about the matter—for he had been anointed king as well as inaugurated. He was to be spiritual leader as well as war leader and ruler. And yet he had done so little. Truth to tell, all he had done was to move Columba's relics and the Stone of Dalriada into hiding for safekeeping. And by so doing had he himself further weakened the faith?

He didn't know the answer, but at least such questionings gave him a focus for his restlessness. He would visit Brother Corbanac at DunStaffness. He had asked the faithful monk to remain there until he could come to him. Now he could go.

It was a day of clear, cold sunshine, as if—the air itself having turned to ice—the sun's rays were reflected through diamonds, bright and almost as cutting. Kenneth went first to Crinan and was greatly heartened by Donald's progress there. Shipments of fine timber from the Island of Mull and from the forested lands above Loch Linnhe had been hewn into strong boards and poles, and Donald's workmen were skilled in the fitting and joining of such into strong, deep-hulled ships with six oars on each side.

"We can hope for a fleet numbering sixty and upwards for our share of the alliance if the weather holds reasonable," Donald assured his brother.

And with such encouragement Kenneth took one of the smaller vessels with a crew of only six and sailed up the Firth of Lorn to DunStaffness, the fort on the Staff promontory. Although this had long been one of the strongplaces of the royal house of Dalriada, Kenneth himself had spent little time here. Was this still one of the most secure places in all the land? What if he found it less mighty than it had seemed to him in childhood? What would he do then? Why had he been so rash as to order his nation's treasures to a place where they might be exposed to even greater danger?

As the boat drew nearer, he hoped that he had not been overly optimistic in his earlier assessment of the dun's strength.

But as the boat rounded the promontory into the glittering waters of Loch Etive and he looked on that massive stone pillar topped with a well-maintained timber palisade enclosing the fortress, the impression of impregnability that Kenneth had long carried of DunStaffness returned along with the added amazement that men could manage to build a structure atop such a great mound of solid rock.

Apparently a guard atop the palisade spotted Kenneth's royal banner flying from the boat, for they had no more than pulled into the marshy harbor than they were greeted with a flourish of horns and an escort appeared on the path above the quay. Unlike most duns, which were built on hills and had long, sometimes intricate, entranceways to be ridden up on horseback, the pillar foundation of DunStaffness stood flat on its promontory overlooking loch and firth. One simply walked to the foot of the rocky column, where a narrow stairway led up the side of the rock to the well-guarded gate. It was something like a broch, only many, many times larger, higher, and stronger.

Kenneth felt himself relax. His relics would certainly be safe here.

Brother Corbanac met him just inside the gate, his face flushed from running, his robe still kilted into its rope belt in the back. "My lord the king, forgive me. If I had known you were coming I would have met you at the harbor. I would have had all prepared. I would have—"

Kenneth interrupted. "Columba's relics. The Stone. Are they safe?"

"Yes, my king. Of course. What could happen to them here?" Corbanac's open face showed amazement that the king should ask.

Kenneth smiled. "That is all the greeting I would have."

"You have come to take them then? You have found a safer place?"

"I am unlikely ever to find a safer place—or a more diligent guardian. I have come to see them, that is all. I will not move them, I think, until it can be to a place of permanence and reverence. A place of greater accessibility to all our people."

"Where will that be?"

Kenneth shook his head. "I do not know where, and I do not know when, except to say that it will certainly not be until we are rid of the threat of Danish attack. We will see what victory God will grant us this spring. For the moment we must settle for security. But for now I would see your charges. Who knows of their whereabouts?"

"The exact location, only myself. Cened, your steward, himself stood guard to the lower chambers under the hall house so that I might carry out your orders unobserved. I judged it best—"

"And so were you right." Kenneth turned to the steward, who had stood aside while monk and king talked. "Cened, I thank you for your careful stewardship."

"My lord king, you will take meat with us? It is almost prepared."

Kenneth considered. Eating would then mean staying the night, for it would be too dark to sail home. But this would then give him more time to arrange matters with the captain of the fort. DunStaffness could be well located to learn the whereabouts of Viking comings and goings and then send vital information on by the chain of hilltop bonfires Kenneth planned to initiate. And it would give him more time to talk to this interesting monk. "I thank you, I will. But first I will make pilgrimage with our good brother here."

Corbanac led the way to the tall, narrow hall house where the steward nightly fed warriors and guests and tonight would offer hospitality to the king himself. At the far end, nearest the well, was the kitchen—not a separate building as was so often found in the larger duns. Perhaps King Ewin, who kept his strongplace here in the days before even the Romans intruded northward as far as the Clyde and onward, perhaps that Ewin had liked his meat and bannocks hot and therefore established his kitchen close to his high table. For so ancient were the claims of this fortress as a place of great history.

Such thoughts pleased Kenneth as he followed Corbanac's brown-robed back. Surely the use to which he now put the place would give it added meaning in the songs of the bards.

Corbanac took a thick, pitch-soaked stick from an iron wall bracket, held it in a cook fire until the end flared brightly, then turned to the darkened mouth of what appeared to be a cave in the floor.

Steps cut into the rock base of the fort led downward to a narrow tunnel that wound under the kitchen with cavelike compartments cut on each side. Here casks of heather and barley beer were stored, great yellow wheels of cheese kept fresh in the cool underground temperatures, and baskets of apples and marrows kept crisp all through the winter months.

"Ingenious! I wish we had such an arrangement at DunAdd."

"You will eat well tonight, my lord. Cened keeps a good table. Far too good for a poor monk." But Corbanac's grin showed that he little objected to partaking of the food that proved to be so much richer than that allowed by the stricter rules of Abbot Dairmait.

At the next-to-last storeroom Corbanac shifted several large baskets of wheat and barley to reveal a small cavity beyond. "If the king would like to wait here, I will bring the relics out."

But already Kenneth was on his knees, crawling into the little cavern. Corbanac held the torch low to light the way.

And then the flickering yellow beam fell across the cherished objects: the carved wooden stool containing the stone that Columba had anointed with his own hand as a reminder that righteousness alone exalted a nation and which veneration Kenneth himself had established by use at his own anointing; the small, house-shaped Brecbennoch of Saint Columba; the simple casket containing the dear bones of the blessed Columba, who had given this land the greatest riches any nation could possess—faith in God and a knowledge of His Son Jesus Christ.

And that significant but pitifully small collection was all that physically remained of three hundred years of the work of saints and kings on the holy isle. That and the accumulation of stones they had been forced to leave behind. Some were incised with crosses, some bore the name of their Lord, a few more were elegantly carved with intertwined plants and animals, but all were sadly broken by the hand of marauders.

If he had not already been on his knees, Kenneth would have dropped to them now. He was awed by a sense of history and of holiness. Here, in this dark, hidden hole, he saw a symbol of Dalriada. For all around the dark was growing. It seemed that everywhere the faith was weakened, the barbarians strengthened. And yet these few symbols of faith shone as light in the darkness.

The torch flickered as a draft from the tunnel caught it. From such flickering beginnings could greatness grow. Columba had been but one man, obedient to the call of God. And so had the apostles been but men—men with recorded weaknesses. And yet they had changed the world by following Christ.

And Kenneth, the restless man of action, the war leader of a nation, lingered on his knees, meditating. The words of Abbot Finguine, spoken months ago, before Kenneth saw the relics of Saint Andrew, and the words of Brother Corbanac, spoken less than an hour ago, before Kenneth came again to the remains of Columba, ran as a single stream in his mind. Surely this small, northern piece of land was doubly blessed to contain the relics of two so holy men. Surely they should blaze as lights set on a high hill, calling all of Dalriada and Albana to follow Christ as Lord. But if it was to be, the time was not yet, for the remains of both men lay hidden away, all but forgotten while their countries struggled for life and faith.

"Corbanac, I would take mass. Can you serve it?"

"My lord king, I am not a priest. I was only a brother—the youngest and lowest of the Iona brotherhood."

"There is something in the Scripture, is there not, about the last being made first? I am king of matters both temporal and spiritual. Cannot I make you a priest?"

Corbanac drew back, and Kenneth saw by the look on the young face beneath its gleaming tonsured forehead that he had blundered.

"My king, it is possible for a priest to make another priest, but it is not usual. A bishop or abbot . . ."

Kenneth smiled. "Yes, yes. Don't be perturbed. It is but my way to rush headlong at what I want. Although I am learning that does not always work best. It will take much practice for me to learn your way of seeking God's will first. If you cannot serve the elements, can you at least pray?"

"Oh, yes." Corbanac's smile was brighter than the torch he held. He placed his free hand on the king's bowed head, and Kenneth felt the warmth of his touch flow outward like anointing oil.

> "Christ be our Savior,
> Father be our Lord,
> Spirit be our Guide.
> O Lord God, fight our fight.
>   Against a faithless people,
>   Against a deceitful people,
>   Against an unbelieving people.

O God, be the King of our king.
Be his strength,
Send forth Your light.
Send forth Your fidelity.
Lead him on.
   Lead him to Your holy mountain,
   To Your dwelling place,
   To Your altar.
Be the God of his strength.
Be the God of his gladness and joy.
Let us give thanks to You upon the harp.
Let us hope in God.
Let us forever give thanks in the presence
   of our Savior and Lord."

And Kenneth went forth with a sense of renewal—and determination.

22

It seemed that they had no more than celebrated the Christ Mass than spring was full upon them with the solemnity of Lent and the glories of Easter. And all across the Great Moss, spreading each side of DunAdd, the silvery waters reflected pale blue skies filled with fluffy white clouds. Tall marsh grasses grew in the spongy ground, giving nest cover to curlews, eider ducks, and water hens.

Perhaps it only seemed that spring came with a special heart-rending tenderness that year because it came as accompaniment to the hosting call for men, arms, and horses from every part of Dalriada. And even as the fields were seeded and the warriors turned to sharpening their swords on the weapons stones of every dun, it seemed unthinkable that there could be those on neighboring shores preparing to kill and destroy.

And yet as the days warmed and flowers bloomed yellow and purple on the south-facing hillsides, there was tension in the air, a sense of waiting, a feeling each day that this could be the day a rider would arrive with word that black, serpent-prowed Viking ships approached. And few in DunAdd went to their beds at night without first searching the horizon for a flicker that could be one of the series of beacons Kenneth had established the full length of Dalriada to warn that the Vikings had struck.

Word was that it had been an early thaw in the land of the Danes and in Orkney. So it would not be long now. If the war fleet under the black raven banners of Ragnar Ladbrok and his fierce sons had wintered in Orkney, as some said, the first attack would come even sooner.

But when the first messenger came, he was not from the north or west as expected. Rather, the mud-splattered roan pony that stood with foam-flecked mouth and heaving sides in the lower courtyard of DunAdd had crossed the Moss from the east.

"Walk him until he is well cooled," the equally mud-spattered messenger ordered the stable lad who ran forward. "And do not let him drink until he is cooled. Well cooled, do you hear? He has done me valiant service. I'll not have him foundered now by ill handling."

The servant nodded and led the horse off.

The messenger turned toward the ascent to the hall house, but Kenneth came to meet him at a run. Already an ox horn sounded a low call to all in the dun to make ready, and a fresh messenger stood ready to carry Kenneth's orders to Donald at Crinan.

"Where did they attack? How many ships? Which way do they sail?"

The messenger shook his head and emptied the drinking horn a serving girl had brought from the kitchen with such haste that she spilled near to half the contents.

"The islands? Ardnamurchan?" Kenneth named the northern areas of Dalriada—most vulnerable to attack.

Again the messenger shook his head. "Ce. Cruithne of Atholl received word yesterday. They say the slaughter is great."

Kenneth was stunned. For all his dire warnings to the Alban mormaors, yet the news came as a shock. "Derile mac Riogan?" Kenneth thought of the youthful mormaor as he always pictured him, with his blue eyes reflecting the color of the Norse Sea, which wrapped around his region.

"Cruithne did not know. But it is not hopeful. It is said a large fleet—sixty ships or more—attacked the fortress at AberDee."

Kenneth nodded. "So. It begins."

Derile, apparently, had been the first to fall. Derile, who would have made alliance with Dalriada if the others would have. Although, truth to tell, it was doubtful even the alliance as Kenneth had envisioned it could have averted this surprise move. But now the longships of the black foreigners would sail unchecked up the Dee, and likely up the Spey as well, and all Ce would be in Danish hands to attack Findach and Atholl and Circinn around them. Certainly this was no mere raiding party. This was a bold attempt to take over a nation. An attempt that might well succeed.

Now the waiting was worse. Knowing the Vikings were on the move, but not knowing where, Kenneth considered sending Donald's fleet northward to patrol. And yet with no information to guide them, such a patrol would steer by little more than blind chance. And if they were then needed elsewhere, the Dalriadan response to any attack would be delayed and weakened. So Kenneth, who was not a patient waiter, waited.

He was not required to bide long. And this time it was no mud-spattered messenger who arrived at DunAdd, but none other than the king of Dublin himself with full escort.

Kenneth welcomed Olaf into his hall house and called for horns of his best heather ale and chunks of his favorite herb-flavored cheese. He thought briefly of sending for Cathira as well but chose instead that his generals be notified, knowing that his sister would not hesitate to include herself in any council should she so choose. A good thing it was that Kenneth's own mother had come from a people who practiced matrilineal descent, so he was not unaccustomed to women who would rule. With such wry thoughts he turned his attention to his guest.

"Olaf, you do us honor. It is in my mind that your coming brings good news."

Olaf smiled, and the whiteness of his teeth matched the whiteness of his hair. "*Ja.* May it be so. I have considered well your treaty offer. And I have consulted with the kings of Ireland I thought likely allies."

"It is good you have delayed no longer. You have heard of the Viking attack on Alba?"

"I have heard. Many would say those lands are far from Ireland—let the Danes have their sport there so they leave us alone. But I can see, Kenneth of Dalriada, that you are farther-thinking than that."

"To give our enemies any land is to give them bases to use against us. We must fight on every front. And we must fight together." Kenneth's dark eyes looked levelly into Olaf's deep blue. He was aware of a slight stirring at the back of the hall that probably signaled the arrival of some of his generals, but he would hold Olaf's gaze for the crucial question. "You will make alliance to fight with us, Olaf of Dublin?"

"Not I only but Cerball of Ossory, Godfrith of Oriel, and Jarl Ketil of the Hebrides. Even now our fleet assembles. One hundred ships meet in Lough Strangford—those to add to the sixty Godfrith has there already. We assemble to defend our lands. We will work with you to protect your lands as well, for we deem it to be better to stop the Viking before he sails south to Ireland . . ."

Kenneth reached for the beaker of ale to refill their horns that the bargain might be sealed with the drinking of the treaty cup, but a slight quiver in the air, the hanging of an unfinished sentence, stopped him mid-motion. "There is more?"

"How many ships can you raise, Kenneth of Dalriada?" It was not quite a challenge and yet more than a simple mathematical question.

"I have not received final count from Man and Gwynedd. Eochaid of Galloway sends twelve ships, which will bring our count to sixty." Kenneth hurried on before his count could sound puny in his own ears. "Plus we have warriors mounted on land."

"And the others, they will bring each twenty ships or more?"

Kenneth shook his head. "It is doubtful. Our assembled count will be somewhat fewer than a hundred ships."

Olaf nodded. "*Ja.* It is as I thought. So it could be said that Dalriada needs Ireland more than Ireland needs Dalriada."

"I believe we need each other. We have more to offer than ships. I have established already a system of beacons across the land as well as horse messengers. We need ships in the right places to strike, but we need more than ships. For example, the fleet you and Ketil Flatnose defeated last autumn was in truth only a small part of the force my informants located in Loch Snizort. We then rid the western waters of these raiders, or they might well have chosen to winter there. In that case your jarldom of Lewis would have been long attacked before you could have assembled your great show of strength this spring." Kenneth would admit to no weakness in his fewer numbers.

"*Ja.* Such is why I consider alliance. That and one thing further."

Again Kenneth held his eyes firm. "And that is?"

"I would have Cathira of Dalriada for bride."

The hall was silent save for the gentle sound of amber beads jangling and the swish of a tunic hem on the floor rushes before the door at the end of the hall slammed. The slamming could have been from the entrance of Barr and Talorgen, who now approached the high table. But Kenneth could tell from the slight smile on the face of Olaf the White that he did not think Kenneth's captains were responsible.

The appearance of the two men made a convenient diversion, however. Kenneth introduced the sturdy Barr and raven-haired Talorgen and reported to them Olaf's terms. All except his last sentence. "Dungal mac Machar is at Crinan with my brother. He returns tonight. After we have taken meat together you will know our answer, King of Dublin."

Barr and Talorgen all but gasped. Kenneth knew they were wondering what could possibly hold their king back from offering the treaty cup now. The promise of one hundred sixty fully manned longships could not be quibbled over.

But Kenneth would not promise treaty terms he could not deliver. And he knew his sister too well to promise her where she might refuse. He left his guest in the care of his captains and went in search of Cathira.

He could form no clear plan of how best to approach her. The last time they spoke of the matter had been months ago, and yet the memory of her angry refusal had not faded. If her visit to Olaf's court had done aught to soften her, she had given no evidence of it.

If anything, she had shown more preference for Talorgen since then. Apparently Dungal had noticed this also, for he had more than once asked Kenneth to set the wedding date of his daughter to Kenneth's dashing young captain. Perhaps Kenneth should not have delayed the matter. Did cowardice direct his reluctance to anger his sister by giving his final blessing to the marriage of Brocessa nic Dungal and Talorgen?

Now, however, there was no time for such maneuvering at court. He must approach Cathira directly and obtain a direct answer. An affirmative answer.

But he was to be frustrated in his attempt. Or was it momentary relief he felt when Sinech, Cathira's favorite serving girl, met him at the door of the women's place and told him that her mistress had gone for a ride?

"Tell her I *will* have speech with her." The slight emphasis Kenneth put on the message made it sound like a threat. Just as well that she should take it so.

The platters of roasted mutton and venison had gone around the high table twice, however, and Cathira still had not joined them. Conory, Kenneth's bard, had begun no song yet but sat on his favorite stool between the high table and the central fire, strumming a harp. Servants and others from the women's place kept the drinking horns filled, and their royal Norse guest seemed well pleased. Kenneth wondered if there was any significance to the fact that Brocessa was the woman to serve the high table. Not for the first time Kenneth wished he were as wise in the ways of women as he was in matters of statecraft and war.

A flutter of movement from the door nearest the women's quarters caused Kenneth to turn in expectation. But it was only the serving girl Sinech. She did not stop at the foot of the women's table, however, but continued to the dais.

"My lord king, the princess Cathira sends word that she will join you after meat." Sinech gave her gap-toothed smile, bobbed a show of respect, and darted to her place at the end of the hall.

Kenneth noticed that Cathira sent no word of greeting to their visitor and begged no excuse for her failure to honor their guest with her presence at the feast in his honor.

Perhaps Olaf noticed too, for he seemed amused. Or was Brocessa's careful attention to filling his drinking horn the source of his amusement?

Red Samian pottery bowls filled with the last of the winter-stored apples, withered but still sweet, were being passed the length of the tables, and Conory had struck the first chords of the sea song he had chosen in honor of their visitor from a great seafaring people, when Cathira made her entrance—not from the women's side but from the far end of the hall so that no eye might miss her.

Even though she was his sister, Kenneth gasped at her beauty. Had she taken matters into her own hands so completely as to come dressed for her own marriage this very night? He stole a sideways glance at Olaf. It was clear from their visitor's look of admiration and amused delight that, if such were her plan, Olaf would have no objection. And Kenneth saw something else in the look in Olaf's eyes and the set of his jaw: if there was any man on earth who could handle the princess of Dalriada, it was the king of Dublin.

Cathira approached at a stately pace, matching her step to the music Conory continued to play, although the bard had ceased singing. At first glance her tunic appeared to be woven entirely of gold thread, but as she came closer and the torches flared brighter, Kenneth saw that in truth it was of the same scarlet material as the cloak she wore flowing down her back. But the fabric of the tunic was cleverly woven to include gold threads like a plaid in the warp and woof so that it shone like a cloth of gold. And on her head she wore the headpiece that the royal women of Dalriada wore only for marriages and enkinging ceremonies. A band of gold encircled the forehead like a torque. Above the band rose entwined branches of gold, each tiny branch hung with a bauble of semiprecious stone. The jewels swayed and danced in the firelight as Cathira continued her procession.

And Kenneth held his breath. What did she intend to do?

She had just passed Conory's seat and was approaching the high table when a disturbance at the back of the room turned every head.

"My lord king!"

Dungal, spattered with mud, his gray hair and beard windblown, his spurs clanking on the flags of the hall floor, entered at a near run. "My lord, your brother sends word—come of sudden from King Huel of Man. The Vikings attacked him, just setting out from Ramsay Bay to answer your hosting call. Eochaid of Galloway hurried full sail to his aid." Dungal stopped for breath.

"And?" Kenneth prompted.

"Disaster. Your cousin of Galloway is slain. Huel wounded, but lives."

"And the ships?"

Dungal shook his head. "Ragnar Ladbrok—for so his black raven banners proclaimed him—outnumbered them three to one or more. He left none seaworthy."

In the hush that followed Dungal's words, for he had spoken so that all could hear, Kenneth made quick calculation. Ragnar must have been sailing with seventy-five ships. And that most likely only part of the story. His son Ivar the Boneless would doubtless have infested their waters with something little fewer than an additional fifty black dragons. And Rognvaldur Ragnarson would be likewise lurking nearby in sea loch or cove with near to that many.

Treaty with Olaf was Dalriada's only hope. Kenneth would take the consequences with his sister later.

The hush in the hall was changing to murmurs of outrage, disbelief, and fear. Kenneth stood and pounded the hilt of his eating knife on the table for attention. "This is grievous news indeed."

Few in the room knew how grievous it was. Merfyn of Gwynedd was now Dalriada's only ally with any fighting strength left—if Ragnar had not since attacked the Welsh. And the Danes had already attacked to the east. How long could either Dalriada or Alba hold?

"But I have heartening news to counter. Even now the kings of Ireland gather a mighty fighting fleet. King Olaf of Dublin this afternoon offered alliance with Dalriada. We accept that offer of alliance—and all its terms."

While the room vibrated with the thumping of fists and sword hilts on tables, Kenneth offered the treaty horn to Olaf.

Olaf stood. He drank with Kenneth, but his eyes never left Cathira, standing stiff as a carving on a memorial stone.

23

Kenneth looked straight ahead at the waters of the Sound of Jura beyond Crinan Bay. A light rain fell, and patches of fog hung around the rocky coastlines and broken waterways. But Kenneth and his men knew the waters well. They could sail in the dark if need forced them, although that was only to be attempted at the most desperate of times—even more desperate than these, if such were possible.

It was good, though, that Olaf had sailed southward a few hours earlier to take word of the Danish attack to the combined Irish fleet that should now be assembled at Strangford. Kenneth sent Donald and Barr and half the Dalriadan fleet with Olaf and had delayed only these few hours to send a message to Merfyn Vrych in Wales and to seek word from his own watchposts to the north.

He had expected the first attacks to be in the Hebrides or lands closer to the Viking homeland. But Kenneth's riders, under the leadership of Talorgen, who would head the land patrols, brought quick confirmation. No warning beacons had been lit anywhere on the entire western coastland. It had been clear weather yesterday, the day before, and last night. Any attack, even on a remote village, would have been reported by now.

So Ragnar must have sailed straight down the Minch, perhaps under cover of night, heading unswerving toward a target. It was unlikely the Isle of Man would have been the goal of such an arrowhead attack. It must have been Huel's bad luck to have been in the way. No, it seemed clear that the Danish raiders targeted an enemy of long standing. The powerful kings of the northland were not content to let the rich pickings from Norse trading centers slip out of their grasp while they filled their ships with the loot of random attacks. Clearly this was to be a war for permanent settlement and established trade routes. A war that would decide the fate of Ireland and the Western Isles—and perhaps of Dalriada.

Leaving Dungal with a minimal fleet of fifteen ships to respond to any need closer to home, Kenneth hoisted sail and signaled his oarsmen to set their course.

Barely out of Crinan Bay, they ran into a thick fog bank in the Sound of Jura. He ordered his men to raise oars and sounded the signal horn to his fourteen following ships to hold as well. There was a light wind behind the rain—the mist could blow on past soon. Better to lose a little time waiting than a longer time reassembling a scattered fleet.

Although a reasonable course of action, waiting was even less easy for Kenneth than usual. It gave rise to thinking about the unsettled matter of Cathira. He disliked leaving her in charge of the dun, especially with Talorgen so near at hand with his land patrol. Ever since they were children, Kenneth had never known what mischief his sister might get up to. And yet there seemed little choice. He needed all his captains at their battle stations, and though Midir was a faithful steward for the daily affairs of the fortress, he needed one in charge. It was all Kenneth could do, and yet . . .

His waiting was rewarded. An increased burst of wind pelted stinging drops of rain down on them, but it also blew the heaviest of the fog ahead of it. He had barely given the order to lower oars when he saw shapes to the south—not the cluster of black rocks they first appeared to be but a fleet of dragon ships headed toward them at full hammer.

He calculated quickly. The serpent prows seemed double the number of his own fleet. It was possible, maneuvering in their own waters as his men would be, and battle-ready warriors as he knew them to be, to win against such odds. But it was foolish to take such risks unless necessary. It would be far better to encounter them on another day when his force was up to its full fighting strength.

He had enough lead time—just—and the wind was slightly to the north—a factor that would aid the Danes should he choose to sail south to meet them now but would help him even more if he turned north. With skillful sailing they could round the tip of Jura and take shelter in the cluster of islands that surrounded it or sail on to more open waters where they could make good time for meeting the others.

Kenneth gave the order to sail north. The wind filled the canvas as the thirty-two oarsmen pulled together. The northeast coast of Jura sped by on their left. They maintained their distance from the Vikings, but just barely. And Kenneth's men could not maintain this pace endlessly. They were fine seamen and warriors but essentially farmers and herdsmen, not full-time seafarers like the Vikings. He must think of something or be overtaken.

He looked at the sky over Jura. Mist hung above An Cruchan like a spider's web. Behind the mist lay the darkness of a lurking bank of fog. And ahead was the narrow Gulf of Corrievreckan between Jura and Scarba, with its treacherous whirlpool waters. Should he attempt it with the fog bank threatening or continue northward to the Garvellachs, where a multitude of tiny, rocky islands required skillful navigation even in clear weather?

And then an idea struck. If the fog would cooperate . . .

Kenneth was not a man accustomed to praying in the midst of his labors—that was monks' work. War was his work. Yet the monks spoke of serving God in all one's life. And certainly only He of the heavens could see to the perfect timing this would require. And there was the precedence of our Lord's commanding wind and waves. So Kenneth offered a short prayer, then gave his orders.

Slow the rowing pace—gradually, so the Danes would think them tiring.

Then turn wide at the mouth of Corrievreckan as if negotiating close to the Scarba coast.

As soon as the tip of Jura blocked them from sight, swing sharply left and keep as close as possible to the shore. If they timed it right . . . if the fog provided just the right cover . . . if the Vikings took the bait and followed . . . it was just possible.

Kenneth felt his rowers slowing. He saw the Danes getting closer, the dragon-head prows now visible against red and green striped sails.

The Dalriadan fleet was past Jura. Kenneth had given the order, transmitted by horn signals from ship to ship, to sail close together. Nearly at the south coast of Scarba, they swung suddenly west almost as one ship.

Kenneth held his breath. Could they then pull back quickly enough to avoid the treacherous sucking of the whirling black waters and yet not betray a warning to the Danes? He could hear the crashing of the riptide on the rocks of the Scarba coast, rocks that would smash any boat caught in the power of the tidal races—any boat not simply sucked to the center of the maelstrom and on down to the depths of the sea. He could tell by the look on his men's faces that they felt the pull on their oars. And yet they were not beyond sight of the Danish lead ship.

And then the miracle happened. Kenneth couldn't have asked for better timing. The fog rolled in. The Dalriadans pulled to the coast of Jura in single file, arced around the swirling vortex, and positioned themselves again near to Scarba, as if they had sailed straight that way in a tight clump. A freshening wind lifted the curtain of mist enough to give the Danes a tantalizing look at their target, sailing ahead at a weary pace.

Kenneth watched. Would they take the bait? As he held his breath, a fragment of the psalm Father Ernan had read at their departure that morning returned to him, words that Kenneth barely heard at the time yet had registered somewhere in his busy mind. *Behold the deeds of the Lord. He gives victory over the enemy. The bow He breaks, He splinters the spears, He burns the shields with fire.* Would He also sink warships?

The Vikings took the bait. Now would they hold course until it was too late to pull back? Or would they too feel the suck of the tide and turn away? The Danes were sailing in tight formation so as to offer a more solid shield wall for battle. If the leaders were slow to notice the pull of the tide, if they thought it not a serious matter because the Scots had apparently sailed through it, or if they mistook the currents for the play of wind-driven surf rather than something more ominous, a great portion of the ships could be destroyed. The litheness of the Viking vessels, which made them so obedient to the sea, could now work against them.

The Danes' lead ships came on at full speed.

Kenneth ordered the rest of his fleet to sail on toward Ireland, keeping back only two ships to observe with him. He noted the moment when the Viking oarsmen reversed their rowing and began pulling against the current. But the wind billowed their sails above, and the water sucked the hulls below. There was little the would-be raiders could do. The first three ships were fully into the maelstrom before the mist descended once more, drawing a curtain over the scene.

The Lord of hosts is with us; our stronghold is the God of Jacob. Kenneth's mind repeated Father Ernan's reading. With lightened heart he ordered full sail for the rendezvous at Strangford Lough. He would have good news for his treaty partners, who would surely be in want of it so soon after the defeat of Huel and Eochaid.

They had perhaps ten hours' sailing to the coast of Oriel—if the weather did not worsen. They would do well indeed to make their goal before nightfall. But Kenneth could feel the vigor of his men's pull on the oars, renewed by their victory. The king took a turn at the oars, as did his other warriors, while those who had rowed so valiantly through the treacherous gulf rested under the canvas awning at the prow.

As they sailed southward the winds strengthened, and by late afternoon, just as they passed between the Mull of Kintyre and the green cliffs of the Irish coast, the sun broke out. Fulmars, guillemots, and kittiwakes whirled in the sky above them as if to give them welcome.

235

But that was the only welcome they received. Kenneth had expected the news of his victory at Corrievreckan to hearten his sword-fellows, but he could have had no knowing how desperate the need for cheering would be.

Red streaks flamed behind gilt-edged clouds in the western sky as Kenneth rounded the easternmost point of Ireland and made for Strangford.

Struan, his chief boatman, was the first to smell smoke.

Kenneth sniffed the air. "Cook fires, no doubt. One hundred sixty ships with no fewer than fifty men each—it will take a good many fires to cook stew enough to fill all those bellies."

But it was no cook fire that met them at the blocked mouth of Strangford Lough. It was the still-burning remains of three ships sending black pitch smoke into the sky. Three Irish ships.

Kenneth ordered Struan to put in at the ferry port. He must know what had happened. It was some time, however, among a population stunned by loss and busy mourning their dead, before he could find anyone to tell him.

"All ships?" He repeated. Surely he had misunderstood, for the man's accent was somewhat different from his own.

But there was no mistake. All the ships were lost.

"But I was told they numbered one hundred sixty," Kenneth continued to argue. It could not have happened. The valiant Irish and Norse ships met here in mighty alliance could not have been burned and sunk even while he was defeating a raiding party of thirty. And yet it was so. All one hundred sixty ships had been lost.

24

Cathira strode the length of the lower courtyard at DunAdd. It was a fine thing to be in sole charge of the fortress of Dalriada. Now was her chance to set all in order, to exercise the gift for ruling that she had been born with. For on her mother's side she came of lines of women that, in spite of the possibility of being bought and sold by their husbands, yet enjoyed high status and much freedom in a society that allowed them to speak at public meetings, own property, get divorces, and take complete charge of their households. And on her father's side ran the blood of the race that had produced such warrior women as Boudiccea and Cartimandu.

The steward Midir and the servants Garbh and Sinech followed close at her heels, making careful mental note of all her orders, for it would be their job to see that her commands were carried out—precisely to the last jot.

"The stones of the courtyard are loose here. They are to be reset before the next rain."

Midir nodded. He would see to it.

Cathira walked on to the miller's site, where several rotary querns ground corn for all the surrounding area. "Come summer the mice will get to those sacks." She pointed to bags of flour sitting flat on the floor of a storage shed. "Order the carpenters returned from Donald's shipbuilding to construct new storehouses set on stones shaped so . . ." She drew a mushroom-shaped stone on a board covered with dust from the milling. "See—the mice cannot run up such."

Midir's enthusiastic nod showed that indeed he understood and was impressed. Sinech gave a wide smile that displayed the endearing gap between her front teeth and said that this was a mistress to be proud of serving.

Cathira turned to the miller. "And in the meantime, store your wheat and barley in clay pots rather than these open baskets. Covered pots. You will have less spoilage."

The miller appeared less pleased at being told how to do his job than Garbh was, but he nodded. It would be done. None enjoyed the consequences of disobeying Princess Cathira.

The inspection tour moved on to the blacksmith. Cathira was gratified by the craftsmanship of the iron-hafted saw he was producing. After a winter of making nothing but swords, spear tips, and war helmets, she could see he was taking pleasure in this new work. They passed on without orders for improvement. A rarity indeed.

The storage sheds in the second courtyards were much in need of re-thatching. Cathira observed them for some time. "At the rath of the king of Dublin the buildings are roofed with turf. Boards are placed over the support beams." She pointed to the rafters buttressing the sagging thatch of one building. "Then blocks of turf are cut and fitted snugly over the boards. It seems a much sturdier roof. I will have these sheds redone so."

Garbh nodded.

"But have the roof beams reset also. Make them steeper and the sides to come down closer to the ground. The buildings will shed water better and stay cooler in the summer."

The princess sniffed a wheel of dark gold goat cheese. "This is perfect. Just ripe. It will remain so longer in a building so roofed for coolness." She considered for a moment. "But do not fail to see to the air vents as well. We must have good circulation to preserve freshness."

She stepped to the other side of the shed and ran her hand through a basket of hazelnuts. "Mold!" She drew back in disgust and wiped her hands on the apron she wore over her tunic. "Hazelnuts we keep as special for feast occasion. They are a particular favorite of my brother, the king. I will not have moldy hazelnuts served to the king of Dalriada. Nor will I tolerate such waste from careless storage." She turned to Sinech. "See that all baskets of hazelnuts are turned out into flat trays and picked over carefully. Then stored flat in a thoroughly dry place."

And Sinech nodded.

The inspection continued to the next courtyard, where the goldsmiths, enamelware painters, and jewelers with trays of glass beads and caskets of jet, garnet, amber, and other semiprecious stones did much of the finest work in all the land. Cathira stood long watching an artisan enamel a fine roundel brooch.

He started to dip his brush in the pot of red enamel.

"Blue next," Cathira said.

He did not look up. He did not hesitate. He dipped in the blue.

Sinech gave her gap-toothed smile again as they moved on toward the poultry byres. "You were right, my lady. The blue was much better next to the purple."

"Of course."

Two days later all DunAdd was astir, carrying out Princess Cathira's commands. She had been over every inch of the dun. She had issued instructions for every improvement she saw to be made. There were no more orders to be given. It occurred to her that she might inspect farther afield in Dalriada and assist their people in improving their animal husbandry and farming methods. But even Cathira had to admit that she knew little of the ways of crop growing. First she would have to become better informed on the matter herself.

But for the moment she sought amusement. Talorgen and his men had not returned from their northern patrol, so there were few opportunities for amusement. The chatter of the women's place bored her. Weaving, embroidery, and the design of ornamentation were of much importance to her, but only so that they might be used to gain power—power she would wield for the good of her country. Knowing what was best, she would use any means at hand to bring it about.

She decided this would be the time to improve her musical skills, for, though she had been trained from childhood on the harp, the strings did not leap readily to her fingers, and always she must practice long for a song to give a sound that pleased her. And yet it was a matter of great satisfaction when she had conquered an agreeable melody. She took her harp of highly polished black bog oak and went in search of Conory.

She found the bard in the courtyard just below the summit fort, sitting at the far end of the inaugural stone, which bore the footprint into which Kenneth had placed his foot at the moment of enkinging. Conory's harp lay beside him, and he traced the print idly with one finger.

"I see you are thinking deep thoughts, Conory the harper." She sat beside him on the east-facing side of the rock. "Think you of a new song celebrating the line of Fergus mac Erc and the house of Gabhran?"

"My lady, I was thinking, indeed, of the sons of Erc and of Gabhran but even more so of the future. I think I would not care much to live subject to a Viking king. My heart is turned to God, asking for victory for our king. Then I will make a new song, when I know that I will live as a free Scot."

Cathira's laughter was almost a scoffing. "A true Scot will be free in his heart no matter whose foot treads the enkinging stone. But do you doubt Kenneth's victory, Conory? Dalriada will triumph over the barbarian—both from the north and from the east."

"The east?"

Cathira shrugged. "I overspoke. Our Pictish cousins to the east are not barbarian. It is merely that they lack a leader with the vision and courage of my brother. They need him for ally and leader. And when the Dane has been sent northward to stay, then can Kenneth look eastward again. Prepare you a song for that day, Conory. And teach it to me that I may sing with you then."

Conory's eyes shone, framed by the small braids he wore on each side of his face. "Yes. And it is not so wild a dream, for so did Constantin and Oengus of the house of Gabhran rule both Dalriada and Alba." He picked up his harp and let his fingers glide over the strings as words at first disjointed, then blending into lines, formed into bard song.

But Cathira's harp lay silent on her lap as she followed the winding silver line of the River Add eastward across the Moss and toward the forest. Yesterday had been a day of slate gray clouds and drizzling rain, but today the sun shone, making all sparkle with newness.

At first she thought the small dark dots of movement she saw on the edge of the forest must be a herd of deer coming to the edge of the Moss for easier grazing. She sprang up. It had been long and long since she had ridden to the hunt. And even emptied of expert marksmen as Kenneth had left the fort, there were many yet whose arrows could take a deer. This was a perfect day, and fresh roast venison would be just the thing for feasting their triumphant warriors soon to return.

Halfway up the path to the summit, Cathira paused and looked back. But surely that was no herd of deer to advance so steadily and in such close formation. Then a flash of silver reflected the sun. And that was no white gull. A mounted party approached, flying silver banners.

Bruide of Findach flew banners of a black boar on silver. Cathira had heard Kenneth refer to them often in council meetings, symbolizing as they did the ancient lineage of his mortuath from the days when Craig Phadrig was the high throne of Alba. And she had heard Kenneth speak of Bruide's desire that it be so again.

So did the mormaor of Findach know that the strongplace of Dalriada and its women, craftsmen, and servants were guarded only by those warriors Kenneth could spare from his battle against the

Danes? If so, she would do her best to show Bruide that they were still none so weak. She ordered the guard at the gate of the summit fort to sound the alert on his ox horn, and she sent the nearest servant scurrying with orders for Garbh and Sinech.

By the time she reached the stables, the horses were already saddled. She chose the four best-appearing guards to ride with her.

Cathira already had her skirt kilted and was astride her saddle when Garbh arrived, wearing a borrowed leather breastplate under his plaid cloak and carrying both the red and white wolf banner of Dalriada and her personal banner of a crouching mountain lion. A warrior would carry the wolf, and Garbh would attend her with the unfurled golden cat above her head.

Sinech arrived last with Cathira's sword and casket of torques. She snapped bands of twisted gold around her forehead, her neck, and each wrist.

And Dalriada rode forth to meet Findach.

A short distance from the foot of the fort they came together.

Cathira was disappointed. After all her preparation, she found herself greeting only Bruide's envoy and not the mormaor himself. But the young man flanked by black boars was none so mean a deputy. She smiled when Kinnart mac Bruide announced himself. So Bruide had sent his son—a son who bore the Pictish form of her brother's name.

"My father sends greetings to the king of Scots and asks that his word be heard."

The lad was so young and struggled so valiantly to appear far beyond his new-made manhood, although it was obvious that he could not have taken valor and joined the man's side more than a summer ago, that he awakened a strange sensation in Cathira. She felt motherly toward him. But she also felt triumphant. Was Alba come to this? Sending boys to the courts of men? She well knew of the defeat of Derile of Ce, whose region lay directly to the east of Bruide's. Did the coming of this child mean that the Vikings had also struck Findach? Her mind raced, and her heart exulted as she led up the entranceway to the fort. Had Alba now fallen to Dalriada's grasp like a ripe plum?

Once in the hall house, with Kinnart sitting beside Cathira at the high table and the formalities of the guest cup finished, she learned the truth of the matter.

"My father Bruide and Cruithne mac Boanta of Atholl send to Kenneth of Dalriada that they have considered. They will have him for treaty friend."

"Excellent words, indeed, Kinnart mac Bruide. But there is no need to rush so at them. Tell me first of news of Alba. I have many friends, even cousins, among the Albannach and hear sparse reports of their welfare." As she spoke she smiled leisurely and refilled his horn. If she talked of womanly, family matters and plied him with heather beer, she had no doubt of her skill to learn far more of the true state of matters than any ambassador would willingly impart.

"Oh, yes." With a visible shake he recalled himself to his duty as guest. Always news was the most sought-for commodity. He must impart his share in exchange for his host's bread and meat. "Reuther mac Galan of Cait—know you him, Princess?"

She nodded. "An old and trusted friend of my father's father."

"It is so. A fine graybeard. But his gray hairs keep him to his bed. He was unable to answer my father's hosting call."

"Your father Bruide hosts against the Danes?"

"With Cruithne of Atholl. You heard, perhaps, of the black foreigners' attack on Ce?"

Cathira nodded.

"Derile mac Riogan was no friend to my father, but he fought hard for his mortuath and fell with a Danish battle-ax in his shoulder."

"And so the Danes attack Findach?"

Kinnart shook his head. "Not yet. Gormr of the horned helm sailed the Don, striking many places along its shore to ensure his victory in Ce. We do not know where he may strike next, whether Craig Phadrig or even at Forteviot."

Even Cathira was awed by such audacity. The strength and courage of a war leader to sail that deeply into the very heart of a country and strike at its strongest fortress showed a daring and command of the Danes' strategy of surprise that demanded respect as well as fear. And it must mean that the horned Gormr knew well the weakness of the Picts.

"And the house of Ferat? King Bran and the mormaor Nechtan?"

If Kinnart thought to be surprised that a woman had such knowledge of affairs, he did not show it. "Bran and Nechtan rode to the aid of Ce. They are slain. Mormaor Fergus of Fife as well. Abbot Finguine of Kilrimont and Princess Maia hold in Forteviot."

Kinnart was not so tongue-loose, however, but that Cathira felt there was something he wasn't telling her. Yet what he did tell was enough. She knew more of Alban affairs than her young visitor could have guessed. And she was very good at keeping score in her head. Seven regions of Alba: the mormaors of three slain by Gormr; one laid low by old age; three in alliance against this fierce, black-horned Dane—and of those three she knew Cruithne to bear no love for Bruide, and Euan to be young and hotheaded. And the royal family all slain or in seclusion.

It was little wonder that Bruide was willing to call on Kenneth of Dalriada for help. There was little doubt that Bruide planned to seize the high throne for himself, but first he must rid his nation of Vikings so there could be a high throne for him to sit upon.

As swiftly as she calculated, Cathira considered the possibilities. She could refuse with the hauteur none but she could so well command. Alba had been offered—and had refused—Kenneth's support. Let them see to their own defense. That would ensure the Albannach defeat, but then Dalriada would have Viking neighbors, a situation Kenneth worked to prevent. Or she could stall, which would not be a stall at all but a mere telling of the truth, saying that her brother was even now battling another Danish fleet to the west and could look east to Pictland when he was finished. If there was any Pictland to be seen then. She even fleetingly considered accepting in Kenneth's name and riding forth herself with what few troops she could muster. If she kept Kinnart here as hostage, she could even claim the throne for Dalriada when they defeated the Vikings.

But even Cathira, who had always been chastised by her brothers for her heated imagination, realized that such a plan was overbold. Her archery skills rivaled any man's, and she had been trained at sword practice with her brothers, but she knew herself to be no Boudiccea.

Yet she could act. This news was of far too much import to await Kenneth's return in the normal course of events. He must know now. She considered who she should send as messenger. Garbh was faithful enough, but this was too important for any mere servant. The handful of warriors Kenneth left to guard DunAdd were needed at their post should any trouble arise. If Talorgen were returned with his horse guard, he could go. But it could be as many days and more until his return as waiting for Kenneth himself, for Talorgen had a long coastline to patrol.

Her decision was partly a result of her own desire for action but mostly of her determination that the message should be delivered with absolute accuracy—and with the proper urging for Kenneth to take action now. What were Ireland and Man when the throne of Alba was within grasp? Certainly her decision had nothing to do with any desire to see Olaf the White again—ever.

"Kinnart mac Bruide, bide you in DunAdd of Dalriada tonight. Midir, our steward, will see to your comfort. I will take your message to my brother the king. Then return you to your father with good assurances. Tell him Dalriada will have no Danish neighbors."

She did not add, *Nor any Albannach either.* But here at last was the chance for her dream. Dalriada could subdue Alba. There would be not a mere sharing of kings as had been done under Constantin and Oengus in times past but the complete subjection of Alba to Dalriada.

She took only Garbh with her. At the loch she would find all she would need of escort. And as it fell out, there was no need of looking, for Talorgen and his men were there, well tired of watching for signal fires that were never lit.

"It was a fine plan of Kenneth's that we should defend on land as well—for the Danes, although fierce fighters, have only those horses they can steal and have no knowledge of the lay of the land beyond that they can see from their ships. Even with the difficulty of defending a shore sliced by sea lochs—"

"Talorgen mac Cetus," Cathira cut in impatiently, "all that I know. Listen you to what you do not know." She told him quickly of the matter of Kinnart mac Bruide.

The captain's dark eyes flashed. "Yes, you are right. The matter must be laid before Kenneth without delay. I will set sail at first light in the morning. You may be assured the matter is in good hands."

Cathira ignored his last sentence, for indeed the matter was in good hands. "Yes, Talorgen. You may accompany me. See you to arranging for the soundest vessel and best seamen in the loch. First light will do very well."

She turned toward the private sleeping chamber at the top of the hall, which had been Donald's those many months he spent here overseeing the assembling of Kenneth's navy. Then she turned back. "Garbh carries my private banner. See that it flies high. I want none to mistake the princess of Dalriada's vessel for that of a mere fisherman."

"Is that wise, Princess? Would it not be better for the Danes to think us mere fishermen?"

"My brother will see that the Danes are well occupied. None would dare raid a ship of the princess of Dalriada."

The next morning the purple banner with the golden cougar whipped above the billowed sail, defying any who would get in its way, while the twelve oars of Talorgen's quickly assembled crew skimmed the ship down the Sound of Jura.

Cathira stood at the prow, feeling the wind in her hair and the salt spray on her cheeks as she loved to do. At the whipping sound overhead she looked up and smiled. Her banner looked fine against the blue of the sky.

They were almost past the mouth of Loch Tarbert, that eel-like body of water that all but sliced the Mull of Kintyre in half, when the boatman standing at the rudder shouted. The billowing sail cut off Cathira's vision, but his words were clear enough.

"Danes! Danes!"

She strode aft. Three dragonships sailed out of Tarbert, the first not more than fifty yards behind.

"Can we outrun them?" she asked Talorgen.

He shook his head. "We have twelve oars. They have upwards of thirty."

She took quick stock of their weapons. Talorgen was armed, as were the four warriors he had chosen for escort. The fishermen hired as oarsmen had only their knives for gutting fish and slicing the hard bread loaves their wives put in the leather satchels the men wore around their waists.

Cathira could see the yellow beard of the man standing fore in the first ship. The sun glinted off his helmet and vest.

"Prepare, men!" Talorgen drew his sword.

"No." Cathira stepped in front of him. She pulled the sharp, long-bladed dirk from the scabbard she wore on her belt. "Sheathe your swords. Up oars."

And now the Viking ship was drawing alongside.

As soon as the boat slowed, she jumped over onto the rowing bench nearest the yellow-bearded Dane. Except for her brief time at the court of King Olaf she had spoken little of the Viking tongue since the death of her mother—and that Norse, not Dane. And yet they were very like. She flung both arms in the air, aware of the sun on her golden wristbands and the breeze taking her scarlet and saffron plaid cloak full behind her. She tossed her hair and lifted her chin.

"Who are you that harries the princess of Dalriada?"

"Einar son of Ragnar Ladbrok."

"Let us pass, Einar Ragnarson. We have no booty for your pillaging that would be worth incurring the wrath of my brother King Kenneth mac Alpin and his allies."

Einar son of Ragnar gave a laugh that was more of a sneer. "The allies of your brother lie deep in watery graves without even the glory of death fires to carry their souls to their gods."

Cathira would not let him see how much his words shook her. "If that is so, what would you with us? We have but five swords among us, the rest are fishermen. Let us pass, Einar, that I may see to my brother's burial if need be."

"You are brave, Princess. But you know well your value as booty."

Cathira smiled. He understood her every word and was falling into her trap. She lowered her arms. Her right hand, which held her dirk, she placed just above her waist. "Then let my men go, Ragnar, and I will be your booty."

Now his laugh was an open challenge. "Why should I bargain for what is mine already?"

"Think you I would be so easily taken?" She twisted the sharp knife to catch the sun. "A dead princess would be of little value to you save to bring the fury of revenge on your head." She grasped the hilt with both hands, the long blade just a few inches below her breastbone, pointed upward. "Hear me, Einar, son of Ragnar. I will be taken alive only at my own will."

Einar inclined his head. "Speak."

"The small island of Gigha lies ahead. I will order my men to put me ashore. When their sail is beyond our sight you may send as many bearded men ashore for me as you think needful." Cathira knew little of Viking ways, but she knew that a reference to a man's beard was a challenge to his courage—one he could let no woman make lightly.

"It will be as you say."

Since the exchange had been carried out in the Viking tongue, Cathira now had to translate for Talorgen and her men.

Talorgen started to protest, but she cut through his words. "Do not waste time, Talorgen mac Cetul. I have stood up to Einar Ragnarson. Think you I cannot stand up to you? Bruide's message must reach my brother. Tell him I said he is to grasp the throne of Alba. When that is done, he can deal with the yellow-bearded Einar. I can see to my own defenses."

For the first time Talorgen smiled. "That I can believe, Princess Cathira."

It took less time than Cathira thought for the sail of the small vessel to disappear from sight. She hoped Talorgen would be clear of Kintyre now.

She turned at the sound of the splash behind her.

Einar Yellow-Beard strode through the shallow water toward her. He had come alone.

She tossed her hair and raised her chin, then stood facing him.

25

Kenneth wiped his sweating, smoke-blackened hands on his leather jerkin, then ran them through his hair, as if the effort of doing such a simple task would help focus his mind. But the facts were all too clear. The Danes—apparently Ragnar Ladbrok, from the impression his black raven banners seemed to have made on the survivors of the battle—had sunk, burned, and otherwise crippled almost the entire fleet of the Norse/Irish alliance. And that after defeating Huel of Man and Eochaid of Galloway, Dalriada's allies.

But he must have more exact information. What of the number of warriors? What of the leaders, Cerball, Godfrith, Ketil? Had they perished with their fleet? And what of Olaf of Dublin? Was he here with all his ships? Was Olaf slain as well?

And then the worse-yet question—what of Donald? When had the attack come? Surely these charred ships had been burning for hours when Donald arrived. And yet there was no sign of the king's brother nor of Barr and Dungal and their fleet. Was Kenneth's small handful of vessels, delayed by the skirmish at Corrievreckan, all that stood as bulwark against a complete Danish victory? If so, the final battle would not be long in coming.

Kenneth's chief boatman was the first to spot the red banner with its howling white wolf. He grabbed Kenneth by the shoulder and spun him around with enough force to rock most men from their feet.

Kenneth thought he had never seen a gladder sight. It was Donald.

He had been scouting the sad remains of broken ships in the lough, and he brought Kenneth his first hopeful news. Herthiofur, Olaf's general, was in the next bay, seeing to the repair of his ship, *Lion of the Waves*. Donald and the Dalriadan fleet had arrived with Olaf close on three hours ago and found the scene much as Kenneth now saw it.

Knowing his brother's first need would be for information, Donald had sent his own ships southward toward Dublin with Olaf and set about to scout Strangford with a handful of his men. Although the Dalriadan longships could not enter the blocked passageway, many smaller fishing vessels plied the waters. One of these Donald had commandeered and so had seen much of the damage. He shook his head. It would be many weeks and beyond before any of the remains here could be made seaworthy.

Herthiofur greeted Kenneth as a long-lost brother. Strange it was what war could do. Were it not for the Danish menace, Norse and Scot would likely be bitter enemies. But now they must band together against that which would be worse. Herthiofur ordered his men to carry on with their weary task of clearing the grievously wounded *Lion of the Waves* of broken timber, dead bodies, and burned canvas.

Herthiofur's Gaelic was none so fluent, but Kenneth had a little Norse from Alpin's second wife, and so he got the story. In the darkest hours of the night, when even the watch were inclined to drowse, the Danes had sailed up-lough in near silent coracles. As many ships as they could they boarded by scaling ropes and grappling hooks. Some crews they put to sword before setting the ships aflame. Other ships they merely fired by flinging burning casks of oil or pitch aboard.

"Oh, *ja*," Herthiofur told the Dalriadan brothers, "we fought back—and valiantly. Many a horned Viking has gone to Odin on a funeral pyre of the ship of his own burning. Before even the dawn broke, by the light of our own burning ships we raised the counterattack.

"Godfrith led first, as much as any man could lead in that melee. When he fell—I think he lives yet, but much wounded—I took his place, for I had taken ship with him when my *Sea Lion* was wounded. We rallied all still afloat to the center of the lough and made to break through Ragnar's barrier at the mouth. Had Olaf been here, he would have commanded we drive at them in a wedge. Knowing that, so I attempted, and like enough would have succeeded but for the shift in wind which broke our forward drive.

"From then on, the fighting was hand-to-hand. Our men returned thrust for thrust, and our swords returned red as oft as theirs. And then our ship swung sideways at a ramming that knocked all from their feet. The next ramming brought the waters flooding in."

And so the picture grew. With the light of full dawn, the mouth of the lough was stopped like a corked bottle and all the fleet disabled.

"And the Danes?" Kenneth asked.

Herthiofur thrust his mustachioed lip forward proudly. "They did not escape without memory of our swords. Many of their ships pulled back with burning sail and broken hull." Then his brave front drooped. "But soon they will return to claim their victory."

"Then we must see that they are given a warm welcome."

Kenneth considered. Certainly the Danes would be back. A day or two to lick their wounds, and they would be ready for their final assault with little doubt that such battle would leave them in possession of the High Throne of Tara. King Maelsechlaind, who had been too proud to make treaty, now had only a very thin shield wall around his royal rath.

But it was not at Tara, near to twenty miles inland, that the Vikings would strike. They would strike Olaf's Dublin, for it was the riches of the kings of Vestvold, their Norse neighbors, that the Danes most envied. Olaf no doubt realized this and was even now making plans for his defense. Two of the alliance Kenneth had not heard from. Merfyn of Gwynedd? Ketil of the Hebrides? Neither Donald nor Herthiofur could tell him of them.

The need was clear. Kenneth must reach Olaf before the black ravens of Ragnar Ladbrok once more swooped down upon these waters. "I would know where Ragnar has made his raven's nest."

The Isle of Man would make the most convenient port and seemed most likely—with Huel wounded and his ships sunk—so maybe Kenneth's earlier assumption that it was just bad luck that placed Huel in Ragnar's way was wrong. But the Mull of Galloway was almost equally convenient to Strangford, and King Eochaid and his fleet likewise defeated. Anglesey lay farther to the south, a greater distance from the attack on Strangford but almost directly across the Irish Sea from Dublin. If Olaf was the target, as Kenneth suspected, Anglesey would make a good base indeed.

"Can you find men to crew three fishing vessels?" he asked Donald.

"Three times thirty, I should think. For all who can hold a sword are ready to strike back."

Kenneth smiled at his brother's enthusiasm. Such heart was much needed. "Three will be enough for this task. I will take on all who are able to fight with me. But get you men who can handle fishing nets as well as swords, for I would have you appear simple fishermen while you see what you can learn in the nearest ports."

At Herthiofur's suggestion, however, Kenneth raised the number to six fisher-scouts so that ports on the Ireland side could be surveyed as well. Carlingford Lough and DunDalk Bay offered likely possibilities.

249

It was too dark to set sail now, especially as Kenneth's men were exhausted after their own encounter with the Vikings and a long day's sailing. Setting a careful watch on his ships, which rode at anchor just outside the blocked mouth of the lough—it would not be beyond the wiles of the Danes to return, if they had reason to suspect new adversaries had arrived—Kenneth made camp on shore.

Even with a first-light sailing, it was midday before he reached Dublin Bay. Olaf was much heartened by his arrival, as they both were a short time later by the sight of Ketil Flatnose and twenty ships with the fresh air of the Western Isles still billowing their sails.

There was agreement among the three war leaders, who would not often agree on anything, that Ragnar Ladbrok meant to rule Ireland, but if not all Ireland, at least Dublin. And Dublin he would strike next, surely knowing that he had destroyed many of Olaf's ships at Strangford.

"*Ja*. With luck he will think he has them all—but he knows he has not me." Olaf shook his fine head like a horse with a white mane. "He would have no sword but his own kill me. That is the leader's privilege."

"And he will not know we have arrived. At least we can hope he will not know," Kenneth amended. "Let us prepare for him a small surprise."

He surveyed the harbor, then laid his plan before them: Olaf with his remaining ships would stay in clear view, deep into Dublin Bay near the mouth of River Liffey. Ketil Flatnose would position his to the north where the headland curved to form a fine shelter. Kenneth would deploy his to the south below DunLaoghaire. When the Vikings sailed in to attack Olaf, sitting like an eider duck on the nest, Kenneth and Ketil would close behind the dragon ships of the black raven, each leaving a few vessels behind for reserve.

Ketil Flatnose suggested only one improvement to the plan—a particularly Viking touch. "*Ja*. And once along shore we will remove our prow heads and cut bushes and branches to cover our ships, so even if he looks with careful eye, Ragnar Ladbrok and his raven sons will see only wooded banks."

It took most of the afternoon to arrange all to the three war leaders' satisfaction, and although it was unlikely that Ragnar would attack at late evening, it was more than likely that he could come at night.

"*Ja*. But he'll not find us so sleepy as he would like."

Ketil, Olaf, and Kenneth held a final council aboard Olaf's *Horse of the Foam*. There was no question but that Olaf would well guard his proud steed. Its high-sweeping double prows, designed like all Viking ships to make turning the vessel unnecessary for sailing either direction, bore lofty horses' heads that echoed his banner. These he had chosen rather than dragons' heads because, Christian at least in name, he no longer believed in the spirit serpents of the sea.

Kenneth was much impressed with Olaf's long, lithe "foam horse," designed shallow to ride high over the waves, rather than cutting through them as the heavier Dalriadan ships did. The wide, overlapping planks of the ship's side were joined with iron nails, except for the lower eight strakes, which were lashed together with tarred rope to provide greater suppleness in the seaway. Such ships had made the Northmen the rulers of the waves.

But Kenneth guarded equally well his deeper-hulled, less sleek, equally valuable fleet. He changed guard every two hours during the night to ensure that his sentinels stayed alert and all got sufficient rest. Even so, nothing more militant than a flock of guillemots and oystercatchers descended on Dublin Bay.

By midday Donald returned. Kenneth's guess had been right. Holyhead Bay in Anglesey held something upward of eighty dragon-prowed longships. Whether it was the entire Danish fleet Donald could not tell, but it was enough.

Kenneth nodded. This was not the first time his men had faced odds of nearly two to one. And they were ready. He explained the plan to Donald.

Later that day Dungal arrived with more news. Port Erin at the southern tip of Man also served as raven's aerie. Perhaps twenty-five ships—most likely under the command of one of the Ragnarsons—looked ready to sail but had made no move while Dungal's men fished the waters and caught themselves a fine breakfast.

So they must look to their backs and hold what they could in reserve when they closed the circle behind Ragnar Ladbrok. Kenneth hoped it would be soon. Restless waiter he was, and his men were little better. He warned them to keep even better watch that night, for Ragnar would not delay long.

But delay he did for another fretful day and unsettled night. And Kenneth worried over the difficulty of keeping his men sword-edge sharp when they had naught to occupy them but games of dice and branfadd and the distractions of Dublin's wineshops and women.

Before the setting of the night watch, Kenneth mounted the fine dappled horse Olaf had given him and rode the length of the shore occupied by Dalriada.

"Hear me, Scots, sons of Erc all. Keep you watch well with your swords sharp and your throw spears to hand. For tonight the raven may swoop. Or he may choose to stay another day on his nest. But soon or late, he will swoop. And when he does it will be with sharpened beak and bared talons. And any dulled with barley beer and women's bodies will be quickly turned to carrion.

"Scots of Dalriada, men of valor, we fight in foreign waters, but we fight no less for our own garths, for our own hearths, for our own bairns. And we fight for our God." Kenneth paused. He wished Father Ernan were with him. He felt the need of strong prayer. Such things must be strengthened in his land when he had peace to see to it. For now he could but do his best.

"We fight a people who would establish their dark, foreign gods in our land. We, who have known the true God through His Son Jesus Christ since the time of Saint Columba and Saint Patrick before him, must not allow our land to sink back into the dark. Let every man look to his own heart. Make there an altar and seek the strengthening of God that when the battle call comes you may fight in His courage and His strength."

Kenneth could only hope that his words had bolstered the courage of his men. For himself, he felt depressed. He knew how far short he had come of all he would do. His words were mere shadows of what he felt he wanted to say. His own faith so pale a reflection of what he would have it be to lead his people. And his actions even less. Instead of boldly advancing with Christianity as Columba had done, he had hidden away the symbols of his nation's faith in a dark tunnel. Instead of protecting and reestablishing Iona as the beacon of faith to shine across the land, he had allowed it to be attacked once more and the brotherhood to abandon it.

Yet through all his dismal thought, one light flickered. There was Corbanac, guardian of the Stone, even now standing faithful at his post keeping Stone and relics safe, as Finguine was faithful at his similar post in Kilrimont.

And that thought further depressed Kenneth, reminding him as it did of his failure to unite the Dalriadans and Albannach. His own envoy had committed treachery, his own attempts at peacemaking had failed, and his conversations with Maia had ended . . .

But no, he would not think on such. He would sleep. And he would polish his sword. And he would pray as he had bade his men to do. For in spite of his failures, he was king inaugurated and anointed. Weak as he might know his efforts to be, he was leader in matters temporal and spiritual. And when the raven descended, he must be strong.

It was good that Kenneth had done his best to prepare his men and his own heart, for at dawn the next morning the raven swooped.

At least it would have been dawn if the sun could have been seen. As it was, the pouncing of the black banners above their black dragon prows was all the more ominous for coming as they did in the sudden breaking from the silence of a fog bank.

Kenneth, pacing the length of his longboat behind its camouflage screen of green boughs, felt his blood rise with a rush of energy that drove the doubts of the night far away. Every muscle poised for striking its first blow. His mind focused on every move of the enemy, awaiting the perfect moment to give the order for his men to throw off their cover and lash forward. But the fog made such judgment, which must be carefully timed to be of full benefit, all but impossible. He could have no idea when Ragnar's ships were all in the bay when he could see neither ships nor bay.

At least the fog bank held just inside the mouth of the inlet, so he could see the movement of the Norse vessels when Olaf, under his white foam horse banner, engaged the attackers. There was little strategy but apparent fierce combat.

Kenneth could see an exchange of throw spears and arrows. And here and there, already a few ships were grappled together and the fighting was hand-to-hand, as Norse boarded Dane, and Dane boarded Norse.

He looked to the east. His heart sank. With the battle already engaged on the far side of the bay, Viking ships were still emerging from the mist, their dragon prows trailing gray fog like the smoke of their breath. It was not yet time to move. But he must soon, or Olaf would be overpowered.

Finally there was a break in the inpouring. Was this the moment to spring the trap and surround the ravens with their net? It was impossible to tell whether this was the entire flock or not. But the water was black with firedrakes, dragons, and serpents. He delayed to let them sail as far forward as he could.

Many were already lowering sail to prepare for battle, so that the ships could be maneuvered by oar only and not blown out of position by a sudden shift in the wind. He must not delay too long. Surprise from the rear would do little good if the front gave way. He could sense his men's impatience like that of a horse in the hunting run.

At last he gave the signal: a low note on the ox horn to be heard by his men only. They threw off their covering bushes, and they plied oars. Kenneth watched carefully the last line of Viking ships. He would not alert them of his presence until they saw on their own. Best it would be if Dalriadan and Hebridean ships could close the gap.

That was not to be. But at least he was many yards across the bay when he saw the oars of a near-to-back Dane ship reverse. He heard a shout. Another reversed.

Now it was a race to close the harbor, for the Vikings well understood what he was attempting. He could see Ketil approaching ahead. The Danes bore down from the left. He could hear the rapid chant of their oar song. It would be a near matter.

Kenneth gave the order for his boatmen to strike the oar hammer louder and faster and his warriors to beat on their shields with their sword hilts. His ship shot forward.

Ketil was closing fast. The Viking ship dashed at the gap.

They arrived all three at the same time, striking hulls with a jolt that sent all asprawl. Kenneth's men were quick to pick themselves up and sort out the tangle of limbs, weapons, and oars.

He ordered his men on the near side to draw in their oars, those on the outside to pull—hard. Again. Harder. Digging deeper. The ship pivoted and moved forward, scraping the side of the Viking vessel full-length, snapping off its oars like twigs and impaling many of the oarsmen on their own broken lances.

Kenneth could see that Ketil's men had boarded the Viking vessel from their side. Crippled as it now was, Ketil would make short work of it.

He looked to his right and his left. The allies' shield wall was in place. A sparse line chained the mouth of the bay. The sparseness worried him. He wished the barrier double strong. But this was all they had, save a pitiful few held in reserve. Still, it would do—because it must.

He gave the forward signal, and they encountered the next ship. For this one his men, now thoroughly sorted out after the jostling of the impact, were ready. Kenneth saw from the thin lines of black smoke that the flints had been struck, the pitch pots burned. They swung within arrow range of the Viking firedrake.

Kenneth's ship received the first flighting of arrows. Most thudded into the hull side or broke against his men's bullhide-covered lindenwood shields. A few found their marks in flesh.

They returned better than they received. Each arrow was bound in rags, and the Dalriadans dipped the shafts in flame pots before they shot. The answering sally was so sparse that, after one more shooting, Kenneth could turn his men to finishing the ship fighting with Dungal's just beyond them.

And then they were in the midst of the full fury. For surprise and strategy were all very good and could do much to gain advantage, but in the end it came to sheer brute force, exchanging blow for blow, returning your own sword dripping red before your enemy did so with his. And Kenneth, although it was his place to command and he did what he could of such, gave most of his attention to the wielding of his own sword.

The next ship drew near, and his men again fired. But the momentary victory shout that rose from his warriors was cut short by the scraping of grappling hooks and the battle cry of Vikings boarding from the other side. The surprised cry of men feeling the final sword thrust in their bellies, or the angry shout of a warrior as a spear pierced his sword arm, mingled with the victory cries and battle chants of those whose weapons found their mark. And overhead the gulls and guillemots circled and cried and swooped, adding their voices to those of men and battle horns.

It was impossible to keep any count in this melee, but Kenneth had a sense of buoyancy, of momentum, among his warriors. Even as he saw his own men fall near him and red streaks appear on their leather breastplates, he could tell that, with the exception of small breaks here and there along the line, the chain held. And slowly they were driving forward.

It was still perhaps a mile across the bay to Olaf's ships. But there was no rush to reach him. As long as both lines held and Norse and Dalriadan outfought the Danes, they would triumph.

The question was, how long could they hold without wearying against numbers that still near to doubled their own? Was this the time to call in their few reserves still waiting under their covering of bushes? Fresh sword companions at their backs would much hearten his men. Kenneth considered sounding the signal.

But before he could fill the horn with air, the harbor filled with fresh-blown sails. The unwearied swords that sailed through the now-lifting mists, however, were not their companions'. A fleet of serpent-prowed ships sailed into the harbor under the wings of yet another black raven banner.

26

These newcomers Kenneth recognized, for he had heard of Rognvaldur, the Ragnarson who flew a black raven with red on its wingtips for his own distinction. This was the eldest and fiercest of the sons of Ragnar. And Kenneth could see him, standing high in the upswerving prow of his ship, as pale sunlight glinted dully from the wings of his helmet and his long, straw-colored hair and beard flowed in the wind of his ship's going.

Kenneth seized his bronze-tipped horn and blew three short, loud blasts. This was no time for their reserves to doubt his intentions or their duty. As he prepared his next order, he heard the signal being relayed by ships to each side. A heartening sound, even knowing as he did how pitifully few were the reserves his horns called forth.

His next command was no less emphatic but had no need to be so loud. It was for his own oarsmen to make for Rognvaldur's ship. The white wolf of Dalriada would bite at the red-tipped raven of Daneland. Kenneth's order was to grapple and board the ship, not to fire it. Engage every man they could. But Rognvaldur was his.

The raven saw them coming, and the first volley of arrows was flighted with raven feathers. But the Scots were ready for exchange. For a time the sky was darkened as with a flock of blackbirds descending on a new-planted field. Then they were too close for arrows, and all made ready with sword and spear. It was unclear who threw the first grappling hook, for clearly the Danes were as ready to do combat as the Scots, and the exchange of warriors over the hulls seemed about even—save for the fact that the Scots had already been long in battle, and many were wearied and wounded.

But Kenneth felt no weariness as he fought his way with thrusting sword toward Rognvaldur. The Viking war prince stood, feet apart, in his own space as if he had given the order that his men were to leave the Scoti king to him—for such a killing would be worthy of the son of Ragnar.

The exchange of throw spears was no more than a formality, the announcing of a challenge, both easily deflected by embossed shields. The clashing of swords was the real language of battle. Close in, so one could look the enemy in the eye. Judge his courage, his fears. And one could see the muscles of the sword arm. Judge the opponent's strength, his skill. Rognvaldur lacked nothing in Kenneth's judgment.

Blow for blow they exchanged, the clash of steel ringing above the rest of the noise of battle. The boat rocked under Kenneth's feet, its sway giving a thrust to his own spring, for always Alpin had stressed to his son the work of the feet as much as that of the arm. And the work of the shield. One must parry as skillfully as one thrust, or there would not be another thrust.

And Alpin had been a good teacher, for the Viking's thrusts were fierce and wild, his sword of a weightier heft than Kenneth's, but Kenneth's shield skill held, and he did not feel the stinging edge of steel. And Kenneth's foot skill held, for he was a broader but shorter man than the raven prince and must rely on the spring of his feet to make up for any shortness of reach. And still they exchanged blow for blow.

Kenneth it was who drew first blood—a cut on Rognvaldur's cheek that let a red stream flow into the thatch of his beard. And with the flow of blood he could see the red mist rise before the Viking's eyes.

With a bull-like snort Rognvaldur drove forward with a blow that, taken full, could have cracked Kenneth's shield and severed his arm.

As it was, Kenneth sprang at the precise moment, even so far as to feel the upward curve of the hull under his feet, and lunged with his own thrust before Rognvaldur could halt his momentum. The blow took the Dane in the side, a blow that could have been telling had not it been deflected by the metal rings sewn on Ragnvaldur's battle sark. Even so, the sark gave beyond the rings, and Kenneth's sword found second blood.

Both men whirled, Kenneth now with the higher position. Rognvaldur struck a swift blow, and Kenneth felt a warmth in his sword arm. Even before, he had sensed himself tiring. They were well-matched in age and skill, but the Dane came fresh to battle. Kenneth knew he must win quickly or not at all. On his next lunge he saw the redness of his sleeve—more than he had thought. The arm would weaken soon. Already he felt it so. A very small amount, but with such an opponent it would be enough.

He thrust his shield at Rognvaldur, using it as a weapon, driving him backward and backward. Then suddenly Kenneth dropped the shield and grasped his sword in both hands for a full-powered lunge. It would have finished the task but that Rognvaldur stepped sideways at the last moment, and the thrust fell inches from its mark. And yet the sword returned red.

Now the Ragnarson thrust his own shield from him and plunged his sword at Kenneth in a killing blow.

It was his father's carefully taught footwork that saved Kenneth.

And it was Kenneth's lightning whirl with a blade held clear at arm's length that took Rognvaldur full across the back.

The Viking, already frontward moving, fell forward, facedown. He did not rise. A red streak spread slowly across his back just below his shoulder blades where Kenneth's sword had sliced deeply.

Kenneth made a dive to retrieve his shield, ready to battle onward if Rognvaldur's men stood to avenge their leader's blood. But all around him were engaged in their own thrust, slash, and parry of hard steel and bossed lindenwood.

He turned to the mast where the red-winged blackbird flew. It was not the fabled banner of Ragnar Ladbrok, which always brought victory when its wings flew full overhead. But it was enough like. With a single slash of his sword Kenneth cut the rope. The raven drooped, then fluttered downward, its red feathers looking like blood.

Then Kenneth saw Dubtach, his armor bearer, who in the shortage of warriors had been made swordsman for the day. "Save it for me." Kenneth tossed him the flag.

The signaling of their leader's fall would take much heart from those who had time to notice. But Kenneth could see that it would take more than even Rognvaldur's death to defeat these Danes. For in spite of the throwing in of their reserves, it was clear that the allies were now losing ground.

All around he saw the black smoke of fired ships, and many times he could not tell whether it was Danish vessel or Dalriadan, but he could tell by the shoreside landfall that his men were being driven backward. They had little distance to go and they would be out of the protection of the bay and into the Irish Sea. They had fought valiantly, but the sheer overpowering of numbers was too great. Rognvaldur Ragnarson had fallen, but the coming of his fleet would carry the day, for they had trapped Kenneth's ships and Olaf's doubly so.

He groped under his jerkin for his ox horn. Should he sound the retreat? Without order to stop, his men would battle on until the last ship was sunk. And then fight in the water until the last drop of blood. But should he pull back now and give them a chance to lick their wounds so that they could fight another day? He hesitated, knowing that waiting would be to fight an enemy even stronger by its holding of the Irish coastline. A coastline but a few miles from the shore of Dalriadan Kintyre.

And then a signal sounded. At first he blinked at the horn in his hand. No, he had thought of blowing retreat, but the horn had not touched his lips. Was that then Ketil Flatnose, signaling his Hebridean men to withdraw?

The horn sounded again. No ox horn, but a bronze trumpet. The kind played by the Welsh. A horn of the kind played by the druids of Maelgwn at his dun in Harlech. Merfyn Vrych ap Erthil ap Maelgwn of Gwynedd and his son Rhodri had arrived. At the moment when fresh reserves were most needful, Merfyn sailed in with upward of twenty longships, banners flying in the midafternoon sun and trumpets sounding.

Kenneth cut a bandage from his cloak and would have bound his sword arm himself but that Dubtach saw to it.

Again renewed, the allies fought on. It was one of the longest battles Kenneth had known, for men could not sustain such heat and fury for long. It had been the repeated adding of fresh forces that extended the hours. And yet, as they now made progress toward the shore, Kenneth saw that Olaf, first to engage, still fought, silver-helmed under his white banner in his brave horse-prowed ship.

And at last, with the sun still bright but dipping in descent to the west, the handful of Danish ships that remained seaworthy escaped through a chink in the Scot and Welsh shield wall. In the center sailed the ship of Ragnar Ladbrok. That bold Viking lived yet, but his brave raven banner drooped.

Ragnar's youngest son, Ivar the Boneless, did not sail away, however, for he had been taken hostage by Ketil Flatnose.

"Goot. It is very goot." Olaf surveyed the hostage, whose plumpness made it appear he had no bones. "We will make present of you to King Guthrif of Vestvold. He can bargain with your Danish lord. It may be that the king of Daneland will care enough for the return of your scrawny beard that he will agree to turn his pirate raiders eastward to the lands of Charles the Bald on the Seine and leave our trading routes in peace."

He looked at the cringing Ivar. Perhaps Ivar's bone-covering layer of fat was not the only reason he was called boneless. "But then maybe he won't. Best for you that you pray to Odin that your Dane lord will make such treaty."

The ring of funeral pyres burning around the bay, some on land, some in high-prowed ships of both Norse and Dane gave added threat to Olaf's words—as did the stench of burning wood and flesh that reached the allies gathered in Olaf's *Horse of the Foam*.

The sky was streaking red when a small vessel entered Dublin Bay. At first Kenneth thought it was one of the fishing-boat scouts he had dispatched from Strangford. Then he saw the purple and gold cat banner. Could it be that his sister sailed here? He pointed out the vessel to Olaf, who ordered his weary oarsmen to make for the small ship.

It was not Cathira's red tresses he saw at the prow, however, but the curling black hair and leopardskin cape of his captain Talorgen. The boats drew aside, each pulling in their oars, and the Dalriadan captain sprang over both hulls.

"Kenneth, my king . . ." For all his energetic beginning, Talorgen suddenly seemed uncertain how to proceed.

Olaf's son Thorstein the Red offered a drinking horn.

After the day of battle with heated men grabbing frequent refreshers, the only ale left was bitter sour and very watered, yet Talorgen lingered over its drinking. At last he put the horn from him and began again.

"My lord, your sister Cathira is taken by Einar son of Ragnar, but she bade me—ordered me—sail on to tell you. The Picts have entreated. Bruide of Findach would have your aid against the Danes. Cathira commands . . . er . . . begs you take the throne."

Kenneth shook his head against this blast of news. Coming as it did at the end of an exhausting day of battle from which he did not yet have his wounds properly bound, he could not be certain he had heard rightly. Much less did any plan of action form in his head.

"My sister taken, you say? By that Einar they call the Ugly? What have the Picts to do with this? Take the *throne*—you mean she would have me back in DunAdd?"

The evening breeze shifted, bringing a new, sweeter smell from the shore. It was not only funeral pyres that burned but cook fires as well. No matter the issues before them, the scent of fresh baked bread and bubbling stew pots could not be ignored.

Kenneth had emptied his second bowl of stew and was ready to hear Talorgen's words again. This time the Dalriadan gave his report in careful detail, recounting just as Cathira had told him of the coming of Kinnart mac Bruide to DunAdd, of the state of affairs in Alba, of Cathira's certainty that Kenneth should seize the high kingship at Scone, and then of her bargain with Einar so that her message could reach him.

And yet Kenneth could hardly take it in. Bruide had sent for him? Sent his son under his banner? It seemed impossible that things could be bad enough that Bruide of Findach would send to Kenneth of Dalriada.

He put his wheat loaf from him, suddenly sated. What should he do? In a choice between his sister and his country, where did his duty lie?

Jarl Ketil was first to speak. "*Ja.* I know this Einar son of the one eye. Word that the brother of his captive killed his father Rognvaldur might do much to soften him. No love there was between those two. Rognvaldur despised his son. Slave-born he called him. Baseborn son of a slave girl he was."

Olaf nodded. "*Ja.* I have heard so also." He smiled, and his white teeth gleamed against his tanned skin in the firelight. "Einar might not think it so bad a trade—his boneless uncle for your red-haired sister, Kenneth of Dalriada. And agree to look elsewhere for plunder as well."

For the first time since hearing Talorgen's thunderstriking news, Kenneth smiled. "If I know my sister well, Einar may be all too glad to be rid of her. She'll soon have every kist in his rath turned out and every thrall in new-polished neckrings freshening floor reeds and roof turfs."

Even Talorgen smiled. "Now that I think on it, Einar did look much in need of a good bathing. That would be worth the seeing."

With the tension-breaking of food and humor, Kenneth now could think more clearly. "Know you where this Einar keeps his rath?"

Olaf shook his head, but his flatnosed former father-in-law knew. "In Orkney. North Ronaldsay."

"Ah. Goot." Olaf got to his feet with decision as if he would set sail that very moment. "It is across Norse Sea, closest island to Vestvold. If Einar will not make exchange for Boneless Ivar, we will take him on to King Guthrif. But be you sure of this, Kenneth of Dalriada: exchange or no, I will bring your sister with me, for I mean to have her for wife. See you to your Pictish neighbors."

Kenneth nodded. It was decided.

27

During the long days of voyaging to the northernmost point of Orkney, Cathira sat proud and silent on a stool under the striped canvas awning at the prow of the ship.

She had met her one-eyed captor in only one confrontation. When first he had carried her to his vessel and dumped her over the hull, she had landed on her feet to meet him face to face after he clambered aboard, none so agile as many. He demanded her dirk, as she had known he would. And she gave it to him, as she had known she would—proudly, without an undignified struggle, which she would have had no hope of winning.

"But hear you, Einar. There are ways and many of taking one's life. I will be a quiet captive, for I would not waste my energy fighting with you, but if you or any of your men lay hand on me you will have no living hostage for the king of Dalriada."

Einar looked her up and down with his good eye, an expression on his lips that would have been a sneer or a smile had his face not been so puckered with scars.

It required all her willpower not to cringe when he took a clump of her hair in one dirt-blackened hand and let the strands fall from his fingers. But she held straight, not changing expression.

Einar shouted something over his shoulder that, judging from the reactions of the men behind him, must have been obscene. He dropped the last locks of red gold hair and whirled with a shout to his men to take oar.

Cathira sat as if in the high place at DunAdd.

The first night she refused fish stew eaten from a communal pot but ate three of the fresh baked barleycakes.

Then she faced Einar once more. "I will sleep under the awning. Your men—all of your men—and you, Einar—" she considered referring to the spottiness of his beard growth, as hair would not grow from his scars, but decided against chancing pushing him too far "—you also, Einar, will sleep ashore."

Apparently Einar also was a careful judge of how far an opponent should be pushed. He turned with a curt nod, picked up his leather sleeping bag, and plopped it down by the fire on the coarse sand. And so it continued for the four days of sailing.

At last they took port below the most barren land Cathira had ever seen. Einar's rath stood on a rocky knoll above the harbor, where flat, open heathland, some of it cut into long, narrow strips of cultivation, ran treeless to the sea in every direction.

Cathira shivered. There was an edge to northern Orkney air unlike anything in her western home. It was as if it blew straight off ice fields—even now with the wheat in the field strips sprouting a tenuous green.

Einar's rath consisted of a collection of round earthen houses. Piers of stone extended spokelike to support the turf roof and walls and divided the floor space, which radiated from a central fire. Over the fire a bronze cook pot hung by a heavy chain from the ceiling, and around it children played a game of sticks and pebbles.

In the house of Einar the women's place was on the far side of the fire amid upright looms and clay and bronze cooking pots. A tall, broad-shouldered woman with thick yellow braids hanging below her woolen cap emerged from the dimness of the house carrying a leather cup of something that smelled like soured milk.

Einar quaffed the drink, wiped his mouth on the sleeve of his woolen shirt, and handed the empty cup back to the woman. "Helga, take you care of this one. She is a king's daughter."

For the first time Cathira felt fear. One look at Helga's fierce blue eyes told her she would rather take her chances with Einar any day than with this Viking wife who had no intention of losing her supreme position at Einar's hearth.

The long apronlike tunic that Helga wore belted over her dark green shift was richly embroidered at top and bottom, and, although all the women wore brooches clasping their short shawls together in front, only Helga sported a fine collection of rings, bracelets, and a beaded pendant necklace—all of which bore testimony to the success of her husband's raiding forays.

But Cathira was not to be given any choice in the matter of dealing with Helga, for the next morning one of Einar's men brought the news that, in Einar's absence, Halfdan Highleg—he who would make himself king of Orkney over Einar's jarlship—had struck at Westray across the North Sound from Ronaldsay. Halfdan had killed all the men in three raths, taken the cattle and women, and returned to his lair in Eday.

Einar rose with a snorting like an angry bull, upsetting horns of sour milk and ale all down the trestle table. He struck the table with his fist. "It is enough. We will make an end of this troublesome son of Harald Finehair. None but Einar Ragnarson will rule in Orkney. Halfdan shall know."

Already Helga and the three other women, who could have been wives or daughters or servants, were packing strong-smelling cheese and dry, flat bread loaves in leather satchels.

When Einar was gone, Helga turned. Hands on her generous hips, she faced Cathira. "You will cut torf."

Cathira did not reply. She would take refuge as long as she could in the pretense that she did not understand the Viking tongue.

"You—" Helga pointed "—will cut—" she handed a spade with a long, L-shaped blade to Cathira "—torf." Helga then pointed to the stack of dried peat squares beside the low-burning fire. In a land with no timber, peat would be their only fuel. The job of cutting and hauling the squares must be a never-ending task.

Cathira did not move.

Without warning Helga struck her a heavy blow on the side of the head. "You will cut torf, fine princess. I know you understand. I care not for hostage keeping. I care that the cook fires burn hot that I may cook my husband's food. It will be safest for you to keep the fires bright. Such work could well prevent your meeting a so unfortunate accident." She thrust a small pouch of food into Cathira's pocket.

Cathira's threat of self-destruction would not work with Helga. Helga would gladly supply the instrument of destruction herself—even wield it herself.

Cathira picked up the turf-cutter and went out. Next to the door was a wooden sledge, its platform set on runners as for traveling over snow or ice. The runners kept the turf wagon from sinking in the marshy land, but they did not keep her feet from sinking. The bog sucked at her every step, and her feet pulled heavy, caked with mud. She kilted the skirt of her tunic, but even with it to her knees, the hem still hung an ugly, spattered brown.

The short handle on her angle-bladed spade required that she work at a back-breaking angle. She soon wore blisters on her hands from gripping the rough handbar. The side of her foot suffered repeated cuts and scrapes from slipping off the side of the blade when she misjudged the setting of her spade. But worst of all was the very little progress she had made by the time the watery sun reached midpoint in the sky and she drew her lump of goat cheese from her pouch to eat with the other turf cutters. She had only begun the second layer of long bars on her sledge. The others had already two or three times emptied their platforms, spreading the water-logged bricks out in the field to dry to solid fuel.

She sat apart from the others, observing the girls and old women who gossiped and laughed exuberantly between bites of their sour cheese and hard bread. Much of their conversation was muttered or spoken too quickly for her to follow. When they burst into laughter, she wondered if they had been discussing her. Especially when they looked her way, at first in sly peeks, then in open stares.

Cathira stared back.

The young girl nearest Cathira on the edge of the cluster, perhaps thirteen or fourteen years of age, was a pretty creature with ice blue eyes in a round face framed by blonde braids hanging beneath a blue and vermilion knit cap. At last the girl ventured a small smile. The gesture revealed a wide gap between her front teeth exactly like Sinech's.

Suddenly Cathira's secure life at DunAdd seemed a lifetime away. Until that moment she had never doubted that her brother would rescue her in a short time. The realization struck her that she could spend the rest of her life a prisoner among these people. Cathira nic Alpin a slave, cutting endless squares of peat. The unthinkable happened, and tears formed in her eyes.

The round-faced girl left the group and came toward her. She sat on a clump of moss. After an uneasy silence she said, "Jorunn."

Cathira understood that the girl had offered her name. If she were to be stuck here forever, Cathira could not afford to spurn an offer of friendship.

"Cathira."

Then Cathira reached for her last crust of bread, and the girl saw the red welts on her hand. Jorunn dug in the pouch she wore on her belt and produced the cloth her own cheese had been wrapped in. "Your hand." She gestured for Cathira to hold it out. Jorunn wrapped the napkin around her blistered palm.

"Thank you." Cathira blinked as she said the words. The simple gesture of kindness was much harder to bear than Helga's scolding and threats.

Jorunn nodded. *"Ja."* She picked up Cathira's spade. "I show you." She demonstrated how to set the blade at just the right distance from the edge of the turf being cut, then to slice smoothly downward and out, tossing the bar of turf beside her on the upward swing. "Like this." She repeated the gesture four times, making a perfect brick the shape of her blade each time. "Now you." She handed the spade to Cathira.

The bending was still backbreaking for the taller Cathira, and the cutting was awkward for the inexperienced princess. But she did manage a reasonably neat square. She nodded. "Thank you, Jorunn." And she almost smiled.

By the time the setting sun signaled the hour for the turf cutters to drag their sledges back to the rath, Cathira had spread her second load of lopsided squares out to dry. She then followed the example of the others and piled her platform with hard, dry turfs from the far side of the drying field to haul back for the night's fuel.

The dry peat squares were lighter than the water-soaked ones she had hauled all day, but the sledge still pulled heavily, and the hemp rope cut through the wrapping on her hand. She turned at a light touch on her arm.

"Like this." Jorunn stood beside her. The girl had pulled her heavy woolen cloak lower to pad her ribs, then slipped the sledge rope around her body to pull it back to her own wheel-house.

Cathira did the same, then thought to unbind her hand and return Jorunn's cloth.

Jorunn looked at Cathira's hands and the streaks of dried blood on her foot. "Soak them in warm saltwater tonight. It will draw out the redness. Then let them dry well. In time they will harden."

Cathira longed to spurn such advice with the haughty reply that she would not be long about such work and that a Dalriadan princess had no need of work-hardened hands. But the day of labor, which had left her mind free for unhappy imaginings, now found her none so sure of such a reply. Talorgen might not have gotten through to her brother. Kenneth might have been killed in his Dane battle—a thought she refused to credit, yet it remained. Even if he were successful in Ireland, she had then urged him to see to the Pictish throne. So with all best speed and fortune, she might still be here many months. She would not submit to the contemplation of years.

After only one day at Ronaldsay, she realized she had far underestimated what she would be subjecting herself to as a Viking captive —and had far overestimated her own ability to control her circumstances.

Yet she was not helpless. That night she did not spurn the stinking fish stew. She knew she could hold up to Helga far better on a full stomach. And it was a good thing she was fortified, for the jarl's wife was none too ready to agree to supplying a basin of warm saltwater for this new captive.

"Einar will not be pleased if the hostage he hopes to exchange for much gold dies of wound sickness before he returns," Cathira reminded her. "And you, Helga, Einar's wife, will not be pleased to have it said of you that you cannot do so simple a thing as keep a slave alive."

Cathira saw the tensing of Helga's wrist that told her the Danewife longed to slap her. But she got her basin of water.

And so the days continued. Cathira cut peat all day, ate fish stew at night, then fell into her straw-filled box bed—the farthest from the fire—too aching to sleep and too tired to care.

On the second week after Einar's departure, a violent Norse Sea storm drove crashing waves far up on the rocky beach below the rath. Cathira, assigned to scrub the bronze cook pots with sand because no one would venture into the peat bog that day, listened to the women gossip around the fire.

Each roar of the wind that tore at the turfs of their roof brought a new worry to mind: Niord, god of the wind, was angry with them; he would blow their rath into the sea. This from the youngest, most nervous, serving girl—or daughter?—earned the child a slap from Helga, who would tolerate no such foolish talk at her hearth.

But the next suggestion—that if Freyr, god of the rain, followed with equal violence, the sprouts would be washed from their seed-beds, and it was late in the year for replanting—was a fear even Helga agreed to.

The third worry—that Einar would find such weather hard sailing and worse—brought gloomy silence to the fireside in spite of Helga's reminder of the valiant sailing successes of the well-built Viking ships.

Cathira's thoughts were not brightened, for such a storm could be no aid to any rescue ship that might be coming to her. The slim, supple Viking vessels, which skimmed the waves, were better suited for such conditions than were Kenneth's heavier, deeper-hulled craft. Even though her brother's ship was well-calked with tarred rope, the overlapping boards leaked even in calm weather, and it had to be bailed constantly. And any from Dalriada would be sailing in unfamiliar water.

The wind blasted the rath, and the crashing of the sea seemed to come closer. She shivered. But even closer was Helga with her ever-ready stinging slap, and today she was wearing an extra assortment of silver rings, as if armoring her fingers. Cathira picked up a fresh handful of sand and scrubbed harder at the bottom of the pot where charred fish and vegetables had dried onto the surface.

By noon the next day the storm had blown itself out, and she found it almost a relief to be returning to the peat field. The fresh turfs did not smell as bad as the burning ones, and here there was no smoke to sting her eyes and make her nose run.

It was noon two days following, and she had her sledge half filled with her second load, when a bleating of ox horns and a thudding of sword hilts on shields called all to the harbor from peat bog, from field strips—where indeed much needed replanting—and from watching herds and flocks in distant garths, as well as those cooking and weaving in the rath.

Cathira looked around. Should she empty her sledge first? Take time to refill with dry turfs? Jorunn and the others had simply dropped their spades and ropes where they stood and were hurrying to the call of their jarl. Cathira was in no hurry to see once again him his people called Torf Einar but the world called Einar the Ugly. Still, she was happy enough to drop her spade.

Five dragon-prowed ships bobbed proudly on the waves beneath Einar's raven banner, surrounding two other ships that had been stripped of their identifying flags—fine booty indeed. By the time Cathira got there—one of the last to arrive—the victorious Einar and his warriors were marching toward the rath surrounded by cheering women, servants, children, and even dogs.

Oddly enough, the focus of the celebrating didn't seem to be so much Einar himself as the bound man who walked a spear-prod ahead of Einar. Cathira caught her breath at the sight of the tall, pale-haired figure.

She felt the blood drain from her face, and for a moment all went dark.

Jorunn caught her arm, or she would have fainted. "Are you ill?"

But Cathira shook the girl off and ran ahead for a better look.

The relief she felt when she saw the prisoner full face was almost as great a shock as her violent reaction when she had thought him to be Olaf. Could she really care that much for the fate of the king of Dublin? She thought she would have been relieved to have him dispatched by a mutual enemy; then she would have no call to marry the Norseman. But now she realized how thoroughly she needed to rethink her feelings for Olaf the White.

There was not time for such thinking now, however, for Helga dashed ahead of the men, shouting orders to everyone within hearing. Einar and upward of a hundred warriors had returned victorious. They must be fed.

Now Cathira understood the frenzy of baking, roasting, and brewing that had occupied the rath for the preceding days. By the time Einar had entered the stone wall encircling the rath, trestle tables and benches had been set up in the grassy forecourt, and servants were bringing skins of mead and ale to fill the drinking horns that hung from the mens' belts.

But to Cathira's surprise, there followed no order to bring on trenchers of meat. And Einar did not take his place at the high table. The men slaked their thirst standing up and grabbed a few kisses from the women who welcomed them home.

In the center of this, the prisoner Halfdan Highleg stood quiet. He did not fight his bonds. Nor did he accept them. He ignored them, as he ignored all celebrations around him.

Only once did he seem to let his eyes stray to the spot they had passed on their way up from the harbor. There the land rose to a high place just before the turfed surface fell sharply to the bay. On the cliff edge a ring of black stones stood watch over the sea, as they had stood long before the coming of the Vikings who drove out the Picts, and perhaps long before the coming of the Picts who drove out the little dark people who lived there before them. Perhaps they had so stood since only gods and spirits inhabited this land, the gods and spirits who still demanded worship there—or their successors.

Jorunn told Cathira, in response to her puzzled looks, that none would eat until Einar had made victory sacrifice to Odin at the altar of the dancing stones.

Einar quaffed a final horn of ale, wiped the foam from his mouth on his sleeve, and with a jubilant shout turned to his wheelhouse. Helga was ready for him. She stood in the doorway with his scarlet cloak and a huge, silver disk brooch set with blue and red stones.

The courtyard quieted as all realized the ceremony had begun. Einar strode to the weaponstone by the entrance to the rath. He drew the sword hanging from a baldric over his left shoulder and honed it to a fine sharpness.

Halfdan, head up, did not watch.

Then to a blast of ox horns, Einar marched toward the stone circle, and Halfdan's guards prodded him forward with their spears. The procession stopped before the stone altar in the center of the ring. The guards tore Halfdan's cloak, leather tunic, and woolen shirt from his back, leaving his pale skin exposed above his wide leather belt and wool trousers.

Cathira did not want to watch, yet she could not turn away.

Now there was a low beat of drums that seemed barely more than an emphasis to the roll of the surf on the rocks below. All else was quiet.

Einar approached Halfdan's back with drawn sword. When he was a sword's length from the prisoner, he stopped. The first tracing

269

of the raven on Halfdan's back was little more than a scratch, a mere blood drawing to mark the pattern of the proud symbol of the house of Ragnar Ladbrok.

Halfdan stood unflinching.

Cathira had heard Olaf's skald sing of such as this. Halfdan Highleg son of Harald Finehair would have his bravery sung of.

Then Einar plunged his sword. Halfdan fell forward onto his knees, his arms spread-eagled across the altar. With quick deep cuts of his sharp-honed blade Einar laid open his victim's back and separated his ribs from his backbone to below his belt.

The sword flashed silver as he flung it to the grass. With both hands he reached into the red cavity before him. His hands emerged, red to the wrists, each holding its half of a spongy red organ. The guards flung Halfdan Highleg's body aside as Einar had flung his sword. Extracting the lungs had been the whole purpose of the bloody exercise.

Now the ox horns began a long, low wail, and the drums beat in a slowly increasing rhythm. Einar placed the lungs on the altar, spreading them carefully into the form of the victorious, swooping raven of Ragnar Ladbrok. He stood back as horns and drums reached a frenzied, mesmerizing pitch.

Then all inside and outside the stone circle began a chant, some clapping and stamping, some with arms extended over their heads.

"Odin, Odin! King of the gods. God of war; god of wisdom. Odin, Odin! Sky god; high god. King of the gods!"

Then the chant changed. The sacrifice was finished, and now the worshipers could look to earthly results.

"Einar, Einar! Warrior and high man of the rath. Jarl and Viking prince. No more jarl. No more prince. King Einar! Einar king of Orkney!"

And Cathira understood. Halfdan Highleg had been offered to Odin as a sacrifice for victory. And with this bloody rite, Einar had established his credentials as ruler of the Northern Isles.

She shuddered that such a barbaric rite could establish a man king. Kingship was a position that should be based on valor and leadership skills, a caring for the people, and right of bloodlines—not on slaughtering one's enemy and proclaiming one's right with hands still blood soaked.

And then her stomach lurched, and she fought down the sickness that rose in her throat. No, she would not be sick. And she would not credit the thought that had produced her revulsion. For her nausea was not caused by Einar's act, rather by memory of her own. She held the thought at bay. No, she would not think it. There was no similarity. The cases were entirely different.

But were they? And Cathira, never a coward, would not run from her own thoughts. How much difference was there between what Einar the Ugly had done and what she had ordered done to Drust of the Picts?

But I did what I did for the good of my country—and of Alba. I did it that my brother might be king of both.

And did not Einar act for the same reasons?

But Kenneth would be a good king.

And Einar? In spite of the ritual he had just enacted, Einar was not simply a butcher. He was a practical man, familiarly called Torf around his own hearth for being first to cut turf for fuel in this treeless world. And he was a strong warrior, as a king must be. A man of honor who had kept the agreement he made with Cathira—and a strong ruler who saw that others kept his word as well. Also, she saw many Picts from surrounding raths among those cheering his kingship. So Einar must be none so bad a ruler over his lands—as the respect given him at his hearth showed he was none so bad a master over his own house.

But Einar was barbarian, pagan. The house of Alpin was Christian.

And with that thought Cathira knew that her act had been the worse. Einar had faced his enemy in open battle, defeated him, and sacrificed him to his god. *A false, heathen god,* she tried to argue. But it would not do: Odin was Einar's god. Einar had obeyed as he understood.

Cathira professed to follow the God of love and peace, and she had acted in treachery. The motive the same, the act much the same, but Einar acted in obedience. She had acted in rebellion and self-will.

As the entire population of Ronaldsay made its jubilant way to Einar's rath for the feast of king-making, Cathira's feet moved with them, but her mind turned inward. Did she honor Christ in her heart? How long had it been since she had truly worshiped? When had she last sought the will of God for her actions?

Now, far from home in this hostile, windswept land, she saw herself and her heart. Always she had believed with her head. Dalriada was Christian. She was a princess of Dalriada, so she was Christian. Now she saw the difference. It was not enough to believe with her head for her people. She must believe with her heart for herself. And not only believe. She must submit not only her heart to Christ for His sin-cleansing. She must also submit her will to Him for His life-leading.

The impossibility of doing such in her own strength overwhelmed her. "Lord, help me," she prayed.

An ancient prayer, some said of Saint Columba himself, carefully taught her in childhood now returned to her:

> "*Jesus Christ,*
> *Man and God,*
> *Sacrificial Lamb who died for me;*
> *Christ cleanse me of my sin,*
> *Christ purge me of my pride,*
> *Christ wash me of my willfulness.*
> *God guide me with Your wisdom.*
> *God chastise me with Your justice.*
> *God help me with Your mercy.*
> *Spirit fill me with Your fullness.*
> *Spirit shield me with Your power.*
> *Spirit lead me with Your grace.*
> *For the sake of Your Anointed Son.*"

As she entered the rath, Cathira's step was as jubilant as Einar's most ecstatic subject. For her heart was right before God.

And then her step faltered. Had she not been held so tightly in the press of people, she might have fallen. She must also make all right before man, and she quailed at the thought. She must confess her deed to Kenneth.

It was perhaps the first time in her life Cathira had quailed. Always she had thought herself equal to anything. She could accomplish whatever was needed by her own strength and intelligence. But here was something she couldn't do in her own strength. She could not face Kenneth mac Alpin with the truth that she had ordered the treachery against Alba. Only in the strength and grace of God could she even think of doing so.

And even with the assurance of His help, she pulled back. Yet it must be done. If ever she had the chance.

28

Kenneth had been in Forteviot less than two weeks. Already the Vikings had struck five times at isolated sites along the eastern coast of Alba. The damage they did had been the usual strike of surprise and fear, pillaging chapel or monastery, burning the surrounding farmsteads, and stealing a few horses. The fact that they could do so at will showed the complete breakdown of government and defensive forces in Alba. Finguine, as the last son of Ferat, sat in the high seat at Forteviot palace, but he would not be king. He was abbot of Kilrimont, a holy man avowed, to which he would return when better days came.

Kenneth struggled to gather a war band from the ravaged numbers still remaining. Many mortuaths were without mormaors to whom he could address his hosting call. Rhodri ap Merfyn, the valiant prince of Gwynedd, true to his alliance with Dalriada, had come with a handful of men, and Kenneth had brought his captains Talorgen and Dungal with as many men as were unscathed from their battles in the west and able to travel swiftly. He sent Donald back to DunAdd in his place, and Barr he ordered to gather what men he could and make for Fortriu overland.

Kenneth, Talorgen, Dungal, and Rhodri had sailed as soon as their ships could be resupplied with water and food and their men could cut new alder branches for shaping arrows. They proceeded up the Clyde, sending word ahead to request free passage from King Roderick of Strathclyde. Kenneth hoped someday to approach the northern British king on the matter of alliance, but for now it would be enough to establish courtesy with this ruler who was harried by Angles and Saxons as thoroughly as Kenneth was by Danes.

At Glasgow they bought horses. Two days of heavy riding brought them to Forteviot, where Kinnart mac Bruide had prepared all with comforting assurances of Kenneth's coming but had done little to advance the war readiness of his devastated country.

"And what of your father? Why is the powerful Bruide of Findach not here to make Dane war?" The Dalriadan king looked at the mormaor's young son. The boy had good spirit in him, but he was inexperienced. Why was Bruide the Granite not taking the war leader role?

"My father is dead these many months." Kinnart spoke without emotion. "He died at Craig Phadrig of wound fever from a Danish sword slash. He bade me not tell those who might prove enemy to Albana."

"And Cruithne?"

"Dead of a Danish arrow."

"So. You would trust my sword skill but not my faith keeping?"

After a moment Kinnart met his eyes. "It was as you say, Kenneth mac Alpin. But now you are come to our aid. We have no choice but to trust all."

It was a somewhat unsatisfactory answer, but it must do for the time.

War readiness must take all Kenneth's attention. And yet he made little progress in establishing the needful spy system and warning beacons he must have if ever he were to catch the Vikings on land—as he must, since the Dalriadan fleet remained in the west, and Alba had nothing to match the sleek Danish dragonships.

Word came. But always one day, two days late—long after the black-burned thatch had cooled and the black foreigners had escaped in their black longboats.

This morning the latest report had come. Two days ago the battle had been, but this morning a messenger arrived with news of the defeat of Euan of Circinn.

Indeed, the dark-haired young courier lad in his tattered cloak and worn-through boots sat yet in the high hall, heather ale still half-filling his horn, when a second news-bringer arrived. This one was white of hair and beard, stooped with age. His scarlet cloak was held with a fine brooch, and his arms were adorned with silver bands that told he was more accustomed to taking his ease in his own hall house than riding breakneck the width of Fife. And the fact that he had come himself rather than sending a trusted servant told Kenneth of the likelihood that this man's hall house was burned and his servants slain.

Kenneth, always one who found pacing a help to focus his thoughts, now strode not just the width of the dais at the top of the hall but the full length of the long room, ignoring rumpled reeds under his feet and any dogs so careless as to stray into his path. "Euan lashed to a stake and used for target practice by Gormr's bowmen, you say?" He looked to the first messenger for confirmation.

"Yes, my lord. They demanded he tell them where the treasures of Restenneth Priory were hid. He would not tell. I doubt he knew, but it would have made no difference."

Kenneth nodded. Euan of Circinn. The young hothead had never been Kenneth's friend, but he was no coward. He would not have surrendered the treasure of his region's holy house. And Gormr would have killed him anyway.

So. Two days ago the Danes were in Forfar, striking the holy house founded more than a hundred years ago by King Nechtan. But they got no gold.

"They would not leave empty-handed. What did they take?"

"Horses, my lord."

Then Kenneth whirled to the new arrival. "And five brothers of Kilrimont tied in tree branches and their robes set afire?"

The gray head nodded with a dignity made stiff with the horror it was acknowledging. "It is so."

Kenneth ran his fingers through his hair and resumed his pacing. So. Gormr's men were in Circinn and Fife, attacking duns and monasteries on both sides of Tay. Then he stopped and whirled again. Restenneth's treasure was safe—for that Euan had died—but what of Kilrimont? What of the beautifully carved casket holding the precious bones of Saint Andrew?

But before Kenneth could form the question, Finguine, who had sat quiet at the end of the high table, asked, "The relics? Kilrimont's treasure?"

Again the aged messenger shook his head. "I do not know. I think they carried little off. Perhaps for that the monks died. I know only that the Danes emptied the stables of their horses."

An idea was beginning to form in Kenneth's mind. He strode to the table and leaned over the roughly sketched map of Alba spread out there. With his dagger he traced the route of the Tay from its mouth at the Norse Sea, up its long firth almost as far inland as Scone, then dividing, with River Tay going north to Scone and River Earn coming south to Forteviot. He traced the narrowing of the Earn, thinking of the Viking ships, those of smaller draught with shallow bottoms. They could sail thus far—he pointed with dagger tip—in rivers still at their springtime fullness. Yes, and then continue on with horses when the river failed them. Why else steal horses, which made such awkward cargo?

Kenneth slammed his dagger point down into the table through the map, piercing the spot marked Forteviot. "They mean to strike at Forteviot. Gormr means to be king of Alba."

He sent a servant scurrying for Dungal and Talorgen. Rhodri ap Merfyn had heard all and now leaned over the map, his copper-highlighted black hair almost brushing Kinnart mac Bruide's dark curls.

When Dungal and Talorgen arrived, Kenneth announced his battle plan. "It will take an hour of riding to the place Earn narrows?"

Kinnart acknowledged that was so.

"Talorgen, I will have every warrior of Dalriada and Gwynedd weaponed and those with horses mounted within the hour. And an ax for every man."

Talorgen had already turned to do his king's bidding.

"Did you hear? An ax and well-sharpened." Kenneth seldom repeated his orders, but this was vital.

He turned next to Kinnart. "There will be fishing boats in the Tay?"

The Pict nodded. "There should be and aplenty—unless fear of the black foreigners keeps them hidden."

Kenneth acknowledged this, then turned to his most seasoned captain. "Dungal, I would not leave the palace unguarded." Kenneth did not allow himself to look to the side of the room where he knew Maia sat with two of her ladies, busy at their weaving, yet hearing every word. "There is much of treasure here. Much," he stressed. "Keep you the Albannach warriors that they may guard well their own high seat."

None pointed out to the Dalriadan king that, although Forteviot was the favored palace, Scone was the highest seat of Alba. It seemed that all took Kenneth's meaning.

Now that he had a lead on Gormr's whereabouts and an idea of his next strike, Kenneth was so anxious to be about setting his plans in motion that he barely held still long enough for Dubtach to gird him in his leather jerkin and brass-studded arm bands and to strap his baldric across his shoulder.

But the sturdy armor bearer succeeded, and then they were off, riding hard through the green curving land and thick forests straight to the mouth of Earn.

Kenneth immediately set his men to work, some to cut saplings into strong, sharp-pointed poles, others to gather stones into a great pile on the riverbank. Kinnart he dispatched to secure what he could of fishing boats. None worked harder at the chopping and hauling than the king himself. And by the time Kinnart had his small flock of five sturdy, wooden vessels assembled, Kenneth was ready.

He directed his men in holding the new-cut poles, sharp points up, slanted eastward in the boats, while others filled each vessel with stones. Enough stones to hold the poles and sink the boats. Sink the boats to fill the mouth of the Earn with sharp stakes pointed at the bellies of Gormr's ships.

Hopefully it would be enough to damage, even to sink, some ships. Certainly it would be enough to block their passage. If he had more time, he would so barricade all of Tay. Farther up where a chain of islands divided the river into narrow passages, that would not be difficult. If he had time enough. Time and men—there were never enough of either, but he must do with what he had.

Already it was too late to set night patrols for other than guarding their own camp. Tomorrow he would establish a system of scouts and signals on both sides of Tay. If Gormr delayed. God send that he would.

Gormr delayed. Kenneth's watch was set. But no black, serpent-headed ships were sighted in the Firth of Tay. And no galloping messengers were intercepted on their way to Forteviot with word of another pillaging.

Was Kenneth wrong? Had Gormr sailed instead up the Forth? And was he riding even now overland on the swift horses he had stolen to strike at Forteviot from the underside? The thought was so dreadful that he turned, fearing the approach of a messenger from the south. Had he left the palace and all it contained—that of supreme value to him—insufficiently protected?

On the fourth day of such wearying, worrisome waiting, Kenneth took the lead scouting himself. He rode eastward along Tay, keeping as far inland under cover of bushes and trees as he could and still hold a clear view of the firth.

It was a fine morning. Bluebells spread an azure carpet among the mosses and grasses, and peewits and whaups chirped and called in the green branches of the larch and pine overhead. Great round bushes of broom bloomed pale yellow. To Kenneth's left the Tay flowed a gently sparkled blue with the wooded hump of Mugdrum Island floating in the estuary like a giant but nonthreatening Viking ship. And around it was a flock of smaller, similarly shaped, tree-covered islands.

Kenneth rode on several yards, scanning the waters curving ahead of him. Once he drew up short at the sight of three boats sailing close together. Then he realized they were Picti fishermen. He paused to watch a man haul in a net of wriggling silver.

It was impossible to say what sparked the thought—perhaps a motion or a sound too faint to be named—yet suddenly he whirled, jerking his horse's bridle far harder than he meant to.

It seemed impossible. If Olaf had not taught him the trick—if he had not done the very thing himself—he would not have credited it. Those were no islands gathered around Mugdrum like ducklings to their mother. Gormr had cleverly disguised his fleet, and by sailing at night and lying hidden along the wooded river shore by day, he had penetrated near to twenty miles inland without being spotted by local fishermen or Kenneth's scouts.

He dismounted and edged toward the riverbank for a closer look. It was impossible to say how many ships were there, for some must be grappled together to make larger "islands," some hidden along the shore where he couldn't see them, and some that appeared to be disguised Viking ships were in fact actual islands. But it must be a fleet nearing twenty. Thirty, perhaps, if some lay hidden along the far side of Mugdrum. Even smaller, oar-powered ships, as these were for river sailing, would carry crews of twenty men or more—plus the stolen horses. Gormr must have nearly nine hundred men. So once again Kenneth fought odds worse than two to one.

But perhaps it need not come to hand-to-hand combat. Gormr was hidden for the day. Tomorrow Mugdrum would appear to a careful observer to be much diminished, and islands farther up the Tay and Earn would be visited by these floating forests. It was clear Gormr was making for a specific target, or he would divide his ships to shelter in protected coves where the crews could pillage at will. This was not a mere raiding sortie. This was war. And Kenneth had these hours of daylight for his use.

The sun was straight overhead when he arrived back at camp.

So for perhaps four days had Gormr made his careful progress, and the care he had taken was proven by the fact that he had come so far undetected. In that time they had had no rain. For four days the larger trees on the vessels had dried. The smaller bushes would be thrown off each night for easier sailing and renewed before dawn each morning. But the Danes would not have time to arrange the entire camouflage fresh each day. The first-cut trees would be approaching tinder dryness.

Kenneth gave a thought for the fine horses that would be lost—he could only hope many of them would jump into the water and swim. But he spared little sympathy for men who tied monks in trees and set them aflame, laughing while the holy men danced at the ends of their ropes.

Kenneth dispersed his warriors in a solid line on shore, ranging the length of Mugdrum. Each man prepared to carry out Kenneth's orders: "Fire your flaming arrows into the camouflage foliage. And continue so firing until you can engage in sword fight those who make it ashore."

With a single bleat of the ox horn it was as if the sun itself had fallen to earth in a violent shower of flame. The islands below them erupted with angry, surprised shouts, wild whinnies, and a frantic flinging off of bushes.

But the ships were too well camouflaged. They were as thickly wooded as the natural islands. Many boats were hampered by being lashed to fellow vessels. As soon as it became apparent that the flames spread faster and the arrows flew thicker than the fueling wood could be discarded, the river was full of swimming men.

Kenneth's warriors now abandoned their arrows wrapped with pitch-soaked rags and sent bare, iron-tipped shafts after the swimming targets.

Some found their mark, but many a strong-swimming Dane made it ashore, a few even to the north side, where Kenneth could only hope that his handful of scouts stationed on that side could deal with them. But most made blindly for the near shore, only to be welcomed by the steel of Dalriadan swords. A few ships—three or four, no more than six—were moored where the arrows could not reach them. And here their double-end design paid off. Without turning, they escaped toward the Norse Sea.

But the rest, black foreign warriors and their ships, fell on the banks of Tay, including three vessels moored farthest to the west that had made it to the mouth of the Earn and fallen afoul of Kenneth's underwater trap. The only thing that prevented the victory's being total was the fact that Gormr himself had been in one of the ships that escaped up the firth.

Kenneth, not forgetting that his sister was held in Viking hands and thinking that hostages might be useful for her return, had given orders to take what prisoners they could. It was by hearing the careless, defiant talk of two such captives, who did not think a Scots king would have the Dane tongue, that Kenneth learned of Gormr's escape and of his likely next target. The Vikings exulted bitterly that the next victory would be theirs, by Thor's hammer. For none would suspect that Gormr meant to strike next at the shore of northwestern Wales.

Kenneth translated for Rhodri. The prince's response was immediate. "Let him come to Gwynedd and welcome. I shall see that his coming is made memorable to him. For the short time that he has memory."

Kenneth nodded. "It will be many weeks—perhaps months—before Gormr has a new war fleet prepared, but go you as soon as your men are rested. We would want nothing to be missing in his welcome." He smiled. "I would keep my men here, but take you Dungal, my best general, and if you meet Barr and his host, make you welcome to their sword arms. I will have all our lands free from Viking threat. And now that we are treaty strong, it can be done."

Kinnart mac Bruide, his black bullhide breastplate splashed red with darkening Viking blood, joined them. "Kenneth mac Alpin, all Alba is your debtor. We will raise here a fine picture stone to tell of your victory, that all ages will remember."

Kenneth bowed his head. "Let it be a cross, that none will forget Him who gave the victory. And tomorrow at Forteviot let Abbot Finguine say mass—a mass of thanksgiving and a mass of remembrance of our brothers who will not be with us."

There was much yet to do on the red-streaked banks of Tay, and already Kenneth's men were about it. Those who fought for Alba would be given Christian burial. Those Danes not already drowned would be piled in what remained of their charred boats and all sunk. And Kenneth was pleased that among the death work of sorting and stripping—for the spoils of battle belonged to the victor and the Danes ever loved to sport their wealth in neck rings and brooches—many well-blooded horses stolen from Alban holy houses and farms had escaped the ravages of fire and sword.

Suddenly he was exceeding weary. A fine gray boulder offered him a seat, and he sank onto it gratefully. Much lay ahead. After the mass he had bespoken would come the council meeting. What remained of the noble families of Alba would meet to choose their new king. And then would begin the hardest part for Alba, as for Dalriada and Dublin and Gwynedd—for winning the battle was but the beginning. Now they must build the peace.

29

"I am the Lord, and there is no other. There is no God besides Me. It is I who arm you, though you know Me not, so that toward the rising and the setting of the sun men may know that there is none besides Me. I am the Lord, there is no other."

Abbot Finguine stood in front of the altar in the little chapel beside the hall house at Forteviot. The room was crowded with those who would give thanks to God for their victory over the Vikings as well as Godspeed to their brothers who died by Viking sword.

All in the room responded, "Give the Lord glory and honor."

But none spoke with greater fervency than Kenneth mac Alpin, sitting near the back with his captains around him. In front sat Kinnart mac Bruide and a hastily assembled handful of Albannach leaders. To the right, serene and distant, surrounded by her ladies, sat Maia nic Ferat, whom Kenneth had hardly seen—and spoken to less—since coming to Forteviot. Could she be as unaware of his presence as she seemed? Was it possible, when he was so aware of hers?

"I am the Lord, there is no other." The white-robed abbot's voice drew Kenneth back. "Though your enemies intend evil against you, they cannot succeed. For you shall put them to flight. You shall aim your shafts against them."

And the people responded, "Be extolled, O Lord, in Your strength! We will sing, we will chant the praise of Your might."

Finguine continued, "Sing to the Lord a new song; sing to the Lord, all you lands; tell His glory among the nations; among all the peoples, His wondrous deeds."

And Kenneth wondered what new song would Alba now sing. For as soon as the service was over, this small, haphazard council, which was all that remained of ordered government in this devastated land, would meet to choose a new high king. And Kenneth knew that there were only two possible choices—himself and Kinnart mac Bruide.

"Give the Lord glory and honor," Kenneth mouthed with the others.

281

"For great is the Lord and highly to be praised, awesome is He, beyond all gods. For all the gods of the nations are things of nought, but the Lord made the heavens." Finguine went on.

But Kenneth's mind had fully leaped ahead to the council meeting. Now, with peace established, was the time to establish the greater vision he had held in his heart for so long, not even looking at it sooner himself for fear of distraction from the more immediate need to defeat the Danes.

But now he saw before him his shining goal of a great land, of Alba and Dalriada working together as one nation, strong in their faith in Christ. He would rebuild the churches and monasteries, and he would establish justice, with laws of rights and property throughout the land, and send all noblemen's sons to the monks to learn their letters so that those laws could be read. And encourage the craftsmen, especially the Picti stonecarvers and silverworkers, who so excelled in their work.

"Give the Lord glory and honor."

Kenneth interrupted his thoughts to respond, then returned to them with a glance at Kinnart. Would Kenneth be given the chance to build such a nation? Kinnart was young, an unproven leader, and his fierce father had made many enemies among the fathers of those now in council. But he was Albannach. What chance was there that the council of Picts would choose a Scot for their king?

"Worship the Lord in holy attire; tremble before Him, all the earth; say among the nations: The Lord is King. He governs the peoples with equity. Give the Lord glory and honor."

The mass was ended.

All around him were moving, but Kenneth, ever the man of action, now sat. There was much he would do. Enough for two lifetimes. But he would take no action until the right to do so was granted him. He thought of how his sister had urged him to seize the throne. He could do so. He had kept his warriors with him, sending only Dungal off with Rhodri. There was little likelihood there would be much battle. The Alban host would offer little resistance. Kenneth played with the idea.

But no, he always came back to the same determination. His goal was not to wield sheer power over the land; his goal was to build a nation, a nation of laws and heart-bonded people. That could not be done at sword point. He would await the decision of the council.

The chapel was nearly empty. Maia and a small group of women knelt at the altar. Kenneth thought of joining them in prayer or of waiting to have speech with the princess. But it would not do to interrupt their devotions. Instead he turned and left.

The midmorning sun shone warm on the cobbled courtyard, and the light dazzled his eyes after the dimness of the chapel. He was aware of a cluster of activity beyond the yard, but it was too soon for word from the council. So he must wait.

The soft, feminine body flinging itself into his arms with a squeal of delight almost knocked him off balance. Could Maia be behaving so?

But even before he held her from him at arm's length for a full view, he realized his mistake. No daughter of the house of Ferat this, but of the house of Alpin. "Cathira! God be praised. Christ be praised. Sister, you are returned to us! Praises be."

"Why, Kenneth, I think you are glad to see me!" She tossed her copper hair and laughed.

There seemed little need to ask, but he did so anyway. "You are returned. And are you well? Your treatment . . ."

Now she was more sober. "I am well. Einar held to his word that I would not be touched. Did you know that they call him Torf Einar for his starting the cutting of turf?" She held out her scraped hands with the broken nails. "Cutting turf is hateful work, but it was the worst that befell me."

Then Kenneth looked beyond his sister and saw the gleaming smile of Olaf the White. "And much good befell you, perhaps?"

Cathira half turned to take Olaf's hand. "I will submit me, brother. I will marry Olaf." Her chin rose, although not so high as she was used to raising it. "But only to preserve your honor, Kenneth mac Alpin."

Since none believed her protest, Kenneth moved ahead to ask for details of her rescue and of matters in Orkney. Cathira told him of the defeat of Halfdan and the king-making of Einar.

"I arrived shortly after," Olaf said. "Einar took little persuading to accept exchange of this one for his half brother, Ivar. And agreed to looking toward the land of the Franks for plunder as well."

Kenneth slapped his plaid, trouser-clad knee. "Excellent bargaining! You gained two concessions for the trade of Boneless Ivar—he hardly seems worth the price."

Olaf shrugged. "I did, I believe, give Einar the impression that without such agreement I would offer my wares to Guthrif of Vestvold."

Cathira laughed. "He gave that impression most clearly, and that in front of Einar's jealous wife, Helga. I ventured something of a smile at Einar, sitting on the side of his good eye as I was, when Olaf suggested leaving me behind. I fear that for all his bold warrior skills, Einar the Ugly would not choose to offend his Helga."

They talked some while longer, for Kenneth would hear more of the strength of the king of Orkney and of Olaf's sailing the length of the coast of Alba.

The coming of Brother Ekeld, Finguine's gentle assistant from Kilrimont, shifted them to matters closer to hand. Kenneth was much delighted to see Ekeld. He had hoped the ever-smiling monk had not been one of those brutally murdered by Gormr.

Now, however, the broad, tonsured forehead was wrinkled in an uncharacteristic frown of concern. "Abbot Finguine sent me messenger. He would have you know from him and not as idle gossip . . ."

Kenneth's heart sank. There was no need for words. The council had decided. And not for Kenneth mac Alpin. He would save Ekeld the pain of saying so. "The council will not have me."

Ekeld hung his head so that his half-moon tonsure with its fringe of gray hair behind was all that showed. "I am sorry. I believe the holy father much favored you."

"So. It is the son of Bruide?"

"No, it is neither. Not yet. They cannot decide. They will hear you speak. There are questions they would put to you."

"Then all is not lost." Kenneth took a stride toward the hall house. "I will speak."

Brother Ekeld placed a restraining hand on Kenneth's arm. "Not yet, my lord. Kinnart mac Bruide speaks to the council first."

In contrast to the monk's gentleness, Kenneth felt jerked around by the strong tugging on his other arm.

"And I will speak to you first, my brother." Cathira pulled him away from the others, toward the chapel door but not into the building. "Kenneth, now is your chance. Be you as bold in the council chamber as you are on the battlefield. Tell them you will be king of Alba. It is yours by right of arms and of blood."

When Kenneth did not speak, she continued, grasping him by both shoulders and speaking forcefully. No one else was on their side of the courtyard, so there was little need to keep their voices down, and Cathira had no inclination to whisper.

"Tell them what they already know. There is none in Alba so fit to rule as you. Without your speedy reply to their craven cry for aid, there would be no Alba today. And as descendant of Fergus you are kin to Constantin and Oengus, Dalriadans who ruled in Forteviot. And for these who think so much of the bloodline of the mother, remind them that your mother came of their own royal house." She paused for breath but not long enough for his reply.

Kenneth, however, would speak. He held up a hand, breaking her grip on his shoulder. "All that and more they know. I will not ding their ears with what has surely already been said in my favor in their council."

"Then tell them what they don't know but should. Tell them your warriors are ready. Tell them you will have by force if necessary what is yours by right."

Kenneth backed away from the intensity of her imploring. "I will not tell them what is not true. I would not shed blood in Forteviot—although there are those yet who think I have already done so. We spoke of this many months ago, sister. I have not changed. I will not force my governance upon Alba. A nation should not be forged by one man or one group taking power over another."

Cathira started to speak, but he held up his hand again. He had just been thinking on this matter. For the first time he would give voice to those thoughts.

"I have considered long on this. Hear me. What makes a nation? Fear of a common enemy? Then what have we left when the enemy is defeated? The marriage of royal houses? Then what of the next generation if there are not daughters or sons enough? A people living on land next to one another for generations? Then what is to be done about in-comers? Such things are elements of nationhood, but they are not enough.

"A true nation must be built by people who believe together, who choose to work together to make a strong country for their families. I would build a nation of laws, a nation of strong faith, a nation of families working together for the same goals. I cannot achieve that by force of arms and spilling of blood, Cathira."

Her green eyes blazed as she once more gripped his shoulders. "Then you will let it slip from you? You will return to DunAdd without the kingship? After all I have done? After the lives already spilled—" She choked on her words and whirled suddenly away from him.

"What mean you, Cathira?"

She turned back, her head down, the fire quenched. "I am sorry, Kenneth. I am doing this all wrong. I prayed much in Orkney. I saw that I had done much wrong and must make it right. I promised I would tell you—confess to you what I had already confessed to God. But it is not so easy. I did not mean it to be a matter of temper."

"Your temper I am used to. This confusing speech I am not. Best you tell me what it is." He spoke evenly, but already he felt cold around his heart. These would be words he did not want to hear.

"The killing of Drust and his guard. I ordered it. In your name."

The words fell like a dagger thrust. Kenneth took a step backward against the chapel wall.

285

"I meant it for good. It was for your kingship." She raised her head. "And I was right about that—all that has happened since has shown so." She dropped her head again. "But I acted from my own will, not seeking God's will. I am endeavoring to do better, but it does not come easily."

Kenneth was silent for the space of many heartbeats. "So, they were right—Maia and those who accused me of treachery. I did not order it. I did not intend it. But I am responsible for commands given in my name. I am the traitor."

He asked her about the order giving—how she went about it, who took it, who else knew the truth of it. She answered all his questions directly and simply.

From the other side of the courtyard Brother Ekeld's soft sandals slapped the cobbles. "Will you come now, my lord? The council is ready."

"And I am ready."

Cathira grabbed him. "Wait! What will you say?"

"I will say what I must. That I am Iscariot. A traitor cannot be king."

30

Kenneth entered the hall house of Forteviot Palace, the palace that he had hoped would be his own. Here he would have worked to forge the great nation of his shining vision. Now he strode the length of the royal hall for the last time.

But he would not enter as a murderer. He would not skulk. He held his head up, his shoulders square, his golden ring brooch clasping his red and saffron plaid cloak in careful folds. For he came not as one who had committed a wrong but rather as one who would right a wrong committed by others for whom he took responsibility. He would make expiation as best he could, salvage what honor he could.

He was halfway to the dais before his heart misgave him. The tall, blue-clad form of Princess Maia with silver combs in her black hair was entering from the women's side. He would not choose to have her witness his humiliation. And yet perhaps it was best. Have the matter all finished in one sword thrust.

"I thank the council for hearing me," he began without preamble. "There is a matter you must hear. It has just come to my hearing, and I bring it straight to yours. Near to a year ago in this very hall was committed an act of unthinkable treachery when guests who came from Dalriada—my own emissary under my banner—slaughtered your king and his guard."

A sharp intake of breath by the council was followed by harsh mutterings and a nodding of heads.

"Much confusion clouded the matter as to who struck first and who plotted first and who was truly traitor. Since your council took the word of my captain, the matter seemed closed. Now I know differently. I know my general, Eoganan, struck first, believing such to be my orders. I could not be your king under such a false cloud."

Now the earlier mutterings grew to shouts and table banging. Finguine fought to bring the council back to order.

Kenneth stood silent and straight, awaiting their response. He had said what he came to say. Finally the abbot regained control, and the questions poured forth, one hot on the heels of another, barely giving Kenneth time to answer each. Yet he did his best to deal with each one clearly and honestly.

For a time it seemed as if the matter would continue so all day and beyond. Many questions were repeated time and again as the mormaors pressed to understand how the seemingly impossible could have happened, probing for anything he might still be hiding from them. At last, though, the questioning slackened.

Kinnart mac Bruide banged the table with his engraved silver dagger hilt. "So. The matter is done. Let us look now to the future. Let us look to my king-making."

The council appeared confused, then shrugged. They had not voted, but there seemed little need. There were no other candidates. Several nodded. Abbot Finguine looked around uneasily, as if hoping for a third applicant to appear miraculously.

It was no supernatural manifestation, however, but the soft swish of fabric and the tinkle of silver bells from the necklace of Princess Maia that stopped the council in mid-assent to Kinnart's kingship. "Men of Alba, you forget. You forget the long tradition of our people. I say to you that the final choice is not yours. It is mine."

The confusion caused earlier by Kenneth mac Alpin's opening statement was but a foretaste of the shock now caused by Maia nic Ferat. Inexperienced as most of the council was, many members had never seen their princess before.

Abbot Finguine did not carry a dagger to bang the table. Instead, as a signal for attention he held aloft the large silver cross he wore around his neck. "Princess Maia, we are honored at your coming. Always the princess of Alba should have full speech before her council."

She nodded in acknowledgment of the correctness of the abbot's words and continued as if there had been no interruption. "We are long and long a people who recognize that the life of the tribe passes through the mother. For it is the mother who gives birth and life-milk to the sons. So gave my mother to my brothers who ruled; so gave my grandmother to my father who ruled, and so backward.

"But I would look forward. Had I sons now, one of your choice would rule. Had I a marriage lord, he would rule."

The mormaors looked at one another and, guided by Finguine, nodded.

"So, I will take a marriage lord."

Now the council members looked at one another in a different light, obviously wondering which of the leading men of Alba her choice would fall on.

But Maia did not look at the council. She turned and stepped off the dais. Slowly she walked to the spot where Kenneth mac Alpin stood.

Kenneth's heart leaped, taking the full meaning of her gesture, yet not daring to believe. He held out his hands, and she took them. "You heard all I said?" he asked.

"I heard all you said in hall. But more important, I heard all you said in the courtyard, standing before the open doorway of the empty-seeming church. The church was not empty. I had remained to pray. When you spoke of your vision for the nation I knew my prayers had been answered."

"But this other matter—this killing of Drust."

"You did right to take the guilt on your own shoulders. Such is the king's responsibility. But all who are truly repentant may be absolved. Alba lost a good king in the slaying of my brother Drust. I will not now let them lose a great king in the blaming of Kenneth mac Alpin."

Kenneth shook his head to clear his thoughts. "I do not remember all I said in the courtyard. But I know I said that a nation should be built by people who choose to work together for a great goal. Maia of Alba, you are choosing to work with me to build a nation? Something that in its sum will be greater than the total of each of our countries on its own?"

"Kenneth of Dalriada, I so choose."

Hand in hand, they turned to face the council.

Approval by the assembly was a formality of mere minutes, but the talking and wine drinking that followed wore on endlessly. Brother Ekeld brought Cathira and Olaf into the hall. Olaf was welcomed and honored as due a neighboring king. Cathira, wisely, stayed to the background, knowing that Kenneth had answered openly the questions about her perfidy.

Olaf's hurry to be on his way back to Dublin made an escape for Kenneth and Maia as well.

In the courtyard Kenneth lifted his sister lightly to her saddle. "Cathira, you go to be queen among a people new to Christianity. When I return to DunAdd I will send Father Ernan to you for support. But keep you the faith strong in your heart that you may build it in your people."

Cathira tossed her hair and lifted her chin. But her smile was far sweeter than ever before. "I am learning, my brother."

The last of the king of Dublin's retinue had not passed out of Forteviot's gate when Kenneth turned and took Maia in his arms. He had not thought the icy, stiff princess could be so warm and bending in his embrace.

They walked slowly toward a little stream, which flowed from the Earn between banks thickly mossed and ferned. Tiny yellow water irises bloomed in clumps at the water's edge.

"This will not be an easy matter—this business of forming one nation of two. There is much that needs to be readied in Dalriada, and I have been away for many weeks. Come with me, Maia. I would have you see Dalriada, for you will be their queen and the mother of their king's sons."

Kenneth sent messengers ahead to Donald to make all ready in DunAdd. Nor had he forgotten the faithful Corbanac, keeping his watch at DunStaffness. At last it was time to bring the emblems of his people into daylight again.

Abbot Finguine, as the highest religious of Alba and brother of the soon-to-be queen, traveled with them. Their guard was half Alban, half Dalriadan, and they flew both the scarlet banner with the white wolf and the white banner with the black boar.

Such compromise was workable for the moment, but Kenneth knew that it could not continue so for long if they were truly to be one nation.

"We must not think of ourselves as Albannach and Dalriadan, as boar and wolf, as Pict and Scot," he said to Maia as they sat late before the fire in the guest hall at Inverary.

"Then how are we to think of ourselves?"

He shook his head. "I do not know. I only know it must be in a new way, and that the weaving of the new way must be of equal strength in the warp and the woof."

A loom stood by the fire, where earlier in the evening the mormaor's wife had sat at her work, sending the shuttle bearing blue filling-in woof yarn skimming back and forth nimbly between the green warp threads. He fingered the strands as he spoke. "This is how I see our new nation—a careful weaving of a distinctive pattern. Some threads will be Albannach, some Dalriadan, but the whole cloth will be something the world has not yet seen."

He playfully set several of the loom weights swinging with his foot before he returned to his seat. "But which strands should be Pict, which Scot? That is what troubles me. I must fix the pattern wisely from the first sett, if it is to be a smooth weaving."

And two days later in the second courtyard at DunAdd, Kenneth began his weaving with the strongest of his fibers—the marriage of Kenneth of Dalriada and Maia of Alba. As soon as Corbanac arrived from DunStaffness, he had been anointed priest by Abbot Finguine, and so the wedding was performed by a priest from each house. Finguine led them in the taking of their sacred vows. Corbanac pronounced the final blessing:

> "The love and affection of the angels be to you,
> The love and affection of the saints be to you,
> The love and affection of heaven be to you,
> As your love and affection is to each other,
> So be it to heaven and to your people."

And then the trumpets blew in celebration as Finguine dipped his fingers in the sacred chrism in the bowl carved behind the enkinging footprint in the Stone of Dalriada and made the sign of the cross on the foreheads of Kenneth and Maia.

Kenneth waited until the cheering quieted. As he stood there with the soft breeze ruffling his thick brown hair and scarlet and gold cloak and bringing the scent of heather to him, he looked out across the green Crinan Moss to the misty mountains beyond. This was the hill where he had been made king, as had his father before him and as had Aiden mac Gabhran and all the kings of Dalriada since the coming of Fergus mac Erc. And he knew that he would be the last to be so enkinged; for as the shuttle wove, the pattern changed.

But he would not have generations to come forget this dun or this rock. Nor would he have them forget the very special act performed there this day—this day that began his weaving of a new nation. He signed to Corbanac. The time had come for the final part of the ceremony.

Corbanac knelt by the stone on the downhill side. A little distance below the footprint, between the print and the cup, he began his careful chiseling, incising a pattern of fine lines with delicate taps of the mallet on the iron chisel. It took some time, for Kenneth had emphasized that this was to be his best work, not to be hurried.

Many guests wandered away, some to their own work, some to await the feasting in the courtyard of the summit fort. But Kenneth and Maia stood hand in hand, watching it all. "Is it fine enough for a Picti stone carving?" he asked.

Maia returned his smile. "It is very fine, my husband—as many a Scoti thing may be fine enough for a Pict."

At last it was done. Corbanac blew the last of the stone chips away and smoothed his hand over his work before standing up. Kenneth signaled the trumpeters to blow a salute to this symbol of unity: a Picti boar carved on the high stone of Dalriada.

Kenneth nodded, and Corbanac knelt again. This time he made only a few slashes of his chisel a little beyond the boar's head. In the long and short lines of the ogham writing the Scots had used for hundreds of years the stonecarver recorded the significance of that day.

And then the weaving of the next sett began, for the high seat of the combined countries could not stay at DunAdd, ancient and sacred though the site was. It would ever be an important strong-place, and Donald would hold it well, but a unified country must be ruled from a more central location, one easier to reach by land travel and one less exposed to attack by enemies from the sea. The next fibers in the weaving would be of Albannach spinning.

And so they traveled back to Fortriu, but not to Forteviot, although that would ever be their favored palace. Nor did they go to Scone, the ancient enkinging place of Alba. They traveled some ten miles north of Scone to the heart of a forested, mountainous setting on the banks of River Tay. For Kenneth had chosen DunKeld, home of the monastery founded jointly by Mungo and Columba, to be the spiritual heart of his new kingdom. Here, only a few miles from the secular center, would be where the religious matters of the land were administered.

This, the religious weaving, required perhaps the most care of all. The choice of site had not been difficult, for it must be central. And it must be a holy house established by Columba. Saint Mungo's having had a hand in it further strengthened the pattern. Nor was the choice of abbot difficult, for the aged father who had served there nearly forty years now served in heaven, and there was none in the run-down monastery to take his place. It was a job for a man of youth and vigor, of proven loyalty and steadfastness. It was a job for Corbanac.

It was an easy choice that here the relics of Columba would be enshrined, far from the clutches of marauders and watched over still by Corbanac.

But the next matter was not an easy one. On the night before the enshrinement ceremony Kenneth called the new abbot of Dun-Keld and Finguine of Kilrimont to him.

It was several moments before Corbanac's shock at Kenneth's announcement could find words. "Saint Andrew? Not Columba? You would make *Andrew* patron saint of this land?"

Kenneth's answer was gentle. "I know how great a disappointment this is to you, my brother. As it is to me, for I have loved and revered Saint Columba from my earliest youth."

"But Columba it was who brought the faith to this land. Columba lived and worked here. Died here. Columba gave us Christ, and Columba gave us his own life. What has Andrew done for Dalriada or for Alba?"

Here Finguine spoke up. "Can it be that you do not know the story? It was our great Picti king Ungus mac Uirguist to whom Saint Andrew appeared in a shining white light. King Ungus was locked in a battle to the death, completely surrounded by the Britons who would have invaded our land, when a divine light shone from heaven and Andrew spoke to Ungus, promising him victory if he would dedicate the tenth part of his inheritance to God and Saint Andrew.

"After the victory of Ungus over the Britons, the Lord led him to Kilrimont, where he was met by Saint Rule, bearing the relics of Saint Andrew, and Ungus knew it for the fulfillment of his vision."

Corbanac was silent. As was Kenneth. He had heard the story before, but it seemed Finguine related it with special power this time. It confirmed in Kenneth's heart what his head told him was right.

"But Andrew is already the patron saint of Russia," Corbanac argued still.

Finguine nodded. "Russia might have chosen Andrew for their saint, but God chose Alba to receive Andrew's relics. And Rule, who bore them hither, ministered for thirty years. Would you go against the choice of our Lord, brother?"

Corbanac looked at Kenneth. "And such is truly the choice of our king as well?"

Kenneth nodded. "Columba is Dalriada's patron saint, Andrew is Alba's. We are to be a united people. We must have one patron saint. Andrew was an apostle of our Lord Himself. Our shores were honored to receive his relics. Surely, brother, you would not have us refuse so special an honor from God?"

Corbanac was silent. This weaving was to be of Alban cord.

The next morning the two abbots, side by side—one Pict, one Scot; one of Kilrimont, one of DunKeld; one of Saint Andrew, one of Saint Columba—officiated at the high mass enshrining the relics of Columba in their new home. It was a pattern of very careful weaving.

Afterward, Kenneth stood in front of the altar and spoke to the congregation of monks and warriors.

"I have chosen to establish DunKeld, here at the very heart of our land, as the spiritual center, because if a land is to be strong it must be strong in its spiritual heart. Strength of heart is necessary in a people before strength of arms. We shall be a great people, we of the Picts and the Scots, great in arms but greater yet in heart. That I entrust to you, our holy men of DunKeld and of other houses. Let you build in all whom you teach people of strong hearts—and people of the joy that follows faith."

The saying of the final prayer fell to Corbanac. "Father, You make Your church on earth. Your house is a house of prayer. Your presence makes it a place of blessing. You give grace upon grace to build in Your Spirit. You create beauty from the holiness of our lives which reflect You.

"You called Your people to be Your church. We gather in Your name. We depart to serve You. As did Columba. Let us ever remember his service to us through a life given wholly to You. And so let us serve others in Your Name."

And then to Scone for the final sett.

From the first it had been clear to Kenneth that the new nation must call itself by a new name and must march under a new banner. But the choosing was a heavy matter. And so he told Maia in the royal chamber that night.

Already the mormaors and leaders of Alba were gathering for his inauguration, and the decisions must be made. And made right. If the regional leaders accepted these new symbols of nationhood, if they took them back to their people with gladness, the weaving would be sound. If not, a raveling would set in at the first snag.

"I would not have the new banner be red or white, wolf or boar. I would not have one kingdom feel subject to the other. We need a new symbol for our new country, neither wolf nor boar. But I do not know what. The horse is Olaf's symbol, the dragon Gwynedd's. A bear, perhaps?"

Maia, in her blue nightshift and with her waist-length hair falling over her shoulders, sat on the bed in the royal sleeping place in Scone and leaned against a cushion covered in softest fur. She patted the place beside her. "Have you thought that it need not be an animal at all?"

Kenneth laughed. "No, I had not thought. Always our people have used animals."

She nodded. "And ours also. Our carvers have a great love for entwined animal bodies. But we also use other symbols on our stones —crescents, mirrors, combs, rods, crosses . . ."

Kenneth was just sinking into comfort beside his wife, but now he sat up straight. "Crosses! Yes, we could have the cross of our Lord on our flag. A fine sun cross with a great wheel of light behind it, like the standing crosses that call men to prayer across our land."

Maia smiled. "Yes, perhaps that would be best."

He noted the doubt in her voice. "Did you have another idea, my heart?"

"You did a fine thing in choosing Dalriada's Andrew to be patron over all. My Picti women say good things about you—even when

294

they do not know I hear their gossip—and always they praise your naming of Saint Andrew. And so I was thinking, when I was a little girl Finguine would tell me often stories of Andrew, of how he worked among the people in response to Jesus' order, and how he ventured far into ancient lands taking the gospel to people who had never heard, and how he was finally crucified, but not as our Lord was crucified. That always captured my imagination—the picture of the saint lashed hand and foot to his saltire, taking days to die so, but preaching the gospel to the very end until weakness overcame him and finally his soul was freed to paradise."

As she spoke she traced the X pattern of Andrew's cross on the skirt of her blue shift, her white fingertip leaving an impression in the fabric spread over the soft furs.

Suddenly Kenneth saw it. He grabbed Maia's hand. "Yes! That shall be it. Neither wolf nor boar, not any animal with its roots deep in pagan meaning, but a cross. The cross of Saint Andrew—white on blue like your tunic. And with this symbol Scotland will be reminded that it is called to be truly Christian." He pulled Maia into his arms and kissed her enthusiastically.

But suddenly she pushed him away. "What did you say? *Scotland*? Where did that come from?"

Kenneth grinned. His enthusiasm had betrayed his next step. But perhaps it was best so. "It came from my head. We must have a new name for our new country."

"Think you the choice might be somewhat one-sided?"

He grinned again. "I had feared you might think so. Yet it sits well on the tongue."

"Scotland, Scotia, land of the Scots . . ." She paused. "Yes, it sounds well . . ."

"It is a thread from the Dalriadan side. The saint, the flag, the high seat are all Alban. This is a balance."

And two days later when he stood on the small mound called Moot Hill in front of the chapel near the hall house of Scone Palace, so he told all gathered there. Behind him stood Dubtach, proudly holding the white-crossed banner that Maia had directed her women to make from the same weaving as her blue shift. And the wind fluttered it bravely.

"And so the saltire—the broken cross on which Saint Andrew died so nobly—shall be our official banner at Scone and at Forteviot and wherever the king of Scotia holds sway. In Galloway and the Western Isles and DunAdd and Inverness, in the highlands of Cait and Atholl and the seacoast of Ce and Fife—over all Scotland. Perhaps even someday beyond that, for united in faith and purpose this Scotland will become a great nation.

"Great because in Christ we have a new nationality—in Him is no Alban nor Dalriadan—we are Christian first, then we are Scotian. Let us show this oneness as we march under one banner."

Kenneth held his breath. Maia had taken some persuading at this point. What about these mormaors, some who had voted for the son of Bruide in the first place, and all who came with regional loyalties? Would Dalriadans march under the banner of an Alban saint? Would Albannach answer to a Scoti name?

They stood now before him, holding boots filled with the soil of their regions—not a few grains as were used at DunAdd, but bootsful. And behind him stood Corbanac and Finguine on either side of the Stone of Destiny. For here, to the enkinging place of Alba, he had brought the Stone of Dalriada in its carved case to be sat upon hereafter by kings neither of Alba nor of Dalriada but of Scotland—a stone of remembrance like that of Jacob's, because Kenneth truly believed that hitherto had the Lord led them.

But would his mormaors agree? Would they now pour out their soil in allegiance to their new king, Kenneth, and their new country, Scotland? Or would they turn away and carry the soil back to their own mortuaths?

After coming so far in the weaving had he pushed too hard? Would they turn away before the final thread was tied?

There was a murmuring in the crowd around the hillock as if many were trying the word on the tongue as Maia had done that night in their chamber.

He turned to look at her now, standing tall, silvery blue under the flag beside the stone. And he saw that she was leading them in repeating the name.

"Scotland, Scotland, Scotland."

More and more took it up, and it lost its strange sounding in the repetition.

There was a movement at the center of the crowd. Slowly the gathering parted as a mormaor dressed in dark leathers pushed his way forward. Kinnart mac Bruide strode halfway up the mound of Moot Hill. For the space of two repetitions of "Scotland" he looked at Kenneth straight on. Slowly he raised his boot and dumped the full contents of the soil of Findach before Kenneth mac Alpin. He shook the boot well that the last grains fell before he joined his voice to the chant, "Scotland!"

Wind riffled the blue and white saltire behind him, and Kenneth, king of Scotland, sat on the Stone of Destiny.

31

Mary sat on the stone. It was a rectangular chunk of old red sandstone, standing at seat-height on cement posts atop Moot Hill in front of the little chapel at Scone Palace. Peacocks strutting on the lawn before her gave their screeching cry, and her friends applauded.

"Isn't it supposed to cry out or something when the true leader sits on it?" she asked.

Gareth cocked his head to one side and grinned. "I dinna think peacocks squawking comes to quite the same thing."

"Well, if it is supposed to, now we know you're a fake," Brad said.

"Certainly not. The stone's a fake." Mary jumped off the cold, hard seat and picked up the packages and umbrella she had laid beside it.

"Ach, no. The wee lassie's nae a fake." Their friend Hamish, whom they had met up with at a storytelling the day before, strode up the gentle mound, his blue and gold kilt swinging below a thick Arran sweater.

Mary turned to run her hand over the stone. The rough-hewn pink block was almost twenty-seven inches long, seventeen inches wide, more than ten inches deep, with a heavy iron ring fixed on each end. "What do you think, Hamish? Is this truly a replica of the one Kenneth mac Alpin sat on?"

Hamish ran a broad hand through his thick red beard. "Well, now, it's a replica of the stane Edward took to Westminster. Most accept that as coming to the same thing."

The breeze blew strands of Mary's hair across her face. She pushed them back. "But what do you think, Hamish? The story you told last night at the ceilidh about how Kenneth united the two parts of Scotland was wonderful, but you didn't say what you really think. I mean, if Kenneth really had the stone encased in a carved casket, it could have had anything inside it."

"Aye, so it could have. Perhaps I was a wee bit begging the question in telling the tale like that."

"Keeping your options open?" Brad suggested.

"That's it exactly. So I was. Not sure about the matter yet myself, ye see, and that's the truth of it. The more I learn, the more confusing it sometimes seems. There are those who have thought carefully about the matter and think the enkinging stone was Columba's altar. If so, it could have been about this size and sat up on posts or something like this." He motioned to the replica before them.

"But this looks so heavy. Wouldn't it be an awful job to carry this around?" Mary asked.

Hamish nodded. "Four hundred fifty-eight pounds, tae be exact. That's why I find myself favoring the idea of a smaller stone. If the original crowning stone was Columba's pillow—or Jacob's, or a piece of the Lia Fail, or some other such—it would have had to be encased in a chest or chair—or be blazing awkward to sit on."

Another group of tourists came up the hill to examine the stone. A little girl with them was far more interested in Hamish with his colorful kilt and fiery hair than in any old rock. At last the child's mother smiled and turned to him. "I'm sorry to intrude, but could we take your picture with Alice Marie?"

Hamish obligingly helped wee Alice climb up on the stone and stood beside her while the cameras clicked.

"Have you had lunch?" Gareth asked when Hamish rejoined them at the edge of the chapel lawn. "Their bakery here is famous. My mum makes soda bread from their recipe all the time."

He held out a hand to Mary. With a smile she gave him the parcels she was carrying. The gesture had become almost routine between them. He grinned back but without the brilliance his smile usually held. That deep wistfulness she had come to recognize under all his fun was close to the surface today. She wondered—for maybe the hundredth time—what was it that seemed to trouble him so?

He took them across the wide gravel drive toward the beige stone palace with its square, crenellated towers and white-framed, arched windows. They went downstairs to the Old Kitchen restaurant, where fresh salmon salad and steaming vegetable soup were being served with freshly baked cakes, bread, and scones.

Mary surveyed the bright rows of copper kettles, pots, and molds lining the shelves and walls. "I love this palace. Its history goes back forever, and it has all the grandeur one expects in a palace, and yet it's really a family home too. Did you notice the family snapshots tucked in between the priceless oils in the state rooms upstairs?"

Gareth gave his brief little jerky nod. "Yup. Sensible lot we are, us Scots. I knew you'd like us when you got to know us."

So many replies flooded Mary's mind that she couldn't choose one. She turned instead to the safer Hamish. "I loved the story about Kenneth mac Alpin you told last night. Where all have you been since we saw you last?"

Hamish, holding a thickly buttered whole meal scone in his left hand, counted on the fingers of the other. "Well, now, let's see. From Dunadd I went up to Dunstaffnage—what I called DunStaffness in my wee tale. The castle there is much more modern than anything from Kenneth's time—somewhere in the thirteenth or fourteenth century—but the amazing mound of living stone it stands on has been there since creation, or perhaps just a wee bit after. A verra fine stronghold it would have been for anything Kenneth wanted tae hide from his enemies."

"Was it old red sandstone—the native rock? Did you see any like the Stone of Scone?" Brad asked.

"Nae." Hamish shook his head, then paused to enjoy another mouthful of scone before going on, "Then I went up to Inverness to Craig Phadrig, the Picti capital before Scone."

Mary nodded. "Where Columba visited Brude. You mean it's still there?"

"Ach, aye. No timbers from Brude's hall house, I fear, but a fine green mountain with traces of the old hill fort wall."

Mary put down her spoon and leaned forward, captivated by the thought of scenes of so long ago.

Hamish went on. "And then I made my way courtesy of our efficient if noisy rail system, then bus, to Saint Andrews."

"Yes, I wanted to ask you—that was Kilrimont in your story, wasn't it?"

"That's right, lassie. Kilrimont was the old Culdee name—holy men of the Celtic church, that is. It became Saint Andrews when it grew to be a power center of the Roman Church sometime in the twelfth century." He took another bite. "Then I made a short stop at Dunkeld, and here I am."

Mary shook her head. "All that in less than a week! You've really traced all the footsteps of your story, haven't you?"

Hamish shrugged. "Seems ye can never trace them all, lassie. One lifetime's far too short. I stop at every standing stane I pass along the roadside or in kirkyard, but ye can nae see them all."

Mary laughed and gave her cousin a playful slap on the shoulder. "Tell that to Brad here. He thinks we can see them all."

"Amazing, aren't they?" Brad adjusted his glasses. "The Picts had such a sophisticated symbol system with their intricate animals and V-rods and zed-rods and mirrors and crescents—it's just so frustrating that we can't decipher them. But the battle scenes are quite clear. Now take the Alberlemno churchyard cross for example—" In his enthusiasm he leaned forward and narrowly missed putting his elbow in his salad.

Mary laughed. "Brad, that salmon is far too good to waste on your sweater. You'd better eat it first." She turned back to Hamish. "You really made Kenneth live for me."

"Ah, now that's a verra fine thing. I hold great respect for the man. It couldna have been an easy job, his."

Mary toyed with her spoon. She didn't want to sound critical. "But I was wondering . . . I mean, Kenneth sounded so . . . so enlightened . . ."

Hamish shrugged. "Aye. The records are heartbreakingly sparse. The best we know of him is the title later chroniclers gave him."

"Which was . . ."

"The Scottish Alfred. I have therefore based much of my tale on what we know of Alfred the Great: a leader in war, in statecraft, in lawgiving, in education, in the arts, and in faith."

Mary's soup cooled in her bowl as she listened. "As you said, enough for several lifetimes."

"And like Alfred the Great, Kenneth's was none too long but well-spent. Like Alfred, after he got the Danes quieted down he was able to concentrate on building a strong nation. So when ye look at the results of Kenneth's reign, I think my tale is none too anachronistic. And the fact is, the truth is nae such a volatile thing as many think. Aye, there's different ways of looking at a thing. But what was true for one age is pretty much true for another."

Mary nodded. That was something she would need to think about. "And so what happened to Kenneth finally?"

"Kenneth ruled well for sixteen years and died in his palace at Forteviot. His brother Donald ruled after him, then the line went back to Kenneth's sons and grandsons. Kenneth and Olaf of Dublin were both buried on Iona."

Brad finished his salad, then took up where he had left off. "Yes, but the point I was making is that those people were such skilled stone carvers. They seem to have put up exquisitely carved stones like we put up hoardings."

"Huh?" Mary asked.

"Billboards to you, outlander. Anyway, does it seem likely a stone so revered as their enkinging stone would be rough-hewn with no ornamentation at all?"

Mary, stinging from Brad's cousinly jab, was unable to reply for a minute. Her blood was as Scottish as his. It wasn't her fault her parents had chosen to emigrate before she was born. And she cer-

300

tainly didn't *feel* foreign here. She had never felt more truly at home. But she wouldn't betray her hurt by defending herself. Instead she pushed back her mane of hair and entered into the discussion.

"Well, it seems obvious to me—the original Stone of Scottish king-making is the one at Dunadd. I was wondering—I mean, Kenneth apparently had such a feeling for symbolism, could he possibly have had a piece of the DunAdd rock quarried and moved to Scone? Not from the end where the carving was, of course—that would have been sacrilege—but from the other end, maybe?"

Hamish and Brad were quiet, considering. Mary saw that Gareth had left the table.

Brad nodded. "Yes, it could probably have been done easily enough. There are deep seams running through the rock face with cracks crisscrossing it. A piece could have been cut along one of those natural lines."

Hamish nodded too. "Aye, and then carved as fully as desired."

Mary picked up the thought with enthusiasm. "And then put in Kenneth's casket—maybe even right alongside whatever stone was already in there from his crowning. If he first had used one of those pillow stones, they would surely have been considerably smaller than any seat." She was quiet for a moment. "You know, I really like that idea. That truly makes it the Stone of Scotland with nothing borrowed from anybody else—and yet linked symbolically to those important stones like Jacob's and the Lia Fail and Columba's pillow . . ."

When neither of her companions answered she continued, speaking almost to herself. "Isn't it interesting how things can take on a wider meaning, something you can feel but can't quite get hold of?"

"Aye, feelings are the verra hardest things of all to get hold of." Mary turned at the sound of the soft Glaswegian voice. She hadn't noticed Gareth's return.

The waitress brought their bill, and Brad and Hamish got up. Mary started to rise, but instead of helping her with her chair, Gareth held out a small brown bag from the Scone Palace gift shop.

"For me?" she asked.

He nodded.

She opened the bag and took out a delicate, silver thistle pin set with an amethyst.

"I thought you should have it—as an honorary Scot."

She wanted to thank him but didn't trust her voice. Instead, her nod was accompanied by a rather wavery smile.

That evening, alone in her tiny room in the B & B—a spotlessly clean room decorated in cheery floral chintz but with barely space to

301

walk around the bed—she sat on her bed with her notebook on her jeans-clad knees. Unlike the more academic approach Brad was taking to their quest for the true Stone of Scone, for her it had taken on the proportions of a good mystery story. She was keeping notes on all their clues.

"Candidates for Original Stone and Composition" headed one list, which included: "Jacob's Pillow—yellow sandstone? meteorite? Lia Fail—black granite? meteorite? Columba's Pillow from Ireland? Later stone of Columba's—green Ionian marble? The Dunadd Roundel—greenish slate; the Dunadd Enkinging Stone, granite; the Westminster Stone—old red sandstone." She looked at her list. So many question marks. So much guesswork.

The harder she tried to concentrate on the question before her the more the questions whirled. And as her puzzles grew, a larger, more important one pushed in. How she wished she could understand Gareth. But she couldn't even form questions. After a moment, she sighed and forced her mind back to her notebook.

On the next page she noted: "No red sandstone in Holy Land, no red sandstone on Iona, no red sandstone at DunAdd, no red sandstone at Dunstaffnage . . ."

The notebook slipped onto her rose and green patterned douvet and lay there untouched. The likelihood of the Westminster Stone being authentic looked slim indeed, but that thought took only a small part of her attention. The stone that held her thoughts was closer to hand—on her hand to be exact—Michael's diamond.

She *must* call Michael tonight. She really didn't have any excuse not to call now that they were out of the Highlands. Of course, she could have called from there. It wasn't that there weren't any phones in the Highlands—it was just that one felt so remote. There was such a sense of being apart from the modern world that she couldn't bring herself to break the spell.

She started to get up to go to the phone in the hall when the light caught the other stone she wore—the amethyst in Gareth's thistle.

She smiled as she turned to the thistle—and thoughts of the man who gave it to her. What was it about Gareth? She struggled with the question as she had times without number. It seemed a more intriguing puzzle than any about the Stone of Scone.

She ran over her past answers again. Intelligence—certainly that; she had seldom met anyone quicker. And yet as much as she admired that, it was hardly a unique trait among the men she knew; certainly Michael was brilliant. Good manners—true enough, Gareth was a natural gentleman, always thoughtful. But there was something else, a better, more-embracing, rather old-fashioned word. She groped for it, but it eluded her.

Oh, well. She looked at her watch. Two o'clock in the afternoon in New York—should be a good time to call Michael. She started to reach for her credit card when her thoughts were interrupted by a rap at her door. "Come," she called.

Gareth stuck his head in, then pulled back rather shyly and rubbed the top of his springy black hair. "I just wondered if you'd like to go for a wee little walk?"

She had her feet in her shoes before she could say, "I'd love it."

They sauntered along the quiet, tree-lined street in the glow of the long evening, not talking about anything important. And yet the talking itself was important—and the spaces of quiet comment, punctuated with the laughter that was never far away when Mary found herself with Gareth. The next street they took was lined with large detached homes one hundred—maybe two hundred—years old, standing behind wrought iron or stone fences or well-clipped hedges. The residential section of Perth was hilly, and the sidewalk rose steeply here.

"How's the leg?" Mary asked when Gareth's pace slowed.

"Ah, it's grand!"

She was surprised at the enthusiasm of his reply.

Then he paused and grinned. "Well, the leg's not exactly grand yet, but everything else is—the evening, being here. I don't know when I've had more fun. I really regret the time I've wasted."

Mary started to ask him what he meant, but at the top of the hill the ground flattened out, and a playground stood there, offering swings, slides, and a merry-go-round just for them, as all the children had long since gone home.

"Oh! Come on!" Gareth grabbed her hand and set out across the broad, green lawn with his little loping run that seemed all the more graceful for including a slight hop on his weak leg.

They reached the swings first. Mary took off with one shove of her feet and was sailing high in three swings.

"Oh, how I love to go up in a swing, up in the sky so blue. Oh, I do think it the pleasantest thing ever a child can do." She quoted the rhyme as she had almost every time she had swung for as long as she could remember. "My mother taught me that when I was about five years old." She stuck her feet out in front of her and leaned back at arm's length until she was lying almost flat.

"My mum did too." Gareth matched the level of his swing to hers. "Robert Louis Stevenson."

"Oh!" She sat up. "He was Scots too, wasn't he? I hadn't thought about that." She kicked a final time. "Up in the air I go flying again, up in the air and down." She finished the poem and let her swing glide to a stop.

Gareth jumped off and led her to a piece of playground equipment Mary hadn't seen before: two platforms maybe fifty feet apart with an overhead cable between. A child could grasp a long vertical bar and swing to the other side, Tarzan style. Smiling, she watched Gareth swing wide and land lightly on the far side. His agility amazed her anew. Even with a recuperating broken leg he could keep pace with a gazelle any day.

He gave a heave to the bar and sent it skimming back to her side. Mary grasped it, pushed off, and rode it, screaming and laughing, to the other side.

Gareth grasped her lightly at the waist and set her on the ground.

"The merry-go-round next," she cried and set out at a run. But when she reached it and turned around, laughing and breathless, Gareth wasn't behind her.

It took her a moment to spot him, leaning over a perhaps six-year-old boy from whom muffled snuffling sounds were coming.

"What is it, laddie? This is nae time for you tae be about."

Between sniffles the child explained that he had stayed too long at a friend's house, then when he got home the door was locked, so he thought his brother might be in the park, but now he didn't know where anyone was.

Gareth knelt down to the child's level, his Scots accent getting broader as he spoke in comforting tones. "Noo there, there's naething tae cry about. I'll take you home. And this pretty lady here will come right along as weel. Would you nae like that?"

The tousled-haired tyke slipped his hand into Gareth's. Then he wiped his nose on his sleeve and pointed to a house across the street. Gareth signaled Mary to join them, which she did, following just a little behind as there seemed to be no need for another person. Gareth had the situation entirely under control as the child trotted happily at his side, chattering about a boat he was building with his mates.

And again Mary thought about Gareth's special qualities. It was such a small thing, something anyone would have done, to walk a frightened child home, and yet it was the complete naturalness with which Gareth did it, his empathy with the child.

In a few minutes the lad was restored to his mother, who had been out looking for him, and Gareth turned to Mary. "The merry-go-round, you said?"

"Sit down and hang on," she cried when they reached it. "I'll give you a ride." She pushed it to a dizzying speed, then jumped on and clung for dear life. After some time the roundabout stopped spinning. But Mary's head didn't. Still laughing, she lay on the ground until at last the earth stilled.

It was getting dark, and soon the grass would be damp, but she didn't want to move. Some kind of night bird sang in one of the trees edging the park.

Gareth sat a little distance from her, his arms around his knees, looking at the lights in the valley beyond. And she knew he would have sat so, not interrupting her thoughts, for as long as she chose. With that realization came the word she had sought earlier—gallant. Sir Gareth the gallant. She smiled at the thought.

She sat up carefully, feeling still a little tipsy. A lavender-pink light in the distance reminded her of something else from earlier in the day. "Gareth, I haven't said a proper thank you yet for the thistle." She paused, warning herself not to gush. "Thank you."

He gave a jerky little dip of his head. "Welcome."

But being an American she couldn't leave it at that. "And for the honorary title. I guess you could tell I hated being called a foreigner."

"No foreigner could get as wrapped up as you are in this business about the Stone."

She thought for a moment. "Maybe you're right. Because it isn't really just the Stone itself, is it? It's really what it represents—all those hundreds of years of history—people living and struggling, kings and armies clashing . . ."

"That's right." He took up her thought. "And beyond the doing there's the believing—people working for something beyond themselves. I think that's what I see more than anything else. In all the places we've been, all the stories Hamish has told, is a sense of God dealing throughout history."

Mary felt herself go cold. Why did he have to spoil it? She tried not to make the situation worse with a harsh answer, but she had to be honest. "Sorry. I guess that 'faith of our fathers' stuff never did much for me."

He was quiet a moment but refused to back off. "But think, Mary, where would any of us be today without our heritage—without the spiritual roots of our country? I could say countries, but it comes to the same thing—the same faith playing the same central role."

She wanted to argue, but as she turned her head the amethyst in the thistle winked at her. Her reply was more conciliatory than she intended. "I don't know about faith, but I do love the stories of justice triumphing."

"That's right. Now, ask yourself, What makes right? What makes justice? What or who sets the standard if there's no absolute right and wrong?"

She turned away. She couldn't—or wouldn't—answer. But she thought. It *was* remarkable that through all those hundreds of years the standards hadn't really changed. Ways of expressing ideas had changed. But right and wrong—decent human behavior really hadn't. Could it be that everything wasn't really relative?"

"Well, certainly no one denies the civilizing role of Christianity." That was the best she could do, so she went on the attack. "So why are there so many different churches if there's one absolute truth?" Now she had him.

But he didn't even hesitate. "That's all right. One truth, but we see different aspects of it because our minds are too small to comprehend the whole. But that doesn't mean there isn't a whole. It doesn't mean truth is different. If it's something different for each person, it isn't truth—it's emotion. The fact that we feel differently about truth doesn't make the truth different."

His calm really was too much. "Are you always so sure of yourself?" She sounded more irritated than she realized she felt.

He gave a startled little laugh, shook his head, and ran his fingers through his hair. "Is that the way I seem to you? I've never been less sure of myself."

She was amazed. "What?"

"The responsibility of being a minister—when I've made so many mistakes. I want to help people, but can helping a hundred make up for causing one to go out unready?"

What in the world is he talking about? She wished she could understand, because he had opened himself the tiniest fraction, and she liked what she saw inside even more than she had thought she would. They had talked about nothing but their differences, yet she had never felt closer to him.

She got to her feet. "I've got to get back. I have a telephone call to make." She started walking without looking back.

BOOK 3

Of Queens and Clerics

Queen Margaret Marries Malcolm III, 1068

32

The Scottish folk music Mary had slipped into the tape deck played softly in the background, and the green, rolling Perthshire countryside sped by as Gareth guided the little red car along Route 26. But Mary, who would normally have been exulting in the morning sunshine that brightened the lush farmland and the little, flower-bordered gray stone houses, pulled further into herself as she recalled last night's phone call to Michael.

Dear, handsome, going-places Michael with his important job on Wall Street. It was hardly to be wondered at that he found her chatter about searching for the truth about the Stone of Scone to be amusing but irrelevant.

"I'm glad you're having a nice vacation, Mary. But isn't that rather a waste of time? I mean, it's really just a block of stone—I've seen it in that beat-up old chair in Westminster Abbey. And I'd think you could read the facts in any decent guidebook—or better yet, *The Encyclopedia Britannica*. Shall I have my secretary photocopy it and fax it to you at your next stop?"

Mary had sighed and politely declined. After all, he was just trying to be helpful. Instead, she had changed the subject and told him about romping in the playground the night before. Well, what did she expect? Of course Michael would think that was silly. He probably hadn't even gone to playgrounds when he was six years old. He had once told her that his father helped him set up his first stock portfolio for his tenth birthday.

And of course she was the one being silly. Her perceptions were just askew because she was so far from home. Other than his failure to understand about the things she told him, Michael had been wonderful. He couldn't wait for her to come home and marry him. He'd even been working on plans for their honeymoon. Would she prefer Bermuda or the Riviera? Bermuda, she had said and let him think it was because it was quieter and more romantic. Michael would never have understood her choosing a place because it was British.

So Michael was wonderful. So why did she feel pressured—trapped? That was ridiculous. No one could possibly be freer than she was at the moment. And yet the weight remained.

And even more ridiculous was her feeling that Michael was shallow. Michael was undoubtedly the most solid, hard-working, successful person she knew. What could possibly be shallow about that?

The tape finished, and she slipped in Vivaldi for a change. The narrow, winding road was rather heavily trafficked today. At least this was two-lane, wide compared with those in the Highlands but without the broad shoulders she was used to at home. The driver in front of them had the irritating habit of speeding up, then slowing down for no apparent reason. He was in his slowing down mode at the moment.

The other lane was empty. Gareth pulled into it to pass. They were even with the other car when one appeared over the next hill coming toward them. Gareth pushed on the gas. They slid easily around and back into their lane.

Gareth looked at her. "I hope I didn't make you nervous, but sometimes in a spot like that it's best just to go for it."

She smiled. "No, I wasn't at all nervous." Of course, there had been no reason to be—there really was enough time. And yet it surprised her to realize how calm she was. Normally passing on a road like this would have her at the screaming point. She realized now that not once during all these days of driving had she felt herself tensing. She had complete, relaxed faith in Gareth's demonstrated skill to judge distance.

She looked sideways at him, his hands steady on the wheel, his thumbs moving in time to the rhythm of "Summer." Such judgment was probably an important part of his skill as a footballer. But he was so unconscious of possessing any special ability. She smiled. That was so much of his charm—the naturalness of it all.

And yet there were the times, and it seemed these came more often lately, when he seemed far away in his thoughts—a very different person from the lighthearted companion he was most of the time. Something troubled him deeply, even more deeply than mourning for a friend. She wished he would open up to her as he had started to that evening on the playground.

With a sudden ruffling of papers, Brad emerged from his own world in the backseat like Badger emerging from the Wild Wood. He stuck his head between the front seats and pointed ahead to a wooded hill with brown craggy rocks thrusting above the trees on top. "That's Dunsinane."

Mary's thick dark eyebrows rose. "Dunsinane—you mean like in *Macbeth,* 'Till Birnam wood to Dunsinane come'?"

"The same. There was an ancient fort there, and historians seem to agree—as much as they ever agree about anything—that it probably was Macbeth's. Birnam Wood, where Duncan's hill fort was, is five or six miles to the west, not at the foot of Dunsinane as Shakespeare makes it seem."

"Wait a minute!" Mary switched off the music and turned to face her cousin. "Professor Bradley Hamilton, are you telling me that Macbeth is for real? There really *was* a Duncan and Macbeth and Lady Macbeth and Malcolm and all of them?"

Brad took off his glasses and blinked in surprise. "Of course. And you the drama major. What did they teach you at Dartmouth?"

"Of course I know the characters in Shakespeare's history plays were for real—even if his plots aren't always strictly accurate. But *Macbeth* is a tragedy. I mean, nobody claims Hamlet or Othello or Romeo and Juliet were real people."

"Well, Macbeth was real enough, but as you say, the historic facts differ from the plot. Brilliant theater though it is, Duncan was not a wise old king—he was thirty-three and killed in battle, probably by his cousin Thorfinn, Earl of Orkney—not done in by Lady Macbeth."

"Amazing," Mary muttered.

"And," Brad continued, "Macbeth's claim to the throne was perfectly sound. Actually he and Duncan both were in the line of Kenneth mac Alpin, although Macbeth's was through his mother and his wife rather than the male line. By the way, Lady Macbeth's name was Gruoch—a fact Shakespeare fails to mention, and the son she babbles about having given suckle to was Lulach. He was by her first husband and reigned for a short time after Macbeth."

"Amazing," Mary repeated. Then, "What kind of king was Macbeth?"

"By all accounts very competent. He ruled for seventeen years until Siward, pressing the claim of Duncan's son Malcolm, defeated him at Scone, and Malcolm killed him—not on the rugged summit of Dunsinane under branches borne thither from Birnam but on the far less glamorous Pell Bog. He was buried on Iona."

Mary scrambled for her notebook. "Cousin, you leave me breathless. Does your Sharon know what a treasure of information she's getting?"

Brad grinned and repeated several of his just-quoted facts for her to write down.

At last her pen stilled. "So go on, tell me about Malcolm. At the end of *Macbeth* I always heave a great sigh, believing the country is in good hands after all that turmoil. Now don't you dare tell me Malcolm was really a snake."

Brad pulled back and raised a hand as if in defense. "Not at all. He was known as Malcolm Canmore—which means big head. That could have meant that he literally had a large head, but it's more likely it means he was regarded as a great leader. At any rate, he ruled for thirty-five years and established the House of Canmore, which ruled Scotland for well over two hundred years. Although, truth to tell, his favorite pastime seems to have been making rather brutal war on England. His real claim to greatness was his good taste in marrying the Saxon princess Margaret, whose ship was blown to Scotland when her family was fleeing William the Conqueror."

Mary's pen was moving across the page again. "Tell me more."

"Better yet, we'll show you," Gareth said. "It's only about thirty miles south to Dunfermline."

"Great." Mary wasn't sure what Dunfermline was, but she was content to go there. She turned Vivaldi on again and settled back to enjoy the ride, amazed at herself that a woman who had always insisted on knowing where she was going and why she was going and when she would get there could be so relaxed.

Well, it would have been thirty miles had they gone straight down the M90. As it was they spent considerable time darting up little back roads to see Picti standing stones to which Brad directed them. And they had to stop in Abernethy because it had once been a Pictish capital and an important center of the Culdee church, as well as the place where Malcolm Canmore did homage to William the Conqueror in 1072.

"Now, let's just hack our way around here and take a peek at the Round Tower. It dates from the ninth century, and there are only three of them in all of Scotland." Brad strode out like a professor leading a class of enthusiasts on a field trip.

They stood on the soft grass at the foot of the gray stone structure and gazed upward seventy-four feet to the top. Round Tower was well-named, for indeed it was a round tower, tapering slightly inward as it rose. Its single doorway was well above head level. Its only window slit was about halfway up, with ventilating louvers near the top.

"The upper parts were rebuilt in the eleventh century, and of course the clock is comparatively modern," Brad continued.

"Yes." Mary wouldn't have dreamed of arguing with him. "But what's it for?"

"A refuge for the monks. This was the most important monastery in Pictland until Kenneth established Dunkeld as his ecclesiastical capital. See, when attackers threatened, the monks could pull the ladder up and lock the door after them. The defense was practically impregnable."

Then he turned. "Now, over here is a class one Picti symbol stone. It was dug out of the foundation of a house in the village. It had been trimmed down to building-stone size." He shook his head at the desecration, then traced the deeply incised patterns in the stone. "The 'tuning fork' is flanked by a blacksmith's hammer and anvil. And here we have a crescent and V-rod—"

"I saw a grocery store back there. How about buying some things for a picnic?" Mary grinned at Gareth.

He took up her suggestion. "Right. Can't come to Abernethy without buying Abernethy biscuits. They're just the thing with cheese. Have you had Orkney cheddar yet?"

In the end, their luncheon picnic ran into more of a late tea. And then there was just one more Pictish symbol stone to see up this road. Fortunately a square white sign with distinct black B & B letters offered them a haven for the night right across from Brad's intricately carved cross-slab.

Mrs. Harris, their hostess, made them tea, and they ate the leftovers of their picnic. Mary went up to her room early. She was unaccountably tired. Gareth said he'd be up as soon as she was through with the bath, but Brad chose to sit longer in the parlor.

"Hope to finish these journals tonight." He indicated a thick stack.

Mary took a hot bath in the wonderful old tub that stood on lion-claw feet, then, snuggled in her knit pajamas under a goose down douvet, was soon asleep.

She had no idea how long she'd been asleep when she was wakened by a cry from next door. She grabbed her flannel robe and ran to Brad and Gareth's room. The door must have been ajar because it opened under her pounding. Brad's bed was still empty.

Gareth tossed, muttering protests, on his bed. She shook his shoulders. "Gareth, what's wrong?"

Still asleep, he turned his head from side to side on the pillow. Suddenly his eyes came open, wild for a moment, then focused on her. "Mary."

He sat up and rubbed his eyes. "Did I cry out? Sorry I bothered you." He attempted to smooth his wild hair.

She saw his hands were shaking and took them in hers. "Gareth, what is it?"

"I dreamed about the climbing accident again. That hasn't happened for more than a month now. I thought I was over it. I'm sorry I bothered you."

She looked at him for a long moment. "Well, I'm not. I'm glad I was near." She dropped his hands and turned to the small shelf where their hostess had provided an electric kettle. "Two sugars?"

"Yep. Thanks."

In a couple of minutes she handed him a steaming cup, noting that he took it with steady hands now. She sat on Brad's bed with her own cup. "Want to talk about it?'

He took a long drink. "I don't know. That is, I think I do, thanks. But I don't really remember much. Just the sense of horror. Alex was dead . . ." After a pause he finished so quietly she could hardly hear him. "And it was my fault."

"Don't be silly. He fell. Slick rocks in the rain, you said. How could it be your fault?"

"He was right above me when he slipped. I shouldn't have come up under him. He twisted to avoid me. He wouldn't have fallen on the boulders otherwise. He would have landed in the bracken like I did."

"Maybe. But you can't be sure. It just happened." She reached out and took his arm to add intensity to her words. "Gareth, it's not your fault."

"I guess I'll never know. But that's not all—not the worst."

"What?"

He shook his head. "You wouldn't understand."

"Try me."

"Alex wasn't ready to die. We grew up together in the church, but we were the two that always held back on spiritual things. Usually me holding back when he wouldn't have. I could have influenced him for good when there was plenty of time. But I didn't. I made the bad choices. And suddenly there wasn't any more time."

He drained his cup and set it aside. "For me, I kept thinking— he did it for me. Two men had died for me. I could tell Jesus thank you—spend the rest of my life saying it. But it was too late for Alex."

What could she say? How could she give spiritual comfort when she didn't even believe there was a God? If she could have prayed she would have at that moment. "But you don't know for sure. He didn't die right away, did he? There might have been time . . ." She buried her face in her cup. She had never felt more of a hypocrite in her life.

There was nothing more to be said, nothing more to be done. The next morning it seemed best to do the British thing and pretend their midnight talk had never happened.

314

That was surprisingly easy as they drove into Dunfermline, a beautiful city with wide cobbled streets and tempting tea shops running up and down its steep hillside. Brad was in full flower as a history lecturer, for which Mary was grateful, but, try as she might, she could only keep so much of the confusing Scottish history straight at one time.

As they approached the church built on the site of the medieval monastery, the first thing Mary noticed was the words "King Robert The Bruce" running in hewn stone around the top of the tower.

"And now, for a free admission ticket, can you tell us who's buried here besides Queen Margaret?" Gareth grinned.

"Shall I take a wild guess and say King Robert the Bruce?"

"Right. Not the most subtle architectural hint, is it? But I'll bet you don't know who else was born in Dunfermline besides all the Canmore royal children?"

Mary spread her hands. "I haven't a clue."

"Then I'll tell you, and I'll get a free admission ticket too—Andrew Carnegie."

"Oh, that is interesting. But you know what, I don't think they charge admission to the church."

Brad led them up the wide stone nave flanked by massive round pillars of the modern—1822—church. Partway up he stopped and pointed to brass strips set in the stones of the floor. "These mark the chapel Margaret built here when she established her Benedictine monastery."

Mary followed the lines, tracing what had been, nine hundred years earlier, a tower-nave, choir, and semicircular apse. It filled less than one-third of the present nave.

"Before she established her monastery there was an ancient Culdee community here. This is where Margaret and Malcolm were married."

Brad's tour was of the bare bones variety, but Mary liked it that way. It gave full range for her imagination to fill in the spaces in the story of the reputedly beautiful Saxon princess who married the burly Scots king, then took on the task of civilizing him and the entire nation.

Beneath the spiral wooden staircase leading up to the elegantly carved pulpit, Brad pointed to a brass plate in the floor showing a chain-mail clad king with a lion on his shield and another beneath his feet. "The tomb of Robert the Bruce."

Then he took them out the small eastern door behind the altar. Here had once stood a splendid chapel that, until the Reformation, had held the body of Margaret in a magnificent casket, which drew

315

pilgrims from all parts of the kingdom. All that remained now was a simple stone slab surrounded by a wrought iron fence. The marker was too small for Mary to read through the grille protecting it.

But Brad didn't need any such cue cards. "The story is that when Margaret's bier was being carried up the nave of the church to be interred, her coffin grew so heavy when they passed over Malcolm's tomb in the crypt below that the bearers had to set it down. Her son rightly interpreted her wishes and directed that Malcolm also be interred in the chapel so Margaret and Malcolm could rest together."

Their knowledgeable guide then led them southward to the buildings of the medieval monastery, which were in varying stages of ruin. An arch took them across the road to what in medieval times had been the abbey guest house but was originally Margaret and Malcolm's favorite royal residence. And nursery, for here all of Margaret's seven children were born, one to become an abbot, one queen of England, and three kings of Scotland.

Brad and Gareth went off to make a closer examination of the ruins, but Mary chose to wander down the steep path below the church, across the burn running through Pittencrieff Glen to the thickly wooded, steep bank of what had once been Malcolm Canmore's park.

As the lush foliage closed over her, Mary felt as if she were entering another world. She walked slowly up a dirt and stone path banked solid on both sides with ferns, bushes, and trees. Wood pigeons cooed overhead. A light breeze blew the higher branches, letting rays of sun filter through onto the black, leaf-strewn path and making a soft soughing to accompany the splashing of the burn below. She could easily believe she had stepped backward nine hundred years to Margaret's time.

She sat on a large boulder covered with bright green moss, longing to capture every detail of this lovely place. If only she could take something of it with her in her heart so that she could enter it at will when the pressures of modern life got too much for her.

She didn't know how long she sat, just listening, looking, smelling, but she gradually became aware of an increased capacity to feel—as if there were suddenly more space within herself. Love— certainly that was a good word, and yet love with greater wideness and depth than she had known before. And there was joy—a kind of harmony, a dim vision of beauty and light breaking just beyond a distant hill. At the same time all was tinged with a weight that was a kind of sadness, a longing, a homesickness for a perfection she couldn't reach or contain.

And she knew that somehow she was more alive just knowing she was capable of feeling this. She was afraid to breathe for fear the feeling would leave and she could never recapture it.

And then she understood something of what Gareth had undergone that night on Skye. She knew she wasn't alone in the universe. There was something bigger than everyday life—something beyond the material. And she could understand why Gareth, perhaps like Columba, would want to give his life to telling others about it. Why, when once one opened oneself to this love, nothing else in life would be truly important.

* * *

Margaret sat on a moss-covered rock beneath a spreading alder beside the burn. Pittencrief Glen offered the solitude and soothing beauty she found so needful for the contemplation her soul craved. Assuredly, the Lord knew best. She would not doubt Him or question Him. Always she sought only to do His will. But she could not help searching her own heart. There must be great wickedness in her that she should so long for peace and beauty when the Lord had so sharply directed her life in other directions. Could a desire for peace be rebellion? Yet it must be so when the Lord seemed to be so clearly leading in other ways.

She had been in Scotland only seven months since last autumn's storm blew them hither—and so much had happened. She had seen so much need—and found so much peace. How she, who loved beauty, could feel at home in the midst of such ruggedness was a wonder indeed.

Margaret tugged at the tails of her moon-colored hair, wishing for at least the thousandth time that it might have been a nun's wimple that would soon cover her head as the bride of Christ rather than the fine linen headrail of Saxon royalty that she must put on as bride of Malcolm Canmore. No, she was not envious of her sister Christina, who had found the fulfillment of her vocation in the monastery of Romsey. She was happy for her sister. She only wished that she could be likewise fulfilled instead of facing the frightful task before her.

She turned at the sound of approaching footsteps on the steep path. "My lady, forgive my bothering you here. I . . . ."

Margaret looked at her waiting-lady. The princess blinked but could not clear the sadness from her eyes.

"What is it, Elswyth?" Margaret smiled at her most faithful serving lady, who had done much to take Christina's place since her sister had taken her vows.

Elswyth stood before her now looking as she had when they were girls together at the court of Margaret's uncle, Edward the Confessor, king of England. Her tiny person and round face with pouty pink lips had never looked more forlorn than Margaret now saw her.

Were they all so sadly changed? Margaret remembered the light skip that had reflected Elswyth's light heart in happier days. Elswyth had been the merriest of the maids at Edward's court, always singing in the deep window recesses of his favorite castle in London or in the sweet green paths of the woods when the court was at Winchester or Gloucester. But the arrows of Norman William and his invaders had changed all that.

Elswyth turned away, her green kirtle and brown hair seeming to blend into the verdant sun-mottled vegetation. "I am sorry. I . . . I should not have come."

"Well, whether or not you should have come, it seems that you did. Now I would have you tell me what is so amiss that you would seek me here."

"Nothing is amiss, my lady." Elswyth spoke quickly, then paused, and her pale blue, wide-spaced eyes took on an alarmed look. "That is, I—"

"Elswyth, I know you far too well for this dissimulation. Ever since we sat at Sister Magdalena's knee at Saint Anne's you could never deceive me. Do not attempt to now."

"No, my Margaret. I would not deceive you. It is just that my heart was so ready to speak, but my mind tells me I must not. You must do what you think best."

Margaret sighed. "Oh. It is that again, is it?"

"I am sorry. I should not have come. I will go."

"No, Elswyth, sit. You did right. But there is no argument you can make that my own mind has not already made."

Elswyth nodded. She sat where a shaft of light filtered through the branches to gild her hair. Always impatient of veils, she had tugged hers off, even though her fine, waist-length hair would never stay in the braid she so carefully plaited down her back. Her impatience carried into her words. "My lady Margaret, to marry a barbarian. It is unthinkable." In the passion of the moment she had slipped to the familiar speech they had used as girls.

"Malcolm Canmore is king of the land to which God has led us." Margaret wished her words carried more passion to her own ears.

"King he is. But also barbarian—if not actual heathen. He is loud, his manners are—are—nonexistent. He is dirty. He cannot read. And he cannot be a true Christian, can he? To take the blessed sacrament from a priest who is married! My Margaret, you would not be wed by such a priest, would you? Surely it could be no true marriage. And Malcolm's wife is not yet cold in the grave. There are even whispers—"

Suddenly Margaret laughed. It was the most exquisite relief to hear someone put into words the thoughts that had been chasing each other around and around in her head. And when she heard them she realized how shallow the arguments were—mere rumors and superficial things. What were they compared to the leading of the hand of God?

Well, not all superficial, of course. The spiritual matters were of the greatest import. It must have been for the righting of these that God had caused their storm-tossed boat to fetch up on the little neck of land in the Firth of Forth when fleeing that royal assassin William of Normandy.

William the Conqueror some now called him. But he had not conquered the rightful heir to the English throne. Their mother, Agatha, would have this remnant of the descendants of Alfred the Great return to her native Hungary. There Margaret's brother, Edgar Aethling—who should be king of England now that King Harold had been slain at Hastings—could raise an army to put himself on his rightful throne. So Agatha had proposed. But God had disposed differently.

God had brought them to Scotland. Wild, rough, barbaric Scotland. And for Margaret Aethling a wild, rough, barbaric husband.

And it was true enough that Ingeborge Thorfinnsdotter, Malcolm's wife and mother of his son and heir Duncan, was so new-laid in her grave as to make a marriage celebration barely decent. But it was nonsense that some whispered of poison in the queen's wine. People always whispered so when an all-too-common fever carried off one of high estate.

Margaret's own father, the elder of Edward the Confessor's two nephews, had died shortly after returning to England from a lengthy sojourn in Hungary, where he had married Agatha of the Hungarian royal house and where Margaret and Christina and their brother Edgar had been born.

Then King Edward died, and Edgar became his successor, but due to the intervention of Norman William at Hastings, Edgar did not sit on the throne of England. And the fact that Edgar Aethling became a rallying point for Englishmen who did not wish to be ruled by a Norman brought the wrath of William the Conqueror on Margaret's family. Margaret's life had been ringed about by battles and storms and political intrigue but not by poison. She would have no talk of such nonsense.

319

"You have helped me immeasurably, Elswyth. I am decided."

"My Margaret, that is wonderful! You will refuse Malcolm?"

"On the contrary. You have helped me see how clearly God has led. I see how much I can accomplish here. Elswyth, we must build a new life here. Will you help me?"

Elswyth's scowl clearly said that she did not want a new life. She wanted her old life, the life that was smashed and gone forever. Her noble father, whom she had rarely seen, and her brother, whom she adored, lay dead at Hastings. All that remained of her former life was this small band of refugees fleeing the Conqueror's violence with Edgar Aethling. And all that remained of Saxon hopes for the throne was that slouching boy who sat beside the skirts of his mother, the sharp-featured, scowling Princess Agatha.

What she would do without Margaret, Elswyth could not imagine. And yet the pale gold girl whom she had known since earliest childhood in the convent school was perhaps the most lost to her of all. It was not just Margaret's incomprehensible decision to marry this great oaf of a Scottish king, who looked more like bear than man with his thick red black hair and beard emphasizing the size of his enormous head and a leather tunic and heavy cloak adding to the size of his body. Elswyth had not been close enough to find out, but she was certain he must smell as bad as a bear too.

No, it wasn't Margaret's decision to marry that separated them. It was her serenity. Always that great calm had been Margaret's chief trait, the one that most drew people to her, the one on which Elswyth most relied when the world was too difficult. But now Margaret had changed.

Still, the change was not in Margaret but in herself. For now Elswyth did not find Margaret's composure a restful thing. Now it angered her. How could anyone be so serene when the whole world had fallen apart? When she was to wed a barbarian?

Yet at the same time Elswyth was annoyed by Margaret's serenity, she desperately coveted such peace for herself. Certain she was that she would never find it in this rough land.

But she must do her best. She sighed, and her scowl changed to resigned determination. "Help you, my lady? Of course I will. I will plait your hair with golden ribbons. I will embroider your finest kirtle with gold and silk. And your red leather shoes I will gloss with sheep's fat. I will help you show these ruffians what Saxon refinement is."

The furrows in Margaret's brow eased, and her face relaxed into its perfect oval as she gave a chuckle of laughter at Elswyth's fervor. "Yes, we shall set this Celtic court an example they won't soon forget. I have no doubt of your being the finest help in such matters, Elswyth. But I meant, will you help me in the greater matters too?"

"Greater matters?"

Margaret's laughter died. She took Elswyth's hand with a sigh. "There is so much to be done. Have you not observed—"

"Certainly I have observed. How could I help not? I have observed dirt, poverty, ignorance, ill manners, irreligion. That is why—"

"No, no more of your objections. Think only of the good there is to be done: to clean the dirty, to feed the hungry, to inform the ignorant, to reform manners. To Christianize the Christianity."

"Can these Celts be capable of such reform? Or worth it?"

Now Margaret's voice lost its earlier hesitancy. She spoke with a ring of conviction. "Certainly they are worth our all—for they are God's creation. And certainly they are capable—for they were created in His image. But think not only of the Scots. Think of what we can do for our own Saxons here."

"You mean at court?"

"I mean in Scotland. Have you not noticed those doing the heaviest labor in the fields? The most menial tasks at court? Their straw-pale hair alone should tell you they are Saxon."

"Yes." Elswyth nodded slowly. "I saw but did not think of it. All the slaves seem to be so."

Margaret tightened her grasp of Elswyth's hands. "Yes, that is so. Simple peasants carried off from their farmsteads and villages as booty of the incessant border wars. All Northumbria is red and black with blood and burning. We must work to free the slaves and to prevent more war."

Elswyth shook her head, and the thick golden brown braid bobbed on her dark green kirtle like a patch of sun through the thick foliage around them. "We are but weak women."

Margaret rose. "Ah, therein lies our power, Elswyth." Now her smile was brilliant. "And Malcolm is none so unreasonable nor so ill-favored a man. And he does not smell—much."

She led the way back across the glen to the clutter of wood and wattle buildings that comprised Malcolm's castle.

33

Two weeks later, at as near to high noon as anyone could judge through the leaden clouds, Princess Margaret stood in her room in the tower of Malcolm's hall house, robed and ready to become wife of Malcolm III of Scotland.

Only minutes before, Elswyth had taken the final stitches in the gold and silk embroidery worked over the heavy padding that made both hem and sleeves of the bride's blue kirtle bell out to display its fine silk lining. Elswyth adjusted the folds of her lady's long scarlet cloak, then placed a fine silk veil over Margaret's pale, gold-bound hair, giving the effect of moonlight shining on a casket of jewels. Margaret's serene, grave beauty had never shone more truly.

Elswyth was indeed happy with the results of her labors. But she was not happy about the ceremony before them. "But my lady, is there no better place for you to be wed? Such a building would not have been used to stable cattle at the court of your Uncle Edward."

"Elswyth." Margaret spoke sharply. "The Culdee church is small, but it is holy. Men have worshiped God and served our Lord on this spot for near to five hundred years. Did not even our Lord preach on a hillside?"

"Well, yes, but—"

"I shall be truly married by Mother Church—my dear Father Turgot shall see to all."

"Yes, but the other—"

"Elswyth, I will hear no more. Abbot Melmore of Saint Andrews is a holy man of God. It is true there is much error in the Columban church, but—"

In the strength of her feeling Elswyth interrupted the princess. "Error? You would call false religion *error?* The tonsure, the celebration of Easter, the celebration of the Eucharist . . . you would tolerate—"

The gold bands at Margaret's wrist clinked as she stepped forward. "Enough. Tolerance of evil is evil. But reconciliation between

322

those reconciled to God is a foretaste of heaven. Can you not discern the difference, Elswyth? Will you not witness for me even now?"

Elswyth bit her full lower lip, revealing a square jaw under her softly rounded cheeks. "I cannot pretend to your goodness and piety, my lady. I will stand for you. But I will not stand beside that Iain mac Euan. Such would be a foretaste not of heaven but of a quite different place. I am told that Malcolm's captain was often the one to carry wine to Ingeborge. I will not stand by a poisoner."

Margaret laughed. "I despair of you, Elswyth. How can I hope to teach these Scots anything when I cannot teach my own ladies? But there is no need for you to stand by Malcolm's captain. You can witness as well standing at the other end of the altar. Come now."

The little Culdee church near Malcolm's hall house—the royal residence could hardly be called a palace—had stood on the hill at the edge of this glen for centuries. In all that time the Culdee brotherhood had lived and worshiped and helped the poor in a manner worthy of their name, "Friends of God." But it was true that of late years much of the fervor had gone out of worship in the land, and the increased number of poor from the nation's almost incessant warring had much dimmed the monks' achievements.

And none was more aware of the shortcomings around her than Elswyth. But she could see that she was not the only one in the small company squeezed inside the dim little church who disapproved of the proceedings. Agatha, princess of Hungary, sat proud and stiff beside Edgar on the front bench. Her sharp dark eyes snapped beneath the whiteness of her fine silk veil—held in place by a band of gold around her forehead lest any might forget that she was daughter of royal blood and mother of the rightful heir to the throne of England.

Edgar slumped beside his mother, doing ill justice to his deep red plush tunic. In spite of the numerous gold rings adorning his fingers and the heavy chain around his neck, he showed little of royal blood in his veins and little of the happiness he might be expected to feel at his sister's wedding.

Elswyth had to admit that, in spite of their disgusting half-moon tonsures and the coarseness of their nut-dyed robes, the Culdee brothers did an exceptionally lovely job of chanting the Psalms. Their soft Scottish voices seemed perfectly suited for the task.

"Happy the man who fears the Lord, His posterity shall be mighty upon the earth; wealth and riches shall be in his house, lavishly he gives to the poor, His generosity shall endure forever."

Elswyth smiled. Malcolm had no idea how lavishly he would

give to the poor if Margaret had her way. And Elswyth suspected that Margaret would have her way.

Then a stir at the rear of the church caused Elswyth to turn, and she looked back at the most handsome man she had ever seen. He was taller and straighter than any other man around, with broad shoulders and narrow hips that made his rough tunic and gold and russet plaid cloak look finer than the cloth of gold and red brocade so favored by courtiers at the English court. And she had never seen such hair. Like the sun sparkling on a riffled pool, the silver coils framed a square-jawed face alive with deep-set dark eyes and a broad mouth. How she would like to see that mouth smile.

She had determined not to speak to Malcolm's annoying captain but found him next to her. She decided to ask the dark-haired young man with the provocatively snapping eyes. "Who is he?" she whispered under the continuing chant and nodded toward the newcomer.

Iain looked in the direction Elswyth indicated. "Liulf Thorfinnson." He turned sharply back to the altar.

Elswyth blinked. Liulf Thorfinnson? This was Liulf, the thane who had reportedly objected so strenuously in council to the marriage of Malcolm and Margaret? He who had accused the king of murder? Surely, by his presence here Liulf was signaling that he had put away his objections. But his face did not soften as the brothers continued.

"Happy the man who fears the Lord; his wife shall be like a fruitful vine, his children like olive plants around his table. His posterity shall be mighty upon the earth."

Elswyth scanned the church. Malcolm's children by Ingeborge were not here. The girls had returned to Norway. But Duncan, who would soon come on manhood, should have been here.

Then her attention was called back to the marriage ceremony by the serving of Communion. At least that was done properly. Father Turgot, who had chosen to go into exile with them so that he could remain as Margaret's spiritual adviser, was a true son of the Roman Church, one trained in the Clunaic tradition and having served at Durham.

"Christ loved His church and sacrificed Himself for her so that she could become like a holy and untouchable bride." The properly tonsured priest in his splendid robes and pure white stole offered the wafer to the marriage couple. Then he elevated the wine and partook for them.

Elswyth relaxed to see things being done the right way. Then Abbot Melmore stepped forward to pronounce the nuptial blessing.

Elswyth turned her eyes from the offensive spectacle of a married priest.

> "The guarding of the God of life be on you,
> The guiding of our loving Christ be on you,
> The blessing of the Holy Spirit be on you.
> The love and affection of heaven be to you,
>   each day and night of your lives.
> The Lord of all keep you from haters,
>   keep you from all harmers,
>   keep you from oppressors."

Elswyth obediently crossed herself, but she would not look up. "Just such a prayer as one would expect from a heretic," she muttered, not entirely under her breath. About the church she could see smiles and head nodding, and all around she heard sighs and whispers. These exuberant Scots seemed to think this was an occasion for celebrating rather than a solemn sacrament. And then she saw Iain mac Euan's taunting smile.

"You would nae begrudge a prayer of the holy Columba in a church of his own establishment?"

"I do not begrudge any man's prayer. No doubt the spirit was sincere. But unpoetical is unpoetical."

It was unlikely that Iain heard her, however, as at that moment he stepped to the altar and stood beside Malcolm. The younger man was almost as tall as his king, but in spite of the broad shoulders beneath his light blue tunic topped with green and gold plaid, he was built on much slimmer lines.

Elswyth drew back with a frown when she saw Iain withdraw an object from the folds of his plaid and hand it to Abbot Melmore. It was a silver casket shaped like a little house. What new profanation were they about to commit?

Abbot Melmore took the casket, and its enameled designs sparkled as he lifted the lid and drew out a vial of oil. He handed the reliquary back to Iain and unstoppered the vial.

Her hands folded in devotion, light from the altar candlesticks playing on her silver gold hair, Margaret knelt. Malcolm stepped back, his brilliant red and green plaid slipping into the shadows, leaving Margaret alone in the center before the highest churchman in Scotland.

"Margaret, you have this day vowed before God and these witnesses to become true and loving wife to Malcolm mac Duncan mac Crinan mac Malcolm mac Kenneth."

"I have." Margaret's voice, always musical, took on a special vibrancy in the little church. Even the most demonstrative of the wedding guests were silenced.

"Do you now vow before God and these same witnesses to become true and loving queen to King Malcolm and to the people of Scotland?"

"I so vow."

"Do you promise to serve your king and your people in love and in justice as the King of heaven so loves you?"

"I do promise. So long as God gives me breath."

"Then, as the prophet Samuel first anointed King Saul, and as our beloved Saint Columba so anointed Kenneth mac Alpin mac Gabhran mac Fergus mac Erc with holy chrism from Columba's own Becbrennoch, I anoint you, Margaret, queen of Scots."

Abbot Melmore poured the amber drops over Margaret's head. Each droplet caught a flicker of candlelight and fell like a tongue of fire. The sweet fragrance of spices filled the chapel.

Malcolm stepped forward, beaming. He raised his bride and queen while the Culdees chanted, "Fill us with Your love, O Lord, and we will sing for joy all our days. May the goodness of the Lord be upon us. May the Lord give success to the work of our hands."

The marriage couple led the way out to the courtyard of Malcolm's dun, where trestle tables covered the open grassy spaces between all the buildings. Hugh, the seneschal, gave the signal as they emerged from the church, and a great wailing and blaring of pipes accompanied the procession as all those gathered inside the stockaded wall of the dun cheered.

Margaret smiled to those on every side as Hugh conducted them to the high table set under a green and gold striped canopy in front of the hall house.

But Margaret refused the seat offered her.

"I pray you, not yet, husband." She turned to Malcolm and placed a hand on his arm. "We must begin as we intend to go on. Fresh come as I am from my vows to show love and mercy to all our people, I beg your indulgence."

Malcolm's broad smile above his dark rust beard lit his eyes and clearly showed that he would not be likely to refuse his queen any indulgence. "As you wish."

"Then let the gate be open that all those beyond the wall who have gathered to wish us well on our wedding day might come in and share our bounty."

Elswyth turned with all those within range of Margaret's voice. Standing on an incline as they were, they could see over the wall to some of the throng gathered in the fields. One hundred at least, undoubtedly more, and when the word spread that Malcolm had opened the gates to his wedding feast . . .

"Aye, you're a kindhearted lass, Margaret. But so many mouths . . ."

Margaret nodded toward the six spits beyond the castle cook house where whole oxen roasting on the turnspits dripped fat into the flames. "If some must refuse a third portion that others might have a first, so be it. You would not want it rumored that the king of Scots kept a meager table."

Malcolm nodded.

Hugh hurried off to give the order.

A train of servers passed near the king, bearing platters heaped with roast geese, baskets of fresh-baked loaves, and pots of honey.

"Aye. Now let's eat." Malcolm's hearty cry was accompanied by cheers of agreement from the courtiers around them.

"But my lord, forgive me, but surely the Scripture calling us to servanthood in the manner of our Lord Jesus is clear"—Margaret's smile was as gentle as her words—"as are the customs of hospitality in this land known for its graciousness."

Elswyth blinked. This was the first she had heard that word applied to their new land.

It appeared to be a new concept to Malcolm as well. He regarded Margaret with caution. "I'm hungry, lass."

"As is fitting, is it not? Since the poor of our land are also hungry." She turned to the abbot. "Father Melmore, surely you know your flock best. Bring to me six of your poorest." Then she turned to her waiting-lady. "Elswyth, a basin of warm water with a linen towel." She paused and regarded Malcolm. "Two towels, and my best lemon herb soap."

Elswyth bobbed a curtsy before turning to issue orders, more sharply than necessity required, that Margaret's latest whim be obeyed. By the time she returned, Father Melmore had six beggars assembled on low stools in front of the high table, and Margaret was removing her scarlet cloak. She took one of the towels and bound it around her waist. She handed the other towel to Malcolm.

He held it between two fingers at arm's length.

Iain stepped up and took it from his hand. "If I might be of service?" The captain's black eyes shone with merriment, and Elswyth was certain she saw a barely suppressed smile on his lips as he pulled Malcolm's flowing cloak back from his shoulders. Although an ample length of linen, the towel could not be tied around Malcolm's more ample middle, so the captain merely tucked it in the gold-studded leather belt that strapped the king's long saffron tunic.

Malcolm was still standing rooted to the spot, so Iain gave him a helpful shove on the shoulder. "The one to the left looks as if he'd spent a wee bit less time dunging the fields."

Margaret was already applying her lemon-scented soap to the second of the stunned ragged paupers before her. This, an old woman who, even while sitting, leaned heavily on the gnarled stick she carried. Margaret took infinite care over the grandmother's mud-caked, work-hardened feet, talking to her in a gentle voice as she worked, inquiring about her family and her living conditions. The fact that the crone was missing several front teeth made her replies difficult to understand.

Margaret then turned to a small boy, who had a nasty sore on his ankle. "Maethilda—" she addressed another of her waiting-ladies "—I will need ointment and bandages."

Maethilda scurried toward the hall house.

Behind them the crowd was becoming restless. None seemed to feel obliged to suppress their impatience or desire for food and drink simply because they were being kept from it by their new queen. Elswyth worried. She knew Margaret meant well. Margaret always meant well. But now even Princess Agatha was scowling at her daughter. And Edgar complained loudly that the meats were cooling rapidly.

Elswyth's frown deepened when she looked at Iain. In the whole company of several hundred observers he seemed to be the only one enjoying himself. He now made no attempt to suppress his broad smile as he pulled the abbot of St. Andrews forward. "Father, will you not take this opportunity to say a wee word to your flock?"

The abbot looked up, either for guidance or to ascertain the likelihood of their all receiving a washing of the rainwater the dark clouds undoubtedly held. He cleared his throat and spread his arms to command the attention of those who would listen. "The Lord Jesus, when He had eaten, poured water into a basin and began to wash His disciples' feet, saying, 'This example I leave you.'"

Maethilda returned and offered to bind the child's running sore. But Margaret insisted on performing the task herself.

Malcolm was still struggling with the chore of cleaning the feet of the simpleminded cowherd seated before him.

"If I, your Lord and teacher, have washed your feet, then surely you must wash one another's feet." Melmore paused and looked at the circle of beggars. He drew a deep breath and declaimed more loudly than before. "If there is love among you, all will know that you are My disciples. I give you a new commandment: Love one another as I have loved you."

He stopped and looked around, somewhat desperately, for help. Father Turgot came forward. "Faith, hope, and love. Let these endure among you. But the greatest of these is love."

The two priests drew breath and nodded at each other as Margaret and Malcolm rose and handed their soiled towels to a servant.

"Now." Malcolm grabbed Margaret's arm none too gently and turned toward the table.

But Margaret knew her own mind. And indeed, she was starting out as she meant to go on. Her small, red-leather-shod feet stood their ground. "My lord king, is it not a shame on so great a kingdom as Scotland that some who come to do honor to their king by partaking in his marriage feast must shiver, ragged in this fine, crisp northern air?" She picked up the long, scarlet cloak she had laid aside before the foot-washing ceremony and placed it around the bowed shoulders of the old grandmother. Without a word she looked at the ring of courtiers around her, smiling confidently.

Iain, returning her smile, reached to undo the large gold brooch holding his green and gold plaid cloak to his shoulder. "Will you bestow it on the most worthy for me, my lady?"

"We are all unworthy," Margaret said softly. "But I thank you, Iain. Has not your captain set a fine example, Malcolm?"

Malcolm glared at Iain. "Aye." It came from between gritted teeth as Malcolm removed his own cloak. He little more than threw it at the nearest beggar, then turned to his men. "Be quick about it, men, before the food's turned to stone."

In a sudden rush, the mormaors, thanes, and sheriffs of Scotland all vied with one another to bestow their cloaks upon the most ragged of the assemblage. In the end, since there were far more nobility there than peasants, many of those who stood farther from the proceedings simply ended up exchanging cloaks.

"May we eat now, Margaret?" Malcolm thundered, his russet brows looking almost black under his scowl.

"Why, of course, my lord." Margaret gave him her brightest smile. "My husband the king must be fed whenever he desires. It is only right."

But instead of taking Malcolm's arm to be led to the high table, she turned to help forward the oldest of the beggars, an ancient man with a gray beard hanging to his waist. Her other hand she held out to the boy with the sore foot. "Come. Our king bids us eat. We must not delay."

Liulf and several of the nobles started toward the high table at her words. By the time Margaret reached the table with her poor, the nobility stood in order behind their seats.

"Is it not a blessed thing, my lords, that our Lord Jesus Christ has promised that the last shall be first? It bodes well for our own placement in His kingdom, does it not? Poor unworthy sinners that we are." Still smiling gently, she seated the ancient grandfather in Liulf Thorfinnson's seat.

Iain strode forward to escort the crippled crone to his place and insisted on filling her goblet from the jar of Frankish wine on the table. "Aye, it's certain the new queen of the Scots knows how to throw a fine feast." He bowed deeply before turning with a jaunty air to seek a seat among the muddle of tables spread across the dun yard.

A considerable time later, after all the scramble the reseating of the high table caused, Elswyth found herself seated near Liulf at a table before the falconer's hut. She bit ravenously into a wheaten loaf, not caring in the least that Edgar's warning had long ago come to pass and the food was chilled. Then she looked up. If there were any other seats to be found in all the castle yard, she would have moved. She did not wish to talk to Iain mac Euan. She turned sharply from his dancing black eyes to speak to Liulf.

But Iain would have speech with her. He leaned across the table with a broad smile. "*Och,* that was the finest play of power I have ever seen. Before today I would have taken any wager offered me that Malcolm couldna be tamed by any woman. But here now she has done it in the space of three hours—before even he has bedded her."

Elswyth flushed hot, whether in maidenly embarrassment or in defense of her queen she wasn't sure, but there could be no turning away from this challenge. "That was no power play, I assure you, sir. Margaret is most sincere."

"Of course she is. That is what made it so fine. It wouldna have worked had her devotion not been pure."

Elswyth nodded. "Margaret would have made a fine nun."

Iain's humor that always seemed just below the surface broke out in a laugh. "Never! Abbess maybe—pope, if she were a man. But never a mere nun."

But Elswyth would not be turned from the topic of ambitions. "Yet I wonder at your motives. It seemed you were always the first to follow her lead. Is your devotion also pure, Iain mac Euan?"

For the first time something more than humor flashed in his eyes, but Elswyth could not tell what it was. Pride? Ambition? Or perhaps it was a form of devotion. But to what?

"Aye, I'm devout." He took a deep drink of heather ale and wiped his mouth on his sleeve. When he looked up, the humor was back in his eyes. "Is it not the job of a captain to show his king the way when he is in need of a wee nudge? But for the most part I was enjoying myself. Is that not the Saxon way? To enjoy yourself at a wedding?"

Elswyth would have liked to return a sharp reply, but she could think of none. She did not know the answer. Humor, enjoyment seemed strange motivators. Ever since her mother died when she was seven years old and her father had sent her to be educated at the court of Edward the Confessor with the newly arrived Aethlings, the models in her life had been King Edward, who was more monk than king, the holy sisters who had guided her education, and the princesses Margaret and Christina. Had their lives not been torn apart by Norman William, Elswyth would undoubtedly have taken the veil as Christina did. And there she might have found the tranquillity that always escaped her and seemed so impossibly far away in this Scotland.

Now she had taken vows of quite another sort, and it was clear that helping Margaret civilize this land would be no light task. At least the flaxen-haired Liulf Thorfinnson had better manners than most.

She turned to him. "I have heard you called thane of Slaley. Where is this Slaley?"

"In Northumbria, mistress, below Hexam. When Malcolm retook the land from the English seven years ago, he bestowed the lands and title on his wife's youngest brother."

Elswyth thought Liulf put just the slightest emphasis on the word wife. Then she followed his gaze as it fell on Edgar, slumped over his wine goblet at a table beyond theirs.

Liulf held his ale mug between both hands and looked deep into its contents. "Slaley is a small manor but one with fine forest and dale before it reaches the broad moorland. I would keep my lands against the Normans. And I think you have as little cause to love them as do I." It was a statement, yet he paused as if expecting an answer.

"Normans killed my father and brother at Hastings. Normans drove me from my home."

He gave a sharp nod. "So. As I thought. And I think there are perhaps others we share no overfondness for." He looked at Iain across the table, laughing with those sitting on both sides of him. When Elswyth didn't answer, Liulf continued. "Beware of that one. He is too ready to do the queen's bidding."

331

Liulf cut a bite of roast boar and ate it off the tip of his knife rather than picking up the whole joint as most did. He followed that with a chunk of cheese and a drink of ale, then returned to his topic. "It is in my mind that you would have your land freed of Normans that you might return there?"

Elswyth let the full force of her homesickness show in her solemn head nodding.

"And so, no doubt, would Edgar Aethling. I have no little influence with my uncles the lords of Orkney. The Saxon prince will have need of such friends if he is to gain his throne. Tell him I would have speech with him soon."

Elswyth nodded again. She would have liked to ask Liulf the same question she put to Iain. What was his purpose? To hold his lands against the Normans, assuredly, but was that reason to support Edgar's cause? What of his accusations that his sister had been murdered to make room for Margaret at Malcolm's side? If he still believed that, would he be likely to support Margaret's brother?

The rain that had begun to fall from the leaden sky did not chill Elswyth near so much as the sense of danger around her. She must warn Margaret. Dear Margaret, who loved everyone, would expect everyone to be as good and loving as she. Elswyth could see there were pitfalls she had held no idea of when she vowed to help Margaret—dangers for which nothing in Sister Magdalena's careful teaching had prepared either of them.

34

The trill of the harvest thrush was first to penetrate her consciousness, then the sounds of uncommon stirring in the yard below the tower. Elswyth threw a shawl around her shoulders and hurried to the tiny window of her room just off Margaret's.

Following her wedding last spring, Margaret had taken one look at the chamber that had been Ingeborge's and declared it unlivable. Malcolm had forthwith ordered another floor added to the tower at the end of his hall house. With the single-minded drive with which she did everything, Margaret had taken full delight in furnishing it with the finest tapestries, silk cushions, and gold candlesticks.

When someone at court had been so outspoken as to express surprise that one so devoted to the poor should spend so much money and effort on worldly finery, Margaret had met the objection head-on. She spoke in a voice that reached not only her detractor but all dining in Malcolm's hall as well. "Wanton ugliness is a form of evil. God created beauty and order. We mock Him when we destroy His beauty or do less than our best to foster beauty around us." There had been no more objections.

Now Elswyth pushed aside the damask hanging and leaned out the window. Sparks flew from the grindstone at the blacksmith's as, one after another, the drengs and bonders held their long-bladed scythes to it. Heavy-footed sumpter horses stamped and shook their harness as they were hitched to wagons. Everywhere women shooed chickens, geese, and children. All activity in the castle yard and the fields beyond prepared for the harvest.

But those were not the sounds Elswyth had heard. She drew in her head. There it was again. How could she not have recognized it at first? She grabbed her wash basin, a pitcher of water, and a clean towel. She entered Margaret's room none too soon with the services of a clean basin and a cool, damp cloth. There was little she could do but hold Margaret's head until the violent spasms passed.

At last Margaret looked up, pale and shaken.

"What is it, my lady?" But even before she asked, Elswyth feared the answer. She grabbed the goblet by Margaret's bed and sniffed its contents. "The wine. What have you drunk? From whose hand? Did you eat oysters last night? I have heard it is possible . . ."

The queen pushed feebly at Elswyth's hand, still wiping her face. "No, no, my dear Elswyth. I have not been poisoned."

"But my lady, you cannot be sure. There are rumors . . ."

"Elswyth. It is not poison. I know."

"Then you are sick, my lady. I shall call the Culdee brother Donal? He has a fine reputation as herbalist."

"No, Elswyth." Margaret grasped her hand. "Can you not guess?"

Elswyth's eyes widened. "Oh. Oh, praises be. You are certain?"

"Yes. I have told my mother also. She says the sickness will mostlike pass quickly. It was so with her. I pray it will." Margaret shook her head.

"Then you have not told the king yet?"

"No. He has been so busy. His brother Donald Bane and the northern mormaors continue to make trouble. And William threatens war to the south. I will choose the right time." She went to the carved chest against the wall and took out a clean shift and a russet kirtle. "Help me dress, Elswyth. I must feed my poor."

"Surely there are those who can see to that for you."

"Yes, of course. I know it is selfish of me to want to keep the joy of such service for myself. But just these twenty-four are special to me." She smiled.

Elswyth picked up a bone comb and began working through Margaret's long tresses, the color of the ripe barley. "You must be so pleased, my lady. You have been queen less than half a year, and yet already you have done so much. Hundreds of poor regularly receive food and clothing now. And the manners of the court are much improved."

But Elswyth's speech, meant to encourage, seemed to depress Margaret. "Yes, the time passes so fast, and there is so much to accomplish. So much I have not begun on. And every day I delay, someone suffers more. Sometimes I don't know how I shall bear the responsibility, Elswyth." She tucked her white linen veil tight across her forehead, then draped its long ends gracefully over each shoulder and across the neckline of her kirtle. "But I must not wallow in the sin of self-indulgence by counting my failures. After mass you will ride out with me to observe the harvest. We will see what may be done for the people there."

Elswyth agreed readily to the ride, but she did not join Margaret at Father Turgot's mass. Instead she hastily drew her green cloak around her shoulders and ran toward the glen. She did not give herself time to think, for she had decided. And Margaret's news made what she would do all the more important. She assured herself for the hundredth time that she was betraying no one by agreeing to work in secret for the cause of both England and Scotland. And Margaret would thank her for her efforts. Certainly she would tell Margaret all as soon as the plans were made. For the moment there was no need to worry the queen.

Unlike the tender spring green of the trees, mosses, and ferns that filled the glen when Elswyth had found Margaret beside Pittencrief burn the day she decided to marry Malcolm, the steep hills on both sides of the valley today were a blaze of red, russet, and gold. Mice scampered from her feet as she hurried down the path, and squirrels scurried along branches overhead.

He was sitting on a rock very near the one where Margaret had sat, his brown tunic, leather jerkin, and yellow hair blending perfectly with the foliage.

"So you have come. I thought you had changed your mind."

"Of course I came. I told you I would. My duties with the queen took longer today. That is all."

"And how is the fair Margaret?"

"She is well. She is at her prayers."

"Ah, yes. When is she ever not? It is good that she has those around her willing to take more practical action, Elswyth." Liulf reached for her hand.

She drew back. "I do not like these hole-in-a-corner meetings, Liulf. Our cause is right. We should speak freely."

"As we will soon, truly. But the Scriptures admonish us to be wise as serpents and harmless as doves."

"That is what troubles me. Is making war, even in a just cause, being harmless as doves? I know that is what Margaret will ask. She is staunch for her brother's rights, but she abhors war."

Liulf's smile was more of a sneer. "Have you heard nothing I have tried to say to you? It is war we will prevent. Malcolm does nothing. Someone must act."

"He will, but now there is trouble in Northumbria."

"Exactly. And it is rightful that he should see to his own kingdom. Let those with the most to gain by Edgar's establishment see to this matter. You would see your father's death avenged?"

Elswyth nodded.

"You would see England free of these upstart Norman overlords?"

She nodded with more certainty.

"You would see Edgar on his throne so you could return to your home?"

Now the nod was accompanied with a smile. She even let him keep her hand when he grasped it warmly.

"Then gain Margaret's trust for me. Malcolm will send me as envoy to the disaffected Saxon lords if she asks. Although allied with those of power, I am but a thane. But if I take Duncan mac Malcolm with me, my words will have authority. Do you not agree that it would be best for the English to overthrow William themselves? Then with Edgar on the throne of England and Dunc—that is, the rightful heritage established in both lands, we shall be secure."

"Yes. I agree that would be best. I will speak to Margaret."

"When?"

"Today if I can. We are to ride out to observe the harvest this morning. It is likely I might get a chance then." She pulled her hand from his as she rose and brushed bits of brown moss from her skirt. "I must hurry. Mass will be ended soon."

The ride was delayed, however, for Father Turgot had no more than admonished his tiny congregation to depart in peace than Princess Agatha and Edgar Aethling confronted Margaret.

"We have been in this barbaric land for almost a year now, and there has been no support raised for your brother, Margaret. I thought surely, once you were established as queen, something of purpose might be accomplished."

"If you spent one-half so much money or effort on my cause as you do on your wretched poor, sister, I might be sitting in comfort in Winchester now instead of abiding in rooms more fit for a monk."

"Mother, Edgar, I do not forget the Saxon cause. Indeed, I have spoken to Malcolm repeatedly, and he is in complete agreement with us as to the right of Edgar's claim to the throne. But there are many claims on the king's attention. The earl of Moray and his thanes are much in revolt over Malcolm's call for troops to defend his Northumbrian lands."

"Northumbria? What good is that? What of raising an army to march to London?" Edgar stuck out his lower lip.

"I am doing all I can, Edgar. Do not think I forget your cause."

"Well, see that you don't. I certainly can't see that much has been accomplished."

When Margaret turned away from her family, Elswyth spoke. "Have you given thought to Liulf Thorfinnson's offer to aid Edgar?"

Margaret tucked in the corners of her mouth in a thoughtful manner. "I have thought. But I cannot like Liulf."

"But surely, if he is willing to offer aid . . ."

"We shall see." Margaret turned at an approaching footstep. "Ah, Iain. Are the horses ready?"

The horses were ready, and a short time later Margaret, at the head of a group of some dozen ladies and courtiers, rode from Dunfermline across the rolling land where the field strips of every farmstead were alive with the activities of reaping and in-gathering. Across the countryside the land lay like the bracelets on the arm of the queen, silver strips of barley alternating with the gold of ripe oats.

Elswyth gave particular attention to a strip close by, where the husbandman in a bark-brown tunic gathered oats with his left arm and cut them with a rhythmic swing of the curved blade in his right. The swooping and swinging pattern continued in perfect cadence to the end of the strip.

Behind the reaper, his wife, in an ocher kirtle, kilted to her knees, white kerchief slipped to the back of her head, gathered armfuls of golden stalks and placed them in a high-sided, two-wheeled wagon pulled by a patient ox.

The workers had a sunny day for their labors. Bees buzzed in the thick clover by the roadside. Horses' harness jangled like bells. Even the quiet Maethilda laughed at a gentle jest from one of the thanes.

Elswyth looked at the blue fringe of mountains beyond the fields. This Scotland was a beautiful country. In some way its ruggedness made it more appealing than her native land.

And—she looked at the riders in their party—not all the inhabitants were as barbaric as she had at first thought. At least not since Margaret had shown them better dress by giving Malcolm finer tunics to set an example. And she was learning what true hearts some had. Such as Liulf, who would take on himself an ambassador's job from sheer patriotism.

Or even Iain, whose manners were none so bad, even though he refused to add gold braid or silk trim to his wine-colored tunic. He observed her looking at him now. She turned away. But not before she saw his saucy smile.

And then the attention of the whole company was turned to a group of children who had been gleaning, catching up the grain their elders missed and adding it to the mounds in the wagons.

The oldest girl, wearing a white apron over her blue kirtle, her long red hair bouncing unbound around her shoulders, was the first to look up and cry out, "Oh, look! What fine ladies and gentlemen." She grabbed the hand of the small boy in an ivory smock who toddled beside her.

The children at first hung back when they realized the fine lady sitting on the white palfrey at the head of the party was the queen, but they soon drew forward, laughing and clapping when Margaret encouraged them with a few friendly words. In a moment the riders were surrounded by a flock of smiling smudged faces.

"I will dismount," she said. The always attentive Iain was quickest to slip from his horse and help her down, then hold her bridle as she moved among the children. She opened the purse she wore at her belt and sent the boys and girls running back to the fields with coins pressed into their hands.

The party moved forward, and Elswyth found herself riding beside Liulf. She would have been happy to talk to him of light matters, but it seemed he was not one for frivolities like some. "Have you spoken to her yet?"

"You can see there's been no opportunity. Why do you not speak yourself?"

"I will when you have prepared the way. I cannot but feel that Margaret has no love for me. I am never as quick to foresee her wishes as that Iain mac Euan. He is a clever one, that. As wily as his father."

Elswyth raised her eyebrows in question.

"Aye." Liulf nodded, a sour expression on his face. "The mormaor of Perthshire. Did you not know? One who wields much influence with Malcolm—and not always to the good, to my thinking."

A few paces along, Iain fell back to ride at Elswyth's other side. "A fine-favored day we have, is it not?"

"And some are quick enough to add to their own favor. It seems the peasants and landowners are not the only ones who would make hay today."

He showed confusion at her sharp tone. "My lady, if I have offended—"

Elswyth laughed. "Never fear. Your worst enemy could never accuse you of willingly giving offense."

"And what would my worst enemy accuse me of?"

She wondered if he glanced at Liulf. "Surely, sir, you can have no enemies. Who would be enemies at court?"

He started to reply, but Margaret had again stopped, this time to observe the threshers at work. In a hollow where tracks from a number of field strips came together, several wide circles of hard-packed earth served as threshing floors. Carts piled high with grain lumbered forward to have their sheaves carried to the circles, where grain, straw, and chaff were separated.

In the nearest circle a young man in a ragged tunic, with hair as pale as the barley, wielded a lengthy pole from which a leather thong held a long flat flail. He repeatedly beat at the stalks by flinging the stick forward and then back over his shoulder, but he seemed to be producing little results no matter how the muscles of his arms strained with the effort. Sweat stood out on his brow and ran into his eyes, but the flail flopped lopsidedly, and the sheaves of barley seemed to slither in every direction.

Disaster came when a small dog, which had been rooting in the straw, bounded into the circle after a grasshopper. The thresher pulled back his pole sharply to avoid hitting the dog. The flail struck the harvester behind him instead.

The crack of the overseer's whip fell across the thresher's shoulders before Elswyth fully realized what had happened. The black lash snapped again. And again. The third stroke knocked the slave to the ground, but the blows did not slacken. A blotch of red showed through a rip in his tunic.

The beating likely would have gone on until the slave lay senseless had not Margaret ridden forward with a sharp cry. Her party had halted in the shade of a small spinney—doubtless the overseer did not realize he was being observed by nobility, though it was unlikely that such knowledge would have softened his blows much.

"Stop! Do not beat that man!"

The overseer started as if the lash had fallen across his own shoulders. "What! Eh? Who bids me not beat my own slave?"

"Margaret, queen of Scots, bids you, dreng," Iain shouted in as harsh a voice as Elswyth had ever heard him use.

In a flurry of movement, the man dropped his whip, dipped a bow, and reached up to pull off a cap he wasn't wearing. "My lady queen, I bid you welcome to my poor farm. I apologize for offending your eyes by chastising my slave before you."

Behind him the thresher struggled to his knees.

"But if I had not been here you would have beaten him senseless with no apologies made?"

"He is hopeless, madam. My ox is a better worker than this Ebert."

At the mention of the slave's Saxon name, Elswyth turned to Liulf. "The queen will be much upset. She has long had the cause of the Saxon slaves on her heart."

"Understandable, as they are her own people. But it is hard to see what she can do. It is the way of things. The man is no harder on his slave than he would be on his ox or his wife."

"Will the overseer beat him harder when we leave?"

339

Liulf shrugged. "Of course, for now he has been shamed before the queen."

"Couldn't Margaret order him not to?"

Another shrug. "She could try. But the man is a dreng—one of the free, property-owning class. Not even the king can tell a free Scotsman how to treat his own freeheld property."

"Margaret would free all slaves if she could."

Liulf laughed at this. "And I would give her the moon if I could."

"Could not she order them freed?"

"I told you. Not even the king can take away a freeman's property—so long as he pays his taxes, of course. And if she could, there would just be more captured when next Malcolm wars across the border."

"Not if Margaret persuades Malcolm otherwise."

Liulf's sneering smile showed how little she understood of men's ways.

It seemed Margaret understood, however. She reached for her purse. But she had emptied it for the children. She pulled off one of her gold bracelets as if she would offer it instead, but Iain stopped her with a hand over hers. "It is too much. Let me." He drew three coins from his own purse and handed them to the owner with a few words.

The man bit each coin, then tucked them in a pouch inside his tunic. He hooked a hand under Ebert's arm and thrust him to his feet. "It's well rid of you I am. See you serve the queen better than you did me, or she'll cut your thievin' Saxon hands off." With a final bow to the queen, the dreng turned to right the chaos that his threshing circle had become.

"You are called Ebert?" Margaret spoke to the man who stood dazed at her feet.

"Sa. I am. My lady, I thank you . . ."

"Where are you from?"

"Berwick."

"I think you were not a farmer."

"No, my lady. Fishing, trading. Always I loved the sea."

Margaret nodded. "I see. Would you go back there now, Ebert?"

He looked confused. "My lady? I am to serve you."

"No. You are free. Would you go home?"

The man tried to speak but choked. He fell to his knees, his head level with her stirruped foot. He made no sound, but his shoulders shook.

"How long have you been a slave, Ebert?" She spoke kindly.

340

He took a deep breath and looked up. "Seven years." His mouth hardened, and his words came out hard-edged. "I was carried off as booty when the soldiers burned our town."

"Scottish soldiers?" Margaret's voice was even.

Ebert shrugged. "Scottish. English. It made little difference to my family lying dead inside our house."

Margaret turned toward Iain.

But he had already dismounted in anticipation of her wishes, and now he raised the former slave to his feet. "Are you any handier with a horse than with a threshing flail, man?"

"I am, but . . . but . . ."

Iain held out the reins of his own fine chestnut. "We canna have you walking. It would slow the whole progress."

If nothing else, seven years of slavery had taught Ebert obedience. He mounted.

"It will slow us almost as much if you walk, Iain." Margaret's smile held just a tinge of mischief. "Ride you with Elswyth."

Elswyth set her full, rosebud mouth in a firm line. So much for her hopes of a quiet word with the queen.

A few moments later, however, she found that the topic she wished to discuss came naturally to the fore.

As the party turned homeward, Margaret turned to Iain, sitting at ease behind Elswyth's saddle. "Long I have known that the slaves must be freed. I do not see how, but I will find a way. Now I see another problem. There must be something for them to do as well. Some will want to return to their homes. We must make that possible. But for those who stay here there must be work." She paused, deep in thought. "I must find a way. And prevent more being taken into slavery as well."

This was Elswyth's opening. "When Edgar is on the throne of England, Saxons will again be welcome in their own land. And there will be no need for Malcolm to make war on the borders to keep the Normans at bay." She did not mention that the Scots had warred over the borderlands long before the Normans arrived.

"You speak true, Elswyth. But I fear restoring my brother's rights will be a difficult and costly task as well."

Elswyth took a breath. This was not the privacy she had hoped for, but such opportunity might not soon present itself again. "There is one who would work for you, my lady. One who holds lands in Northumbria and would see it won by diplomacy, not war." She turned her eyes meaningfully toward Liulf, not wanting to name him in front of Iain. "Will you not speak to Malcolm? It would cost little of men or money to let a loyal thane work for him."

Margaret's mind was clearly deep on this problem. "Perhaps. I must give the matter careful thought. And prayer. Come with me tonight, Elswyth. Help me pray." She pulled ahead to speak to another of her ladies.

Elswyth rode in silence for some time, relaxing to the clop of her horse's feet on the hard dirt road. She started when Iain spoke. She had nearly forgotten he was there, so natural the motion of his body felt to the rhythm of her horse.

"You will nae like this, Elswyth, but I must speak. Do not trust Liulf."

She turned so sharply their heads almost bumped, and her wayward veil slipped over one eye. "Do not be ridiculous. There is no reason I should not trust Malcolm's thane. I believe you are jealous. Do you think you are the only one who can serve the queen?" She pulled the veil the rest of the way off.

"Now who is being ridiculous? I know that one. I dona know his game. But I know he is playing for his own ends. And he is using Duncan as a pawn. Be careful, Elswyth."

"I will not listen to this, sir. You may be quiet, or you may walk."

"Alas, the queen bade me ride."

Elswyth was glad she could not see the sparkle she knew was dancing in the dark eyes behind her.

35

Restlessness, scuffling, and murmuring pervaded the hall. The rushes on the floor crackled dryly under the stirring feet of thanes and courtiers. A harshness growled in voices that normally burred softly. Malcolm gave a brittle cough and thumped his empty goblet. "What is the matter with you, man?" he growled at his seneschal. "Charge the beakers, Hugh."

The steward twisted the hem of his tunic as if wringing a cloth. "Er . . . my lord king . . . er . . . that is . . ."

Malcolm slammed a fist against the table and opened his mouth to shout his orders, but a soft white hand closed over his.

"Do not yell at Hugh, my lord. He is but following my instructions."

"*Your* instructions? What mean you, Margaret? To parch the court of Scotland for some penance?"

"No, my lord. My ladies and I would do you honor."

Malcolm sputtered.

"We would serve the first cup by our own hands as our loving service."

Malcolm gave a jerky nod. "Well, be you about it then before we're too athirst to be sensible of your honor."

"Immediately, my lord. After prayers, of course."

This time the sputter was a small explosion, but Malcolm obediently crossed himself as Father Turgot rose at Margaret's nod.

"May almighty God bless you in His mercy and make you always aware of His saving grace."

"Amen." Malcolm crossed himself with one hand while reaching for the platter of roast fowl with the other, then froze midway in his reach.

"May the God of all strength strengthen your faith with proofs of His love so that you will persevere in good works."

"Amen." This time Malcolm got a crisp golden pullet halfway to his plate.

"May He direct your steps to Himself and show you how to walk in charity and peace."

"Amen." Malcolm dispensed with crossing himself and reached for the oatcakes and honey with both hands.

"May Almighty God bless you, the Father, and the Son, and the Holy Spirit."

"Amen." This time Malcolm resignedly did a thorough job of crossing himself and refrained from reaching for the food until Margaret smiled and rose gracefully to fill his empty goblet.

"I do hope you enjoy it, my lord. I ordered the very best for you."

Elswyth smiled too as she took up her duty, just as Margaret had instructed her ladies. The matter of prayers before meals had long been a problem to Margaret. Although she always had Father Turgot pray at meals, the men would not refrain from beginning their eating and drinking before, and often even during, the prayer. But as all liked to clear their throats with a cup of wine first, this simple expediency would go far to improve manners and increase devotion.

And Elswyth had no doubt but that, before the meal was over, Margaret would have convinced Malcolm that the whole brilliant idea had been of his devising.

Once the feast was in progress, however, Malcolm's attention quickly returned to affairs of state. The king quaffed a full goblet of wine and set it down with a thump. "The matter can no longer be borne. It is too dangerous," he thundered to all the captains and thanes within hearing. "This English overlordship of Northumbria cannot continue. The lands were my Uncle Siward's, and mine after him, by decree of King Edward the Confessor."

A growl of assent followed his recitation of old rights and grievances. "If we allow William these lands, it will not be long until his greed extends to Lothian and beyond."

The growl grew to a rumble.

"William must be stopped."

The warriors thumped their tables and shouted.

Her widening blue eyes and furrowed white brow showed how deeply these words distressed Margaret. Elswyth thought once she even saw the queen's hand move as if she would cross herself. The distress remained in Margaret's face, but never did she betray her turmoil by the least inattention to her king or faltering in her duty as hostess.

Elswyth had expected her to rise after the second of the sennachie's tales, but Margaret stayed, smiling graciously, through the third, this a harp song of the ancient days when Fergus and Lorn, the sons of Erc, first came to these shores. Then, with a bright smile for her husband and only the slightest nod to Elswyth to accompany her, Margaret led her ladies from the hall.

Maethilda, Ethelfled, and the others retired to the ladies' bower, but Margaret and Elswyth continued on behind the hall and slipped through the gate in the stockade, with only the briefest wave to the watch, which told Elswyth how accustomed the guard was to his queen's nighttime vigils.

"Come with me to my prayers," Margaret had said, so Elswyth assumed they were going to the Culdee church. She knew what great fondness Margaret held for this church and its small community of brothers, even though she disapproved of some of their eccentric practices.

But the queen walked beyond the little church. Even in the dim light her feet followed naturally along the narrow path to the clifflike edge of the glen. For perhaps five minutes they walked steeply downward between thick bushes and under heavily boughed trees, while little night creatures scurried and chirped in the thick dusk.

Suddenly it was as if Margaret had disappeared. Then Elswyth realized she had entered the mouth of a small cave to her left.

The queen was already on her knees, striking the flint to light candles stuck in niches in the walls. An ornate golden crucifix stood in the center of a small altar flanked by more candles. The altar cloth was of finest red silk, and Elswyth recognized the embroidery as being Margaret's own work. A thick Turkish rug covered the hard dirt floor.

"My lady." Elswyth fell to her knees as much in surprise as in reverence.

"Is it not beautiful? My own cashel. Only Father Turgot knows. And now you. One day, when my heart was much weighted with longings for God to move in this land, He guided my footsteps here. It is my special place to pray for the soul of Scotland."

"My Margaret, I do not understand."

Margaret shook her head. "Neither do I. It is my heaviest burden and my greatest privilege—praying for this land God has given me. And yet I do not know what He would have me say or how He would have me pray. I only know that there are times when I feel the weight so great that I can only bring my tears here and ask God to use them for Scotland. If I were not so weak, if my efforts were not so poor . . ." Her voice caught as her throat choked.

"You? You are not—"

Margaret shook her head. "I get so discouraged. I set out with such high goals. I was so sure of God's leading."

"But you have accomplished so much."

"Just enough to show me how much there remains to do. For every hungry person I feed, how many starve? For every slave I free, how many suffer under the overseer's lash? For every reform I make in manners, how much do morals fall short?"

"You judge yourself too harshly."

Margaret's focus was too deeply on her own soul and the soul of her country to hear her lady. "I know what people say. I know I am accused of being too headstrong, too sure of myself. But I am not strong and sure. I am strong in reliance on God. I am sure in wanting only His way. But I do not know. I know the way of peace and love is His. But even in the Bible He often led His armies to battle. So how do I know when battle is right? I know I hate war because people are killed, beauty is destroyed. But it cannot be right to let another conquer our country. Oh, if only I knew. If only God would speak to me."

She grasped Elswyth's hand. "Pray with me. The weight is so heavy." She released the hand to cross herself and turned urgently to her prayers.

At first it seemed silent in the cave. Then Elswyth seemed to sense a gentle rustling, as if angels' wings fanned the flickering candle flames. The tiny cave filled with an unearthly harmony that was beyond human melody. The benediction of peace.

It was perhaps a few minutes, perhaps several hours, later when the queen looked up, her face radiant. "My God! How I search for You. How I thirst for You in this parched and weary land. How I long to find You. I would go into Your sanctuary to see Your strength and glory. At last I shall be fully satisfied."

She turned to Elswyth. "I have seen the Lord's sanctuary. We must prepare the way for the fulfillment of this vision. It will be a fulfillment for Scotland and for all people of all ages, who will be able to look to this land to see what God has done."

"What will He do?" Elswyth felt barely able to breathe in the face of Margaret's luminance. Yet she must ask.

"I do not know what our God in His majesty and His strength will do. But I know that we must prepare. We must chop the firewood. We must till the soil. We must build the church. So all will be ready for the outpouring God will make upon this land. For the battle must be spiritual. That is the only true victory. Faith must be planted firm. Truth must be in the hearts of the people. The deadwood of unbelief must be cut out. Pure practices of faith must be established. I will build a church to show the way. I will speak to the leaders that they may catch my vision."

"How will you do that, my lady?"

Margaret looked at her swollen abdomen and caressed it gently. "I cannot travel far. The church leaders must come here. From Saint Andrews, from DunKeld, from Iona. Malcolm will call them. They are good men, but there is much error. Many weeds choke the good that they would do. Truth must shine forth. It must start with the leaders, but it must not end there. It must reach every corner of the land; the poorest peasant, the smallest orphan, all are creations of God. His vision of glory encompasses all."

"And the English?"

Margaret gave a flash of humor. "I suppose even William the Norman is a creation of God—no matter how wayward he seems."

"But the embassy—Liulf and Duncan. You will speak to Malcolm?"

Margaret closed her eyes. "War is awful. It is so at odds with all that I would have for my country. We must try for a peaceful solution. I will speak to Malcolm."

36

Margaret, ever a woman of action to match her strength of prayer, wrote the next morning to her old friend Archbishop Lanfranc of Canterbury.

"I will build the finest church in Scotland that it may serve as a beacon of truth, calling all men to pray. It will be a testimony of my vision, Elswyth. Not just a church, but a priory with a community of holy Benedictine brothers to guide the scattered Culdees."

The queen's face took on a radiance reminiscent of that in the cave. Then she sealed her parchment in a leather pouch and called for Ebert to be sent to her. "A church of timber and wattle will not do. We must have a fine, high tower nave with a choir and a semicircular apse for the high altar." She turned back to Elswyth. "We must build in stone as they do in France. I am sending to the archbishop to send me a master of works to guide in this building."

Elswyth's mouth had fallen open. "Lanfranc? But, my lady, he is Norman. He will send Norman workmen. You would bring the enemies of Scotland and Saxon England to Dunfermline to build a church?"

"Was it not Scotland's own Columba who said, 'Your enemies are not God's enemies'? Perhaps if we can work together to build for God, we can cease to be enemies."

"But—but, my lady queen—"

Margaret stood. "I will not allow fear or prejudice toward any man to keep me from doing my best for God. Lanfranc is my friend. He is a godly man. Norman builders are the best."

The errand boy entered, bringing Ebert. The former slave stood straight and tall, his lash wounds no longer making him cringe. His blue eyes were clear as he looked at the queen who had freed him.

"Ebert, you spoke of your fondness for sailing. I have an errand that requires a seaman, for I would have you take this letter to Canterbury for me."

The joy on Ebert's face was as if the sun had burst from behind heavy clouds. There was no doubt that the first step of Margaret's plan was in good hands.

It was also obvious, however, that her plan to have Malcolm call a council of church leaders must await a calmer day. Malcolm was much taken up with councils of war to which he had called his earls and mormaors from all the regions of Scotland. Even now voices of the leaders from Atholl, Angus, Fife, Mar, and Strathairn thundered from the hall and reached the queen's bower.

"Aye, we can raise five hundred men—seven hundred from Galloway." That was Earl Waltheof, cousin to Malcolm through his Uncle Siward.

"We'll have no Norman foot treading our fair Fife." Mac Duff, the hardy, gray-headed warrior, thumped the table.

"The wily William's seen no battle yet. He thinks to burn Northumberland into submission, but we'll have our lands back." Was that Cospatrick, the former earl of Northumbria, or Liulf, who had been likewise dispossessed when William claimed for England all the land between the Tweed and the Tees?

Margaret shifted her thinking from church matters to those of state.

When Malcolm came to her room before the hour for eating, she made him comfortable with a cup of wine. "My lord, I think the concerns of war and peace are heavy upon you. I would not have you march from me to battle if it can be avoided."

Malcolm set his cup down with a bang. "What! Woman, would you make a milksop of me? The king is war leader. Of course it cannot be avoided."

"No, certainly not—if there must be war. But have you considered other ways? Ways that might obtain your lands for you without the cost of having them burned over yet another time? Ways that will leave the houses still standing and the people and cattle living? Would not that be better?"

Malcolm nodded grudgingly. "Aye. It would."

"Have you considered that if Edgar were on his rightful throne, you would not have that grasping William plundering your northern borders?"

Malcolm looked at her. "What do you propose?"

"There is one—your thane Liulf—who has offered to go south as your envoy to rouse the Saxon nobles to Edgar's support. He would take Duncan with him as a sign of your sanction."

"And why did not my thane come to me? Why would he hide behind a woman's skirts?"

Margaret pushed aside the thought that Liulf's first approach had not even been to her but rather to her waiting-lady. "He would speak to you, Malcolm, but you have been much caught up in your councils. And this is a plan perhaps best laid not too openly."

"Perhaps. I wonder if enough support could be raised among the Saxon lords to bring pressure on William? Hereward the Wake is still strong in the fenlands, gathering warriors to him and harrying William's forces with considerable success. There may be others . . ."

Margaret sat on a small stool near Malcolm's chair. "Would not that accomplish double—to turn William's attention from Northumbria and to gain support for Edgar?"

"Mayhap. Or perhaps it will further anger William to march against Scotland. If there is to be war, I would choose to be the one to march first."

Margaret persisted. "But if there must be war, would it not be better that it be farther south—away from our borders?"

Malcolm shrugged. "Aye, if Saxon and Norman are to fight only. But if Scots are to fight, it is best done near to our own supplies of men and food. Also I like not sending Duncan. He is young."

"But he is son of the king of the Scots. Will he not add weight to Liulf's words?" Then before Malcolm could answer she grabbed both his hands in a sudden inspiration. "Malcolm! Let us make pilgrimage!"

"Pilgrimage?"

"Yes, to the shrine of Saint Andrew. Is it not Scotland's holiest shrine? Would it not be a good thing to go there and pray for our land at this dangerous time?"

Malcolm shook his head in confusion. "Are you daft, lass, to propose such a journey in your condition and that I should leave in the midst of war preparations?"

"And when is prayer more needful than when facing matters of life and death? If you insist, I will travel in a litter, and we can take the journey in easy stages. Would it not be a fine thing for your people to see their king so devout that he puts prayer before all other considerations?"

Malcolm made a rumbling "Hrumph," then nodded. "Verra well."

Margaret rose and planted a kiss in the middle of his broad forehead. "You are a good man, Malcolm Canmore."

She had less success, however, with her own family.

She found Princess Agatha and Edgar in her mother's chamber off the far end of the hall. Clad in a purple kirtle with fur-lined sleeves and a snowy linen headrail, the princess sat by the window, bent over her meticulous embroidery, while Edgar slouched in a cushioned chair, fondling the ears of a small dog with one hand and the stem of a wine goblet with the other. Agatha's scop strummed a small harp in accompaniment to the "Song of the Wanderer."

"What a dreary land this is." Edgar's voice was just short of a whine. "I shall be glad to have this behind me when I have my throne back."

Agatha looked up and sighed. "Perhaps we should have gone on to Hungary after all. My uncle Emperor Henry would not have treated us so shoddily."

"As I recall you were happy enough to take refuge here when Malcolm offered it, Mother." Margaret spoke sharply, then turned to her brother. "Edgar, do sit up and try to look more of a king. I have just come from Malcolm. He is considering more than one plan to deal with William. It does seem that you should be more active about your own affairs."

"But what can I do?"

"That is what I have come to speak to you about. Malcolm and I are to make pilgrimage to the shrine of Saint Andrew in Kilrimont to ask the Lord's blessing on these matters. Would you come with us?"

Edgar frowned. "That sounds an uncomfortable journey. Could you not pray as well here?"

Agatha laid aside her embroidery. "What is this shrine of Saint Andrew? Surely it is not of the Roman church?"

Margaret swallowed her impatience. "Abbot Melmore is of the Columban church, Mother. But we pray to the same God."

"To be sure. But does God receive such prayers the same? You, daughter, baptized and raised in the true faith, would pray at a shrine of those who commit an impropriety every time they serve mass, who fail to keep Sunday a holy day, who observe Easter wrongly?"

"There are errors, to be sure. I am working for their correction as the Lord gives me opportunity, Mother. But there is more about which we agree than about which we disagree. Much more."

"The devil goeth about in sheep's clothing, daughter."

Margaret sighed. "Then you will not go?"

For answer, Agatha picked up her embroidery and returned to her work.

Margaret looked at Edgar.

"I shall stay with our mother."

"Very well. But I do think you could stir yourself more in your own cause." She did not wait for his answer.

Margaret left her mother's chamber in such agitation she barely noted two figures in the shadows of the alcove behind the tower stairs. Indeed her foot was on the third step before she turned back. "Elswyth! What do you think you are doing lurking in dark corners?"

The pair pulled apart.

"Liulf! The two of you—behaving no better than peasants behind the cattle byre."

"My lady, I am sorry. We were talking, and . . . and . . . it just happened. Never before—"

"That is enough, Elswyth. I would speak with both of you on another matter. In two days the king and I shall make pilgrimage to Saint Andrews. You will attend me, Elswyth. We will be seeking special blessing for the matter of your embassage, Liulf. Perhaps God would have you spend your time in more fruitful preparation."

He bowed low. "Yes, my lady queen. I thank you."

Elswyth continued to apologize once they reached Margaret's bower, but the queen stopped her with an impatient gesture. "You behaved improperly, Elswyth. We shall say no more on the matter."

Margaret wondered why she had reacted so strongly to the sight of Elswyth and Liulf kissing. In truth, they were not being openly indiscreet, and they were well-matched, she the daughter of a Saxon earl, he a Scottish thane, the son of the earl of Orkney . . .

Ah, that was the source of the niggling Margaret felt at the back of her mind whenever she thought of Liulf. He made nothing of the matter—it seemed certain he would as soon have it forgotten—but the fact remained. Liulf was brother to Ingeborge, Malcolm's first wife. The wife the gossipmongers accused Malcolm of poisoning to make way for the fair Margaret. Ingeborge, who was mother to Duncan, whom Liulf would take to England as his showpiece to the Saxon lords.

She must be careful. Duncan was the rightful heir to the throne of Scotland. But when her child was born, and all the children she hoped would follow this one . . . yes, she must consider carefully.

"My lady, which cloak will you wear on the journey?" Elswyth was on her knees sorting items from Margaret's kist into a traveling chest of woven rushes.

"Oh, the blue beaver-lined one. It is warm but not overly heavy. We will take warm but serviceable garments. This is a holy pilgrimage to be done in true reverence, not for show." She turned to the small prayer bench in the corner of her room. "These I would take with me. Pack them carefully."

She ran her hand over the engraved surface of the silver casket containing her most precious possession—the Black Rood—a fragment, she believed, of the true cross. It had been brought from the Holy Land by a devout pilgrim. So she would take it on her pilgrimage.

She turned to the other item on her bench, a book of the gospels. It was a most beautiful treasure. The figures of the four evangelists were painted in brilliant colors outlined with gold. Every capital letter glowed in gold, crafted in flowing shapes of intertwined knots with tiny birds and animals peeking out from the intricate lacing. Seldom a day had passed since her father gave it to her that she had not studied the words of Christ from that book. "I shall want this by me to read from."

She turned to survey other items: exquisitely wrought tapestries and silk hangings, jeweled crosses, golden candlesticks. "I must choose the very best gift for the church there."

Elswyth frowned. "Yes, my lady, but there are . . . er . . . problems . . ."

"Oh, don't you start too, Elswyth. I have heard it all from my mother. The Columban church is not in line with the church of Rome. And how are we to lead them into line if not by showing them the right way, I ask? Ignoring them in righteous anger will do no good. We must lead in love as our Lord does us. What if He spurned us every time we committed error?"

The many considerations still weighed heavily on Margaret the next evening as she served Malcolm's wine—after a most orderly prayer by Father Turgot. And they stayed with her throughout the meal. She ate little of her roast venison and boiled marrow.

At last she turned to the king. "My lord, if you would forgive me, I would leave the rest of the serving to the care of my ladies."

"Margaret, lass, are you unwell? Is it the babe?"

Margaret smiled and touched her rounded abdomen. "He is snug and well, have no fear. It is that my mind and heart are so heavy. I feel unworthy to undertake a pilgrimage. Please excuse me to my prayers."

"If you are unfit, Margaret, there is no hope for the rest of us."

"Indeed there is none. Save in the blood of Christ. Let us all rest in that hope, Malcolm."

He shook his head in wonder but smiled fondly at her.

Margaret slipped out the side door of the hall and across the yard, where the brown grass crackled under her feet. The path to the cave was carpeted thick with fallen leaves, most of the branches overhead now bare, but the thick bushes still provided a cover of privacy. She moved silently with hands folded and head bowed, her mind already turned inward as a monk going to prayers. It was some time before the voices penetrated her consciousness.

"We will have Malcolm's approval soon, then we can move." That was Liulf's voice.

"Yes, but what if my father—"

"Do not be daft, Duncan, lad. We will speak true for the king. Malcolm is as anxious to regain his lands as we." That voice was of a much older man. Cospatrick, the dispossessed earl of Northumbria, perhaps? Well, that would make sense. He would have much at stake in any negotiating regarding that land.

The speakers moved on, crashing through the bushes above Margaret. There had been nothing disturbing in the words she heard. And yet the conspiratorial tone in which the men spoke made a tingling at the back of her neck. And why were they choosing to talk in the woods beyond the castle rather than at meat in the hall as all the rest of the court?

37

The small party set out after mass the next morning. Liulf and Iain attended Malcolm. Elswyth, Maethilda, and Father Turgot attended Margaret. A few servants accompanied them to see to the animals and their luggage.

Though Margaret had promised Malcolm she would travel in a litter, she would have far preferred riding her gentle white Bryne. The early November day was crisp and gray, but it was not raining, and the truth of the matter was that the litter, borne between two horses, jostled far worse than the little palfrey, which followed at the back of the party bearing the Black Rood, her gospel lectionary, and the golden candlesticks for the Church of Saint Mary's Mount, among other things.

In addition to the jostling, the view from the litter was much restricted, even when she gave orders that the curtains on all sides be raised to the top and securely tied.

But Margaret observed carefully. The land lacked the lush greenness she had so much admired when she first saw it. And now the golden splendor of the harvest was past. Yet there was a strength in the brown soil with its thrusting rocks and barren tree branches that well-suited these people she had taken to be her own. In looking at this harsher landscape, she could better understand their fierceness to resist English encroachment and the determination to find their own way. She reminded herself, not for the first time, of the care she must take in any changes and improvements she would make.

And nearer to her she noted in the smiles and glances passing between Elswyth and Liulf another matter in which she must exercise care. It was little wonder they were taken with each other: Elswyth, with such warm, flowerlike delicacy, and Liulf, whose brilliant Nordic looks, like the sun sparkling on a glacier, never failed to attract every eye. They made the far most attractive couple at court, and yet . . . Margaret turned to the view from the other side of the rocking litter.

They stopped for a noonday picnic in Carden Forest. When they resumed their journey, Margaret asked Elswyth to bring her gospel book to her. One advantage a litter offered was that reading was far easier than on horseback.

That evening they spent in a castle beside the River Leven. It belonged to Mac Duff, the earl of Fife, but as he was not there at the time, his good nephew Iain served as host.

It was the next morning, just as they were preparing to ford the Leven, when they met a band of pilgrims. They were a small group, five adults and two children, poorly dressed and hungry looking. Margaret was immediately gripped by the devotion of such people that led them to undertake a holy journey.

"Have you come far?" she asked the nearest woman.

"From Edwin's Burgh, lady. We have been traveling two weeks."

Margaret looked blank. She turned to Iain. "I do not know this Edwin's Burgh. Is it far?"

"A small village around a great rock. There is a castle there, not much used now. It is but across the Forth from Dunfermline."

"Then why have they been traveling for two weeks?" She turned to the woman, who was now holding the smaller of the children in her arms. "Oh, did I mistake? I thought you journeying toward Kilrimont. You are traveling homeward?"

"No, lady, you did not mistake. It is the journey around the Forth, you see. The nearest bridge is at Stirling."

Margaret was horrified. "But are there no boats?"

Iain shrugged. "The rich have boats. But with so many wars of late years, there are few rich."

"And where is this Stirling?"

"As the crow flies, about fifteen miles west of Edwin's Burgh. More afoot, of course."

Margaret turned from Iain back to the pilgrims. "You mean to say that you people have walked thirty miles out of your way?" She shook her head, still in disbelief. "But that is as far as the entire journey from Dunfermline to Kilrimont."

The child squirmed and fussed in her mother's arms, but the woman nodded. "That is so. The journey to the bridge is half again the length of the traveling."

"But that is not right. It should not be so difficult for people to express their devotion. Something must be done." And then Margaret looked at the feet of the pilgrims.

Malcolm followed her gaze. He threw up his hands, gave a resigned shrug, and dismounted. "You best send back to the castle," he called to Iain. "We've nae soap and towels fine enough with us here."

356

Malcolm was already on his knees before one of the male pilgrims when the basins of water arrived.

Having been informed that this was no less personage than his king, Malcolm Canmore, the peasant pulled back in horror when he saw that the monarch meant to wash his feet. "Nay, nay. It canna be. It's no' fitting."

"Hush, man, and stick your foot in the basin, or we'll none of us see Kilrimont today," Malcolm growled with a vehemence indicating that lack of obedience would result in the man's being lifted physically into the vessel.

But Margaret was not content merely to wash and bind feet that had already walked forty-five miles over rough ground in holy pilgrimage. Nothing would do but that the women and children should ride in her litter.

Malcolm shook his head but did not argue when she ordered the packs removed from her palfrey so that she might ride; without being told to do so, Iain and Liulf took the men up behind them on their mounts.

By midday the group reached a pleasant glade surrounded by fir and holly. While the servants set out cold meats and cheeses, Margaret asked that her gospel be brought so that she might use the time for devotional reading.

In a few moments the servant, Finn, returned white-faced. "My lady queen, I do not know how it happened, I cannot think . . ." He held up the cloth binding that had held the precious volume. It was empty. "The book was there when the packs were moved. I am certain. Oh, my lady . . ." He fell to his knees.

The loss was so great that even Margaret did not know what to say. She stood still while the color drained from her face and her eyes became bluer and rounder.

"Is Finn right, Iain?" Liulf asked loudly. "You were the one who moved the packs, were you not?"

"I was." Iain stepped forward. "Surely it has simply slipped from the pack. We have come no more than six miles from the ford. I will go back for it." He mounted, then looked back at Margaret. His concern was written clearly on his face. "Dona fret. It will be well."

Elswyth turned at Liulf's touch on her arm.

"More than likely that one put the book aside so he could play the hero and recover it."

Elswyth gasped. "He wouldn't. He couldn't. Could he? Surely not. It would be too awful."

Liulf shrugged with a cynical smile. "Who knows what one will do to curry royal favor?"

But the direction of Elswyth's thoughts changed sharply as she felt Liulf's hand slide up her back. She shivered deliciously, then moved a safer distance from him with a small smile playing around her lips.

The party sat around the cold repast, but none had much appetite. Margaret looked over her shoulder at every sharp sound.

When one such noise proved to be a cow driven to a cotter's field rather than the rider she so awaited, Malcolm placed his broad, battle-roughened hand over her small white ones clasped so tightly in her lap. "Dona fret, lass. I'll order you a new book. The Culdee brothers are fair copyists. And I'll have it bound far finer for you than this one."

Margaret forced a smile. "You are good, Malcolm."

Only a few minutes later the sound behind them could not be mistaken for any cotter's beast. Iain galloped toward them, his bay horse breathing hard.

Even before he drew rein, Margaret jumped to her feet with a cry of delight.

Iain held her lectionary in his arm.

"Oh, well done, Iain. Where did you find it?" Then her joy turned to dismay. The volume he held out to her was dripping wet.

"It fell into the ford, my lady." He shook his head. "I found it at the bottom of the river with the motion of the water riffling its pages. I regret much that I was not sooner, for just as I reached for it one of the sheets of silk covering the golden letters washed away." He held it out to her with bowed head.

Margaret took the book in both hands and pressed it to her heart. "There is little to hope that even one letter remains visible." She closed her eyes as if in prayer. After a few moments she looked up. "Thank you for recovering what you could, Iain."

She opened the book.

At her sharp outcry, Malcolm put his arm around her shoulders. "Nay, Margaret. I told you I'll order another. I'll—" The king caught his breath and pulled back, his broad features stricken.

Tears rolled down Margaret's cheeks. She held the open volume for all to see. The pages were perfect. Not a letter was smeared or blotted. Even as drops of water ran down the page, the sun gleamed off the gold of the swirling capital letter on the page across from *ses Mattheys Evangelista*. Saint Matthew, his red beard and green robe brilliant, sat sideways at his high desk, writing in a golden book. The vellum was still smooth to the touch. The black letters of text varied by lines of scarlet or gold were unblurred.

358

"It is a miracle," she whispered.

She handed the book to Father Turgot. "It is a mark of our Lord's favor on this pilgrimage and on this land for which we have come to pray. Let us give thanks now."

At the end of the father's prayer, Margaret's face glowed. "This volume, which I cherished more than any other I owned, is now doubly precious to me. I will build a chapel at the Leven ford and establish there a priest to help pilgrims on their way."

She looked at the small band of pilgrims now accompanying her. "And I have been thinking much. I will also establish houses of rest on either side of the Forth beyond Edwin's Burgh so that pilgrims and poor might turn aside there to rest after the labor of their journey. There they will find ready attendants and everything necessary for the restoration of the body."

"Aye." Malcolm nodded. "With towels and fine soap aplenty for the foot washing."

But Margaret was not finished. "And I will provide also ships to carry pilgrims from Lothian across the Forth, both going and coming. Never with any fee to them but all to be done to the honor of Christ and to the increase of devotion in this land."

"Aye. That's fine, lass. You'll do it fine as you do everything, without doubt. But now let's be on our way." Malcolm picked her up and set her on her horse.

As the party moved ahead at the best speed Malcolm could urge them to, Elswyth turned to Liulf, riding nearby. "I do not think it was a purposeful thing. I do not see how it could be."

Liulf shook his head. "Nor I. But if it was a trick, I'd like to know the way of it."

By late afternoon it began to rain. The whole party, except those in the litter, was as wet as the book recovered from the Leven by the time they rode up the muddy path along which the shops and houses of Kilrimont straggled.

They went first to Abbot Melmore's residence. Liulf referred to it as a castle, but Elswyth could hardly think such a grand word suited the heather-thatched wattle building whose tower was barely taller than the hall roof. The abbot's hot meal served by the Culdee brothers, however, was greatly welcoming.

Margaret was never one to let any opportunity go by, so as soon as the meats were served she turned to Melmore. "My lord abbot, we are indeed grateful for your hospitality."

He nodded his tonsured forehead and beamed in beneficence.

"We look forward to returning your graciousness."

"I thank you, my lady queen." The abbot looked a little confused, as if he had missed something in the conversation.

"Oh." Margaret looked at Malcolm sitting on Melmore's right. "Have I run ahead of you, my lord? Forgive me. But perhaps it is as well that I spoke, for I am sure you meant to take this time to invite our good bishop to your church council."

Malcolm's eyebrows rose, but the eyes under them twinkled. Apparently he had become accustomed to his wife's ways. "Indeed. I am certain I did. But as you've made so good a start, why do you not go ahead with the invitation in my name?"

This happy arrangement left Margaret free rein to talk and Malcolm free to eat.

"My lord king and I are much pleased with the devotion and good works we find among the Culdee brothers and the Columban church in general. Particularly the piety of your hermit brothers who so devote themselves to prayer—they are an inspiration we should all follow more closely. So the king would do what he can to foster such strengths by calling a council of churchmen at Dunfermline this spring."

"Oh, aye?" Melmore looked at Malcolm.

Malcolm waved the fat goose leg he had just bitten into and nodded.

"The king hopes that, by bringing together all the spiritual leaders, true piety might be strengthened in the land, errors corrected, and devotion increased. As abbot of this holiest of shrines, you will, of course, take a leading role."

But Melmore was not to be moved by flattering words. *"Errors* corrected, you say?" He looked at Malcolm.

Malcolm did not bother lowering the beaker from which he was drinking the abbot's mead. He merely gestured toward Margaret with his free hand.

"Is it not natural, my lord abbot, where churches are so scattered and in a land so removed from the rest of the world that variations of practice might slip in? Through no ill will or lack of love for our Lord, of course. But should not the strength and beauty of this country be reflected in the strength and beauty of its service to God who made it?"

Melmore bowed his head. "As you say, my lady queen."

Malcolm let Margaret have her head with the abbot, but he would not be overruled in the care of his wife and unborn child when she suggested they go to the church. "If you start now, Margaret, you will pray all night. I know you too well, lass. It has been a long day, and our son needs rest even if his mother doesn't. The abbot can say evening prayers as well in the hall tonight. We will go to the church tomorrow."

Margaret submitted.

The next morning they walked through a heavy mist rolling in from the harbor and blanketing the North Sea, which lapped gently against rocks and sand at the foot of the cliff beyond the village. It was a cold, steep climb to the little Church of St. Mary on the Rock. But once inside, the pilgrims were enfolded by the shelter of richly painted walls and the glow of candles freshly lighted. Even on such a dim day, the little eastern window shone with a silver light.

All held back and let Margaret lead the way around the benches that filled the room to kneel before the richly carved sarcophagus containing the relics of Saint Andrew.

Malcolm knelt beside her, Abbot Melmore beside him, Father Turgot to Margaret's left.

After a time of silent prayer, Melmore prayed aloud. "O Lord, in Your kindness hear our petitions. You called Andrew the apostle to preach the gospel and guide the believers in faith. May he always be our example as we strive ever to feed Your sheep."

With considerable bustle and stretching of joints, discomforted from kneeling on the stone floor, Malcolm led the party in rising. He offered his hand to Margaret to help her up.

Her eyes closed, her hands folded in prayer, she did not see him.

Malcolm cleared his throat.

There was not the slightest motion of her white-draped, bowed head.

The king turned and banged his shins against the front bench. With a creaking of the leather jerkin covering his heavy brown tunic he strode to the back bench and sat to await his wife. He clasped and unclasped his hands. Folded and unfolded his arms. Crossed and uncrossed his legs.

"What can the lass find to pray about so long?" he murmured. He went through the clasping, folding, and crossing procedure again. "One wouldna think there were so many sins in the world to be prayed over."

Malcolm added to his routine by running hands through his hair, adjusting his cloak, and fingering his scabbardless belt and was on his fifth or sixth time through the course when Margaret rose.

Her face glowed with the sheen of moonlight on a pearl. She blinked at first as if surprised to see others in the room with her. Her voice was soft with a strange harmony of joy and sorrow.

She spoke with the homesickness of one who has visited a much-loved place and longs to return to it. "I have seen a land. A land in which faith plays a vital, public part. A land in which the importance of faith—of man's spiritual nature—is recognized.

"Not just he who is richest or smartest, not who is strongest, or whose forces can smash all others—but he who is best in his heart and truest in his spirit will be honored.

"Much of this country is parched—spiritually dead and barren. God wants to move mightily here. He wants to give a fresh outpouring of His spirit, to move His people with boldness and courage. The Lord showed me the key. Just now as I prayed for His wisdom, He revealed the way to me."

The room, which had been quiet, now grew totally silent.

"It is prayer. The Lord would pour His blessings upon us, but first the people must pray. It will not happen otherwise. Father Turgot?" She held out her hands in a groping gesture as one who is sightless.

He took her hands. "Yes, daughter."

"You taught me the way long ago. Do you not remember? The Jesus prayer. You taught me the way of the early Fathers who learned to pray without ceasing. But in my weakness and my sin I forgot. I had the key. But I forgot. Always I would pray more, but it was not enough." She was silent.

Turgot turned to those sitting on the benches as if she had directed him to speak. "The early Fathers who went alone into the desert to learn more of God and how to live more truly for Him and in communion with the Lord Jesus Christ considered long the commandment to pray without ceasing. They struggled hard to learn how to obey such a command. At last they learned the Jesus prayer, 'Lord Jesus, have mercy on me.'

"This prayer they learned to say until it became as natural as breathing. To pray this prayer with their heartbeat until they were in constant communion with God, giving an ever-open channel through which He could speak to them and direct their ways. This prayer, this way of life, can be practiced by any who would truly be one with his Lord."

Turgot was quiet.

Melmore crossed himself, his lips moving silently.

Malcolm's leather creaked as he looked around uneasily.

Margaret spoke, her hands folded before her, eyes focused upward, but it was clear that she spoke to no one in the room. "I would be a perpetual choir. I would have my life be a prayer. I would have every breath I draw be a prayer for Scotland. When I cannot enunciate the words, Lord, let Your Holy Spirit make intercession for the salvation of this land."

She turned then to Abbot Melmore. "I will establish a perpetual choir here at the shrine of Saint Andrew—the shrine of Scotland—that at all times of the day and night there might be someone praying for the salvation of this land, of these people."

Perhaps she would have said more, but Malcolm rose to his feet, seemingly filling the back of the room. "Aye, lass. That is a fine thing. You do that." With which approbation he strode from the church.

The mist had given way to drizzle. Malcolm leaned against the church wall, sheltering under the narrow overhang of the roof.

Liulf followed at his heels, Elswyth behind him. "My lord king, have you given thought to the matter of my embassage?"

Malcolm grabbed both his shoulders. "Ah, a man of action. I'd go with you if I could. Tell all the Saxon lords who will listen to you that Malcolm of Scotland will have his lands back, Norman William agreeing or no."

Margaret rounded the corner of the church and stopped at his last words.

"And I will need money, my lord. William has left little to the Saxons, even those who still hold their lands. Hereward's men live as exiles in their own country. I will need coin to show them and more to promise."

"And you shall have it." Malcolm thumped him on the back.

"My lord, are you sure of this?" But Margaret's worried voice did not carry through the rain-sodden air as Malcolm and Liulf strode down from the church on the rock.

38

"But, my lady, it is but the second week of November. No one else is beginning their Advent fast. Brother Appin is the holiest of the Culdees, and he told me the brotherhood does not begin their fast for a week yet. And many do not begin until Saint Andrew's day, which is the last day of the month."

Elswyth held the goblet of wine and plate of honeycakes closer to Queen Margaret.

The queen shook her head and sighed. "Indeed, Elswyth, I am all too aware of the truth of what you say. And it troubles me deeply. How can we expect the Lord's blessing on a country where His holy observances are kept in such haphazard manner? Mother Church is most precise in calculating the time for fasting and the time for feasting. Such must not be taken lightly." She pushed the rich food away with a pale hand.

"But my lady, the babe—"

"The babe and I will both be well enough sustained with plain cider, boiled fowl, and porridge, Elswyth. Did not our Lord fast for forty days in the wilderness with far less than that to sustain Him? Should we, His children, do less when we have His Spirit to sustain us? And is not spiritual sustenance far greater than mere food and drink?"

"Yes, of course, my Margaret. None would argue with that. But it is not yet forty days to Christmas."

Now Margaret's countenance glowed with the zeal of a reformer. "Elswyth, Elswyth, have you been in this land little over a year and already forgotten the way of truth with which you were raised?" She shook her head. "If so, what hope can there be for these who have never known the proper way?"

"But Brother Appin is most careful. He assured me—"

"Careful, perhaps, but mistaken. Can being careful over a mistake make it less of an error? Elswyth, the Sabbath is a day of rejoicing throughout the year, whether in Advent, Lent, or ordinary time. It would be a denial of our Lord to fast on His day. Therefore Sundays may not be counted as fast days. Those who do so calculate, fast only thirty-four days, not the prescribed forty. This is one of the gravest errors I have observed in the Columban church. We who have been properly taught must teach others by our example. Then the matter may be brought before the council."

Knowing when she was beaten, Elswyth sent a servant scurrying to the kitchen for a bowl of porridge for the queen. She picked up one of the rejected honeycakes and licked its golden sweetness.

"Elswyth! Have you heard nothing I have said to you? The Advent fast begins today for *all* in my command."

"Finn!" Elswyth turned quickly so that Margaret should not see the look of disgust on her face as she called the servant back. "Bring you porridge for myself as well—and for all at the queen's table."

Margaret rose. "Yes, that is good, but we may not eat until the poor have been fed. You will help me today, Elswyth, in place of Malcolm, as the king has gone north to confer with his mormaors. It seems Donald Bane is making trouble there again."

Elswyth picked up a basket of oatcakes to take to the twenty-four poor people Margaret sustained at court throughout the year and fed daily by her own hand. She walked quickly to the foot of the hall. Porridge was bad enough. Cold porridge was unthinkable. And theirs was sure to be stone cold by the time Margaret's charity was finished.

Elswyth handed out oatcakes and poured beakers of fresh milk as rapidly as she could. But it was to no avail, for Margaret would not be hurried. She spoke to each pensioner, taking time to observe the healing of the sore on one hand and to inquire after another's toothache. And then each of the orphans who were likewise sustained at court had to be petted, their hands inspected for cleanliness, and their educational progress checked with a recitation of the catechism.

Elswyth looked toward the high table in the middle of the hall, where heavy pottery bowls sat filled with porridge congealing into a solid gray mass.

It was a fine thing that the Lord had called so many of the early saints to a hermit's life where they might practice their asceticisms alone. But God help those whose place it was to serve such sanctity. And yet at the same time Elswyth rejected Margaret's holiness, she envied it. Was it possible to adore and dislike someone at the same time?

At last the queen turned to her table.

With a grimace Elswyth took up her horn spoon and attempted a bite of the unappetizing blob. The grimace changed to an amazed smile. The boiled oatmeal was warm, creamy, and slightly sweet. Was it a miracle? Elswyth raised her eyes to the smiling face of Iain sitting beside her.

"If it is right for the queen to be so careful over the feeding of her poor, surely there can be no wrong if one of her household bespeaks properly prepared food for our lady's table."

In spite of her determination to dislike this flippant Scottish courtier, Elswyth could not hide her appreciation of the tasty food. "You had the cook sneak honey into the queen's porridge?"

Iain looked sincerely shocked. "Nay. I would no' have her break holy fast by subterfuge. Do you really think so poorly of me, Elswyth?" When she did not answer, he went on. "I merely told Hugh of my mother's method of preparing fast-day porridge with the top-skimmings from the milk basin."

"Thank you." She could not resist a smile at him.

"Aye, 'tis a good thing to be prepared. With Ingeborge, though, it was buttermilk and boiled whitefish. There was little could be done against that."

Elswyth tensed at the name of the previous queen. "You would do well to forget her, sir. It's clear enough the king has."

"I meant no disrespect to our lady Margaret." The laughter in Iain's eyes now took on a dark foreboding. "But there is still much talk behind stairs that I nae like. The whispers that the Norse queen was poisoned will not go away."

"Who would say such a thing?"

He shook his head. "They are but rustlings on the wind. If there were anything that could be got hold of, I would report it to Malcolm —or deal with it myself. But I am glad of this chance to warn you. Take care for the queen."

"Surely you are wrong. Margaret is universally loved—adored. Her popularity with the people grows daily. And when she has given Malcolm an heir—"

"When she has given Malcolm an heir there will be one to replace the line of Thorfinn on the throne."

Suddenly the porridge tasted less sweet, and the chill at the back of Elswyth's neck had nothing to do with any cooling of her food. But surely this was nonsense. This must be another of Iain's attempts to stir up trouble. If there were whispers, he was more than likely the one doing the whispering. Were not Ingeborge's brother and son at this very moment seeking to strengthen Malcolm's hand in the south?

Elswyth had little time to puzzle over the possibility of court intrigues, however, for Margaret was not content to mark the Advent season, whether calculated correctly or incorrectly, with mere fasting and added prayers. She had transformed her bower into a beehive workroom and set all her ladies to a flurry of cutting, stitching, and embroidery that had necessitated a doubled order of candles from the chandler's hut on the far side of the dun yard.

Margaret shook her head over the poor quality of the yellow tallow candles, made from the fat skimmed off boiled pig's carcasses. They smoked and stank of burning fat. "We shall have fine white candles from purified beeswax for Easter. There is so much—so much to be done, but that is a matter I shall not overlook. There is not time to send to France before the Christ Mass, but we shall have them for Easter."

She turned to the nearest lady. "No, no, Maethilda. The red silk is for the king's tunic. It is to be cut long, below the knees as the kings wear in the courts of Europe. And the ermine must be cut wider than that."

The queen turned next to Elswyth, who was teaching a wife of one of Malcolm's thanes the Saxon method of padded embroidery. "That is fine, Jonet. You'll soon be skilled enough to work on altar cloths. When you have finished your husband's tunic and your own, you may begin on one of these for the unmarried thanes. Elswyth, that aquamarine silk would make a fine tunic for Iain. You may begin on his."

Elswyth so recoiled that she pricked her finger with her needle, increasing her displeasure at Margaret's orders. But she did not give the displeasure voice.

If the queen was not ordering the court to stricter adherence of a holy life, she was ordering them to give more attention to finery and rich display. Even Elswyth, who had known Margaret from girlhood, did not understand. And she could see the confusion on the faces of those around her. Even those, like Jonet, who enjoyed needlework and would take up the adorning of a new kirtle without question—no matter how surprised they were at royal directives to decorate the men's tunics with gold embroidery—shook their heads over the queen's seemingly conflicting orders.

At last Elswyth spoke. "My lady, I do not understand. You insist on the most rigorous of fasts, indeed even as we stitch our stomachs growl and our fingers tremble from hunger. And yet you drive us to lavish yet more care and effort on worldly adornment." She dropped her embroidery hoop in her lap and sucked her pricked finger.

"Indeed. Is it so strange that I would have you give honor to God in all things? Does it honor the Creator of all the beauty of the universe to have His own children go about in faded tunics and soiled leather? Did not King David, returning from battle, first bathe and adorn himself in fine raiment before he offered to God his praise for the Lord's victory? Can we do less in imitation of the One who adorns the fields with lilies?"

Elswyth sighed and picked up her hoop. She should have known Margaret's answer would be complete in its logic and its devotion.

But Margaret was not finished. The patriotic fervor that completed her answer was new to Elswyth. "And did not God direct me here that I could be His handmaiden in making Scotland a model to all nations in its purity and its strength? Surely we please God by showing outwardly the richness of His blessings to this land."

Elswyth opened her mouth, but Margaret went on. "Especially at this season, when God directed that His Son should be welcomed to earth with gifts of gold, frankincense, and myrrh."

Elswyth closed her mouth and stitched with more energy.

From the first, the queen had made clear that she was determined to reform the manners of Malcolm's court. Yet always she would find a gentle way to do it. So far she had had but limited success, even with Malcolm's attire. But no one would refuse the queen's gift at Christmas. All would accept, and all would wear the new clothing in her honor, and so she would win. What would be next?

And why must Elswyth be the one to stitch the impertinent Iain's tunic? Then her mouth twitched with mischief. She would sew the inner seams of his fine blue green silk garment with horsehair rather than with thread. The seams would hold as long as the stone walls Margaret would raise in her new church. And they would itch as if made of heather thatch. She would wipe the self-satisfied smile off his face.

So the preparations for the Christmas festival continued in the most fervent of sacred and secular terms. As soon as Malcolm returned from Moray, none too pleased with the results of his dealing with his difficult, power-hungry brother, Margaret insisted that he sign a royal decree that all Scotland would observe the full twelve days of Christmas, as decreed by her ancestor Alfred the Great. Jugglers, singers, and storytellers from across the land were bidden to Dunfermline for entertaining at the feasts, and messages sent out that the poor of the land who could not be cared for at court were to be fed in thanes' and mormaors' halls and Culdee churches. All Scotland was to celebrate the Lord's birth.

The week before Christmas turned bitterly cold. Elswyth found Margaret looking out her small tower window toward the site of the great church she had planned. Snow covered the piles of rough-cut stones the queen had ordered quarried but none knew how to build with.

Margaret turned with a sigh. "How I wish we could celebrate the Christ Mass in the new church. Will it ever be accomplished, do you think, Elswyth?"

"Of course, my lady. I have never known you to fail in anything you wished to accomplish."

Margaret shook her head. "I fail in so much, Elswyth. So much. I would pray more, fast more, but I am so weak. And now I must add to my other failings the sin of impatience. I do hope Ebert has come to no harm. I had hoped he would have returned from Lanfranc long before now. Elswyth, will you come with me to my cave?"

Elswyth was happy enough to accompany Margaret to her prayers, although why they must needs be accomplished in a cold, damp cave, reached only by treading a snow-packed trail, Elswyth could not understand. Surely God could hear just as well prayers offered from Malcolm's tower or the Culdee brotherhood's church. She considered pointing out to Margaret that in the tower they were considerably closer to heaven than in a cave on the side of a cliff.

The thing she did point out once they reached the main door of the hall, however, was the unsuitability of their soft leather shoes for tramping through the snow.

Margaret's face lit with delight like that of a child offered a treat. "How wonderful that I ordered boots such as Malcolm wears for just such a time as this. They arrived from the cobbler only three days ago, and now we may wear them. There are two pair in the kist under my window. Will you fetch them, Elswyth?"

Elswyth sped lightly up the tower stairs, but she paused at Margaret's door. She was certain she had closed it tightly behind her. She peeked in the crack, then drew back sharply.

Iain was in Margaret's private chamber.

Elswyth held her skirts that they might not brush against the door and peered again.

He lifted each item on Margaret's writing table, examined the three books lying there. Then he turned to the chest by the queen's bed. Here he seemed to find what he sought. He carefully replaced the heavy carved lid and turned with a book in his hand.

Elswyth drew back and hid under the stairs leading to the next level of the tower. She could not believe what she had seen. Iain was stealing one of Margaret's books. But not just any book. The volume he had so carefully sought was her gospel book, the one which, always her favorite, was now doubly precious to her because of its seemingly miraculous recovery from the waters of the Leven.

She waited, scarcely breathing, until she heard his steps descend the stairs, then slipped into the room and grabbed the boots. Her first instinct was to tell Margaret all she had seen—to denounce Iain loudly in front of all who chanced to be in the hall. Perhaps Malcolm was by the central fire with his counselors.

But then a better thought came to her. Let Iain carry on with his plan. She would denounce him when it would have the most effect. If he meant for Margaret to miss the book so that he could produce it once again after a 'miraculous' recovery, just let him try.

"Here are your boots, my lady." She handed them to the queen as if nothing had happened.

So Elswyth accompanied Margaret to her cave, but she did not pray for Ebert's embassage, as Margaret supposed. Rather, Elswyth prayed for Liulf and his delegation. Elswyth had missed Liulf much in the weeks he had been gone.

Sometimes it had seemed he was the one person at court she could understand. Liulf—who had always been in the shadow of others, yet strove to do his best in their service. Liulf, she was sure, felt many of the same inner conflicts as she did in admiring the good qualities in those she served and at the same time mocking their impracticalities. Liulf, she knew, admired and served Malcolm at the same time he envied and disdained him.

And Elswyth, kneeling beside the queen she so admired yet envied and contemned, prayed fervently for the success of the mission she hoped would bring to Liulf the honor he so deserved. And let him return soon to court.

As they crested the path leading back to the dun, Elswyth shivering against the cold that Margaret seemed not to notice. Then, at the sound of jangling harness, Elswyth's heart bounded. God had heard and answered her prayers! A small contingent of horsemen was just entering the gate of the wooden palisade.

"Oh, my lady, let us hurry! They are returned." She ran the best she could through the ankle-deep snow.

But once inside the gate, she stopped. She should have known. It was not her petition that had been answered, but Margaret's.

"Ebert." Margaret moved forward to greet her returned servant. "Praises be, you have returned in time for Christmas. And you were successful?"

"The archbishop received me most courteously once he had read your letter. He expressed great interest in your project and promised to send a contingent of Benedictine brothers to establish a monastery when the building is ready."

"And I see you have brought newcomers to our court." Margaret smiled graciously at a man and young woman, heavily swathed in fur-lined cloaks, who had just descended from their horses. "But let us go into the hall where we may talk in comfort."

She led the way and ordered Hugh to bring bowls of mulled cider for the travelers.

Before the fire, Ebert presented Cyril de Vailly and his daughter to the queen and others.

Margaret bade them welcome, then perused the parchment Ebert brought from Lanfranc. She looked up with a smile. "His grace assures me you are the most skilled of his master builders," she said to Cyril. "I am grateful that he should spare you to me when I know the good archbishop is much involved in building his own cathedral in Canterbury. And your daughter is most welcome too." She turned to the girl Ebert had introduced as Alys.

Elswyth, standing somewhat in the shadows, scrutinized the new arrivals. Cyril de Vailly was the epitome of the sleek facile style she so despised in the Normans. His curly dark hair close-cropped, his olive skin smooth shaven, he seemed to smile far too easily, as if only to show off his white teeth. Finer-boned than the Scottish and Saxon men around him, he wore his brocaded, fur-trimmed tunic with an easy air.

When it was Elswyth's turn to have the newcomers presented to her, she duly held out her hand to be bowed over, but her responding curtsy was the merest sketch.

Alys appeared to be only a year or two younger than Elswyth herself and, although shorter than even the petite Elswyth, was soft and plump like a pigeon. Alys's hair, dark like her father's, had escaped its round veil and hung in damp ringlets around her face. Her skin was very white. Her wide blue eyes held a frightened look.

Iain bowed deeply over her hand and apparently said something comforting to her because she lost her look of an animal cornered by hounds and gave him a small smile.

A fine thing, indeed, Elswyth thought. *Margaret has brought our enemies to Scotland for Christmas.*

39

Two days later Liulf returned.

Elswyth was in the front of the company to greet the Thorfinn-son but drew into the background with the other waiting-ladies serving welcoming cups of hot wine when the party moved into the hall to report fully to Malcolm.

She would have liked to capture Liulf's attention, but even the simple task of filling his cup was performed by Maethilda, and Elswyth was left to serve Edgar, who was complaining in his high-pitched voice about the devastation William had wreaked on Northumbria and Yorkshire.

"My throne will be worth little enough if I ever do get it back. What can the man mean to be doing by burning the whole country?"

"I expect that the Norman means to see to it that the north submits to him and stays submitted," Malcolm said. "He also means to see to it that we will find little enough to aid us there should we venture over the Tweed. But what did you find of Saxon resistance?"

"Hereward holds strong in Ely. Although he has not repeated so great a victory as he had at Peterborough last summer, the dispossessed English lords flock to him. His tactics are to strike, then fade back into his fen fastness with the slipperiness of one of its eels."

"Yes, yes." Malcolm pounded the arm of his chair. "But will he fight for us?"

Liulf's eyes gleamed. "The Saxon lords will rise. But certain inducements will be necessary."

"Inducements? You mean they want the sight of Scottish gold?"

"It costs much for men and arms, my lord."

"And do you think I dona ken that? But how strong is the support? I'll not be throwing my men and money away." Suddenly Malcolm stopped and looked around, frowning. "And what of Cospatrick? Did he not return with you?"

Liulf glanced around uneasily at the other envoys.

Edgar slumped in his chair and took a deep drink of his spiced wine.

It was fourteen-year-old Duncan who spoke up. "He did not return, Father. He has gone to his own lands. Cospatrick made his own peace with William. William reinstated him earl of Northumbria."

"What!" Malcolm came out of his chair with a bull-like bellow. "That turncoat has sworn fealty to William again?" He pulled his knife from his belt, brandished it over his head in his huge fist, then slammed it into the table. The blade sank a good two inches into the solid oak. "That man can change his coat quicker than a snake can shed its skin."

"I did not think you would be pleased, my lord." But Liulf looked extremely pleased. "It will be an inconvenience fighting Cospatrick as well as William, but undoubtedly worth it in the end to be rid of both of them."

"Waltheof—Waltheof should have been earl of Northumberland. He was Siward's son."

Liulf looked askance at Malcolm's pronouncement, as if this was not the one he would have named, then shrugged and nodded. "So you will raise the army, my lord king?"

"There can be no peace and no honor in Scotland with such men installed as our nearest neighbors. Aye, we'll fight."

Throughout Malcolm's outburst, Margaret sat frozen, her hands clasped as if in prayer, all color drained from her face. Now she placed one hand lightly over his, which still clutched the hilt of his knife. He looked at her as if he had forgotten her existence. "Margaret, lass. You should not be here, and in your condition."

"It is all the more needful that I be here, Malcolm. Is it not my land, my people, my husband, and the father of my babe that you so rashly pledge to war?"

Malcolm opened his mouth to speak, but Margaret placed one white finger over his lips. "My lord, it is but two days until the eve of our Lord's birth. Must we talk of war at the very time when God saw fit to send peace to earth? Must we talk of destruction when here we will be laying the cornerstone for the construction of a great church?"

"Oh, your church." Malcolm turned to Liulf. "Aye, now there's gold—money laid aside for the building. So. We shall begin our preparations the day after Christmas."

Elswyth would not have thought it possible for Margaret to blanch any whiter than she had at Malcolm's initial outburst, but she did at those words.

She never faltered though. "The Twelve Days, Malcolm—you have decreed a full twelve days for the feast."

Malcolm dipped his big head in submission. "Aye, I have."

The next two days were given over to an even more furious pace of preparation than all the other weeks of Advent. Recently Margaret had been so busy she had little time for reading and therefore did not notice that her book was gone.

Elswyth considered telling her, then pulled back when the servants entered with armfuls of strewing herbs. But soon. She would choose her time carefully, but soon she would denounce Iain for the thief she knew him to be.

The beaten dirt floor of the hall had been swept clean of its old rushes and laid with clean straw. Now came a thick carpeting of sweet-smelling thyme and rosemary. The rafters were draped with dark green yew boughs and holly branches. And Margaret carefully instructed Iain in the choosing and bringing in of a yule log.

"It must be a bole of oak or ash—a hard wood—no less than a rod long, for it must burn for the whole twelve days."

Fasting, which was to hold strictly until the midnight Christ Mass, was harder than ever to observe with the fine smells issuing over the frosty air from kitchen and brewing house. Already pots of brown ale were being spiced and simmered with tart apples for the wassail for which Margaret had issued careful orders.

Before the Christ Mass, which Margaret had tactfully arranged to be said cooperatively by Father Turgot and Brother Appin, she arranged for all the court to gather in the hall for the lighting of the yule log. While pipe and drum played, the great log, stripped of its branches, was pulled the length of the hall by means of ropes and placed, surrounded by twigs and dry leaves, in the central fireplace. Malcolm then stepped forward with a lighted spill and set the twigs ablaze. The assemblage cheered, and the skirl of pipes reached a crescendo.

Elswyth cheered with the others, but the intense warmth she felt was not due only to the merry burning of the great log. Now was the time she must speak. This was the moment she had waited for, before all the assembled court she would tell what she had seen.

But Margaret was not ready to yield the floor to anyone. Earlier that day she and her ladies had carefully smuggled into the hall the fine stitchery on which they had labored for so many weeks and covered their work with bearskin robes.

Now Margaret took Malcolm by the hand and led him to the first of the stacks. "My lord, I have a Christmas gift for you." She pushed aside the heavy cover and drew out the red silken tunic she had worked over so carefully. She placed it in his large, rough hands. "Is it not beautiful, my lord?"

"Er . . . yes. Certain it is." Malcolm's wide brow knit.

"And you will look fine in it. You will look the finest king in Christendom, which of a certainty you are."

"Oh, aye?"

The other women now presented their husbands and the other thanes and mormaors their finery. All received them with as much confusion as their king had.

"We are to wear gold and silk?" Jonet's husband held at arm's length the tunic adorned with her exquisitely embroidered bands. "Woman, I am a warrior—as we all are, not popinjays and peacocks."

"It will please our lady queen. And you will look very handsome, Dungal." Jonet smiled at him.

"Well . . . if the king does. It can hurt little to wear such for the feast days." Dungal trudged off to change from his sweat-stained tunic.

Elswyth, with a sour look at Maethilda, who was presenting Liulf with the saffron tunic she had trimmed in rich brown fur, turned to do her duty to Iain.

"The queen bade me sew this for you."

Iain's eyes twinkled as he performed an exaggerated bow. "A most gracious speech—its memory will warm my heart, even if this light fabric lacks aught of warmth." He looked across the hall where Cyril and Alys stood watching the procedures. "We shall all look as fine as any court our Norman friends are accustomed to. I must thank our gracious queen."

Cyril wore a jeweled belt and sleeveless tunic above a longer undertunic with tight-fitting sleeves and embroidered cuffs. It was not Cyril's finery, however, that piqued Elswyth. It was his daughter's soft smile for Iain that spurred Elswyth's sharp retort.

"I count no Norman friend of mine. Nor do I count any as friend who would steal from the queen." She was vaguely aware of those around her falling quiet and turning her direction, but Elswyth was so annoyed with the whole situation she hardly knew what she said. "Do not think you were unobserved when you stole into the queen's bower, sir. I saw you take her gospel book."

Elswyth heard sharp gasps and saw horrified looks all around her.

But the assured smile never left Iain's face. He offered no excuse for his behavior.

His arrogance infuriated her. She pulled back her hand to strike him.

At that moment, however, even Elswyth's attention was taken by Malcolm's re-entering the hall, splendid in his new clothes. The red silk overtunic fell well below his knees. Its hem and the sleeves, ending at the elbows in a wide bell, were lined with thick bands of ermine, enhanced by the queen's exquisite embroidery, which incorporated a design of little furry animals in trailing vines. All the court stared. No one would have guessed their warrior king could have looked so elegant.

Margaret walked to him, then stopped as he held something out to her in both hands. "My lord, what is this?"

"And did you think, lass, that you were the only one clever enough to prepare a Christmas surprise?"

She hesitated, and the light from yule log and torches glinted off the gold and jeweled object he held.

"Take it, Margaret. It is yours." He put the gift into her hands.

The queen's emotion was clear to those who stood near as she opened her gospel book and tenderly turned the pages. At last she looked up. "Malcolm, thank you. It is so beautiful." She looked again at the gold leaf and rich reds and blues enhancing the delicate tooling of the leather cover, at the cut stones encrusting each corner. "But how did you ever manage?"

Malcolm beamed his pleasure at having arranged such a satisfactory coup. "Weel, I bespoke the making of the cover right upon our return from Kilrimont. The binding was a wee bit more tricky. If you must be knowing, I set my best thane on burgling your room."

Margaret clasped the volume to her chest, and the look she gave Malcolm was as good as any kiss.

Elswyth turned away in confusion. That this barbaric Scot, who thought of little but war, who could not even read, could show such devotion to a holy book because it was dear to his wife . . . and that Iain, so far from being traitor, could have been performing an act of service . . .

She looked up.

He was still standing there, smiling at her.

"Iain, I must apologize . . . I . . ."

"Nay, lass. You spoke in loyalty to your queen. She has much need of such devoted friends. But it's nae fair, you ken."

Elswyth shook her head in confusion. "What isn't fair?"

"You look sae helpless, as if you'd break. A man nae expects such strength. See you use it wisely, lass."

She could think of nothing to say.

Bells tolled across the dun, signaling that the Christ Eve Mass would begin in only a few minutes. Malcolm's men hurried away to change to their fine new raiment.

A short time later Elswyth walked alone through the frosty night to the little church. Maethilda and Ethelfled beckoned her to join the other waiting-ladies, but Elswyth preferred to be alone with her thoughts.

> "The light of the star shine upon you,
> The song of the angels sing around you,
> The care of the shepherds enfold you,
> The blessing of Christmas be upon you."

Father Appin was beginning the service as Elswyth found a seat on a back bench in the little square room.

She felt no warmth from the Christmas blessing. She remembered her last Christmas in England. She remembered the time before William the Norman had smashed their lives and driven them into this cold, rough land. They had celebrated the Christ Mass at the fine new West Minster that Edward the Confessor had built on the bank of the Thames. In her mind she saw again the candlelight flicker on the stone arches that vaulted overhead like angels' wings. She heard again the melodious chanting of the Benedictine brothers, the ringing of bells, the soft English voices untainted with Gaelic. With all her heart she ached for her home that no longer existed.

At least the next prayer was pronounced by Father Turgot. In proper black robe with proper round tonsure, Margaret's confessor prayed in proper Roman manner. "God our Father, we pray that Christmas morning will find us at peace. We rejoice as we look forward to this feast of our salvation. We keep vigil for the dawn of salvation and the birth of Your Son. We welcome Christ as our Redeemer . . ."

She followed his clear Latin without even realizing she was translating, until Father Turgot switched to English for the homily and a slight movement in front to her right caught her eye.

Iain was bending over to translate the priest's words for Alys. Light caught the red and gold braid of the circlet holding the Norman girl's veil as she nodded understanding and her eyes grew wide at the beauty of the words.

Elswyth jerked impatiently at her own veil.

"At this time was the wondrous Nativity. The Goldbloom came into this world and took man's body. The queen of all maidens gave birth to all peoples' Comforter, and all earth's Healer, and all spirits' Keeper, and all souls' Helper. Through that bearing we were healed. Through that birth we were set free. Through that coming we were honored and made rich and ready . . . "

Gradually the poetry of the words transferred their meaning to Elswyth's heart.

"Men's hearts were all of stone, and their eyes were blind so that they could not understand what they heard, nor know what they saw, but Almighty God took the harmful veil from their hearts and shone in their minds with light, that they might know Him who came down to this world bearing healing and help and food."

The final "Depart in peace" closed the mass, and Elswyth turned once more to the darkness of the night. But her path did not become dark when she left the church, for Iain walked behind her with a torch. At the ladies' bower, a small building separate from the hall, she turned. "Thank you for lighting my way."

"It was a small enough service. Much smaller than went into your stitching of my tunic. It is very comfortable."

And then she remembered the horsehair. She blushed and started to stammer as she thought his words must be sarcasm. Then she realized. She had made but an overtunic, worn atop a narrow-cut garment of soft wool with long, tight sleeves. He would feel no barbs from her stitches.

And she was glad.

40

Throughout the finishing months of winter all Dunfermline bustled with the fervor of war preparations. And rumors flew so fast one would sometimes hear the counter rumor before one heard the starting news: William had spent Christmas in York, all the better to attack Scotland at the first thaw . . . William had bided snug in Winchester . . . Ely had fallen to William . . . Hereward was taken, Ely held . . . The powerful English earl Morcar had fled to Hereward, adding to his forces . . .

Now all making of fine tunics was put away for the sewing of metal scales on leather jerkins. Across the dun, torches burned late into the night in the huts of cobbler, armorer, and blacksmith.

All seemed caught in the frenzy except Margaret. She was making quite a different preparation. She spent hours in her bower pouring over plans presented to her by Cyril de Vailly. "And will the stone hold firm in such an arch?" She pointed to his drawing of the entrance to the nave.

"Indeed, my lady. The arch is the strongest of structures; as the stones bend together they support one another."

Margaret nodded. "Yes, I see. And the design is repeated in the circular apse." She rose to her feet gracefully in spite of her advanced state of pregnancy. "Oh, it is beautiful—it is just what I would build. But all the money in Malcolm's treasury is to be diverted to this war effort. It distresses me so, and yet I would see my brother returned to his throne. Oh—" her hand flew to her mouth as she realized she spoke to a Norman "—oh, but William is your king."

Cyril shook his head. "True enough, I am Norman. But I am a builder. I would build to the glory of God, not destroy to the glory of men."

"But what if one must go to war to stop destruction? I cannot bear to think of the reports we have heard of William's laying waste to the north of England—they say he has destroyed all means of life in large areas so that the desolation may last for upwards of twenty years. And yet I must think of it. For if he should do that to Scotland . . ."

She choked and turned away. "I pray so hard. Every moment I pray that there will be no war. I pray that Malcolm and our men will not march away from me into battle—some of them never to return. But it may be that God will not grant my prayers. I do not know."

After a silence broken only by the swish of her kirtle and the rustle of the reeds she paced over, Cyril spoke. "Indeed, it is distressing, but perhaps we can counter a little of the tearing apart in the world with our building up."

"Yes." Margaret turned again to the plans. "Whatsoever things are lovely, if there be any virtue, and if there be any praise, think on these things." She sighed. "I would begin with it all tomorrow, Cyril, but there is no money. I am even short of money for food and clothing for my poor and orphans. And with Lent approaching I had meant to do so much more." She paused in preparation for one of the swift shifts her conversation often took. "If we mean to do good and do it not, is it then sin?"

"I do not see how it could be if there are no means, lady."

"But is not all failure sin?"

Cyril shook his head. "I am no priest—"

Just then Ebert entered with a knock and bow. "My lady, the king would have you come to him. If it is convenient with you, he says."

Margaret smiled, recalling how, when she first came to court, Malcolm would merely bellow his orders from one side of Dunfermline to the other. Indeed she had made some progress in her reform of manners. And here was Ebert before her, a fine, free man who had once bowed under the whip of slavery. And yet the very memory of her accomplishments brought to mind how much more there was she would accomplish.

"Thank you, Ebert. Certainly it is convenient." Yet she hesitated. "But, Ebert . . ."

"Yes, my lady?"

"You are happy in your life here?"

"Yes, my lady queen." He smiled. "There is a maid who works in the dairy . . ."

Margaret heard the doubt in his pause. "You may speak freely."

"I would not have you think me ungrateful. You paid my ransom . . ."

"Another paid the ransom for us all. Speak."

"When I traveled south on your errand last autumn I saw many fine things in London and Canterbury. But I also saw that there are

380

some finer here—Scottish woolens, the furs from your trappers. I expect it's the harsh winters—the animals grow luxurious pelts for warmth . . ."

"Yes, yes. So?"

"So, my lady queen, I would return to my trading business if you could spare me—and your dairymaid Gwynn."

"And you would return to Berwick and build a trade with England?"

"With England, yes. But if our furs are finer than theirs, how much finer must they be than those on the continent . . ."

"So you would establish trade with Brussels and the Franks and others?"

"I hope I am not too bold, my lady."

"You are bold, Ebert. But there may be much good in that. Let me think on the matter."

She went then, as bidden, to the king's private chamber below hers. "Malcolm—"

He looked up from the papers he was pouring over with Liulf. "Ah, Margaret. I am in need of ten thousand merks."

Margaret smiled ruefully. Perhaps the credit she had taken for reforming manners owed more to her servant's wording of the message than to any lessening of Malcolm's abruptness. "Indeed, and I would be glad of a similar amount."

"What of the jeweled crosses and the gold Communion plate and candlesticks you have collected?"

"*Malcolm!* They are for the new church. You would not have sacred vessels turned to instruments of war? Would you take the silver casket from the Black Rood or the very jewels from my gospel book?"

Malcolm looked alarmed. "Dona excite yourself, lass. Remember the babe. I wouldna touch your book nor the Holy Rood from Jerusalem. But there are other things, which could be replaced."

"I would ask *you* to remember our babe and all the babes that may be harmed in this war of yours, Malcolm. The Scripture speaks of turning spears into plowshares; you would do the reverse. I have not enough to feed my poor, and yet I would do more for Lent."

"The poor you will always have with you. But I'll not attempt to match you quote for quote—I would be soundly beaten. But think of the harm that will come to your poor, of the number of your people who will be taken into slavery, of the children who will be made orphans if William lays waste to Scotland."

Feeling all had been said yet nothing accomplished, Margaret walked to a far corner while Malcolm gave his attention again to Liulf's battle strategy.

"Leave Duncan in my place when we march south? Nay, man, he is too young."

"But he is your heir. It would accustom him—"

"He will not long be my only heir, and I would needs leave a regent with him."

Liulf cleared his throat. "I am his uncle, my lord. It is not uncustomary . . ."

Malcolm waved the suggestion aside. "Aye, you'd do your duty —I know that. But I'll nae have it. Euan, mormaor of Perth, is aging; it will not harm old bones to miss a battle. He shall keep the king's dun in my absence."

Margaret could see that Liulf was none too pleased with the naming of Iain's father, but she would rather have the kindly gray-haired mormaor seeing to the running of the castle if Malcolm must be gone. She absently fingered the brass fittings of the heavy carved chest she had chosen to sit on.

She would escape to her prayer cave if she could, but it was not practical at this moment, so she turned inward to the Jesus prayer that she had endeavored to make part of her every breath since the pilgrimage to Kilrimont. Today she was in such turmoil she found it difficult to frame a coherent sentence, but as she focused she found herself repeating, over and over, *Lord, have mercy on Scotland; Lord have mercy* . . . Her breathing steadied, her heartbeat slowed, her natural serenity returned in rhythm with the words.

And with the return of inner peace she was able to focus again on her surroundings and the problems she must deal with. She became aware of the chest she was sitting on. It held the Maundy money, the gold coins struck especially for the king to lay on the altar at high mass and to distribute to the poor on Maundy Thursday.

With a small cry she knelt by the chest and raised the lid. The dim light of a winter afternoon struck the gold disks. "Malcolm!" She dipped her hands in and let the coins fall through her fingers. Her laughter chimed as the coins clinked against each other.

"Malcolm, I had prayed that we could feed six more poor, then felt my prayer puny, so prayed the Lord would give me means to feed twenty-four. Here He has done abundantly above all I could think or ask. He has provided ample for three hundred! Praise the Lord of all abundance!"

Malcolm came and caught her hands. "Hold, madam. Is this not my coin of special minting? And would it not feed three hundred warriors as readily as three hundred poor?"

Margaret's laughter died like an extinguished flame. "Malcolm, you would not. This money is consecrated. To use holy money to make war . . ."

He shrugged. "It is but struck gold. It is not consecrated until I take it to church and Father Appin blesses it."

Margaret shivered against the cold that seemed to close in on her. She found no words to argue against the horror she felt. To use the Maundy money for war . . .

"Margaret. Margaret, lass."

Malcolm's voice came to her as if from a distance. Then she felt his arms tight around her. He clasped her extended roundness in an awkward bear hug.

"I yield me. Feed your poor—I'll help you with my own hands."

"Oh, Malcolm." She leaned her head on his shoulder. "You are good." She touched his auburn beard. "But now, how are you accustomed to providing for your warriors?"

"My mormaors collect taxes. They raise their men for king's service. But with Donald Bane troubling the north and the years of trouble in Northumbria since Siward died—and now William—there is little enough left to be taxed."

"So it is simple." Margaret squared her shoulders and spoke in her most common sense manner. "We must find a way to provide more income for the people. Then more taxes may be collected—for war if necessary, but far better for building churches and feeding the poor."

Malcolm laughed. "If it is so simple a matter, why not provide sufficient income that there will be no poor?"

"Yes!" Margaret clapped her hands. "With ample useful employment, only the sick and elderly will need to be provided for, and the religious houses can easily do that!" She stopped suddenly and turned in his arms. "Oh. You mock me."

"I am sorry, Margaret. It was but a small jest. But it is nae so simple a matter."

"Not simple in the doing, I am sure. But simple in the understanding—and that is the first step."

"And what magic will you work to provide this employment?"

Margaret thought. What were the occupations of the Scottish economy? Farming, fishing, hunting, weaving, crafts . . . "Perhaps more land could be put to the plow . . . our craftsmen encouraged . . ." It sounded trivial to her own ears. Then she recalled her conversation with Ebert. "Malcolm, I know! Trade. Establish trade routes to the continent. I am told Scottish furs, wool fleeces, fabrics will be much in demand. I am told that such fur-bearing animals as martin, miniver, and ermine do not flourish in gentler climes as they do here. And other weavers are not as skilled as ours. Our merchants can exchange such for fine fabrics and spices not available here."

Malcolm threw back his great head and laughed. "And the king can tax it all! And thereby equip his warriors."

"And thereby build great churches."

The talk of a great trading center for Scottish goods at Berwick put new hope and energy into the court. It would be long—perhaps years—before Margaret's vision would become a thriving reality, but the very vision was enough to spur Malcolm's mormaors to come forward with the needed men and arms. And Margaret was able to wheedle enough to start the building of her church as soon as the winter storms eased.

Thus she entered the season of Lent that year with greater devotion, greater rejoicing, and greater need of the Lord's help than ever before. To be sure, many eyebrows were raised and many heads shaken both in the court and in the Culdee community when she again began her period of fasting a week before the others. But she had explained her reasoning fully at the time of the Advent fast, and she had, as always, the support of her dear Father Turgot. Malcolm went along with her. The fasting he minded not, for rich food was not important to him. He could work as long, or longer, on a bellyful of good plain porridge.

He did begrudge the extra time spent in prayers but agreed to the schedule. "Aye, I'll nae waste time arguing with you, lass, when I know it will be as you would have it in the end."

"It is not what I would have, Malcolm. It is Holy Church following our Lord's example. Did He not fast forty days—"

"Aye, aye. So you've reminded me."

"And the council, Malcolm—you will call the council soon that we may remind others? If we allow them to persist in error we will share their sin."

Malcolm blinked, obviously trying to recall what she was talking about. "Oh. The council. Aye. When William is well and finally taken care of." When Margaret started to protest at this delay, he hurried on. "You'd nae want our church fathers en route to your council to be carried off by marauding Normans. Would you, lass?"

Margaret had to admit she wouldn't. So the council was postponed, but not the beginning of the Lenten fast. In agreement with the Roman Church, the fast would begin on Ash Wednesday.

There were no Culdee brothers in attendance, but the glow of the candles Father Appin had lit welcomed the small party of Saxons as Margaret led her mother, brother, and waiting-ladies into the cha-

384

pel. On the center of the altar stood her most precious possession, the gleaming, cross-shaped, silver reliquary containing what she believed to be a splinter of the true cross. Margaret had placed it there with her own hands as part of her Lenten self-denial. She would not keep such a beloved sacred object for her own devotion during this time of penance.

They were barely seated when a stir at the back attracted her attention. Vailly and his daughter were taking a place on a back bench, followed by Iain mac Euan. No other of Malcolm's mormaors, thanes, or warriors had chosen to attend, but this was a beginning, a small victory. Margaret smiled at Iain, then turned forward at Father Turgot's words.

"Let us pray in quiet remembrance of our need for redemption."

As Margaret crossed herself, her mind immediately focused on her own need for redemption and her constant prayers for the redemption of the land she so loved.

Turgot continued, "Lord, protect us in our struggle against evil. May this season of repentance bring us the blessing of Your gift of light."

The priest then held the basin of ashes heavenward. "Let us ask our Father to bless these ashes which we will use as the mark of our repentance." He lowered the vessel as he prayed, "Lord, bless the sinner who asks for Your forgiveness, and bless all those who receive these ashes, for You do not want sinners to die but to live with the risen Christ, who reigns with You forever and ever."

And all in the little church said, "Amen."

In silence Father Turgot sprinkled the ashes with holy water.

Margaret was the first to go forward and kneel. The father dipped his finger in the ashes, then pressed a small black dot on the queen's forehead between her eyes. "Turn away from sin and be faithful to the gospel."

"Have mercy on me, O God," she replied.

And thus began Margaret's keeping of Lent.

After her sustaining bowl of porridge that evening, Margaret went to her bed for a few hours.

"I would have you sleep in the side chamber tonight, Elswyth. If I do not waken before Father Turgot begins matins, you must rouse me. I normally have no trouble waking, but I find I sleep so much heavier with the babe."

"You sleep heavier with the babe, my lady, because you and the babe have need of your rest. Nature intended it so." Elswyth knew her words would have no effect, but she must try.

Margaret nodded. "You speak truth, Elswyth. The flesh is indeed weak. Were it not so, we would have no need of penance."

Elswyth suppressed a sigh as she looked at the thick flakes of snow swirling against the window. "Yes, my lady. But to cross the courtyard in the darkest hour of the night, with the snow piling ever deeper . . . surely it is no part of your penance that you must also take a chill. Could not the office be as well said in the hall?"

Margaret looked horrified. "Elswyth, it is not consecrated. Must I preach conversion to my own people even before I take such matters before Malcolm's council? The Columban churchmen have not been taught the right way. As a daughter of Holy Church, you know better."

Elswyth clamped her jaw tight and set out Margaret's heaviest cloak and thick boots before going to her bed. A few hours later, however, there was no need to rouse Margaret. She was already pulling on her boots when Elswyth entered from the small chamber beside the queen's bower.

Elswyth thought longingly of her bed. She could go back. Margaret would not require attendance at her private devotions. And yet Elswyth knew she could not return to the warmth of her sheepskin mat and thick woolen brychans. Whether it was the result of her early training in a house of holy sisters, her devotion to duty to her queen, or the strange mixture of envy and longing with which she always viewed Margaret's holiness—which she knew sprang from the depths of her prayer life—Elswyth would accompany Margaret.

Disgusted with her own decision, she jammed her feet into the spare pair of boots, these not fur-lined as the ones she had set out for Margaret, and flung her hooded cloak around her. She picked up the candle from the queen's bedside table and pushed aside the curtains covering the door.

At the moment she flung the door open, a gust of wind blew up the stairway, extinguishing her candle. Already in forward motion, with Margaret close behind, Elswyth stepped into the pitch blackness of the landing.

Rather, she sprawled headlong as her feet tripped over a large object on the floor in front of the door. She shrieked as she dropped the candle and crashed onto the hard floorboards.

Elswyth pushed herself to a sitting position. Behind her she heard Margaret groping for a flint. "Who could have been so stupid as to leave a bundle in front of the door? Of all the ignorant, muddle-minded—"

"*Och*, I am sorry."

Elswyth started at the sound of a sleepy male voice. She drew her cloak around her and huddled against the shadowy far wall. Who would dare lurk outside the queen's chamber? What could he be meaning? She drew breath to scream for the guard who should be on duty at the foot of the tower.

Her scream came out a muffled "*Mmumph!*" as a large hand clamped over her mouth.

"Dona scream."

Denied her voice, she lashed out with hands and feet from her crouching position. Her flailing fists glanced off the hardened chest and shoulder muscles of the man holding her, but she felt the triumph of her knee landing solidly in his stomach.

"*Oomph.*" He rocked backward.

Elswyth scrambled to her feet, sputtering with rage.

At that moment Margaret reappeared in her doorway, holding a lit candle. The light fell on the face of Elswyth's attacker, still on the floor.

"*Iain!* What are you doing here?" Margaret knelt beside him, the candle lighting the concern in her face. "Are you hurt? Has there been a battle?"

"Only here, my lady." Holding his midriff, Iain clambered to his feet. "I meant it as a service, but all seems to have gone awry."

"A *service!* What do you mean lurking outside the queen's room? Did you come to steal something you saw when you fetched her book for Malcolm? Do not try to blame your errand on the king this time." Only the queen's presence stopped Elswyth from attempting to slap this infuriating man.

"Nae, it was not the king's idea. It was my own."

"Well, then?" Elswyth turned to Margaret. "My lady, will you not summon the guard and have this man arrested?"

Margaret smiled. "I hardly think that necessary, Elswyth. Explain yourself, Iain."

He rubbed his lip, and Elswyth thought with satisfaction that perhaps not all her blows had gone so far astray.

"I knew you would be going to the church as you did at Advent. But the night is colder and the snow deeper now. I thought you'd be glad of a torch to light your way. I didna think I'd fall asleep, though —I've stood the night watch often enough before battle." He grinned at Elswyth. "And risen to meet a foe no more formidable that the one here, it seems."

In spite of herself, Elswyth smiled. But she carefully walked beside Margaret, not him, as they crossed the snow-choked courtyard, their way well-lit by his flaring pitch torch.

And thus passed the early weeks of Lent. Every night Elswyth told herself she would not get up that night, but she did. And every night Iain lit their way to the church. And although Elswyth often dozed off through the long night watch, she knew Margaret never slacked in her prayers, completing first the Matins of the Holy Trinity, next the Matins of the Holy Cross, and then the Matins of Our Lady.

Sometimes Elswyth would rouse, numb with cold and cramped with kneeling, to hear the queen reciting the Offices of the Dead, and then be lulled back to a shallow sleep by the soothing rhythms of her musical chanting of the Psalter. Sometimes Margaret would finish the Psalter before Father Turgot returned to the church to say Lauds. Only when the Office of Lauds had been completed would Margaret allow Elswyth and Iain to lead her back across the still dark courtyard.

"Was it not glorious! Does not the time spent in prayer speed like the very wings of angels?" Margaret's face and voice glowed with joy after the long night.

But Elswyth urged her to her bed where she slept for the few hours remaining until Prime.

Even Malcolm rose for Prime, for after this first office of the day he and Margaret girded on towels to wash the feet of six beggars, feed them at their own table, and send them on their way with warm cloaks and scrips full of food and coins.

Whether it was the natural accustoming to a new schedule, or the fact that the next week the Culdee community began its period of penance so there were more in attendance for the night offices, or because the snowstorm the night of Ash Wednesday was the last of the season and a gradual thaw set in during the early days of March, Elswyth found herself at first less resentful of her self-imposed penance and then almost accepting of it. She doubted whether she would ever actually welcome such strictures as Margaret did, but the keeping of the night hours in prayer were no longer an agony. She even began to stay awake through more of them and spent some of her time truly praying.

And even though the winter ground cleared, and the nighttime sky lightened, Iain continued to accompany them.

It was but two weeks before Easter. Margaret was full of plans for the keeping of Holy Week, beginning with a fine Passion Sunday service—perhaps it would not be too sacrilegious to use yew branches in a place where no palms were to be found? And then the Chrism

Mass on Holy Thursday. Father Turgot must be supplied with the rarest of spices for the oil of the catechumens—the oil that would be used for anointing in symbolism of Christ's baptism. And then the distribution of the Maundy money.

"Oh, Elswyth"—Margaret grabbed her hands as she had done when they were girls and had just been told of a special treat—"it must be the most wonderful Easter ever. We have so much to celebrate. Life is so good. All is so beautiful!" Margaret spread her arms as if she would embrace all of Dunfermline.

Elswyth looked around her at the mud-choked huddle of wattle huts. Their heather thatch dripped with the reminder of the rainstorm that had just fallen from a sky alternating patches of black and gray. A young boy and girl dressed in rough, homespun brown tunics prodded a herd of swine through a mudhole in front of the chicken house and dovecote at the lower end of the yard.

"Is it not beautiful?" Margaret repeated.

Elswyth raised her eyebrows. "Yes, my lady. If you say so."

41

It was two days later when—the path to the castle slick with mud and the sky hanging heavy with rain—a messenger arrived from the south. Liulf heard the news first, then ushered the man into Malcolm's presence. William had gathered five thousand men at York. There was no doubt about it. He who had conquered England meant also to conquer Scotland.

He would march north soon. Perhaps he would wait until after Easter. Certainly no longer. Already he had ordered burning in Cumbria, so there would be nothing to support Malcolm's troops should the king of Scots choose to march down the western border of his land.

At the messenger's words Margaret's eyes grew round, and her hand flew protectively to her abdomen. "No. Surely he cannot. God could not allow it at this holiest of seasons."

"Perhaps it is not God from whom William takes his orders." Malcolm strode from the hall to call his counselors.

Margaret gripped Elswyth's hand until her fingers dug into the flesh. "War. It cannot be. There has been so much talk of forging swords and renewing armor, but I did not think the terror would come upon us." Then she turned with a jerk that almost pulled Elswyth off her feet. "Perhaps it is not too late. It has not happened yet. There is still hope. I must pray."

If Elswyth had not dug her heels into the rush-strewn floor Margaret would have dragged her out into the cold drizzle without so much as a cloak around her shoulders. "Wait, my lady. I will get our wraps."

"Yes, and the Black Rood—bring it also that I might focus better on His cross as I pray for salvation for our land."

"It is at the cashel, lady."

"Oh, yes. My gospel book then."

In a few minutes the women more slithered than walked down the steep path to Margaret's cave. Elswyth focused all her attention on staying upright herself while at the same time supporting Margaret, heavy and awkward in her advanced pregnancy. Where was Iain now that they really needed him? she wondered. Undoubtedly off planning for war with the rest of them.

Inside the tiny prayer grotto, Margaret quickly struck a flint to the candles set in niches in the walls and opened her book to the picture of Saint John with his thick red beard and his intricately draped robes. She read for some moments the words on the opposite page, then folded her hands. "O Lord, I trust in you, let not my enemies triumph over me. All the nations shall bow down before You, O God, for dominion is Yours, and You rule the nations.

"Upon Your people be Your blessing. Lord, hear me—" Margaret's voice caught on the word as if her breath had been knocked out of her. She doubled over, arms wrapped around her middle.

"My lady! What is it?" Elswyth huddled beside her and placed an arm about the queen's shoulders.

In a few seconds the spasm relaxed. Margaret looked up, pale but excited. "It is the babe. I had a few twinges this morning, but I thought nothing of them. I did not think the time would be until after Easter. Apparently I was wrong."

"Come, we must get you back to your bower."

"Yes." Margaret leaned heavily on her lady to rise. Tiny beads of sweat shone on the queen's lip.

They had taken only two steps toward the mouth of the cave when another cramp took Margaret so hard she could barely stand.

"My lady, they should not be coming so fast. Not yet."

Margaret shook her head as the pain eased. "My mother warned me, but I fear I did not heed her words. She said it is so with the women of our family. She went very fast when it was her time."

Elswyth was horrified. "My Margaret, what shall we do? You cannot give birth in a cave. But the path is so treacherous—"

"I will wait here. You must go for help. Malcolm, my mother . . ." She caught her breath at the twinge of a returning contraction.

Elswyth backed toward the mouth of the cave. "Yes, my lady. I will go. You be easy—if you can. I will hurry." Outside, her feet squished in the ooze of the path. The ascent required all her concentration. The drizzle had now turned into full-fledged rain. She grasped the bare branches of trees and bushes to help pull herself up and hold her while she sought a relatively firm footing after each step.

She had been struggling along for several minutes when she heard a sob behind her. Not Margaret? Surely she would not have left the cave. She glanced over her shoulder but saw nothing.

After a few more steps she heard it again. Above her now. Perhaps a small animal. Except that the sound seemed human. She grasped another branch to hurry onward. But the bark was wet. It slipped through her hand just as her feet slipped on the trail.

She cried out, felt herself falling backward, and cried again. Then she was off the path and sliding straight down the steep glen toward the burn, foaming brown and full in the spring thaw. She grabbed at a bush but missed it. Her fingers closed on the next branch. She struggled upward, then fell back again as the rocks under her feet dislodged and tumbled down the hillside. She heard them splash in the water below and knew she would be next.

She reached out. Her fingers closed on a handful of mud. Her foot hit the cold swift water. The spate sucked at her, pulling her downward. Her other foot went in. Now the water tugged at the hem of her kirtle. The waterfall could be only a few rods downstream.

She clutched at a rock on the bank, but her nails slid across the slick moss. Then they slid no farther.

A strong hand gripped her wrist and pulled her upward. She fought to find footing. In a moment, soaked, muddy, and bleeding she stood upright, supported by her rescuer's arm around her waist. She wiped her face with the somewhat cleaner lining of her cloak and looked up. She gasped.

In the past months she had said not one kind word to this man. She had never missed an opportunity to show her displeasure that a Norman should be welcomed at court. And yet, at this moment when the armies of their two countries were preparing to fight, Cyril de Vailly had saved her life. And thereby not only hers but also the queen and the child she bore.

At that thought all care for her own plight fled. "The queen! She is in the cave." She pointed wildly. "It is her time. We must hurry."

Fortunately the man's English had improved much in the time he had been working with Margaret on the church. And Elswyth knew some French, so she needed repeat herself only twice before he understood. "Yes. Yes. The queen. She gives birth now. You return to her. I know what we need. You will trust me?"

Elswyth had no choice but to trust him even though he represented their sworn enemy. She nodded.

Cyril boosted her up to the path. The trail seemed far less treacherous now that her inner frenzy was calmed with the knowledge that help was on the way.

In a few minutes she was back, kneeling by Margaret, who was hunched on her knees as her lips moved in keeping with the prayer beads slipping through her fingers. As always, Margaret's serenity reached out to calm Elswyth.

And always it was so, no matter how Elswyth might resent Margaret's inner peace, it never failed to do her good. Her desperate dash up the hill, her panic as the world gave way beneath her feet in a mad drop toward the rushing waters, all could have been a bad dream were it not for the state of her clothes and the mud and blood on the hands she now tried to fold in prayer. Margaret's tranquillity had never reached her more forcefully.

The queen smiled at her and placed her own hands over Elswyth's before the waiting-lady could report what had happened. "It is well. Help is coming." Margaret did not make them questions.

"Yes . . ." Then Elswyth was quiet as the queen gripped her in the strength of another contraction.

Margaret breathed deeply, held her breath at the top of the pain, then released it in a slow exhalation.

Much sooner than Elswyth had thought possible, Cyril returned with three workers from the construction site. Between them they carried a heavy leather sling borne on poles, used for carrying building stones.

"My lady?" Cyril indicated the conveyance.

"Yes. That will do fine." Margaret lay on the rough stretcher as if she were reclining on a fur-cushioned bed in her own bower. "Has my mother been notified?"

"Yes. Alys was on the path. It was she I sought when I found your waiting lady. I sent her ahead to tell the Princess Agatha to prepare what is needful."

Elswyth paused to pick up the gospel book and extinguish the candles before following.

When they entered the hall there was no need to question whether the formidable Hungarian princess was in full command. Servant girls scattered astringent-smelling lemon grass among the floor reeds. Hugh directed the boiling of water over the central fire. Servants hurried in from the kitchen, bearing basins of brewed herbs and pots of salve. Finn rushed across the hall from the direction of the wash house with a stack of clean linen.

Agatha's voice floated down the stairs from where she directed Margaret's women in the queen's bower. "No, no, not the bearskin. Do you think my daughter is giving birth to a cub, girl?"—Elswyth hoped the smack that followed had not been on the girl's ear—"No. That linen is much too harsh. Have you no sense at all?"

Margaret smiled weakly. "Malcolm should let Mother captain his troops." She jerked with the beginning of another pain. When it eased she rose from her litter to walk, supported by Cyril, up the narrow stairs. "My husband. Has he been told?"

"He has ridden to Dunsinane to confer with the Mormaor mac Duff."

Margaret nodded, then stopped, bending almost double. Her face gleamed with perspiration when she looked up. "The babe comes!"

Cyril de Vailly carried her up the last flight of stairs. He all but flung the queen on her bed right under the long, sharp nose of Princess Agatha.

"Sir, what do you mean, entering the queen's chamber in muddy boots!"

"Mother—" Margaret began, then caught her breath on a gasp.

"No men are permitted in here at such a time!"

Agatha shoved Cyril toward the door.

Elswyth flung aside the crimson drape that it might not impede his expulsion.

"Cyril was—" But Elswyth miscalculated in drawing attention to herself.

Agatha turned on her. "And what can you be thinking of? You, the gently bred daughter of a Saxon nobleman. The swineherds were never so filthy at my uncle's court in Hungary."

Behind them on the bed Margaret's breathing had changed to shallow, rapid panting interspersed with moans.

But the blood of emperors ran in Agatha's veins. She would not be deterred. "We have been in this barbarian land barely over a year, and we have come to this. If I could have but foreseen—"

A high, thin cry wailed across her speech, accompanied by an ecstatic "Ooh!" from Margaret.

Agatha whirled. Maethilda and Alys had delivered the queen of a fine, red, bawling boy. Maethilda saw to the cord tying. Agatha snatched the babe from Alys, who held the squirming bundle with a look of amazed rapture. "Give him to me. The very idea! A Norman holding my grandchild." She held up the babe in triumph. "Have I not done well? I have given Scotland a fine, strong heir to the throne." A few drops of golden liquid fell between the fingers of the hand that supported the princeling bottom.

"Malcolm and I did none so ill either, Mother." Margaret held out her hands for her son.

Elswyth looked on in amazement from the doorway. Margaret and Malcolm *had* done exceedingly well. Especially Margaret, who had given birth under difficult circumstances with the same equanimity with which she did everything else.

But perhaps Elswyth was the only one who knew the identity of the true hero of the hour. Without the services of the Norman, who was even now clattering down the stairs to ride to Dunsinane to tell Malcolm the joyful news, the report the king received might have been very different indeed. Elswyth's mind filled with fearful images of herself being swept down the rushing burn toward the waterfall while the queen gave birth alone in a cold damp cave.

"It is most fortunate that you and your father happened to be in Pittencrief, Alys. More than fortunate—I would say nothing short of miraculous that you would be out for a stroll in such weather."

"No, my lady," Alys tucked the unruly black curls that had fallen around her face back under her veil. "It was not happenstance. Nor was I out for a stroll." She moved closer to Elswyth so she could speak quietly. "I am so unhappy. I was so desperate. If my father had not found me, I do not know—I was making for the burn—but I do not know . . ."

"Alys, what is it?"

"I had just heard. Iain told me. Of the war." She choked on a sob. "Oh, my lady, I must tell someone, or I shall die. And you always look so kind . . ." Alys looked like a small frightened animal.

Feeling a hypocrite, yet having no heart to turn the girl away, Elswyth pulled her out onto the landing and tugged the heavy crimson drape closed behind them. "You may tell me."

"It is Robert, my brother. He is one of William's household warriors. He is certain to be among those gathered in York to march northward. And Iain, he is my only friend here. He is so kind. Yet he tells me he must march south." She dropped her face into her hands. "I cannot bear it."

Elswyth closed her eyes and saw Malcolm's troops battle-ready, the sun glinting off their helmets, spears, and brass-bossed targes. She tried to shut out the picture of a pair of laughing black eyes framed by a crested helm. Why should she think of Iain so, other than that Alys had mentioned him? She should care only for Margaret's brother, whom she had some difficulty picturing astride a war horse next to Malcolm. The only outcome she should care for was that many Normans be killed—enough that Edgar could be returned to his throne and she could return to her civilized southern home.

But no, she would not wish that the son of the man who had just rescued her and her queen should die of a Scottish sword thrust. She took Alys's hand. It was very small. She was afraid to squeeze it for fear of crushing the fragile bones. "The queen prays ever for peace. We must join our prayers to hers. Although how it can be, I cannot see."

42

Prince Edward mac Malcolm was christened on Easter Sunday at the Culdee Cashel in Dunfermline. Margaret, too weak to walk to the church so soon after giving birth, was borne in a litter. At her special request, Cyril was one of the bearers.

The next day Malcolm and his men gathered to ride south.

Elswyth was at the dovecote at the foot of the yard seeing to the birds, which were the queen's personal property and a symbol of her wealth and influence. One of the first things Margaret had done after her marriage was to see to the building of a sturdy, well-stuccoed dovecote and stocking it with the best soft gray, round-breasted doves for eating and carrying messages.

Elswyth was busy selecting the plumpest to be stewed for the queen's dinner when the ashwood door creaked on its hinges behind her. "Take care. I'll not have the doves disturbed." The sharpness of her voice, however, was more likely to cause disturbance among the gently cooing birds than the intruder's quiet entrance.

"I meant nae perturbation. Canna you bid me Godspeed, Elswyth?"

"Oh, it's you, Iain." She ignored his question. "You may as well make yourself useful, since you're here." She pointed to a fine round dove perched on the highest rafter. "That one will be fine for the queen's table. Get you it."

Motes of dust and bits of down danced in the thin streaks of golden light falling through the high round openings of the small, dark building. One beam highlighted the bird Elswyth had selected.

Even stretched to his fullest height, however, Iain was unable to grasp it.

"Wouldna another do as well? There's a fine one." He pointed to one with shining white feathers and a gray ring around its neck, perched to his right within easy reach. "My mother always preferred white-feathered doves."

"I don't think it's likely she would have preferred a scrawny white bird to a plump gray one. Will you extend yourself to serve the queen or no?"

The birds cooed and rustled gently in the background.

Iain gave her a long look as if deciding whether or not to speak something of moment. But all he said was, "Aye."

A wooden crate, used to carry feed to the dovecote, stood in one corner. Iain dragged it to the middle of the cote and turned it on end. The boards creaked as he put his weight on them. On instinct Elswyth held out a hand to steady him. Iain could easily have snatched the bird's legs with one hand, but it was best to take doves by enfolding them gently from the back with both hands over their wings.

Just as his hands came around the dove, the crate wobbled. He pitched forward and seized the bird with far more ferocity than he intended. The bird let out an exceedingly undovelike squawk. It managed to free one wing and set up a furious flapping. The twenty or thirty other doves in the cote responded with like squawks and flaps, filling the air with dust, feathers, and beating wings.

Iain sneezed and fell off the rickety box, crashing into Elswyth. With a cry she landed on a floor well-carpeted with bird droppings. Iain landed almost in her lap, still holding the flapping dove.

"Get off me!" she managed to order before she was choked with flying dust and down.

Instead of the lightning removal of his large person and the abject apology she expected—and certainly deserved—the infuriating Scotsman sat there, pinning her skirts to the floor, as the doves beat a mayhem above his head. And he laughed.

A surge of fury rose in Elswyth's throat. She opened her mouth to give him the scolding he merited. At that moment one of the birds above them let fall a prodigious dropping on Iain's head. Her fury evaporated as she saw the situation for what it was. A small chuckle broke from her. At first she tried to maintain her dignity, but a fit of sneezing and giggles overcame her. In the end she was laughing so hard she had to lean against him for support. He offered little help, however, as he was laughing as hard as she.

"It's a fine thing for you to laugh," she choked out. "You're sitting on my kirtle—not what I lighted on."

"Och, but Elswyth, pity my frustration. Here I have you alone in a dark place—and both my hands full with this daft bird."

Elswyth made the quickest work she could of delivering the dove to the kitchen and changing her unspeakably soiled kirtle, but by the time she was returned to the courtyard, Malcolm had already clattered down from taking his leave of the queen in the tower. He mounted and spurred forward.

The troop was almost to the palisade when Elswyth spotted Iain close behind the king, the spring sunshine glinting on his helmet. She waved and was starting to call out when she saw that his returning wave was not directed to her. She looked to her left and saw the fair Alys in blue kirtle and crisp white veil, waving to the man she had sobbingly confessed a few days before to be her best friend in Scotland.

So. Alys's tears had been for more than homesickness and fear for her brother. Something far more personal perhaps.

Elswyth turned sharply away. A small group before Princess Agatha's bower had not yet mounted. She strode to them and stood near Liulf. She would bid her last farewell to one who did not turn his coat so readily as the son of Euan.

By their jingling of the bridles they held and their glances toward the gate it was obvious that Edgar, Duncan, and Liulf would willingly be on their way. Agatha, however, would not be stinted in her charge to those she clearly considered her household cavalry.

"Edgar, remember that you are rightful heir to the throne of England, so named by your Uncle Edward and proclaimed by the council. Therefore conduct yourself as the Aethling, and do not let Malcolm settle for less." She turned her authority on Duncan. "None can understand the situation better than you, Duncan mac Malcolm. You battle this Norman upstart for your own throne and that of your good brother. Ride forth with valor."

It was clear that there was nothing the two young men would rather do than ride off beyond the hearing of Agatha's strident voice, but she continued.

Liulf turned to Elswyth and spoke almost under his breath. "She has no need to bid the king be off. Did you note the rush with which he spurred forth? As if he would hurry to get an unpleasant task over with that he might the sooner return. In the days before, he was none so loath to lead his men to battle."

Elswyth caught the edge to his voice that seemed to say Malcolm had been a better king when married to Liulf's sister. It chilled her— as did Duncan's choice to ride beside his uncle rather than his father when finally Princess Agatha came to the end of her harangue. Yet surely Elswyth was being fanciful. They all rode for a common purpose—to defeat a common enemy. Did they not?

As she turned her steps toward the hall, she saw Cyril de Vailly leaving the blacksmith's hut carrying a freshly forged mallet. She stopped with a frown. Suddenly all her softened thoughts of him for his helping Margaret turned as hard as the sledgehammer he carried. There was the enemy. How many knew he had a son in William's service? Would Malcolm have been so complacent to leave the master-of-works in their midst if he had known? Perhaps she should tell Euan of Perth, now holding Dunfermline for Malcolm in the king's absence. At a minimum she would keep an eye on this Norman who had such free entrance of the royal household.

But now her place was beside Margaret. Elswyth lifted her skirts to hurry across the yard and up the tower stairs. She fully expected to find the queen melancholy at the departure of her lord, but Elswyth was in no way prepared for the hollow look of the tear-streaked face and desolate eyes that turned to her from Margaret's bed.

"My lady! The babe—"

Margaret managed the flicker of a smile. "He is well, praise God." She turned her eyes toward the tiny bundle sleeping in a cradle beside her. But when she turned back to Elswyth, the haunted look had returned. "They are gone then."

"You need have no fear, my lady—we will be safe here. Euan is old, but a fine mormaor. He will oversee—"

"I have no fear for my own safety." The queen's voice was flat, lifeless. "It is not for myself or even for my babe I fear."

Elswyth smiled and bent to smooth the queen's bedclothes. "My Margaret, Malcolm is a fine warrior. He has survived many a battle unscathed. So he will return to you whole this time. You are but dismal from childbirth. It is common. Let me fetch a harper to cheer—"

"No. No." Margaret's voice was more disconsolate than before as she turned her head from side to side on the pillow.

Elswyth had been with Margaret in the aftermath of the Battle of Hastings, when the Conqueror marched into the Saxon court with his men behind him and took the throne of England. She had been with her through the fearful storm at sea when, fleeing for their lives, the small band of refugees was blown into what waters they knew not until they found harbor in Scotland. She had been with the queen through the crisis of a precipitous childbirth. But never before had she seen such desperation, such hopelessness, on Margaret's face.

It struck fear to Elswyth's heart. Always Margaret's calm, Margaret's strength had held firm for those around her to draw upon. Now that it wavered, Elswyth found herself adrift. "My lady . . ." She stood by the bed, wringing her hands.

Margaret seemed unaware of her lady's presence. "They have gone. Scotland has gone to war. I prayed that it would not be so. Through all the offices of the night. With every breath I drew, I prayed. Why did God not grant my petition? Was I too weak? Were my prayers not enough? Should I have fasted more?" She crossed herself, then folded her hands. "My God, my whole heart is Yours. My whole life is Yours. What more can I do?"

Elswyth backed quietly toward the door. This was beyond her. She must get help. Father Turgot, Father Appin, even Princess Agatha—someone. She had no more than slid the rings of the curtain aside when the door behind it opened.

Father Turgot, comforting in his familiar black robes, entered, carrying the small silver case that held Margaret's cross.

"The Culdee brothers thank you for the loan of this most precious relic, my lady."

"The Black Rood." Margaret held out her hand. "I would hold it. I am in much need of comfort."

But Turgot could not spring the little catch that held the cross inside its casket. Perhaps he too felt some of Elswyth's desperation at the queen's hopelessness, for he fumbled even his third attempt.

Margaret moved her fingers over her coverlet. "Oh, wretch that I am and unworthy. Am I to be judged unworthy to see the holy cross?"

Then the catch sprang up. Turgot took the relic out of its case and placed it in Margaret's hand. She seemed calmed.

Elswyth backed to the door, just to the edge of their murmuring voices in case the queen should call for her.

Turgot's voice took on more strength as he answered Margaret's whispered question. "God is faithful, daughter. Leave it in His hands. Do you have the faith to do that?"

Margaret's head turned on her pillow. "I do not know. I want to be strong—strong for the faith, strong for Scotland. But I am so weak."

Turgot opened his psalter to the fiftieth psalm, and Margaret spoke the words with him: "Offer to God praise as your sacrifice and fulfill your vows to the Most High: Then call upon Me in time of distress; I will rescue you, and you shall glorify Me."

Margaret ran her fingers over the cross. "We are so blind in this life. I know what I think is best. I pray God for what I believe to be His will. But I do not *know*. I cannot *see*." She paused long. "O God, take my groping blindness and transform it with Your light."

By the following week they had still received no word from the south. And indeed, the word they did receive two days later was from an entirely different direction. Cyril had taken a group of his workmen into Perth to look at a quarry of what was rumored to be the

400

finest stone in Scotland—fine red sandstone that could be easily cut into smooth, straight blocks for special parts of the church, such as arches and windows, that must be joined with precision for sure strength in the building.

It was a day of April sunshine. The sun warmed a sheltered angle of the courtyard where a clump of brave narcissus grew against the hall, and there Margaret sat in a cushioned chair holding a nursing Prince Edward in her arms. Maethilda sat on a stool, strumming a light tune on the lute while Elswyth read from a chronicle of Anglo-Saxon history.

At the sound of approaching horsemen the queen signaled Elswyth to quit reading. "See who approaches, Elswyth. Perhaps it is a messenger from Malcolm."

Elswyth hurried around the corner of the building, then slowed when she saw it was only the Norman builder returned from his stone seeking. Yet Cyril approached the hall entrance with purposeful stride.

"The queen is here, sir," she called.

Cyril removed his green plush cap with the padded roldeau and side swag—the most obviously Norman item of his attire—and bowed. "Thank you, lady. But I seek the mormaor Euan." He fidgeted as if distressed.

"If aught is amiss with the building you should speak to the queen."

"Yes—"

Euan himself strode from the hall and settled the matter. "I am at your service, de Vailly. You may speak to us both." He joined the ladies on the south side of the building.

But Cyril was reluctant. "I would not trouble the lady queen."

"You will trouble me more by keeping secrets from me, Cyril. Come. I will have your report."

Cyril bowed. "The stone we sought is fine, even excellent, lady. But this very morning on our way back, we had turned aside by Loch Leven to view some of the fine Pictish standing stones in that area— the carving is wondrously done. But as we would retake the main path, we were all but swept aside by a great host of armored men."

"*What!*" Euan bellowed in a voice that left no doubt about his strength in spite of his gray beard. "Do you mean to tell me, man, that a weaponed troop passed through Perth without my leave? How many were they? Did you recognize any devices?"

The master-of-work shook his head. "Upwards of two hundred, I'd say. Perhaps as many as three. I'd not be knowing any of their marks, but one of my stonecutters is a Northman. He said the black boar was of Moray."

Euan slammed a fist into his other hand. "Donald Bane."

Margaret frowned. "Does the king's brother go to join him in battle?"

"Engage him in battle is more like, I fear." Euan shook his head. "Donald is well-named Bane."

"That will be very troublesome for Malcolm." Margaret handed the sleeping babe to Maethilda.

"It will be more than troublesome. If Malcolm is engaged with William to the front, it would not be a happy thing to have Donald attack from the rear."

"But how would Donald know of this? Malcolm would not have called him. I know he bears his brother no trust." Margaret took three paces forward, then turned. "The king must be warned. But can two hundred or more men expect to travel undetected through the land? Will they not pass by here?"

Euan shook his head. "Nay. It is a lucky thing they came so far down as Loch Leven before turning west to Stirling. Perhaps they are so confident of success they think there will be no need of stealth once the thing is accomplished."

Margaret paled but held steady. "What do you mean? What thing?"

"Donald has made no secret of his desire to rule Scotland. Whether he means to help Malcolm defeat William and then demand more land as reward or whether he means to entrap Malcolm—and mostlike Duncan with him—and claim the throne, either would be unhappy for Scotland."

"Malcolm must be warned. Can you reach him in time, Euan?"

"Och, aye. One man may outride an armored troop any day, and I have no need to go around Stirlingway to cross Forth. I can use the ferryman you established yourself, my lady."

"Godspeed you." Margaret bowed her head, and the men left.

Elswyth knew the queen's next words would be that she was going to pray, but Elswyth spoke first. "My lady, can you believe the word of a Norman in this matter?"

Margaret frowned. "What do you mean, Elswyth?"

"Cyril de Vailly is a fine builder, but he is of people who are unfriendly to us. None know that better than you, Edgar Aethling's sister. Think, my lady. Who else reports these Moraymen? Only this one who stands to benefit by Malcolm's defeat."

"How would that benefit Cyril? If Donald means to entrap Malcolm, would that not aid the Normans?"

"Yes. But such is mere conjecture. If Cyril's report is false, may not such news turn Malcolm from fighting William, leaving the Norman the freedom of Northumbria with open gateway to Scotland?"

"Do you truly dislike all Normans so deeply, Elswyth?"

"Why should I not? They have taken our home. Now they fight to take this, our second refuge. If you send Euan to Malcolm, my Margaret, who will there be to guard us and the new babe?"

At mention of the babe, Margaret caught her breath but for a moment only. "We have Hugh and many loyal servants. But far better, we have our prayers and those of the holy brothers."

Elswyth shook her head. She knew Margaret could not be dissuaded.

43

"Lay the brambles more thickly over the cabbage sprouts," Margaret directed the bent-over, brown-tunicked gardener. "I'll not have the birds eating my seedlings." Dunfermline's kitchen garden, one of her many projects for improving the diet of her people, was green with sprouting onions, leeks, beans, peas, and cabbages. "If this sunshine holds, we shall have need of frames for the peas in another week or so. The king will be greatly surprised at our progress when he returns." She nodded and walked on.

She had managed to keep any note of worry from her voice. It was becoming increasingly important that she show no sign of wavering as the days of Malcolm's absence lengthened. The queen was aware that her ladies and servants, even the Culdee brothers, were watching her. As long as she held firmly confident, so would Dunfermline.

At least she held outwardly. But why did they hear no reliable reports? Surely Malcolm would send messengers?

And the reports they did hear from passing travelers were so muddled and uncertain they were worse than no news at all, giving rise to panic or elation with next to no foundation for either. Unless carried by a direct messenger, anything heard this far north of the Tweed was merely rumor based on gossip based on murmur, whereby one wounded man could grow into a defeated army or one fallen foe could grow into a great victory.

Margaret sturdily shut her mind to all such. She would rely on her communication with heaven until she could hear directly from the king.

She turned her steps toward the church. The foundations all dug, and stonelaying begun, in places the walls of the nave rose almost to her shoulder. Surely Malcolm would return before the walls grew much higher.

Father Appin and two Columban brothers walked along the path of the great structure that stood beside their humble church. Margaret greeted them and commented on the fortunate weather.

But it was apparent that Father Appin saw through her veneer of calm. As the others continued up the path he held his hand up in a blessing of peace. "Take your care to Him, my lady. He is sufficient for all."

"I do not doubt. I have no lack of faith in Him, Father. I lack faith in myself. How can I ever be good enough?"

The monk wrinkled his tonsured brow. "Never."

Margaret blinked.

"We can never be good enough. There is none worthy—only the Lamb of God. We can have secure faith only in Him. Never in ourselves."

Margaret sighed. "Yes, I know. But I fail so often."

"As we all do. But He never fails."

Margaret smiled. His were such comforting words. Turgot would likely have laid another penance on her, but Appin beamed grace.

The sun seemed warmer on her head as she continued the length of the new building. She was just rounding the corner when she heard the pounding of hoofbeats. Perhaps this was the long-awaited messenger. She turned toward the gate.

Then she stopped as the guards heaved open the heavy portal and a rider entered at a furious pace. His head bent forward, he was flecked with foam and blood from the horse, his own sweat staining his leather armor. She barely recognized the wild-looking man who all but fell at her feet.

"*Malcolm!*" She flung her arms around him for support. "Are you wounded? Where are the others? Are they slain?" Could the whole army be lost? Scotland defeated?

A Culdee brother rushed from the cashel behind them with a tankard of ale for the king.

Malcolm drank it at a single gulp, then pulled off his helmet and shook his head, more massive than ever now with weeks of growth of dark red hair and beard.

"Praise God you are returned safe to us, my lord," the monk said. "The battle went well?"

Malcolm shrugged. "The men are happy enough. They bring more booty than they can carry. They ride half a day behind me." He turned suddenly and grasped Margaret as if he could not believe she was really there. "But what of Dunfermline? There has been no trouble? Donald—"

"He did not come this way. We thought he rode to entrap you. Did not Euan warn you?"

"Aye, he did that. God be praised. We beat Donald easily

enough at Hexham. My only regret is that my brother escaped with his head intact on his shoulders."

"Malcolm, you cannot mean that."

"I warrant it would save trouble enough later, lass. But I'd nae shed his blood by my own hand, no. Except when Liulf's scout reported this morning that the Moray men rode for Dunfermline." He pulled Margaret to him again. "If he'd touched you, Margaret . . ."

She pushed gently on his chest to gain a little breathing room, although he smelled so strongly of horse, sweat, and wet leather that she refrained from breathing too deeply. "We are fine here. Why should the man report such, I wonder. But never mind, what of William?"

"Nothing of William. We marched south as far as Cleveland on the Tees and west to Harterness in Cumbria. A few Norman troops from York gave us battle. Cospatrick's men we defeated, but the turncoat lives. I am told he fled to Flanders. It's well enough to have seen the back of him."

"But you gained nothing to settle matters with William?"

"If anything they are worse. If William so chooses, he can now claim we invaded his land. He has excuse to march north if he pleases."

"But what of the English barons who were to rise in support of Edgar?"

Malcolm shook his head again.

"So many false reports, Malcolm. Is it not strange? Can you not as a rule trust your messengers?"

"Aye. It is strange. At least de Vailly's brought by Euan was aright. Things might have been far different had he not brought word."

A shiver ran down Margaret's spine at the thought. Strange— their one accurate report had come from a Norman. Could there be that much error and misjudgment in their own ranks? Or was the king purposely being given misinformation? But why would anyone do that? Now the shiver she felt was not for what might have been. It was for what might yet be.

But she would not speak of such now. Malcolm was returned to her. His war had accomplished nothing he set out to do. But their men returned safe. And his new son had grown much in that time. "Come, see what we have accomplished in your absence, my husband."

Princess Agatha was attending her grandson when Malcolm and Margaret entered. Her eyes grew wide at the sight of the battle-stained king. She flung a hand over her mouth and nose.

"Is it not wonderful, Mother? Malcolm is returned."

"I can see that very well. But what of Edgar? Is he to have his throne?"

Malcolm inclined his head to her. "Your son is well, madam. But the English throne was not an issue we encountered."

"Not an issue? What can you mean? Was that not the whole point of the war? Did you not march on William? Why did you return if the Norman still rules? Are you cowards?"

"The issue was the safety of Scotland, Mother. That Malcolm is sworn to." No matter her personal feelings about war, Margaret would defend Malcolm to her last breath. Especially to her mother. "He would have been happy to do Edgar a service. He already devoted men and money to an embassage south, you will recall."

"To little enough effect," Agatha snorted. "Margaret, you speak as if your brother were a side issue. Edgar's throne is the whole point—" She interrupted herself with a scream and made a dive for the prince's cradle.

Malcolm had stooped to pick up his son.

"Sir, it will not do. My grandson is a prince. And you have dirty hands."

"And my husband is a king . . ." Margaret began.

But Malcolm held out an admittedly dirty hand to silence her. "Nay, she is right. I'll go wash."

That night in hall Malcolm's men were returned. Well-washed, the usual retainers ate in their accustomed places. Those who would stay at Dunfermline only a day or two and then go on to their own duns or farmsteads were served in the courtyard or wherever Hugh could make room as he directed servants and cooks at a furious pace.

Margaret looked about her and smiled while she led her ladies in pouring the accustomed first cup of wine after Father Turgot's prayer. Only those new to court had to be nudged by their neighbors to await grace before beginning. And many had done honor to their return feast by wearing their finest tunics. Those who were traveling on had at least donned clean cloaks or plaids. And Malcolm, washed and his hair and beard trimmed, had had his full time holding his son.

If only William would not take too great an offense at Malcolm's foray, perhaps they could now continue in the peace and prosperity Margaret craved for this land. Now that she was strong enough for long rides again, they could plan a progress through the land to encourage the people and help the holy houses in their work. She had heard much of the holiness of the anchorites, which were a great part of the Columban tradition. She would like to visit these hermits who lived in mountain caves or on islands in the center of lochs. And see the trading centers at Berwick and elsewhere. There was so much to do.

First of all she would ask Malcolm to call the council of churchmen. She had not forgotten for one day her longing to bring the Columban church into universal Christian practice. Indeed, the longing grew. The more she came to love and respect Father Appin and the Culdee brothers, the more she wanted to correct what she saw as error there. Her heart sang with gladness as she filled a cup at the end of a long table.

Then she stopped.

Huddled in a miserable group beside the wall of the weaving and dyeing house, their pale blond heads bent over bowls of stew, was a collection of the saddest-looking people Margaret had ever seen. Her heart went out to them immediately—to the two small children, probably a brother and sister, who clung to each other so desperately; to the young woman who would have been very pretty were it not for the angry bruises splotching her face; and to the men, whose muscled arms exposed by torn tunics showed a strength of body that was not mirrored in their hopelessly slumped shoulders.

"Who are those people?" she demanded of the nearest thane.

He lowered his knife with a succulent cut of roast venison still on it and shrugged. "Just some slaves, madam. Part of the booty."

Slaves. More Saxon slaves. And after she had made clear that she wanted no more such inhumanity in Scotland. She had made every effort to free any she heard of. She had recently sent several, whom Father Appin had told her of, to work with Ebert in his newly established trading company, after exchanging with their owners geese and milch cows from her own byre. And now Malcolm's Northumbrian raid had brought another flood of defenseless victims into the land. It seemed that every farmstead north of Tweed must be worked by English slaves.

She would not have it, and God would not have it. She could scarcely ask God to pour His blessings upon a country where such atrocities were common practice.

"Malcolm, I will not have it." She approached the king with an unaccustomed ferocity that caused him to lower his tankard with a clatter. "Did not you make it clear to your men they were not to take slaves as booty? They must be set free. *Now.*"

Malcolm looked along the table at his captains. "Would you tell me how to order my own men, madam?"

Margaret swallowed and inclined her head in a gesture of apology that she did not feel. She did not apologize for speaking against slavery. But she did apologize for her passionate manner, which could have diminished Malcolm before his men. "My lord, in my deep concern for our people I misspoke."

Malcolm gave a jerky nod. "Aye. You'd nae get far telling my warriors they're no' entitled to their booty."

Margaret reached to refill his cup, then realized her pitcher was empty. She turned as if going for a refill, but in truth she sought her brother.

Edgar sat at a table against the far wall. It was apparent from his manner that his cup had been kept well-filled. As she approached, he drained it again and plunked it on the table. "Ah, just in time, Margaret." He shoved the tankard toward her.

"My pitcher is empty, Edgar, but I must speak to you. Did you know the soldiers took slaves?"

He shrugged lopsidedly. "Slaves, gold, cattle—'tis but the victor's due. It's the way of things."

"But Edgar, these are *Saxon* slaves. Your people. You are their king proclaimed. Cannot you serve these few, at least? Granting them freedom would be a kingly act indeed."

Edgar looked around him. Up and down the table, sturdy warriors, well-fortified with strong ale, cut hefty chunks of meat with their knives and speared them with the sharp tips. "Aye, I could claim power over these men's booty. If I had no care to keep my head on my shoulders."

Torn with compassion for the slaves and frustration over her own impotence, Margaret turned to her bower. It was clear. The slaves could only be freed by purchasing them. She would not claim right to control a man's gold or his cattle. No more would he allow control over his human property. But where would she find so much gold?

In one corner of her room stood the chest where she kept the precious vessels she was collecting for the new church. One candlestick would easily be worth several slaves. But these were God's, sanctified for His holy house. True, she might use them to purchase freedom for His created ones, but there must be another way. She ran her hand over the small cross encrusted with Tay pearls that she had bespoken from a local craftsman. No, it had not been consecrated by any priest—only in her heart. She paused. Such thoughts reminded her of an earlier conversation.

The Maundy money—the chest of gold in Malcolm's room. It was not yet consecrated, he had argued when he threatened to use it to finance his war, the very war that had produced these unhappy slaves. Already her feet were moving as she argued with herself. It had been Malcolm's idea to use the money to pay his warriors. Of course, he meant it to provide equipment to go to war, not for a booty exchange afterward. But there was little difference. And Malcolm would choose that his people be free and happy. He kept no slaves himself—at least not since she had talked him into granting freedom to all at Dunfermline.

The carved wooden chest stood just as it had the day she sat on it many months ago. The cupboard in which she kept her church plate had been made by the same craftsman in their own carpentry shop. Her key, which she drew from the satchel at her belt, opened the king's kist. With a smile she dipped both hands in and let the golden disks fall through her fingers just as she had before.

No more than half the coins slid in their golden shower, however, before the others were knocked to the floor by strong hands grasping her wrists in an iron grip. "And what is this, madam? Would you steal from your own king and husband?"

She looked into his blue-black eyes. "Malcolm—I—I meant no harm. I—"

"Guard!" He thundered. Before the footsteps on the stairs reached the room he continued, "Thief! I caught you in the very act. I'll have you arrested, tried, and condemned."

The booted treads stopped just inside the door. "My lord?" The guard's voice showed his uncertainty at the scene before him.

Still holding Margaret's hands, Malcolm swung around. "Aye. And what do you think of a wife that would steal into her husband's chamber while he is at his meat and take the very gold from his chest?"

The guard shuffled his feet and cleared his throat.

"And what will the justicar say, do you think?"

"Er . . . um . . . my lord?"

Malcolm raised his hands, still holding Margaret's. "Will he not say it's a fine thing for man and wife to think sae alike that she precedes him to his duty?" He let out a great guffaw.

"Er . . . um . . ."

Malcolm released one of Margaret's wrists to wave the man away. "Dona stand there hemming and hawing at me, man. See to your duty before a real thief decides to try our defenses."

Margaret blinked as if to get a better view of her contradictory husband. "Malcolm . . ."

The guard gone, he swept her into a hug, still laughing. "And how did you know what I was thinking? Had you been a few minutes later you would have found me in like posture."

"Oh, Malcolm." She collapsed against him, laughing, crying, and shaking.

He held her at arm's length. "What? Margaret, lass? You nae thought I meant it, did you? You kenned I was just having my bit of fun, did you nae?"

"Oh, Malcolm." She wiped her eyes and kissed him.

It was some time later before Margaret's thoughts returned to the matter of slaves and gold. Wrapped in Malcolm's length of red, black, and green plaid, her moonbeam hair a soft tangle around her face, she bent over the chest with the king beside her.

This time it was Malcolm who reached in for a handful of coins. He held them out and turned to her gently, now with no jocularity. "Margaret, lass, I dona mind you taking the Maundy money for your poor. But if you keep this up, *I* shall be the poor."

Margaret frowned. "What do you mean?"

"The chest was more than half full, even after my queen's generous Easter bounty. Margaret, I dona mind your using the money, but you should tell me."

"Malcolm, I did not."

They looked into the depths of the dark chest. The gleam of gold filled it less than halfway. "Then who did?" Malcolm looked around as if he should find the thief lurking behind a wall hanging. He rose to his feet. "I mean to find out. I canna abide a thief."

A soft word from Margaret turned him to her. "Oh, aye, lass. Take it all. Buy your slaves and feed your poor. I'll see to this other matter." He picked up his belt from the floor and fastened it around his tunic before striding from the room.

Margaret carefully searched the floor to rescue every coin that had been flung there earlier. She gave a few worried thoughts that there could be a burglar at Dunfermline, but her mind was soon taken with plans for an organized effort to free all the slaves in Scotland, not just those whose plight happened to come to her attention. She would make a systematic search through Lothian, Strathairn, Atholl, Buchan, Angus . . . She would establish a system of spies through all the provinces to ascertain who were oppressed with the cruelest bondage or were the most inhumanely treated. She would ransom them and restore them to freedom.

Her plans put wings to her steps, and she sped down the tower stairs clutching a small bag of gold. She would perform her first emancipations in her own courtyard. At the foot of the stairs, however, a conflicting duty presented itself in the person of Elswyth.

"My lady, the babe. We gave him honeyed water, but he will no longer be pacified. Would you have me seek a wet nurse? The Princess Agatha—"

"No, Elswyth. I am much aware of my mother's opinion that I need not nurse my own babes. That is not the only point upon which our views differ."

"No, my lady."

"I will come." Margaret looked at the bag in her hand. Most of the warriors would remain at the castle tonight—with their booty. But those who lived near might return to their own farmsteads yet. And she would have no human being held in bondage one hour longer if she could be the instrument of his release.

Elswyth's voice interrupted her thoughts. "Be you off, Iain mac Euan. I bade you welcome. I've no time for more."

"Iain," Margaret said. "I have a task for you."

"Gladly, lady."

"Take this gold and purchase for me all the slaves held as booty. See that they are comfortably housed for the night and tell them I will see to their needs in the morning."

Iain took the bag with a bow. He loosened the drawstring and drew out a coin. He looked at it with a frown.

"What is the matter? Will it not be enough?"

He weighed the bag in his hand. "Oh, aye. Gold aplenty. I'll get you good bargains. But these coins—"

"The king's Maundy money. Malcolm gave it for my use."

Iain nodded. "As you say, a special minting of the king of Scots. So why, I'm wondering, did I see it circulating in alehouses in Northumbria?"

"No. Surely you mistake."

He held out a coin. "There's little mistaking Malcolm's impressive head. I noted it at the time but did not think of its being the special coinage."

"In Northumbria. What can it mean?" Then Margaret felt a familiar warm wetness at her breast calling her to her mothering duty. She left Iain to sort out the matter.

44

That autumn the fields of Fife and beyond grew a rich silver and gold with ripe barley and oats, so that one riding across the land could think that the moon and sun shone at the same time. Pheasant and grouse ran in the lowland fields, salmon and trout jumped in the wide rivers, and deer bounded across Highland hills. At Dunfermline the king and queen and their mormaors, thanes, and courtiers sat late after long harvest dinners, while the dogs under the tables gnawed contentedly on fat bones and Malcolm's sennachie told stirring tales of adventure and love accompanied by tunes on harp, drum, or pipe as suited the mood of the story.

Tonight the firelight danced on the storyteller's red hair as his fingers danced on the harp strings. He told the story of Fiad, the son of the Lord of the Isles, who fell in love with the beautiful daughter of the King of the Fisherfolk. Often he would watch the maiden Galbrenza at play with her ladies, would smile at her golden laughter, and hum with the harmony of the songs she loved to sing.

But the girl was silly and vain, preferring her own amusements to the love of the prince and choosing to go her own way. And so the prince went back to the land where his duty lay. After his father died, he served his people well as a just and mighty king, but he never forgot the fair maiden to whom he first offered his love.

One day when he was returning victorious from a skirmish with rebels in an outer isle, King Fiad thought to sail apart to look once again upon the fair face and golden tresses that had remained in his heart all those many years. He went to the beach and walked on the white cockleshell sands, thinking of how they had been blessed by the footfall of his beloved.

An old bent crone with wrinkled skin and gray hair hobbled toward him. "What do you here, young man?" she croaked. "Do you not know that this is a place of sorrow?"

"It may be so to you, old mother, but to me it is a place of great joy, for here I loved a beautiful lass. But she was a princess and chose the pleasures of her people rather than my love."

413

A sob broke from the woman, and he looked at her more closely. "It cannot be. Galbranza?"

She hung her head. "It is I. I who was once your beloved. But in my silly thoughtless way I spurned all you offered me for the amusements of the moment. When you left, great unhappiness came upon our people—famine, disease, suffering."

He grasped her hand and held it, rough and wrinkled as it was. "Yet I have found you again. Come with me now. It is not too late."

She looked at him in amazement. "What? You would still have me? No, no. Do not jest with me. I am ugly and broken."

"I do not jest, Galbranza."

"But why?"

"It is true you are sadly changed. But my heart is not. You are still the one I love. My heart has not changed, but it has been broken too. My heart has bled with pain for your refusal of me."

He opened his arms, and she walked into them. Fiad bent to kiss her. And at his touch the wrinkled skin became silken smooth, the cracked lips rose-petal soft, and the thornbush hair shone like spun gold.

The strains of the harp soared heavenward. Margaret dabbed at the corners of her eyes.

Later, when the music had changed to a lively pipe song, and she felt the tightness in her throat diminish sufficiently so that she could speak, she placed a hand on Malcolm's arm. "My lord, I am much remiss."

Malcolm smiled and shook his head. "If you are remiss, lass, there is nae hope for any of us."

"But that is exactly my point. Because I know better, more is demanded of me. To whom much is given much is required. If I allow others to continue in error and do not attempt to teach them better, then the sin is mine, not theirs."

"Your council meeting again, is it?"

"Oh, yes, Malcolm!" Then she drew back. "But you—you do not wish it?"

He took a long drink from his cup before he answered. "Our Columban church and our ways of worship have suited us well for five hundred years."

"But Malcolm, do you not hear what you say? 'Our church.' 'Our ways.' It should not be a matter of our way, our church, but God's way, God's church."

"And only Rome can know the mind of God?"

"I should think that any who read His Word would know such commands as 'Remember the Sabbath day to keep it holy.' Malcolm, you cannot deny that hunting, revels, even drunkenness, are none so uncommon among the people on the Sabbath day. You cannot think that pleases God." She choked and clasped his arm in her urgency. "Oh, Malcolm, you who—"

"Nae, lass." He patted her hand. "I meant not to distress you. Only a little testing to show you the arguments our churchmen will make. I doubt not that your answers will be fine. In the end, though, it will not be your words but rather your life that will answer loudest. Many may dispute your logic of the counting of the days of Lent. But none can dispute your devotion in their keeping."

"Then you will call the council?"

"I will call it."

Malcolm was as good as his word. Within the week the king's messengers rode to Iona, to Glasgow, to St. Andrews, to DunKeld, to Melrose, bidding the leading churchmen of the land to council at Dunfermline that autumn.

In the end, however, it was not in the golden fall-of-the-leaf time that year but in the tender green-budding time the following spring before all could be gathered. Malcolm's messenger returned with the word that Co-Arb Donchad of Iona, chief abbot of the Celtic church, had gone on pilgrimage and retreat to the monastery of Kells in Ireland and could not be expected at Dunfermline until after Easter. And it was unthinkable that the council could be held without the abbot of the cradle of Scottish Christianity.

So throughout the winter Margaret worried and prayed for the great task ahead of her. As always she was lovely, outwardly happy, and complaisant, sharing in others' joy, yet always there was a slight sadness behind her eyes that bespoke the burden she carried for her people to turn their hearts to God.

By the beginning of Lent, Margaret realized she was pregnant again. Neither that joyous fact, however, nor the rigorous schedule she undertook of prayer, fasting, and charitable works kept her from meticulous preparation for the council. She spent long hours in study and meditation on the matter before her—and even longer hours closeted with Father Turgot in her bower, discussing the case she would lay before the leaders of the Celtic church.

"I do not wish them to misunderstand me, Father Turgot. I have great respect for their tradition of worship—Columba, Mungo, Aiden—the founders of the church here I hold in much reverence. They planted the faith well, and such men as Cuthbert, Wilfrid, and the Venerable Bede flowered from the soil they nurtured. I would not do violence to such a heritage."

"No, of course not, daughter. But you must point out that much was lost during the dark times of the Viking invasions. Many of their strongest trees cut down to the roots, if you will. The shoots that have returned have been in many cases fervent and well-meaning but wild. Will such an analogy not hold?"

"Yes, perhaps it will." But Margaret looked doubtful.

"Now, I have here—" Turgot drew a leather-bound volume from his satchel "—the *Decreta Lanfranci*, the monastic constitutions which our great archbishop has written."

Margaret nodded. "Yes, and I have no doubt they are most holy and most complete. But these Celtic bishops and abbots will not readily accept the rules of a Norman."

"Archbishop Lanfranc is achieving great success transforming the old English monasteries. They are much revived and reformed by following this model." Turgot continued to hold out the book.

"I do not know, Father."

"Well, then, perhaps we must settle for second best." Turgot produced his secondary plan in the form of a slimmer volume. "If they will not accept a Norman constitution, perhaps they will consider a Saxon if offered by the hand of their own Saxon queen." He offered her the *Regularis Concordia*, the directory drawn up for England by St. Ethelwold and promulgated by King Edgar, Margaret's ancestor.

She took the book. "Thank you, good Turgot. I will study these well."

And so it was that, three weeks after Easter, Margaret of Scotland sat before a council of the highest churchmen from all of the kingdom. She had ordered for Malcolm and herself tunic and kirtle of the finest white wool, belted and banded with gold and scarlet embroidery, and for new cloaks as well, his of the deepest purple, hers of lavender. Malcolm's auburn hair and beard gleamed beneath a slim, gold coronet while Margaret's silver blonde tresses curled demurely around the edges of a white silk veil held in place by a golden circlet.

The walls of the Abbey Church of the Holy Trinity were not risen high enough to shelter the company, so Margaret and Malcolm sat on high seats halfway down Malcolm's hall.

Co-Arb Donchad, his gray hair curling behind his half-moon tonsure and wearing a simple brown monk's robe adorned only with a golden sun cross hung round his neck, pronounced the opening blessing.

"The embracing of God be upon us,
The guarding of Christ be upon us,
The guiding of the Spirit be upon us,
The compassing of the Three shield us,
The compassing of the Three lead us,
The compassing of the Three aid us.
God before us; God behind us; God above us;
God below us. Keep us ever on the path of God."

Malcolm spoke a few words of welcome.

Then all looked to Margaret, for no matter that the invitation was issued in Malcolm's name and all proceedings couched in terms of the king's leading, everyone knew this was Queen Margaret's council.

She spoke slowly and clearly, for several were aged, and she would have none misunderstand her. Malcolm served as translator where there was need of Gaelic phrases she did not have. She spoke pleasantly with a note of melody in her voice, for these were holy men and she but a handmaiden of the Lord. But she never veered from her careful list of arguments: the calculating of the Lenten fast, the marrying of priests, the keeping of the Sabbath day, the taking of the blessed sacrament at Easter, the coronal tonsure of St. Peter in memory of our Lord's crown of thorns . . . All her arguments were orderly, backed by Scripture or by precedence of Holy Church.

The council was polite. They listened. A few scowled. A few shifted on their stools. But they all listened. And none agreed.

Margaret could tell as she continued her planned speech. Her fine arguments of law and logic were not reaching them. And it was little wonder, for though she passionately believed every word she spoke, she found the contentions dull herself. She was speaking of matters of a truth so powerful, of a faith and a love so all-encompassing it could transform lives and nations, and she was striving to condense them into a matter of stultifying laws. It would not do.

And then she knew. She longed for a harp to accompany her words, but there was none in the room. She hoped her smile could reach them. "My lords, the saddest of all the bard tales are those of unrequited love. It makes my heart ache to think of our Lord—how much He loves His unrepentant creation, and they love Him not. How His sacred heart must break for love of them who return not His love."

The scowl on the tonsured forehead of the wraithlike Abbot of DunKeld slowly smoothed.

"Just as God will never truly give up on a child of His who has turned wayward, so God will never truly give up on a nation that was formed in His name. Where holy men and women have toiled and prayed—where people have believed and worshiped—God will work among them through the ages.

"The faith may go dormant for a time—as seed in the ground or a tree at winter—but where the roots are, the flowering branches will follow. Yet as a tree with one strength can be improved by grafting with a tree of another strength, so can the faith be strengthened. So may it be with the two branches of our faith. The Columban tradition is strong in its understanding of God's grace and in the importance of faith. The Roman tradition is strong in understanding and practicing the holy living to which Scripture calls us. Would we not be stronger to have both grace and holiness? Should not the strength of your faith be borne out in such matters as reverent keeping of holy days? Do we all not need to repent as we see ourselves in the light of the truth of God for the careless way we have treated the faith revealed to us?"

Now none shifted on their seats. Margaret even thought she saw a slight nod from Abbot Melmore of St. Andrews.

"Did not Christ come to earth and die on the cross that we might be reconciled to Him in love? Should we not then as His children be so reconciled to one another?" Now she was certain she saw, if not smiling, at least accepting faces before her.

"Where there is truth there should be no division. The truth is the same from age to age. It ever has been and ever will be, because truth is of the nature of God Himself. The core of truth should unite us rather than our allowing superficial differences to separate us."

Margaret sat back in her chair next to Malcolm.

All eyes turned to Abbot Donchad, who as the highest churchman present sat on the other side of the king. Donchad sat in silence for several moments as if seeking deep inside himself—or, more likely, praying. At last he spread his hands wide. "Come, let us reason together, saith the Lord."

45

The success of Margaret's council spurred new vigor in the building of the abbey. That fall a small group of Benedictine brothers arrived, sent by Lanfranc. The monastery that would support the abbey was not yet ready, so the monks must be housed at the Culdee cashel—with considerable suspicion and reticence on both sides, no matter what agreements the church leaders may have reached. But in spite of uneasy ripples, the work of castle and church continued apace at the dun above the waterfall.

Into the third week now the sun had shone an autumn gold, growing the sugar in the small, round red-and-gold-striped apples in the orchard beyond the palisade, while at the same time the nights were sharply cold, developing their crisp tartness.

Today the fruit was at its peak. All the castle except King Malcolm and the highest nobles would take a hand in the in-gathering and cider making, if only to observe the labors of others and taste the product of the cider press. For the cidering was something of a festival, and all knew that even tomorrow, or certainly next week, dark clouds would roll in from the North Sea and the autumn storms would begin.

Elswyth's chief job for the day was to watch Prince Edward. He was a lively toddler, precocious far beyond his less than two years and bent on exploring all the world had to offer at breakneck speed. It was a full-time job for Margaret's ladies to see to it that the neck he broke was not his own.

She and her ladies stood uphill of the orchard, watching the bustle below as servant lads vied for the honor of climbing to the highest branches while the maids picking from the lower branches kept a sharp lookout for apples that might fall on them none too accidentally. Of long-standing privilege, the pressing was done by Father Appin and the brothers, who took the firstfruits of the brew house for celebrating Communion.

Three of the black-robed Benedictines standing behind the

queen's group had apparently just had the matter explained to them by the Columban monk serving as their guide.

"You mean to say to you drink the juice of *apples?* Not grapes?" Brother Roger pinched his nose in displeasure, which made his French sound oddly high-pitched.

Brother Cynad, the only Culdee who spoke French, nodded. "And did not our Lord make the apple as well as the grape? Of a certainty we serve the juice of the vine for the most of the year, but when the Lord provides such a bounty of sweetness as you see before you, would we not be ungrateful creatures indeed to spurn His offerings?"

Brother Roger's reply was given in a formal Latin, which was lost on Elswyth. She had cared little for her Latin studies and had her attention much distracted at the moment by the insistent tuggings of the princeling.

"I am very weary today." Margaret put a hand on her protruding abdomen. "The babe feels so heavy. Maethilda, I will return to my bower. Elswyth, stay here with Edward as long as you wish it, but do not be ruled by him. I would have you curb any signs of waywardness in him, by force if necessary, for how will he learn to obey God if he does not obey earthly masters?"

"Yes, my—" Elswyth began.

But Margaret was not finished philosophizing. "You are sometimes too soft with him, Elswyth. Remember that you are molding a future king. It is only in learning obedience ourselves that we can then teach others to obey us. And obedience is the only path to serenity."

"Yes, my lady." Elswyth bowed her head, and the queen went on her composed way, her ladies following. "Here endeth the first lesson," Elswyth muttered not quite under her breath.

"What? Did you speak?"

She looked up into Iain's lively smile. She wasn't sure which irritated her more, Margaret's tranquillity or his unshakable good humor. "Not to you, sir."

At that moment Edward slipped from her grip and started toward the orchard as fast as his short legs would carry him over the rough ground.

Iain caught him and scooped him into the air with a flourish that brought a chuckle from the child. "You'll find the view much improved up here, you young nuisance." He plumped the child onto his shoulders and gave him a polished apple to hold, then turned his attention back to Elswyth. "Forgive me—I know your concern is for the queen. I thought she looked much distressed. That is what I wanted to speak to you about."

"Distressed? Margaret? You jest. She who just delivered a lecture on serenity is ever her own best model."

"If you are right, perhaps it would be wrong of me to speak and disturb her calm, especially so near her time as it is. On the other hand, if she were distressed, I'd not be wanting to add to her troubles."

"What troubles could the queen have? The people love her. The king loves her. God loves her." Elswyth did not want a note of bitterness to edge her words. Margaret deserved the love of all. Elswyth herself loved her. She did not begrudge Margaret the love she received. Elswyth would simply like to have her own share.

Love and tranquillity, Margaret's supreme qualities, along with her goodness, had been those most sought by Elswyth and those which most eluded her grasp. Even now she eyed Liulf near a wagon of apples ready to be carted to the press in the brew house. He and Duncan appeared deep in conversation. For a moment the thane glanced her way. She smiled, but the smile was not returned. Probably because Iain stood nearby. It was no secret that there was little love between those two.

Iain, amusing the child on his shoulders, apparently awaited an answer from her, although she had asked the last question.

"You surprise me, sir. I've never known you to be overguarded in your speech. If you seek advice, you may as well speak—if it's a matter of import—for it will reach the queen's ears anyway, and mostlike in larger proportions by then."

Iain shook his head. "It does not seem a matter of such great import. More rumors and grumblings."

"Then why do you bother? Was there ever a time when such were not rife at any court?"

"Aye, that's true enough. It is but the nature of these, striking closest where Margaret cares most—her charities and her churches."

Elswyth sighed. If she was to spend any of her freedom today with Liulf, she must rid herself of Iain's company. "Then speak to the queen. She has gone now to her bower." She motioned impatiently up the hill. "Or to the king. Surely the son of his most trusted mormaor could have Malcolm's ear for a matter touching the queen." She started to turn away, then realized her charge Edward was still with Iain.

"I would rather speak with you."

"Oh, fine. Be out with it."

"You are too gracious. I will seek not to impinge on your time overlong." The fact that Prince Edward was now hammering on

Iain's head with the apple added a certain sincerity to his pledge of brevity. "There is much speaking behind stairs against the queen's hoarding of gold and jewels."

Elswyth gasped. "But they are not for herself. They are for the church. Surely no one can begrudge a gift for God?"

"The building of great abbeys with rich ornamentation is not our way. We have ever, since the time of Columba, preferred to worship God in the great out-of-doors which He created. Many say the ornamentation is of man's works and idolatrous. Others say the gold and jewels could better be used to feed the poor."

Elswyth gave a disparaging laugh. "A scriptural argument indeed. But think which of the disciples made just that complaint when a costly offering was made to our Lord."

Iain smiled. "A quick-witted reply, that, my lady. And there is much truth in it."

Elswyth saw Liulf walk away at a brisk pace, leaving Duncan alone by the apple cart. Her chance to talk with the Thorfinnson was lost, so she might as well turn her attention to Iain, who was at least doing an admirable job of amusing Edward by keeping two apples aloft with one hand while holding the child with the other. "With a little improvement on your skill there will be no need to hire a juggler for the harvest feasts."

"A strange accompaniment to a serious conversation, I fear." He gave her a rueful smile. "But I would hear your mind."

"You need not fear disturbing Margaret with the matter. She is well aware of the gossip and complaints—usually made by those who least wish to contribute to her poor fund, I might add. But she is never disturbed when she knows she is right."

"That is what I ask you—what is right?"

"Margaret would say that such adornment is but a poor attempt to show the spiritual in earthly terms. We must somehow express our love and adoration of God. We show how much we value Him when we give what we most value—and poor weak creatures that we are, we do value material worth."

In exuberance over the juggling show passing before his nose, Edward reached out to grab a flying apple and knocked it off course. Holding the boy by his legs, Iain bent to retrieve the fruit. He settled the child again before asking, "But are we not to value the spiritual things more?"

"Certainly. But not all do so. By such giving to the church we show to those of a less spiritual bent that our true treasures are in heaven. It is but an acting out, an allegory, of the life to come. Does not Scripture refer to streets of gold and gates of pearl? Is it wrong for us to want to reflect this splendor of God's in our pale way?"

Iain nodded without taking his eyes off the leaping apples.

Edward chuckled and clapped his hands.

"Aye, you make fine arguments. Perhaps it would be wrong if Margaret gave gold only for adornment and no charity. But no one in need is ever turned away. Indeed, they are sought out and ministered to by her own hand."

"We were always taught that God cares for all aspects of life. Perhaps in caring for the material as well as the spiritual, Margaret is teaching us that all of life is God's."

Edward, who had never been known to sit still so long before, suddenly tired of the arching apples and began kicking his host.

Iain dropped the apples and set the toddler on his feet. "You may run as far as that tree, you wee pest, but see you come when I call you."

The princeling bounded off, then tripped over several apples strewn on the ground and plopped himself down to chew on one.

Iain turned back to Elswyth.

She was not sure whether the seriousness of his expression was for herself or his concern for the queen.

"I value your conversation, Elswyth. Thank you. My concern for our lady queen is not spiritual but political. It would seem the complaints are more than questions—rather almost an attempt to discredit the lady and her works. I can use your arguments in answer, but I fear they will serve only so far."

"But who would try to discredit Margaret? I could understand a Norman seeking to undermine Malcolm's queen, but she is good even to those who have usurped her brother's throne. It is the very church built by Norman direction that she seeks to adorn. I do not see who—"

"Perhaps those who would have the gold spent on neither church nor poor, but for their own ends?"

Elswyth frowned. "What do you mean?"

"I do not know. That is what I would discover. I do not know who or why, but there are those at court who cannot be trusted."

It was unfortunate that at that moment Edgar, munching on an apple and accompanied by Duncan mac Malcolm, should come sauntering toward them from the far side of the orchard.

Elswyth sprang to the defense of anything that could be a slight against her people. "I hope you do not imply blame on Edgar Aethling. It is true he would have Malcolm provide greater support for his cause, but—"

Iain held up a hand to calm her. "No, no. I would not accuse Edgar of slandering his own sister. I was thinking of such matters as the Scot's king's Maundy money showing up in Northumbria, apparently financing Norman troops. And the promises of English nobles, backed by Malcolm's purse, that reportedly promised to rise to his aid but did not. It seems that nothing but loss came of Liulf's embassage, and still he urges—"

"What! Is *that* the purpose of your conversation, sir? Would you have me believe you came seeking spiritual counsel when you meant only to cast aspersions on one placed higher than yourself? It is despicable to think there are those at court who gossip and quibble because they are jealous of gold. It is a far more contemptible thing that there are those who plot because they are jealous of others." She stalked over to Edward, now with hands, face, and tunic sticky with juice and bits of apple and grass, and jerked him to his feet so sharply that he howled.

Her cross mood extended to everyone she saw around her— especially to Alys, who now emerged from the orchard with a basket of apples to dump in the waiting cart. Frowning, Elswyth watched Iain turn to the daughter of Cyril de Vailly.

"Didn't our mother ever tell you if you scowled like that your face would freeze that way, and then you'd catch raindrops in the furrows?"

"Edgar." Elswyth looked at the Aethling and Duncan mac Malcolm standing beside her. "What nonsense," she snapped. "I was just thinking of how clever it would be of William to have planted a spy in Malcolm's court."

Edgar followed the line of her gaze. "Alys? Pretty little thing. But I don't think it's likely she's a spy. That's a silly notion, Elswyth."

The heir to the Scottish throne was quicker than his English counterpart, however. "I think she means Alys's father," Duncan said. "I can't think of a better place for a spy, Edgar. He has the run of the entire dun. I never did have any love for him—or for half the other notions my father's wife brought with her from the south. But Father hasn't listened to me since Margaret set foot on these shores."

"Well, now—" Edgar began.

Just then a harsh cry broke from the orchard. "Watch it, lass! And is it the de'il chasin' you?"

Followed by angry demands that she come back and pick up the apple basket she had turned over, a serving girl from the hall sped up the hill to Elswyth. "It's the queen, my lady." The girl bobbed a curtsy and gasped for air. "She's brought to bed. The Princess Agatha sent me to fetch you."

424

Elswyth bent to pick up Edward. "Oh, what a lug you are." Edward howled his protest at being disturbed. "No, you must be good now. You've a baby brother on the way."

"Or sister." Duncan shrugged. "Leave the lad here."

Elswyth hesitated.

"The Princess Agatha said to hurry, my lady," the servant girl urged.

"See you watch him good, then." Elswyth handed Edward to Edgar, who looked totally surprised to have a squirming toddler deposited in his arms.

Duncan waved her off with the back of his hand. "No harm can come to him here."

Just over two hours later a thin wail from the queen's bower announced the entry into the world of Prince Edmund, red-faced and impatient to be fed.

Margaret's tired oval face relaxed in a smile as her greedy son found her nipple. "Mother, I know Malcolm is waiting below. I can almost hear the thud of his pacing. Bid him come meet his new son." She turned to Elswyth. "And Edward. He must see his brother."

Elswyth stifled a gasp. She had been so occupied with the birth she had not given another thought to the toddler. "Yes—yes, certainly, my lady. I'll fetch him." She pulled her kirtle and undertunic well above her ankles so they wouldn't hinder her speed and ran down the stairs and through the hall.

She came to an abrupt stop at a small table by the door. Duncan and Edgar sat there playing chess. Liulf was lounging nearby, watching.

"Oh, thank goodness. I was afraid I'd have an awful time finding you." She looked around. "Where is he?"

Duncan looked up, his fingers toying with his bishop's miter. "Who?"

"*Who?*" She tried not to shout. "Who but Prince Edward? Who else was left in your keeping?"

Duncan moved the chess piece to take Edgar's rook. "Oh, yes. What did you do with the brat, Edgar? I think he was with one of the Culdee brothers last time I saw him."

Elswyth slammed her hand on the board, scattering pieces every direction. "What do you mean, you *think*? The last time you saw him? Do you mean he's lost? You said you'd take care of him!"

Liulf was the only one to show proper concern. "But that is terrible! I will help you look for him." He wrapped his gold and russet plaid around his shoulders. "You go to the cashel. I will organize a search of the orchard."

Duncan began picking chessmen off the floor. "I'm sure he's fine. Probably at the cashel like Liulf said."

Elswyth ran blindly from the building. She tried to think of the places he could be, the things that could be happening to him. Two hours he had been unattended. He could be . . . the images were too terrible. She was better off not thinking.

She went to the cashel because she could think of nothing better. Father Appin and Brother Cynad were quick with consolation and offers of help, but, no, they had not seen the child since leaving the apple picking. Cynad, who was younger and could run faster, would check the orchard. Father Appin would go to the brew house. Perhaps the youngster had followed a cart being pulled there.

Elswyth turned to the half-finished abbey. Scaffolding scaled both sides of the west wall, where tiers of platforms were lashed to strong poles by leather thongs. Edward loved to climb. If he were up there somewhere . . . she shaded her eyes and looked upward. She saw no movement but could not see all the layers of platforms. She stepped backward for a better view. Was that something just where the arch of the window curved inward? She was sure she saw a movement.

She stepped backward again and tripped on a building stone. With a cry she fell backward. Her head struck the stone floor.

Elswyth couldn't have been unconscious for more than a few minutes, but the dark was very deep. And her head hurt as if it had been struck by a sledgehammer.

"My lady Elswyth. Lie still. You have had a hard fall."

"No." She struggled to get up, but a wave of nausea made her drop her head back into the lap that held it. "The prince," she protested. "I must find Edward."

"The princeling is missing?" The voice seemed to hold genuine concern. "You think he came here?"

Elswyth forced her eyes to focus on the man who supported her. Then she wished she hadn't. In her clumsy haste she had fallen into the hands of the one man in all of Dunfermline who would be the least likely to help her. Cyril de Vailly. She could not expect his aid again.

She struggled to sit up, but dizziness overtook her once more. It seemed she had little choice but to tell him the truth. "Edward wandered off from the cidering—perhaps two hours ago. I was told he might be with the brothers, but they've not seen him. I thought I saw something on the scaffolding . . ." She waved a hand toward the unfinished wall.

Cyril laid her head gently on the flagstones and stood to look more carefully. "I do not see anything. But perhaps such a little one would not be seen from under the platforms."

Elswyth watched as he began climbing the ladder. Was it possible? Could one not yet two years old climb such a thing? Even one who was such a monkey as Edward? What if he had made his way to one of the upper platforms and fallen asleep? Her heart lurched at the thought.

She forced herself to sit up. Her head throbbed, but if she moved slowly she could control the giddiness. She must watch Cyril. Was she putting Edward in more danger by sending the Norman after him?

Cyril was at the top of the scaffolding now.

"The planks by the window. There." She pointed to the spot where she thought she had seen movement.

Cyril shook his head. "There is nothing. Perhaps you saw a bird."

Could she believe him? She could see nothing from below. She would have to believe him. She certainly couldn't climb that scaffolding. She could barely stand. "Look around. Do you see anything from up there? He was wearing a green tunic. Bright green with yellow embroidery . . ." Her voice caught as she remembered Margaret's joy in adorning the tiny garment for her son.

Cyril surveyed the castle area inside the palisade, then turned to look beyond the wall to the glen of the waterfall. He shook his head and descended the ladder. "Perhaps we should search the glen."

"Did you see anything there?" She wasn't sure whether to be hopeful or fearful. The thought of a toddler in that tangle of underbrush, the craggy rocks lining the steep drop of land, the tumbling burn and waterfall . . .

"I see nothing now. But earlier I recall seeing a man in a bright plaid on the path."

"With a child?"

"Not that I saw, but the youngster could have followed—perhaps attracted by the gay colors."

Elswyth put down the niggle at the back of her mind warning that, if Cyril were the un-friend she suspected him to be, he could be leading her in the wrong direction purposely. "Yes, let us look." She had no better idea, and she was getting frantic. Margaret would be wondering why she had not brought the prince to her long ago.

The thought of searching the glen was daunting. It would take all of Dunfermline to do a thorough job. And it would be dark long before then. Perhaps she should send Cyril for more help now. Usually there would be builders, monks, observers at the church to be called on, but today all were on the other side of the hill. Then she heard footsteps running toward her on the path. A messenger? They had found him? She turned, her eyes shining with hope.

But she could see by the look on Iain's face that he did not bear good news. For once even his mischievous sparkle was gone. "Elswyth, I have just heard. Brother Cynad said Edward—"

"It's true. We must search the glen, but it's so big—"

"Yes." He gave a quick nod and looked around. "The water. We'll do the most dangerous parts first. I'll go up here." He pointed to the rim of the valley where the stream began its rapid descent over the rocks. "You go down." He pointed to the waterfall, then crashed through the brush on the shortest way to the stream.

Elswyth went the way directed. Her head still ached, but the dizziness was gone for the most part—if she moved gently.

Cyril reached the waterfall well ahead of her. They had had little rain lately, so the water was low. But that made the black rocks jutting out of the swirling water look all the more ominous. And accessible. Just at the top of the fall, a row of boulders appeared to offer almost a bridge across the burn.

At first Elswyth thought the fifth rock out was covered with a particularly lush patch of moss. Then a scream rose in her throat. *Edward!* Had he fallen in above and been washed there?

No. He moved. He was watching the water swirl around him. Elswyth started to call out to him, but Cyril held up a hand. "No, do not disturb him. He might move. It would be very dangerous."

She swallowed hard. Yes. Dangerous indeed. Cyril was already in the burn, making toward Edward, when she saw a log swirling down the rushing waters, heading straight for the child. This time she did not stifle her scream.

Cyril saw it at the same moment. He plunged forward. Would he try to push the log away or grab the child? There was barely time to do either as the water swept all toward the fall.

Cyril lunged like a leaping salmon, grabbed Edward in both arms, and took the full blow of the log squarely on his back.

Elswyth, watching in horror on the bank, could feel Cyril's pain. He was in water to his waist, leaning against the rock. His tunic was ripped and his back bleeding. He seemed unable to move, but he never slackened his grip on Edward, who was now squirming and howling.

Elswyth doubted her ability to aid the injured man back through the tumbling water. *Oh God, don't let his back be broken,* she prayed. At least she could take the child. She tucked her skirts high into her belt and stepped into the water. It was barely to her knees, but she had had no idea the pull of the current was so strong. And the rocks were slick underfoot. She grabbed at a bush for balance as her head whirled.

Before she could take another step a crashing of underbrush behind her stopped her.

"The child! Is he—"

She turned to see Iain, ashen faced, running down the bank.

"Thank God," he cried as he spotted Edward in Cyril's arms.

Without pausing, he ran into the stream, and in a few splashes he held the prince secure.

Cyril collapsed onto the rock.

Elswyth held out her arms to take the child. "Cyril. Help him."

Moments later she had Edward warmly wrapped in Iain's cloak, and the Norman was lying on a bed of leaves. "The log hit from the side. I think it twisted my back. I'll just rest a bit." He nodded at Elswyth. "Go on. Take the child to his mother."

"Yes, yes, I must—but—" She looked at the injured man in a turmoil of confusion.

Iain pulled off his tunic and knelt to cover Cyril. "Go on. I'll care for him. Send you help back."

Elswyth nodded and turned up the path. Her feet found the way easily, but her mind was awhirl. Cyril the Norman had saved the Scots princeling at risk of his own life. Cyril, whom she had suspected of spying and subterfuge and perhaps even wishing harm to Edward. Cyril was now lying hurt and bleeding from the great service he had done for a Saxon queen and prince. It made no sense.

She was almost to the top of the glen when she heard a rustle just below her. Could Iain and Cyril be coming so soon? Then she glimpsed bright plaid through the autumn leaves.

"Liulf!" What good fortune. He could aid Iain far quicker than she could send help from the castle.

But there was no reply to her call. She looked again, but this time saw nothing. Had she mistaken? Perhaps she only heard an animal and had mistaken russet and gold leaves for Liulf's cloak. It mattered little, for she met Dungal and another man outside the palisade and sent them hurrying toward the waterfall.

When Elswyth reached Margaret's bower, her remaining fear was relieved, for the queen had fallen asleep immediately after congratulating Malcolm on his fine new son. There was plenty of time to clean and feed Edward before presenting him to his mother. And in the end, by the time Margaret awoke, the princeling himself was sound asleep, having been adventuring all through his nap time.

Elswyth knew Margaret must eventually be told the truth, but she would not distress the queen today. So instead she confessed all to Malcolm, stressing full well the valor of the Norman builder and knowing the king would reward him fully.

With Edward safely asleep in the royal nursery and her own culpability confessed, Elswyth turned to the cashel where she knew Iain would have taken Cyril for nursing by the brothers. She found the Norman, with Alys and Iain by his side, in the room the brothers used as an infirmary.

"Brother Cynad has just given him a draught of poppy juice and honey. He will sleep soon," Alys said.

Elswyth looked at the strained, olive face under the dark, close-cropped hair on the pillow. "Sir, I must thank you—I must apologize—I—"

"No, no. You need do neither. I am thankful I was able to avert disaster."

"But, you—you are sorely hurt?"

"It pains much just now." He shifted one shoulder. "But I will mend."

Elswyth gave a sigh of relief. That was what she had wanted to hear. She glanced at Alys for confirmation.

The girl gave a small smile and nodded.

But Elswyth was too confused to let the matter drop. "I am thankful for that. More thankful than I can tell you." She paused to cross herself. Later she would light a candle and say many Our Fathers. But now she wanted to understand. "But you—you are Norman, and yet you risked all for one who is Scots and Saxon—Normans kill my people."

The voice from the bed was soft but clear—the poppy juice was not working yet. "There was a battle at Hastings, yes. Many Saxons were slain. For that I am sorry, but—"

Even in her present grateful state, Elswyth could not let such understatement go unchallenged. "But, sir, do you truly think that is *all?* Thousands died in the north of England as well when William scorched the earth and slaughtered whole towns."

"You are right. William is my king, but he has done much of which I disapprove. But I serve also a higher King, and He bids us to love one another. As His created ones, we are to be reconciled to Him and then to each other. In such there is no Norman or Saxon or Scot." Cyril's speech slowed. Now the poppy was working. "That is why I build. I build places of worship to serve for reconciliation in a world where so much would tear men apart . . ." His eyelids fluttered, then closed. His breathing smoothed.

"Oh, I should not have said that. I tired him." Elswyth took a step backward.

"No. Do not worry." Alys looked at her father and stroked his cheek. "I am sure you made him happy. It is his favorite thing to say. The first words I can remember from him were that love is more powerful than hatred; building up is stronger than tearing down." She looked from Iain to Elswyth. "Go on. I will sit with him." She held her hand out then to Iain. "I am so thankful—so very thankful that you happened to be there. If you hadn't . . ."

He raised her hand to his lips. "I, too, am grateful."

But outside the small building, he turned to Elswyth. "Elswyth, you must know. I nae just happened to be there. Let Alys think so, but you must know the truth."

"What?" Her head was still aching. So much had happened. She had so much thinking to do about Cyril's words. Could she have been wrong in all that she felt so strongly?

Iain put his hands on her shoulders. "Elswyth, you will nae like this. I dona like it much myself. But you must know. I saw him do it."

"Who? Cyril? You saw him do what?"

"Nay, lass. Not Cyril. Liulf. I saw him."

She stiffened but said nothing.

"That log did not wash down the burn by happenstance. It was lodged by the bank. I was searching for Edward. I saw Liulf push it into the current with his foot."

"But Liulf—" She started to protest that Liulf hadn't even been there—he had gone to the orchard to search. But of course he had been there. She had even called out to him. So why had he hidden rather than answer her? "But why would he do that?" The question came almost under her breath. No. Iain was wrong. Liulf was there, but probably for an entirely unrelated reason. He likely meant to cross the burn near the log and dislodged it by mistake. Of course he didn't even know Edward was there, or he would have come to help.

Wouldn't he?

46

The spring of 1073 was a fair time across Scotland. Bluebells bloomed in thick carpets by woodland edge, lambs tottered in the fields, and everywhere husbandmen and bonders plowed their field strips and prepared the good earth to receive the seed that would grow in another season of bounty.

Likewise the Margaretsons grew sturdy in the nursery, watched over at the moment by Elswyth, who sat winding silver thread around an intricate pattern of pins on a lacemaking pillow. She observed the princelings tumbling with a big yellow dog on the floor. It seemed that all that Margaret put her hand to grew and flowered. The Church of the Holy Trinity, the first stone church in the land, had been dedicated at Easter—although much work remained to be done, under Cyril's guidance.

Elswyth smiled with relief as she did every time she thought of his recovery, although she suspected that his back still pained him at times.

Her litany of Margaret's successes continued. Hundreds of English slaves had been freed under her sponsorship, and many who did not choose to return south, or to work on the land, now worked in the growing merchant trade such as that engaged in by Ebert at Berwick. Already Margaret's ladies commented on the ease with which they were now supplied with fine velvets, silks, and brocades for the vestments, altar cloths, and courtly raiment they stitched.

Manners and worship changed slowly, but Elswyth noted that this year Lenten fasting had begun on Ash Wednesday as a matter of course, and there was rarely any evidence of drinking or dicing on Sabbath days. And she noted that although the poor and orphans still received regular bounty from the queen's hand, fewer showed up at Dunfermline's gate since Margaret had made clear that she expected all who could, especially the churches and cashels, to follow her example of charity.

All in the land was content, it seemed, except Elswyth. Frowning, she interrupted her thoughts to untangle one of the knots that incessantly appeared in her threads but in no one else's. With a cursory glance at the boys, she turned her thoughts inward again. She had never felt herself truly satisfied, especially when she measured her serenity against Margaret's. But she had always told herself that, if she stayed true at her prayers, God would grant her fulfillment.

Such faith seemed much flimsier, however, as doubts about Liulf had grown in her mind since last fall. He was always ready to flirt with her. And she had had much pleasure laughing with the Thorfinnson when he sat at table joking with Edgar and Duncan, or commiserating with him when he complained about the loss of his lands in Northumbria—usually a counterpoint to Edgar's grumbling about the English throne when he was egged on by Princess Agatha. But lately Elswyth found herself even more desolate as doubt that he would ever ask her to be his wife clouded even those small pleasures.

She was convinced that only marriage with Liulf could bring her the happiness she longed for. The thought occurred to her more and more frequently of late that perhaps she should have chosen a religious life after all. She could have taken the veil when Christina did, rather than following Margaret to this land—she seldom thought "barbarian land" anymore—but she sensed no vocation for a religious life.

Truth to tell, she had often wondered how spiritual Christina's call had been. Princess Agatha, however, had already received word that her daughter had been appointed to an important office in her house in Romsey. It seemed certain Christina would become abbess someday.

Elswyth made an impatient gesture, which knocked out three pins holding the delicate filigree of silver thread on her lacemaking pillow. The threads unwound. Now she must begin all again. Better to have gone to Romsey. At least she wouldn't have had to make lace there.

She jabbed a pin back in the pillow. She aimed it at an awkward angle, however, and stuck her finger. Red drops marred the silver lace and white cushion. She stifled her impulse to angry words by sticking her finger in her mouth.

At that moment Margaret entered with her aura of silver serenity. It was all Elswyth could do to keep from throwing the pillow at her, complete with pins.

Margaret sat beside her on another low stool. "Oh, you've stuck yourself." She took the pillow onto her own lap. "Do you mind if I work a bit? I have always found lacemaking so soothing, and I have much on my mind just now." Margaret replaced the pins in a perfect pattern and began winding silver threads around them with the ease of a spider spinning a web.

Elswyth kept her finger in her mouth as a defense against speaking.

Margaret continued. "Father Appin was just here to see me. There is much talk among the Culdees that the heritage of their faith is being taken from them. I tried to make him see, as I did those at the council last year, that I mean to take nothing away except error, and I mean to add much." She looked out the window and continued as if Appin were still there. "Heaven and earth are full of the glory of the Lord. So should we do our best to make all beautiful." She smiled at the lace lying like a moonbeam pattern on her pillow. "The Eucharistic mystery should be a reflection of all redeeming beauty."

Elswyth removed her finger, which had quit bleeding several minutes ago. "Did Father Appin disagree?"

Margaret sighed. "No, but he says their way has beauty in its simplicity. It seems there is much fear, not so much here as at cashels farther away. They say that just as the Vikings destroyed so much of what Columba built, I will destroy what remains. I, Elswyth, I who would only build and beautify and help all to worship God better. Yet I am seen by some as a destroyer."

So all was not the serene perfection in the land or in the queen that Elswyth had imagined. "Perhaps if you could tell them yourself, my lady."

"But I already spoke to the council."

"No, not to the leaders only. But to the small brothers in their cashels, to the hermits, even . . ." Elswyth shrugged. "I do not know, but the common people love you so. Perhaps you could explain your ways to the lesser brothers better than the abbots and bishops could. It is they who complain, is it not, rather than such as Abbot Melmore or Abbot Donchad?"

"Yes, Elswyth. You are right." Margaret's blue green eyes shone. "That is exactly what I must do. We will make a progress to the cashels and hermitages in the near mortuaths. Elswyth, you are such a comfort. You make it all seem so easy, when I can see no way to turn. I thank God daily that He has given me such a friend as you." She put the pillow aside, then turned to embrace Elswyth before leaving the room.

Elswyth shook her head in amazement—amazement that Margaret could be disquieted, amazement that her own few simple words could be significant—amazement that the queen had finished the whole row of lace in those few moments.

Two weeks later Margaret, Malcolm, the princelings, and a goodly group from Dunfermline set out on progress to visit the ancient holy places of Fife and Perth that Margaret had not yet seen. She did not mean to go so far east as Kilrimont, which she had already visited, but did not want to slight the highest house in the land, so she requested Abbot Melmore of St. Andrews to accompany her. Father Turgot and Brother Appin were to go, perhaps as an object lesson that Roman and Columban could worship together.

Elswyth and Maethilda, with several other ladies of the court, attended Edward and Edmund. Iain, Liulf, Duncan, and Edgar were among Malcolm's bodyguard. Princess Agatha had been invited to join them, but she sniffed at the very idea of the discomfort of being dragged about the country in a litter. And of course she would not think of such an undertaking on horseback.

The party set out in a misting rain but with high spirits, for although Margaret had made clear that this was to be in the nature of a spiritual pilgrimage to the holy places, there was much of holiday festival about it as well. The blue and white banner of Scotland and the colorful pennons of Malcolm's thanes fluttered overhead while Malcolm's sennachie played a merry tune on a small pipe.

This was to be a mission of reconciliation, a bringing together of those with different viewpoints. Elswyth smiled. What better time than this to settle the uneasiness that had grown between her and Liulf? Perhaps on this journey to promote love and fellowship she could make progress on the relationship she had desired for three years and more.

He rode ahead of her now, talking quietly with Duncan.

She pulled forward, hoping for the chance of a pleasant word.

"But are you certain, uncle?" Duncan asked.

"Aye. And when it's done we should be at Scone. Convenient for you, I'd say." Liulf laughed.

But it was not a sound that warmed Elswyth. She pulled her mount back. She would talk to Liulf later.

The first night they stopped at Loch Leven, where, Father Appin told Margaret, a very holy anchorite lived on Saint Servanus's Island.

"And who was this Saint Servanus?" she asked, looking across the gently lapping waters of the loch to where one could just make out the form of a small isle.

"It was he who reared the blessed Mungo, first bishop of Glasgow. Mungo, or Kentigern as he was then called, was of royal birth, but his mother was cast from the royal dun when she was found to be with child and unwed. Her tiny coracle fetched up at Saint Servanus's cashel at Culross. There she was given shelter and her son taught the ways of our Lord."

"But why is Servanus's island here? We are many miles from Culross, are we not?"

"Indeed, but the holy men of our tradition have always been much given to seeking time alone with God—in imitation of our Lord Himself, who went apart forty days into the wilderness. Columba had his desert on the Island of Hinba. Servanus had his here, and so have many anchorites made hermitage here, as the blessed Chad, on whom we shall call in the morning."

"I hope he will not mind our interruption. He has gone to such great effort to find solitude. But I would much like to seek his counsel."

Appin pointed to a small flat-bottomed boat nestled in the reeds at the shoreline. "The blessed Chad turns away none who seek in sincerity. This small boat is here for just such purpose."

"All who are sincere—how does he know?"

"Chad lives in close, holy communion with our Lord, who promises that His Spirit will have fellowship with our spirit. The Christ in one believer does well recognize the Christ in another believer."

"And if the solitary Chad deems a visitor unworthy?" Margaret felt her heart skip a beat at the thought.

Father Appin shook his head. "He does not come out of his hut."

"I see." She bit her lip and turned away.

They were entertained well that night at the hall house of a loyal thane. The meats were roasted crisp, the oatcakes brought to table steaming beside orange wedges of sharp cheese. But Margaret ate little.

That night the royal couple was given the thane's room at the top of the hall. Fresh reeds were on the floor and colorful tapestries on the wall. Margaret lay on the wide bed, cradled in Malcolm's arms, but she could not sleep. Tomorrow she would put all to the test. What if she failed? What if the Holy Spirit, who guided the sainted Chad, should deem her unworthy?

Always she had sought to do her best. Yet none but she knew how often she fell short of her goals. What if her best was not good enough? She slid from the bed to her knees. The air filled with the tangy scent of lemon and rosemary as she crushed the strewing herbs she knelt on. Perhaps the scent of the herbs rose to heaven. She did not feel that her prayers made it so high.

The next morning she spent a long time closeted with Father Turgot, making confession of all the shortcomings she could bring to mind. His absolution did little to comfort her.

Father Appin rowed Margaret to the island. All the way she sat in profound silence, listening to the dip and splash of the oars, to the gentle call of wood doves and the trill of larks, and to the hum of small insects just above the surface of the water. The world was fresh and crisp, and the sun gave promise of coming warmth. But Margaret shivered inside her cloak.

At the island Father Appin pulled the boat well up on the shore and handed her out onto the wispy grass. Then he led the way to the clay-daubed, thatched hut where the hermit lived. A small cook fire gave a gray curl of smoke, evidence that Chad had been about that morning. But that was the only sign.

The island was silent. Father Appin approached the hut and lifted the leather doorflap. He shook his head. "Not here."

"Could he have gone ashore for supplies?"

"He does not do that. All he needs is brought to him from the cashel at Abernethy. Perhaps he is still at morning ablutions in the loch."

Margaret nodded. She hoped such a simple explanation would prove true. The fear of a more profound meaning sat like a weight on her. "I will go apart into this grove to pray. Please come for me when he returns—if he will see me."

The last was added under her breath. Without waiting for a reply she walked to a spinney of newly leafed birch and alder trees and fell to her knees. What would she tell Malcolm? How could she face Father Turgot? How could she go on, should she be judged unworthy?

The touch on her shoulder was so light she thought it was only the wind ruffling her veil. When it came again she opened her eyes. She blinked at the apparition of a young child standing beside her. Surely the boy could be no more than ten or twelve years old, and he had the brightest eyes she had ever seen. But no, not a child; he was bearded. An elf or wee person then? She had heard many sennachie tales of such but had not thought they existed.

"You have come to see me, daughter?" When he spoke his voice was that of any elderly man, except softer, more harmonious, as one who had no need of shouting and spent much time singing.

"Father Chad?"

"Nay, daughter, Brother Chad only." He held out a hand to help her rise, then indicated that they should sit together on a fallen log. "I have been waiting here for you."

"But how did you know I was coming?"

"I saw the boat approach."

"Oh—"

He smiled. His teeth were surprisingly white and strong for one of his age. Only two or three were missing. "You are disappointed in such a mundane answer? There is little need for God to reveal what we may learn through the senses He has given us already."

"Yes—"

Chad nodded at the hesitation in her voice. "God reveals Himself to us in the world of His creation and in His holy Word. There is not as much need for special revelation as some would think. Many are too lazy to seek the answers He provides so abundantly for all."

"Yes, or too weak of faith to believe when they find the answers."

Margaret almost shouted her reply, for she had the answer to her own doubts—had had it since that day long ago when Father Appin had told her that indeed she was not worthy—only Christ was. And God would accept His worth for her worthlessness. Her failure to accept this had been her faithlessness.

She blinked at the anchorite as if the sun had just burst from behind clouds. "Yes, yes. Thank you for helping me see." And yet, even as her heart sang for her own epiphany, the ache within her increased. How could that be?

"You bear a great weight, daughter. Do you wish to share it?"

"Yes. Yes, I am so happy, and yet . . ." She paused, groping for words. "I have such a desire for all I would have God do here—His love and peace spread abroad, the land prosperous spiritually as well as physically. Sometimes it is so heavy . . ."

"God would not give you the desire did He not intend you to use it for Him or did He not intend to fulfill it."

"Then it will be of use? This weight of longing I carry?"

"In heaven, yes. That is the ultimate longing. But until then you must be satisfied with the hunger. For the longing is more satisfying than any fullness. You would be less alive without it."

"And the land?"

"Continue your prayers, daughter. Let the weight take you downward to your knees that the longing might rise upward in prayer."

Yes, that had been her pledge at St. Andrews—that the pain of her longing might be a perpetual prayer for Scotland. She had tried to pray without ceasing but so often had forgotten and failed, as all were doomed to fail in this life. But God would accept her poor efforts because He loved her and because Christ was worthy.

Margaret's heart was so light that she felt she could have flown back across Loch Leven to Malcolm. Brother Chad had refused all she in her gratitude could offer him. He truly had no needs. But she had come to him with great needs, and they had been met. She could not just go on as if nothing had happened.

"It was wonderful, Malcolm. He understood. He put into words my deepest feelings. A man who lives alone on an island—yet he knew my secret heart. He is truly a man of God. Malcolm, let us endow a cashel here on the shores of Loch Leven."

Father Turgot, who had been standing beside her, cleared his throat. "Surely you mean a priory, daughter."

"No, good Father, I do not. I mean a Culdee cashel in honor of this Columban brother." She gestured toward the island. "Father Appin—" she turned to the other side "—perhaps one or two of the Dunfermline brothers would come to establish the work here?"

He bowed his head. "Gladly, I am sure."

"Yes, well. That's settled then." Malcolm looked at the sun nearing midday. "Let's be on our way then. We've a far ride to make Euan's castle by nightfall." The king began urging everyone to horse, then more threw Margaret into her saddle than merely assisted her and set out at a fair pace.

In spite of Margaret's best will to keep up with her impatient husband, however, she would not ride by those in need without doing what she could for them. She emptied her own purse first, then relied on whichever courtier happened to be closest to supply coin, cloak, or cap to the needy who flocked to them from field and village.

And she stopped as well for those who were not needy. For many a prosperous peasant farmer bowed low at the side of a field strip to present his king and queen with a basket of eggs or pot of honey. Margaret accepted these with great pleasure, knowing that they would soon feed one who might otherwise go hungry that night.

But her favorite of all were the children, who ran from meadow and farmstead with handfuls of bright blue and yellow flowers for her. These she wound in Bryni's bridle, gave to the princelings to play with, or bade her ladies carry for her. But none were discarded until all their bloom was gone, for she cherished and returned the love her people gave her.

She had visited only one hermit so far on her pilgrimage, and already the whole goodness of God's grace seemed increased to her a thousandfold. It was hers, a special shining gift from God to His beloved child. Therefore she must not keep one shred of it for herself. One to whom He had given so bountifully as to herself must give to all. She was merely a channel through which God's blessing could flow to this land, which He loved even more than she did.

Now all lay clear before her like a glowing path. In her mind she saw the land washed clean of envy, strife, and war, and all the people as free and light of heart as the smiling, red-headed girl skipping toward her with a handful of bluebells just the color of her eyes.

Margaret checked her horse and leaned forward to accept the offering.

47

It was late the third day before they reached DunKeld. Elswyth's frustration was near to exploding. Never had she seemed nearer to her goal. Never had Liulf been more attentive or charming. He who had always seemed stiff, withdrawn, and preoccupied in spite of his handsome person and polished manners was suddenly almost elated. And Elswyth was happy to be the recipient of the widest smiles she had ever seen on his square-jawed face.

The wraith-thin Abbot Oswold of DunKeld, with skin as gray as his hair, had received warning of their coming. He welcomed them to his table and then showed them around the cashel with great pride. It appeared to Elswyth much the same as the other Columban communities she had seen—a huddle of clay and timber thatched buildings within a stockaded enclosure. Gardens and orchards lay beyond the wall. Yet it was clear that this was regarded by many as a place of importance and holiness.

Malcolm explained part of it. "My grandfather Crinan was abbot here. He was killed in battle aiding Duncan, my father."

Margaret was startled by that information. No one was more aware than she of the differences in their church traditions, and yet . . . "A holy man—married and fighting?"

"And does not the state have need of holy men as much as the church? Abbot Melmore of Saint Andrews took much part in battle until he grew so aged." Malcolm nodded toward their accompanying churchman, who was now talking to a group of the DunKeld brothers.

"And I myself was married," Father Oswold added. "Alas, my dear wife is dead these many years, but her herb garden is still carefully tended." His glance rested on a small area filled with clumps of plants of varying shades of green, then seemed to force his mind back to the present. "But come, there is much you must see."

The party moved on, but Elswyth held back, admiring the mingled scents of mint, thyme, and lavender while keeping her eyes firmly on Prince Edward. Suddenly she felt a delicious tickle down her spine as a masculine hand gave a tug to her slipping veil.

441

"Aye, the state has much need of holy men, I'd say. And Malcolm Canmore is never one of them."

"Liulf!" Elswyth smiled into his deep, unreadable eyes. "How dare you mock your king?"

Liulf made a sweeping bow and presented her with her veil. "I mock not. I said nothing Malcolm would not say of himself. But I will not say more if it displeases you."

"It displeases me." It did, but she wasn't sure why. She had thought the same thing of Malcolm many times.

"And would it also displease you if I asked you to walk by the Tay with me?"

Elswyth thought longingly of the smooth-flowing river, its banks lined with yellow green willow and small flowers in lush grasses. Then she looked at the rambunctious Edward gathering stones to fling at birds or—worse—to cram into his mouth. "It does not displease me, but I cannot."

"Cannot someone else mind the lad?"

Elswyth recalled the near disaster that had occurred when she slacked her charge last autumn. She would take no more such risks. She shook her head firmly, more against her heart that implored her to accept than against the implied meaning in the gaze of Liulf's dark eyes.

He gave a curt nod. "Then tonight. After the brat's abed. Meet me south of the enclosure. I've something to say to you."

Elswyth caught her breath. "Yes, I will." Then she turned and ran to catch up with Edward before she should weaken and abandon her duty.

She stayed by the child, but it was impossible to keep her mind on him or on Abbot Oswold's tour. How soon could she hope to be free tonight? Could she bear to wait so long to hear what Liulf had to say? What could it be? Could this important speaking to her be the reason for the strange elation she had noted in him of late? Oh, she did hope so.

"Edward, don't run off." She ran to where he hid behind a standing stone depicting a number of kilted men with pointed beards playing pipes and harps.

Oswold had led the group beyond the small church to a cemetery, where several graves were marked by elaborately carved rock slabs. He pointed to a rock depicting men and beasts apparently marching into battle. In the lower corner a small figure lay, beheaded.

"The tombstone of Abbot Crinan, who fell in battle," he explained.

Margaret bent to examine the back of the stone, which was carved with a simple cross. Several other stones were likewise sculpted with crosses and figures commemorating battles or other important events in the life of the country or of the people buried beneath them.

"Our most precious relic is in here." Oswold led the way into the church. Beneath the small eastern window stood an elaborately carved stone casket. "This once held the dear remains of the blessed Columba, brought here for safekeeping when Viking raids made holy Iona an unfit place. Sadly, DunKeld itself was later raided, and we have now only the casket, which tells his story."

Oswold ran his hand lovingly over the carved surface, then pointed to the engraving of a small sailing ship with several figures standing in it. Edward was taken with the picture and strode forward in a manner reflecting his father to trace the pattern with his finger.

"The man in the front, holding the book, is Saint Columba," Oswold explained to the child. "He was a prince in Ireland, but he was responsible for starting a great war where thousands died. He felt so bad about the war that he vowed he would never set eyes on his beloved homeland until he had taken the new life of Christ to as many people as those whose deaths he had caused. So he set sail northward with his helpers. At every island he came to, he put ashore and looked back. But he could still see Ireland. Finally he came to the most beautiful island of all, which we now call Iona, but people then just called I. Columba could not see Ireland from there, so he knew that was the place God wanted him to build his cashel."

Oswold pointed to a picture of a man praying in front of a building with a cross beside it. "From Iona, monks went to all parts of Scotland, telling the people about Jesus."

"Why is the horse in the water?" Edward jabbed at a barrel-shaped head emerging from a wavy line of water.

"That is the water horse, a fierce monster which lives in one of our lochs. Saint Columba raised a man to life who had been killed by the water horse. Then he rebuked the monster so it wouldn't bother his monks who were doing missionary work around the loch."

Oswold pointed to the fourth panel. "Columba preached to the heathen King Brude of the Picts. King Brude became a devout believer and granted Columba the freedom to preach in all of Pictland."

Edward frowned. "King? He doesn't look like my father."

Malcolm tossed back his head with a roar of laughter and swung the boy into the air. "Nay, lad. That was long ago. But I'll have you know I'm well and truly descended from that Brude of the Picts as well as Fergus mac Erc of the Scots—and so are you. And you'll be a mighty king someday too."

A harsh sound behind her made Elswyth turn. She just caught the cold look in Duncan's eyes before he strode from the church.

But Margaret had seen nothing of that; she was far too entranced by the abbot's story. "But that is wonderful! This whole land Christianized by the work of this Columba."

"Yes. And Columba himself founded our own cashel. Columba and Mungo together. So DunKeld is doubly blessed in its founding."

"And this cashel has been here five hundred years—since the time of Columba?"

Oswold nodded. "That is true, my lady."

"And what of Iona?"

He lowered his gaze and shook his head sadly. "The kings of Scots are buried there still, as you doubtless know, since MacBeth rests there. There is a small church, a few huts for brothers who serve there part of the year."

"A few huts only? But Abbot Donchad—"

"The Co-Arb and the brothers spend most of their time at Kells in Ireland."

Margaret persisted. "But I do not understand. The Viking danger is long past. Why do they not return?"

Oswold shrugged. "The place is little more than a ruin."

"And yet it is so holy." Margaret said it like a prayer, her hands clasped, her eyes shining. "Malcolm, this is wonderful. Such holy men, such holy places. Why did no one tell me? We must endow this DunKeld. A new church—a fine stone one like we are building at Dunfermline. Would that not be a fine thing?"

"Aye, lass, we'll think about it. Perhaps when Dunfermline is finished."

"Oh, yes, Malcolm. You are so good. And you are right. We must finish Dunfermline first. But Iona must not wait."

"Iona?"

"Oh, yes. Was not your heart moved when you heard the story of the great work for the faith that was done there? When you think of the centuries of Christianity in this country—and it all started on that island. And does not your heart weep when you think of it all in ruins—destroyed by the evil men wreak? We must begin immediately on Iona, Malcolm."

"Hmph. It's a great distance."

"But not too far for Abbot Donchad to travel for your council, Malcolm. Surely you could send workmen?"

"Oh, aye. Aye. It could be done. At great expense and effort. Will you not be content with feeding your poor and washing beggars' feet?"

"Oh, Malcolm! You are so good. And I am so remiss. I had not thought. Oh, thank you for reminding me of my duty." She turned to Oswold. "You will gather the beggars from your district that we might minister to them?"

Elswyth thought Malcolm groaned, but it could just have been a noise he made playing with his son.

In any case, it was late, after a prolonged foot washing and serving of soup to the poor, followed by prayers, followed by meat, fish, and fowl, before Margaret left the abbot's table with Father Turgot to hear him recite Compline, as that was an office the Columban monks did not observe. By the time Elswyth had Edward in bed and Maethilda had agreed to stay with him until he was asleep, so that Elswyth could slip out the wicket gate at the rear of the enclosure, a new-risen moon was shining on the Tay.

She stood by the flowing waters, her heart thumping in her throat. Where was Liulf? What if he did not come? Had she been too slow? Had he changed his mind?

She walked slowly along the dark path beside the river, enjoying the beauty, listening to the night sounds, but most of all, longing for Liulf. At last she heard steps behind her.

"Hello," she began, then gave a tiny shriek of surprise as masculine arms came around her. He silenced her cry with his lips. She started to pull away. Then a delicious dizziness swept over her. She nestled against him and returned his kiss. She had dreamed of this ever since those stolen moments below stairs long ago. And the reality was far better than the dream.

At last he raised his head but held her snuggled in his arms. "Oh, lass, forgive me. But I've wanted to do that for sae long."

She wrenched from his embrace. *"Iain!"*

"Aye, and who did you think you were kissing?"

But already she was running up the path, tears stinging her eyes. How could she have been such a fool? So long she had dreamed of Liulf—and then he went off and left her with that . . . that superficial, insincere . . .

"Elswyth? Here. Will you run right past me?"

She stopped and pulled back at the sound of Liulf's voice. She did not want to repeat her mistake. "Liulf?"

"Aye. Who else?"

"I have come."

"So I see. And I am grateful."

"I thought you were not here. I was returning to the cashel."

She could hear amusement in his voice. "It would have taken you some time to get there, even running as you were. It is the other direction."

"Oh."

"I will walk you back. But first I must tell you—ask you. I would have you for wife."

She caught her breath. First the shock with Iain. Now this. It was too much. She sat on a mossy rock.

Liulf stepped toward her, and the moon struck his hair, making it more silver than ever. In the dark his eyes were deep hollows. "I know this is abrupt, but you know well enough that I have long admired you. I could not speak while I had no property. But I have received word. I will soon have my lands back. Events—" He stopped.

"What has happened? I have heard nothing."

"You will soon. All will know soon. But I ask you now. Will you come with me?"

"Tonight?" She probably would if he insisted, but she would rather have time to collect herself first.

"No, no. When all is settled. In a day or two."

"I must speak to Margaret."

"Yes, yes." He sounded impatient. "When the time comes. But we will keep our secret for now, will we not?"

"Yes." She would have likely agreed to anything he asked in her present euphoric state, although she could see no reason for secrecy.

"Good, good. That is settled then. You will like Slaley." He bent forward—she thought he was going to kiss her—but he had more to say, this in an intense, hushed voice. "There is one thing more."

"Yes?"

"Tomorrow we go to Scone. There the palladium of our land is kept. Perhaps you have heard of the Stone of Scone?"

She shook her head.

"It was Jacob's pillow, carried by an invader to Ireland where it served as coronation seat for their high kings. It was brought to Scotland by Fergus mac Erc, who was of the royal Irish blood. It has served as enthronement seat for all the kings of Scots since then."

Elswyth blinked at this fervently whispered history lesson, delivered on the heels of a proposal of marriage and spoken with a far greater sense of urgency. "Oh." It seemed that some response was expected of her. "Yes?"

"Yes. The stone is kept at Scone since Kenneth mac Alpin took it there two hundred years ago and more."

"Oh?"

"Yes. It is kept there in secret. Great secret. For it would not do if enemies of Scotland were to do harm to her great palladium."

"No, of course not."

"Aye, but the queen should see it. Sit on it even—for then she would be more truly queen. Such would do much to help quell the murmurs against her for her Roman ways. But Malcolm is unlikely to think of it. Why do you not suggest the bringing out of the Stone? It could do much to promote the purpose of this progress for the queen to honor Scotland's ancient Stone of Destiny."

Elswyth nodded. She could see the sense of what he said. "Yes. That is a fine idea. I will."

"Good. But do not tell her who suggests it. Let my future wife take the credit. Perhaps you will be rewarded."

Elswyth smiled. She would do as he asked for now. But when it was over and all said what a good idea, then she would tell whose idea it was. That would shut up such as Iain mac Euan, who ever brought to question Liulf's motives.

Liulf talked of his Northumbrian lands all the way back to the cashel. And Elswyth was glad to let him talk, for she had much to think of. He left her at the guest hut where Margaret's women were lodged. Only after Liulf had melted into the shadows of the night did she realize he had made no attempt to kiss her.

447

48

"Aye, here it is. Tom a Mhoid—the Hill of Vows." Malcolm extended his arm toward a gently rounded grassy mound.

Margaret tried to look impressed to match her husband's obvious pride. "Oh, yes. It's very nice."

"Nice? Lass, do you not understand? It's magnificent."

Margaret nodded. Perhaps she was expected to kneel. Elswyth had spoken of a stone of great importance here. Perhaps she had got it wrong. Perhaps it was this little green mound that bore such historic import. She started to sink to her knees.

Malcolm stopped her with a hand under her arm. "Not here, lass." He propelled her up the mound. "Here, on the top. That is where they kneel. But you have no need to. Did you not pledge your fealty in your marriage vows?"

"Yes, truly. But Malcolm, I don't understand. Is the Stone buried in the hill?"

"Nay, nay. The abbots bring the Stane forth from its keeping-place, and the king sits on it atop the hill." He strode to the highest spot, which was in truth not very high, and turned to face her, his stance wide, arms akimbo. "Just here I sat. All the landholders of Scotland came here to swear fealty to their king on their own land."

"On their own land?"

"Aye. They fill their boots with their own soil for the swearing. Is that not better than for the king to ride to each holding?"

"Yes. Yes, indeed."

"And when the ceremony is over they empty their boots. So the hill is built of their vows."

"Oh." At last Margaret understood. This was no natural hill. It had been built up over centuries of loyal Scotsmen—and before them Picts, she supposed—swearing fealty to their chosen king. "Oh, yes." Now her voice was warm with the enthusiasm Malcolm had expected. "It is a grand thing indeed. There are grains of all the freely held soil in Scotland here." Her throat closed as she lifted the hem of her kirtle to observe the spot on which she stood.

Perhaps for the first time she grasped something of the fierce sense of freedom, of rugged independence, even wild energy, that had been much of her initial attraction to Malcolm—even before she discovered the kindness and generosity inside the man—and his strange sense of humor, which she never completely understood but which always made her smile.

"Do you truly see?" His eyes were shining like Edward's when the princeling was greatly pleased with a new puppy. "That is why I am king of Scots—not of Scotland. The mormaors, thanes, and drengs accept my overlordship. But the land is theirs, not mine. It is my job to lead them in keeping it free."

Margaret nodded. She did not truly see, but she realized that it was a profound concept. She had not seen before that there were different ways of being king. "And the Stone—that is of importance also, I am told. Could it be brought forth? Could I see it?"

"Oh, aye . . ." Malcolm sounded hesitant, as if he did not want to disappoint her but was uncertain about granting her request. "It is short notice. Abbot Melmore and the abbot of Scone could bring it out, but it is usual to give them more notice."

"Perhaps I could just look at it then. I would not choose to inconvenience them. Just show it to me, Malcolm."

"Yes, a good idea. But do you not want to visit the cashel first? Did you know they care for a number of orphans here? The brothers teach them their letters, and many choose to become priests or sisters themselves." As he spoke he turned toward the cashel wall behind the hill.

"Malcolm!" Margaret caught his arm and laughed. "I believe you are stalling. Do you not know where the Stone is?"

Malcolm spread his hands wide and shrugged. "I never thought to ask. Kenneth mac Alpin brought it here for safekeeping at a time of much danger to the kingdom. It was important that such be well hid from the Vikings. So the hiding has continued."

"But the abbot would tell the king, surely."

"Oh, aye. I've but to ask. I'll see to it. The brothers are waiting now, though."

All morning Elswyth had been hoping to talk to Liulf, but he seemed preoccupied, looking over his shoulder at the sound of an approaching rider or even a bonder driving his cow to pasture along the beaten dirt road in front of the cashel. Maddeningly, it seemed that every time she sought to catch his eye, she wound up looking full into Iain's smiling face. The mocking twinkle in his eye made her blush and turn away in anger.

449

At last the messenger Liulf apparently watched for arrived, for a man she had observed much in his company of late clapped him on the shoulder, and he turned quickly toward the road. Her heart soared. It must be the news he awaited of his property. Had William agreed to recognize his rights? Was Liulf again master of his own manors and free to take a wife?

In her excitement she followed Liulf, for surely the news was now as much hers as his. She got as far as the group standing outside the orphanage, where Margaret was being read to by a well-scrubbed child. Suddenly she was brought to a stop by a firm hand on her arm.

Iain. Her anger flared. She opened her mouth with a sharp dressing-down on her tongue.

But he gave voice first. "Elswyth, I must speak with you. I meant you no disrespect—"

"I don't know what you speak of, sir. I'm sure nothing could have occurred between us. Unless you refer to the time you pulled me to the floor of the dovecote. But that is long forgotten, I assure you."

"Aye, that's the best way. So long as you do not hold me in displeasure."

"I assure you, sir, I do not hold you at all. You need have no fear I'll say anything your Alys would upbraid you for." She started to brush past him, but he held her arm.

"Alys? Lass, do you think I played false? I'd nae do that. Alys is promised to a man in London." He smiled. "A Norman. But even if she were not, it would make no difference."

Elswyth wasn't listening. She wanted to reach Liulf. She wanted to hear the happy news that would secure her future. She wrenched her arm free and hurried on. But it was too late. Liulf was nowhere in sight.

Margaret led the party back to the little hill where, sure enough, an elegantly carved casket stood atop the Tom a Mhoid. Through the openings on the sides Elswyth saw a large, dark stone, itself carved with interlocking lines. So this was the Stone of which Liulf had spoken with such reverence and which she herself had urged Margaret to have moved into public view.

She walked around the case. Was that a cross carved on this side of the Stone? If so, it must have been added later in the Stone's history, for neither Jacob nor an invader of Ireland would have used such a device. Perhaps that was part of the power and mystery of the Stone —that it had been used as an object of importance, even reverence, through so many generations, with each age leaving something of its own mark upon it.

A fur cushion covered the top of the case, so apparently Margaret meant to sit on it. The queen approached now, walking slowly up the hill, talking to Malcolm.

The king and queen were only a few feet from the Stone when Liulf erupted from the crowd, his sword drawn. Rough-clad warriors, their own swords glinting coldly, rushed from the woods, surrounding the small group of courtiers and monks.

"Duncan, the Stone awaits you!" Liulf gestured with his left hand. His right, holding the sword, never wavered.

"What is the meaning of this?" Malcolm roared. His hand went to his scabbard, but as he had just come from the monastery, it was empty—as were the scabbards of all his men now standing at the mercy of the steel pointed at their necks by the warriors that had charged in from the forest.

"Did you think that a son of Thorfinn would let the murder of his sister go unavenged?" Liulf shouted.

A gasp escaped Margaret. Her face drained as white as her veil. But she stood firm by Malcolm, her head high.

"Did you think I would allow a son of this Saxon wh—Saxon woman usurp the rightful place of my own nephew?" Even in his frenzy, Liulf could not pronounce Margaret impure.

"You're mad! You can't hope to get away with this, man."

"I *have* gotten away with it! Donald's men surround you now, even while William's forces claim Fife."

"What?" Malcolm's thundering voice shook the Hill of Vows. "William has crossed Forth? And I not know it? Impossible!"

"And I tell you that William's forces are at Abernethy on Tay!" Liulf gave a shout of triumph. "Agree to Duncan's enthronement or feel my blade—you and your 'queen,' she who took the rightful place of my sister, along with her mewling brats you think to put in Duncan's place."

Elswyth clutched Edward to her protectively, just as she knew Maethilda beside her did Edmund, asleep in her arms. It was the cry of the prince as he clasped her knees that more than anything else brought all into focus. Liulf had not cared for her. Iain had been right all along. The stolen Maundy money used to buy sword service, the reported uprising of the English lords that never occurred, the log that almost killed Edward, and the whispered words by the moon-silvered Tay last night—all were a plot to bring about the downfall of Margaret and her sons, to enthrone Duncan and have Liulf, whom William would probably make earl of Northumberland, rule as regent.

Infatuated fool that she was, she had played along at every step. Iain. He had been right. She must apologize. If she lived that long.

Her hand moved protectively over Edward's dark curly hair. At the same moment she felt the warmth of a hand at her waist. She knew the touch. It had felt just such a warm comfort when he held her last night. She did not turn, just relaxed the slightest bit against his arm, bringing her ear near his lips. She nodded at his whispered words.

The next instant her fingers that had been fondling Edward's hair so gently tugged sharply at a handful of the princely locks. Edward opened his mouth and let out a howl that could only have been bellowed by a son of Malcolm Canmore.

It caused but a moment's distraction to the Morayman pointing his sword at Edward, yet it was enough. Iain pulled his dirk from under his cloak, dispatched the traitor, and armed himself with the man's sword. In the ensuing fracas, Elswyth could not see the top of the mound clearly, but it appeared that at her son's scream Margaret had turned on Liulf with such force that he retreated a step—one step backward to where the Stone of Destiny caught him in the back of the knees. Liulf stumbled over it and fell to the foot of the hill built by the loyalty of generations of men true to their king.

Malcolm seized the blade Liulf dropped and made quick work of the man who had dared to hold Margaret of Scotland at sword point. "Iain!" he shouted at his captain. "Call your Perthmen. See to my brother Donald that he keep to Moray if he would hold his head on his shoulders!"

Iain called his men and charged to action even before the king's words were finished. Already the Moraymen were melting back into the woods from which they had sprung.

"And now we'll see to William!" Malcolm roared, brandishing the sword still red with Liulf's blood.

A cheer rose from his warriors, running for their horses. But Malcolm did not run. He stopped mid-stride at Margaret's grip on his arm. "My lord, would you ride to battle without bidding me farewell?"

"I ride that I may rid Scotland of tyranny and return to you the sooner, lass."

"Yes, ride you well, and rid you our land well. But will you consider for a moment that there may be more than one way of ridding?"

"Aye, there are many." Malcolm half shouted, half laughed. "There are swords and dirks and arrows, to name but a few."

"Malcolm, I do not jest. There is also entreatment."

"What? Woman, would you have me beg William for my own land which he invades illegally?"

"I would not have you beg. I would have you make treaty, as rightful king to rightful king."

"I'd remind you that Norman William is none so rightful a king."

"And that is why he will make treaty—to get you to agree to his kingship."

Malcolm still held his sword aloft, but he hesitated. "You would have me agree to that—in spite of Edgar's claim?"

"If you do battle with William's troops and beat him to the sword point, what will come next?"

"Next? Why, I'll have him swear never to invade Scotland again. I'll demand gold to repay the damage he's done my land. I'll—"

"Exactly. You'll make a treaty with him."

"Aye." Malcolm lowered the sword. "That's the way of it."

"So why not make treaty *before* lands are burned and men slaughtered?"

"And why do you believe he'd do that?"

"And why do you believe he'd not? As you said, you hold Edgar —focus of Saxon rebellion—under your protection. William is expecting Donald Bane to rise to his support. You've already cut that off. He's expecting revolt in your household troops—perhaps even that Duncan will be the king he deals with, not you. You've stopped that."

"Aye. We have him half beat now. Why should we stop longer than to gather a troop? A few days only. A few skirmishes to keep him occupied while my mormaors gather their men. He'll not likely expect any resistance. It would be an easier thing if my men'd had more warning, but it can be done, never fear."

"Malcolm, I do not doubt the possibility of the matter. I doubt the right of it."

The king gaped at her.

She turned then so that she addressed not only Malcolm but also all his men not yet mounted, her ladies, the abbots who accompanied them, and the brothers of Scone. Standing on the very top of the ancient Hill of Vows beside the Stone of Destiny, as a breeze rippled her soft blue kirtle and white veil, Margaret of Scotland spoke in a voice barely louder than that she used at her prayers, and yet in her intensity it reached every ear.

"Search you your heart, I pray, for what is right. For someday we each must stand before God to receive His judgment as individuals. But that is not all, for also Scotland will be judged as a nation— as all nations will be. And as it will be for individuals, the question for nations will be, What did you do with Jesus Christ? Did you receive Him and then give His love to others? Did you serve Christ as He serves?

"As a Christian nation, marching under the cross of Saint Andrew, was Scotland a loving servant? Or was it mad for power and material wealth? Holy Scripture is not clear on how such judgment will be made—but what if you, my lord, as earthly king, are required to stand before the heavenly King and answer for your nation?"

Margaret trembled as if the breeze that blew her veil shook her as well. She turned and knelt at the Stone as if at an altar.

Malcolm jammed Liulf's sword into his scabbard almost absently. "Hear me, men—Dungal, Alwayn, Morgair, and the household guards shall ride with me. All others go now to gather the Scots host. We will try this matter of treaty. At the least it will serve as a helpful delay. But we will bargain with strength, knowing your sword arms gather behind us. If William will not treat in good faith, he will soon wish he had."

Margaret arose from her stone altar. "You have chosen wisely, my lord. I knew you would. Would not it be a fine thing for the princes and me to ride with you as well as your warriors?"

"To battle? Are you mad?"

"Malcolm, did you not just choose to entreat rather than battle? What better warrant can you give to William that you come in peace than by bringing your wife and babes with you?"

Malcolm shook his head, but then he smiled. "Aye, and Duncan and your brother, Edgar. I would keep them under watch."

Margaret's voice dropped so that only her ladies standing nearest could hear. "Do you think they conspired with Liulf? Not Edgar—"

"I think they needs be watched."

"But could the plot have worked? Would setting Duncan on the Stone have held such power?"

"It would nae have been enough—for declaration by the ri, the subkings of Scotland, anointing by the highest abbot in the land, and the fealty swearing are all a part of the king-making. All that is necessary to be true king of Scots."

"But Liulf knew all that—surely?"

"Aye, he knew. And he knew that part of a ceremony—the most ancient part—was better than none. Once his sword dripped red with my blood, there would be few to oppose him. It might well have served."

Malcolm turned to his troops.

Margaret again fell to her knees at the Stone. "Dear God, I have no words. The ache inside me is too great. Take my pain as a prayer for Scotland."

Malcolm's warriors had not ridden out on progress in battle armor, and the Scone fortress yielded but poor stores. They were enough, however—crested steel helmets to cap the men's flowing hair, a few leather tunics sewn with steel rings to cover their saffron undertunics, and some heavily bossed round targes to shield against Norman sword thrusts should it come to that. In little more than two hours they had forded the Earn and ridden southward until the gray stone top of Abernethy's round tower showed through the trees.

"Aye, the cashel brothers are no doubt glad of their tower about now. It's sure they'll have taken refuge in it at the first sight of William's metaled warriors."

"Shall I ride ahead with Andrew's cross?" Abbot Melmore glanced upward at the blue and white banner he carried. "It will bring comfort to the brothers there and serve as sign to William that we come in peace."

Malcolm nodded. "I'd hate to have him fire the brush he's undoubtedly piled against the tower. No need to heat the brothers unseasonably."

"And how is your French, Abbot Melmore?" Father Turgot looked down his thin nose at the Columban churchman.

"It is very ill, good Father. It would not serve to address the Norman conqueror. Would you accompany me? We can ride together in peace in the hope of bringing more of it into this world, we who both serve the Prince of Peace."

Turgot, bearing Margaret's banner, purple with a red cross, pulled aside Melmore. The path was very narrow, but they rode side by side.

In a short time they returned, and Melmore smiled. "You were right. William has brush piled the height of two men all around the tower, but he has not touched flint to it."

Melmore would have continued, but Turgot apparently thought it was his turn. "The Norman king will talk, but he bids me warn you that if you come not in good faith he will first fire the tower, then he will fire the rest of Scotland."

"Yes, yes. We are well enough aware of William's fondness for scorched earth. I'll none of it in my land if it can be avoided." Malcolm thundered and spurred his horse forward.

The two kings approached each other on the flat meadowland beside the high stone tower that guarded one of the oldest and holiest cashels in the land, for here had once stood an important Pictish capital. Each approached beneath banners born by a captain and followed by a handful of guards. Farther back, their troops edged forward in hopes of coming within earfall of the proceedings. The Scots made a strange-looking assemblage in their hastily collected armor, bright cloaks, and short tunics, their legs bare or clad in cross-gartered hose. The Normans presented a solid wall. Their hair was close-cropped under conical helmets with strange nose pieces, their knee-length chain-mail hauberks protected by long, egg-shaped shields.

Elswyth watched in a state of numb shock. Liulf, whom she had pledged to marry, lay a fallen traitor. His fine words had all been a trick to use her for his purposes. If one held in such fondness and admiration for years could be so false, his promises so empty, what hope could there be for words spoken between kings who were known enemies?

In spite of her inner turmoil, she followed the drift of the exchange, which the monarchs carried out in loud voices, undoubtedly for the sake of having adequate witnesses to each stage of the agreement and the better to gain the support of their men.

It was evident from the first that Margaret had been right. William was none so loath to treat. The first stroke went to Malcolm as soon as it was made clear that William's Scottish support had been dispatched. William would retire south of Tweed.

But there Malcolm must bow, for William would not cede his Northumbrian lands. The best Malcolm could accomplish was the naming of an earl endorsed by the Scots—Waltheof, son of that Siward who had stood in place of father to Malcolm after Duncan's death. Waltheof would make a far trustworthier neighbor than the turncoat Cospatrick.

Malcolm yielded Scottish claim to Northumbria. William must yield English claim to Lothian. So it was. But the exchange was not equal. England had in truth held no Lothian lands for perhaps a hundred years. Northumbria was yet nearly as Scots as English. William acknowledged this. He would give manors in Huntingdon and Cumbria to Malcolm. Rich manors. Twelve in all.

But in exchange, surely Malcolm realized that it would not do that he should harbor the pretender to William's throne at the Scottish court. There could be no true peace between them while Malcolm held the figurehead of dissent. Malcolm argued that Edgar was his wife's brother. All the more that he could not be tolerated, William replied.

Elswyth knew Malcolm well enough to see that his resistance was token only. It took no great force on William's part to wring an agreement that whatever Saxon threat Edgar represented should be exiled to Flanders. Elswyth smiled. It was unlikely that Malcolm cared much one way or another about Edgar. But Princess Agatha would surely go to Flanders with her Aethling son. Let this appear a triumph for William; she knew the truth of it.

William's next demand, however, brought gasps from the Scots. "The weight of Scottish swords has long been heavy on Northumbria. It is our way to demand surety for an agreement to keep the peace. Malcolm, king of Scots, I would have your firstborn son as this surety."

Elswyth felt as if the breath had been knocked from her. She looked at Edward picking wildflowers in the meadow beyond them under Maethilda's watchful eye. Malcolm would never agree to that. It would kill Margaret. Would the armies crash targe to shield even here on this peaceful green field?

Then she smiled. Of course. Not Edward. Duncan was Malcolm's firstborn. Duncan who, whether willingly or innocently, had been the focus of treachery in Malcolm's court. Again, William was solving a problem for Malcolm with his demands.

But Malcolm could not be seen to give in too easily. "My son? Man, that is barbarian. Is not the sworn word of a king good enough for you?"

"I can assure you, Malcolm, your son will be treated ever as a royal prince. He'll be no prisoner but raised as a son in my household."

After a few more exchanges Malcolm nodded in agreement. Duncan rode forward stoically.

Elswyth wondered what the boy was feeling. Resentment? Relief? Excitement? Perhaps a bit of all three.

Malcolm nodded and signaled his bearer to dip his banner in salute. "So. It is done. There will be no smoking thatch in either land. It is well done."

"It is well done," William agreed. "When it is done. One matter more remains. The fealty swearing."

Malcolm laughed. "Aye, a fine jest. I wish I'd made it myself. But you've no need to swear me fealty, William. Your word before witnesses is enough."

William did not smile. "I do not jest, Malcolm. I will have fealty sworn *me.*"

Malcolm's heavy brows met over his high-arched nose. He leaned across his saddle until his full-bearded face was inches from William's clean-shaven jaw. "My son will live obedient in your house. That is understood. But he is Prince of Scots. He will no swear fealty to another crown. The idea is absurd. You made a jest whether you intended or no."

Malcolm started to rein his horse aside, but William's hand on his bridle stopped him. "Not Duncan. I think you purposely misunderstand me. It will not do, Malcolm. *You* will swear me fealty."

Malcolm's face turned an alarming red. It seemed certain that the grass under their feet would soon be a far brighter red.

457

Elswyth backed her palfrey away. She must look to Edward. Take him on her saddle and ride—where? Where would there be safety in all the land once William's fury was let loose on it? To have come so close to peace and then lose all was heartbreaking.

But Margaret did not ride backward. She nudged her horse ahead to take her place beside Malcolm. Her hand rested on his arm for a moment only. "My lord William, I know you will forgive the interruption of a mere woman in man's affairs, for you Normans are much famed for your chivalry. I would only wish to say that you have done my husband great honor in the granting of such fine manors on English soil. I am but newly learning of your Norman feudal system whereby all land is the king's and the nobles do him fealty for their holdings. The Scottish system, it has been explained to me, is much different."

William looked as stunned at Margaret's speech as at her interruption. It was probably her beatific smile, which always made her look like Our Lady, that won the day. For no man could offer discourtesy, much less war, in the face of that. William floundered in gallant speeches that did not trip easily from his warrior's lips.

But the time had been enough. Malcolm had taken Margaret's hint regarding his newly granted manors in England. While William was still wrestling with his speech to Margaret, Malcolm dismounted, drew off his gauntlets and tossed them to Dungal. "Well, will you stay nattering to my lady queen all day, man, or will you get on with the swearing?"

William hastily dismounted and clasped the folded hands which Malcolm extended to him. "I, Malcolm mac Duncan mac Crinan mac Malcolm mac Kenneth, swear to do loyal service to King William for all my lands in England and to hold the same in peace for him."

The satisfied smile with which William had greeted Malcolm's extended hands faded in confusion as the import of the wording of the oath sank in. Malcolm gave him a hearty slap on the shoulder. "We have done a good day's work here, William. Thirsty work. Let us repair to the cashel. I am sure the brothers, once down from their tower, will be all too happy to serve us their best wine."

William held back for a moment longer, then jerked his head in agreement. "Aye. It will serve." Whether he referred to the brothers' wine or to Malcolm's oath mattered little to the troops on both sides, who were now free to break out their own wineskins.

49

By the time the saying of mass in the cashel, much lengthened by many heartfelt prayers of thankfulness for peace, was over the next morning, the Normans had departed from their encampment in the meadow.

Edward set up an enormous fuss to be allowed to climb to the top of the tower from which the brothers had descended with such rejoicing the night before. Elswyth looked at the ladder leading to the small doorway high in the wall and extended her gaze on upward along the narrowing shaft to the tiny window in the top. She pictured the narrow stairs winding their way around and around the inside of the dark tube, undoubtedly filled with dust and dove droppings, and she swallowed as Edward tugged at her kirtle.

But Margaret's firmness rescued her. "We have a good two days' ride to Dunfermline, Edward. Come along like a sensible lad, and you may ride with your father." The jolt of delight that suggestion brought cut the princeling off in mid-howl. Besides, he well knew what the alternative would be should he attempt to disobey his mother.

Malcolm's custody of his son left Elswyth free to enjoy her own thoughts on the southward trip. But *enjoy* was hardly the proper description. For now, with the prospect before her of life's returning to normal, she realized the full impact of her misjudgment. Iain's smile now haunted her as she alternated between chagrin at how she had misjudged him and despair over how she would miss him now that he was gone from her life. She was uncertain just how much he understood of her conspiracy with Liulf, but it was unimaginable that Iain's affection for her—for now she saw it in its true light—could have survived her spurning.

But return of his affection or no, she fretted for the return of his dear person. For peace might reign like the sunshine across the verdant Fife that they traversed, but Iain had gone northward at his king's command. Northward, ill-equipped, in borrowed armor, and with far fewer men than Donald Bane commanded, to do battle with the king's rebellious brother.

It seemed impossible that swords clashed, horses screamed, and men died in this land even now. She closed her eyes to shut out the horrible image. But she opened them even quicker when her mind filled with Iain's impish smile beneath his snapping black eyes and tumbling copper-highlighted dark hair. No. Such could not be gone from her life, gone from the world. Not now that she knew how little life would mean without him.

It was late the second day, as the horses' shadows were stretching long to the east, when Margaret revealed that she, too, was dwelling on matters of war and peace. "Malcolm, the Treaty of Abernethy —it was well done."

"Aye." He nodded. "With your help, lass. I'll admit I'd not seen the way out available in swearing fealty only for lands in England until you pointed it out."

Margaret smiled. "Oh, but you would have, my lord. You needed but a little time to think."

"Harumph." Malcolm cleared his throat.

"But Malcolm, this peace with William—will it last?"

"Aye. For a space."

Margaret nodded somewhat sadly. "Yes. That must be the truth of it. I would wish it to last for always." She looked at Edward riding proudly before his father, and at baby Edmund, asleep in Maethilda's arms. "But no earthly peace lasts for long, does it? It will be for our princely sons to win the peace for their time. We can but hope to give our children a secure land. We cannot do their work for them."

"Aye, I've been thinking much the same. There's something I would show you, Margaret. You're not too tired to ride on a bit, are you?"

Elswyth, riding close behind Margaret's palfrey, followed the queen's long look to the right. It should be soon that they would turn toward Dunfermline. Elswyth could only guess about Margaret, but she knew how thoroughly she longed for her own bed. Last night's borrowed pallet had been a lumpy affair indeed.

And perhaps word of Iain would await them at Dunfermline.

"Why, no, my lord. I'm not the least fatigued. Is there another cashel I should see? Or have you heard of some poor in need of ministering to hereabouts?"

"Oh . . . er . . . aye." It was clear Malcolm had given little thought to the charities that were never far from Margaret's mind. "Would you not like to inspect your ferries and pilgrims' shelters on the Forth?"

"Oh, Malcolm—" her eyes shone like a child offered a special treat "—your goodness ever amazes me. We could send most of our company home and stay at the ferry. I would much like to reward the ferrymen myself. Abbot Melmore has told me how pilgrimages to Saint Andrews increase now."

Elswyth nodded. That would be fine. Let them go on. Just so she was among the party freed to go to Dunfermline.

But it was not to be so. Maethilda, indeed, would return with Edmund, but it seemed Malcolm was enjoying his son's company as much as Edward was his father's, so Edward would go on with them. And so would Elswyth.

The attendant who pushed back the leather door flap of the wattle and thatch building and hurried out to greet the new band of pilgrims fell to his knees speechless when he saw that his guest for that night was to be Margaret herself. The king went all but unnoticed, but Malcolm, who cared little for ceremony anyway, seemed perfectly content with his heather ale, oatcakes, and sour cheese— the usual provision for pilgrims. Father Turgot, who had continued with them, said evening prayers, and Elswyth, at least, was happy with a bed softer than she'd had for several nights.

In the morning a boat large enough to accommodate all their party transported them across a Forth tossed with a stiff wind. Edward enjoyed the ride best of all their company, and he clapped his hands at the swooping gulls and leaping fish. When they rowed near enough to a small inch to see that its mounding rocks were covered solid with fat brown and gray barking seals, Elswyth had to grip the lad with all her strength to prevent his climbing the hull for a better look.

Then they reached South Queensferry, which passed the royal inspection as well as its northern sister. Now Elswyth thought they would be free to return. But she had reckoned without Malcolm's energy. "Aye, it's only two hours' easy ride."

"What is, Malcolm? I thought we had come to see my ferries," Margaret asked.

"Oh, aye, lass. That too. But did I not explain about the fortress of Dunedin above Edwin's Burgh?"

Margaret's wide blue green eyes showed that he clearly had not.

"Oh, well, you'll see it soon enough for yourself. A fine spot. Much derelict now. But it can easily be made the strongest fortress in the land. I was thinking much of this when you were speaking of leaving the peace of the land to our sons. If William or his sons—and that William Rufus, I like nae much—should break treaty, I'd want a

461

stronger keep than Dunfermline for you. And now that Lothian is clearly declared Scotland, we need such a stronghold here."

As they drew closer to the monumental cliff of sheer rock that rose above a straggling village, Elswyth could tell by the look on the queen's oval face that she found the prospect no more pleasing than Elswyth did.

But Malcolm was in raptures about the invulnerability of such a fortress. "The fortress was won for the Scots by King Indulph a hundred years and more ago—in the days when all of Lothian was part of Northumbria. We shall see that does not happen again, for this is fine land, is it not?"

Margaret heartily agreed that it was. They rode along the north side of the craggy hill, where marshland and a narrow loch lay between them and the fortress. On the east side they made a slow ascent through the settlement named Edwin's Burgh by early Saxon settlers, who had become more numerous since the conquering Normans had prompted many to flee northward.

Many such in-comers had cleared forest holdings and built homesteads in the green land spreading out beyond the hill. Others settled in huts of timber and clay along the lower reaches of the slope that spanned upward to the dramatic escarpment. When they reached the top, Elswyth felt herself on the top of the world.

Malcolm directed their gaze to the northwest from which they had come. The waters of Forth spread blue and shining as far as she could see. Then he strode to the western edge of the precipice, so close to the sheer drop of the rock that Margaret spoke with far greater sharpness than usual to remind Edward to hold tight to his father's hand.

Malcolm pointed down the hill to the green, lion-shaped crags that would have been impressive did they themselves not stand on higher ones. "Arthur's Seat they call it, for a prince of Strathclyde who ruled here—some say in Columba's time." He lowered his arm to direct their gaze to the foot of the crags. A cluster of small buildings was just visible. "There's another clutch of monks for you to visit, lass."

Margaret looked, then pulled back from the edge as a blast of wind all but tore her veil from her head. "Malcolm, do you really mean to build in this awful, desolate place?" The thatch had long fallen through the roof timbers, and many of the walls crumbled of what had once been the dun of Indulph.

"But of course. Can you not see what a fine stronghold it will make?"

Margaret nodded. "Oh, yes. A fine fortress indeed. But not a home."

Malcolm's face fell with a look of stricken concern. He grasped both of Margaret's hands—Elswyth darted forward to grab Edward before he could make for the edge of the cliff. "Can you not love it, Margaret? I do mean to build here."

"I can see you do. I cannot love to order, Malcolm, even for you. But I will abide it if you say I must."

There came a sharp tug at Elswyth's hand. Edward's young ears were better than hers, or perhaps it was that, lower to the ground, he was less in the howl of the wind. But either way, he had detected the pounding of an approaching horseman making up the slope from Arthur's Seat. Her heart lurched. Was this the messenger she had awaited ever since Iain had ridden off to battle?

She did not like the speed with which he approached, the almost desperate spurring of his horse, which she could see even from this distance. Why was it that good news could be brought at leisure, but bad news must be spurred forward? The rider still wore his crested steel helmet, so she could not make out his identity. Malcolm had not yet seen him.

She turned to tell the king of the rider's approach. But her news must wait, for Margaret was speaking.

"Build you your fortress, my lord. I will build here a chapel."

"Oh, lass, another abbey? Surely not a great church in a fortress?" The groan was loud in his voice.

Margaret smiled. "No, my lord. Only a chapel. A very small chapel, where I may pray for your soul if you must needs go to war again."

Malcolm's shout of laughter was almost enough to shake the rock of Dunedin. He folded Margaret in his arms. "Aye, lass, you do that. For war or no, I'm sure to need it."

The king was preoccupied with holding the queen, so it was Elswyth who turned to the messenger. If the news was bad, let them have this moment of joy. Margaret might have need of her prayer chapel even before she had time to build it.

50

"Victory, my lord!" the rider shouted above the scrunch of horse's hooves on rock and dismounted with a leap. "Donald's not muchlike to attempt your harm anytime soon."

Malcolm gave an appropriately hearty reply behind her, but Elswyth could not hear with the roaring of the rush of blood to her head. And it's doubtful that Iain heard either as he pulled off his helmet and stood grinning at her.

The grin that she had so long attempted to avoid now held the whole world for her. He opened his arms, and she started to walk into them. Then stopped. She was firmly anchored by the prince's grasp. She returned Iain's grin. "Just a minute. I'll come to you unencumbered."

Elswyth shooed Edward to his father's side and turned to Iain—so patient, so trustworthy, so valiant. And her heart shouted a great *Yes!* Yes to God, yes to Iain. In one breath she quit fighting them both.

She would never be the saint Margaret was, never so utterly tranquil. But in ceasing to strive for her own way, in saying yes to God for His way, she felt a relaxation she had not known was possible. A great calmness grew within her, followed by the seeds of joy.

Margaret had moved to the far side of a broken wall. "Here is where I would build it, Malcolm, this very spot. Small, but very strong. I would build it of stone as strong as this mountain. Because I would have my chapel shine a beacon from the strongest fortress in Scotland for a thousand years.

"I would have this small stone chapel stand a symbol that righteousness alone exalteth a nation. I pray that Scotland will be a truly exalted land."

Behind the wall of Margaret's envisioned chapel Elswyth came to Iain.

* * *

Behind the wall of Margaret's chapel, Mary turned to Gareth. "What an absolutely fantastic place! The view is incredible." She

464

shaded her eyes to look out over the stone ramparts of the castle to Old Town, running higgledy-piggledy down the cobbled streets of the Royal Mile to Holyrood Palace at the foot of Arthur's Seat below. Then she turned to her left and looked across the green valley of Princes Gardens, growing where Nor'Loch had been drained some two hundred years ago.

"There, that's Prince's Street." Gareth pointed to the bustling, flag-lined street up which she had come when she first arrived in Edinburgh. From here she could even look over the top of the Scott Monument and on around to the Forth River Bridge, spanning the Firth at the exact place Queen Margaret had established her ferry nine hundred years before.

They entered the tiny chapel, the oldest building in Edinburgh Castle. Outside, it had looked like little more than a stone block; inside, Mary was enchanted with the dollhouse structure. The first room was plain enough. It had four white walls, but the eastern wall was divided by a fine, pillar-supported, double arch decorated with zigzag carving. Beyond that she stepped up to a semicircular apse. A vase of yellow flowers stood on a wooden altar in front of an arched stained-glass window picturing Saint Margaret in a gold-embroidered purple gown.

Words from the guidebook in Mary's hands jumped out at her: "Above all, she loved God; and, loving her people, she wanted them to love God, too." Her throat tightened, and she had the strongest, strangest urge to kneel.

Had Brad and Hamish not come in just then, she might have done so.

"Is this the actual building Margaret built?" she asked her cousin.

Brad shook his head. "Probably not. This was most likely erected on the spot of her chapel by her son David I. When Robert the Bruce ordered Edinburgh Castle destroyed in 1313 so that it couldn't be used by the English, he ordered that Margaret's chapel not be touched. On his deathbed sixteen years later he issued orders for its repair."

"And so it's come down to us nine hundred years later." Mary shook her head. "What was it Margaret said about wanting the prayers of her people to pour out on the land like an anointing oil in a blessing that would last a thousand years?"

"Aye, lassie, that's about it. Seems you were listening to my wee tale better than yon cousin of yours."

Brad started to protest, then grinned sheepishly when Hamish went on. "It's nae use denying it, laddie. I saw you nodding in the corner." Hamish stroked his fiery bush of a beard thoughtfully. "Aye,

465

nine hundred years. Seems she came pretty close to her thousand—but I ken we've about run out. Seems it's time for a new anointing."

Mary turned away from the altar. History was fine, but such talk for today's world made her distinctly uncomfortable, especially after she had come so close to embarrassing herself by kneeling. "Hamish, you didn't tell us the end of the story, though. What happened to Margaret? Did the peace of Abernethy hold?"

"Aye, it held for twenty-one years. Until the Conqueror's son William Rufus came to the throne. He was as hard a man as his father but not sae strong—a bad combination in a ruler—weakness and cruelty. William Rufus revoked title to the manors his father gave Malcolm at Abernethy and claimed Cumbria for England. He insulted Malcolm and enticed the Scots into a Northumbrian war."

Hamish led them from the chapel as he talked and stood looking down toward the Portcullis Gate and the Esplanade beyond—filled now with temporary seats for the Tattoo. "Can ye nae see the fine auld king, like a grizzled bear, leading his troops off once again with bright plaid cloaks billowing and banners flying?

"It must have been a proud thing, for his sons Edward and Edgar rode with him as well. But Margaret's heart was like to break, for she was sore ill, much due to her overfasting. Now she knew she would have need of her chapel. And there she prayed night and day for the husband, sons, and country that she loved sae dear.

"*Och*, but it's a heavy-hearted tale, for the nephew of a Northumbrian earl, a 'sworn brother' of King Malcolm's, killed the good king by treachery deep in Northumberland. Edward, a fine warrior prince, was killed in the same battle, protecting his father's body from the English.

"Margaret lay already on her deathbed in the castle here. Edgar returned from battle and knelt at her bedside. She demanded the truth from her son, who would have spared her. But she had no need of words, for she had foreseen Malcolm's death. Margaret died four days later, holding the Black Rood."

Mary swallowed. "That's amazing. How do you know so much detail nine hundred years later?"

"Turgot wrote her biography—hagiography, I suppose I should say, because Margaret was destined for sainthood. The only Scot to be made saint in the Roman church."

The group walked on. Mary felt the rough paving cobbles even through the soles of her walking shoes. She surveyed the battery of eighteenth-century cannon looking out over the rooftops of Edinburgh and the Forth sparkling blue in the distance. She imagined Margaret's standing here amid a much different castle and looking at the same blue water. The wind riffled Mary's hair, perhaps only a shade more golden than the Saxon queen's. "So Edgar was king next?"

Hamish's blue eyes sparkled brighter than the Forth waters, and Mary could see a tale coming on. "Nay, lassie, things are seldom so simple. Donald Bane seized the throne, aided by Margaret's second son, Edmund. 'Tis hoped that Edmund later repented and became a monk or some such thing. But Donald Bane was quickly enough run off by the thoroughly Normanized Duncan with a force supplied him by William Rufus. Duncan held the throne for almost a year until he was murdered by one of Donald Bane's mormaors. Then Edgar captured and blinded Donald—did I nae tell you it was a fine bloody tale?"

Mary shuddered, but Hamish continued. "Donald was the last Scots king tae be buried on Iona. Edgar ruled peacefully for ten years, then the throne passed to his next brother, Alexander. Alexander ruled for seventeen—and that brings us tae David."

Mary could tell by Hamish's voice that she was supposed to be impressed, but she knew nothing of King David. "Oh?"

"Aye, aye. Do you nae ken David—the best of the Margaretsons? He wed a fine rich lassie. The daughter of Waltheof, she was. And he ruled as king of Scots for twenty-nine years—one of the best reigns in all Scottish history."

"Well, don't stop. I want to hear about it!"

Hamish laughed. "Nay, lassie. I'd nae be true Scots to be giving it to you for free. It's the tale I'll be telling at the storytelling tonight. You must buy a ticket."

"We wouldn't miss it, would we, Brad?" She nudged her cousin, who was gazing abstractedly over the ramparts.

He removed his silver-rimmed glasses and gestured with them. "This site was originally formed by the core of an extinct volcano. But the action of glaciers moving from west to east left the west side of Castle rock less steep than the north and south faces. Notice how the rock descends here in a series of terraces—"

"Earth calling Bradley Hamilton." Mary gave him a sharp prod, then waved her hand in front of his eyes. "Is anyone but the computer home?"

Brad grinned and pushed his blond mop off his forehead. "Sorry. Was I being a bore? I thought we came on this jaunt to look at rocks."

Mary laughed helplessly. "I'm sure you did. But don't let it come as too much of a shock to you that there are other things in the world. Hamish is telling a tale about King David tonight. I said we'd go. Right?"

"Sure, go. I've got a few things to see to before we leave Edinburgh again, but no reason you can't attend."

"'A few things to see to.' Does that translate 'Sharon is calling'?"

"You got it."

"Well, thank goodness for Sharon. Maybe you aren't so hopeless after all—rescued by the love of a good woman." She turned to Hamish. "I'll be there anyway. Thanks for the tour of the Castle. This place is magnificent."

"Aye, it is that. I need to be getting on just now, but ye'll nae leave without seeing the Honours?"

Mary blinked. "Er . . . huh?"

"Oh, they're verra fine. The oldest complete regalia in all of Europe. A fine sight, a fine tale—I'll tell it ye someday."

Mary felt Gareth's hand warm on her arm. "I'll take her, Hamish, no fear." He paused, then turned to Mary. "And to the storytelling tonight, if you nae mind?"

Mary gave him her special smile that was more a crinkling of her eyes.

Hamish nodded and walked off down the steep cobbled driveway. The billowed sides of his plaid swung above his red and black argyle socks and brogues.

"Um . . ." Brad began, then hesitated.

Mary and Gareth laughed and together gave him a hearty shove on each shoulder.

"Go on. I'll bet this is the day your next issue of *Mineral Mania* comes," Mary said.

"Now that's unfair. But I have been away from my desk for quite a spell, and if we're going to Stirling Monday . . ."

"Go." She turned to Gareth. "You can too, you know. I don't want to be a nuisance."

"You're nae a nuisance."

She caught her breath at his grin. Hamish must have been thinking of Gareth when he told the tale of the young warrior at Margaret's court who had such a saucy smile. The one who was true all the way through.

She was silent as they walked up the slope past grim-faced stone buildings toward the heart of the medieval castle. The climb was steep and the paving stones rough. Two small boys, separated from their tour group, barreled down the way toward them.

Gareth had taken Mary's arm to steer her to the side when one of the boys veered and cannoned into him. Caught off guard on his weak leg, he fell against her. They both sprawled against the stone wall.

"Are you hurt?" He turned instantly to her. "I'm sorry to be sae awkward."

"You're nae awkward." It was a moment before she realized she had so imitated him. She started to laugh, then saw him blush. Whether it was her imitation or his stumble that produced his vulnerability she didn't know. But she walked in even deeper silence to the Scottish National War Memorial.

Gareth pointed to the carved plaque: *The souls of the righteous are in the hands of God. There shall no evil happen to them. They are in peace.*

She nodded, and they moved on. Her lighthearted sightseeing had suddenly taken on a solemn air.

Especially, it seemed, for Gareth. The sparkle faded, and she saw the hollow look in his eyes that told her he was thinking again of the friend who had died unprepared. He was so deep in thought she wanted to take his hand as if to guide a child. She thought of his helping the child home that night at the park. That was it—Gareth looked as if he needed help finding the way home.

Now that she knew the burden he carried, she wished she could help him. But what could she—of all people—do to help someone with what amounted to a spiritual problem?

At the Palace they took their place in the queue of tourists waiting to view the Honours. The approach to the display wound through a history of Scottish kings and queens. Mary paused before a replica of the crowning of Robert the Bruce.

"When Bruce took the throne, the Stone of Scone was nae available—whether away at Westminster or in closer hiding. So he had a crown fashioned as a new symbol of kingship. That was probably the first time a king of Scots was crowned."

Mary nodded at Gareth's explanation, then followed him into the room where the magnificently displayed Honours rested in state.

The golden, gem-encrusted Scottish crown lay on a pillow of red velvet and cloth of gold with gold-embroidered thistles. "Gold from Bruce's crown is in that one. It's the only original crown in Britain—because Cromwell couldn't get his hands on it tae melt it down."

Mary moved on to the beautifully chased silver sword and the elegant gold and crystal scepter, but her mind wasn't really on these symbols, which, oddly, seemed too modern to her. She wanted to go back to Margaret's simple white chapel.

Could all the stories that were told about Margaret be true? Not all of them could be fact, she knew, but the essence of the matter—the strength of Margaret's faith, the beauty of her inner life? Mary, who had felt such inner turmoil of late, could only wish that serenity such as Margaret's was possible. Maybe she would learn more tonight in Hamish's tale of Margaret's greatest son—the one reported to be the most like his mother.

As on her first night in Edinburgh, which now seemed months ago, Mary felt enfolded and warmed by the soft green walls and mellow wood of the old meetinghouse. It was lighted by golden candle glow, and Hamish, sitting at the front in his ancient green and brown plaid, grasping a tall oak walking stick, his wild red hair tonight tied back with a leather thong, could easily have been Malcolm's own sennachie.

She and Gareth took a seat on the front row of chairs. He returned her smile, but she couldn't help sensing a distance in her companion. The thought troubled her, but she had little time to pursue it as the harper began a gentle tune full of the rustle of forest leaves. He left off harping to play a bird call on his tin whistle, then horses' hooves on the drum. And as Hamish began his narrative, Mary closed her eyes and saw a king and his attendants riding through a thick wood.

"King David, the third and greatest of the Margaretsons to reign as king of Scots, was enthroned upon the Stane of Scone. And truly, in his kingship he fulfilled his mother's dream of a nation exalted by righteousness.

"It could fairly be said that he hurled Scotland into a new age— organized, law-abiding, and productive—by the force of his own energy. But best of all, he was a great builder of abbeys. He built Jedburgh, Kelso, Dryburgh, and Melrose, all that Scotland might be strong in the faith he loved. But David built none greater than the Abbey of the Holy Rood at the far end of Edwin's Burgh beyond the fortress of Dunedin. And no abbey's founding could be more wondrous than that of Holy Rood.

"David had called his counselors, mormaors, and thanes to a council in Edinburgh. They sat obedient at the council table, nodding over affairs of state. But they were nae judges or monks; they were warriors and men of action. They could no' sit for long. So David promised them a day of hunting in the fine forests of Lothian. And then Father Alwin, the king's priest, reminded him that the day set for the hunt was the Day of the Holy Rood, the Feast of the Exaltation of the Holy Cross.

"David was much distressed that he had promised a hunt on a day proclaimed by Holy Church as one to be set aside for the feast of the Eucharist. And yet he had made promise to his men—given the word of a king. So he decreed that all should attend high mass, then the hunt.

"There was nae kneeling space in Margaret's chapel for sae many men wide of bulk and clad in wool and leather, so many knelt in the courtyard of the castle. Father Alwin walked among them all, elevating the Black Rood, that all who gathered might see the silver reliquary containing a piece of the True Cross of our Lord sae beloved of David's mother."

A gentle harp song lilted upward like winged prayers.

"And then, tae the hunt."

A pipe trill called all to horse, and drummed hoofbeats clattered from the castle in haste to catch the hart before the morning was sped.

"And as the hunt swept through the woods, David, his mind still filled with thoughts of his mother and her holy example, pulled aside from the rest. For he recognized the patch of wood he was in. It surrounded the tiny blue oval known as Margaret's Loch, some said so-called because the waters were the exact shade of her blue green eyes.

"David was sitting at loose rein on his horse, his arms folded, his thoughts deep on the needs of his land, when there arose a great thrashing of the underbrush behind him. Birds cried out sharply and took to frightened flight. Small animals squeaked and darted across the path. The earth shook with thudding hoofbeats. Only a wild boar could make such a clamor. A maddened, deadly boar.

"David gathered his reins to spur his horse away, but at that moment the creature broke through the trees. No ugly, snorting wild boar with spearing tusks but an elegant stag with a great span of thrusting antlers. More deadly than boar's tusks, those branches of angry daggers—all aimed at David. For the mighty creature, crazed by an arrow wound, plunged blindly forward.

"David's horse snorted and reared, then lunged with a twist that sent the king crashing to the ground. The stag was so close that David could feel the warm moisture of the animal's snorted breath. The king had only time to cry, 'Lord Jesus!' as preparation for his death.

"But the sharp plunge of dagger horns did not come. David felt still the stag's breath, heard the animal's rasping, labored breathing as well as his own, but that was all. All else in the forest was silent. He opened his eyes, expecting to see the enraged stag preparing a final lunge at him.

"But David could nae see the creature. He saw naething save a bright light, which filled all the woods as if the sun had come to earth. And in the center of the light was the Holy Rood—the Black Cross so cherished by his queenly mother.

471

"The stag, no longer in pain, backed away into the wood. David, who hadna moved from where his horse dumped him, rose to his knees.

"'My Lord,' he prayed, 'as You sent the cross into the world that by Your death You would save all who looked to You, so You sent this cross to save my worldly life. Make me worthy, I pray, of this great miracle. Let me be a good king in Your name. And in memorial of this great miracle You have done this day, let me build a great Abbey of the Holy Rood. All in Your will and Your name, O Lord.'

"And King David so did. And it was good."

Mary wasn't sure whether it was the beat of the small drum or of her own heart that cadenced her thoughts as she sat still with eyes closed. Almost all had left the room by the time she opened her eyes. Gareth waited quietly beside her.

She gave him her hand, and they walked from the room.

BOOK 4

Of Priests and Patriots

William Wallace Defeats English at Stirling Bridge, 1297

Robert the Bruce Defeats English at Bannockburn, 1314

51

"Scots, wha hae wi' Wallace bled,
Scots, whom Bruce has aften led,
Welcome to your gory bed,
Or to victorie!"

The tape player boomed the stirring tune, and Gareth and Brad sang at the tops of their voices as the car rolled up the motorway toward Stirling. Mary regarded them with wide-eyed bemusement. Though neither could ever be cast as the stereotyped "dour Scotsman"—which Mary had yet to meet—she had never witnessed such a burst of patriotic fervor from them.

"Now's the day, and now's the hour:
See the front o' battle lour,
See approach proud Edward's power—
Chains and slaverie!"

By the time they reached the sixth verse her head was ringing.

"Lay the proud usurpers low!
Tyrants fall in every foe!
Liberty's in every blow!
Let us do, or die!"

As bagpipes skirled forth on the next number, Mary reached weakly forward to turn down the volume. "You're mad, both of you. I'd been warned about Scottish nationalism, but I've never seen anything like this."

"What, lassie, would you nae have us enjoy a wee little singing of our national anthem?" Gareth grinned as he broadened his brogue for all it was worth.

"*Och,* now! That's nae our national anthem. 'Scotland the Brave' is." Even Brad, whose Scots dialect lay buried under years of university scrubbing, brought out the act for her. "Unless you're thinking it's 'Flower of Scotland' because you sing it at your daft football matches."

Mary laughed, but there was enough honest fervor behind their words that she forbore suggesting that "God Save the Queen" just might be the national anthem.

In their best football stadium voices they took up Brad's suggestion. "Oh, Flower of Scotland, when will we see your like again? That fought and died for your wee bit hill and glen . . ."

Mary didn't understand a word of the history the songs referred to, but the love of country and freedom behind them translated loud and clear. Besides, the melodies were stirring. And Gareth had a beautiful tenor voice. She closed her eyes.

"And stood against him, proud Edward's army, and sent him homeward tae think again."

She opened her eyes when the song came to an end and looked up to see a high wooded hill topped with a monolith of soft gray stone. Its tower was capped with the most magnificent crown dome she had seen in Scotland.

"What's that?"

"The Wallace monument," Brad said from the backseat.

"Oh. As in 'Scots, wha hae wi' Wallace bled'?" She did her best with Burns's dialect.

"That's right. Grand, isn't it? Or grandiose—depending on how tolerant you are of Victorian excesses." Brad pushed his papers aside, preparatory to getting out when Gareth pulled into the parking lot. "But I guess it would be pretty hard to overstate a tribute to Wallace."

"But who was Wallace? I've never heard of him." Mary emerged from the car and looked upward again. "Whoever he was he must have been pretty important to have merited a monument like this."

Brad banged his door shut behind him. "In terms you could understand, cousin, William Wallace was Scotland's George Washington."

"Oh. I didn't know you had one." She frowned, still trying to sort it out.

Gareth spoke softly, coming up slowly on her left. "You're right to ask who was Wallace, rather than what he did. He did plenty all right, but more important was the man he was. He was a man of great determination and vision, a man of loyalty and faith. Of all Scotland's story, his is one of the most inspiring. And one of the saddest. "He's the kind of man we need today to lead against our enemies."

Now Mary was really confused. "Enemies?"

The gravel crunched under their feet. "Far more subtle than

the ones Wallace faced. Not southern knights in impenetrable armor. Unseen enemies, whose destruction can be much worse."

Mary stopped breathing as she looked at the man beside her. She had no idea what Gareth was talking about, but the intensity with which he spoke and the passion sparking his eyes gripped her. She could easily imagine him in shining armor, leading men into battle against overwhelming odds.

She forced herself to move with her companions. A narrow dirt path led almost straight upward from the parking lot to the monument. They had climbed probably less than a hundred feet when Brad spotted an interesting rock outcropping. He started toward it, then stopped. "Er . . . you don't mind if I just dart over here for a bit? I'll see you at the top. And keep your eyes open for Hamish—he said he'd probably meet us here. Not that you could likely miss him if he's around."

"Off you go. Don't give us another thought." Mary and Gareth's conspiratorial grins showed they clearly knew he wouldn't.

And Mary didn't give him another thought, for it was soon clear they had made a mistake in choosing to climb to the monument rather than take the shuttle bus. Gareth was limping badly, his face white and strained. The sparkle was gone from his eyes. There was little hint of the light-footed agility she so admired.

She was deeply concerned for him. She couldn't bear the idea of Gareth in pain, much less the thought that too much strain might cause permanent disability.

But she was even more overwhelmed by her own feelings. She stopped dead on the trail. Her heart cramped so that she could scarcely breathe. She grabbed a tree for support. "I need to sit down." Her voice sounded strangled.

She stumbled to a fallen log offering a seat beside the path. What was this? How could she care so much? And even as she asked, she knew—had known ever since that incredible night of falling stars and streaking comets on the Isle of Mull. She was in love with Gareth Lindsay.

This confusing, maddening Scotsman who talked with such passion about things she didn't understand at all and would probably disagree with if she did understand—this man who was building his whole life on principles she considered outmoded and unenlightened was the one person in the world she wanted to be with more than any other, cared about more than any other, loved more than any other.

And yet as quickly as the thought came, she rejected it. She had known him such a short time. They were nothing alike. And she was in love with Michael. She was going home to marry Michael. Soon.

She glanced at Gareth sitting at the other end of the log. *This is impossible,* she thought. There was no way. No way a bright, success-oriented woman like herself, engaged to a brighter, even more success-oriented man such as Michael, could have fallen in love with someone whose prospects were worse than hopeless. *Infatuation,* she argued. *A kind of shipboard romance.*

"Are you all right?"

The concern in Gareth's voice made her realize she had been holding her breath. She must have turned an alarming shade of puce. She nodded and tried to laugh, but the laugh came out as more of a squeak. "Tired. That's quite a climb. Er—" she was quite sure her knees wouldn't support her yet "—tell me about Wallace." If it were a long enough story, she'd have time to recover. After all, this was only temporary insanity.

"Well, let's see how much I can remember of my history lessons. We don't get much Scots history, you know. It's mostly English."

"But that's iniquitous!"

"Yep. That's one reason I've enjoyed these jaunts sae much. I've learned so much about my own heritage. I can use it in my ministry."

She closed her eyes and set her teeth. He certainly knew how to twist the knife.

"I think the last descendant of Margaret and Malcolm to rule Scotland was Alexander III, one of Scotland's noblest monarchs. I remember my teacher telling how he was returning from Edinburgh to his wife in Dunfermline in the middle of a wild March storm." He stopped; the twinkle was back in his grin. "I always liked that part—she was young and beautiful, he riding through the ice and dark, his cloak whipping in the wind to reach her side. But for all the grand romance of the thing, he never made it. His horse stepped in a mole hole or something. Anyway, he was thrown and killed."

"Ooh," Mary made the appropriate commiserating noises with more intensity than she had intended. Her heart was still thumping, and she had little concentration for a king who died more than seven hundred years ago. Almost none, actually, when Gareth was sitting there with his strange combination of vulnerability and strength, of dedication and humor.

"The heir to the Scottish throne was Alexander's granddaughter," he continued. "She was a three year old whose father was king of Norway. She died on board the ship carrying her to Scotland. Scotland was a kingdom without a king."

"But good law-abiding sort that we are, the matter was to be settled by a Court of Claims. Only trouble was, the man who instituted the court was Edward I, soon to become 'Hammer of the Scots.' Talk about setting the fox in the henhouse.

"At that time he was just calling himself 'Overlord of the Land of Scotland.' In truth, though, Edward's hammering had begun. He insisted that all those wishing to be considered for king swear fealty to him as their feudal superior. And he set English constables, well-backed with English troops, in all the key Scottish castles—to keep the peace, you understand."

Mary tried to follow it all. History made a fine antidote—a distancing from the turmoil she was feeling. But Gareth's voice was so dear, his face so appealing as he wrinkled his forehead to recall what he knew of those long-ago times . . .

"There were thirteen contenders for the throne. The strongest were John Balliol and Robert Bruce, both descended from daughters of King David, I think. Anyway, Edward chose Balliol—he who has come down in history as 'Toom Tabard'—the empty coat. He made about as good a show against the ambitious Edward as an empty coat would have. A month after he was enthroned, he did homage to Edward at Newcastle.

"Seems he tried a bit of resistance, made an attempt at a treaty with some French king to renew the 'Auld Alliance' with France. But John's ill-armed warriors were no match for the English longbows. Besides which, Edward was well supplied with heavy cavalry, which you may translate as Sherman tanks."

Mary was only half listening. Part of her wanted to cling to every detail of Gareth's speech and appearance, while the other half of her mind fought desperately—but with little success—to recall Michael's face and voice.

"Get a good history lesson?" Brad's voice, accompanied by his rustling through the woods, came from behind them.

"Oh!" Her surprise betrayed the fact that she had forgotten her cousin's existence. "Oh, yes. Very good."

"I'm sure you did. Our Gareth's a verra bright lad."

"Bright? He's brilliant." She hadn't meant to say it, but amid all her inner turmoil it just slipped out. "He's the most brilliant—and the *stupidest* person I've ever met!"

Her warring emotions spurred Mary to her feet. "Gareth Lindsay, you need a good smacking. To give up a legal career when with a mind like yours you could go to the very top!"

It had sneaked up on her. The soft speech, the twinkling eyes, the happy-go-lucky grin had masked the absolute brilliance underneath it all. Brad's words had snapped the realization into focus for her. This man could do anything—and he wanted to be a *preacher.* "It's ridiculous."

But the distressed eyes he raised to her made her stop her storming. "Yep."

"So you're not sure?"

"I'm sure I want to—I'm not sure that's enough—or rather, that *I'm* enough." He shrugged and dropped his gaze.

Mary was amazed to realize that he could have doubts. She felt an impulse to reassure him. Silly—after she'd just told him what a dumb choice he'd made.

"Well, not that it makes any difference to me, of course. But I have enough good Scots blood in me that I hate to see waste."

The energy of her confused emotions took Mary to the top of the hill without pausing. She went on to the 246-step stairway that wound to the top of the tower. Let Gareth climb the stairs if he wanted to. It didn't matter to her. She didn't want anything to do with any part of his life.

She paused at the first of the vaulted chambers dividing the tower, the Wallace Sword Room. She stood before the glass case displaying William Wallace's mighty broadsword, but her mind wasn't really on the man who became Scotland's George Washington. She was still back 225 years before Wallace. And her sympathies were with Elswyth. At no time in her hearing of the story of Queen Margaret had she so strongly identified with the serving lady who was disgusted with the saintly queen's serenity at the same time she herself longed for it. But that was just poetry—a sennachie's tale. Such tranquillity wasn't possible. Was it?

She turned from the sword display to enter the round, leather medieval field tent in the middle of the room. She stopped with a gasp when a magnificent bearded figure within, clad in leather jerkin over a long hauberk of chain mail, spoke in a ringing voice as if addressing his troops. In truth, the stirring speech came from a hologram portrayal, yet it was so lifelike it was as if the man himself had come alive.

* * *

William Wallace emerged from his deerhide tent on Abbey Craig. What was that ruckus of men and horses marching southward on the road below? Could Edward's army be returning victorious from Moray so soon?

He scrutinized the banners. It was certain they were English. But this was not a contingent intent on battle, apparently. More on

480

celebrating, it seemed, from the jubilant shouts that echoed against the hillside. Certainly they had no interest in keeping their progress secret.

Boasting and swaggering, they passed beneath him, mere soldiers but lording their presence over the land they conquered, as haughty as if they were proud Plantagenets themselves.

Wallace reached behind his neck and fingered the hilt of the hefty broadsword he wore sheathed on his back because it was too large to carry at his side. Was this the moment to draw it?

His fingers ached to curl themselves around the cold steel and rasp it from its sheath. A battle shout rose in his throat. His legs tensed with the impulse to hurl himself down the hillside and take what toll he could upon those arrogant rapers of his country.

And if he did, the thirty men who had followed him into this forest fastness would be as quick to take arms as he. John Graham, who had just buried his slain father, and Jock Brice, although a Benedictine monk, would like as not outrun him to join battle if he were to give the word. But what would it avail?

The brief pleasure of giving in to the rise of hot blood would be of little value when that loyal Scots blood soaked into the earth along with all the other that had already been spilled. And yet much, much more must be spilled if Scotland were to be a nation again.

With an act of focused will, Wallace forced his hand to return to his side. He walked a few feet deeper into the thicket. Were it not for the turmoil of his mind and the desolation of his country, he would have exulted in the fresh Maytime beauty of the spring-green woods carpeted with bluebells and chorused with bird song. As it was, he was barely aware of his surroundings.

He allowed his mind to flick only briefly to his home in Renfrewshire. Were his parents and brothers still there, planting the rich, black earth with seeds for a late summer harvest? Or had Edward's men. . . . No, that wasn't helpful. He had to keep his thinking clear if he were to lead his men to any useful purpose.

And yet he could not force his mind to battle plans, for his heart sped his thoughts on southeastward to its true haven—the home of his Marion. His mind filled with a picture of his tall, lithe bride to be, walking under apple trees heavy with bloom, the sweet-smelling petals dusting her golden hair. Marion Braidfoot, who would now be his wife had it not been for Edward's ravaging of Berwick.

Although sunshine filtered through the trees on Abbey Craig, the big man shivered with the remembered blast of a March wind coming off the North Sea two months before. Wallace had gone with a message from James the Steward to Sir William Douglas, commander of Berwick Castle, and Wallace had been only too happy to carry a message for his father's overlord.

But when William Wallace arrived at Berwick, no greater contrast could have been imaginable from the heart-singing peace and beauty of his days with Marion in Lanark. Two days before, Edward had crossed the Tweed and marched into the greatest seaport in Britain. Here was centered Scotland's vast wool trade. Through Berwick's harbor poured in the wealth and culture of all western Europe. The customs of Berwick alone were reckoned to be worth a quarter of all British ports.

A cosmopolitan city of trade and culture, Berwick was unused to war. The castle itself was fortified by only a rampart of earth. The Douglas put up a spirited defense against the English invader, but the town soon fell, and Edward set about teaching the Scots a lesson they wouldn't soon forget. Instinctively Wallace put his hand to his nose to block out the remembered stench of blood.

All was quiet the evening he rode into the devastated city, for even the looters had finished quickly and fled the grisly scene. The slaughtered lay everywhere—mounds of heads, impaled bodies so mutilated that their blood ran in rivers along the streets. Neither age nor sex was spared.

Whether the fatal toll was seven thousand or ten times that—and the truth was probably somewhere in the middle—it mattered little to the desolated city and its butchered inhabitants.

A young man in his early twenties, William Wallace was not likely to sit long at such a scene awaiting his battle blood to rise. He would have plunged immediately to join the Scottish army, rumored to have gone south over the border seeking revenge, but he had a prior commission to discharge. So he had headed west again into Douglas lands in Strathclyde to deliver the documents that, as he suspected, were now of little import, although it encouraged his heart that the hardy Douglas was at least talking of raising an army from his own vast lands.

Duty discharged, William Wallace sought the troops marching under the gold banner with the rampant red lion to lend his sword to the freeing of his land. But once again he arrived in time only to see the desolation left by Edward's longbowmen and heavy cavalry. Spottismuir field below Dunbar was dotted with the bodies of the poorly led, overeager Scottish soldiers who had been scattered in a brief battle.

There it was that Wallace met John Graham. Together they searched out the body of John's father, one of the wisest of Scottish barons. Together they wrapped the noble body in the tattered red and gold and bore it home.

After Spottismuir, three earls and seventy knights, the principal leaders of the nation, fell into Edward's hands and were sent to English prisons. So ended Scottish resistance. Grinding the Scots' submission in their faces, Edward marched north through eastern Scotland, planting garrisons in the towns and castles and receiving, almost without exception, the homage of the Scots leaders.

Seemingly bent on removing all symbols of nationhood, Edward ransacked Edinburgh Castle of wagonloads of official records, charters, and other documents. He packed Queen Margaret's Black Rood off to London. He stripped the royal treasury of its crown, scepter, and ring and sent the Honours of Scotland southward. He clapped King John Balliol in chains and sent him to exile.

The nation of Scotland lay inert.

But it lived in the minds and hearts of William Wallace and the small band of freedom fighters gathered around him in the forest.

52

The snap of a breaking twig behind him brought Wallace to his feet in a lightning move astonishing for one so large. He crouched, battle-ready. His sword slipped from its sheath in a single slice.

"S-s-sorry!" A young man with red gold hair and surprisingly blue eyes held up both hands and stepped back a pace, cracking several more twigs in the maneuver. "I didna want to bother you, but the man on guard—in a monk's robe he is—" the blue eyes widened in even more amazement "—he said I should speak to you."

Wallace grinned slowly as he let his sword slip back into its sheath. He ran a broad hand through his red-tinged dark beard as he calculated that the youth before him, although tall and broad-shouldered, was not yet old enough to grow a beard. "Well, then, let you be speaking rather than sneaking up on a man in his meditations. You are . . ."

"Jamie. James MacInnes. I've come from Scone. From Sir Kenneth Corvan, whom I serve."

Wallace frowned. "I know no Corvan. How did he know of me? And where to find me?"

The young man grinned, extending his square chin and showing his fine teeth. "But all know the name of William Wallace." He paused and looked down. "Well—all who whisper in dark corners that Scotland must be freed of the tyrant Edward, that is. It is rumored that you gather men for battle."

"It cannot be many who speak so. But how did you find me?"

"It was thought that you follow Edward northward. Had you been at Scone for his great act of vandalism, your sword would not have stayed sheathed. So my lord thought you still southward in the forest. Beyond that it was luck."

He paused to survey the last of the English army unit rattling down the road below, the heavy wheels of their supply carts lurching at the ruts. "Or not so lucky. For I am too late—and by only a hair's breadth it seems. There was hope that you might ambush them and regain the Stone."

"The Stane? Edward has taken the Stane of Scone as well?"

Jamie pointed to the last of the baggage train disappearing around a bend in the track. "Perhaps if we ride after them now? It's certain to be in one of those carts. No man could carry such a great chunk on a horse, even fitted with rings as Edward ordered it."

Wallace shook his head of dark curly hair. "Nay. If we had known sooner perhaps. But thirty men canna attack two hundred from the rear. What do you mean, Edward had it fitted with rings? Have you seen the Stane?"

"Oh, aye. A massive chunk of red sandstone this wide and long." Jamie MacInnes spread long-fingered hands to a width greater than himself. "So thick." He placed one hand above the other, about the span of his hand apart. "Or a bit more maybe."

Wallace thought for a moment. He ran his tongue between his teeth as he often did when trying hard to piece things together, especially things that didn't make sense. Suddenly his brown eyes lit and crinkled with humor at the corners. He motioned to a boulder a little beyond the stump he had earlier been sitting on. "So. I think I see. Tell me about this Sir Kenneth of yours—he has lands hereabouts?"

Jamie nodded and sat. "From near Forteviot. It's said the earldom goes back to Kenneth mac Alpin. My great-great-grandfather Angus held our lands from their family—and as far back beyond that as anybody remembers. It is tradition in the house of Corvan that they are Guardians of the Stone. Appointed by Saint Columba, they say. But Sir Kenneth was not at Scone when Edward's men came. We rode as hard as we could, but when we arrived they had already ransacked the chapel and had the Stone ringed with heavily armed guard. Even then I expected Sir Kenneth to give battle. It was strange . . ."

"Yes. Such would have made an excellent display. But why spill his own blood when mine would do as well should Edward want surety of the authenticity of his booty? I think your Sir Kenneth calculates closely."

Jamie's blue eyes shone wide with innocence. "I dona know what you mean."

Wallace leaned forward. "What I mean is that four years ago I was present at the crowning of King John. The Stane he sat on was inside a fine carved case, but even so I could see enough to know it was no chunk of rough-hewn red sandstone such as you describe. It is in my mind that a shrewd man whose family has guarded the Stane for centuries would not be likely to crumble at a single order from Edward but might send an order of his own ahead to those at Scone Abbey."

Jamie slapped his leather-breeched knee in delight. "So you think my lord pulled a switch on Edward?"

"I dona know. But I know the stane you describe is not the one I saw John Balliol set his royal bottom on."

"So where's the real one?"

Wallace shrugged. "Hidden in the palace? Buried somewhere? Carried to a safer place?"

"Couldn't have been carried far. They didn't have much warning. And Edward's men are everywhere." Jamie drifted off in thought, then sat upright suddenly. "But Edward will be furious when he finds out. He'll wreak worse punishment on us than he did on Berwick."

Wallace's face lost its glimmer of humor. "Nothing worse is possible." He paused. "But how's Edward to find out? He never saw the Stane. He sent his men riding in with orders. They rode out with a stane. That is enough. So you can go back to your master and tell him that even without the charade of Wallace's blood baptizing the Stane, his role of guardian has been fulfilled."

After a moment he asked, "Will Corvan fight for Scone?"

Jamie looked surprised at the question. "His land is not at Scone. It is near Forteviot. His role in Scone was only to protect the Stone. Edward emptied the abbey of its books and charters and appointed an English justiciar—Ormesby, I think his name is. Sir Kenneth would fight for his own land."

Wallace ground one massive hand into the palm of the other. "*Scotland* is his land! When will we see that? As long as each man stands for his own land, each clan stands for its own territory, never caring whether they fight Scot or English for their own bit, Scotland will never be a nation.

"If Edward's invasion will teach us that we must work together as Scots for Scotland, perhaps it will be worth it. If not, Scotland is as dead as Edward says it is. Much good it will do Sir Kenneth Corvan to have saved our palladium if our children and our children's children are born Englishmen. As well he send the true Stane to Westminster and kiss Edward's feet as the rest of our nobles have."

Yet the thought of Edward gloating over even a substitute palladium galled Wallace. He had been awaiting the right moment to strike his first blow for freedom. Perhaps Corvan's message was his call to arms.

"Graham! Brice!" His long legs carried him to the path to the camp in two strides, and his deep voice rolled down the hillside.

His captains were by his side in a matter of minutes.

486

"I've just received word—" he indicated Jamie still sitting on his boulder at the edge of the clearing "—Edward has raped Scone Abbey and installed his own justiciar there. Would it not be a fine symbolic act to remove this personage who continues Edward's humiliation of Scotland in the heart of our land?"

John Graham's fair skin paled even whiter under his freckles, but he never blinked his gray eyes. "Do we ride now?"

Wallace considered. "Our first blow must be a telling one. If we mean to give the call that Scotland is not dead, it must be a clear one. The force of Edward's army will have moved on, but he will have left a garrison behind. Scone Palace is not built for fortification, yet it is strong. It is too large a task for thirty men. The hardy Douglas was seeking to gather his men when I left him. I know of no other Scots lord doing so save Moray in the north. Graham, ride to Douglas. Tell him I will await him at Perth. Brice, gather the men for prayers."

When his men had left to do his bidding, Wallace recalled young James, still sitting on the rock. "I will take you back to your master."

Jamie mac Innes looked squarely at Wallace for several moments, then drew himself to his feet in a stalwart stance that made him seem much older than his perhaps sixteen years. "I would fight with you."

"You will fight for all of Scotland, not just your own lands?" Wallace did not mean to mock the earnest lad, but he would teach a point while he had opportunity.

"I do not know. It is a new idea. But at least I would have Edward out of Perthshire. And if we would then remain free of him there, he must also be beyond Lothian and Strathclyde. So it seems we might as well clear the land of his scourge while we're at it."

Wallace's bear-claw hand ruffled Jamie's bright hair, and the trees above rang with the giant's laughter. "A clever lad, Jamie mac Innes. I canna take you without your lord's permission—I'll nae be accused of kidnapping—but come with me to Scone, and we'll see what may be done."

Wallace turned to the men Blair had assembled on a lower spot on the hill. "Patriots of Scotland, hear me. Edward Plantagenet has stolen the Stane of Scone."

A shout of protest rang against the hillside.

Wallace raised his arm, brandishing his massive sword, far too heavy for a lesser man to wield, and the men silenced.

"Scotland is England's vassal state."

Again, a shouted protest interrupted him.

"But it will not be. Let the 'Hammer of the Scots' meet the 'Hammer and Scourge of the English'!"

Now the hill shook with the sound of men's shouts and of swords hammering on targes.

"Does Edward really think that by robbing Scotland of her Stane he can truly deprive her of her palladium? Scotland's history is in the memory of her sons. Her palladium is in their hearts. Edward will find that Scotland needs no talisman to give her freedom."

Again the hillside shook, and the sun glinted off upraised swords.

"We march against far greater numbers than ours. Their numbers are greater, but not their might. For right is on our side. Scotland will not yield to tyrant sword. For God armeth the patriot!"

Across the hillside, with a voice sounding many times their small number, the men took up the cry, "God armeth the patriot! God armeth the patriot! God armeth . . ."

It had been a stirring scene, good for men untried in battle who had waited long in hiding and were now riding to their first testing. But the next day, in the gray of a cloudy morning and the chill of a spring rain, Wallace considered the cold facts as he led his troops by back trails through woods and fields to Perth.

If Graham had to go all the way to Douglasdale in southern Strathclyde, it would mean days, if not weeks, of waiting. And his men were ready for battle now. Once lost, it would be hard if not impossible, to regain their fervor. And it would be impossible to hide thirty men in the farming fields near Perth as securely as they had sheltered in the forest.

Wallace hoped his men had listened more to Jock Brice's prayers than to his own words the day before. They were sure to have more need of the prayers before they saw the end of this. He doubted they had. He could hope God had, though.

He pulled his woolen mantle farther over his head for what protection it could give him against the rain and tried to form a plan.

"And a fine bracing day, is it no'?"

Wallace shook a spray of rain from his head and turned to look at the speaker, who trotted up beside him. Jamie mac Innes's usually brassy hair gleamed pure copper, and the damp on his cheeks and jaw emphasized the strength of his bones.

"*Harrumph,*" Wallace returned. "I've been thinking we may have many days to wait in this fine bracing weather before Douglas can meet us." *If he comes at all,* he added under his breath. "We're heading toward your lands. What do you know of a place where thirty men can shelter securely?"

Jamie looked around at the rugged hill country they were traveling through, almost without aid of trail in order to avoid the English. "I don't know this side of the Ochils verra well, but I'm thinking—" he pointed off through the mist to the right "—that might be the draw that leads down to Dunning where our lands are."

In the dim distance Wallace could just make out a notch in the hills. "You're suggesting we could await Douglas there? How far is it from Perth?"

Jamie shrugged. "Less than a day's ride. The land's verra secure—thick wooded hills to the back. And verra beautiful." Youthful pride sounded in his voice.

Wallace nodded. He could plant scouts at Perth to await word of Douglas while he kept the body of his men in the hills outside Forteviot. It would be perfect. "Thank you, young Jamie. I believe we'll be accepting your invitation."

Although not easy riding or walking, the trackless Ochil Hills made perfect cover for men who did not wish to be discovered, and the rich abundance of game and birds kept the little band's cookfires dripping with roasting meat, even as the flames sizzled against the rain. Wallace kept their pace steady but did not push, since the men's spirits stayed high and they had a wait ahead of them anyway. Fewer than half his men were horsed, and nothing was to be gained by exhausting his foot soldiers.

Therefore it was several days later that they reached the bottom of the draw between the hills Jamie had pointed out. It was the first clear day they had had, and the promise of approaching summer gave a lift to all their spirits. Most of Wallace's troops were younger sons like himself or small landholders whose farmsteads had been plundered by the English, so few among them had need to worry about spring planting at home and could enjoy the warmer weather.

Murdo Grant, who had been with Douglas at the fall of Berwick Castle and was one of the first to gather around Wallace, rode up beside him. "Would you have me scout ahead a bit? Doesn't appear there's been a southern within a hundred mile a' here, but you can never tell about the sneaky dogs." Although his voice held a note of sarcastic bravado, his small dark eyes darted to each side as if he could see around the trees, and restless fingers danced on the hilt of his sword.

"Aye, Murdo, take Jamie. He knows the way. See that it's clear, and find a likely spot we can pitch our tents. I'd like the men to have cover if we have to wait through another rainy spell."

The sound of their horses' hooves on the soft earth had barely faded when an uneasy feeling came over Wallace. He held up his hand for his men to halt. He could hear nothing in the woods save the rustling of small animals and bird song. Reassuring sounds, surely.

They had encountered no sign of Edward's men in their near week of travel. He had complete faith in Murdo's scouting skills. One of the very few seasoned soldiers in his band, the little man was also one of the oldest, with a few gray hairs in his black beard to signify his status. The wily Murdo was not a man to ride unaware into an English trap, should the English have any idea there was need for setting one.

The bulk of Edward's army had surely moved northward swiftly after subduing Scone. By now they would be well into the Grampians. Unease was not reasonable. Yet the unease persisted.

Wallace lowered his arm, and the march continued forward. That morning, while eating slabs of cold roast meat and oatcakes from the night before, washed down with mugs of spring water—their supply of ale had long ago run out—they had surveyed a map hastily drawn by Jamie. If it had been correct, they could be no more than a mile or two from Dunning Innes, which in the time of Kenneth mac Alpin had been the dun of Angus. They must keep their eyes open, for they could soon encounter small folk driving their pigs into the woods to root among the trees. They would not want to startle anyone who might dart off and give an alarm of armed soldiers approaching.

They had ridden perhaps another mile when Wallace again halted his men. The sound of other horses' hooves pounding up the dirt track was unmistakable. But it sounded to be only one horse.

In a few moments Murdo broke through the underbrush. He was, indeed, alone. "You'll need to come, Wallace. The lad will nae move, he's that distrait. It's a wee Berwick."

Wallace's stomach lurched at the memory. Many a night he awoke in a sweat and lay long, trying to clear his mind of the pictures of destruction. Now the images of spoilage were no less disturbing in warm daylight. He barked an order to Jock Brice to bring the men on slowly. With set jaw and narrowed eyes he nodded to Murdo to lead the way.

Breaking through the fresh-scented intense green of the newly leafed wood to the charred timbers and stinking corpses of Edward's handiwork was like falling from heaven to hell.

The field beside them lay brown and mud-soaked. It had been half prepared for spring planting. To the other side was an orchard that should be passing from blossom to tender new-leaf stage but was instead a cruel expanse of charred snags.

The pasture beyond reeked with the stench of rotting, bloated carcasses of sheep, cows, and horses. Geordie MacInnes had been a prosperous man, husbanding wide fields and fine herds. Until Edward.

Wallace forced himself to ride to the hall house. At least to what was left of it. Shells of barns and outbuildings, thatched roofs burned and fallen, ringed the scorched and broken tower that had housed the family.

And now it was not the rotting bodies of cattle that Wallace turned from but that of the servants and tenant farmers who had stood with their master. At least the rain of past days had washed away much of the blood, and the cold weather had slowed the decay.

Wallace turned to Murdo with a set face. "Gather the weapons. We'll use them against the—" He swallowed the end of his sentence with a gesture toward an English arrow protruding from the body of a child.

He dismounted and walked on toward the house. Jamie was just inside the door, standing as if at guard over the hall. The body of a young girl with hair just a shade lighter than Jamie's hung half off the trestle table, her bodice ripped from neckline to knees.

"Agnes." Jamie pronounced his sister's name in a stiff, toneless voice. "My mother." He indicated a similarly ravaged body among the rushes under the table. Here there had been no cleansing rain to wash away the blood of slit throats. The reeds and strewing-herbs lay matted in blackish brown pools on the earth floor.

Jamie continued on around the long, high-ceilinged room, naming each person. Family member, slave, servant, steward, pet dog—each received the same careful monotone identification, until they came to the end of the hall. There Jamie stopped, unable to name the horror. The tall gaunt form of Geordie MacInnes swung from a rope flung across the rafters.

Wallace drew his broadsword and cut the body down. Only when father, mother, and sister were lying on the long table in as decent order as Wallace could make of them did Jamie give vent to the piercing cry that was within him.

Wallace stood until the sound died in a choking sob. Then he clasped the young man to him in a bearlike embrace. "Jock Brice will be here soon. We'll give them Christian burial. It's all we can do for them now."

Jamie nodded. "And kill the men who did this. My sister Aline. They must have taken her. Rather she were dead." He looked around the hall once more, at first standing still beside the table bier, then walking slowly about, looking carefully behind every stool and

491

upturned bench. "Rory—my older brother. He's with Sir Kenneth. He will fight. Is that why Edward did this? Did he know we resisted his rule?"

Wallace shook his head. "I doubt it. And it would have made little difference. It made none at Berwick. Edward means to teach a lesson none will ever forget. He cares naething how much slaughter it takes to do the job."

By late afternoon all the buildings and fields had been searched, all the bodies that could be were brought to the hall. They did the best they could to wash those who had fallen where the rain had not reached them for cleansing. But there were only the standing pools to work with, for the well was choked with bodies, most thrown in headfirst. They pulled out those they could reach. The ones deeper down would just have to be buried there.

Jock Brice, the warrior monk, stood at the head of the hall. The strong light of the northern evening came through the long windows, and the few candles that had been unearthed from the chaos flickered in broken holders. He crossed himself and cleared his throat.

"The prophet Isaiah foresaw such a time of desolation as this:

'The land is emptied and laid waste.
It is turned upside down.
Its inhabitants are scattered.
The earth is utterly laid waste, utterly stripped.
The earth mourns and fades.
The wine mourns, all the merry-hearted groan.
Stilled are the cheerful timbrels,
    ended the shouts of the jubilant,
    stilled is the cheerful harp.
The city is chaos.
    All joy has disappeared
    and cheer left the land.

But the Lord of Hosts will reign
    on Mount Zion and in Jerusalem,
    glorious in the sight of His elders.
The Lord will open up the gates
    to let in a nation that is just—
    one that keeps faith.
A nation of firm purpose He will keep in peace;
    in peace for its trust in Him.

O Lord, mete out peace to us,
    for it is You who will accomplish all we set to do.
Increase our nation, O Lord.
Increase our nation to Your own glory.'"

The rest of the service for the dead was more conventional—as conventional as it could be under the circumstances.

Then Wallace set his men to work digging graves. The work was easy in ground softened by spring rains. And so by evening the kitchen garden that should have been sprouting green with parsnips, peas, and cabbages had only rows of rough-hewn wooden crosses to break its barrenness.

The next day the men did what could be done to clear away the bodies of the animals and to salvage any tools or wagons remaining in the wrecked buildings. Although grim, it was useful work. And none worked harder than Jamie MacInnes, who was much in need of taking out his rage in physical labor. It was useful as well for the men to be actively employed while remaining in hiding.

Wallace calculated how soon he could hope to hear from Graham, then shook his head over the enforced delay. He must not lose all by a too-precipitous strike. But neither could he delay too long—it would be equally disastrous if he were to miss his rendezvous with the Douglas.

Perth, the nominal capital of Scotland, was a great religious center, housing large monasteries of Black Friars, Gray Friars, White Friars, and Carthusians. Therefore Brother Jock, the devout if fiery Benedictine who had joined Wallace at the encouragement of Robert Wishart, bishop of Glasgow—the only leading churchman in open opposition to Edward—could blend in readily and would arouse no suspicion by spending several days in the city. Wallace sent him as scout.

In the meantime Wallace set his men to finishing plowing and planting the few bags of unscorched grain they found in one corner of a byre. There would be no one to tend the crop—and likely no one to harvest it. Yet William Wallace could not abide waste and disorder. He would set his hand to fruitfulness wherever he could.

The south field, however, was only two-thirds planted when Brice returned with John Graham three days later. Graham had met Douglas just as he was preparing to ford the Forth above Stirling Bridge, certain that the bridge itself would be guarded by Edward's men. The Douglas, too, had been moved to action by Edward's pillage of Scone and had hastily gathered near to two hundred men for the march. They would be in Perth tomorrow.

Wallace gave Graham a hearty clap on the shoulder that almost sent the slighter man reeling. "Good news, indeed! Aye, ye've done well. Both of ye." His broad grin above the curly beard included both of his captains.

"And what did you learn of Edward's justiciar?" he asked Brice as he led the way into the hall house.

"William de Ormesby holds court in Scone Palace. It seems his brief is to seek out and bring to Edward's allegiance those of lesser importance whom Edward desires should swear fealty to him. Apparently the hand kissing by all the magnates in the land isn't enough for Edward's vaunted vanity." He all but choked on the note of bitterness, then quickly dropped his head and crossed himself as if repenting his uncharitable attitude.

"Much value there is in fealty sworn at sword point," Wallace scoffed. "But what success has he?"

Brice shrugged. "Rumors vary, as rumors will. Those who show reluctance, however, are sentenced to fines or outlawry—a plan much calculated to improve his success rate. Those who do accept are required to pay the clerks a penny. It is said the clerks are becoming wealthy fellows."

The Wallace's huge fist slammed against the trestle table at which they talked. "So, Edward's humiliation goes on and on. If we can overthrow his justiciar we will, in sign if not in fact, overthrow the usurper's authority in the land."

He sent Graham and three other men to intercept Douglas's march to Perth and bring him and his men to Dunning. And two days later, the fine gray head of Sir William Douglas bent close to the broad dark one of William Wallace at the same table.

"Blair got no reliable report as to the number garrisoned at Scone. Rumor had it all the way from two hundred to double that."

"Ah, that's a fine thing," Douglas rubbed his chest as if after a good meal and leaned back in his chair. "Enough for a good tussle but nae more than two to one outnumbered. I'd be saying two Englishmen to one Scotsman should give us odds of about three to one. And my men are aye ready for a good fight."

"I think our men will have no trouble with Edward's troops. But Ormesby is rumored to be a slippery fellow. Capturing him will be the crucial part."

The two leaders talked late over strategy. They would divide at Perth, Douglas going round to the northwest, Wallace approaching from the southeast. Should the weaselly Ormesby attempt to run, he would find both ways blocked.

Jock Brice said prayers at daybreak.

No man had to be urged to step lively. Indeed, Wallace thought he was going to have to restrain Jamie MacInnes, who would have charged the entire twelve miles to Scone if given free rein. At last they were to take the initiative. The Scots would be attacking, not defending against Edward's attack. Edward would know Scotland was not dead yet.

Jamie fingered the sword hanging heavily at his belt. Although he had had considerable instruction in wielding such a weapon as part of his training with Sir Kenneth's men, this was his first time to wear one into battle. It was his father's.

He was glad for the hatred that washed over him whenever he closed his eyes and saw again the desecration of his family and home. Such overriding emotion precluded any possibility of fear hindering his actions. Yet he would be glad when his first encounter was over and his valor had been forged in the heat of battle. Teeth gritted, he curled his fingers around the sword hilt and vowed that his family's blood would not go unavenged.

In the thick woods outside the village clustering about the walls of the palace where King John Balliol had once lived and where Scottish parliaments had once sat, Wallace called a halt. He ordered Murdo to slip through to the other side to tell Douglas they were in place, while Wallace arranged those he led. His men would stay with him in the center. Those of Douglas's who had marched eastward with him he divided into right and left flanks.

Since surprise was their best weapon, the leaders had agreed on a simple, full infantry charge on the English troops garrisoned outside the palace. And since Wallace had the farthest to march to get into position, he was to give the signal. Evening shadows were beginning to lengthen. The English would soon be at their cookfires—a good time to catch them unaware.

Jamie tried to conjure up the face of the first Englishman he would hold at the tip of his sword. Would he be old or young? Would his eyes show fear at the last moment? How would the sword feel going in? He recalled the satisfying swiftness with which his blade sliced into the sawdust-filled practice dummies once he had pierced their leather skin. Would it feel the same?

He had been concentrating so hard it was a moment before he recognized the horn blast for what it was. But then suddenly he was thundering from the shelter of the woods across a small pasture. Geese and hens fled amid great squawking and flapping as his squadron of fifty men pounded toward the round tents and thatched huts that sheltered the occupying army.

Jamie's blood rose with every stride. A few more yards and surely the enemy would hear them and engage. Then he could draw his sword. Then he could take his revenge and kill.

A small figure appeared in front of him so quickly he barely had time to dodge. He missed the child by a matter of inches. It was mostly luck that Jamie's first kill in battle was not a wee Scottish bairn.

And where *was* the enemy? Ahead he could see men surrounding the English tents, stabbing at their walls to make certain none were hiding inside. But there was no answer to their challenge. The English had simply left the field.

Beyond him Jamie saw Wallace, broadsword drawn, enter the unguarded palace gate. Jamie ran ahead to follow on the heels of John Graham. But there was little following to do.

Serving girls ran screaming from the hall as the soldiers entered. An old crone, head and shoulders swathed in a white mantle, bent lower over her broom and continued sweeping the floor rushes in a far corner.

Wallace strode to her. "What is this, grandmother? Where are the English?"

The old woman turned her head to look up, her eyes bright. She gave him a gap-toothed grin. "Aye, and they're gone, are they noot?"

"Gone? Where? When?" Wallace straightened and looked around over the heads of his men.

The old woman shrugged her stooped shoulders and resumed sweeping. "Sped like chicks afore a fox they did. E'en oot the window." She inclined her head toward an unshuttered back window and gave a cackle of laughter.

Douglas and his men now burst in from the back of the hall in similar bemusement. The old cleaning woman was the only one who found the situation laughable.

Jamie suppressed a desire to draw his sword and beat it against the empty chair at the center of the dais where Ormesby should have been sitting. Wallace stood in the center of the hall, a full head above the other men, his discouragement showing plainly in the slump of his mighty shoulders.

Theirs was a defeated victory. The patriots had cleared Scone of the English but had been denied the telling blow they intended to strike. It was impossible to claim a victory when not a single blow had been given. By sneaking off into the dusk, Ormesby had denied them a means of issuing their clarion call to Scotland to rally for freedom.

And Jamie MacInnes was denied the sweet taste of revenge. This was yet another addition to his store of hatred, a store that could only multiply by waiting. His family was unavenged. Scotland was unavenged. Now another time must be awaited. Another opportunity sought. But when? Where?

"Murdo—" Wallace barked his order, his voice thick with the frustration Jamie felt "—see to the treasury. Take three men, gather all ye can safely carry. No sense leaving it for the English. Then see to the men's pay. Scots treasure it is—it shall pay Scots patriots, not English invaders."

"Aye, better to pay the English with the point of our swords," Jamie rasped through clenched teeth.

53

Jamie's hand went to the dagger at his belt even before he lifted his head from its pillow of floor rushes near the kitchen door. He had the weapon unsheathed before his eyes were open enough to see that it was an old woman who stood over him.

He sheathed the blade and rubbed his eyes. Pale morning sun glimmered at the windows. The rest of the hall was awake. He blushed that youthful sleep had held him past the waking of his companions. Then he looked back at the stooped figure with wisps of gray hair escaping her white headrail.

"Morag!" He came to his feet in a single bound and grasped her gnarled hands. "I thought all died at Dunning."

The aged servant hung her head. "I had gone with Luke that day. The lad asked my help driving the pigs to root for acorns in the hills. The flames of our thatch were burnt low by when we got back."

Jamie nodded, picturing the tidy cottage where Morag and her grandson lived on the edge of the orchard.

"There was naething we could do, Jamie. There were still Englishry about, or I would have seen to . . ." She covered her face with work-worn hands. "We made for Forteviot."

"Forteviot? Then you've come with Sir Kenneth? Corvan is here?" Jamie rushed toward the hall, then turned back. "Morag, I'm verra glad to see you—glad that someone remains." He grasped her arm more roughly than he meant to. "Morag—do you know aught of Aline? We found no body. Did you see her taken?"

"Nay, lad." The faded eyes in her deeply wrinkled face rested kindly on him. "Nay. The smoke from the byres was fierce. We saw little."

Jamie went on to the hall of Scone Palace with an aching throat.

At the dais end of the hall Sir Kenneth Corvan approached the table where Wallace and Douglas sat at morning ale and oatcakes. Corvan was a short, stocky man whose pale hair fell almost into his gray green eyes. He was somewhat older than William Wallace, yet not above thirty-five.

"So you have driven the interloper Ormesby from Scone—and his rat troops with him. Excellent work! I regret that I was not here for the fun."

"There was little fun in it. The rat went down his hole and left us with an empty victory." Wallace frowned under his thick eyebrows.

"So what will you now? Give him chase to Northumbria?"

Douglas regarded the newcomer. "How do you know that's where he has gone?"

"Only logic. That's where his lands are. Mostlike go to raise more men."

Douglas nodded grimly. "Aye, it's for sure he'll be back. I'm for going westward to join Wishart. I'd be there now if events in Scone hadn't drawn me northward. The good bishop of Glasgow is gathering a resistance."

"Aye, I've heard." Corvan took the mug of ale handed him by one of Douglas's men. "Who else joins him?"

"Few enough. I've heard Sir Richard de Lundin has yet to bow his knee to the English king. James the Steward was raising men for the bishop when I turned north. And there's rumor of the earl of Carrick rising."

Wallace's guffaw turned every head in the hall toward the dais. His words followed a bit more quietly but with no less vehemence. "What? Robert Bruce? Edward's darling? Surely it's unlikely that the grandson of Balliol's challenger for the throne would take arms in King John's name."

Douglas nodded. "Aye, true enough. But he might take arms in his own name."

Wallace hit the table. "And there lies the crux of the trouble. None will take arms but in their own name. And when they do gather, what will they do but squabble among themselves for precedence and over whose lands they'll defend? They'll be far too busy fighting among themselves to find time to fight Edward."

The scraping of horses' hooves on the hard ground outside followed by the pounding of running feet drew Jamie's attention from the dais in time to see a messenger hurry in. After a brief word, the man Wallace had set to guard the door pointed to the top of the hall, but he did not admit the man.

Jamie recognized Hugh Danduff, one of Corvan's squires, and started to vouch for him when he saw Sir Kenneth moving to the doorway, followed by the Wallace.

Hugh began his report without preamble. "Sir, you bade me

follow the Stone. Edward's men are like to have crossed the Esk with it by now."

Corvan gave a satisfied smile. "So, it is well on to London?"

Hugh nodded and opened his mouth to speak, but Wallace was first. "Aye, I'd just have a wee word with you about that stane, Sir Kenneth. It seems you had some notion of my doing battle over a chunk of sandstone. It might be that I value my blood a mite higher than that. I'd like to be hearing more of the story if you wouldn't mind."

Sir Kenneth Corvan almost grinned. In the end he kept his mouth straight, but his peacock-colored eyes flicked across to the rising ground before the chapel. Jamie remembered the last time he had seen Moot Hill, ringed about as it was with English soldiers, swords drawn, guarding others who hefted a huge chunk of sandstone off the ancient knoll.

Now the gentle hillock stood bare; spring grass and a few harebells covered any boot marks the marauders might have left in the soft earth. And Jamie saw what he had not seen in the midst of the earlier melee. He walked a bit apart from the others to get a better view but not so close as to draw unwonted attention to what Sir Kenneth would surely want kept secret. It certainly looked as though the sod on the north side of the hill had been disturbed and then tamped back into place. Perhaps it showed more now than it would have earlier because no harebells bloomed along the line of the apparent cut.

Or perhaps it was his imagination. Perhaps there had been no hasty digging in Moot Hill at all.

He turned back to hear Corvan's exclamation over the rest of Hugh's report. "What? Rory taken? And the English turned all their prisoners over to the sheriff of Lanark! Why would they do that?"

Hugh shrugged. "Heselrig is said to be Edward's true man. Rules by fear and hatred just like Edward. The ideal man for the job if you want your prisoners punished cruelly and think it too much nuisance to march them all the way to London. Besides, a Scottish execution would serve little enough object south of the border. Better to make a show of them here to serve as warning."

Jamie's hand curled around his knife handle. His brother prisoner of this English sheriff and about to be executed? He opened his mouth to urge Wallace to action.

But William Wallace needed no urging to ride to Lanark. "Why did no one tell me of this man Heselrig? Edward must have installed him just after I was last there. He is much persecuting the citizens?" He did not name Marion or the Braidfoot family, but the lines of his face deepened. His fingers went to the sword hilt at the back of his neck.

It was a brave messenger indeed who could face William Wallace with hand on sword hilt and continue unswerving in his report of cruelties, oppressions, and crushing taxes. "His men take the women of the town at will. None are safe. Any who oppose him are hung after the barest mockery of a trial."

Wallace turned to Douglas, who approached their group slowly. "Go you to Wishart if you wish, Sir William. I am for Lanark."

And Jamie MacInnes would go to Lanark as well, for Sir Kenneth readily granted the request that Rory's brother become Wallace's man. Corvan gave Wallace a score of men in all, including Hugh Danduff.

Morag, ancient but faithful, with her grandson Luke, would return to Dunning Innes to do what they could there. It would be little enough, but it was an encouragement to Jamie that if Aline should return there would be a fire on the hearth waiting for her.

That night he sharpened his father's sword. Soon or late it would find English blood.

So William Wallace set his face toward Lanark. His original band of thirty men now numbered three times that. It was still a pittance against Edward's horde, but it was a strong, loyal pittance.

Although absolute secrecy was not so essential as on the northward trip, it was still wiser not to make open display of themselves, so, keeping to the back ways, it was the better part of three days before they arrived at the Fords of Frew to cross the Forth.

If there was one place the English would be likely to attempt to halt their progress, it would be at Stirling Bridge. So Wallace led his men west, hoping that the fords would not also be guarded. If they were, they must fight for their crossing or continue on far westward into the Highlands. And Wallace wanted no delay to keep him from Lanark.

He told himself, and it was true, that he would have sped as readily to the defense of any Scottish citizenry so oppressed by English hand. He would as gladly strike his blow for freedom in any venue offered. But the added incentive of seeing Marion again, the fact that he would be fighting for her personal safety and the immediate freedom of her family, added a sharpness to the nudges with which he spurred his horse forward.

Wallace's stout-hearted mount, Gallus, was as bold and tough as his name implied. Since the sturdy short-legged garrons, favored by many lowlanders and of a necessity by all highlanders, were impractical for one with legs the length of William Wallace's—and yet a heavy charger such as the English rode would be inefficient in Scotland's hilly, often-boggy country—the young William had set himself to horse breeding in the long-ago sunnier days in Elderslie. Gallus, longer-legged but as high of heart as the hill garrons other men rode, was the result of many seasons of work.

Now, three days after the crossing at Frew, Gallus carried Wallace through the May green countryside outside Lanark. In the looped and folded ground beneath the rugged Cartland Crags, where steep hillsides were covered with deer grass and heather, Wallace drew up his men.

"You'll have me scout ahead?" The lean, dark Murdo materialized at his leader's side with the unnerving stealth that made him such a good spy.

"Nay, but I'd have you set a careful watch here. The crags are fine for lying hidden but no place to be taken unaware. I'll go to Lanark myself."

Brice was the first to object. "Is that wise? Known as you are hereabouts?"

"And kenspeckled," Graham added.

Wallace laughed. "Aye, my size is a sore nuisance for one who would choose to go unnoticed. But here I have means of learning the facts of the situation, means which outweigh other inconveniences."

"Still, you may be glad of a friendly dirk at your back. I'll come with you." Sir John's blue eyes glinted with a determination Wallace would not oppose.

"Two dirks." Jamie drew his from the sheath at his belt.

Wallace regarded them levelly. He knew nothing of the defenses of Lanark. He had no desire to lead two of his men into a trap. But he would, indeed, feel better with them at his back. And it was Jamie's brother that Heselrig held prisoner. "Aye. Two dirks." He gave a jerk of a nod and mounted.

A prosperous, bustling market town, made a royal burgh by David I one hundred fifty years earlier, Lanark was only partly walled and therefore easy enough to enter under cover of darkness. But they would leave their horses outside the wall beyond Castlegate, where Wallace knew a spot low enough for a man to vault it.

The next day was to be a market day, so even after nightfall there was plenty of coming and going to blend their movements with others. The three walked past the sheriff's sleepy guard behind a lumbering cart of squealing pigs and squawking chickens without earning so much as a glance.

"Go you to the inn." Wallace nodded up a curving, cobbled street to a thatched building from which golden light and rowdy noises were emanating. "See what you can pick up there of use. I'll join you behind Saint Kentigern's before the monks sing compline." A smile softened his stern features. "Aye, Saint Kent's—where Marion and I shall one day be wed."

With light heart and step Wallace set off for the Braidfoot home. He slipped through the gap in the hedgerow surrounding their garden that he had found useful more than once in the past. He rapped at the back door.

Marion herself answered his knock and, after a gasp of amazed disbelief, hurled herself into his arms.

"William!"

His big hands all but spanned her waist. He lifted her off the floor and spun around. Dizzy with delight and the sheer joy of being together, they collapsed on the settle, neither willing to let the other go.

Marion's younger sister, Rhona, peeked around the corner just long enough for William to see the sparkle in her black eyes. Then she scurried off, presumably to tell their father what the disturbance was.

Marion snuggled closer in the shelter of William's arm. "Will, this is what it will be like every night when this dreadful fighting is settled and we're man and wife with our own fire to sit before. How long must it be, Will?"

Wallace shook his head. "Ah, Marion, I fear it will be long indeed before a loyal Scotsman may rest easy by his hearth, knowing his wife and bairns are free from threat. You must be brave, my sweeting."

He felt her nod against his rough tunic. "Yes, Will. I know. And I am sae proud of what you're doing. But I miss you sore. I just hoped that after your victory at Scone . . ."

"So word has reached here already?"

"Dougal heard of it at the inn. He would have been off to join you long ago but that Shona is so near her time." Her brother and his wife lived just on the other side of the Braidfoot land.

"It much eases my mind that Dougal's sword arm is near for your protection, Marion. We hear much of the cruelty of this Heselrig. Has he bothered you?'

Marion sat up now, pulling slightly away. The firelight danced on her smooth cheeks and full lips. "Father is not well. He has seemed to grow frailer with Scotland. He is fined—well, taxed, they call it. But no more heavily than the other burghers."

"That is good, at least." Wallace let out a long sigh. "Then you do not think they know of our connection? It has been a fierce worry to me that I might bring danger on your house—on your dear person."

Marion shook her head, and the glistening of reflected light on her hair was as if she had stirred the fire. "No. It is Rhona I fear for. She will not stay confined to the garden, and yesterday one of the sheriff's men followed her home." She lowered her head. "Oh, Will, I should not speak of such things, but she has just come upon her womanhood. If she should be taken by force . . ."

"Aye." Wallace shut his mind against the scene of the women at Dunning Innes. "Marion, I must know of other things too. The prisoners Edward's men brought from the north—it is said they were turned over to Heselrig."

"Yes. The trial was two days ago. Three were executed this morning. Three more tomorrow."

"Executed?" This was worse than he thought to expect. Already they were too late.

She turned away, and her thick golden braid fell over her shoulder. "Hung, drawn, and quartered, as a warning to traitors."

Wallace struck the seat of the settle with a blow that rocked them both. "Traitors? They had sworn no loyalty to Edward. They cannot commit treason against one they never swore fealty to. John Balliol is their king."

"It seems Edward says otherwise." Marion gripped his arm with both her small hands. "William, you see why I fear so for you? You would make the same argument if you were taken. And you would be listened to just as well. And swing just as high." She buried her face in his tunic with a sob and shuddered in his arms.

He held her, feeling the fragility of her bones, smelling her herb-fresh hair.

But even as he held his love, his mind turned to the job he must do. Here indeed was the place to strike a blow for freedom. They were too late for some, but the rest of the prisoners must be freed. The injustice of this tyrant was not to be borne. Let the word go out.

"So what is to be done must be done quickly."

Marion sat up and pushed away the tendrils that had escaped her braid. "William—be careful."

The kiss he gave her was long, full of tenderness and passion. A remembrance of the past, a promise for the future. It might be many a long month before he would kiss her again. This must last for as long as need be.

"Aye. I'll be careful. For your sake."

Marion smiled at him from under her long lashes. "For my sake, and for Scotland's. We both have need of you, Will Wallace."

He would have kissed her again but for a banging at the door that nearly rocked the whole house. Marion started to rise, but Wallace pulled her back. "No, Marion. Do not unbar the door at this hour."

"But father is unwell. I should see to it."

Wallace was indeed shocked when he saw Duncan Braidfoot going to the door. He had no idea the man had been so unwell. The formerly sturdy burgher of Lanark had become a mere shadow of himself in the past months. Apparently the weight of the sheriff's hand had fallen heavier on the family than Marion would admit.

"Open the door in the name of the king's peace."

"This is a peaceful house, sir." Duncan's voice lacked the vigor of his earlier days, but it did not waver. "We have no need to open to your demand."

Marion pushed William toward the back door. "They must have followed you here, Will. Quick, run through the garden. You can be over the wall and away before they catch you."

Wallace shook his head. "I do not think I was followed. I will no' leave you defenseless."

"Open, I say! You may have no need, but I do." Now the slur of liquor sounded in the knocker's voice. "Do not deny it—you have a daughter here, ripe as a plum, with hair as dark."

"What! Rhona is a child. And would ye rape my daughter in my own house? Is this your king's peace?"

But already the heavy blows of the drunken soldier and his companions were shaking the door. It would splinter in the next minute. Over Marion's protest, Wallace stepped forward and lifted the oak bar so that the door gave with such suddenness that it sent the three intruders reeling.

Sword drawn, Wallace lunged after them into the street. It was a matter of only three or four exchanges with Rhona's would-be ravisher until the man was disarmed and clasping a flesh wound in his sword arm that would keep him from action long enough to rethink the wisdom of such behavior in the future. The other two sped off into the night. Wallace turned.

Marion stood in the open doorway, and the pale candle glow was like a halo around her head and shoulders.

He took only the briefest of kisses, just enough to renew the feel of her lips, the sweetness of her scent to his senses. "Bar the door." It was a command, a warning, a prayer.

It was long past the hour he had told Graham and Jamie he would meet them at St. Kentigern's. Keeping to the shadows, watching for anyone who could give an alarm, Wallace approached the church from a narrow lane. Would they still be waiting? Could they have somehow been discovered by the sheriff's men? What of Jamie's brother? Had he been in the first group executed and so beyond their help? Or were there still a few precious hours?

A shadow moved along the rough stone side of the church where the thatch hung almost to the ground. Wallace slid into the darkness beside his men.

"Have you heard?" Jamie demanded in a hoarse whisper. "Tomorrow morning in the market square. They're to butcher Rory and two others of the Perthshire men."

"Aye. I heard. But are you certain for Rory? We're no' too late?"

"The first murdered were the older ones, men with lands and families—more like to recant, Heselrig'd be thinking." Jamie bit the words off with bitterness.

"The lad's got the right of it," John Graham continued. "They're held in the tolbooth."

Wallace considered. The tolbooth—not a fortified castle dungeon but a sturdy wooden structure, undoubtedly well guarded. With the sheriff's house nearby. Should they ride back to the crags for their men? There would be time enough if they slipped out now. But near to a hundred armed men could not enter Lanark unchallenged. There would be a battle at the city gates. Then another at the tolbooth. Wallace had no doubt of his men's ability to win such encounters. But the plan would give Heselrig too much warning—time aplenty to put his prisoners to the sword. So even when they succeeded in capturing the English sheriff, they would have lost the battle.

Surprise now was their best ally. And they had little enough time to achieve it before one of the whoring soldiers Wallace encountered in the street described him to someone who recognized him and spread the alarm among the English that William Wallace was in town.

At the tramp of booted feet on cobbles the men drew farther back into the shadows. A group of four or five soldiers passed at the end of Kirk Lane.

"It's too early to make our move. We need two or three hours yet till all are settled for the night." Wallace rose to a crouching position and looked around him. "There's a barn in the Braidfoot orchard. We can lie up there undetected until after midnight."

As he led the way stealthily through the twisting wynds, a plan formed in Wallace's mind. They would need to draw the guard away

506

from the tolbooth. A good blaze in the sheriff's thatch across the street would be just the thing. Graham and Jamie could slip in and free the prisoners while he took Heselrig at sword point. Then they would see if the Englishman liked submission to a Scots court any better than the Scots liked trial by English justice.

For the second time that night Wallace slipped through the hedgerow. He saw a faint glow at the upper window that he knew marked Marion and Rhona's room. The iron hinge creaked as he pulled the barn door open. A few hens flapped on their nests, then settled at a soothing sound from Wallace.

"Might as well get some sleep." He pointed to a pile of hay in the corner. "It's to be a long night. I'll stand guard."

Jamie curled into a ball and was asleep before Graham crossed the beaten dirt floor.

"Wake me in an hour, Will. I'll take second watch." Sir John loosened his sword belt but kept it beside him.

The night settled into a lull of soft sounds. Wallace closed his eyes but did not sleep. It was maybe three quarters of an hour later that he jumped to his feet at the sound of thudding steps and growled commands. Did Heselrig know they were there? Had the English surrounded the barn even as he watched?

But then he realized the sounds were farther off, carrying clearly on the night air. He peered out the unshuttered window. Armed men at the house! The flare of torches lit the street in front and the garden behind. Was it Heselrig himself? Come looking for William Wallace? These were no drunken soldiers bent on debauchery.

Wallace shook his companions awake. His instincts were all to rush the soldiers, broadsword flailing. But would that be to put Marion and her family at even greater risk? If the sheriff searched the house and found him gone, would Heselrig then leave as well? He hesitated.

The crash of splintering wood followed by a cry of alarm ended all hesitation. He burst from the barn, Jamie and Graham at his heels, and pounded through the dark across the rough ground.

But even as they leaped the garden wall and raced for the back door, hanging half open on broken hinges, they could hear the sheriff and his men marching out the front. Graham darted back through the hedgerow to follow the departing men.

Wallace, frozen in the silence of fear at what he would find, dashed through the door and up the narrow stairs to Marion's room.

She lay peacefully in her bed. At first Wallace thought she held a scarlet-petaled flower to her breast. Then he realized. The red stain on the white shift was blood.

54

Jamie lurched to a halt behind his leader. Wallace's broad back blocked his view of the room, so at first he saw nothing. But he heard the anguished cry that broke from the big man with the sound of a soul being ripped from a body.

Jamie stumbled backward. For days he had been fighting his own anger, his own bitterness, his own grief. But even the dreadful sights at Dunning Innes had not been more terrible to him than the rage and grief that shook William Wallace.

A soft rustle on the stair turned him about. "Marion? What—"

A soft female voice rose in alarm at sight of him. Then she looked past him. "Oh. Will. How did—"

Jamie caught at the small arm under the shawl-covered night-shift. "No, dona go in."

"Wh-who are you? You're not English." The dark eyes were wide with fright, the skin whiter than her bleached muslin shift.

"Nay. Jamie MacInnes. Wallace's man." Even in these circumstances he could not keep the note of pride from his voice. "You are Marion's sister?"

"Marion!" The girl turned again toward the door, but Jamie held her.

"Nay. Let him mourn."

"*Mourn!* You mean—" She swayed against him, and he held her until the spasm of sobbing passed. At last she looked up.

Jamie led her to sit at the top of the stairs that descended from the loft where the two sisters had slept together for fifteen years.

"Marion said if any soldiers came back I was to hide in the kist. But they were not looking for me. I heard them accuse her of helping the rebel Wallace escape. They said she was his leman . . ." She buried her face in her hands as she choked on another sob. "I should not have stayed hidden. It was cowardly. But I was so afraid."

He took her tiny hands in his. They were ice. "No. You did right."

"But Marion—I could have helped."

He shook his head. "No one could have done anything. Not even Wallace had he been here, although I doubt he'll be easily convinced of it. We must get you a blanket."

She nodded toward the bedroom.

But that was not a good idea. Jamie led her down the stairs. And at the doorway of Duncan Braidfoot's room, another dreadful sight met them.

"Father!" This time Jamie did not restrain her from throwing herself on the body. He merely stepped over the fallen figure to pull two heavy blankets from the bed—one to warm Rhona, one to cover her father, who would ne'er be warm again.

At that moment a belatedly wakened Dougal Braidfoot arrived from the house beyond the garden, irritated at the barking of his dogs and unprepared to see the fate of his family. At the same time John Graham returned from following the sheriff.

Jamie stuttered and gestured helplessly, unable to find words to speak to the man who would have been William Wallace's good-brother.

"Dougal."

The little group huddled at the foot of the stairs jerked to attention at the commanding voice of the man who seemed even more gigantic than usual, standing above their heads.

"See to what must be done here." Wallace clattered heavily down the steps. "Sir John, Jamie MacInnes, it is time to be about the plan we have set."

Wallace gave only the briefest glance at the body of Duncan Braidfoot as he strode toward the door. He had said good-bye to Marion. Now his mind and body worked in an icy calm. He had left behind him all emotion that could cloud his judgment.

At the door he turned. "When the guards run to the blaze of the sheriff's barns, take your prisoners and make for the crags as we planned. There is only one change. We will no' take the sheriff prisoner. Heselrig is mine." His voice rasped with an edge as cutting as his sword.

Their success was as inevitable as the flooding of a river at a great thaw after heavy snow. For nothing could stop the awful measured precision of William Wallace's burning and breaking or the force of the back and forth, figure-eight swing of his mighty sword.

He barely noted the angry, confused cry of the soldiers when they discovered their jail broken into behind their backs. He allowed himself only the briefest grunt of satisfaction when his sword re-

509

turned red from the bowels of William de Heselrig. He gave little thought to whether or not he was followed through the night streets of Lanark. He would fight and kill as many English as chose to challenge him. But none challenged.

Onward from that late May night in the year 1297, the nature of the conflict changed. There would be no more mere sending of messages that Edward was opposed and that the Scottish people should not lose heart. William Wallace no longer would lead his men in mere resistance fighting.

This was war. Nothing but full-scale battle would do. Now William Wallace was determined to expand his band of freedom fighters to a full army, an army to stand sword-to-sword against Edward. And defeat him.

That meant two things. Edward's strongest leaders in Scotland must be opposed. And the Scottish lords who had not gone over to Edward must be convinced to fight under one banner. Edward himself was preoccupied in the south, preparing for a campaign on the continent. But he had left the northern matter in the cruelly competent hands of Anthony de Bec, bishop of Durham.

Bec had sent Sir Harry Percy to Ayr to suppress the unrest there. Perhaps the disruption of English rule at Carrick meant that young Robert Bruce, earl of Carrick, was mustering troops for the Scots. It was to be hoped that if he was mustering troops it would be for the Scots, in spite of the fact that he despised King John, who had taken the throne instead of Bruce's grandfather. And in spite of the fact that Robert the Bruce had been raised as a brother to Edward—and that Edward still paid the Bruce's gambling debts. It was to be hoped that loyalty to native soil would weigh more with the young earl than his debts.

But at the moment the loyalties of Robert Bruce were a side issue to Wallace. The more important fact was that Bec's general, Hugo de Cressingham, had been ordered not to scruple spending all the money in Edward's treasury if necessary to repress the disorder in Scotland—which primarily meant Wallace. The only Scots lord openly in the field was Andrew de Moray, who fought far to the north. Robert Wishart urged revolt, while James the Steward and William Douglas refused to come into Edward's peace but dithered on the sidelines in needless negotiations with Percy and Clifford.

Wallace sent emissaries to the Scots lords, urging that they act together. But he would not stay his sword in waiting for the others. He swept through the country between Forth and Tay, not now in stealth but openly challenging the English to battle and calling the Scots to rally to the banner.

510

And always, it was not the banner of William Wallace he called them to but the banner of John Balliol—king in exile but nonetheless true-crowned king of Scots.

As word of each success spread, and at the continued energetic encouragement of the bishop of Glasgow, knights and nobles at last rallied to the call for Scotland. Sir Richard de Lundin, Sir Robert Boyd, Henry de Haliburton, Sir John Stewart of Bonkyll—the Steward's brother—and Sir Alexander de Lindsay, each with hundreds of men at his command, gathered to lend weight to the negotiations in Irvine above Ayr.

"Should we not be joining them as well?" Jamie sat next to Wallace before the cookfire, huddled under a woolen blanket as a defense against the late June rain.

They had all listened with rising spirits as Murdo, newly arrived from Wishart, reported on the latest lord to join the cause. Bruce indeed had rallied to the defense of his own lands, if not to the banner of King John.

"Aye, it will be a fine thing," Murdo urged. "The English lords wear muckle gold into battle. There'll be spoils for the taking."

The spy's small dark eyes glinted as with humor, but Wallace wondered. The energy with which the Welshman gathered booty seemed somewhat to exceed that required of his role as Wallace's treasurer. But many others were industrious for their share too, and they had little enough pay.

"Aye." Wallace nodded. "There will be if the Scots engage in battle. Have they chosen a leader yet?"

Murdo dropped his eager gaze. "Well, Wishart is the highest churchman there—but he is a churchman. James the Steward holds the highest office but has few men. Douglas is superior in age, but it is Bruce's lands they fight on . . ."

Wallace nodded grimly. "Aye. It is as I thought." He caught his tongue between his teeth and considered well. At last he rose and tossed his hood back in spite of the rain. He would have nothing block his voice from any of his men who would hear his reasons.

"In the three weeks we've spent north of Forth—" his pause was all but undetectable. He never referred to that night in Lanark or the driven ride he had made back to the Ochils, noting little and caring less whether or not his men followed him. But they had followed. And fought valiantly. And their numbers had grown to nearly five times the size of the band that had gone south from Scone.

"—in these three weeks we have driven the English garrison from Doune and from Castle Glowry. We have driven Edward's sheriffs from Crieff and Dunblane and more. We have defeated no fewer than twelve English patrols. And we have cleared six—no, seven it is—churches of English priests placed there by Edward and returned the benefices to good men under the see of Saint Andrews."

A cheer went up.

Wallace continued, detached and shrewd, as he was always now. "And in that time, how many sheriffdoms, how many castles, how many kirks have our assembled Scots lords taken?"

Derisive laughter met his calculations.

"I will join my countrymen when I see that they are ready to fight the English and not each other. I did not take arms against Edward to fight with words."

Jamie, though he sat a little apart, cheered with the others. They had achieved much indeed.

Rory, well-trained in service to Sir Kenneth Corvan, had quickly become one of Wallace's most trusted fighters. He was in charge of one of the small flying squadrons Wallace used to hurl themselves against the enemy wherever most needed. Jamie found it good to be in company with his brother again.

His family was much on his mind. For at last it had happened— Jamie had killed. They surprised English troops raiding a priory and plundering its sacred vessels, and Jamie had killed. He could still feel the jerking of the man at the thrust of his dagger and the heaviness of him as he slumped to the ground, leaving the blade dripping in Jamie's hand. The man was a simple foot soldier like Jamie himself— not one of the chivalry, or he would have been armored beyond the capacity of Jamie's weapon to pierce its plating. Jamie had turned from the man with a triumphant thought for his father, hanging from the rafters of his own hall.

And yet he was unsatisfied. Would more killing staunch the pain inside him? If so, how much? Could he hate enough to overcome the ache?

And what of Aline? Was she somewhere now in this black night, hating and hurting like himself?

He felt a large hand on his shoulder before he heard or saw the man.

Wallace sat beside him. "You fought valiantly tonight, young James. But your first killing is no' an easy matter, is it?"

"I would it had been ten of them—twenty." The bitterness almost strangled the words. "There's not enough English blood to pay for my family. I would kill all Englishmen, could my blade reach them."

"Ah, Jamie. Is your hate so large as all that?"

"Of course. Is not your own?" He would not name Marion.

Wallace shook his head. "Nay. I do what I do for love, not for hatred."

It was a moment before Jamie could answer. He couldn't have heard aright. "Love?"

"Aye. For love of Scotland, for freedom, for justice. I hate what Edward has done—and never mistake, his cruelty is a calculated thing, for he well understands the power of the fear he raises in a subdued people. We must hate such cruelty, such tyranny. But we cannot act out of hatred alone. When Scotland is free, England will still be our neighbor. We will live best with peace along our border. And in our hearts."

They sat long, side by side, staring into the burning embers. But Jamie could make no answer.

Two weeks later Wallace's toll against the enemy continued to mount. That day he cleared Rumbling Bridge of its English guard. That night Adam Wallace—William's cousin who had joined him shortly after Lanark, bringing the welcome news that his own family at Elderslie was well at least—now brought, if not welcome news, at least confirmation that Wallace's evaluation of the Scots lords had been accurate.

Sir Richard Lundin, one of the few who had never bowed to Edward, had declared that the jealousy and dissension among the Scottish leaders made effective resistance hopeless. In disgust he had gone to Percy with all his men. "I will no longer serve with men who are at discord and variance," Adam quoted Lundin, for the man's words had been much repeated among those at Irvine who had witnessed the collapse of the Scottish resistance.

But Adam Wallace had more dire news to report. On July 7 the Scottish army had capitulated in the long, drawn-out talks they had held with the English leaders. The Scots had made their submission to Percy and Clifford as King Edward's representatives. The earl of Carrick had been required to surrender his infant daughter Marjery as hostage. William Douglas and Bishop Wishart surrendered themselves as hostages and were imprisoned.

William Wallace's heart sank. In spite of all their small victories, this was the lowest Scottish hopes had been since the defeat at Spottismuir. The sacrifice had been so great. So great. And now Wallace alone commanded the only active Scottish force south of the Highlands.

Their only hope lay to the north. There Moray marched in triumph. Leaving Aberdeen secure behind him, in spite of John Comyn's support of Edward, Moray now moved south.

The only remaining English stronghold north of the Forth was Dundee. Here, in the beautiful town on the banks of Tay, Wallace had gone to university in days so long ago they seemed almost beyond recall. And yet he did recall them with an ache. The carefree camaraderie of his student days would come no more. He could only pledge to work even harder that the freedom Scotland had known under King Alexander, last of the House of Canmore, would come again.

He turned his troops to Dundee. They had no siege engines, but there were other ways of taking castles, as his experience had well taught him. They had barely begun the siegework, however, when word came that the English army under Surrey and Cressingham was moving northward to cross the bridge at Stirling. They were but a few days' march south, perhaps ten thousand strong.

Wallace had fewer than a thousand men camped in the Ochil Hills behind him. He could send to MacDuff for perhaps another thousand, for the nephew of the earl of Fife had not accepted defeat and had been vigorously mustering men to the ancient banner of the hereditary inaugurator of Scotland. And he would speed a message northward within the hour to Andrew de Moray. If de Moray could arrive in time, that should bring their numbers near to four thousand. Would it be sufficient?

It would be because it must be.

The Scots spirit, which had risen higher and higher with each castle taken, each churchman or sheriff sent south, each company of Edward's troops destroyed, would sink more suddenly than it had soared if Scotland's last army in the field were defeated and dispersed. The moment must be seized quickly. Even a minor defeat could cause all hopes to crash at this uncertain juncture. All belief in Scottish freedom might die forever if an English justiciar were to lord it again at ravished Scone.

Engaging Surrey in battle was bold to the point of rashness. And yet, with four months of unbroken success behind him, and with Moray's victorious force fresh from the north, Wallace could never hope to meet the English army with better chance of victory.

Still, the odds were daunting at best. And it was far more than a matter of Surrey's sheer superiority of numbers. While the matter of thousands of simple English foot soldiers was not to be taken lightly, Surrey also commanded a strong contingent of Welsh—fierce, hardy mountaineers bred to war and superb bowmen. And, as always, there was the pride of England, its heavy chivalry, armed knights on armed destriers, to be considered. But perhaps the greatest contrast lay in the fact that the core of Edward's army were seasoned soldiers, well armed and thoroughly experienced—veterans of France and Palestine and having a long tradition of firmness and discipline. And a tradition of winning complete, crushing victory over their enemies.

Wallace's men were absolutely without any kind of military experience except strike-and-run raids and ambushes, brief breathless charges and wild hand-to-hand encounters between small bands of men. They were lightly armed. Swords, dirks, and twelve-foot spears were almost their only weapons.

The son of a knight, Wallace himself had been trained in all the arts of war, but, saving Sir John Graham and Rory. MacInnes, almost none of his men knew even the theory of an ordered line of battle and advancing and retreating according to the tactical scheme of an experienced commander. Their discipline was effective solely because they had learned to trust a general who had led them from one side of Scotland to the other, from small successes to ever greater ones during a whole spring and summer.

The men trusted William Wallace. They trusted him with their dreams for the freedom of their homes. They trusted him with their lives.

55

Wallace and Moray sat their horses on Abbey Craig, looking southward. Behind them the rocky Ochils rose in a steep, formidable wall; before them swept nearly a mile and a half of smooth green haugh, its September-thick grass hiding the swampy ground that made it so ill-suited to an English cavalry charge. To their left the Forth made one of its serpentine loops that formed almost a complete circle. The English would be able to do little with their right flank, walled in as they would be by the river.

Straight ahead, about five miles to the south, Stirling Castle sat atop her proud mountain, at a level almost equal to Abbey Craig. From this secure stronghold, perhaps the mightiest in Scotland, Cressingham and Surrey would soon march forth to lead the thousands of men camped on the plain beyond.

But before they could reach the Scots they must cross Stirling Bridge. This narrow wooden structure was the only crossing of the river for at least three miles in either direction. And few, if any, of the English knew where the fords were. Here the Forth was nearly thirty yards wide, not swift but deep, unswimmable for armored men and horses. From the bridgehead a paved causeway led across the swamp toward Abbey Craig.

Last night Murdo, slipping back from Stirling town, had brought news for hope and for caution. The earl of Surrey, who had fresh marched his thousands from Berwick, was elderly, ill, and made no secret of his irritation at Cressingham. And it seemed that Hugo de Cressingham, fiercely hated in Scotland for his cruelty in collecting King Edward's revenues, was almost as vigorously disliked by the English for his greed and hauteur. This fat churchman was especially unpopular with his own troops because, as Edward's treasurer, he had withheld their pay.

And yet there remained the weight of their numbers and superior strength, added to, Murdo reported, by the presence of James, steward of Scotland, Malcolm, earl of Lennox, and other Scottish barons who still adhered to the allegiance they had sworn to the king of England.

It was as always it had been in the past months. The Scots must make the land fight for them, and they must turn the vast English numbers to their own disadvantage.

"Aye!" Moray struck his saddle with such suddenness that Wallace, intent on his own calculations, started. "If Scotland is to be freed of yon invader we must strike a mighty blow. And quickly."

Wallace nodded but did not speak. He was not a man to be hurried from his thoughts. And he would give one more thought to the fact that he was back almost to the exact spot where he had been when it had all started: when young Jamie had brought him word that Edward had raped Scone of its Stone. Then he had been the head of a band of only thirty men. Then Marion had been alive. Then the first blow for freedom had yet to be struck.

Now all was different. All had been set in motion. Now events carried as of their own momentum. Now, even if he could see what lay ahead, there could be no turning back. And it was as well, for Wallace would not turn back if he could. He had set his hand to the helm.

"Aye, a blow they'll not soon forget." Even as he spoke, the late afternoon sun glinting on the road from Stirling to the bridge caught the movement of a small band of men. Wallace squinted to make out their banners, but it was too far even to be sure the horsemen carried banners, let alone to read the devices.

It was not long, though, before Jamie MacInnes, who had been set as courier for the guard at the village at Causewayhead, came crashing through the trees, much as he had on that afternoon so many months ago. "It is the Steward and Lennox. They carry a white flag."

Wallace and Moray exchanged long looks with eyebrows raised. "So. And have they seen sense before we rub the English noses in it? Or do they think to talk us round to their traitorous ways?" Moray's words sounded harsh for one so usually cheerful.

Wallace shrugged. "We shall see. Jamie, get you to my captains behind the Craig. Tell them to stay well hidden. I'll not have Surrey know our strength. But send Sir John Graham to us—he shall like to parley. And Scrymgeour with the standard. The rampant red lion shall meet Edward's gold leopards."

To the front of them the Craig fell in a precipitous drop. The Scots turned to ride down the somewhat gentler slope to the west. The two groups met in the middle of the mile-and-a-half-long causeway.

The Steward rode forward.

Wallace met him. "These are strange times indeed, my lord, when the Steward of Scotland would ride out under the English leopards."

Sir James shook his long head of graying dark hair. He had a slight speech impediment, which made him hard to understand, but Wallace had been listening to his father's overlord all his life. "Better to be riding under them than to lie trampled under them. The leopard's claws gouge deep, my son."

"Aye. For that reason I would have Scotland free of him."

The Steward licked his thick lips. "You always were a brave laddie. Brave and true and good. Scotland needs your life, not your blood. Listen to sense. You've seen the strength massed against you. Surrey will grant honorable terms. Live to fight another day. You and all your true Scotsmen."

Had Wallace not been bred with full respect for the nobility of his land—whether or not they lived up to their calling—and special deference for his own overlord, he would have laughed in the Steward's face, or worse. As it was, he drew himself up to his full height in Gallus's broad saddle, well dwarfing the Steward, who was forced to look upward at him, squinting against the sun.

"Say this to Surrey." He took a deep breath so that his voice might have carried to the general himself had he not been immured in Stirling Castle. "Tell Edward's men that we have not come here to gain peace. We are prepared for battle to avenge and deliver our country. Let them come up when they like. They will find us ready to meet them to their beards."

There was barely room to turn Gallus on the narrow causeway, but Wallace spun the magnificent animal on his hind legs and rode off without looking back, Moray and the others falling in behind him. He did not stop until well into the fastness of the tree-covered slopes west of Abbey Craig.

Jock Brice was the first to meet him. As it was approaching the hour for evening prayers, the monk had pulled his cowled robe on over the battle clothes he usually wore.

"Jock, well met." Wallace reined Gallus to a stop. "Bishop Sinclair from DunKeld joined us this morning. Find him, and say that I would have all the men hear evening mass. Let no man go to the battlefield unshriven." He paused. "Myself included."

Hearing confessions and serving the Host to nearly four thousand men was no small task. But Wallace knew William Sinclair could handle it. Young, impetuous, active, high-born, the bishop of DunKeld was not a typical churchman. In truth, he was acting bishop

518

only, as the aged bishops of DunKeld and St. Andrews had both taken voluntary exile in France rather than live under Edward's hegemony. With the valiant Wishart in prison, that left Sinclair as the only high churchman active with the Scots army. Wallace had been much heartened by his presence. He knew how sorely they needed all prayers.

The last rays of the red gold September sun, sinking behind the Highlands to the far west, cast long shadows across their tree-encircled camp. Red and gold streaks had just begun piercing the green when Jock Brice rang the small bell to call all men to prayer. Bishop Sinclair emerged from his deerhide tent, head bowed, hands folded, as properly robed as if to say mass in his own cathedral. Before him on a cloth-covered table was the heavy silver cross he had brought from Dunkeld and the elements.

He raised his hands and spoke in a strong, carrying voice. "This is the word the Lord spoke against Moab in times past. The glory of Moab shall be degraded despite all its great multitude."

An undertone of muttered agreement met his words. The parallel was lost on no one, and the men inched forward to hear better.

"There shall be a remnant, very small and weak."

The men looked at one another and nodded.

"But on that day the Lord of hosts will be a glorious crown and a brilliant diadem to the remnant of His people—a spirit of justice and strength to those who turn back the battle at the gate."

In Wallace's own mind he saw not a gate but a bridgehead. Truly, if strength and justice were to reign in this land, the battle must be turned back there.

"Woe to those who depend upon horses, who put their trust in chariots because of their number and in horsemen because of their combined power, but look not to the Holy One of Israel nor seek the Lord.

"He will rise up against the house of the wicked and against those who help evildoers. The enemy are men, not God. Their horses are flesh, not spirit. When the Lord stretches forth His hand, the enemy shall stumble, the evil shall fall."

When all was ready, Wallace stepped forward first. He readied himself to receive the sacrament but instead felt the bishop's hands on his head in a blessing. He opened his eyes in surprise and looked into the face of William Sinclair, his eyes closed, his face lifted toward heaven.

Wallace bowed his own head lower in humility at the words Sinclair spoke. "Gird your sword upon your thigh, O mighty one. In your splendor and your majesty ride on triumphant in the cause of truth and for the sake of justice, and may your right hand show you wondrous deeds."

Wallace was so overcome he could barely open his mouth to receive the Host.

The benediction of that service remained in a small part of Wallace's mind the next morning when he rode out to survey the valley. Would the English take the message he had sent them? It had been clear. "Let them come up when they like, and they will find us ready to meet them." The English could advance as they wished. The Scots would defend.

He could feel the woods behind him alive with his waiting troops. This was the hardest part of all. And it was certain to get more difficult through long hours. And if Surrey and Cressingham chose to accept his challenge, it would be many hours before their troops could be in place for battle. Would the English come? Would his own men hold firm and hidden?

It was not long before he knew the answer to the first. The fields between Stirling and Forth gleamed as one solid sheet of metal overflown by a forest of waving, colorful pennons. The first company approached the bridge.

Mounted knights under the yellow and black banner Wallace recognized as that of Sir Marmaduke de Twenge, a brave and determined soldier of much experience, were the first to mount the narrow wooden bridge. Wallace could only imagine how it must thud and shudder under the inexorable pounding of the heavy horses' hooves.

They came with all speed possible, but that was slow for men itching to charge down the hill shrieking wild battle cries. Slow indeed, as the knights could cross the bridge only two by two, and the causeway was little wider.

As the prolonged filing continued to the beat of English drums, Wallace would not allow himself to move so much as to flick a fly. For he knew his men waited with every nerve taut. Never had he relied more completely on the discipline of his troops. It was imperative to the success of the entire battle that no movement on the wooded slopes dispel the illusion that the Scots were waiting to be attacked when the whole strength of their enemies should have crossed the Forth.

Now the first companies of great horses were over. Next came endless row after row of the superbly disciplined English spearmen, like a moving coppice with their long spears high above their chain-mailed heads. Next the Welsh archers. Wallace held his tongue tight against his teeth. Valiant Wales, homeland of his own ancestors. Wales, which had so recently been hammered into resignation by Edward, now fought for the suppressor. He renewed his vow that Scots spearmen would not someday be so used.

Again Wallace renewed his calculations, praying that he was correctly estimating the strength before him.

56

Jamie MacInnes stood in the front lines of the Scottish foot through the long hours, just able to see over a sheltering boulder. As each unit plodded across bridge and causeway to take its battle station on the sloping green haugh, Jamie felt the heat of his hatred rise. Somewhere down there were the men that raped his little sister, that butchered his mother, that hanged his father from the rafters of his own hall. Perhaps one of those men still held the pale, fragile Aline as his whore.

Jamie felt a burning rush of hot blood to his head. Darkness swirled before his eyes. He leaned against the rough granite to keep his balance. His hand tightened on his spear. He would kill. He would kill and kill and kill again. He would go on killing until the Forth floodplain ran red with Southern blood. He would spill enough English blood today to wash away the stains of his family's blood on the boards of Dunning Innes.

He was so gripped by the passion of his vision that he didn't hear the blare of the horn until the shriek of Moray's piper catapulted him forward. With wild Highlanders shrieking on either side of him, Jamie plunged straight down the hillside.

Reveling in his fleetness of foot, he leaped from stone to stone, balancing sometimes on one foot, sometimes on another. He loved the sense of his own speed, his own strength.

Not until he thrust his foot ankle deep into the bog and yanked it out of the sucking black mud did he realize where Moray was leading them—not to attack the head of the causeway but straight into the waterlogged salt marsh beside the crossing.

To his left he saw the red St. George's cross of England. That must be Cressingham. The heart of the enemy. Most of the destriers he led were now over the bridge and spread along the mile of causeway. Jamie lunged forward, mud to his knees, sloshing and stumbling, while Edward's superbly disciplined columns marched on, sun shining off their armor.

Jamie flung splotches of mud from his eyes. Behind him he heard a double horn blast. Wallace sending MacDuff's troops to engage the enemy at the causeway head. That would turn the attention of the dreaded bowmen away from Moray's men in the bog. Then they could move within range.

Jamie raised his hide-covered wooden targe to protect against the arrows sent from any longbows not turned the other way. Just ahead a wiry Black Highlander who, with many of his fellows, had dropped his plaid to cope better with the mire, thrust forward, leading a band of clansmen. He leaped into the air, then cried out and plunged into the muck as an arrow found its mark.

But Jamie drove onward—only three more sodden leaps—dragging his feet from the engulfing mud each time. He reached the bridge.

The nine-foot spear he carried was of no use at such close range. He tossed it into the mud and pulled the long-bladed dirk from his belt. A fully armored knight riding a fully armored warhorse was impregnable except for two places: the knight's eye-and-mouth holes beneath his helmet, and the soft underbelly of his horse. Jamie couldn't come close to reaching the helmeted heads passing proudly above him. He heaved himself onto the swaying side of the wooden bridge.

The knight with the red and purple devices on his shield couldn't have known the Scottish lad was there until Jamie's dirk sank deep into the hard-muscled flesh behind his destrier's front leg. To keep from being trampled by the flailing hooves, Jamie darted between the railing poles of the bridge and back into the mud.

He watched as the great creature lunged and kicked. His blow had not been fatal to the animal, but the wound would incapacitate him for a battle charge. More important at the moment, the frenzied animal created chaos on the bridge. As did the blows of hundreds of other Scots all following the same tactic. The bridge was a seething melee of thrashing horses, many as severely wounded by their fellows' hooves as by Scots dirks.

Now the advance had been halted, and the Moraymen could attack with swords and spears. Jamie's own spear was lost in the bog. He grabbed one from the hand of a Scot who would need his no more. The lunging, falling horses had unseated their riders on a bridge too tightly packed for any to turn and retreat. Now English eye-and-mouth sockets were within range. Now Jamie's blood lust, which was little satisfied with the blood of horses, could be slaked.

The knight before him opened his mouth to issue a battle cry. Jamie lunged. The cry died in a coughing gurgle. The knight, who sprawled backward across his battle horse, was larger, better equipped, and more experienced than Jamie. But the tide of battle was with the Scots.

It was clear they had done what they had set out to do. The bridgehead was cut. English forces to the north could not be reinforced from the south. Those who had crossed the river and were now taking a battering from Wallace's forces could not retreat across the bridge. Nor could they swim. So they stood and died or ran off into the forest or turned and trampled their fallen fellows in the panic of retreat.

Victory was at hand. But the battle was not done. Again the fighting was too closely engaged for an effective spear thrust, so Jamie drew his blade and lunged. He had lost any count he had thought of keeping, but he was sure he had avenged his family's deaths double at least. And yet he felt unsatisfied, as if he could continue thrusting and slashing and dipping his sword again and again in English blood until there was none left to drain.

And then he saw, to his right, the cross of St. George, blood red on a field of white, fallen and ripped, its field no longer white. And beside it the grossly bloated body of Hugo de Cressingham. His armor had been ripped from his fat, pallid flesh, and Scots soldiers on every side were venting their hatred for the cruelty the man had inflicted on their land. They were flaying the skin from his body and hanging strips of it on their belts as souvenirs.

"Ha, Jamie lad!" Murdo held up a dripping, flaccid piece. "Have your trophy!" He flung it toward Jamie.

Yes! The blood of the vile Cressingham as exchange for the blood of his family. Jamie didn't look where he leaped. He could not have seen if he had tried, for swirling red vengeance lust filled his vision. Jamie sprang.

At the same moment, Cressingham's destrier, on its side, wounded, lashed out with an iron-shod forefoot. The force of several tons of frenzied horseflesh smashed full into Jamie's right knee. He slammed backward against the bridge railing. The shock of pain seared up his leg. He collapsed into blackness.

A wailing pipe tune some distance away pierced Jamie's consciousness. After a moment he fluttered one eye open. Total blackness. "No!" He cried out and jerked upward, one hand groping the dark.

No, he couldn't have been blinded. A stab of pain from his leg thrust him back on his pallet. What had happened? The mournful song of the piper rose and fell. Surely they had won. It was coming back now. They had been winning. He had killed. Many Englishmen. For a moment he felt the sweet glow of revenge as he savored remembrance of his sword scraping on bone and metal and returning to him red. That for Agnes. That for Mother, he had thought. And then he had gone on and on without thought.

And then, the tattered English flag, Cressingham sprawled as if held down by his own fat, the men skinning him. Jamie shifted his position slightly, and the shout of pain reminded him. His knee. He could feel nothing beneath it. Was the intensity of pain shutting off all other feeling? Or had he lost his leg?

His eyes were fully open now, adjusting to the black. He could see he was in a tent. "Hey!" he shouted when he heard someone stirring outside.

The heavy hide flap lifted, and Rory stuck his head in. Even as well as Jamie knew his brother, he would not have recognized him in the dimness but for his voice. "Aye, well, you're awake, are you? Thought you'd just have a wee doze so you'd not have to help with the cleanup, did you?"

Jamie recognized that jollying tone. It was the same one Rory had used at home, usually on Agnes, when there was something unpleasant he didn't want her to think about.

He made his own voice as no-nonsense as he could, although the pain throbbing up his leg made it impossible to speak evenly. "What happened?"

"Oh, you missed all the fun, you did. You'll be knowing an armored destrier carries upwards of three-hundredweight of steel. You can imagine the sight of so much pride sinking in the muck. And those were the lucky ones who managed to get off the bridge."

"So we did win."

"Oh, aye, puddin'head. You weren't thinking otherwise, were you? They are saying that we made the end of some five thousand foot and a hundred cavalry. Near to none that crossed Stirling Bridge lived to cross south again. Surrey's men cut and burned the bridge so we couldn't pursue, or we'd be away south now. But we've plenty to do here, killing stragglers and rounding up the Southern baggage."

Jamie bit his lip against the pain that was overtaking him. He mustn't pass out again until he knew the rest. "And our losses?"

"Light. They say Moray was wounded." Rory shook his head. "A grievous loss if it's severe."

A buzzing rose in Jamie's head. He could put it off no longer. He would soon be forced to cry out against the pain. He had to know the extent of his own loss. "Rory, my leg . . ."

525

"Oh, aye. Well . . ." In the dark his big brother groped awkwardly until his hand came to rest on Jamie's shoulder. "*Och*, Jamie, it was a hard blow. That destrier's hoof made a fair mess of things. He was a massive brute. I was fighting just down the bridge from you. It was my own sword that slit his windpipe."

"Rory—" the buzzing grew louder. He was slipping into blackness "—Rory, is my leg gone?"

"Nay, Jamie. You've all your parts. But it's not so certain just how much use that leg will be to you in the future." Rory stretched out beside him on the pallet. "Jock Brice got a powerful dose of poppy juice down your gullet. Best not try to talk more till it wears off."

Jamie allowed unconsciousness to overtake him. But near morning he floated back up close enough to the surface to ask himself what he could do now.

For months the drive to kill the Englishry, to avenge his family, had given him a reason to live. Now he had killed. But not enough. The pain in his chest over his family was worse than the pain in his leg. He had not killed near enough to assuage that pain. But with a useless leg he could fight no more. If he could not live to kill, what could he live for?

57

Later that week Jock Brice directed the carrying of the Scots wounded to Cambuskenneth Abbey, enclosed within a loop of the Forth just a mile south of Abbey Craig. The monastery had been founded by David I and named for a field where Kenneth mac Alpin defeated the Picts four hundred fifty years before.

Jamie ate when food was spooned into his mouth. He drank when a mug of ale was held to his lips. He swallowed the foul-smelling black liquid one of the monks poured down his throat when the pain made him cry out in his sleep. In the daytime he could clench his teeth on the ash twig Rory gave him before riding out with Wallace and the army to secure the victory. But in his sleep he had no defense against the pain.

Or against the images that filled his mind. He lay now, his eyes forced wide open, staring hard at the rough thatch over his head in hopes he could blot out what he had just seen: Marion Braidfoot so peaceful on her bed—except for the crimson stain on her white shift. Then the pale fabric began to peel, and it was the white skin of Cressingham, being flayed by Scottish dirks. Then it wasn't Scottish soldiers ravaging an enemy leader—it was an English soldier ravishing his family. Then the scene twisted, and he was not looking around the hall of Dunning Innes searching for Aline but was at Lanark, looking down high, steep steps at the small dark-haired Rhona cowering wide-eyed at the foot of the stairway.

He started to cry out against the images but strangled the sound. He did not want any more of Brother Simon's poppy juice. The only shard of brightness in the whole jumbled dream had been his glimpse of Rhona looking up at him, hopeful for help. But then the agony in her face increased his own pain. He would have no more of such sights.

Brother Simon, black robe swathing his sturdy frame, kind intensely blue eyes shining above his close-cropped black beard, bustled in.

Before he could speak, Jamie held up a hand. "No. No more of your medicines, if you don't mind. I can bear the pain better than the sleep."

Simon smiled and lifted one eyebrow, which made his eyes sparkle brighter. "Ah, so you're better today, are you?"

Jamie couldn't grit his teeth and answer at the same time. So he didn't reply.

"Och, that's fine, for I've good news. And the Holy Scriptures tell us a merry heart doeth good like a medicine."

Jamie looked at him. His own heart was as bleak as ever.

But Brother Simon's was merry enough. And it was not so bad a thing. "We've had word. Wallace has completed the siege of Dundee Castle, which he'd started before yon battle. The garrison at Stirling Castle has surrendered, and the English leaders are made prisoner at Dumbarton—now also firmly Scots."

"Aye. That's good."

Simon nodded. "We'll be saying a mass of thanksgiving now. I could help you to it if you'd care to attend."

Jamie looked at the monk. Middling height but broad shoulders, Brother Simon had perhaps done heavy farm work before taking the cowl. Jamie was tall but lightly built. He supposed someday he would have to get up and make an attempt on his shattered leg. When he did, he would be in good hands with Brother Simon.

But not today.

"Aye. I'll just leave the door open for you to hear, then. The abbey stands right by."

The open door let in a shaft of autumn sunshine and the chatter of birdsong as well as the sound of the brothers chanting their thanks for the fall of Stirling Castle: "The castle of the insolent is a city no more. Therefore a strong people will honor You, our God. You are a refuge to the poor, a refuge to the needy in distress. Lord of hosts, You will provide for all peoples."

As the litany of God's goodness to Scotland continued, Jamie's anger rose against the horrors he had seen. Horrors that God had permitted.

"Behold our God, to whom we looked to save us. This is the Lord for whom we looked. Let us rejoice and be glad that He has saved us. For the hand of the Lord will rest on this land."

Jamie hoped so. Somewhere there had to be something hopeful—some reason to go on with life. For so long his hatred of the English had driven him. But it had not been a satisfying thing to build his life on.

The monks next door seemed to have no such doubts. They increased the fervor of their chant: "Open up the gates, O Lord, to let in a nation that is just, one that keeps faith. Let this nation be of firm purpose which You, O God, keep in peace; in peace because of its trust in You."

After everything that had happened, could a nation be built on peace, justice, and faith in God? Could one, Jamie wondered, build a life on such?

Thoughts of peace and love brought again to his mind the dark-haired sister of Wallace's Marion. At least the freeing of the country of its oppressors would be good news to Rhona, if anything would ever seem good to her again. Somehow the thought helped a bit to ease the ache of his emptiness.

But then he thought of his own sister. His parents and Agnes he mourned and felt great bitterness at the cruelty of their deaths. But he knew them dead and in the better place Brother Simon assured him of. But Aline. Was she dead or alive? And if alive . . . His first flush of hope at that thought was always twisted to immediate despair. If alive, what kind of life? Had she been simply raped and cast aside? Or carried off to live as whore-slave to a hated Southern? Surely she would have killed herself in such circumstances.

If Jamie could ever walk again or at least sit a horse, perhaps he could search for her and send her abductor to his judgment.

The monks' jubilant thanksgiving echoed in sharp contrast to Jamie's dark thoughts of vengeance: "O Lord, You mete out peace to us, for it is You who have accomplished all we have done. You have increased the nation, O Lord, increased the nation to Your own glory."

Two days later Brother Simon came in with a white ashwood crutch, carved smooth and carefully padded with lambs' wool. "Brother Infirmarer says it's time our wee Jamie was up and about."

Jamie glared at him.

"Er . . . can you no' try, man? Would it no' be a fine thing to sit in the sun? The breeze is sharp. But there's a bench in the nook of the wall."

Jamie wondered how long it had been since he had felt the sun on his head. Yes, that was it—the morning on the hillside above Stirling Bridge, standing by a boulder, watching the enemy assemble. Two months ago, nearly, that had been. He had felt warmth then. Warmth beyond his own battle lust. Warmth from above. "Aye. It would be fine."

Jamie had not realized that Brother Simon could be so gentle as he unwound the old bandages and bathed the leg in a decoction of

529

dock leaf and witch hazel. Jamie gathered his courage to sit up and look. The bruising, the skin abrasions, and the swelling were gone. But that made the mangling of bone, muscle, and ligament underneath all the more apparent. He took only the briefest look, then turned away before Simon rewrapped it firmly in clean cloth strips to hold the splint boards.

Simon stood on Jamie's good side, turned him, and lifted. "Now, put all your weight on me." He tucked the crutch under Jamie's right arm. "Maybe in time the leg will bear some weight."

Physical pain, frustration, humiliation fought for supremacy as Jamie hobbled his slow progress across the room.

"You're doing fine, lad. Fine. Just a wee bit more now to the south end."

In spite of the cool breeze, sweat was standing on Jamie's forehead. He bit his lip to keep from moaning against the pain of each step. Only Simon's unwavering support made progress possible. Ahead of them two figures appeared on the path coming from the abbot's cell. But Jamie was concentrating too hard on his own struggle to take notice. He was within two dragging steps of the bench. Brother Simon was all but carrying him.

Rory's vigorous voice brought such surprise he would have fallen had it not been for Simon's solid support. "Ah, Jamie lad. A fine thing to see you up and about. I've brought grand news and a visitor to cheer you."

Swaying in spite of Simon's sure grip, Jamie looked toward his brother. But it wasn't Rory's blue eyes that met his. It was the wide dark eyes he had seen so often in his dreams.

Rhona Braidfoot stood before him, her blue gown and dove gray mantle blowing in the breeze. Her black hair was even more luxuriant, her skin whiter, her eyes brighter than in his memory.

His humiliation could not have been more complete. Not only had she witnessed the ignominy of his graceless progress, but now he could think of nothing to say to her. And his strength was so far gone, he feared falling.

Simon covered the moment. With a seemingly effortless gesture he deposited Jamie on the bench and draped a woolen blanket over his lap, concealing the injured leg. "I'm sure Father Abbot has bid you welcome, but may I also? Your brother is an exceptional patient, Master MacInnes. Brother Infirmarer is happy of his progress. We'll be sad to have him leave Cambuskenneth."

For a moment Jamie lost track of the conversation. Leave the abbey? Where would he go? What would he do?

"Ah, that's fine to hear," Rory said. "I've much news for you, young brother. When we marched back from Dundee, I stopped at Dunning Innes to see what I could do about setting things in order."

Jamie set his jaw and turned his head away. He was not at all sure he wanted to hear what Rory had to report.

But in the sum, it was not so bad a hearing. Morag and her Luke had seen to the place since their parting at Scone. Old Padric MacNair had come down from the high garth with his sheep. Rory set him and Luke to building a bothy for the creatures, rethatching the burned roof of the hall, and setting things aright as best he could.

"I'm off south now, when I've finished this errand for the Wallace." Rory waved a hand in Rhona's direction. "I'd hoped to be in at the siege of Berwick Castle. But Jock Brice, who travels with me, received word yesterday that Berwick is ours. Now will word go out to foreign nations that the iron power of Edward is broken in this land, and Scotland can once again lift her head among the free nations of the world."

Jamie looked at his brother. Rory was not usually given to such flowery words. Mostlike these were the words of the monk he had been traveling with.

"Now Wallace carries the war across the border. We shall meet him in Northumbria, where he has gone to teach the English the important lesson that a war that can be waged on one side of a border can be waged on the other side as well. We'll see how Edward likes having his land scorched as he scorched ours."

"Would I could have a part in it." Jamie's clenched teeth made his words almost inaudible.

Rhona raised her eyelashes to look at him, then flicked them downward again.

"Jamie, I've come to ask you. When you're up to a bit of travel—will you go again to Dunning Innes?"

Jamie looked at his brother. Could he face that pain again? Could he turn to farming when all his being had been set on fighting? And yet underneath, the thought of going home tugged strongly.

"Just for a time," Rory urged. "Padric will soon finish the tasks I've set him to. He's steady but has no imagination. He needs guidance beyond Morag's reminding him to clean his hands and eat his stew. We'll need new tenants for spring planting. Many will be moving northward from the burnt lands below Forth. You'll need to choose wisely."

"But Dunning Innes is yours now."

"Aye, that's why I'm asking you. To hold it for me. I must be with the Wallace. What good are sheep, oats, and tenants if Scotland's no' secure? William Wallace is our only hope."

"But we won the war."

Rory shook his head. "Nay, Jamie. We won the battle. Edward is still across the water, busy about his Flanders expedition. But he'll be back by spring. He'll no' give up so easily. We have this space of time to make as much secure as we can. But it's not over yet.

"And think you—this one man Wallace has done all, not only unaided, but actually thwarted and opposed by the nobility of our own country." Rory shook his head. "Nay, it's no' over yet."

There was much more Jamie would have asked about the affairs of the land, but Father Abbot and Jock Brice now approached from the abbot's lodging, and Rory and Simon turned to join them.

That left Jamie and Rhona alone in the sunny corner while the rest of the world roiled and talked of war.

"Would you have a seat, Mistress Braidfoot?" Jamie shifted to the end of the bench, hoping he didn't appear too awkward.

"Thank you." She sat.

"I am much surprised to see you so far from Lanark, Mistress."

"You must call me Rhona." Her gaze had been steady on her folded hands, but she looked up at him fleetingly.

He had the most inappropriate desire to reach over and take her hand.

"Yes, it's a surprise to me too. But dear William stopped in Lanark on his way south. I thought it exceedingly good of him to take care for one orphan when he has the care of the whole nation."

She twisted her hands. "He saw all was not well in my situation and had his men bring me here to Saint Margaret's house of holy sisters."

Jamie caught his breath. His throat worked for a moment. "You are to take the veil?"

"I don't know if I have a vocation. But my brother's wife is to have another babe, and there seemed little room as it was. Oh, Shona was kind enough—and glad enough for my help—but it was very dismal with Marion and Father gone." She took a deep breath and rushed ahead as if she did not want to say the words that bade expression. "I kept waking in the night screaming, thinking soldiers banging at the door . . . I'm sorry, you'll think me a terrible coward. After all you've gone through—" Her hand barely brushed the blanket over his leg extended straight before him. It was as if a butterfly had rested momentarily on his knee. "Does your wound hurt awfully?"

He wanted to lie, to appear brave and stalwart. But her honesty deserved equal exchange. He nodded. "The leg is painful, aye. But not so much as the burning here." He thumped his chest with his fist. "Sometimes I think I could defeat a whole English army with the strength of my hatred."

Now she turned to face him more fully and held out both hands, not quite touching his arm. Her round eyes shimmered. "Oh, no. No, Jamie, you mustn't. You mustn't hate so."

He blinked. "Don't you? After all they did to you? Marion . . . your father . . ."

Now she did hold his arm. "I don't know. Perhaps I should, as a sort of loyalty to my family." She shook her head. "I'm very confused. But if I hate the men who do such terrible things, then I'll be as ugly inside as they are. And then in a way they will have won in a greater strength than even winning a battle."

She dropped his arm and turned away. "I wish I could understand. It makes so little sense. That is why I wanted to go to the nunnery. Perhaps the sisters can help me understand."

Through the long winter months Jamie gained little in understanding. It seemed that each report of Wallace's successes in Northumbria increased his own frustration at not being able to join the battle.

But his physical strength did increase. From the day of Rhona's visit he did not let a day pass that, no matter how painful, he did not make an attempt to hobble about on his crutch. Gradually the searing pain subsided to a dull ache. Brother Infirmarer removed the splint and said he could put what weight on the leg he chose. But when he tried, the results were the most dispiriting of anything he had ever attempted. The leg would bear little or nothing. The muscles would not move on their own. The leg was useless.

With immeasurable patience Brother Simon came to him every day, usually many times a day. Faithfully he massaged unguents into the mangled, twisted limb. Staunchly he supported Jamie's stumbling attempts to walk. Finally, in the new year when the brothers were beginning the long Lenten fast, he came to Jamie with a twin for the single crutch. "I know you'd rather hold to the one, and I'd not discourage you. But I think you'll find the balance easier with the two."

Jamie nodded. He knew, but he'd fought hard against the acceptance. With one crutch he could think of himself as lame, perhaps someday to recover to the use of a mere stick to aid his balance. With two crutches he must admit to being a thorough cripple. He had worked so hard, determined that when next—if ever—he saw Rhona, she would not see him in the humiliating hobble of before. But now it would be worse, because permanent.

Now he could never present himself to her with the offer his heart longed to make. If he got Dunning Innes working well and Rory returned to spur all to vigorous husbandry, there would be land and enough for two families . . . he staunchly pushed the picture to the back of his mind. It would be far better if she should choose to take the veil. He clenched his fists against the pain. He would not see her the wife of another.

58

At least Jamie could move about freely, no matter how ignobly. And he had found it inexpressibly good to be back at Dunning Innes. Seeing the turf green over his family's graves gave him a semblance of peace he had never thought to find. He had pondered long on Rhona's words about hatred and had come to no conclusions. But the feeling that Mother, Father, and Agnes were in some way under his care here gave him a sense of comfort.

As did the knowledge of Rory's success in the field with Wallace. Word reached him from time to time during the winter of Northumbrian towns falling, of plunder being sent back from England—which greatly helped Scots living on burned-out lands to survive the winter—and of holy houses saved from ravage and granted writs of protection. All of which fired Jamie's imagination for the feats of his brother following the great leader and increased his own hurt at not being with them.

But as always, his greatest hurt was his thought of Aline and the fact that now he could do nothing for her.

Daily life was not so bad. Under Padric's gentle shepherding, new lambs tottered on tender green hillsides, and the apple orchard showed a promise of swelling buds to come.

And Jamie's seventeenth birthday approached. He rubbed the sheet of polished tin on the wall and peered at it. His youthful features were still unfinished but strong and boldly modeled. His broad high cheekbones and long straight nose were not badly formed. He ran his dirk over the sharpening stone. The red gold fuzz on his square chin demanded little shaving. But the ritual must be performed for his birthday. He leaned his crutches in the corner and balanced on his good leg as he lathered his face with the lye and goose-grease soap that old Morag had made for him.

He had barely finished wiping his cheeks on the rough flaxen towel when he heard the clatter of a horse in the yard. He put his crutches under his arms and swung himself forward without thinking. Almost. He hesitated, wondering who the newcomer might be.

535

He did not meet new people easily now. He who had formerly been so open, so welcoming and welcomed by all, now drew back from human contact.

But not this contact, for a single boisterous shout told him that it was Rory. Jamie had heard last week that Sir Kenneth was returned from the English wars but had given little thought that it might mean Rory's return as well. Jamie moved toward the door at the end of the hall.

Rory burst in, crashing the door back, his boots scattering the floor rushes. At sight of Jamie he stopped.

Jamie froze. Was the look on his brother's face surprise, discomforture, or rejection? It could be no proud thing for a warrior like Rory to have a brother so twisted.

But Rory had merely paused. He came on with an embrace that near knocked Jamie off his feet. "Ah, Jamie, it's grand to see you. You've done fine with the farmstead."

Jamie shrugged. "It's nature—and Padric and Luke. I've done naught. God greens the hills, and the ewes give birth."

"I'll have none of that, brother. I saw Padric in the yard. He said you've ordered it all fine, bought new seed grain, and all is set for the spring plowing." When Jamie didn't answer he went on. "So, will Morag be having some of her ale to wet a traveler's throat?"

When they were settled at the trestle table, new cut at Jamie's orders because he would not eat on the old one that had been so defiled, Rory began on tales of the Scottish army south of the border.

"And when we came to Hexham, the priory was still in ruins, but three canons with more courage or more faith than their brethren had crept back and rebuilt an oratory. A band of Scots who had slipped the tight rein Wallace would keep on his men chased the canons into their building, brandishing weapons, and threatening the holy men with death if they did not surrender the church treasures.

"At that moment Wallace himself came into the chapel. He drew his great sword and turned it on his own men, making them stand against the wall. Then with great courtesy he bade the monks to say mass. The service went forward until the moment of the elevation of the Host. Out of reverence Wallace stepped outside to remove his weapons.

"Once his restraint was removed, the rogues rushed forward, pulled the very vestments off the priest, snatched the chalice and ornaments off the altar, and even stole the missal so that the service could not be finished. Wallace returned in a great rage and ordered that the criminals be hunted and brought to him for beheading."

Rory paused to take a long drink of ale. "They never found the men. It's doubted their fellow soldiers made overmuch effort to find them. Wallace made what amends he could, though, and gave the priory a written protection in the name of himself and Andrew de Moray."

Rory set his cup down with a sigh. "I suppose you've heard the sad news. Andrew de Moray has since died of his Stirling Bridge wounds." He shook his head. "He was an aye fine man. We have not so many that we could afford to lose one. Wallace is now the sole leader of the army."

He was quiet for a moment. "That's all the more why Wallace must be made Guardian of the Realm. There's no hope of King John returning from exile, and we must have a leader. Wallace is the only man who can lead without splitting the land apart."

Jamie frowned. "But what of the great nobles? What of the Steward? Or Comyn? Or Bruce?"

Rory shook his head. "The Steward is no' a strong leader. No man trusts the loyalty of one who stood south of Forth at Stirling Bridge—although he came round soon enough afterwards with a tale of being there to try to talk Surrey into softening his approach. And if we elect Comyn, who supported Balliol's kingship, we will lose Bruce, who believes Balliol stole the crown from his family. Likewise, to choose Bruce would be to set the Comyns at war on us."

Rory thumped his pewter mug on the table. "We canna fight the English if we must war amongst ourselves. Only Wallace can save us from that. And so you must go and raise your voice with mine."

Jamie blinked. He couldn't have heard correctly. "Go?"

"Aye, to Kirk Forest. An assembly has been called at the Cistercian monastery near Carluke."

"And you want me to go? Are you daft?"

"Wallace will need all the voices that can be raised for him. You've a good strong voice, lad. At least you did the last time you shouted at me."

"And the last time I shouted at you I had two good legs as well. Or has it escaped your notice that that kick by Cressingham's destrier was not so healthy a thing?"

"I see you need a bit of a prop to help you walk. But I'd not noticed that it affected your voice. Or your brain, come to that. You'll not be telling me the beast kicked you in the head as well?"

"No, but something must have kicked you. You are daft. Only the great nobles can elect a guardian."

"Aye, but they'll be guided by the voice of the people. None will be excluded from the proceedings. Your cheers for William Wallace will ring as loudly as those of a Comyn or a Bruce."

Jamie shook his head.

Rory looked suddenly worried. "Can you no' sit a horse?" His voice softened with concern.

Jamie squared his shoulders. "I can sit." He refused to mention, or even think, of the pain the activity cost him. The torture of bits of crushed bone moving around where his knee had been was something he would just have to get used to. And then there was the matter of balance. "Whether I can stay on is another matter."

"Perhaps a wee strap around leg and saddle?"

Jamie looked for a moment as if he might hit his brother. But in the end he submitted to good sense over stubborn heroics that would likely leave him in the dust.

They set out that day, for there was little preparation needed above telling Padric to carry on, filling their saddle bags with Morag's cheeses and bannocks, and figuring out how to strap Jamie's crutches to the saddle. At last he settled on carrying them on his back in a scabbardlike sling, much as Wallace carried his great broadsword.

The first five or so of the eight hours' ride to Cambuskenneth were among the most grueling of Jamie's life. Last winter Brother Simon had arranged for his travel to Dunning Innes to be in an abbey oxcart—a humiliating mode of travel for one who had ridden into battle with William Wallace but gentle enough for an invalid seated on mounds of straw to cushion jolts from the rutted tracks. But now it took almost all of his strength just to hang on against the pain, and as Rory was pressing to meet up with Wallace there was little conversation.

Once he decided to undertake the journey, Jamie had determined not to be a drag on Rory's progress. But now he had to fight hard against requesting they pull up for just a short rest. His good leg was aching almost as badly as the injured one, since it had taken all his weight on the stirrup for several hours over the exceedingly rugged terrain of the Ochils. He set his jaw. When they reached yon burn running through the glen below, he decided, if Rory didn't stop then, he would speak out.

They were halfway down the mountainside when his brother, several paces in the lead, suddenly reined his horse in. As Jamie drew up beside him, Rory raised his arm and pointed to a rocky crag high overhead.

Jamie had never seen a more beautiful sight. The sky above the rugged brown rock was an intense blue with a few white clouds. Soaring against that background were three enormous eagles. Their mighty wings spread, they dipped, circled, and soared in a great exhibition of freedom and majesty.

The riders sat for perhaps ten minutes, watching the display, while their horses nibbled at the spring fresh grass beside the trail. Their gentle tearing and chomping accompanied the occasional eagle's cry that echoed down to them from the rock face.

At last Rory gathered his reins and spurred his horse on up the trail. Jamie sat for a moment longer, his spirit soaring upward with the great birds, then obediently followed his brother.

He had ridden for some time, still watching the eagles in his mind after sight of them had been blocked by thick firs and several bends in the trail, when he realized how easily he rode. The tension was gone from his neck and shoulders. His back swayed effortlessly against the tall saddle with the motion of his horse. His left leg, although still doing the work of two in the matter of balancing and shock absorbing, no longer ached from the strain. And his right leg? Perhaps it was easier too.

The foremost difference, though, was the lightness of his heart. Perhaps for the first time since the battle last September, he had focused upward with his whole attention.

They reached Cambuskenneth before nightfall. As if he had been alerted to their coming, Simon came to meet them. Rory turned to help his brother dismount, but Jamie had thought this through. He was determined not to be pulled off his mount like a sack of oats. He unbuckled the strap around his right leg and stood in his left stirrup, with intense effort pulled his right leg over the high saddle back, and, kicking free of the stirrup, jumped to the ground. The pain of the jarring made even his teeth hurt, but it was almost with pride that he unsheathed his crutches and swung forward to meet his old friend.

"Well done." Simon's eyes shone blue even in the dusk. "You're doing fine, I see."

"Aye. I am." And Jamie realized he was.

Brother Simon, deputizing for the brother hospitaller, saw them fed in the refectory and accompanied Jamie to the guest house while Rory went off to check the horses once again for the night. "As you've no need of poppy juice, I've a finer thing for your sleep," Simon said as Jamie gratefully approached the narrow cot.

"Aye? It's good to see you again, my friend. Won't you sit?" Jamie himself sat on the straw-filled mattress.

"No, it's time for Compline and past. Father Abbot bade me say my own office tonight as I had duties. I'll just leave you with a word of holy comfort." Brother Simon folded his hands together inside the copious sleeves of his robe and crossed them over his chest. But as he began to speak, Jamie felt as if the monk's hands rested on his head in a benediction.

"Do you not know or have you not heard? The Lord is the eternal God, creator of the ends of the earth. He does not faint nor grow weary, and His knowledge is beyond scrutiny. He gives strength to the fainting; for the weak He makes vigor abound. Though young men faint and grow weary, and youths stagger and fall, they that hope in the Lord will renew their strength, they will soar as with eagles' wings; they will run and not grow weary, walk and not grow faint."

Jamie did not even hear the door close as he soared with the eagles. He would never run, but he would not faint.

Three days later they rode into the little town of Carluke in the Selkirk Forest. The fact that it was just a few miles from Lanark made Jamie think of Rhona. Now he wished he had asked Brother Simon about her. Was she still at the nunnery? Was she finding the peace she sought there? Then, when the next question formed in his mind, he knew why he had not asked. He did not want to know the answer: Had Rhona taken the veil?

But now affairs closer to hand took his attention. The sheltering forest, its village of timbered, thatched buildings, and the plain but solid stone monastery where they were to meet thronged with people. The call had gone out from John Comyn, earl of Buchan, lord high constable of Scotland, and Lord James Stewart, fifth high steward of Scotland. And it seemed that all the lords and a good representation of the commons of Scotland had responded to this opportunity to flex their muscles as free men in control of the destiny of their realm.

The MacInnes brothers barely squeezed into the abbey by a pillar where the men of Sir Kenneth Corvan stood their ground. It was soon apparent that the great ones had divided themselves into two camps, the two camps that could so easily split Scotland in half and leave each piece open and exposed to Edward's attack. At the front and to the left were the supporters of Sir John Comyn, lord of Badenoch, chief of the great House of Comyn. Ranged to the right was perhaps a slightly smaller but no less vigorous group, the lords and earls supporting Robert Bruce, earl of Carrick.

Head and shoulders above every other man in the room, about halfway down the center aisle, William Wallace leaned against one of the massive support pillars of the abbey. Amid the sea of nobles in their richest velvet tunics and fur-lined cloaks, Wallace stood with his arms folded over a woolen shirt and leather vest. And looked better dressed than all the others.

Bishop Sinclair opened the proceeding with prayer. "The Lord is the strength of His people, the saving refuge of His anointed. Save Your people, Lord, and bless Your inheritance; feed them, and carry them forever . . ."

Hearty amens followed the bishop's thanksgiving for their deliverance from the enemy and his pleas for defense against repeated attacks. But when the prayer ended, so did all unanimity. The Steward, as highest officer of the land, presided in the name of John Balliol, king of Scots. Reference to the exiled king never failed to bring an undercurrent of protest from the Bruce contingent, although Jamie suspected that, if forced to choose, the Steward himself might prefer a Bruce candidacy for the guardianship.

There were numerous nominations for the office of Guardian of the Realm, each accompanied by lengthy speeches recounting the prestigious pedigree and acts of valor of the nominee. As the chorus of shouts rose after each speech, Jamie began better to understand Rory's insistence on the importance of strong voices.

And more than once Jamie wanted to cry out after a proposed name, "And where was this noble lord when we stood at Stirling Bridge?" But he held his tongue. How much longer must he hold, though? Was Wallace not to be nominated? Had they come all this way to be mere bystanders at the elevation of a Comyn or a Bruce? If so, who would he use his voice for?

He was quite certain that all the things Robert Bruce's detractors said against him held truth. He had been raised with Edward, was more an Englishman than a Scot; he still held vast estates in England, which he might value above his Scottish holdings; even his manner of dress in fur-trimmed scarlet velvet with cloth of gold spoke of ties to the English court. And yet Bruce had taken his stand for Scotland. His very presence at this gathering evidenced the value he put on his Scottish roots, for his mother was of ancient Celtic stock.

But Comyn was older, more experienced, from a mightier family. And when Edward turned his face northward again, as he was certain to do, experience and might would count for much. Perhaps all.

Others must have been toting up the choices likewise and finding the prospects dim, for the next nomination was for William Sinclair, coadjutor-bishop of DunKeld. There was some support for this proposal. Such a compromise would at least prevent splitting Scotland into two camps. But mollifying Comyns and Bruces was not the point of this assembly. Preparing to stand strong against Edward was.

At last the Steward rose. He left his seat as presider of the assembly and stood aside where any free man might speak. Suddenly Jamie could see the strategy. Surely everyone in the abbey was feeling the hopelessness of the situation. Every possible name in Scotland, save one, had been proposed. And as each name was put before them, all could see why that particular candidate would not do.

Now the highest officer in the land held the attention of all as he nominated the only possible man who could lead Scotland out of its own political morass, just as he had led them to victory against Edward's army. James the Steward was elderly, his speech slurred by the impediment of a too-thick tongue, and yet this day his words, bouncing off the stone walls, rang to the back of the abbey.

"My lords, think you. Remember well the days when Scotland cowered and chaffed as England's vassal state. One man, and one man only, rose to stand against the Hammer of the Scots and become in his turn the Hammer and the Scourge of the English. He who hammered the English out of Scotland must now hammer us into a nation.

"A man not of the nobility but a man who carries in his veins, as any Guardian must, the tradition of authority and leadership, a long attachment to Scottish soil, and hereditary service to the royal household. A man with a love of freedom and a zeal and firmness in the cause of freedom.

"I name to you William Wallace!"

At long last Jamie could give voice to those feelings that had driven him to undertake the grueling ride to this assembly. Now he could raise his voice with the greatest in the land. A free Scotsman voicing who he would have rule him.

"A Wallace!"

"A Wallace!"

The building rang.

But William Wallace did not charge his way through the throng to stand beside the Steward and accept the acclaim of the crowd. He remained where he was, arms folded, leaning against the stone pillar. His only motion was when some of his men plucked at his sleeve and urged him forward. Then he shook his head at them.

Could this be? Was Wallace refusing the nomination? Was it possible he could fight so valiantly on the battlefield but refuse the harder leadership in the council hall? If Wallace would not lead them, what could they do? The other possibilities had been looked at and discarded.

Then off to Jamie's right he saw a movement among the Bruce delegation. The auburn hair and scarlet tunic of Robert Bruce shone in the dimly lit abbey. Men shoved their neighbors and pushed aside to make way for the earl of Carrick. He made his way, however, not to the platform where the Steward stood, now at a loss as to how to proceed, but toward the center of the room where Wallace still stood immobile.

Jamie's gasp was not the only one in the church when Bruce drew his sword. Such a thing should not have been worn inside a church or to an assembly. Had the Bruce broken the double rule because he expected trouble? Was he now going to challenge Wallace?

Robert Bruce grasped the point of his sword and held it high over his head, as if raising a cross. "Men of Scotland! Do none of you see the hindrance here? Wallace sees it, or he would not hold back so. In all our giving voice to our approval of William Wallace's valor, none of ye, nor I myself, have thought to bestow on him the title to which his leadership of the only successful army in Scotland entitles him—the title which will make it possible for him to accept the honor and burden of the office you have so rightly thrust upon him.

"This ceremony I perform of right as a knight of the realm is a mere formality. The title I now bestow was won on the soggy ground by Stirling Bridge. Kneel, William Wallace, esquire."

Wallace knelt and bowed his head.

Bruce lowered his sword and clasped it by its golden hilt. "I, Robert Bruce, knight and earl of this realm, do hereby dub you knight. In the name of God and Saint Andrew." He brought the flat side of his blade down on one wide, leather-clad shoulder and then the other. "Rise and go forth in the strength of God to the service of your country, Sir William Wallace."

Jamie had not thought it possible to shout louder than he had at Wallace's nomination. But now he thought his lungs would split with the joy of his own shouting. If ever knighthood had been earned, this younger son of a cadet branch of a not very prominent family had earned his. Now William Wallace could take his place in the rank of noblemen. And as such, he could become Guardian of the realm he had led to freedom.

Now Wallace allowed himself to be led to the altar by the earl of Carrick, and Jamie relaxed, for Scotland had a strong leader, a sure hand to hold against Edward. And as Jamie heard the strength of his own voice and looked around him, he saw how many untitled men like himself had pushed their way into the abbey and were shouting even louder, and he realized Wallace's true strength.

Wallace was far more than the compromise choice between Bruce and Comyn. He was far stronger than the victorious war leader. He was the choice of the people. For Guardian was not king. If his guardianship was to have any more meaning than Balliol's empty coat, he must carry the people. Only this man could so raise the commons to march united with him to secure the safety of Scotland.

When the shouting quieted, Wallace spoke, his voice so naturally strong he hardly needed raise it to be heard. "I pledge to you all that I can: to use all my strength of mind and body to protect and strengthen Scotland and to do all in the name of our rightly crowned King John."

The response to this was mixed, more enthusiastic from the Comyn side than the Bruce.

Wallace looked levelly at the mutterers. "For I would remind ye that a kingdom is its king." Then he hurried on, giving voice to an idea so new that it made his hearers gasp. "But the true realm is not embodied in the king alone. A kingdom is all the king's free subjects agreeing with those who govern them."

Now Wallace spoke to a wholly rapt audience. "We would be but outlaws and marauders if we acted aught but in the name of King John, but we act as free men preserving the royal dignity of our nation."

Jamie could not see clearly from so far back, but even from that distance it seemed that of all men in the abbey, Robert Bruce was most intent on William Wallace's words. Educated at the English court as Bruce had been, such ideas as Wallace spoke, nurtured in the free, hardy soil of Scotland, would not have been taught to the young earl. But the nodding of his auburn head showed that Robert Bruce was as much impressed by William Wallace's political ideas as by his military prowess.

Late that night Jamie lay in the dark of their tent, hearing Rory's rhythmic breathing beside him. Now what? he wondered. He had undertaken a journey that had resulted in a personal victory. And he had been part of a great national victory—perhaps almost as great as the victory at Stirling Bridge. And it had been good to be back in the world he thought he had left forever. The world of men and arms and events.

Tomorrow or the next day he supposed he would ride northward again, perhaps with Rory or some of Sir Kenneth's men. But life at Dunning Innes with old Padric and the sheep, oats, and apples would seem quieter, more isolated than ever before. He was only seventeen. The uneventful, lonely years stretched long.

And yet what else was there? He closed his eyes against the black of the tent, and sleep overcame him before any answers presented themselves.

The dream came slowly, as if he were experiencing it through a mist. Then, as he flew higher, the sun burned through, and he was borne up in a breathlessly blue sky. Soaring with the eagles.

Afterward he was never sure whether he was awake or still dreaming when the words came to him. They had arrived too late to pitch their tent on the softness of the wide green meadow beyond the town so instead had taken a spot of hard earth near the abbey. Yet were they so near that he could actually be hearing the brothers at their night office? Or did the voice that rang so clearly in his head come from beyond the eagles?

"I bore you up on eagle wings and brought you here to Myself. Hearken to My voice and keep My covenant. This shall be My special possession, dearer to Me than all other people, though all the earth is mine. This shall be to Me a kingdom of priests, a holy nation. That is what You must tell the Israelites."

Jamie sat up on his pallet. What had he heard? The night was quiet. *Special possession . . . dearer to Me . . . a kingdom of priests . . . a holy nation . . . tell the Israelites . . .* It made little sense. The commandment, however, was clear: *Hearken to My voice and keep My covenant.* Was the voice talking about Scotland?

Jamie shivered with the cold and lay back down under the covers. But sleep wouldn't come. At last he pushed his blankets aside with disgust and felt in the dark for his crutches. If the brothers were about, perhaps there would be someone who could tell him what it all meant.

The air outside was sharper than in the tent. It was not unlike diving into a cold loch. Jamie shook his hair out of his face and looked up at the clarity of the stars. No one was about. If it had been the brothers he heard, they had gone back to their dormitory for a few hours' more sleep before beginning the gentle pattern of their day. Guards would be posted somewhere, but Jamie didn't see them.

For want of anything better to do, he turned toward the church. He had taken only a few steps, moving carefully in the dark, when he saw a large figure entering the building. Little wonder that William Wallace couldn't sleep tonight either. Seldom in all history had a more difficult task been thrust upon a man so suddenly.

Jamie moved forward quietly; he would not disturb the Guardian at his prayers. A flicker of candles lighted the abbey, so empty and silent now after the shouting throng that had filled it only a few hours ago. Big as he was, Wallace looked small kneeling beneath the massive stone pillars. Unable to kneel with an unbending leg, Jamie sat on a bench and bowed his head.

Moments later he shifted restlessly. How did monks manage to stay at their prayers for hours? The clatter of his crutches falling onto the stone floor echoed like the boom of a drum in the silent church.

Disturbing Wallace was the last thing he wanted to do. But perhaps the great man was finding it hard to concentrate also, for he sprang up instantly.

"Who goes there?"

"It's Jamie MacInnes, Sir William. I dinna mean to bother you."

"Ah, wee Jamie, is it?" Wallace came to him. "I was told you acquitted yourself well at Stirling but with some cost. How are you, lad?"

"Verra fine." And he meant it.

Wallace nodded. "Aye. Good." He looked at the crutches. "You're young for so severe a badge of courage, lad. I've not forgot 'twas you who sounded the call to our first action. You're a brave lad."

Jamie's cheeks burned with pleasure.

After a moment Wallace spoke into the silence. "Is aught amiss with you?"

"I don't know. I don't think so. I'm just verra confused." The dim quiet abbey, with only a few flickers of gold breaking the dark, made the telling of his dream almost like experiencing it again.

Wallace made no comment, so Jamie asked, "What do you think it means?"

Wallace shook his head. "A kingdom of priests, a holy nation . . . fine sounding, that is. But for now we've to concentrate on survival. A realm we are while we give fealty to the same king, but while many give that fealty for selfish and diverse purposes we'll no' be a nation. A nation must work with common purpose." He was quiet for a space. "A holy nation would, I suppose, work for God's purpose. Aye, a fine thing that would be."

He clapped Jamie on the back. "If it can be only in our dreams, I'm glad you've dreamed it, lad. Such is worthy of sennachie, and such must be dreamed before there's hope of accomplishing it."

The chill of the stone around him was sinking into Jamie. "Perhaps I'd best be getting back." He reached for his fallen crutch.

But Wallace's words stopped him mid-motion. "Lad, I'm a man of action, chosen Guardian to be war leader. But I value men of vision like Jock Brice and Bishop Sinclair. When the warring's done,

Scotland will have need of sennachies and visionaries. But for now, Father Brice has need of an assistant."

"Yes! I'd like that." Then Jamie realized he'd answered before he'd been asked.

But the man of action took no offense. He slapped Jamie on the back again. "Aye. That's settled then. And a fine thing. My first appointment as Guardian of the Realm. Master James MacInnes, clerk to Father John Brice."

59

A month later, in an office in the same abbey, his fingers stained with ink, Jamie looked up from the parchment he was inscribing at Brice's direction. Immediately after his election, Wallace had begun work on policies aimed at bringing all the magnates of the land under his sway and overthrowing the English remaining in Scotland. He set about raising troops, sending the call to arms far and wide, then organizing and drilling them into a disciplined army. At the same time he saw to putting men of ability and proven patriotism in offices of influence. This was where Jamie's work came in—writing endless letters and documents.

Jamie had been taught well enough by the Cistercian brothers at the small monastery at Forteviot. But reading and writing had never been his favorite activities. He had certainly felt no call to the life of a religious. Father Jock, however, could work through a long day and on until nighttime candles guttered, seeming to draw energy from his work and from his regular breaks for prayer.

"Sir William Wallace, Guardian of the kingdom of Scotland, and general of the army of the same . . ." Brice dictated.

Jamie's nose itched. But if he raised his quill to scratch, he would lose rhythm with the smoothly flowing words. Worse, he was likely to drop a blob of ink on the parchment. Then he would have to scratch it off carefully with his penknife and start over.

Best to keep at it, no matter how one's hand cramped.

". . . in the name of the noble prince the Lord John, by the grace of God illustrious king of Scotland, by consent of the community of the same kingdom, to all good men of the said kingdom to whom this present writing shall come, eternal salvation in the Lord . . ." The charter went on to appoint Alexander Scrymgeour the hereditary royal standard bearer.

"Ah, that's fine, lad." Brice looked over Jamie's shoulder. "A right fine hand you have."

A bell tolled from the abbey tower. Father Jock placed on the table the stack of documents he held. "Time for Vespers. After supper we will see to this matter of the unseating of William Comyn as bishop of Saint Andrews. The highest see in the land is no place to tolerate a strong supporter of Edward. Wallace would have the canons elect William Lamberton, who has served so well as chancellor of Glasgow Cathedral. No man could have better training than to have worked with Bishop Wishart."

The bell tolled more insistently.

"Yes, well, time enough for that later. Are you coming to prayers?"

So desperate for fresh air was he that Jamie didn't even answer. A side water from the Clyde curled around the meadow beyond the monastery. A moss-covered boulder on its banks beckoned. A week ago he had discovered the favorite evening feeding spot of a blue heron.

He paused only long enough to snatch his cloak from a peg by the door. Late March evenings could chill to the bone, in spite of the brave primroses that bloomed on south-facing banks.

The setting sun dazzled patches on the inlet. The heron stood so still, blue gray bird against blue gray water, that it was moments before Jamie spotted it. Then with a sudden lightning flash, the long-necked bird dipped into the water, came up with a dripping, wriggling fish in its slender bill, and flew off.

At first Jamie thought the sigh he heard from the far side of the rock he sat on was the wind. Then the grass rustled, and he leaned around to look. A young woman with a thick black braid down her back sat on a fallen log.

It was the space of five heartbeats before he realized the impossible was not impossible. He was almost too choked with surprise to speak her name.

"Rhona."

Her startled laughter was as light as the whir of the heron's wings. "Jamie. Can it be? Is it truly yourself?"

"Aye. And you. You're not at Saint Margaret's?"

She scrambled up the boulder. He held out a hand to help her, and she ascended as gracefully as the heron. "I've come on an errand with Sister Richilda, the sacristan. As I am well acquainted with this area and with the Guardian, Mother Prioress thought it best that I come. If I had had any idea you were here, I would have . . ."

"What would you have? Refused to come?" He grinned and raised one eyebrow.

"Ridden faster."

He barely caught the words, as they were muffled by a maidenly ducking of her head. But it was enough.

He put his hand over hers, resting on a patch of soft green moss. "Ah, that's fine. But your errand—to see the Wallace. Is there trouble at Saint Margaret's?"

She nodded and turned her round, dark eyes on him. "The silver gilt plate from the chapel—"

"Stolen?"

She nodded again. "At first even Sister Sacristan didn't notice. She thought Mother Prioress had taken the candlestick and salver for her own devotions. Then last week Father Andrew from Cambuskenneth came to say mass for us, and the golden monstrance set with Tey river pearls was gone."

"Surely that's a matter for the sheriff. Wallace set a fine man in charge at Stirling town, and his contingent still guards the area, does it not?"

"Yes, that's what Mother Prioress thought, but Brother Simon said—"

"Ah, Simon was there too?"

"Yes, come with Father Andrew. And it must have been the hand of God, for it was Brother Simon who saw the truth of the matter. It could be no common thief. Such a one would have taken all he could carry and run far away, not taken items one at a time over many weeks. This must be the work of someone who comes and goes at will as above suspicion."

"One of the sisters?"

"That's what we feared he was suggesting. But there have been no new novitiates or residents of the guest house. I am the newest come of any, and it could not be any of the longtime sisters."

Jamie's hand tightened over hers. "Outlaws? Men displaced from their land by Edward's ravages? Rhona, you must take care. Wallace is doing all he can to restore order, but there are still reavers living outside the law—"

She shook her head. "Anyone like that would have been seen in the area. We live in very quiet seclusion. Saint Margaret's has few casual travelers."

"But then—"

"Brother Simon set to watch with Mother Prioress's permission."

"And he saw—"

"Nothing." Again her sigh was as light as the breeze. "But he feels certain it must be one of the men Wallace set to guard us from such outlaws as you suggested. He has no evidence to present to the Guardian, but he says it is the only answer."

"Ah, so Simon has come here too?" Jamie's smile at thought of seeing his friend was almost as bright as that at seeing Rhona.

"Yes, Mother Prioress thought he and our Sister Sacristan the best to explain the situation. They must speak directly to Wallace, you see, as they suspect his men."

Jamie nodded. Yes, he saw. But surely they were wrong. Because of its supreme importance, Wallace had set some of his best men to duty at Stirling. Some of those who had been with him the longest. When they went back to the office, he could look at the rosters.

The last rays of the sun sank in the west. The next brush of the breeze was markedly colder. Rhona shivered.

"We must get back. It will be time for supper," Jamie said. He slid down the boulder and landed on his good leg.

Rhona sprang down as lightly as a bird flying.

Then came the moment Jamie hated. He reached beside the rock and pulled out his crutches. She had not seen him for so long. She would think him fully recovered. She would not be knowing that he would never recover.

And yet she seemed not to notice his awkwardness as she skipped lightly beside him, holding the hem of her soft gray gown above the long, evening-damp meadow grass. She chattered about their journey from the priory, and Jamie was glad that she seemed so freed from the haunting images that had goaded her to seek refuge with the holy sisters. But he did not ask the deep questions his heart held. He just let her talk for the pleasure he took in listening to her voice.

They were about to enter the refectory, where monks, visitors, and the Guardian's men all ate together, when he realized he had not told her. "Oh, but do you know? Wallace himself is not here. He's gone north to muster more troops."

Rhona clapped her hands and turned with a bound. "Yes, I do know. And Brother Simon says we must await his return. Isn't that dreadful?"

"Aye. I can think of nae worse." He returned her grin just before Simon joined them.

The satisfied smile above Simon's neat dark beard and the twinkle in the monk's bright blue eyes told Jamie that all might not be the happenstance he had thought it to be.

"And was the heron feeding?" Simon asked after their greetings.

Jamie nodded. "Aye, you knew."

"Father Brice did just mention something of the like, and I thought it might be more to the lady's amusement than our poor chanting."

"You're a good friend, Simon."

The three parted to take their places at the long, scrubbed oak table, agreeing to meet before Compline to see what they might learn from the troop lists.

Half an hour later Jamie held a parchment sheet near a wavering, smoking candle. He shook his head as he perused the list. "Of course, there are some here I don't know. And many known only by reputation. But the officers are among Wallace's best. Some of the infantry could be sneaking out at night, I suppose . . ."

Rhona shook her head firmly.

Simon agreed. "Saint Margaret's is a well-walled enclosure. And isolated. It would hardly be worth the risk for a sneak thief to range so far. Much easier pickings in Stirling town—and less danger of being caught. I'm convinced it's one who's been there on duty with some regularity. Someone above suspicion."

Jamie ran down the list again. "Aye, there's the rub. They're all above suspicion: Sir John Graham, Murdo Grant, Robert Boyd, Henry de Haliburton, Hugh Danduff . . ." He read a few more names and put the list down. "These are men who have been with Wallace from the first. They should all be above such petty thievery."

"Aye, they should," Simon agreed.

A sudden incessant pealing of the bell turned all three heads toward the abbey.

"It's too early for Compline, surely," Rhona said.

"Aye, and that ring's nae call to prayers." Jamie felt chilled.

They had heard rumors that Edward's Flanders campaign was ended—in a great victory for Edward, of course. But it was too soon. Wallace had mustered only half the troops he would need to meet Edward—and only begun their training. The land was far from consolidated. Comyn had sent a small body of cavalry under the command of his son John Comyn, called the Red; some of Andrew de Moray's men still rallied to the cause for which their leader had died; and the gallant MacDuff of Fife drilled his men for Scotland. But only one of Scotland's great earls was now active in the field against Edward—Robert Bruce kept strong the castle of Ayr. But he was many days' ride away.

"It's too soon," Jamie said.

"Then one way or the other, it had best be a call to prayer." Brother Simon led the way to the church.

It couldn't be happening yet. But it was. John Graham, whose name had headed the roster at Stirling, stood at the front of the long aisle where only a few weeks before William Wallace had been proclaimed Guardian of the Realm.

Graham had ridden in haste from Stirling Castle. The word had come to him there, carried as it was by a messenger arriving by boat from Berwick. Graham had thought to find Wallace here. But as no one was certain as to the Guardian's whereabouts, his captain would give the news that all might begin what preparation they could.

They would have two months, perhaps a space more, for the messenger had told of trouble Edward was having in the south with his own barons. But it was certain the English king would soon set that to rights. And then he would turn his face northward.

He would bring his own troops, fresh arrived from the continent, with him. But he already had enough massed at the border beyond Berwick to make any man less than William Wallace quail: three thousand heavy chivalry, four thousand light cavalry, eighty thousand foot, and many archers—very many.

Jamie turned to Rhona and gripped her shoulders so hard he was afraid afterward he might have hurt her. But at the moment he had to give expression to the intensity of his feeling. "Rhona, you must get to safety. Simon, get her back to her nunnery and guard her well. Now. As soon as it is light enough to travel."

"Jamie," Rhona held out a small white hand in protest. "He said two months or more. And the priory plate, Mother Prioress said—"

"The plate be hanged." Jamie could have shaken her. "When word gets abroad, this will be a land in uproar. There'll be almost as much danger from Scots as from English. Get to the sisters and make what provision you can. Edward is sure to burn all the ground he marches over, just as he did last time. There will be terrible hunger. Dig holes and store what you can."

Then the commotion in the room around him fell back. Jamie felt he was standing in a bright light. He could hear nothing but the sound of his own voice, and that coming as if from a distance. No, not his voice but that of another, as if speaking through him.

"Ar of Moab is destroyed; laid waste in a night. Every head is shaved, every beard sheared off. In the streets they wear sackcloth, lamenting and weeping. The soul of Moab quivers within him, the heart of Moab cries out. The waters have become a waste; the grass is withered. New growth is gone, nothing is green. The waters are filled with blood."

His hands fell limp at his sides. The light faded. The sounds of the room returned.

"Jamie?" Rhona's eyes were wide with something like fear, but she did not shrink from him. Instead she put a hand lightly on his arm, then withdrew it. "Is that what it will be like?"

He shook his head. "I dona know. I—I had another dream once. It was very fine. I told it to Wallace. He said I should become a sennachie, for the land had need of such. But I've had none since. I do not think he would be much pleased with this hearing."

"No. It was fearful—and awesome." Her hand returned to his arm briefly. "I'll do as you say, Jamie. At first light."

"Aye." He could not comprehend how much he hated to see her go. Their time together had been so short. But she must. "Get you to safety, Rhona. And stay safe. If it happened to you as to Agnes—or worse, to Aline—I . . . I don't know what I would do." He set his teeth, but his jaw still worked. He would have turned from her but hated exhibiting his awkwardness.

"Do you think I don't know, Jamie? Marion was my sister. But I will pray every day. And when at last Edward is driven from the land . . ." It was she who turned from him.

Only after she disappeared through the crowd did he realize he had not asked her if she meant to take vows.

60

In the end the Scots had more time than they could have hoped for. It was July before Edward had secured his barons at his back by offering them the equivalent of another Magna Carta. Then he turned north.

The church was the first to rally to Wallace's support. Wishart at Glasgow, Sinclair at Dunkeld, Lamberton at St. Andrews all emptied their coffers for the aid of a free Scotland. And Wallace now commanded some fifty thousand troops. Perhaps more.

But that was half the English strength. And the problems remained. Although Wallace kept the bulk of his army in the Selkirk Forest, his troops were spread wide across the land, garrisoning castles and protecting towns. With such dispersal, the numbers shrank alarmingly.

And in spite of the arms from captured English castles and armories, the chronic problem was the same. No heavy chivalry and very few archers, none with longbows—the ash tree from which such weapons were made did not grow in Scotland. And there was rumor of a fearsome new weapon Edward brought with the troops from Gascony—a crossbow, which shot level at its target with far greater speed and strength than anything yet faced on the field in Scotland.

"And then there's the English sea power." Jock Brice piled an armful of documents in the leather pouch Brother Simon had long ago given Jamie for carrying things over his shoulder. "Wallace much fears attack at his back from the sea. And Edward feels aye free to burn our land when he knows he can feed his men from supplies brought in by sea." Brice picked up his own armful of books and charters and led the way from the room.

Wallace was holding council in the refectory. What documents he did not need would be burned or buried to prevent their falling into English hands and later used to condemn those whose names appeared there. If things went wrong.

The normally quiet churchyard thrummed with energy. Armor-clad couriers marched in and out of the council room, and monks and servants scurried every direction, making what preparation they could.

But Jamie entered the hall quietly. With all the energy and excitement around him, he felt excluded. This turning over of documents would end his work. There were no more charters to draw up, for Wallace had no more time to make civil appointments; no more letters to write, because Jock Brice, returning to his military role, had no time to direct correspondence.

The hard-won acceptance Jamie had come to over his crippled leg was put to sore testing. He could imagine nothing worse than sitting on the sidelines and watching the Scots army march out, banners flying, bagpipes skirling.

Two days ago Sir Kenneth Corvan had arrived from Forteviot with his contingent, Rory among them. It had been good to see his brother and hear the news of Dunning Innes. The brothers had sat late and talked. But since then, Rory, too, was occupied with military affairs.

Murdo Grant, who had ridden south from Stirling a week ago, now brushed past Jamie, almost knocking his pack off. He strode proudly by in his full plate armor, taken from the Stirling armory.

But the leader he approached still wore his rusty chain-mail hauberk and an old leather surcoat, for in all the captured armor there had been nothing of a size to fit William Wallace. Murdo's errand dealt with, Wallace turned to those from his clerk's office.

Jamie stood by while the Guardian directed Brice in the disposition of the documents. One ledger had only a few figures at the top. It was the account for the securing of books and writing supplies. Wallace paused in the way he had of focusing totally on the matter at hand. Jamie saw him run his tongue between his teeth and knew William Wallace was thinking of things that mattered much to him.

At last he looked up and spoke to Jamie as if he were the only other person in the room, and yet his words were entirely impersonal. "It takes arts of valor to protect a realm and to build a nation. But they are of little use to the future unless forged into stories to bring men's hearts together and to teach the next generation. Of such tales, of the knowledge of common heritage, is a nation made.

"I have many men with sword power. And they are sorely needed at this hour. But I have few who possess such a gift as yours—" now he looked directly at Jamie "—a gift of hearing words not your own, of seeing things beyond your own eyes. Jamie MacInnes, I would have you come with me. Not to bear arms but to bear a mightier weapon. Watch the battle and write the story for the nation we are to build."

Jamie nodded and placed the empty ledger in his pack.

"We have heard of the pride of Moab, how very proud he is, how he lords over the nations, scattering them over the desert."

Jamie tried to focus on the empty sheet before him. But his vision would not clear. He could not write of the battle for the strength of the words in his head.

"I weep with Jazer. I water the land with tears. For on the summer fruits and harvests the battle cry has fallen. From the orchards are taken away joy and gladness. In the vineyards there is no singing, no shout of joy."

The voice subsided. Jamie's candle flame steadied. He dipped his quill and wrote the account as he had seen it and as it had been told him.

Wallace was up before the early summer dawn began to break. Fully armored, he stood on the south slope of the hill, looking toward the winding Avon water, the woods of Slamannan Muir behind him. This was the most likely ground he would find south of the Forth. This was ground he could use—ground that could be made to fight against Edward as always he had of necessity done to help offset Edward's vast advantage of numbers.

It was not as advantageous as Stirling Bridge had been. But Edward was not Cressingham. The wiliest warrior in Christendom, there was no chance of tricking and trapping Edward as he had Cressingham.

Always it was Edward. Edward himself. Not the English people, who were their cousins, but Edward, the First Knight in Christendom, who strove with an obsession beyond all reason to crush Scotland and hammer all memory of nationhood into dust. And Edward was out there somewhere. Waiting for him.

Edward with a hundred thousand men.

Of habit, Wallace's hand went to the sword at his back when he heard the dry grass crunch under approaching footfall. But he did not draw. He had been awaiting the report of his spy. Perhaps this would be the day to end the waiting.

Murdo's report did nothing to dissuade Wallace of that idea.

"Desperate for food they are—starved and half mutinous."

So should he offer battle? Or should he draw back and wait? A few more days of delay and the demoralized English troops might mutiny and break ranks in search of food. But he could not wait long, or his own volunteers, already anxious to be home to harvest crops that would keep their own bairns from starvation, would also break ranks.

Murdo's next words decided the matter. "Aye, and panic in the camp as well." Even in the dim light, Wallace could see white teeth flash in the face of the dark little man. "Edward gave the order that the horses were not to be picketed in lines as usual but each tethered by his master. Edward's page fell asleep. The massive brute he was to be watching trampled on the sleeping king."

"Edward? Trampled by his own charger? Was he hurt grievous?"

Now Murdo laughed outright. "It spread like wildfire through the camp that the wounds were dangerous—even fatal. Pity it wasn't true. But the panic was a treat to see. Two ribs broken, mostlike. Won't be enough to stop Edward."

"Aye. Not sufficient to stop. But slow a wee bit, perhaps." Wallace wheeled into action. His strategy had been to draw Edward through an empty, foodless country, twice burned by English and once by Scots. Now he must take what advantage that course had produced.

By the time the sun was high enough for men to recognize one another readily, his strategies of the last days and weeks were under way. With speed born of careful planning, John Graham's men hammered into place a palisade of long, sharp stakes pointed toward the enemy, interwoven with ropes. That would slow the English cavalry charge and protect the schiltroms into which Wallace now arranged his men.

On the hard ground of the hillside sloping up from the river, Wallace formed the Scots army into three giant hedgehogs of perhaps four thousand men each. Not unlike the Roman squares Wallace had read of at university, these vast human war machines were circular in form, each consisting of a double rank of men facing outward, crouching with their twelve-foot spears slanting upward. The rear rank stood with weapons inclined over their comrades' heads, ready to step forward to fill the places of those who might fall.

The spaces between the schiltroms Wallace filled with bands of Border archers to break the impetus of chivalry charges on his infantry. For always the Scottish commander had to rely on infantry armed with spears against an enemy whose strength lay in heavy cavalry.

Wallace put his own horse troops to the rear—in reserve for pursuit when the enemy should be broken, he told their leader, the Red Comyn. But in truth it was because he doubted their firmness.

Jamie recounted in his mind all that Wallace had told him of his strategy, while watching from his vantage point atop the hill. The

558

sun, now fully risen, shone on the spear tips of the vast metal hedge-hogs below and, across the narrow winding Avon, on the mighty mass of Edward's chivalry. The horses' long, colorful caparisons fluttered in the breeze. Trappers, they were called, because their function was to trap enemy weapons in their flowing folds. The knights, covered in steel from head to toe, held equally bright, long, pointed shields and waited beneath their flying banners. And behind them, rank upon rank of archers.

The enemy advanced.

"I have brought you to the ring. Dance the best you can!" Wallace's proud encouragement to his men echoed off the hillside.

It was met by a resounding reply of cheers and the rumble of spears beating on targes.

"A Wallace! A Wallace!"

"For God and Saint Andrew!"

The rampant red lion danced on a field of gold. The white saltire fluttered against the blue sky. The Moraymen and MacDuff's fifers skirled pipes.

Edward's battle horn echoed from across the river, signaling the first cavalry charge. The hillside trembled with the pounding feet of some thousand fully armored heavy destriers. Jamie felt the tension in the schiltroms as they leaned forward to repel the attack, yet moved not one step from their positions.

Wallace's guard rail of sharpened poles did its work. The front row of thudding chargers wheeled suddenly westward to avoid impalement and plunged into the marshy moss that lined the floodplain. While the forward ranks plunged and floundered in the mud, those behind them pivoted to seek a way around.

A vast cheer rose from the Scots hillside at the sight of the enemy retreating in confusion. The first attack had been repelled without a single sword thrust.

But Jamie did not raise his voice with them, for he sat at higher vantage and could see the thousands yet to come. And he saw what few in the field, intent on the enemy, had seen. At the first enemy charge, the sight of the huge horses and their mailed riders thundering forward had been too much for Comyn's cavalry. Even as the English sank in the swamp, the Scots horse turned and fled into the woods.

And now came Edward's second line, glorious with the banners of dozens of barons, commanded by Bishop Bec of Durham, a man as hated for his cruelty as Cressingham had been. Bec had seen the failure of the first charge. He was prepared. He led his troops sharply to the east, avoiding palisade and bog alike. At the same time another attack fell on the Scottish right from cavalry that had circled the Moss.

Jamie threw his whole heart into watching the battle, as truly as if he held a spear inside a massed hedgehog himself. A great cry broke from his throat as the schiltroms held firm as rocks against the massive attacks. Scottish courage and discipline were unbroken. The charges were repelled into fragments like chaff off the steady circles of spears.

And suddenly, in Jamie's mind, the Scots spearmen were no longer hedgehogs but giant, bristling bushes. The field spun with a confusion of baffled horsemen swirling around a deadly unbreakable hedge of sturdy Scottish thistles.

Now the English infantry advanced. For a moment it was as if the field held its breath. Even the confusion of knights on whirling destriers seemed to fade. Then sounded the twanging of hundreds, thousands of arrows being loosed. To Jamie looking down on them, it was like the flight of innumerable crows pulling a curtain over the hillside. For an instant all below him was blocked from view.

And when the sky cleared and the arrows had fallen, so had hundreds of Wallace's brave men. The thistles shook as if whipped by a great wind, then reformed and stood again, bristling to the defense of their country.

But there was little they could do. Spears could not touch longbowmen. The Scots archers did their best, but their marksmanship was no match for the English. And the shortbow of the Borderers, designed more for hunting than for warfare, had little power against a longbow that could send a shaft through a coat of steel mail.

In vain Jamie looked toward the wood. Now would be the time. Now, if the Red Comyn had regrouped his fleeing cavalry beneath the trees of Shamannan Muir, they could sweep down the hillside and disperse the deadly longbowmen. But no reprieve came. The Scottish thistles were ground into the rough turf of the hillside beyond Falkirk.

Jamie's own wound had never seemed less to him than that late July afternoon as he worked among the fallen patriot army, sorting those to whom they could give comfort from the corpses. Jock Brice, his armor laid aside, directed the salving and bandaging. It would take days to bury their dead. Ten thousand fallen at least—chief among them the noble MacDuff and the gallant John Graham.

Wallace himself directed the carrying of Graham's body to the Falkirk churchyard. "Aye, Jamie, come along, lad. You were one of the first group too. And where is Murdo? He should be here as well."

Father Brice's abbreviated burial service was almost over when the Grant arrived. He left his bag behind a whin bush, but Jamie, standing back, heard the clink of metal and knew what had delayed Murdo. Well, they had none received overpay, and it was certain none of the fallen had need of their worldly goods. As well it go to one who could use it again. He turned back to Brice's words.

"And so is our companion, with his brave fallen fellows, now in God's kingdom, with their robes washed clean in the blood of the Lamb." Father John threw the first handful of dirt over the hastily prepared body.

"Sir John the Graham, of the chief who fought to rescue Scotland. A better knight never to the world was lent."

They covered the grave.

The others moved away, but Wallace stood. Jamie had not seen the great man so still and withdrawn since the night Marion Braidfoot was murdered. Jamie did not know how to approach him, but he would not leave his leader alone. He made his way quietly to a stone bench and sat.

He had no idea how long they remained so—Wallace standing by the new-made grave, only the slight rising and lowering of his broad shoulders indicating that he breathed, and Jamie sitting on the bench. A few night animals stirred. Stars came out.

Then the kirkyard seemed to slip away.

"All mankind is grass, and all their glory like the flower of the field. The grass withers, the flower wilts." Had Jamie's voice not come like the stirring of the breeze, he would have startled himself.

As he spoke aloud the words he heard in his head, the big man standing by the grave turned slowly. Jamie was concentrating on the words and on the green flowering land he saw in his mind, but with another part of his consciousness he saw Wallace's shoulders relax. His face looked immeasurably tired and sad, and yet, as Jamie's words continued, some of the strain seemed to leave him.

"I will lead the blind on their journey; by paths unknown I will guide them. I will turn darkness into light before them, and make crooked ways straight. These things I do for them, and I will not forsake them."

The tension continued to drain from Wallace until his knees bent and he sat on the rough, bunchy grass at the foot of his friend's tomb.

Jamie paused, but an almost imperceptible nod from the Guardian bade him continue.

"This is a people despoiled and plundered, all of them trapped in holes, hidden away in prisons. They are taken as booty, with no one to rescue them, with no one to demand their return.

"But fear not, I have called you by name; you are Mine. When you pass through the water, I will be with you; in the rivers you shall not drown. When you walk through fire, you shall not be burned; the flames shall not consume you. Fear not, for I am with you."

The quiet descended on them so completely that Jamie started when at last Wallace spoke. "Aye. We'll bed at Glenellrig House tonight. There will be much work tomorrow. Work for many tomorrows. Edward has won a great victory. But he has not won Scotland. If he thinks Scotland can be won by might of arms, he must think again. Right is on our side. Scotland will not yield to tyrant sword. For God armeth the patriot."

That night in a corner of the loft at Glenellrig, Jamie dipped his quill and began writing by the light of a single candle. For Scotland would be a nation yet, and a nation must find itself in its history. There would yet be a need for sennachies.

61

And so it was that the struggle for freedom continued. The next year Wallace and the remnant of the Scots army returned to fighting in burn channel and forest fastness. Robert Bruce was still active with a small but hard-hitting force in Galloway. And most important of all, true to Wallace's declaration that Scotland's spirit was not dead, many of the great nobles now joined the fight for their kingdom. Poor, devastated kingdom that it was, as Edward Plantagenet strove to crush all under his heel.

"Use all cruelty," he ordered. And his armies took the directive to heart, burning and slaying. No mercy. All destroyed. Town and church alike. Village and monastery. All left a smoking waste. Soldier and priest. Man and woman. All felt the thrust of Edward's sword.

But Edward overplayed his hand. Far from breaking the Scots' resistance, such brutality spurred their patriotism.

His attempts to reimpose his control on Scotland aroused the most lively spirit of defiance that the land had seen since the Battle of Spottismuir two and a half years earlier. After the period of freedom Wallace's victory at Stirling had given them, the nobles were none so willing to bow again to Edward's yoke. More important, the young knight of obscure origins had demonstrated, by fighting two pitched battles against the most formidable army in Christendom, that tyranny could be resisted. Buchan, Menteith, Umfraville, Brechin, Soulis, Keith—great names that long should have been in the lists—at last took the field to stand with courage and unity.

Jamie lay his quill aside and shook his hand to uncramp his fingers, then took it up again to add the names of Sir Malcolm Wallace, William's elder brother, Sir David de Graham, and Sir William de Balliol to the account he was keeping of those fighting for Scotland's freedom.

He had taken a guest room at Cambuskenneth Abbey, as its position near Stirling on the banks of the Forth made it the ideal location to keep abreast of the news of the nation's struggles. If William Wallace could be said to have a headquarters other than the forest, this was it.

He was becoming somewhat more accepting of a life that demanded long periods of sitting. Some, but not much. A clatter in the courtyard gave him an excuse to lay aside his pen. The clatter came his way, and his face split in a wide grin when the door burst open and Wallace strode in.

"Ah, Jamie lad, I've a fine tale to add to your store. Stirling Castle is ours again. Soulis holds it for the Community of the Realm of Scotland."

"What a grand sight that must be—to see the red lion flying in place of the golden leopard."

"Aye, it is. A sight fit for a sennachie. Will you ride out with me to view it?"

Jamie didn't need a second invitation.

The August day had been cool and rainy, but now evening winds blew the clouds on toward the sea just in time for the westering sun to shine golden across the land. Although the rebuilt Stirling Bridge offered a nearer view, the riders turned by unspoken assent toward Abbey Craig. They pulled up very near the spot where they had awaited the English advance two years before and looked across the wide green valley, cut by the twisting, looping Forth, toward the castle.

"Aye, a fine sight."

In truth it was too far to see what flag fluttered from the battlements, but since Jamie had opened his mind's eye to the task of recording stories, his ability to see the truth of things, unhampered by bare facts, had grown. Now, knowing that he was viewing Stirling Castle returned to its rightful lordship made the view one at peace with the realm.

"It's a fine day that Scotland holds Stirling again."

Wallace nodded. "The whole summer we spent keeping their supplies cut. But it paid off. The garrison was only ninety men. They ate their last horse three days ago. It's likely they were more happy to be freed than even we were to set them at liberty."

"And now with the lords uniting, you'll be gathering an army to march against Edward again?"

Wallace shook his head. "Nay. Famine in England and Edward's restless barons have him busy enough in the south once more. Let him bide there. We've work to do here. The normal business of government needs to be set to rights once again. It's time and beyond for the holding of a real parliament, not just the ad hoc assemblies we've made do with these past years. The church needs strengthening and organizing. Aberdeen, Forfar, Stirling, Lanark, Roxburgh—all over this country there are sheriffdoms needing good Scots officers. A regular collection of revenues . . ."

His sigh was so heavy that Gallus shifted under the motion. "And our relations abroad must be looked to. Lamberton has gone to King Philip of France with some encouraging results, but the bishop needs support. And the pope must be applied to if we would have his continued aid in consecrating our bishops . . ."

"So as Guardian you—"

Wallace brought his hand down on his pommel hard enough to make Jamie's mount prick up his ears. "No. That is what I'm saying. I am not the right man for the job. Not now."

"What?" Jamie almost choked at the idea. "You're the only man for the job. Only Wallace can hold Scotland."

The big man shook his massive head. "Nay. After Stirling there was truth to that. But now—since Falkirk—no."

Jamie couldn't believe what he was hearing. The idea of anyone but William Wallace guarding the Community of the Realm of Scotland was unthinkable. "Losing a battle against such odds is no disgrace. Commanders do so many times and fight on. As you've done."

"Aye. As I'll always do. While William Wallace breathes he'll fight for Scotland. But not as Guardian. I've betrayed the confidence the people had in me."

"No." Jamie fought for words. He had to make Wallace see sense. "Your men still follow you. You just took the greatest castle in Scotland. Can you no' see—"

"Jamie, lad, dona fash yourself. Can you no' see? One who is nae a great noble could be Guardian only by right of military success. I knew it always. The guardianship I did not want, but while none other held sway in the field it was my responsibility. Now the earls are active for Scotland. Now I can do what I do best, unhindered by the burden of governing."

Wallace spoke calmly, detachedly, as if all had been thought through long ago. Emotion was there only when he spoke of the needs of his country and in response to Jamie's heated outbursts.

But Jamie felt no calm. Would the man listen to no reason? Did he mean to resign the guardianship? He must be stopped. "The folk love you."

"Aye. And so I must no' betray their love. I have held long enough for the nobles to take their rightful place."

"But who would be Guardian? Bruce and Comyn are most powerful, but if one is chosen over the other, the unchosen house will revolt. Civil war would mean giving Scotland to Edward."

"Aye." Wallace sighed. "And so they must take the burden jointly."

"Jointly? Co-Guardians? But they hate each other. They cannot work together."

"They can if they will. And they must."

Everything within Jamie cried out in protest. He must do something to stop this. But for once no words came to him. His mind, which he had trained to fill so readily with pictures, was dark. The brave sight of Stirling Castle before them brought nothing to mind that he had not already said. "Then all is lost."

He turned his horse and rode back down Abbey Craig.

Two weeks later Jamie joined the others from Cambuskenneth who went to Scone for the naming of the new Guardian.

Wallace was no longer in power, and yet it was his spirit that ruled. James the Steward called the assembly to order as on that day two years ago. Again Bruce and Comyn factions separated on opposite sides of the church. But this time there was no third throng to cheer the election of William Wallace.

Now all they had before them was William Wallace's example of selfless patriotism—Wallace, who had put his country before all personal considerations. And they had Wallace in person. His great size, his inner strength, and his achievements exerted an influence that more than once kept the debate from breaking into open warfare.

And in the end they agreed. It was as Wallace had said. They must, so they did. Robert Bruce, earl of Carrick, and John Comyn the Red, lord of Badenoch, were Joint Guardians of the Community of the Realm of Scotland. So help them God.

Two days later Wallace told Jamie of his intention of turning his hand to the diplomacy that was so needed. He would go to France to aid Bishop Lamberton at the court of King Philip. And the sennachie's vision, which had been inspired by his hero, left Jamie.

That night in the field beyond Scone Palace he stared at the blackness of his tent roof. The absence of the pictures that would before have filled the space left him with an emptiness he had not thought possible. Once before, he had thought his life over. Then the pictures and words had come to fill the void of the active life he must leave. But now the inner void was greater than before. He missed his pictures far more than he missed the use of his leg.

Without even thinking the matter through, he knew that he would return to Dunning Innes. He gave fleeting thought to the fact that Scotland would have as much need for its tales under the joint guardianship as before—indeed it would have more.

And the idea crossed his mind that now he would be free to search for traces of the lost Aline. Impossible as it seemed, he never entirely lost hope of one day seeing his golden-haired sister again. But now he had no heart to face the impracticalities of such an undertaking.

And there was the matter of St. Margaret's unrecovered treasure. Although what was that among so many abbeys and holy houses ransacked? And what chance was there that the thief, even if one of the suspected officers, had survived Falkirk?

As on that other black night after Stirling Bridge, the years stretched before him long and empty. He was three months from his twentieth birthday. He supposed Rory could find some use for him on the farm. He hoped he wouldn't be viewed as a nuisance.

There was nothing more to think about. And yet one thought kept pushing, the one above all others that he would avoid. Rhona. She was still at St. Margaret's. And unveiled. He had seen her twice in the past year, once when he accompanied Brother Simon on a task to St. Margaret's and once when she had come to Cambuskenneth to share in the Eastertide Mass. Each time their visits had been full of joy and laughter and the parting hard for him.

No, he decided. There was nothing to be gained by one more such. Indeed he would have the memory to cherish. But he would have to live again with the pain of parting. He rolled onto his side, automatically using his good leg to shift the shriveled one.

In the morning he joined the group riding back to Cambuskenneth. Wallace and six of his closest men—almost all that were now left alive of the thirty who had been with him on that first assault on Scone Palace—had ridden out before dawn, so they were a much diminished group. It was a long day of quiet riding.

They arrived at the abbey after the monks' supper was finished, but Brother Hospitallier bade them eat. He had anticipated their return and held a pot of stew for them.

Jamie hungrily wolfed his first bowl of venison in thick broth with root vegetables and gratefully accepted a second. He had just bitten into a chunk of crusty wheat and barley bread when Brother Simon came to him.

"Ah, Jamie. I've so eagerly awaited your return that I sang entirely off-key at Vespers. It's a miracle Father Abbot didn't discipline me."

The monk's open, friendly smile and the warmth in his blue eyes touched a chord in Jamie. He smiled for the first time since

Wallace had told him of his decision to resign. "Aye? What has you so fashed?"

Simon dug in the folds of his black robe and pulled out the little leather pouch that he often slung around his neck for carrying small objects. He loosened the drawstring and dumped a tiny white item into the palm of his hand.

Jamie poked at it with one finger. "Tay River pearl. A very nice one. Small, but exquisite sheen. I didn't know you'd been to the Tay recently."

Simon shook his head. "I haven't. My duty today was to clean the guest house."

Jamie ducked his head. "Sorry about that. I left in some agitation. I've come back to clean out anyway."

"Nay. Not your room, clod pate. Would I be likely to find such as this there?"

Jamie raised one eyebrow. "Och. I wish. That's valuable, that is."

The tonsured head nodded. "Aye. That's what made it so surprising."

"What?"

"I found it while cleaning the room where Wallace's men slept."

Jamie frowned. "But who among them would have such a thing? They were common men to start out, and none has made any fortune following Wallace. Save the picking of some war booty, I suppose." He looked closer at the tiny gleaming jewel and shook his head. "But this seems an unlikely thing to be adorning a dirk hilt."

"So Father Abbot said. A fine memory our Father has. He recalled that Saint Margaret's was robbed of a pearl encrusted monstrance. I'm to take this to them tomorrow. You'll go with me?"

"But that makes no sense. I know all those men. They've followed Wallace with absolute loyalty for three years. Besides, whoever stole such a thing would have disposed of it long ago." Then Simon's question sank in. "Go with you? To Saint Margaret's?" He paused. "Nay. I've only come for my things. I'm leaving in the morning."

Simon raised his dark, expressive eyebrows. "Aye? Well then, you'll be in the saddle anyway. You may as well see me on my errand." He ignored Jamie's head shake. "It'll no' take long."

It took Jamie far longer to ready his leave-taking than he could have imagined, however. While living in the guest quarters he had attempted to match his lifestyle to the brothers' vows of poverty, chastity, and obedience—indeed, it had been little trouble to do so, because there was little opportunity for anything else.

568

Still, he had acquired a great many possessions—mostly books and writing equipment. Might as well make a gift of it all to the abbey. He would have no need of such at Dunning Innes. Perhaps some monk whose inner vision was not sealed could fill the remaining vellum leaves. He ran his hand over the slightly rough surface of the calfskin. This was an especially fine leaf. He could feel how the quill tip would glide over it with almost no scratching. He could see the words shiny and black on the pale ivory page.

He uncorked a bottle of ink, picked up a pen, and wrote what he saw. "Who is this that comes forth like the dawn, as beautiful as the moon, as resplendent as the sun, as awe inspiring as bannered troops? Fair is my beloved . . ." And for all that he would concentrate on the words themselves, behind them he saw Rhona's face, beautiful as the moon, the breeze blowing her cloak like a banner.

And then the scene shifted, as if he were seeing through another's eyes. "Hark! My lover—here he comes, springing across the mountains, leaping across the hills. My love is like a gazelle or a young stag. My love is mine, and I am his."

Only when the quill snapped under the pressure of his fingers did Jamie realize the force with which he had been fighting the images. Far better a black void.

The next morning Brother Simon came to his room shortly after Prime. With his quiet, thoughtful manner he set about helping clear out the chamber. But in light of Jamie's decision to give the books to the abbey, little was left to pack into his saddlebags.

"We'll just leave them here. I'll sort it out when I get back. It'll be a pleasure. The scriptorium will be aye glad of the supplies." Simon rolled up the sheet Jamie had left on his table the night before.

"No. That's just scribbling." Jamie's voice was harsh.

"Aye. Well, I'm sure one of the brothers can scrape it off."

"On second thought, I'll take it." Jamie stuffed the sheet in his shoulder pack. He did not want some monk reading that.

Birds sang over their heads, and fish jumped in the Forth on their right. Unless a storm blew in later, the day would be warm. But now the world was dew-fresh and bright.

"Father Abbot gave me leave to miss Mass. But if we hasten a bit we'll be at Saint Margaret's in time for their prayers." Simon, walking beside Jamie's horse, kilted his robe and strode forward.

Jamie nodded but didn't answer. It had seemed easier to go with Simon than to argue. Certainly easier than trying to explain. He would just ride this way and then go on.

"It's a fine thing you were here for this, as you know so much more about the men and all. Mother Joanna will be glad of anything you can tell her."

Jamie thought of the worried blue eyes in the thin face of the prioress. He had met her only twice but had seen clearly the care she had for her small community. He had thought of the loss of the treasure as affecting more directly the vigorous, outspoken Sister Richilda, who gave the impression that she could cope with anything. But Mother Joanna—if he knew anything that could be of help to her, he could not refuse.

"Aye," he said and set his shoulders.

The skin on Mother Joanna's hand was as thin and white as that on her face. The pearl Brother Simon placed there held far more color. The gentle eyes misted as the fragile nun enfolded the pearl in both hands and clasped them to her heart. "Oh, praises be. Praises." She unclasped one hand to cross herself, then returned it to encasing the pearl. "Our Lord is so good. Is He not good? After so long a time, when there seemed no hope."

"It's only one pearl. We've naught else," Simon said gently.

"Yes, but it's something, when all was gone. Oh, she will be so pleased. So pleased. Bless you. Bless you both."

The delicate wrinkles of the forehead beneath her white veil smoothed with something like a smile.

Jamie felt as if a ray of sun had struck him.

"You must come with me to give it back to her. She will be so pleased." Still clasping the tiny jewel to her heart, Mother Joanna led the way from her office, across a small yard, and to the thatched, wooden priory church.

Who are they taking it to? Jamie wondered. *One of the nuns must be praying in the church.*

But Mother Joanna did not take them to the altar where three sisters knelt at their prayers. Instead she turned to a tiny side chapel where two candles burned low beneath a small, beautifully carved statue of the Virgin Mary. The prioress knelt and lovingly placed the pearl at her feet.

After a moment of silent prayer she turned to the two men standing quietly behind her. "It was hers, you see. It was our greatest treasure because it had once belonged to Saint Margaret herself."

"You mean the pearl isn't from the monstrance?" Simon asked.

"Oh, no. Those pearls were never so fine as this. Larger, they were, more showy, but not of so perfect a quality. No, Saint Margaret's ring—which she gave to this house herself when she established

570

it under her own protection—it was all of perfect pearls around a pink ruby."

"Saint Margaret established this priory herself?" Jamie was awed. He had supposed it merely named for Scotland's most revered queen.

Little wonder that even a single pearl could bring such joy. If only the whole treasure could be recovered. The thought of so sacred an object in the hands of a common thief made him recoil.

The sound of a bell interrupted his thoughts.

Mother Joanna's face took on a luster like that of the pearl. "Oh, is it not glorious? Does not our Lord do all things well? Today is the feast of the Assumption of Mary. Come."

She turned from the side chapel and walked into the sanctuary so lightly that it appeared her feet barely touched ground. And the whole room seemed filled with her radiance as she led in the intercessions.

In spite of his wholehearted participation in the prayers, Jamie could not quite free his mind from the awareness that Rhona sat to his far right, just two benches behind him.

When the service was over there was no escaping her, especially since only his head wanted to, and his heart was much in competition.

"You are returning today to Dunning Innes?" Rhona asked in response to his explanation of his presence there as they entered the sun-warmed courtyard. She bit her full, red lower lip and looked up at him under drooping eyelashes. "Then it will be long and long until I see you again."

"Aye." There seemed to be no more to say. Yet they would not part. Silently they turned their steps to a path beyond the enclosure that led through the woods to a meadow where the sisters often brought their sheep and milk cows to graze.

"So what of affairs in the great world?" Rhona at last broke the silence.

And Jamie found himself relaxing as he told her of the events of the past days. "Och, but it was a fine sight at the end, the Wallace standing head and shoulders above them both—with Bruce and Comyn, the great lords, like boys caught robbing birds' nests. They would each clasp Wallace by the hand but no' each other. At last Sir William took their hands in each of his, rammed them together, and pumped them up and down.

"Bruce took it in good part, but Comyn's face swelled up like an overextended cow's bladder. It's no wonder he's called the Red."

Rhona clapped her hands at the story and laughed, and Jamie

laughed with her. It had not seemed funny at the time, but now he could see the humor.

"Oh, Jamie, you must write the tale just as you've told it. The tale of the great lord who blew up like a bagpipe when he was agitated." Her clapping startled two small yellow butterflies off a clump of heather.

She turned, her hands extended as if she would catch them, and in so doing brushed the parchment Jamie had so hastily stuffed into his pouch. "Oh, what is this?" The roll slipped from the pack at her slightest tug. "Your latest tale?"

"No! Give it to me!"

But she laughed and held it beyond his grasp, skipping backwards just ahead of him.

He swung forward. She danced and laughed, just out of reach.

He increased his pace and raised his crutch to bat the page from her hand.

She ducked and darted to the side. "You'll have to catch me."

She turned to speed ahead, but Jamie moved faster than even he knew he could. He was almost beside her when he reached again for the roll she brandished.

The crutch dropped. Rhona's feet tangled in it. Off-balance himself, Jamie had no way to avoid her sprawling form. He barely managed to avoid falling flat on top of her.

A fat green frog leaped from the long grass with an enormous croak. They rolled in the grass laughing so hard they could make no attempt to get up.

At last lack of breath forced Jamie to make strangled attempts to quit laughing. "That's nae fair. You tripped me."

"I tripped you? Jamie MacInnes, you'll need seek absolution for such a faradiddle."

Then the frog croaked, and they laughed again.

Jamie had forgotten all about the scribbled sheet that started the whole affair, until Rhona sat up and recovered the crumpled manuscript from behind a tuft of deer grass.

He sat up. "No, Rhona. Please—" But he knew it was no use. Already she had it unrolled.

Her peal of laughter caught in her throat. Her face grew intensely solemn. Then a single tear rolled down her smooth round cheek. The parchment rolled shut in her lap. "Oh, Jamie. It's the most beautiful thing I've ever read." She reached out and rested her hand on his arm.

"What a gift you have. How could you have known? Always you

wrote tales of what had already occurred. But you knew ahead, didn't you?"

"Knew what?"

"That we'd go leaping and romping today." She dropped her eyes. "And that I love you so dear."

He shook his head against the impossibility of it all. But he could not fight his own heart and Rhona as well. He took her hand. "Rhona, I—"

With a mighty croak the frog leaped from his sheltering clump and into Rhona's lap. She screamed and sprang to her feet, flinging the creature toward Jamie. He ducked and fell backward, laughing and flailing his arms.

He opened his eyes, and the laughter faded. He looked straight up at the broad, towering figure of Sister Richilda, standing with her hands on her hips. "You're scaring my cows." She waved a sturdy arm toward three red cows watching them from across the field.

Jamie scrambled to his feet with fair alacrity considering the awkwardness of his position, and Rhona unobtrusively tucked a crutch under his arm. "I am sorry, Sister. We were just . . . just . . . we were just laughing."

"Humph. Fine way to act when the Lord has given you such blessings."

Jamie could think of no reply to such a non sequitur.

"Mother Superior bade me give this to you." She held out a scrap of parchment bearing a drawing of a ring. "Saint Margaret's ruby, that is. Mother Joanna seems to hold some notion that you can recover it for her." Her voice was thick with skepticism.

Jamie looked closely at the sketch. He saw that the ruby had been cut roughly in the shape of a heart and the pearls were set around it in clusters resembling flowers. A unique piece. "If I ever see it, I shall certainly recognize it, Sister. But I much doubt—"

"Precisely. So I informed Mother Joanna. She, however, persists in her notion. I am to tell you that you will have her prayers." Sister Richilda sniffed. "That is enough to make me think your failure less certain. Mother Joanna's prayers are very powerful."

"Thank you, Sister. I'll do my best."

"Aye. See to it that you do." She began herding him before her as if driving geese from the pond, the wide sleeves of her robe flapping as she steadily advanced.

Jamie put all his energy into crossing the meadow with as much dignity as the situation allowed. He was not helped much in that, however, by the fact that Rhona, following a few steps behind them, let an occasional giggle escape.

62

How could the time have sped so fast? In spite of the ache of missing Rhona, which he always carried in his heart, Jamie held to the laughing tenderness of that golden day in the meadow through five summers. Often, as he looked back on it, the common green grass would grow to the verdant thickness of a water meadow and the two yellow butterflies to a flock of soaring, golden flutterers that would then light in the greenness and become flowers.

And always he thought next month. *Perhaps next month I will ride south to the banks of the Forth. And I will see Rhona. And I will speak what is in my heart.*

But always there was the work of the farmstead, for Padric had died, and Rory, who was courting a distant niece of Sir Kenneth, was much at Forteviot. And although he never doubted Rhona's farewell, whispered under the piercing eye of Sister Richilda—"Come when you can, Jamie. I'll wait. Never fear, Jamie, I'll wait"—the fact remained that he had nothing to offer her beyond his crippled self. And when Rory brought home a bride, there would be little room for two mistresses at Dunning Innes.

If Wallace would return, perhaps also would Jamie's sennachie skill, and he would have a place at court. Also, perhaps he could learn something of the man who had lost the pearl, perhaps recover the ring. But he doubted it.

And although the pictures did not return to his head, news of the world beyond Dunning Innes reached him, and he continued to make record of it. Edward remained south of the border. Rains watered the scorched earth between Forth and Tweed. The sun shone on it. The crops grew. Cotters renewed their burned thatch. Baby lambs were born, grew, and birthed more.

The Scots held two parliaments. Government was maintained invoking the authority of King John and the Community of the Realm. Foreign trade resumed. And although the Scottish leaders could by no means be characterized as a happy band of brothers, they maintained a dour and dogged persistence in working for the common good.

Then Edward invaded again. Bruce rallied his troops and harried him, slowing his progress and winning a few battles. Still Edward rolled northward. Stirling Castle fell again to English control. For the first time in six years English troops penetrated beyond Tay. Edward spent the winter at Dunfermline. Before departing in the spring of 1304, he turned his wrath against the stately abbey where Queen Margaret and her valiant Malcolm lay buried. Edward marched toward Moray while St. Margaret's abbey burned behind him.

Robert Bruce resigned his guardianship and made truce with Edward. The other leaders accepted terms of submission and sentences of banishment.

Wallace alone refused to enter the king of England's peace. Edward offered a reward of three hundred marks for William Wallace's head.

Rumors flew everywhere that Wallace had returned. But Jamie, chafing against the chores of farm life thrust upon him, had no direct word from his leader. Undoubtedly the great man had forgotten him or had no need of his services. Perhaps Wallace had acquired a new sennachie in France—a Norman troubadour in particolored tunic who sang his tales of valor and romance to the accompaniment of a lute.

Jamie slung the bag of oats onto his shoulder, adjusted his balance on his crutches, and started back toward the house.

He was halfway across the yard when he saw a figure riding up the road on a little garron. It was impossible to be sure from this distance, yet the black robe was unmistakable, and surely something about the way the sturdy figure sat the short-legged horse . . . But it had been so long since he had seen his friend Simon, and cloistered monks seldom ventured so far from their enclosures.

Yet the similarity was so strong . . . Jamie dumped the grain sack on the ground and swung forward. "Simon! I wasn't mistaken! What fortune brings you so far?"

Brother Simon jumped from his mount and embraced his friend. "Fortune indeed. Fortunate for Scotland as well as for us. Wallace is returned. Murdo came to Father Andrew with a message. Father Abbot sent me to bring you to him."

"To Cambuskenneth?" Jamie couldn't imagine why the abbot would wish to see him, but the summons was nae bad news—the monastery being so near St. Margaret's, where his heart dwelt.

"No, to Glasgow. I'm to take you to Wallace."

"Oh. Aye. Gladly," Jamie continued as they moved slowly toward the house, Simon leading his horse. "That's fine. Verra fine. But—have you other news for me, man?"

Simon threw back his tonsured head and laughed. "Ah, so you've nae forgotten the lassie." He turned to dig in his saddlepack. He emerged with a folded letter, which he held tantalizingly just out of Jamie's reach. "Well, she's nae forgotten you either. I came by way of Saint Margaret's—just as happenstance, you mind."

Jamie grinned. "Happenstance. It's two miles out of your way." He took the letter. "You're a good friend, Simon."

"I'll just take Jesse here on to the byre." Simon pulled his horse aside as Jamie loosened the wax seal on the letter with his thumb.

When he looked up some time later he had to blink to remember why Simon was standing before him with a sack of oats slung over his shoulder. His mind had been full of pictures of his dark-haired Rhona, his ears full of her voice and golden laughter. Always he saw her as she had been that morning in the meadow, dancing backward in the grass with butterflies fluttering around her.

"The lassie is well?" Simon grinned and raised an eyebrow.

"Aye, she's well." Jamie lowered his gaze. The joy of remembrance was painful.

Simon placed a hand on his shoulder. "Dona keep her waiting much longer, my friend."

Jamie shook his head. He could not see what he could do. "The summons from Wallace—"

"Aye. That first."

Later that week they neared Newton Mearns below Glasgow, where Murdo had indicated to the abbot that Wallace was taking refuge on the farm of one Ralph Rae. The early August morning had begun fresh and misty on the borders of the forest, but now the sun burned through and, filtering between overhanging boughs, streaked golden on the vapor rising from the forest floor.

A small brown rabbit scampered across the path, causing Jamie's mount to prick his ears. A flock of wood pigeons rose suddenly ahead, uttering startled squawks much unlike their normal gentle cooing. Then to their left a young stag bolted through the brush and ran headlong into the forest fastness. Jamie and Simon barely had time to rein their mounts off the path and into the thick undergrowth to the right before pounding horsemen thundered down the trail in front of them.

The three riders, clearly identified as English by the blazons on their sleeves, fled with torn, stained surcoats, the second one missing his helmet, the third clutching an arm wrapped in blood-soaked rags. Behind them a wide-eyed pack pony, half unloaded of its burden, stumbled as it stepped on its lead rope, then crashed onward.

Jamie pulled farther into the shadows and smiled. "Aye. Wallace is sure to be near."

Simon nodded. "Successfully cut a supply train to Dumbarton Castle, I'd say. Perhaps 'twill be enough to make Sir John Menteith rethink his newfound allegiance to Edward."

"Mentieth? I'd not heard he turned his coat again."

"And with some vigor apparently, for Edward has made him governor of Dumbarton Castle."

Jamie shook his head. "Even when he was fighting for the Scots, that one bore Wallace no love. It is said he blames Sir William for the death of his nephew at Falkirk."

The travelers deemed it wiser not to chance encountering more fleeing English on the trail, so made their way carefully through the woods, then over fields to the farm where Simon had been directed.

"Can this be right?" Jamie surveyed the alternating green and gold field strips, a pond where a flock of geese watered, and a cluster of thatched buildings beyond. "It looks so peaceful."

"It would nae serve for hiding if it didn't." Simon urged Jesse forward.

The farmer, Ralph Rae, came to meet them from a nearby pulse field where the pea vines grew in trailing mounds. "Peace, Brother. May I offer ye refreshment and water for your mounts?"

"Peace to you," Simon responded and drew a dried thistle from the pouch around his neck.

The farmer eyed it levelly. "Aye. Ye'll be wanting to put your mounts in the far byre." He returned to his pease harvesting.

Wallace was not there nor were any of his men. It was likely they would not return until after dark for fear of being followed. Simon and Jamie pulled cheese and bannocks from their packs and settled down to wait.

Evening shadows had turned to black before the waiters heard approaching feet. Jamie scrambled to stand up. It would not do to meet Scotland's greatest hero sprawled in a strawstack.

The door burst open before he had his full balance. "Ah! Wee Jamie is it?"

A dozen figures followed the big man in: Ralph Rae, Jock Brice, Hugh Danduff . . . But Jamie could see no more, for he was engulfed in a great bear hug that lifted him off the ground, then set him down in better balance than he had left it.

Wallace's men shuttered the windows and lit lamps.

577

Wallace drew Jamie aside to the light of a lantern hanging on a peg above an empty horse stall. For a moment Sir William, who had always been so good a judge of men, studied his sennachie. "Aye, you have nae lost the passion. It burns in every line of your face." He paused. "But you have nae lost the hatred either, have you? Jamie, lad, can you no' love Scots without hating English?"

"I have not forgotten what they did to my family, if that's what you mean."

Wallace shook his head. "Jamie MacInnes, if your fire can burn for good, you'll someday be a great man. But if you let your hatred take control . . ." Then Wallace laughed. *"Och,* but I'm neither priest nor sennachie."

Further discussion was interrupted by Murdo Grant's entrance. He hung his cloak on a peg and quaffed a mug of ale before turning to his leader, now sitting on a stool at the back of the barn. Murdo bent close to speak something for Wallace's hearing alone.

Jamie recoiled. The movement of shadows in the lamplight made it look as if Murdo had kissed Wallace.

"What news?" Sir William asked.

"Edward has repeated his demand for your surrender. He does not take kindly that one man in all Scotland holds against him."

Wallace ran his hands through his thick dark hair. "Aye. A sad state it is: Bruce in Edward's peace, Soulis fled to France—at least he would not make terms—Comyn, Lindsay, Fraser, all offered bribes if they would deliver me to Edward . . ."

Murdo, who had been pacing the small straw-covered floor, turned suddenly and grasped Wallace by the shoulders. "Can you not see sense, man? Edward holds all but three of the great castles of the land. There is no lord in Scotland who stands with you. The matter cannot be won. Edward has repeated his offer of three hundred marks for your capture. Submit, man. Seek Edward's peace as all the others have done."

Murdo's voice had risen with intensity in the course of his speech. Now the silence in the building was a thick, breathless thing.

"No!" Wallace jumped to his feet and hit his fist against the wall. "Hear me. And let there be no mistake of this. I say that if all the people of Scotland yield obedience to the king of England—if each man of this land would depart from his own freedom—I and my companions who are willing to cleave to me in this matter will stand for the liberty of the kingdom. I will serve no man but God and my king."

A clatter sounded at the far end of the byre, and at first Jamie thought it was the men thumping their agreement by pounding on wooden planks. Then he felt a blast of cold night air and realized the truth.

English soldiers filled the barn.

The slither of swords unsheathing sliced the air.

"No." Wallace's voice was calm, his command clear. "Sheath your swords. It is I they want." He turned to the mailed leader. "Let my men go, and I'll come peaceably."

The activity of the room fell away from Jamie, sitting in a dark corner by the manger. He was on a lonely dark hillside covered with scrubby twisted olive trees. Torches flared in the hands of mailed soldiers leading their victim away. "Woe is me. The traitors betray; with treachery have the traitors betrayed. Terror, pit, and trap are upon the inhabitants of the earth . . ."

When his vision faded and Jamie returned to the byre, it was as to a dead body from which the great heart had departed, for Wallace was gone.

The door stood swaying on its hinges as the sound of mailed boots faded into the night. Most of Wallace's men stood frozen, their hands on the hilts of their undrawn swords. One or two dashed into the darkness to follow.

Without giving thought to the foolishness of his action, Jamie grabbed his crutches and hurled himself forward. He had no clear idea of what he was doing, how he would catch the invaders, or what he would do if he did overtake them. He only knew that Wallace had once called him, and he must follow now.

It was not, however, a wise choice for a young man on crutches, alone in the dark and unfamiliar with the terrain. He stumbled repeatedly. Once he fell headlong when one crutch caught in a deep furrow. It cost him precious time groping in the dark to recover the crutch. The flaring torches of the armed band were far ahead. There was no chance of catching them, little of even being able to continue following.

And yet he pressed on. His breath came in heavy gasps, sweat stood on his forehead. His arms and good leg ached with the effort, his armpits felt bruised. Still he swung forward into the darkness, following the wavering lights that ever pulled farther and farther ahead of him. Where were they going? Surely they had not started straight out for London tonight. It seemed they were going the opposite direction for that, but Jamie's sense of direction was much confused. What were they doing with Wallace?

"Have no fear. We'll hold him secure at Dumbarton. Mentieth's not likely to let his prize escape easily."

Jamie halted so suddenly at the sound of the harsh voice that he almost threw himself off balance.

A growling reply came from behind the thick clump of bushes to his right. He let his breath out slowly, realizing that the speaker had not been addressing him. He inched forward. A shaded lantern revealed two faces: one English, in the familiar small pointed helmet; the other, the sharp, dark features of Murdo Grant.

Murdo, one of Wallace's original followers, one of his most trusted circle, the paymaster for the Guardian's men. And even as Jamie recalled seeing Murdo collecting spoils on the battlefield, he heard the clink of coins and the growl of the English voice. "Aye, there it is. Three hundred marks, as agreed."

The dawn chorus was breaking over Jamie's head before he had dragged his way back to the byre. It was not so much the physical effort but the fact that he had no heart left in him that made the journey so painful.

Always it had been Wallace. Through all the eight years' struggle, William Wallace was the one man who had stood firm. Other knights, lords, and earls had joined in the fight at one time or another. Some, like Bruce, had fought valiantly and won great victories for a space of time. But all had scurried back into Edward's peace in the end. All save Wallace.

And now Wallace was taken.

What hope remained for Scotland?

Brother Simon came to meet him. Jamie all but fell into his arms in exhaustion and grabbed with both hands at the tankard of mulled ale the monk offered. When he had drunk deeply, he paused for breath. "They've taken him to Dumbarton."

Simon nodded. "Aye, I thought it likely. I'll go to him."

"Will they let you in?"

Simon fingered his cowl. "The cloth has many uses. A monk may enter if any can."

"And a crippled storyteller?" Jamie smiled ruefully. "Surely less of a threat than even a monk could be." He thought fleetingly of the long-gone days when he had charged wildly into battle with sword and spear, following the Wallace's battle cry.

Simon smiled. "I'd be glad of your company, my friend." He lowered the arm that still supported Jamie, easing him to the ground. "Rest here. I'll bring the horses."

"And all the bannocks you can carry. I could eat a horse," Jamie called after him. He had no clear idea of what he could do, but two goals fired deeper in Jamie's breast than the physical pain in his limbs. He wanted to free Wallace. And he wanted to get even with Murdo.

It was a day's journey northward across Clyde, then west to the great rock where Dumbarton Castle guarded the Clyde Estuary. The two weary travelers took shelter that night in a small house of brothers built almost against the towering two-hundred-foot rock atop which the castle sprawled.

"Aye, aye." The ancient prior nodded his hairless skinny head at breakfast the next morning. His eyes were bright, his nose sharp, and his teeth clacked as he spoke, so that the effect was for all the world like talking to a plucked chicken. Listening to him brought the first smile that had come to Jamie's face since the taking of Wallace.

"Aye. Our house is but a poor one, but more than once Sir John Mentieth has taken comfort from our ministerings."

"As well minister to the devil himself," Jamie muttered, but no one appeared to hear.

Instead, the clacking continued in bright agreement to Brother Simon's suggestion that the prior give him a letter of approval that the monk might minister to the new-taken prisoner.

The travelers deemed it best to approach the castle humbly, so left their mounts at the priory. The guard at the foot of the rock barely gave them a nod. Little threat a cowled brother and his wobbling companion could pose to Edward's peace.

Then began the arduous climb up the daunting flight of steps that scaled the cleft between the two summits of the rock. But no effort was too great for Jamie. As long as he was acting, there was hope. Somehow they would do something for Wallace. And he would find a way to repay Murdo.

He thought his ears would burst from the pounding of blood in his head as he hauled himself up step after step, always having to check carefully how he placed his crutches on the rough-hewn stone.

At last they reached the guardhouse. This time Simon was required to make full exposition of the document he carried and give defense of his errand.

"You would minister to the Scottish dog? Let his soul burn in hell."

Simon crossed himself. "Surely that is not for you to decide, but God."

The guard growled but franked the document with a crude mark and waved them through. "Guardhouse on your left."

The turnkey led them into a small stone room with one window slit high in the wall. The space ached with the chill and damp of

581

stone that had not seen the sun for hundreds of years. The door clanked shut behind them.

"What? Have they taken you too?" Wallace put a hand on a shoulder of each of his companions.

"Nay. We've come to help. There must be some way to free you."

Wallace gripped Jamie's shoulder and laughed. "Ah, Jamie MacInnes, you were ever a tonic to me. Have you nae seen the defense of this castle?"

"Yes. I saw. But—"

"No." Wallace shook his head. "There is naught to do. I am in Edward's hands. Edward's and God's. And we know whose are mightier, if Edward does not. I'll gladly hear your prayers, Brother Simon."

Even kneeling, Wallace came above Simon's waist. Simon placed his hands on the patriot's head and prayed.

But Jamie could not pray. He could not accept all so calmly. "It was Murdo. Murdo betrayed you to Mentieth's men!" he blurted out before the prayer was ended.

"Aye. I thought it so. He was once a good man. But he cared overmuch for silver."

The calmness of Wallace's voice increased Jamie's fury. "Augh, that I could smash his teeth in his mouth. Let his arrows be headless shafts. Let him shrivel and dissolve like the worm he is."

"Colorful cursing that is, lad. But you'd do better to pray for him. God's judgment will be far more fearsome than that. But best, pray for Scotland, that all will not be lost for one man's treachery."

Jamie turned away as Simon continued his prayers. If he dared, he would have put his hands over his ears. As it was, he simply allowed the anger inside him to shout louder than the monk's petitions. Forgive? Pray for his enemies? Never.

63

The intensity of Jamie's hatred continued to fire him through-out the grueling two weeks of forced travel to London. Wallace and Simon had both urged him not to make the journey. But their urg-ings that he return to Dunning Innes held no power, even when Wallace thrust on him the importance of writing the account of the former Guardian's capture.

"Aye. I'll write it, have nae fear. But not yet."

Murdo would not have stayed in Scotland. He had money enough to live in comfort in the city. Jamie burned with the desire to meet Wallace's betrayer. He would have his vengeance.

Only once did his determination waver. It was when Brother Simon said, "Aye, make for Dunning Innes as the Wallace bids you, lad. But go by way of Saint Margaret's. Would you have the lassie wait so long? Has she no' been faithful beyond all?"

Rhona's image rose so fair and bright before Jamie that he al-most cried out. But he stamped the picture down by taking a firm grip on his hatred.

And now he clung to his wrath more strongly than ever. It was all he had to hold to.

The trial had been a mere matter of form. Wallace's English judges had resolved upon his death long before his capture. On Monday morning, the twenty-third of August, Jamie MacInnes was among the throng that followed, some on foot, some on horseback, as William Wallace was led from the house where he had been lodged for the night, set on a white charger with a scarlet robe around his shoulders, and led through the streets of London to Westminster Hall with a mocking royal retinue.

The great hall was crowded with those who had come to jeer and exult in the downfall of the man who for eight years had stood against the mightiest warrior in Christendom. Wallace was led by rough guards to the south end of the hall, where he was seated on a high bench. A great derisive cry rose from the crowd as a velvet-clad noble placed a crown of laurel on Wallace's head.

Jamie thought he was the only person in the building not shouting.

"Rebel!"

"Robber!"

"Outlaw!"

He would have shaken his fist in their faces and shouted back at them if he could have been heard. For no matter how much they hated Wallace, Jamie hated them more.

Wallace sat impassive throughout the reading of the long indictment charging him with rebellion, sedition, homicide, robbery, arson, sacrilege, and a number of other felonies. The only specific offenses named were the slaying of the sheriff of Lanark and the raiding of Northumberland.

Then Sir John de Segrave's voice rang from one end of the hall to the other. "Whereas, King Edward has by conquest brought all the Scots into submission and subjugation to his dominion and royal power; whereas, after Edward had conquered the said William in mortal war, Edward had mercifully caused the said William Wallace to be recalled to his peace; whereas, Wallace has refused to submit himself to come to the peace of his said lord the king: Thereby be it declared that William Wallace has placed himself in treasonous rebellion against King Edward."

Since Wallace was declared outlaw, he was not allowed to plead. Only once in the entire proceeding did he voice the defense to which none would give ear. "No! I am no traitor. I have sworn no allegiance. I have broken no oath. I have never been subject to the king of England, therefore could not be traitor.

"For eight years I have carried on war against the invaders of my country by every means at my disposal. And I have encouraged my countrymen to do the same. As well you, loyal Englishmen all, would do if your country was invaded by a foreign power. I am traitor to no one. Least of all to him to whom I never swore loyalty."

Wallace sat again, holding his head up with great quiet dignity against the scorn and derision of the throng. His expression did not change as the sentence was read out in the same tone of mocking superiority in which he had been charged. To be taken from this hall to a place of execution. To be hanged, drawn, and quartered . . .

The sentence went on describing in detail the disembowelment with which William Wallace was to be punished for his immense wickedness against God and Holy Church in burning churches, vessels, and biers.

No! No. It cannot be. The room swirled black before Jamie's eyes. He held to the edge of his bench, or he might have fallen, so intense was his anger against Wallace's tormentors. And at his own inability to smash them all.

Refusing to accept the reality of it, Jamie followed the throng as they spilled out onto the street, cheering the sentence and anticipating the sight that was to come. For Edward's great foe would not be allowed to go to his grave quietly. The goal of his captors was to make his execution as pompous, public, and agonizing as they could devise.

It was now afternoon, and the August sun beat down on the humid air being shared by hundreds of observers packed tightly along the muddy streets. Now the mocking robe and crown were torn from the prisoner. He was not to be allowed even the dignity of walking. Leather-clad soldiers thrust him onto a hurdle made of rough-hewn poles. The upper end ran to the harness of a massive destrier, the bottom dragged deep gouges in the street. Wallace's face lay directly beneath the swishing black tail of the huge creature. Its heavy back hooves jarred the hurdle with each step.

Jamie struggled and shoved, using his crutches as ramming devices to propel himself as close to Wallace as possible. He would have the great man know he had one friend in all that mob if he could. The journey was arduous. More than once his sweat-soaked hands slipped on the crutches and all but pitched him into the refuse-choked gutter. But he refused to think of his own discomfort. His every thought was for Wallace. Every jar of the cruel hurdle he felt far more than the shoving of the crowd.

At last they reached Aldersgate at the eastern edge of the city. The destrier came to a halt at the foot of an inordinately high gallows. Minutes or hours could have passed while Jamie continued his internal struggle—refusing to accept what must be. Then he heard the creak of the gallows as the valiant body rose high over the heads of the jubilant throng. Forcing his eyes to look on the sight was the greatest act of willpower Jamie had ever undertaken in his life.

But then the image blurred, and Jamie was uncertain what he saw. The roar of the crowd rolled over him like a dark cloud, blocking sight as well as sound. He tried to yell back at them, to give voice to his outrage, but the words stuck in his throat, and he thought he would choke on them.

He would call God to see these people. He would call God to punish them. But not in prayer. Rather in curses. "Rise up, O God, rise up against these people. God of vengeance, show Yourself. How long? How long, O God, will You permit this? How long shall the wicked glory? Mouthing insolent speeches, boasting of their evildoing. O God, trample them down. Destroy the wicked."

A forward surge of the crowd told him that the rope was being loosened. Wallace was being let down so that while he yet lived his bowels could be torn out and thrown in the fire that even now added to the heat of the day, roaring and crackling just beyond the gallows.

Weak with the spending of his anger, Jamie could take no more. He turned and pushed his way blindly through the crowd. They were glad enough to let him pass, eager as each one was to get a nearer view.

He was almost to the back of the mob when a plump infant in a mud-streaked tunic toddled in front of him. Through his blurred vision he caught only a glimpse of the golden curls as he swung forward. Then he felt his foot thud against flesh. He twisted to miss falling on the howling, tumbling ball.

The little girl's mother scooped the child into her arms while making soothing noises, then turned to Jamie and offered her free arm to help steady him. "I'm sae sorry. I was nae watching the wee bairn close enough."

Jamie was upright in a moment. The woman turned back to an older child who tugged at her skirt, pulling her into the crowd. It was only after the wave of humanity closed between them that some vague reference clicked in Jamie's mind.

It was more her voice than the appearance of the woman. It had been eight years. Surely it wasn't possible in the midst of all these people. And yet the likeness persisted to ring in his ears.

"Aline!" He spun around and started back into the throng after her.

But then a great shout went up from the crowd, drawing Jamie's attention toward the gallows platform where the grisly execution continued. He looked, then knew he would regret it the rest of his life. He was the veteran of many battles and had watched many more, but never had he seen so terrible a sight—the head of William Wallace on a pole, dripping red.

Jamie gripped his crutches so hard it was a wonder they didn't break. He thought he was going to be sick. He looked around him for something else to focus on. To his left he noticed a figure moving away from the crowd as all others pushed forward for a closer look at the quartering, which was to follow the decapitation. In all this mass of humanity was there one other person who was as horrified as he was?

Jamie moved after the figure. It wasn't until he broke free of the mass of the throng that he saw who he had been following. He was not surprised to see Murdo here. He had expected as much. But

586

he was surprised that the traitor should have been disgusted by the abomination he had caused.

Jamie had played the scene many times in his mind. Always he had felt himself grow hot with rage, shaken with passion for revenge, when he imagined meeting Wallace's betrayer. But it was not so. He was the calmest he had been since Wallace's capture. He felt cool and steady. He hardly hurried as he moved resolutely forward. Murdo Grant was his. He felt his sheathed dirk rubbing against his side. He had sharpened it for this occasion.

He followed Murdo into the dim sanctuary of a building. A heavy oak door shut out the hubbub of the crowd.

"Murdo."

The man was only three paces ahead of him. Murdo turned to meet the challenge.

The pinched ferret face had time only to register recognition of Jamie before the crutch smashed into his temple and knocked him to the stone floor.

Jamie was on him in seconds. His dirk in his hand. His arm arced back. He had begun the downward plunge when a sound reached his ears—the soothing, swelling line of the plainsong. Jamie looked up and realized they were in a church.

He completed the swing of his knife in a feeble drop. It was another of God's cruel jokes. He could not kill in a church.

Murdo groaned and twisted under him.

Jamie couldn't kill, but he could hit. He slammed Murdo's head against the stones again. Then he saw a thong around his unconscious victim's neck.

Feeling the same sense of inevitability with which he had followed the man, he drew the pouch from under Murdo's tunic and emptied a jewel into his hand. He sat for several moments admiring the glow of the heart-shaped, dark pink ruby surrounded by clusters of tiny perfect pearls. He ran his finger over the spot where one pearl was missing.

Edward might still hold Margaret's Black Rood in London, but at least her ring was recovered.

The young brother who stood last in the row broke off from his prayers and came to the men on the floor. "Are you in need of aid?"

Jamie shoved himself to his feet and poked Murdo's limp form with a crutch. "*He* is."

The brother more dragged than carried the unconscious man out a side door.

Jamie stuffed the ring into his satchel and turned to go. Then the words of the chanted lesson caught his attention. He turned toward the front of the church where candles flickered on carved stone and shining metal. And he sat on a bench and let the echoing words come to him.

"I am the Lord who made all things, who alone stretched out the heavens. It is I who bring to naught the omens of liars. It is I who confirm the words of My servants. I carry out the plan announced by My messengers. I say to Jerusalem, Be inhabited; to the cities of Judah, Be rebuilt. I will raise up their ruins."

It was time to go home.

64

Wallace was dead. Perhaps the most valiant heart that ever beat in the land was stilled. And all their hopes for freedom stilled with it at the end of an English rope.

Wallace was dead, but not the Scotland he had given new birth to. Not the land to which he had given a new concept of nationhood. Never had man so loved his native land as William Wallace. No purer patriot ever lived or ever did more for love of country and freedom of his people with less thought for personal gain than William Wallace.

And Wallace was dead.

But not the nation. The nation could not die. The kingdom of Scotland might die—there might someday cease to be a king, as some people believed when John Balliol abdicated. But the nation could never die so long as there were Scots in the land who loved it as William Wallace did.

It was the end and yet a beginning. For seven months the land lay dormant under Edward's mailed fist. But it was a false calm. Until the butchering of William Wallace, Edward had been feeling his way towards a new relationship with the Scottish leaders, which would be based on mutual trust. Edward's vindictive retribution wreaked on one man tore to shreds any bonds of trust he might have established.

Now the torch passed. The torch lit by Wallace shone on the greatest of the Scottish lords. And Robert Bruce did not turn from it.

Sickened by the wanton brutality dealt this man whom he liked and admired—a man only three years older than Bruce himself—Robert the Bruce set his hand to the task William Wallace had first undertaken.

The matter was God's doing, not his own. The mantle settled on his shoulders. He was no longer the spoiled darling of the House of Bruce—and of King Edward himself. Robert the Bruce was the man for Scotland.

Jamie lay his quill aside and rubbed his eyes. Should he light a candle to go on and record the efforts Bruce was now making to establish the nation? He fingered the flint, but he did not strike it. What would he write? It was less than six months since Wallace's execution. In that time Bruce had risen and gathered a fighting band, but they had taken no castles.

The idea of the Community of the Realm of Scotland was not dead. It lived in men such as Robert Wishart and William Lamberton. But the idea had no power. The idea of the community must be put once more into action.

The old answer had been guardianship. But that would not serve against Edward's strength.

The only possible answer was a revival of kingship. The Scottish kingdom must cease to be the disembodied ghost that it had been since Toom Tabard had been stripped of his insignia ten years before. The kingship must be turned into a living reality.

But at that thought Jamie shook his head in despair. Here was again the problem that had set them on the course to disaster at the death of King Alexander. Although in exile and standing firm in his abdication, John Balliol was alive and well. Furthermore, he had a grown son and heir. Yet no one sought the restoration of a Balliol, however rightful his claim might be.

John Comyn the Red still held all the power of his mighty house and rightful descent from King Donald Bane, brother of Malcolm III. Comyn had been active in the war of independence and had served as Guardian of the Realm. And yet Jamie could think of no success to lay to his credit.

Conversely, whenever he heard the name, the one image that filled Jamie's mind was the sight of the Red Comyn and his cavalry fleeing the field of Falkirk at the first English charge—fleeing into the woods with the cavalry that might have later saved the day for Wallace. How could one so powerful be such a failure? Was it possible that Scotland could flourish with such a king?

The fact was that, of late, Comyn had made his stance clear. The Red Comyn was pro-English. He would not work for Scottish independence. If Scotland were to be free, Robert the Bruce must be king.

And yet Robert Bruce, of an equally powerful house and equally fine lineage, could have no chance of leading a united kingdom— and the kingdom must be united—if Comyn did not support him. The quill bent under the pressure of Jamie's ink-stained fingers. He could not write when the way looked so blocked. Bruce was in the field, yet it seemed that he faced stone walls on every side.

Jamie heard the sliding of soft kid slippers on the rush-strewn floor and smelled fresh lemon herb scent before he saw her. When he looked up and saw Rhona skimming across the room toward him, all thoughts of kingdoms and revolutions fled from his mind. He spun on his stool and held his arms out to her.

She laughed, leaped toward him, and settled in his lap.

A time later he lifted his head from the softness of her hair, but he did not loosen his arms from around her. They had been married for five months, and every day his delight in her grew with the wonder of being together.

"Will you not come in, Jamie? I have a fine mutton pie and fresh bannocks. And it is February-cold in here. Surely your pictures cannot be more bright than your own fireside on such a night."

"No place could ever be more bright than where you are, my love."

She slid from his lap, and they went together from the little hut where he did his writing into the cozy thatched cottage that she had chosen to make their own rather than take rooms in the hall house where Rory and his bride lived.

And Jamie shook his head again in amazement that she should be content with so little. Standing before the hearth, warm with the rich scent of mutton pie, he put his arm around his bride. "My Rhona, if ever once I'd thought you could be content in such a place, I would have asked you to wed long and long ago."

She sighed and nestled against him, her arm around his waist. "So many times I despaired of you, Jamie MacInnes. But I was determined. I would no' take the veil unless I saw you wed to another." She paused. "And then you were gone so long I feared that was what had happened."

She clung to him as if he would escape her grasp even now. "The day you came riding into Saint Margaret's bearing the stolen ring and shining as if you'd found the Holy Grail was the happiest of my life." She stood on tiptoe and kissed his cheek. "As every day has been since then."

Jamie had finished his second slice of mutton and potato pie, oozing with rich brown gravy, and was contemplating a third when a knock sounded at the door.

Rhona moved to unbar it, but Jamie held up his hand. "Who comes sae late?" he called.

"Naught but your old friend Simon."

Rhona flew to lift the bar, and Jamie poured a cup of ale for his friend. "So late you come, and with snowflakes in the air. It must be important news." Jamie pushed the pie plate toward Simon.

"Aye, the most urgent."

Jamie felt suddenly chilled as if had been he who had ridden through the winter evening. "Not Edward? Would he march so far before spring to smash so small a force as Bruce's?"

Simon shook his head. "Edward is ill. It is unlikely Edward Plantagenet will set foot in Scotland again. But when it falls his son's turn, we must be ready." The monk's blue eyes sparkled. "And when the time comes, we'll be in far better stead to stand against him. Comyn is dead."

Jamie blinked at the hearing. "John Comyn? The Red?" Among members of such a numerous family, one must make certain.

Simon nodded his head of short-cropped black hair, and the firelight gleamed on his tonsure.

"How is that so? Death can come to any, but he was a young man and sturdy."

Simon finished his bite of Rhona's meat pie and took a deep drink of ale before launching into his tale. "That is what I've come to tell you. Father Andrew said I must come straightway—that this hearing will be your first, straight from the messenger he received from Greyfriars. For of such a deed there will be many a tale, each embroidered finer than the last, and the written record must needs be clear."

But even clear of embroidery, it seemed to Jamie the tale was fantastic enough. Robert the Bruce had slain the Red Comyn before the high altar of Greyfriars Kirk in Dumfries.

He shook his head. "In the church? You're certain, man? Bruce struck down Comyn in the *church?*"

"Before the priest and brothers. It was one of the brothers who came to Cambuskenneth. There is no mistake. An eyewitness."

Always Jamie had favored Bruce over Comyn, as had Wallace. Now Bruce would have a clear path to the throne. And yet Jamie could not rejoice in such a deed. He could not accept it. "But Bruce is a man of knightly honor. He would do no such thing."

Brother Simon chewed a piece of bannock and made no answer.

At last Jamie sighed and nodded. "Aye. An eyewitness, you said. Then tell me how it came about. If it must be told, let it be told true."

"I think it can be truth to absolve the man of premeditation," Simon began.

Jamie relaxed a bit. That, indeed, did help.

"Comyn was residing at his castle only nine miles from Bruce's when Bruce sent for Comyn to confer with him at the Greyfriar's— just across from the castle where Edward's justices were holding session. The church was open with priests and brothers going about their normal duties—hardly a scene set for murder."

Again Jamie shook his head. "And yet it happened."

"Aye, it happened. Bruce had conferred with Wishart and Lamberton not long before. Many believed, mostlike Comyn believed, they had formulated a plan which Bruce would now put to Comyn."

"Such as?"

Simon sighed. "No one knows, for the meeting had barely progressed past Bruce's greeting kiss before tempers flared. But it is thought likely to have been some such scheme as the one Bruce's grandfather put to a rival of his when he bid for the throne awarded to Balliol—that one man take all the other's property and one take the throne."

"Is it likely Bruce would have offered to help his old rival—a relative of Balliol—to become king of Scots?"

Simon laughed. "You know that answer better than I. And the outcome seems to indicate that Bruce proposed himself for king. Whatever the suggestion, it fired Comyn's anger—never a very hard thing to do in the best of times."

The question did not want to be asked, but Jamie must know the truth. "But Bruce drew first? He struck the first blow?"

"The first blow of cold steel. Comyn's blow was with fiery words. He called Robert the Bruce traitor."

"Ah, I see. And Bruce, likely unmindful of where he stood, pulled sword and struck." Jamie hit the table. "But why would he wear his sword into a church in the first place?"

Simon touched his arm. "He did not. It was a dagger he stabbed with. Then apparently gathered some of his senses when he saw Comyn fallen before the altar. He ran from the church and shouted, 'I have killed the Comyn.'"

Jamie leaned forward and gripped Simon's hand. "In what voice?"

"What do you mean?"

Jamie shook Simon's arm impatiently. He had to know. It made all the difference. "In what voice did he cry, 'I have killed the Comyn'? Was it of exultation or horror?"

Simon's answer was such a surprise that Jamie leaned back to his own side of the table to consider.

"Neither exultation nor horror. He cried in doubt."

"Doubt?"

"Aye. He saw the man fall but did not know what he had done. It was his man Kirkpatrick who struck in cold blood. 'Then I'll make certain,' he said. And he did."

"So." Jamie drank thirstily from the tankard Rhona filled while her free hand rested lightly on his shoulder. "So now there is no rivalry for the throne of Scotland."

"None save Edward's, and it seems Bruce has set about with a vengeance to clear his path to Scone. Already the torch has been set alight throughout the land. Kinsmen of the Comyn are fled before his murderer, and Englishmen flee as fast as they might to safe castles or the border."

"So Bruce comes to Scone?"

"All say he is set upon taking the throne."

"With blood on his hands? He will be excommunicated. This is worst of all. Now there is none left to rule."

"Nay. That is why the message was carried to every abbey first. Wishart has absolved Bruce of his sin in being a party to the killing on the grounds that it was necessary for Scotland and for Bruce's person—Comyn having plotted against Bruce more than once before. But Wishart made Bruce swear an oath to abide under the direction of the clergy of Scotland. Father Abbot has a copy of the document."

Jamie nodded and smiled with memories of Wallace's old friend and stout supporter. "Aye. Strong as Wishart held for the freedom of Scotland, the bishop would in no wise support a king who would not uphold the Scottish church."

A block of peat crumbled on the hearth, sending pale ash onto the floor and a heavy, earthy scent into the room. Rhona moved to place a fresh square on the fire. Jamie sat still, staring into the kindling flame.

And then it was not a block of peat he was looking at but a stone. And it was not fire on the stone but a bright white light. A young man sat beside the stone as if he had just been dreaming, with his head on the stone for a pillow. Only Jamie and the man in the vision heard the voice.

"I, the Lord, am the God of your forefathers. The land on which you are lying I will give to you and your descendants from east to west and from north to south. I will be with you constantly until I have finished giving you all I am promising. Know that I am with you."

The vision faded but left in its place the memory of an earlier voice: "Though all the earth is Mine, you shall be to Me a kingdom of priests, a holy nation . . . ."

"Jamie?" Rhona laid her small soft hand on his cheek, and only then did he realize his face was burning.

He took her hand in his and brushed it with his lips. "Do not fret, lassie. It was a wee picture, but a good one, I think."

"What did it mean?"

"I dona know. But it was good," he repeated. "Aye, Simon, I will write as you say. And then I will go to Scone." He felt Rhona's hand tighten in his. He turned to her. "You will come with me, my love? The Bruce will be crowned. He will need a sennachie. And there are preparations I would make if I can."

Later that night with Rhona's small warm body snuggled against him in their bed, Jamie gently stroked the thick black hair that fell over his arm as he thought. Bruce was now set on his course to complete Wallace's work and restore to Scotland all that had been taken from her by Edward. He would do it not as an outlaw, as Wallace had been forced to do, but by right of kingship. And all the kings of this land had been enkinged sitting on the Stone of Scone.

The stone Edward had stolen.

Or had he? Jamie recalled again that long-ago day when he had gone to Wallace. And their raid on Scone with the English justicar fleeing out his bedroom window ahead of them. And afterward when Wallace had talked long with Sir Kenneth, hereditary keeper of the stone.

Wallace had not told him the result of that conference, but Wallace had seemed satisfied to leave then and had talked no more of winning back Scotland's palladium. What had Sir Kenneth told Wallace?

If the real stone was still in Scotland, it must be recovered for Bruce's coronation. Jamie would seek out his overlord. He would search Scone and the surrounding area if need be. He had seen Jacob's pillow in his vision this evening. And some said that was the Stone of Destiny itself. Perhaps his pictures would show him where to look.

He did not know. He could only try. But he was determined to do all in his power that Robert the Bruce might be enkinged on the ancient stone.

65

Six weeks later, March 25, the tenth anniversary of the first blow of Edward's hammer on the Scots, Jamie stood in Scone Abbey to witness the crowning of King Robert the Bruce. Setting his jaw against the knife edge of disappointment that threatened to choke him, he strove to take in all the ceremony. For this was as glorious a spectacle as all the might of the war-ravaged country could make it.

Or at least that portion of the might of Scotland that adhered to Robert Bruce. For his seizing power, necessity though he saw it, was not an act of the Community of the Realm. And although the commons were in enthusiastic support, no more than one-third of the earls had declared for Bruce. Many were in open hostility.

But the fact remained that no such spectacle had occurred in Scotland for near to half a century, and Bruce was determined to give Scotland a royal coronation to remember. The fair green meadow by the silver blue Tay beyond Scone Abbey hosted a tented city where lords and bishops held place in their silken pavilions next to the canvas and skin lodges of lesser men. Beyond that, religious orders set up canopied shrines where all could pray. And then came the booths of merchants and craftsmen, giving all the excitement and gaiety of a fair.

Rhona had clapped her hands and danced at the sight of it all, bustling beneath the myriad colorful banners and pennons flying over every tent and stall. Taking Hannah, one of the Dunning Innes serving girls, as companion, she went off to watch the tumblers, musicians, and trained animal acts. Beyond that stretched race courses and playing fields. None who attended the coronation of King Robert would lack for entertainment.

But Jamie turned his back on all the gaiety and glitter. He had work and enough to do. Was he the only one in all the celebrating throng who worried about the ancient tradition? Was he the only one determined to set matters right if it could be done? His first action was to seek out Sir Kenneth Corvan in his knight's pavilion of green and white striping.

His overlord was happy enough to see him but uncommunicative on the matter of the sacred stone. "Ah, the stane Edward took south, is it? I've nae doubt he keeps his sandstone secure in Westminster. But what would you with it, lad?"

"You know it's not Edward's rough-hewn block I look for." Jamie considered telling Sir Kenneth about his vision of Jacob's pillow but thought better of it. It was not every man who took kindly to tales of showings and dreamings. "Two-thirds of the barons and earls of the land refuse to proclaim Robert Bruce king. Our ancient honors are in English hands. Without the Community, without the crown and regalia, without the Stone, how many will say Robert Bruce's crowning was a true enkinging?"

"You argue well, Jamie MacInnes. But think you on this: because the barons of Scotland are not secure, because even now the earl of Pembroke gathers a Southern army under Edward's banner, because it would be no wise thing to further enrage Edward, would it be best to make so public display of calling Edward fool?"

"But the ancient—"

"Scotland is the most ancient kingdom in Christendom. Its very soil at this most sacred place will suffice."

Jamie swallowed his frustration. He briefly argued his role of sennachie. Surely one appointed to record for the ages should be privy to all. But he did not press the matter. Wallace had named him sennachie. Bruce had not. It was unlikely Robert Bruce knew of his existence. Jamie had come at the urging of the abbot of Cambuskenneth and his own inner determination. He could invoke no right of office.

"And the honours—the sword, scepter, ring, spurs . . ."

Sir Kenneth nodded heavily. "Aye, as you say—in English hands. But I have had conference with Abbot Henry of Scone. Bruce is determined that this ceremony shall bear as close a resemblance as possible to the ancient inauguration. Sacred items have been gathered. Bishop Lamberton has directed the melting down of gold from the trimming on three saint's images to fashion a gold band for Bruce's brow. For Bruce shall add a crown to the honors as well. And Abbot Henry has unearthed a rare treasure indeed from his hidden storehouse—the Brecbennoch of Saint Columba himself will house the vial of anointing oil."

The good knight landed a hearty slap on Jamie's shoulder. "You're a fine patriot to take such care over the matter. But have no fear, lad—all is in good hands."

Jamie knew his dismissal when he heard it. He thanked his overlord and left his tent. But the urging inside him would not let the matter rest. He found Abbot Henry in the abbey seeing to final preparations for the coming day. Short and round, the abbot looked like a man much more disposed to overseeing an orderly brotherhood engaged in work, study, and prayer than to hosting the finest spectacle in the land.

"What do you think?" He turned to Jamie simply because he stood nearby. "We've a twenty-voice boys' choir to stand in front of the chanting brothers. Yet there's nae room for half that many to sit."

His agitation seemed much soothed by Jamie's suggesting the simple expedient of adding a bench in front of the choir rail for the smaller boys, who would, indeed, be too wiggly to stand throughout the entire ceremony.

But Jamie was less successful at getting Abbot Henry to focus on the matter of the Stone.

"Oh. The Stane of Scone . . . yes, to be sure. A sair loss, indeed." He peered shortsightedly at Jamie. "And what is your interest in the matter, lad?"

"I was here with Wallace when he sought to avenge Edward's ravishment. We were too late, but we ran off Ormesby." On impulse he added, "Later Wallace made me sennachie. I've continued . . . on my own." And then, because Henry seemed truly interested, he told of seeing Jacob on his pillow.

Abbot Henry nodded. "Aye. A rare gift you've been given, lad. Guard it well."

"Yes, sir. But the Stone . . ."

Henry sighed. "A sair loss indeed," he repeated. "But if the MacDuff does not come, perhaps the seating would be of little value anyway. For always it has been the privilege of the house of Fife to seat the monarch on the Stane. Mayhap it's best not to make a spectacle of the fact that Duncan of Fife is completely in Edward's power . . ."

The abbot's voice trailed off, and all his energy seemed to go into wringing his hands. "Although there are those who might protest the whole ceremony cannot be valid without the MacDuff . . ." The hand wringing again absorbed him for a moment. "Still . . . best left in the hands of Providence, such matters are. Best left, I say." He looked to the high altar where two tonsured brothers were raising a row of pennons strung on a long rope. "No, no, no. Not in front of the apostle's window. You'd not block Saint Peter's view of the proceedings, would you?"

His wooden crutches thumping on the stone abbey floor, Jamie followed the abbot. At last his persistence won the day. Abbot Henry granted permission for him to search the church's crypt and cellars.

Perhaps he should have known by the abbot's offhanded manner of granting permission that there was nothing to be found hidden beneath the abbey where the Stone of Scone had for centuries been kept. And it was no easy task for one for whom bending, kneeling, and maneuvering in tight places were next to impossible, especially while carrying a burning torch. But indefatigable determination to be true to his vision carried Jamie through the evening and most of the hours of the night.

And now all he had to counter his disappointment was the knowledge that he had done all possible. That knowledge and the shining distraction of the scene in the abbey.

Certainly the list of nobles not there was longer than the list of those present, but there were sufficient for a dazzling spectacle. Four bishops, three earls, and numerous knights entered the church arrayed in their best. Bruce's closest companions—young James Douglas, whose father had been a valiant Wallace supporter; Earl Malcolm of Lennox; Sir Neil Campbell; Sir Gilbert la Hay; and Sir Christopher Seton, Bruce's brother-in-law—filled the front seats, wearing fur and jewel-trimmed, knee-length tunics of green, purple, and saffron velvet and silk.

Farther back, in seats slightly elevated so that they might see better, Jamie and Rhona watched amid Sir Kenneth's company. Rhona, so bubbling with excitement that he could feel her quiver, wore a fine new gown of peacock blue embroidered in scarlet and orange silk. And Jamie's own emerald green cloak was lined with fabric that matched his red-lighted golden hair.

But as Jamie surveyed the splendid company, his spirits sank even lower. In spite of the hope he had held out against all odds, Duncan of Fife had not come. For all the splendor of the ceremony, Robert the Bruce would be made king of Scots without the Stone of Scone and without the hereditary inaugurator.

A blast of trumpets from the back of the long stone nave, bringing all in the abbey to their feet, announced that the details over which Jamie agonized would be the only elements missing. And if MacDuff was not there, there were plenty to see the new king of Scots to his throne. Bishop Lamberton of St. Andrews, primate of all Scotland, led the procession, robed in gold and purple, wearing a jeweled miter and carrying his staff. Behind him came Bishop Wishart of Glasgow and David Murray, bishop of Moray, bearing the richly embroidered cloak with which the king would be robed. Abbot Henry followed with the Brecbennoch, the most ancient and sacred relic of the land.

The monks and choir boys began their chant: "The King in His might loves justice. Our God has established justice and judgment in the land. Extol the Lord our God, and worship at His footstool."

King Robert and his queen entered the abbey. She wore a gown of white silk, cut tight at the bodice and flaring full in the skirt with long, slim sleeves, likewise flaring to points at the wrists. The dress was embroidered with gold and sewn with pearls. Pearls were also entwined in the rope of golden hair falling down her back. Beside her strode the king in a tabard of cloth-of-gold, the rampant red lion of Scotland embroidered in scarlet picked out with rubies. Behind them walked acolytes swinging censors that puffed spicy-scented clouds.

Bishop Murray placed the royal robe on Bruce's broad shoulders. He sat on his throne and Elizabeth on one just lower beside him.

The choir began a new chant as the aged patriot Robert Wishart took the crown from the altar: "Let justice descend, O heavens, like dew from above, like gentle rain let the skies drop it down. Let the earth open and salvation bud forth; let justice spring up in the land of your anointed."

Wishart placed the simple gold circlet, ornamented only with strawberry leaf points, on the broad forehead of King Robert Bruce.

"Long live the king!"

The abbey rang with the shouts.

Other symbols of kingship followed, each accompanied by cheers that were as much for the reemerging nation as for the king who would lead it: scepter, book of laws, sword, ring, spurs. Alexander Scrymgeour, made royal standard bearer by William Wallace, stepped forward with the great red and gold lion banner, and the choir began another chant.

But Jamie did not hear, for at that moment he felt an urgent tugging on his sleeve. He looked down to see one of the small pages who had been stationed near the altar to run errands should there be any need.

"You are Jamie MacInnes, the sennachie?" the lad with the earnest round face inquired.

"Aye."

"Abbot Henry needs you."

Jamie gathered his crutches and attempted to follow the child as quickly and with as little disturbance as possible.

He need not have worried. The chant ended, and the standard bearer dipped the flag over the king's head, signaling a time when the crowd might again cheer. The reverberations off the stones were

600

so loud Jamie could hardly hear what Abbot Henry came to say in his ear.

But at last he understood, and he felt himself pale at the request. Was it possible that in all this detailed planning such should have been forgotten? Was it possible that he should be called on for such a crucial performance unprepared? Could he do it?

"There is no one else. Scotland is without a King of Arms. There is no High Sennachie." Abbot Henry stepped back for Jamie to ascend the platform.

He took his place beside Alexander Scrymgeour. The red and gold banner fluttered just above his head. The king was so near he could have reached out and touched him.

The crowd silenced. This was the moment.

Jamie took a deep breath and began in a voice that he hoped would echo to the back of the abbey. He might be unsure of his ability to get through the complicated list, but he would not have it said that the sennachie sounded unsure of Robert Bruce's right of birth to sit on the throne of Scotland. For proving birthright was the sennachie's role, as had been done at every enkinging from time out of mind. And almost it had been forgotten.

"Robert mac Robert mac Robert mac Robert . . ." At least the first four were easy enough. "Mac Isabel, nic David . . ." He kept his voice steady. He must not sound ashamed that Bruce's lineage came through a daughter of David the First's younger grandson. "Mac David, mac Malcolm, mac Duncan, mac Malcolm . . ." Now he was on solid ground. There could be no arguing with the right of one of such lineage to rule. And so he continued back through Kenneth mac Alpin and Aiden and Gabhran to Fergus mac Erc.

The recital ended to another round of cheering, this enhanced by a fanfare of trumpets. But even as Jamie rejoiced in the triumph, the proclamation served to increase his weight of sadness over the loss of the Stone and the absence of the inaugurator. For all those he had named—all who had ruled in Scotland for almost eight hundred fifty years—all had sat on the Stone of Destiny as a central element of their enkinging.

Still, the ceremony was not over, and the ritual that was to come was perhaps even more ancient in its inception. And certainly more holy. For just as the prophet Samuel had anointed King Saul as a sign of God's blessing poured out on him, so was Robert Bruce to be anointed.

Bishop Lamberton turned to the altar, where Abbot Henry had placed the small house-shaped casket, and removed the vial of consecrated oil he had put there. As he closed the gabled lid he crossed himself, for a relic of Saint Columba, who had brought the faith to Scotland, also rested in the sacred vessel.

Then primate turned to king. "Your throne, O God, stands forever and ever; a righteous scepter is the scepter of His kingdom. You, O king, have loved justice and hated wickedness; therefore God, your God, has anointed you with the oil of gladness above your fellow kings."

A rich, sweet scent of spice permeated the air as Lamberton emptied the vial over Bruce's head, increasing the shine of his dark auburn hair.

Only one aspect of the ceremony remained. That of homage giving. Bishop Lamberton went first to Queen Elizabeth. He raised her from her throne and led her to her king.

She knelt before him, the first to do homage, as she took his hands between both of her own. "I, Elizabeth de Burgh, do take thee, Robert, my liege lord . . ."

And then the long procession began, headed by the highest earls there: John of Atholl; Malcolm of Lennox; Alan of Menteith; then, even though he was but a boy, Donald, earl of Mar, Bruce's ward. Next the knights: Campbell, Hay, Seton, Douglas . . . on through the lists to Corvan.

The ceremony was well on into its second hour, and still Jamie stood by Scrymgeour. He did not know the protocol for a sennachie, and no one told him. But he thought that if the standard bearer should stand by the throne, so should the lineage giver. He resisted the inclination to lean on his crutches. If the others, especially one as old as Bishop Wishart, could stand straight, so could he.

At last the line ended. All the earls, knights, and office holders had sworn to be King Robert's leal men. All except Scrymgeour, who had been occupied with his banner. Now he fixed it in a bracket and knelt before the king. "Your leal man of heart and arms."

Robert's gaze followed the officer as he returned to his place. And it came to rest on Jamie. "Well done, my sturdy sennachie." The king smiled. "And, assured as you are of my lineage, will you not swear me loyalty?"

Jamie could not believe his own hearing. Of a certain he was loyal, as loyal as any in the room. But it was not for the younger brother of a minor landholder to swear fealty. And yet the king had asked.

"With great pleasure, my lord king." Jamie swung forward.

He fell to his left knee and grasped the broad hands of Robert the Bruce between his own. "I do take Robert Bruce for my sovereign and liege lord . . . with all my heart."

Now came the awkward moment. In his eagerness to kneel, he had dropped both crutches. Now he had nothing with which to hoist himself to his feet.

Then he felt himself being propelled upright with the king's hands under both his elbows. The king did not release him until a page had returned the crutches. "I am told you served Wallace."

"Aye. With my sword until Stirling Bridge." He nodded toward his crippled leg. "Then with my storytelling."

"Would you serve me so? As none knows better than you, it is an office I have need of filling."

Unable to reply, Jamie dipped his head in assent.

The festivities continued for two days with feasting, jousting, and entertainment. Rhona's great joy at Jamie's part in the ceremony overshadowed his own deep disappointment at the missing elements. Almost. And her unspeakable delight at his new appointment and the pleasure of enjoying the amusements with her were enough to chase away the cloud hanging over all the land. Almost.

For however much the company here cheered and delighted in their stalwart new king, the fact remained that the earl of Pembroke, Edward's commander in Scotland, was gathering an army just below the border at Carlisle. All knew Pembroke to be a fierce and able soldier—and brother-in-law to the slain Comyn.

On top of that, rumors flew that Edward Prince of Wales followed Pembroke northward with a second army. And King Edward himself was preparing to come north.

But perhaps that was all the more reason to celebrate in the brisk but sun-gilded days of late March, for who knew what summer would bring? The next day was Palm Sunday, and Jamie and Rhona were among the many who crowded into the abbey to join the prayers that Scotland and the new king of Scots would long enjoy peace and justice. They were just emerging when Jamie saw a band of newcomers, riding at an urgent pace. He took one look at the banner the first man carried and grabbed Rhona's arm in an instinctive effort to pull her to safety.

"I know that device. I've seen it often enough when it opposed Wallace. Comyn. John Comyn, earl of Buchan."

Rhona moved closer to Jamie, but she sounded more surprised than worried. "But why would he come here? The men are not mailed."

He looked again. He had seen only the armed outriders who served as guards. The inner group was arrayed as guests to a wedding—or a king-making.

603

And in the center of the company rode no avenging earl but a young woman in a sky blue gown with a cherry red cloak. Ringlets of corn-silk gold sprang out from under her white linen headrail. She had a pert-looking, small-featured face. And a firmly set, determined jaw.

"The Countess Isabel."

"Wife of Comyn of Buchan."

"Sister of MacDuff."

The lady's name and titles sped through the crowd as each person emerging from the church must needs be informed of this surprising turn of events.

Perhaps even more surprising was that King Robert himself pushed through the crowd with long-legged stride and took both the lady's hands in his to assist her down from her white palfrey.

She leaped lightly to the ground with a chime of laughter that immediately faded to stricken concern. "My lord king, I am come too late. I made all haste, but it is for naught."

King Robert extended his hand, palm downward, and the countess placed her hand on his wrist to be led toward the palace. "The joy your presence brings our company cannot be for naught. But Isabel, does your husband know what you do?"

Jamie did not consider whether or not his position of sennachie entitled him to eavesdrop. He simply followed, as did Rhona and many others.

At Bruce's question, the countess's jaw became more resolutely square, and her small chin rose. "My lord of Buchan is on his Leicestershire estates. I chose his finest horses and strongest guards to accompany me. There was no need to disquiet him over the matter. He is not MacDuff. This is a matter that touches my house only."

"You are a brave, loyal lady, Isabel. There are not many who would have done what you have. I fear you may yet suffer for it."

"I did only what right and duty required. If I am to suffer for the Community of the Realm, I am content to place the matter in God's hands." She gave a little shake of her head, making the golden ringlets around the white linen dance in the sun. "But I am desolate that even with all my haste I am too late."

Just then Abbot Henry bustled forward. "Well come, my lady. I had not given up hope of seeing one of your ancient house. I have a room for you."

"The countess bemoans her late arrival." Bruce turned to the abbot. "But it strikes me that Palm Sunday would be no' so bad a day for a special ceremony, a seconding of the first."

The abbot folded his hands over his round belly and heaved a great sigh of satisfaction. "Aye. And if I had ever doubted that the Lord hears and answers prayers, I would never doubt again. We shall have a confirmation."

He looked across the yard to the green mound that had been the site of so many ancient inaugurations. "On Moot Hill. In one hour's time. There is little preparation needed. You will excuse me, my lord king and lady . . . " He bobbed his tonsured head and turned away, calling to one of the monks to find Sir Kenneth Corvan.

An hour later a throng almost as great as the one that had filled the abbey two days before stood in a semicircle around the foot of the ancient enkinging hill.

The preparations had, indeed, been simple. A choir of brown-robed brothers stood behind the mound. Alexander Scrymgeour stood to one side holding the lion banner; Lamberton, Wishart, and Murray to the other. And atop the gentle rise sat a small, intricately carved stool that looked more like a chest than a stool but for the fact that one could see through the openwork to observe that it contained nothing.

Fixing everything carefully in his mind so that he could write about it later, Jamie puzzled over one fact. Assuredly the preparations had been hasty—yet surely not so hurried as all that. Did it not seem odd that the stool was set, not centered on the rounded summit, but slightly to the back and northeast side? The more he considered, the stranger it seemed, especially since the placement required the stool to sit at a sloping angle.

But no one seemed the least concerned about such a detail. A fanfare of trumpets from the palace announced the approach of the king. This time Robert Bruce had his hand on the wrist of her who had been Isabel MacDuff before her marriage into the house of Bruce's enemy.

The crowd parted, and the sister of the earl of Fife led the new king of Scots to his enkinging seat. The king's powerful frame, robed once more in the gold and purple cloak, fully covered the slanting stool.

Bishop Lamberton stepped forward with the simple gold crown resting on a crimson cushion.

Isabel, countess of Buchan, lifted the circlet with both hands and placed it on King Robert's head.

"I am bringing on my justice. It is not far off. My salvation shall not tarry. I will put salvation within Zion, and give to Israel My glory," the monks chanted.

As Jamie joined the cheering that followed, he thought once more what a pity it was that the one final piece of the ancient ritual had not been there.

Or was it? His mind filled with the picture of a similar afternoon eight years earlier when he had stood here with Wallace and noted the apparently disturbed sod. Was it possible that Robert the Bruce had indeed been en-kinged on the Stone of Destiny?

66

Barely three weeks later word reached the new king that Edward had ordered his commander Pembroke "to burn and slay and raise dragon in Scotland." The terrible dragon banner, which meant there was to be no mercy, no restraints, was sweeping northward.

Bruce had made the best use possible of his time. Immediately after his coronation he set about putting the nation in a state of defense. He had ridden throughout the country as far as time allowed, quelling Comyn sympathizers, taking the sometimes-forced homage of recalcitrant earls, seizing castles, and rallying his army. But Bruce had fewer than a thousand men with him. Pembroke reportedly commanded six thousand chivalry—and how many thousands more infantry?

The Scots king sent out his call in every direction and turned northward. He would await the gathering of his troops above Perth on the banks of the River Almond.

He had not long to wait. Indeed, a great army did gather. It did not, however, come to fight for Bruce. A massive English army mustered to fight against him. Pembroke, the English leader, marched to Perth, and behind Pembroke—a few days? a week? The messengers were uncertain—came the earl of Buchan to pit all the strength of Comyn against the new king.

The week before, Rhona had ridden with Jamie to Perth that he might be on hand to give personal account of Scotland's deeds. But now Bruce would move his troops.

They stood by Jamie's fine brown horse, named Clarsach at Rhona's suggestion because a sennachie needs have a harp, though Jamie played none.

"Must you go, Jamie?" She clung to him tighter than ever before.

He unwound her arms gently from around his neck, but it was like the tearing of his own flesh.

"Aye, *mo briagha,* my beautiful." He touched her hair. "You know I must."

"Aye. But Jamie . . ." Still she held to his hand. The words that would not come from her mouth shone in her brimming eyes. At last she dropped the hand. "Mount you, then." She held his crutches while he gripped his garron's saddle and boosted himself up with the springing hop from his good leg he had learned long ago. The high wooden back on the saddle was a considerable barrier to haul his useless leg over, but a great help in maintaining balance on horseback. Long ago he had suffered many degrading spills before he managed it. Now he accomplished mounting almost without thought, seldom bothering with the strap Rory had added to his saddle.

She handed him the smooth white ash sticks, and he strapped them on his back.

"Rhona . . ." He put his hand over the small white one that rested on his thigh. Now it was his turn not to be able to speak what was in his heart. "Go to the castle. The queen is there with her ladies. You'll be safe—no matter what."

"Haste you back." She stepped away.

Bruce moved their camp only about three miles west to the southern banks of the River Almond near Methven Castle. Like Wallace before him, who had always had to fight armies that far outnumbered his own, Bruce would choose the strongest ground available from which to fight. Here was a high ridge with the ground falling away to either side, a wood to the back and a river to the front. The position taken, King Robert sent a large number of men out to forage for food. The morning would likely bring battle, and he would not have his men fight on empty stomachs.

Jamie tethered Clarsach to a small sapling at the edge of the camp. There was grass for the sturdy beast to munch, and, since he had come as observer, there was no need to be close in, although that would have perhaps been warmer and more companionable.

He rolled in a blanket and closed his eyes, soothed by the rhythmic tearing and chomping of the grazing horse. His eyes were no sooner closed than he was deeply asleep.

The coming conflict pressed on his mind, however, for he had little more than slipped into darkness before he rolled and tossed to the sound of trumpet blasts and shouted alarms. In his sleep he saw men less than half awake groping for their weapons, stumbling in confusion, staggering to their mounts.

"To arms!"

"The English!"

Again the trumpet rally. Jamie pulled his blanket around his ears and turned on his side. Tomorrow's battle would come soon

608

enough. Why must his sleep be disturbed with foretastes of chaos and alarms?

The pounding of the earth under him jolted Jamie awake. In the gray half light of predawn June, he saw that he had not been dreaming. The rally and call to arms was real.

English heavy chivalry thundered by, not twenty yards beyond him as he groped for his crutches. Where was Bruce? Had the sentries wakened the king in time? Had Jamie been the only one lost in sleep, or had the entire Scots army been swept upon while they dreamed? Surely the foraging parties could not even have returned yet. It had been near dark when they made camp last night. Bruce and his captains could not have even made a battle plan yet.

The clank and scrape of metal, the screams of horses and men, the insistent shouts of warriors and trumpets so shook the air that he could not feel the crutches under his hands. He must have passed over them several times in his desperate haste before he gripped them firmly and lunged to his feet. He was even slower fumbling with Clarsach's tack. In all the years since Stirling he had never been so near to cursing his uselessness.

But in the end it was his slowness that saved him. By the time he was finally in the saddle, the thrust of the battle had swept past. And he could see by the terrible litter across the field that if he had been in the way earlier, he would have been cut down like the hundreds of Scots soldiers left in the wake of Pembroke's dragon.

There was nothing to be done. They had left no wounded, no captured were being sent to the rear. All were put to the sword. Jamie followed, keeping to the edge of the woods. As horrible as it was to look upon, looking was his job, and he at least would not turn his back on this.

Could the rout be so complete? Could King Robert the Bruce lie somewhere in that heap of human rubble even now being barely lit by dawn's first light? The English swept on as swiftly as if unopposed. And yet Jamie could not accept that his king had fallen. He would not accept it until he saw with his own eyes the dark auburn head fallen beneath the red and gold banner.

He urged his mount forward until he saw a pocket of resistance where battle was still joined. Here a handful of Scots, fewer than a hundred, matched the Englishry blow for blow and far better. But for every Southern to fall under Scottish sword, three rose up. There was no hope of victory. Yet Jamie's heart leaped at the valiant sight.

Then, as morning light crested a hill and flooded the valley, he saw the truth of the matter. Those fighting stood in a ring, the inner ones on foot, the outer still mounted. And they would not move. Not until the last man of them was dead. For at the center of the brave group lay the form they protected.

The Bruce was fallen. Wounded. Perhaps gravely. But that his best men fought on said that he was not dead. Yet.

And the banner was not fallen. Alexander Scrymgeour sat his horse bravely, fighting with sword in one hand and using the banner pole as a lance with the other. The sight of the flag served as a rallying point for the Scots.

But also for the English. From far across the field a contingent of English chivalry, having dispatched what would have been the left wing of the Scots army had they had time to form such, now whirled and thundered toward the struggling ring.

Torn between fear and elation, Jamie saw at the same moment the most heartening of all sights. The king was on his feet. Apparently he had just been dazed by his unhorsing. Now he was wielding his two-handed sword, although it appeared that the men nearest him—Jamie thought them to be Lennox, Campbell, Douglas, and Hay—seemed to be urging him to retreat.

Such glorious stoutheartedness could not last long, however. Pembroke's destriers had only a small ridge to cross before they swept down on Bruce and his circle. The horses' brilliant caparisons whipped in the wind of their going. Knights' armor dazzled in the sunrise. Banners snapped over their heads. And a hundred lances pointed at Robert Bruce.

"To your right! Take to the right!" Jamie knew his shouting was futile, but he could not contain it. The woods were but a few hundred yards away. If Bruce broke now, he might make it. It was just possible. And yet the king drove forward, unaware of the doom pounding down upon him.

Jamie's heart sank, for a small band of horsemen erupted from the woods and made straight for Bruce. Now the way was blocked in both directions. And then, as the fighting Scots opened their circle before the flying arrow formation of the smaller band, Jamie realized that the newcomers were Scots. The green, yellow, and purple surcoat of Sir Christopher Seton, Bruce's brother-in-law, at the arrow tip of the formation was unmistakable. His size was likewise unmistakable. He could have been a match for William Wallace.

Seton thundered into the ring—as much in danger from the sword thrusts of his own men, fighting to ward off the enemy, as from English steel. With one lunge he swooped sideways in his saddle, caught Bruce under the arms, and pulled the king up behind him.

Seton whirled, his horse's hooves striking out as weapons, and made for the woods. The ragtag remnant of the Scots army followed him as best they could. It was inglorious, but Seton had saved the king. He had saved them all, for none in that band would have deserted his king. They would have fought until they fell.

And then Jamie saw that even the doubtful victory of succeeding in retreat was not clearly theirs. For Seton's horse, carrying two heavy men and forced to flee uphill, was slowing. Once he stumbled, and Jamie cried out in alarm, feeling helpless to avert the disaster that played so clearly before his eyes.

Suddenly he saw what to do. As always, riderless horses in battle sought leadership and charged toward the heart of the action. And there were riderless horses aplenty. Significantly few English destriers, but of Scots garrons and light chargers there were hundreds, adding to the chaos on the field.

Without thought to the danger of breaking cover and riding headlong into a field of warriors, Jamie plunged.

The first horse he grabbed for tossed his head with foaming mouth and crazed eyes and lunged away. The next animal within reach was bleeding grievously from a deep cut just above his withers. He would not be long on his feet. Then a fine black stallion galloped straight at Clarsach to Jamie's right.

Ignoring the difficulty of holding a plunging warhorse on his weak side without the support of a strong leg to counterbalance the animal's pull, Jamie seized the animal's dragging reins and spun his own mount toward the woods.

The thrust threw him off balance. For a horrible moment he felt himself falling. He would be crushed beneath the pounding hooves of both horses, and Robert Bruce would fall to the English.

Then he saw the red and black pennon in the lead of the enemy charge bearing down on Seton's slowing mount. Comyn. The earl of Buchan was in the field! The shock made Jamie grab a handful of Clarsach's flying black mane even as he held the extra reins. He righted himself and spurred forward, shouting. "A Bruce! A Bruce!"

He and Comyn reached the king at the same moment from opposite sides. Bruce slashed out in a figure eight motion of flashing steel, which checked his opponent for just an instant. That instant was enough. Seton interposed his sword between Bruce and Comyn, and Bruce leaped to the extra horse.

Suddenly lightened of the king's weight, Seton's mount plunged ahead as Seton's sword cut deep into Comyn's horse's throat. The Scots reached the safety of the woods while Comyn's band, directionless with the unhorsing of their leader, scattered.

611

The Scots barely slowed their pace until they were north of the Almond and into the fastness of the Highlands.

The safety of the Sma' Glen enfolded them. It seemed that all heaved a sigh of relief as the looming crags rose, dark and sheltering, over them. Now they could breathe. Now they could see to their wounds. Now the shock of what had happened overtook them.

Jamie felt the blow of a gauntleted hand on his shoulder. "You saved your king, man. But it would have been better to let him die."

Jamie started to protest. Then he saw the dead hollows of Robert Bruce's eyes. They looked like the eyes he had seen in faces covering the field below Methven.

"I should have died with my men. I was their leader. I wasn't ready, and they paid the price for my failing."

Jamie shook his head. "Pembroke was unchivalrous to strike before dawn. And on a Sunday."

"Aye."

Jamie had not thought the Bruce's eyes could look deader while he still breathed. And yet they did, as if pushed back in his head by charcoal sticks. "Such is God's justice for sacrilege. I struck Comyn in a church. God has struck me on a Sunday."

Jamie wanted to offer some words of comfort. And yet there was terrible logic in what the king said. Perhaps it was not Edward's order to raise dragon, not Pembroke's brutality in carrying out that order, not Comyn's vengeance that had defeated Robert the Bruce. Perhaps it was the pope's excommunication that had directed the outcome of the battle.

They had received word only last week. Bruce had not appeared to give it much thought. It had been expected. But because the cut had been too deep to be seen, it had been the more deadly.

And then Jamie had his own deadening thought. "The ladies. Your lady queen, Countess Isabel—" in his horror he could hardly name her "—Rhona."

Bruce answered as if from a great distance. "I sent them to safety in care of my brother Nigel. Pray God they make it."

Jamie tried to pray, but no words came.

Two weeks later Edward Bruce and the valiant Seton slipped from camp early one morning. Jamie could not muster the strength to ask why these two had joined the growing list of the departed. Could even they have abandoned the ragged hope of these few patriots?

In the days after Methven the few hundred men remaining around the proud red lion rampant had slunk deeper into the hills. Now they huddled beneath the mist that clung to the top of Ben

More even in early July. There was food and enough for forage, and the blazing purple carpet of bell heather made a soft enough bed even for men recovering from wounds.

But it did little good for men to heal their blood wounds when they had no hearts left to pump the blood. And with the heart gone from the king, it was gone from the land. How was it possible that their defeat could have been so total? Jamie wondered.

Since Methven, two messengers, canny Highlanders from the clan Campbell, had melted into camp with news and melted out again as silently. And each time, spirits that one thought could sink no lower dropped deeper yet. Of the more than four thousand men who had rallied to their king's call, almost all were dead. A few had been taken prisoner, but these were the unlucky ones. Alexander Scrymgeour, who had held the banner high until his capture at the last moment, had been led to London and hanged, drawn, and quartered in the same manner as the Guardian who had bestowed the standard bearer title upon him. Lamberton and Wishart were sent to London in chains. And still Pembroke persisted in spreading a reign of terror that was worthy only of one carrying the banner of Edward Plantagenet.

Jamie could not bestir himself to ask what would happen now to the nation. He could not think beyond his fear for Rhona.

On a quiet mid-morning with sun burning through the mist, Jamie sat on Ben More's slopes. In former times he could not have asked for a better place to have his pictures come to him, but now he stared blankly at the rugged sweep of land to the camp below and the small loch beyond.

A few figures moved on the sketchy track leading from the west. Perhaps the hunting party returned sooner than expected. He did not bother to look closely.

Nothing seemed worth the bother these days.

"Jamie!"

At first he thought he had conjured a vision from the depths of his own longing. Surely the purple gown that climbed the hill toward him was an extension of the heather underfoot. Surely the chiming voice was not human but that of the lark that sang so sweetly every morning by the loch.

"Jamie! Will you not greet me?"

"Rhona!" He jumped up so fast he pitched forward and landed in a rolling heap at her feet.

Laughing and crying and calling his name all in the same breath, she threw herself on him. They locked in a tangled embrace while fat yellow bees buzzed threateningly around their heads.

"Oh, Rhona!" At last he pushed himself to one elbow in order to get a better look at her. "I didna dare to think it you." He reached to pull a sprig of heather from her hair, but she grabbed his hand to kiss it, and they were tumbling again.

It was long before they could lie peacefully still and drink in the wonder of being together again.

"You're alive . . ."

"I was so afraid . . ."

They began at the same time, then both stopped on half sobs, half laughs.

"But how does this miracle come? How is it that you're here?"

"Edward Bruce and Seton—they came for the queen. Edward says the king has much need of her."

"Bless Edward Bruce. Our king is not the only one with such needs."

Jamie rolled to his side, and she let him pull the heather from her hair. "Ah, Rhona. You're so beautiful. I can never get used to it." His hand moved from her hair to stroke her cheek.

Then he fell back sharply as if one of the bees had stung him. "But I've no right to be so happy. The battle . . . the king . . . all is lost, Rhona."

Now she turned and traced his sharp cheekbones and firm jawline with her fingertip. "Perhaps not all, love. I heard the king's brother tell the queen how matters stood here. Elizabeth is a very resourceful lady. She has brought a remedy of her own."

Jamie sat up and shook his head. "If any sight can gladden the king's heart, it will be that of his lady. But I fear he'll nae be so easily heartened as I was."

"No. I mean she brings more than her wifely charms, although she is not short on those. You know she is daughter of the earl of Ulster. The Irish were unreformed by any such as our Saint Margaret, and so there are places where the old church is still strong there."

Jamie ran his long fingers through his hair, showering bits of bracken onto his shoulders. "What are you talking about, lass? What has the state of the Irish church to say to Robert the Bruce?"

"That not all are under the domination of the pope. Not all hold the Bruce excommunicate. She has brought Father Dunchad, a holy man from Inchaffray."

"From where?"

"Did you not know? That was where Lord Nigel Bruce took us to shelter when the king moved his army from Perth." She gasped and put her hands to each side of his face. "Oh, my love. My poor love. I can see by your face you did not know. You had thought us still in Perth—under Pembroke's dragon."

They clung to each other wordlessly for long minutes, holding the warm reality to push away the terrible specter of what might have been.

At last Jamie found his voice. "You were in a holy house. On an island?"

"Yes. But not Roman. Of the old church—Culdees they call themselves. Of the order of Saint Fillan."

Jamie nodded. "Aye, a very holy man. But long dead." He sighed.

"But not his memory. Nor the power of his blessing, I believe. Nor the comfort of Holy Communion."

"What?" Now Jamie sat up straight, all attention. "You mean this holy man from Inchaffray has brought an ancient Celtic blessing for King Robert and he will serve the Eucharist to one excommunicated?"

"I told you, he is not bound by Rome. He says one may serve God in his heart without the office of Holy Church."

Jamie stared. "Dangerous talk, that. But if it'll cheer the king, I'll nae gainsay it."

Jamie crawled back up the hillside to where he had left his crutches before his joyous tumble to Rhona, and they walked slowly back down to where all in the camp were assembled before an altar of piled stones.

"Has it been consecrated?" Jamie asked.

"Father Dunchad says that such was good enough for Moses and the prophets. It is not for us to spurn God's ways," Rhona answered.

Jamie raised his eyebrows, but a few minutes later when the king and queen emerged from the Bruce's tent, Jamie could see that the lightness of his countenance ran deeper than the washing and combing he had undertaken in preparation to receiving the sacrament.

The ceremony, stripped of all ritual, vestments, and chants, seemed crudely straightforward to Jamie.

The king knelt before the altar.

"This is My body, broken for you. Eat you all of it." The Culdee gave Robert Bruce a morsel of bread. "This is My blood, shed for you. As often as you drink of it, do so in remembrance of Me." He gave a cup of wine to the kneeling figure, as was the Columban tradition.

But the next elements in the service were a surprise indeed. Father Dunchad took a vial of oil from the altar and poured it over the head of him who had already been anointed king. Unnecessary at best, Jamie thought. He hoped it not sacrilegious.

"Then Samuel, with the horn of oil in hand, anointed David in the midst of his brothers. And from that day on, the Spirit of the Lord rushed upon David." The holy man spoke in a flat, unhurried voice and offered no comment on the meaning of what he did.

Finally he drew a long, narrow bag on a thong from around his neck and took out a slim white object. "This is the most holy relic of our house—the arm bone of Saint Fillan himself, holy man from Ireland who loved his adopted land of Scotia best of all and showed many the way to life everlasting."

He held it out for Robert Bruce to bow over. "The blessing of Saint Fillan rest on you, King Robert Bruce . . ."

He tucked the gleaming white bone back in its suede bag and buried it in the folds of his robe. "It may be many years yet before the fullness of the blessing will be truly yours. The relic of Saint Fillan I will keep always with me as a reminder to pray constantly for the fulfillment of the promise, King Robert."

Jamie felt like mentioning that this would be none too bad a time now, as it hardly seemed likely that King Robert's enemies would ever be much stronger against him. But he supposed Father Dunchad knew his business.

Whatever Robert Bruce thought, when he stood Jamie could see that his eyes were blue again instead of the black they had been since Methven.

The time could not have been better for the hunters to return with a red deer. Elizabeth had brought honey and heather ale with her from Inchaffray, and they made ready to feast. Jamie could see that Robert Bruce would eat well tonight for the first time in many weeks, although meat had been plentiful before. And Jamie felt he, too, would have a much better appetite.

But first, Rhona insisted that they walk apart by the small loch. It was ringed with tall water grass and spindly yellow flowers. A cuckoo called from his heather hillside, and evening moths hung low over the smooth water—smooth until a trout rose to snap at his dinner and descend again, leaving widening rings to spread across the surface.

Jamie stooped to pick up a small flat pebble and sent it skimming across the surface. "Seven!" He gave a cry that would have startled any fish near the shore. "Let's see you do as much."

But Rhona did not rise to the bait. "Sit you down, James Mac-Innes. I've something to say to you."

He grinned. "When you speak in that tone, perhaps I'd best take it on my feet."

"You won't stay there for long, and I've no wish to fish you out of the loch."

"That bad, is it?" Surely she was teasing?

"It's that good. You're to be a father." She pushed at his chest as she said it.

Relaxed as he had been, then with the shock of her words, he went down under her push, but not before he grabbed her hand and pulled her down with him.

For several moments he said nothing.

"Jamie—what is it? Are you no' happy?" Worry creased her forehead.

He gathered her into a tight bear hug. "That's the problem. I'm trying to figure out how it's possible to be so happy in such dreadful circumstances. Oh, Rhona!" He buried his face in her hair, then turned his head to cover her cheek with his kisses. "Oh, Rhona, it's so wonderful. It's fantastic. I can't believe it. Are you sure? When?"

"Aye, I'm sure. After Christmas. Early next year."

"Oh, Rhona," was all he could say again. The storyteller, gifted with words, had suddenly lost all power of speech.

They sat a little apart from the others, eating their fill of crisp roast venison and licking the honey off each other's fingers. Then, with the moon making silvery streaks on the loch, they made their way slowly to Jamie's tent, Rhona carrying one crutch so they could walk with their arms around each other.

Their happiness lasted until just past noon the next day.

67

Bruce had learned his lesson at Methven and posted a secure ring of sentries around their camp and scouts at all the passes farther out. It was a good thing he did, for one of Campbell's Highland men rode in just as the sun topped the peak of Ben More.

"A thousand men—more. MacDougall, lord of Lorn, leads them."

Bruce set his jaw. "MacDougall of Lorn—wed to Comyn's sister." He shook his head. "Then all of Argyll will rise against us."

Jamie thought of how the land lay. Here they were in the very center of Lorn's lordship. To the north was the lordship of Badenoch, passed to the heir of the murdered Red Comyn; behind them, Pembroke held Perth and Fife for Edward; Bruce's own lands of Carrick and Annandale were far to the south.

"Lennox, my lord." Jamie spoke without thinking. It was his place to record, not to advise his king.

But Bruce nodded. "Aye."

Malcolm, earl of Lennox, was one of Bruce's closest companions. But he had been wounded at Methven, and none had seen him since. It was hoped he had won through to his own lands just this side of the Clyde. If he had been captured by the English, surely they would have received word of ransom demands. Or of his execution.

"Aye. We'll to Lennox."

It was a good choice. The only choice.

Jamie felt Rhona's hand on his arm, but as he started to turn to her he was checked by the king's next words. "Nigel, take Christopher Seton and a strong guard and escort the women to Our Sister of Mar at Kildrummy."

Jamie's arm went around Rhona. He clutched her to him as he thought of the long journey over rough land far to the northeast. How long would it be until they were together again? And with Rhona expecting . . .

Isabel, countess of Buchan, gasped, then covered her mouth with both hands. She stifled her sobs but could not control her shaking. The Lady Margery, Bruce's twelve-year-old daughter by his first wife, clung to her stepmother.

Elizabeth, daughter of a great lord and wife of a king, folded the girl in her arms and raised her chin. "Yes, my lord king. We will be ready as soon as your men bring our horses up."

"But—" Margery lifted her small frightened face from the queen's skirts "—but it's so far."

"Margery." Elizabeth's voice was stern but not unkind. She spoke so that all the women could hear. "We would impede the men by staying here. They have a mighty enemy to fight and can do so better unhampered by considerations for our safety. This is our duty for Scotland."

Rhona's face was white, but her eyes dry. "Jamie, you could come with us. Nigel Bruce is choosing escort."

His face felt so tight he could hardly speak. "Aye. I could. I could not provide strong escort, but Bruce would send me north with the women if I asked it. Do you ask it?"

She looked at him long and steadily. "For myself I would ask it. For our child I would ask it. For your own self and for Scotland I would not ask it."

And so he must choose. Between wife and country. Between love and duty. He had not known anything in life could be so hard.

And yet it was no choice. He knew what he must do. But Rhona—would she forgive him?

And there was so little time to talk. To explain. Even now he saw some of the younger men, tough, valiant fighters as he had once thought he would become, leading up the women's horses.

He turned to his wife, but he did not speak. For as he opened his mouth, hers met his in a kiss. A kiss of infinite sweetness and depth. A kiss that would have to last for many months.

She clung to him, her head nestled against his chest. "I know, Jamie. I should not have said what I did. I would not love you so, were you not the most valiant man I know. And always you do what is right. Forgive my weakness. While we are apart, I will draw strength from knowledge of your strength."

He longed to sweep her off her feet and carry her to her horse. Instead he stood by and watched a sturdy infantryman toss her into the saddle.

Nigel Bruce shouted an order, and they were off. He had not even told her to take care. He had not wished her Godspeed.

And just as quickly, Bruce's army was on the move, for this was no place to stand for battle. The ground was too steep and rough, the glen too narrow to allow cavalry to maneuver. Even as the king rode, he questioned Campbell and la Hay as to the terrain between them and Lennox land. But none could tell him.

"Ah, ye must be heading west, unless ye've boats to cross the loch."

The gray-bearded Culdee priest had spoken hardly a word since yesterday's service. Jamie had forgotten that he was still there. If he had given it any thought, he would have supposed Father Dunchad had already turned east to his holy house on Inchaffray.

The king showed his skepticism. "We're a long way from your cashel, Father."

"Aye, but not far from Saint Fillan." He pointed to a tiny silver streak far to the west. "Yon is River Fillan. Just beyond is Saint Fillan's pool, where lunatics are dipped for healing. Beside that, his chapel—the hermitage where he died."

"Aye, a fine omen!" Bruce shouted. "We'll to Saint Fillan."

The king set guard parties ahead and behind his main body of nearly five hundred men, but as they knew MacDougall's forces were behind them, they were free to press forward with as great speed as they could.

In less than an hour they reached the tiny stone chapel, built in the Irish style of cleverly piled stones sloping upward and inward to form walls and roof.

Bruce reined in. He was still riding the fine black stallion Jamie had brought to him at Methven. "Douglas, Campbell," he called, "lead on, and look you carefully for a place we can stand. I'll not have these Highlanders run us into the sea. I'll just pause here to give thanks."

James Douglas started to pull aside as if he would go with his king to prayers, then turned to his orders. The army moved away with the clank of mail, creak of leather, and thud of horses' hooves.

Jamie and Father Dunchad circled the small pool, following the king. The three of them almost filled the tiny chapel. Bruce knelt at the bare stone altar.

It could not have been ten minutes, barely five, when wild, piercing shrieks penetrated the silent chapel. At first Jamie thought it hundreds of birds taking flight or wounded animals shrieking in pain. Then he knew. He had heard tales of wild Highlanders who ran shrilling into battle, clad only in a strip of plaid or less.

In a stumbling run he did his best to follow Bruce to the tethered horses, then at a headlong gallop toward the fray. Leaning close to Clarsach's neck to increase his speed, Jamie could not tell where the pictures in his head ended and the actual frenzied scene began.

But it was all the same. Hundreds of blazing-haired wild men clad in bright plaid, so that it looked as if the heather were on fire, were flinging themselves on the remnant of the Scottish army. Naked men, armed only with swords and knives against armored, horsed knights.

And yet the advantage was with the Argyll men. With the momentum of their frenzy, in far outweighing numbers they swept over the hills and into the narrow pass where the horses had no room to maneuver or charge. The army had set guards ahead and behind but not overhead.

Bruce charged into the mad throng, his sword flashing to right and left. The enemy was so thick he could not slash without hitting something. He drove forward into the steep-sided pass, walled with dark boulders, leaning forward, slashing from one side to the other and behind in a mad, spinning rhythm.

Suddenly Jamie saw—as if a giant red eagle swooped down—a red-haired savage, clad only in leather brogans, fling himself from atop a rock, straight at Bruce.

He landed with an impact that must have dislocated the king's shoulder. For a moment they swayed together in the saddle. The man was too close for the king to get the swing of his battle-ax at him.

Jamie grabbed the dirk from his belt and spurred forward.

The warrior clung to the massive brooch at Bruce's shoulder for balance and leaned backward to give more momentum to the plunge of his long-bladed *sgian dubh*.

Jamie lunged with his knife. He felt the blade strike bone, then lodge between shoulder blade and spine.

The attacker plummeted sideways, still gripping the king's brooch. Cloak and brooch came away with a tearing.

Then Jamie saw the streak of blood down the king's right arm where the man's dirk had scored deep, even through chain mail. And the left shoulder, torn from its socket, hung useless. The king could not fight and control his horse in such condition. And if the flow of blood continued unchecked, he would not be able long to sit.

Jamie pulled the king's sword from its sheath. It was of a far greater heft than any he had handled in his fighting days, but, as he had learned long ago under Wallace, he cut a path down the steep side of the trail away from the melee. If they could make it to the river and then to the other side, they might live to fight another day. Few Highland men had spilled so far that direction yet.

Bruce followed, the slashing hooves of his horse serving as weapons against those fighting on foot.

"A Bruce!"

"A Bruce!"

The cry sounded behind them. Thinking the enemy observed their escape and rallied to chase them, Jamie increased the desperation of his own slashing and thrusting. He made firm contact with very little, probably wounded few, and killed none, but he knocked awry many a sword thrust and caused many a lunging Highlander to draw back.

"A Bruce!"

"A Bruce!"

The cry rang nearer. Then he realized it was their own men, those who were left of them. He thought he recognized Douglas's voice. The cry that would normally be used to rally troops forward into battle was calling them away. "A Bruce!" —fleeing the enemy.

But it was that or stand and die. And little good their blood would be to Scotland in this remote place, caught in an inglorious ambush. If the time came to die for Scotland, they would sell their lives for higher price.

The removal of their targets from the field broke the impetus of the Highland charge. The object of their game fled, and the men turned to looting the fallen bodies that filled the narrow pass. The small band of survivors straggled toward a thicket offering shelter in a draw where the muddy burn curved to the west.

Jamie was more than glad to yield leadership of the group to Neil Campbell, who pulled ahead. Edward Bruce rode beside his slumping brother, steadying him in the saddle.

When they reached the shelter of the trees, Gilbert la Hay took charge to medicine the king. As a lad he had made friends of the brother herbalist who served the monastery where he learned his letters—and had also learned the skill that had proven useful in the aftermath of many a battle. With a swift maneuver that grated bone, followed by a cracking pop that set Jamie's teeth on edge, la Hay set the dislocated shoulder. He bound the king's arm to his side with strips torn from his own cloak, then turned to binding his cut with witch hazel and dock leaves.

"Aye, it's deep but none too jagged. Give it time. You'll wield a sword again."

Bruce shook his head. "Who would follow me? Two battles. Slaughters both. Surprised both times. Once, men might excuse. Not this."

One of the foot soldiers snorted. "Oh, men'll forgive you, my lord. Those that love Scotland. But Saint Fillan will have some explaining to do."

Jamie cringed. Expectation of the saint's blessing had been the king's lifeline. Now he would see himself doubly cursed, by pope and celtic saint alike.

"No!" Bruce struck the ground with his unbound arm. "I'll hear no such ingratitude. Do ye not see? Had I not stopped to pray, I would have been in the advance group—they who took the brunt of the ambush. For whatever purpose, God has saved my miserable head. Better though it would have been had He not bothered."

All through the night and the next day, for they lay hidden to gather food and let their wounds heal, more stragglers found their way to the sorry band. Among those was one of Campbell's best scouts, a man whose mother came from Argyll.

He shook his head firmly. "Nay. There's no chance of winning through to Lennox. MacDougall has been before ye. All the cotters along Loch Lomond have been warned—hide their boats or he'll burn them, he said. He'll no' have Robert Bruce crossing his loch. We must go farther west."

Bruce made no response.

Douglas surprised them all with his knowledge of the land so far from his own. "Loch Fyne. Could we make it there? Then take boats to the sea? There's no safety here."

Campbell and his man agreed on the principle, and the men fell to arguing among themselves as to the best place to take refuge. Several of the western islands were candidates. Some thought that, once free of land, they should set sail for the Orkneys or, better yet, Norway, where a sister of Bruce's was queen.

The king, who had appeared to be slumbering, surprised all by his firm decision. "Ulster."

Campbell turned and stared as if one of the trees had spoken.

But Jamie saw it at once. "Yes, that's fine. To the queen's home." Elizabeth's father, Richard de Burgh, earl of Ulster, had been a longtime friend and companion of Edward, so none would expect Bruce to flee to him. And yet Ulster was far away from those setting traps all around King Robert, and none in Ireland would be likely to betray the husband of Elizabeth de Burgh.

Robert Bruce smiled. "I've a farsighted sennachie."

Jamie ducked his head. He did not want his sovereign to see his own aversion to the plan he had put forth. The journey would be long and arduous, every mile offering dangers of ambush, inhospitable land, and rough seas. But that was little consideration. The problem was the direction. Every mile they gained toward safety for Robert Bruce would take him that much farther away from Rhona and the child growing inside her.

623

It was such a wonder to him, this of birth—the birth of a child to which he had given life. He wanted to be with Rhona every moment. To help her, guard her, and watch the child grow within her. He closed his eyes and imagined her gently swelling white belly. How he longed to cup it in his hands and hold their child. He knew little of such matters. How big would she be now?

Then he smiled and shook his head. It had been only a few days since they parted. Was that possible? It had seemed a lifetime. Pray it not be a lifetime until they were reunited.

68

The trip to the northeastern coast of Ireland was no less difficult than Jamie had imagined. In the month or more they spent skulking across the rugged countryside, lying hidden while some foraged for food, seeking caves to shelter from bad weather, and wandering lost when their guide's skill left him, their original band of fifty dwindled to less than twenty. Some died from wounds that refused to heal. Many simply melted away, unwilling to face the hardship of exile with their king.

They lay at Dunaverty, Bruce's own castle, on the southernmost tip of the Mull of Kintyre for the better part of two weeks, waiting for a fierce autumn storm to subside. The two deep-hulled galleys they had stolen at the top of Loch Fyne were leaking badly, both having been battered against a rocky stretch of coastland when they entered Kilbrannan Sound and were caught in a violent blow.

With the help of local people still loyal to Bruce, the men cut trees with battle-axes and repaired the cracked boards while others hunted and prepared strips of roast meat.

They set sail for Ireland on a golden late September morning, a morning made for walking with Rhona beneath trees just starting to turn yellow while being serenaded with bird song. June, July, August, September . . . Jamie counted on his fingers. By now she would be increasing. Jamie felt a warm flush of pride as he pictured her walking toward him in a blue gown, her belly gently rounded, her eyes shining.

"Jamie, man, row!"

He flushed at Douglas's words and leaned into the oar that had stilled in his hand. The rowing was easy, for a stiff wind billowed the sail, and they moved at a good clip almost directly westward.

Father Dunchad, in offering his parting blessing, had given a single word of advice. "Rathlin," he said, even as his hands were still warm on Bruce's head. "The blessed Columba once had cashel there. The peace of the Dove will rest on the true son of Scots."

The fact that Rathlin was the closest Irish point to Scotland, would offer securely hidden sanctuary to one unsure of his welcome in another country, and was less than ten miles from Richard de Burgh's castle of Dunluce—albeit across treacherous waters—made the small, stocking-shaped island seem an ideal haven.

It looked less than ideal, however, as the rowers approached its northwest corner. A sheer cliff of forbidding basalt towered three hundred feet over their heads. Innumerable seabirds, especially fat black and white guillemots, circled and dipped against the windswept blue sky.

Bruce, standing astern in the first galley, pointed southward, and his boat turned along the sole of the sock, sailing toward the toe that pointed to the mainland. Once around the toe they entered a blue bay. Its peaceful appearance was misleading, though, and Jamie soon realized the strength of the strong undertow on his oar. And here they had no wind to help them, so the sail was lowered and all leaned more heavily to their oars, pulling against the tide to take them back up the cliff-bound coastline.

Surely the entire coast couldn't be so inhospitable, Jamie reflected. If Columba had a cashel here, there must be some place to land. At last, just where the foot of the stocking turned westward up the leg, he spotted a small strip of sand.

They beached the boats as high as they could, every man pulling on heavy ropes to make their way across the beach to the shelter of standing boulders above. It would not do to have the galleys give away their presence nor for the boats to be battered or lost in a storm. Once the boats were securely lodged, they covered them as well as they might with what bracken the sparse vegetation offered.

Jamie shook his head. No doubt Columba had held hermitage here. The place was perfect for those ancient holy men who sought the most inhospitable situations possible. He hoped de Burgh would receive them. He couldn't imagine having to live long in this desolate place.

It was good the men had brought strips of cooked venison with them, for apart from a few birds' eggs one of the men was able to rob and the single fish la Hay managed to spear, their supper would be meager indeed.

At least the basalt cliffs offered shelter, riddled as they were with caves. Leaning on his crutches, Jamie watched Bruce scramble up the steep crags, sometimes leaping from one ledge to another like a mountain goat. The king explored several dark openings in the rock face. Then, choosing a slightly less severe route to the west, where some of the ground had sufficient slope and soil covering so that a thin layer of scrub vegetation could cling to it, he made his way down to report.

"Aye, we'll sleep dry. And warm if we can gather driftwood enough. Campbell, you and your Highlanders can take the eyrie highest up." He pointed to a ledge far up the hillside with a yawning cavity behind it. "Ye'll think you're at home in your own bedrooms."

Neil Campbell guffawed. "I doubt it, Your Grace. Our Highland halls offer certain amenities ye may be a mite short on in your lowlands."

The men leered and nudged one another. But none dared think too long on those left behind.

Bruce pointed to another cavern farther down and assigned la Hay to captain a contingent to the right flank, his brother Edward Bruce to the left.

"Douglas and Jamie, I'll have ye with me." He pointed to a spot almost straight above their heads. No opening showed, but there was a shadow behind a tall boulder.

The men turned to gather the few belongings they had been able to bring with them.

Bruce turned to Jamie. "It's nae so bad on up, man, but you'll have to let me help you over the rocks here."

Jamie set his jaw against the ignominy of being carried like a toddler.

"I'd not take kindly to losing the sennachie who saved me from battle twice. I've said naught, but it's a valor I won't soon forget." Bruce's words eased the disgrace.

The cave was deep and miraculously free from bird droppings. The men gathered moss and piled it on the floor to make sleeping pallets while Jamie grilled the fish and roasted the eggs in a fire built near the mouth of the cave but behind the sheltering boulder so that its light wouldn't give away their presence to any boats passing below.

In the coming days, which grew into weeks, the life of the fugitives settled into a routine that Jamie would have found none too unpleasant could Rhona have been with him. The sound of the surf washing the cliffs below and the calling seabirds above brought a much-needful soothing after the rigors of battle and flight. Once past the treacherous rock face—and he soon found a path he could maneuver if he took it slowly—the island offered unlimited scope for exploration of its beauties.

But King Robert Bruce did not find the situation soothing. The day after their arrival, he had appointed la Hay, Campbell, and three others, including Wat Foyle, who had been born in Ulster, to approach

Dunluce and scout out what could be learned of de Burgh's sentiments without giving away their own situation.

Before they could embark across the four-mile strip of water to the mainland, however, a fierce storm blew up that splashed waves so high against the rocks that Jamie all but feared they would flood the caves. The storm lasted a week.

Wat Foyle insisted on an absolutely clear day for their crossing. The channel was narrow and none too treacherous looking, "but not to be trusted," he insisted. "That's known as *Sloch-na-Marra*, the Valley of the Sea. Taken at flood, the race of the tide canna be pulled against. Brecain, son of Niall of the Nine Hostages, was lost here with a fleet of fifty curraghs."

And so they waited until Wat should declare the waters safe.

The turn of the calendar into October brought colder nights. The king paced like a caged animal. The men hunted when they could, although the storm drove what small game was available to take cover. Empty bellies increased the irritability of the men. At last the water smoothed, and the scouts set sail.

Their departure, however, served to increase rather than slacken the king's impatience. How were they faring? Would de Burgh uncover their secret and send men to trap them in their caves like rats in a hole? And Scotland. What was happening in the land they left behind? Was Pembroke still burning and slaying? Had Edward marched north yet? It seemed that every day they tarried, the English strength must increase, the Scots' decrease. And yet they waited.

Edward Bruce, younger and more hotheaded than his brother, was even worse. He not only fumed over his own frustrations, but he also stirred up unrest among the men already distressed, discontented, and embittered. They all had wives, bairns, homes, crops behind them on that distant shore they could just glimpse on a clear day. And yet seeing that dark outline against the horizon seemed to make home that much farther away.

It was when the mist settled over them like a blanket, holding them close with a sense of coziness, that Jamie felt nearest home. Then Bruce would sit on a heap of moss by the smoking fire and ask his sennachie to tell him tales of home. And Jamie, in the melodious voice he had learned to cultivate—not singing but speaking with great color and variety of tone—would recount the early days of the resistance and his own exploits with Wallace.

He would tell tales of valor he had collected from far back in their history: tales of Columba taking the faith of Christianity from these Irish shores to the land that wasn't yet called Scotland; tales of

Kenneth mac Alpin defeating the Danes and uniting the Scots and Picts; tales of those who had cared for the Stone of Scone from Jacob of the Old Testament down through Sir Kenneth Corvan of their own day.

Such tellings seemed to ease the king's heart, as they did Jamie's. And they were drawn together by the unspoken worry they shared. Had Nigel and Seton won through to the Countess of Mar? Were Elizabeth, Rhona, and the others safe in Kildrummy Castle? Or had Edward's men . . . That thought was too terrible to think.

November brought frosts, turning the thin grass covering the island brown and brittle.

"I tell you, la Hay's been taken," Edward thundered at his brother. "De Burgh will figure it all out soon enough and send a force against us. He's King Edward's closest companion. He'll no' support you, Robert, even if you are his daughter's husband."

"*I* was once King Edward's closest companion, little brother. Sit yourself before you crack your thick skull on the roof of this cave."

Robert's words did nothing to soothe Edward. "Let me go see. Just me. One man. I can blend in among the fishermen and villagers well enough."

"No! If things have gone wrong, the presence of a Bruce will only make matters worse."

The same argument had been fought every day for a week. Edward stamped from the cave.

Robert dropped his head in his hands. "Why did I ever come here? I could have gone north to Norway. I could have stayed in Scotland and fought. I could have . . ."

Jamie shook his head. Such would have made poor choices, but he would not argue.

Then he heard a shout from the rocks below. Before he could get to the mouth of the cave to look, Campbell, la Hay, and Foyle came in—returned from Ireland. One glance at their faces told Jamie that the news was not good.

"It took us long and long to win the confidence of the village folk. We picked up bits in the alehouses first, then talked to castle servants." Campbell shook his head.

"De Burgh is still Edward's man. Nor is he likely to forgive Bruce for renouncing his allegiance to Edward. De Burgh thinks your entering into Edward's peace five years ago was a ruse to get his daughter. So claiming him father-in-law would only increase his ire," la Hay added.

"Especially *now*," Wat Foyle blurted out.

Jamie could see by the warning looks the captains shot him that there was more news. Bad news.

Apparently Bruce saw it too. *"Now?* Now what? Tell me!"

Campbell hesitated.

Bruce advanced on him threateningly.

"Well, sire, it might not be true. You know how rumors—"

"Tell me!" Bruce looked as if he would choke the information out of his men if necessary.

And so the terrible story came tumbling out. Edward's men were following a deliberate policy calculated to terrorize the Scots into submission. Disaster piled on top of disaster: Kildrummy Castle fallen. The women taken in custody—the queen, Lady Margery, the Countess of Buchan, Bruce's sisters Lady Mary and Lady Christian.

Jamie clenched his teeth to keep from crying out. If the other ladies were taken, then Rhona . . .

Still the calamity mounted. Bruce's men—his brother-in-law Seton and his brother Nigel arrested. Marched to Berwick in chains. And executed.

Bruce's face took on a look of cadaverous horror as the details mounted, yet he would hear them: Executions such as the brutality inflicted on Wallace. Hanged. Cut down still living. Organs ripped from their bodies and burned before their eyes . . .

At last Bruce had enough. "Out!" he thundered. "All of you. Leave me."

Jamie stumbled to his feet with the others. He had taken two steps toward the mouth of the cave when he felt a hand on his shoulder. "Not you, man. You stay. Your wife was with them."

Jamie stayed with his king as he had sworn to do. He had sworn the oath that had separated him from Rhona. But for that allegiance, they might be safe at Dunning Innes now.

Jamie stayed, but he did not turn.

Behind him Robert Bruce paced. "Nigel. The best of my brothers. Of all four of them the liveliest, the quickest wit, the bravest heart. And Seton. He bore me from the field at Methven. Elizabeth . . . Margery . . ." He groaned and fell silent.

Jamie had been staring out at the harbor for some time before he realized the dark spot he had vaguely thought a chunk of driftwood was coming closer. And it was no driftwood, but a curragh. "Sire, I fear your men were followed."

Bruce groaned again, then swore and reached for his sword. "De Burgh. He'll not take me cheap."

The solitary figure that the guard led to the king's cave many minutes later, however, was no Irish earl. Rather, he was an ancient,

630

stooped man with skin as wrinkled as a prune, his monk's robe a motley assortment of patches. His thin gray hair was tonsured in the archaic half-moon fashion of the Columban church, which left the head bare above the ears.

"I am Brother Comhgall. I keep Saint Columba's desart at the western end of Ranklin. Last night Saint Fillan came to me as I slept."

The slightest spark returned to Robert Bruce's haunted eyes. "Saint Fillan, you say? Aye . . ."

King and hermit talked. Jamie tried to follow the conversation, for he wanted to be of help to his king. But his own anxiety overcame everything else. No matter how important his loyalty to king and country, he wanted more to be with Rhona. He must find out where she was. How she was. *If . . . if only she's still alive. Oh, God . . .* The anguish was so great he doubled over.

He stayed thus for several moments in a fog of darkness and pain. Then it began gradually to clear, and Jamie realized that if any hope remained for any of them it centered, in earthly terms, in the person of Robert Bruce. The king must be fortified to action. He must have a clear vision of what was required of him.

As the king was now—defeated, in hiding, surrounded by bitter men, incapable of action—there was no hope.

If only this Brother Comhgall could do something—say something. If not . . .

Before he focused on the monk's words, Jamie looked at King Robert. He appeared to be listening intently, yet he was not looking at Comhgall. Jamie followed the king's gaze. He was watching a spider that hung from a long, silken filament almost to the floor of the cave. Its web shimmered on the rocks far overhead. The spider was making a slow ascent up the thread.

Then Jamie turned his attention to the monk. He was not merely speaking but reading from a large volume he had apparently brought with him in the leather satchel now lying open on the cave floor.

"And David left Gath and escaped to the cave of Adullam. He was joined there by all those who were in difficulties or in debt, or who were embittered, and he became their leader." Comhgall looked up from his reading. "The prophet had told David, 'You shall possess the land.' David was possessing a cave."

Bruce made no comment.

Comhgall returned to his reading. "But the prophet Gad said to David, 'Do not remain in the refuge. Leave, and go to the land of Judah.'"

A slight nod of his head showed that the king was listening to the Culdee. But his eyes never left the spider. The tiny creature had climbed several feet up the long way he must travel to his home, but now he fell backward, plummeting lower than before.

"And then Saul called all the people to war." Comhgall's voice was soft, but it echoed insistently against the rocks. "And Saul's war host gathered to besiege David and his men . . ."

The spider was almost a third of the way up his thread. Then his strength gave way. With flailing legs he fell again.

"But Saul's son, Jonathan, came to David and said, 'Have no fear. You shall be king of Israel.' David took refuge in the desert near Engedi. And Saul took three thousand picked men from all Israel and went out in search of David and his men in the direction of the wild goat crags . . ."

Again Jamie's attention wandered to the spider. How many attempts was this now? Three? Five? More? He had lost count. But the slow, determined ascent continued.

And equally determinedly, Brother Comhgall continued. "From dawn to sundown David attacked them. And David recovered everything that had been taken, and rescued his wives . . ."

Only a foot or less from the top now. The spider had almost made it to his gossamer home. The whole scene blended in Jamie's mind: David's struggles against Saul, Bruce's struggles against Edward, the spider's struggles against arduous difficulties. He began to see the spider's success as a symbol of Bruce's success. And the spider was almost triumphant. From repeated defeat, he had tried again and again, and now he was almost there.

A gust of cold wet sea wind blew into the cave, sending smoke from the fire into Jamie's eyes. When his vision cleared he saw that the blast had also blown the spider down once again. If this was to be taken as an omen, it was none too good a one.

But the monk paid no mind to omens. "And the Lord said to David, 'It was I who made you commander of My people. I have been with you wherever you went. I will make you famous like the great ones of the earth. I will give you rest from your enemies. I will raise up your heir after you. I will make his kingdom firm. If he does wrong I will correct him, but I will not withdraw My favor from him. Your house and your kingdom shall endure forever before Me. Your throne shall stand firm forever.'"

With each line of the reading, the spider had inched upward. Now it was barely a handspan from its goal. Jamie held his breath. The spider hung there, tantalizingly close to the safety of its web.

Now the movement of air was gentle, just making the thread turn slowly, catching a pale glimmer of light in the dim corner.

Brother Comhgall's voice fell silent, and he, too, joined the vigil.

The spider remained motionless for the space of three more heartbeats, then, quicker than the eye could follow, it leaped to the very center of its web.

Jamie had to restrain himself to keep from slapping the floor in triumph. What a fine sennachie tale could be woven from the exploits of that tiny creature, whom the eyes of the king had never left.

Bruce stood. It seemed to Jamie he was several inches taller than before, his eyes brighter, his voice firmer. "We will go to Scotland."

Brother Comhgall raised his hand in a blessing. "Faithful is He who has called you who also will perform it." The monk drifted out of the cave like the smoke from the fire.

King Robert the Bruce strode forward and called his men.

69

"No, they did not harm me. I was no one—not worth Edward's notice. But the others, Jamie . . . in cages like animals . . ." Rhona shuddered in his arms. This beautiful, delicate creature who was all the world to him had seen horrors men hardened to battle had not dreamed of.

He placed his hand on her belly as he had so longed to do for all the past months. "And perhaps even Edward would not harm a woman with child."

"Perhaps, but Jamie—" she drew a wavering breath, then held it to steady herself "—Jamie, I must tell you about the others. You must know so you can tell their tale. It's important, Jamie. It will give meaning to what they suffered . . . are still suffering. And only God knows for how much longer they must yet suffer. It cannot be for nothing—it must have meaning."

Jamie nodded, his cheek against her hair. "Aye. The telling can lend significance—make the meaning last."

He did not want her dwelling on such things so near her time. But he also knew that the telling would help her get the horrors out where she could see them. Things that could be seen and spoken of could be put behind. Rhona had talked much of Marion in their early times together. And they still talked of Wallace, the two of them together and Jamie in his tales. But he had not talked of Aline. Perhaps someday he would.

For the moment, however, it was the darkness inside Rhona that mattered, not his own. "Aye, tell me. The queen . . ."

Three weeks ago a lashing winter tide had tossed Robert Bruce and his men up on the Galloway shore. The returning king spent but little time in thanksgiving to be again in Scotland. He had landed in his own lordship of Carrick, but it was held firm in Edward's grip. All the strong castles housed English garrisons, and although the common people—Bruce's own—were loyal to the lord of Carrick, they were afraid for their homes and lives.

Bruce despatched a party to cross to the isle of Arran to forage for supplies, and their band again sought rough shelter. Robert Bruce was a fugitive in his own lands.

That same night he called Jamie to him. The king looked his sennachie up and down, then nodded. "A fine man you've grown. Sturdy in spite of all. And best of all, stout of heart. Such a man as I've sore need of. But I'll not keep you by me here."

Much as Jamie rejoiced at the king's words, still his sense of duty and loyalty protested. He shook his head. "Sire . . ."

But Robert Bruce held up a hand. "No. I've no doubt of your loyalty. Be now my leal man. Get you to your Rhona, if, God grant, she be free, as la Hay supposes. And continue to collect Scotland's stories—the stories of the victories we will win over Edward. When our work is done, come to me at Stirling, and we will rejoice in your brave tales."

Waiting through the night to begin his journey had been one of the hardest things of Jamie's life. He would have thrown himself on a garron from the nearest paddock and ridden north through the dark if he had possessed any knowledge of the lay of the land. As it was, he contained his impatience until the next day, when Bruce was able to secure him a mount. And Jamie had wasted not a moment in choosing his direction, for he had thought it all out long ago. If Rhona were free, he knew where she would go. If she were not free, he knew where he would find friends to help find her.

It took him the better part of four days, riding through a light snowstorm, sleeping in barns, and trading tales for food and ale—for a sennachie could find welcome at any hearth—all reaching toward his goal of Cambuskenneth.

And Rhona had been there waiting for him.

It was long before they could settle to sensible talk. But now, as much out of concern for his king as for the lady herself, Jamie would hear the story of the queen and her ladies.

Rhona shook her head. "No, they didn't torture Elizabeth—beyond the torture of making her watch others suffer, which I often think is the harder part." She ran her hand over Jamie's arm holding her. "When the castle fell—the report was that traitors inside burned the stores and opened the gates to the Englishry. But however that was, when Kildrummy fell, Seton and Lord Nigel led us to escape through the postern gate at night. We made clean away. They would take us to Norway, although I was loath to leave Scotland, no matter how safe the refuge."

She turned in his arms and ran a gentle finger down his cheek. "I thought always of you. You were never from my thoughts and prayers for a moment. Always you sustained me. And the farther north we went away from you, the more fiercely I clung. Oh, Jamie . . ." She bit her lip and grasped him. "Oh, Jamie, hold me. Always. Do not let go again."

He held her long, rocking gently and murmuring softly. And inside he prayed that he would not have to leave her again.

At last she relaxed to his soothing and continued her story. "We traveled for days and days. Weeks. Mid-October, it must have been— a driving rainstorm that lasted for days—we took refuge at Saint Duthlac's shrine. There it was Edward's men took us. Then we were marched south again."

"Oh, Rhona—" His arms came tight around her again.

"No. It was all right, Jamie. Truly it was. Except for my fear I'd never see you again. The weather turned fine, and our guards were not cruel. We had food aplenty and beds at night."

"But you—" His hand slid over her tight-stretched abdomen. It rested there until he pulled back in alarm. "Did I hurt you?"

She laughed. "Nay. It's the babe. He's but greeting his father."

"He? Do you think—"

"I'm certain. Robert Wallace." Then she ducked her head shyly. "That is, if you don't mind waiting to name the second one after you."

Jamie was so filled with wonder at it all that it was several moments before he could speak. He blinked fiercely. "Aye. Robert Wallace. After Scotland's two greatest men."

She nodded. "I call him Rabbie when I talk to him." She gave a shy smile. "I've told him all about his father."

Jamie grimaced. He'd never thought before—he hoped his son wouldn't be too disappointed in him. Embarrassed before the other lads.

But Rhona hastened on. "Ah, the riding was fine. Fresh air, good exercise. As I said, they were not unkind. Then. It was not until we reached Berwick. It was the Countess Isabel. Edward would not forgive her for crowning Bruce. That made a far worse sin than Elizabeth had in marrying him. Isabel and the Lady Mary—whose only crime was in being sister to Robert Bruce . . ."

Again she caught her breath for courage to go on. "Jamie, the English—I'm sure it was at Edward's express orders—made cages for them. Cages of iron and wood like for a wild animal. In such as this these gentle ladies were hung from the walls of Berwick Castle like beasts. They had contact only with the Englishwomen who brought them food and took them to the privy. And all who came by stared and mocked. Small boys threw mud balls and worse at them. And the rough language hurled at them . . ." She covered her ears and shook her head. "They may still so hang . . . maybe for years . . ."

Again Jamie held her and crooned. When this was over he would tell her a fine tale filled with love and beauty, one of rainbows and gossamer wings. He would replace the evil pictures in her mind with ones of his own making, crafted of his love for her. But first she must get the painful ones out.

"The Lady Margery? And the Countess of Mar?" Jamie knew what had happened to their stalwart Scots escort. He hoped Rhona didn't yet know the awful fate of Margery's favorite uncle and Christian's husband. It was a telling that could await another day.

"They made a cage for Margery too."

"What!" Of all the atrocities this seemed the worst. Margery was such a delicate child, much as Rhona must have been when she was but twelve years old. And yet with an even more ethereal quality. Less lively than Rhona, who could be a delightful tomboy at times. To put that angelic creature in a cage . . .

"They made it for her. But I do not think they ever caged her. She was sent to a nunnery somewhere in Yorkshire, I think."

Jamie breathed a prayer of relief. A nunnery Margery could endure. Perhaps even like, in time. If she could know that the father she adored was safe.

"And the Lady Christian—to a nunnery as well. Further south, I believe."

It was as well. Twice a widow, the countess could make a new life in religion if she chose. "But the queen?"

Rhona shook her head. "Confined. Somewhere in England. That's all I know."

"Yes." Jamie's tone was bitter. "Edward will not hesitate to use so powerful a tool against Bruce. His love for the fair Elizabeth is perhaps his one weak point."

Rhona looked at him under long lashes. "As it should be, no?"

He kissed the upturned tip of her nose. "As it should be, aye."

"But you will tell it, will you not, Jamie? Tell it and write it down that it'll never be forgotten. Make it part of the story of Scotland—how these women stood strong. They could have cried mercy to Edward. But they would not. Tell it, Jamie."

"Aye, I will."

He agreed wholeheartedly. But there was some delay in the doing, for that night wee Rabbie Wallace MacInnes made his way into the world.

Rhona wakened Jamie just after midnight, and he set off in the dark, almost too distracted to think to take a lantern, to fetch the goodwife from the village. Had Simon not come to the guest house to keep him company after Lauds, Jamie would probably have gone crazy listening to the heavy panting and moans from the next room.

He gripped Simon's arm. "Will she be all right? She canna be dying! Pray, Simon. I canna lose her now."

Simon smiled, then ducked his head in a brief prayer. "She'll be all right, man. Have you never helped at the birthing of a lamb? You know it's a bit of a struggle. But it's the way of things."

Jamie knew. But he could not relax. There had been a few birthings on the farm he did not want to think on—difficult ones where something went wrong.

Five hours later, just as the bell was ringing for Prime, a lusty squall sent him hurtling into the next room. The auld wife was possessive about cleaning and wrapping the bairn. She allowed the father only the briefest peek at his son.

Jamie turned to the bed. Rhona lay beneath the white sheet, paler than the muslin, her dark hair wet with sweat, streaking back from her face, dark circles under her eyes from lack of sleep. She was the most beautiful thing Jamie had ever seen in his life.

He sat on the edge of the bed and kissed her hand and wrist, afraid to go farther, so great was his sense of awe in the presence of this woman who had given birth to new life.

She smiled up at him. "Did you see him, Jamie? Is he no' beautiful?"

"Yes. But not as beautiful as his mother." He shook his head, afraid he might cry for the sweet pain of looking at her.

Then the midwife crossed the room with a tiny swaddled bundle in her arms.

Jamie felt himself go stiff and cold all over. What would he do? What if he dropped the bundle? What if the wee bairn did not like to be held by him?

The woman loomed over him, scowling severely.

He held out his arms as if they were wooden sticks. She placed the warm, sweet thing in them. His heart rose to his throat as if it would choke him. His arms enfolded his son.

Wee Rabbie opened one eye a slit, the corners of his mouth curled in a reflex smile, and he relaxed into sleep.

Feeling he held the whole world, Jamie leaned forward so that Rhona could hold them both.

It was a brave beginning, but there was much to be done if this wee lad was to grow up in a nation of freedom and peace. And now all the things Wallace and Bruce had fought for, all that he would record and teach in his tales, took on a magnified importance he had not thought possible. For always he had believed in peace and freedom and justice. Always he had worked for those with his whole heart. But now the stakes were higher. He had a personal goal beyond a vague image of the future of Scotland, beyond his own life, even his life with Rhona. Now he was working for Rabbie's future.

When Rhona could travel, they returned to Dunning Innes. Now, as Jamie recorded the events of the nation, it was Rabbie he imagined reading them one day. Perhaps even, in a day far more distant, Rabbie to his son. It was as if Rabbie were sitting on his shoulder, listening to all the tales in Jamie's head as he wrote them on the parchment leaves.

And at night he would sit by the hearth, holding the babe and telling him the most stirring stories he knew. And it seemed that his son was none so disappointed in him. At least not yet.

70

And the tales he now had to tell were none so disappointing either.

At first the news had been bleak enough, to be sure. Bruce had settled on the isle of Arran to plan his initial landing in his ancestral Carrick—the land of his Celtic forebears on his mother's side from as far back as any could recall. Jamie, who knew Bruce well, pictured him waiting in caged impatience, each night looking back across the water for the flaring of the beacon that would tell him all was in readiness. Then he would cross the water with his band of men and take Tunberry Castle, where he had been born. A fitting signal, indeed, that Bruce had returned.

But matters had gone awry. Jamie could not learn the exact truth of it, but the beacon had been set afire by mistake. No, the next messenger said, a traitor had lit it on purpose. Nay, another declared, it was but a farmer's byre set ablaze by a careless boy bedding the animals—or more likely one of the dairymaids.

Whatever the truth, the attempt was a failure. And worse followed. The first flush of exultation that the king's brothers Alexander and Thomas Bruce had joined the seasoned captains Robert Boyd and James Douglas for a campaign to take Galloway changed quickly to dismay. On the heels of the first message came the word that Alexander and Thomas had both been wounded, captured, and sent to Edward. And Edward hanged and beheaded them.

Jamie mourned with Robert, his friend and king. Thomas Bruce he had known little; but what he had seen of Thomas, he had been courteous and valiant. Alexander he knew only by reputation. But what a reputation: the best scholar of his day at Cambridge. They were now both gone to join the lighthearted Nigel. Robert Bruce had only one brother left to him: the courageous but hotheaded Edward.

Perhaps it was that final disaster that brought home to Robert Bruce the truth that he must have known but failed to acknowledge all along: he could not win a pitched battle against Edward Plantagenet. William Wallace had known it. That wily freedom fighter had fought by night, by ambush, by secret. He had marched swiftly with small bands, struck fiercely, then melted back into the woods or hills. And always he had made the land fight for him. His only defeat had been at Falkirk, when he was forced to abandon such tactics.

Now Bruce, trained in the chivalric code by the First Prince of Christendom, Edward of England himself, must fight from unknightly ambush if he and his cause were to survive. A nation fighting for its very existence could not afford the luxury of adhering to a polished code of honor. Bruce would take and keep the initiative. He would strike from ambush. He would dismantle, rather than garrison, the castles he took, as he had not men enough to hold them. And he would not have the English refortifying them at his back.

And yet for all this careful planning, it seemed to Jamie, when he received word on a gentle April day, that Bruce's first victory was more a result of his enemy attempting such tactics against him.

Bruce had been surprised by a major force of English horse coming up the narrow passage of Glen Trool in search of him. He had little choice but to send his Highlanders into the hills to wait in ambush and then hurl a hailstorm of boulders down upon the thousand armored knights who would have crushed the Scots force.

And the ink was barely dry on Jamie's page but that even better news followed, this brought post haste by a most welcome messenger. For always, no matter what stance others took, the Scottish church was strong for Bruce and Scottish independence. Father Andrew at Cambuskenneth was no exception and so sent Brother Simon to Dunning Innes with the fresh-arrived word.

"Simon! Well come." Jamie grabbed his crutches and swung across his small writing room to greet his friend. "I can see by your face that the tidings are good." He held up a hand. "No, do not tell me yet. Come to the house that Rhona might have the first hearing with me. And you some refreshment, my friend."

Simon was quickly ensconced by the hearth with a plate of fresh oatcakes and a mug of foamy milk. Rhona settled in her favorite corner to nurse four-month-old Rabbie. But Jamie was too excited for the hearing to take refreshment. He barely managed to do his duty as host and allow their visitor his first mouthful before he was asking, "Bruce. He is well? The war is fortunate?"

Simon lowered his mug and wiped a fringe of foam from his upper lip with the back of his hand. "Aye. At Loundon Hill, some fifteen miles below Glasgow. An unqualified triumph. Methven is avenged. Pembroke had gathered a great host. Bruce set upon him while he was yet sleeping."

Jamie slapped the table. "Ah, Methven avenged indeed. What works for one may work for another."

Simon nodded. "Bruce forced the Englishry to fight on a narrow front, so that their great superiority in cavalry and numbers were no advantage."

"Aye. Like Wallace." Jamie could not imagine more satisfying news.

"Bruce and his men set upon the van so fiercely that Pembroke's rear fell back in panic. There was little fighting for the Scots. Many struck no blows at all. The English trampled themselves in retreat. They say Pembroke has flown to Bothwell."

"At last. Now Bruce has shown what he can do. Now the Scots will rally to his banner. The red lion rampant will roar mightily."

"It appears truly that God is with King Robert. Much remains to be done. The war will be bloody and long yet. But already he has destroyed Edward's power both among the English and the Scots. Now we will see a rallying to the banner."

It was the next day, after an evening of good fellowship with Simon, when the monk was on his way south again and Jamie once more immured in his scriptorium, as Brother Simon called it, that Jamie's reaction to the news set in. He could not have been more surprised when the elation he felt at such good news for his country, his king, and his former companions in arms should turn to feelings of isolation and bitterness.

While all the country was rallying to Bruce, Jamie was exiled. He who had taken word first to Wallace. He who had for so long worked for and always dreamed of triumphing with the Scots army, sat on a stool in a shed before a flickering candle, ink staining his fingers, his crutches leaning in the corner.

He thrust the quill aside, sending splatters of ink over paper and desk. He had taken it kindly when Bruce sent him to Rhona. But had it been no kindness—rather a mere getting him out of the way, like sending women and children to sanctuary?

Old emotions that he had thought long dead and buried boiled to the surface. Old pictures he thought erased danced before his eyes, blocking out all else.

The happy ones came first. He saw a twelve-year-old Agnes running across a bright field to him, her yellow hair streaking behind her. He caught her and spun her around at arm's length over his head as he had done since she was an infant.

He bit his lip. Aye, he could do such things then. Before the Englishry crippled him. And before they raped and murdered his gay-hearted sister.

642

And Aline, the gravely serious housewife even at fifteen, admonishing them to clean the mud from their feet before they trod her freshly rushed floor . . . Of Aline he had not even a picture of horror to tell him what had become of her.

But his parents . . . he slammed a fist against the table, making the ink pot bounce.

Two months later Jamie had a new story to write, for little over a year after Robert the Bruce was crowned king of Scots, sitting on Moot Hill and whatever secrets it might hold, Edward of Caernarvon was crowned king of England at Westminster, sitting on the stone his father had carried there from Scone.

For Edward Plantagenet was dead. He had died massing his troops for another assault on Scotland and cursing Scotland with his last breath. The Hammer of the Scots would strike no more.

Edward died but not his hate. His hatred remained. And his army.

Edward Plantagenet's determined hatred filled his last orders to his son to boil his body and bury the flesh where he might, but his bones were to be carried before the English army when it marched in ravaging triumph into Scotland.

Such were Edward's orders. But Edward II directed that his father's body be buried decently in Westminster. And Scotland waited. For soon this new Edward would march northward with his father's army, 200,000 strong. First, however, Edward must consolidate his own English lords.

So Robert the Bruce was granted a breathing space—a space sorely needed, for he had his own lords to look to. Bruce had nothing less than civil war on his hands. He must unify his nobles before he faced Edward again.

And the news that reached Dunning Innes was not good. Bruce was fallen ill. Fever. Itching. Weakness. The stories that reached Jamie differed in their description of the symptoms but not in the crucial fact. Bruce was on his bed in Inverurie on the banks of the River Don. He was in the loyal earldom of Mar, supported by the burghers of Aberdeen but tightly circled by rebel lords who bore no love for a Bruce kingship. Buchan was on his right, Ross on his left, and Argyll below.

Such was not the tale Jamie wished to record. But his was not a tale made up for children's delight, as he would tell wee Rabbie by the fire. His charge was to tell the truth. And so he must. But before the end of the year—indeed, on the very day Rabbie took his first toddling step to his father—news arrived that the tide had turned.

As always, the faithful ones—Lennox, Neil Campbell, James Douglas, Gilbert la Hay, and Robert Boyd—captained patriot troops. And now a new strength was added, for the MacDonalds of Islay came with their Islemen, and that notable lady Christia of the Isles, chieftainess of her branch of the Clan Donald, joined Bruce. And the best news of all, Bruce had regained his health and was once more leading the field.

In the year 1307 Christmas celebrations could be the more joyous for true Scots as word spread that, on Christmas Eve, Bruce had won the battle of Inverurie against the rebel lords.

Edward Bruce carried notable success with his ever-vigorous harrying of the Comyns, gaining great spoils as he plundered this richest, proudest house in all Scotland. James Douglas, in his own lands south of Clyde-Forth, recovered Douglasdale, Annandale, and the Selkirk forest for Bruce. By autumn of the following year that great Celtic lord William, earl of Ross, confessed his trespasses against the Scots crown, made his peace with Bruce, and was graciously pardoned by the king. He who had betrayed Robert's queen, daughter, and sisters to Edward's brutality was taken back in peace— a telling sign of how truly Robert Bruce desired unity.

And Jamie dutifully recorded all in as careful detail and as fine a style as he could. But he felt little of the glee he had hoped for. It was good that his king was winning such. He would not have it otherwise. But triumph over rebel Scots did nothing to assuage his own pain.

The English were the enemy. Triumph over and revenge upon the English were all that mattered. Revenge for his mother, father, and Agnes dead; for Aline dead or alive. Revenge for Wallace's brutal murder. Revenge for his own crippling.

But it seemed that Jamie in his isolation and anger was the only one who felt so. An almost festive air rested over Scotland that spring. Now it was time for Robert Bruce to put to rest the complaints of those who held out longest against him—that he was no true king, could not have been rightfully crowned, albeit by a Mac-Duff at Scone, and anointed by a mitred abbot, because no parliament had confirmed him king. A call went out to the Community of the Realm: King Robert Bruce would hold parliament at St. Andrews. And Jamie, in his exile, was sent notice to attend.

When the messenger had spurred on northward toward Scone, Jamie turned to Rhona with the news.

She sat by her wheel before the door of the cottage, where the afternoon sun warmed her thick dark hair, spinning a fine thread from the newly sheared Dunning Innes sheep. At his approach she looked up, her brown eyes still beautiful but perhaps lacking the sparkle they once held for him. Had the English robbed him of this too, in robbing him of his vigor?

"Robert holds parliament at Saint Andrews. I am bidden to attend."

"Aye. You must go."

Her calm matter-of-factness irritated him. Would she be glad to see the back of him? Did his hobbling irritate her? "You bid me go, then? Even so near your time?" He looked at her full belly. They had longed so for another child, planned so excitedly for this. A playmate for Rabbie. A James to be called after his father. Or a daughter for Rhona, perhaps. And yet the coming had held little of the delight they had shared over Robert Wallace's coming, even with the long separation they had had to endure then. What was the matter?

"I shall go and leave you then? And good riddance is it?" He flinched at his own irritation.

Rhona rose stiffly, one hand on her back, the other held out to him. "Jamie, don't. You know I could never feel that. But it seems that of late there is a barrier between us." She groped as at a locked door. "Jamie, what is it? I can't reach you."

His heart twisted at the sight of how he had hurt her. He couldn't understand why he did such things. He moved forward and started to reach out to her.

At that moment, two-year-old Rabbie waddled between them on his short fat legs, chasing a clucking red hen.

Jamie was off balance, reaching for Rhona, and the tangling with child and chicken sent him reeling against the rough wall. "Robert Wallace, watch what you do, boy! You're old enough to have some sense!"

It was not so much the words that he instantly regretted; it was the harsh tone in which he shouted at his son.

The child turned hurt, bewildered eyes on him, brimming with tears.

"Aye." His voice to Rhona, standing frozen, was as harsh as his words to Rabbie. He did not want it so. With all his heart he wanted to reach out and gather them both into his arms. Yet he could not. The pain inside was too great. To hold these loved ones to him would be to rub salt on the old, old wounds. "Aye. I will go."

He banged the door open with his crutch and entered to gather his pack.

71

"I confess my errors and trespasses. I submit me to the royal dignity of King Robert of Scotland and promise forthwith to serve my liege lord well and faithfully."

A murmur that rose to almost a roar filled St. Andrews Cathedral as the earl of Ross, still clasping King Robert's hand, rose stiffly to his feet. Of all the fealty swearing that was to precede the opening of parliament, this, the public restatement of what had occurred in the Highlands a few months earlier by the Bruce's staunchest, most powerful foe—save Edward—was most important.

The list was long, and none of the homage payers unimportant: Alexander Comyn, sheriff of Inverness; Sir Alexander MacDougall of Argyll; Sir John Stewart of Mentieth—the man who had handed over Wallace to King Edward . . .

From his seat in the left flanking aisle, Jamie had a good view of the eastern limb of the great cathedral where the king sat on a throne before the high altar. On one side of him was the aged, stooped James, hereditary high steward; on the other side, Bernard de Linton, Robert's newly appointed chancellor and abbot of Arbroath.

Although the cathedral had been somewhat damaged by the English invaders, as an ecclesiastical town St. Andrews had escaped much of the ravaging that others had suffered in recent years. Now the damaged parts were overhung by brilliant banners, and the fine clothing of the nobles and high churchmen filled the long nave with rich color. And none was more striking than King Robert himself in his cloth-of-gold tabard with rampant red lion set with rubies, which he had not worn since his crowning at Scone, and with a purple velvet cape trimmed in fur around his shoulders. He wore on his brow, also for the first time since Scone, the plain gold circlet topped with strawberry leaves. The symbolic regalia—sword, scepter, and spurs, substituting for the Honours, which Edward still held in London—lay on a table to his left.

As at the coronation three years earlier, no amount of possible preparation had been spared. In his youth Robert Bruce had been a

646

man greatly fond of finery and display. Indeed, that had been one of the things the Scots had most criticized him for. But recent years of war, living the life of a fugitive and ambush fighter, had allowed for none such kingly accoutrements. Robert Bruce, however, fully understood the importance of royal pageantry. In a land of such divided loyalties as Scotland, he would use every tool at his disposal to bring his people together.

So Jamie noted each detail with care.

And there was no worry that this time his observation might be interrupted with a call to service, as it had been at Scone. Today Lord Lyon, king of arms, robed in as brilliant red and gold as the monarch, performed his duty of high sennachie of Scotland in declaring the parliament and council of the Community of the Realm duly constituted and in session.

His announcement was followed by a blast of fanfare and shouts, up and down the nave and from the flanking aisles.

"God save the king!"

"God save the king!"

"God save King Robert!"

At last the king rose and held up his hands for silence.

All resumed their seats but did not quiet until Robert began to speak.

And from his first words he made his goal plain. "My lords and ladies, my people—my united people of Scotland. I greet you and in God's grace congratulate you on the unity we have achieved. For that is our greatest achievement, our greatest need, our greatest hope. That is what we have worked for these long war-torn years—to forge ourselves into a united nation as we have not been since the days of my forebear King Alexander III twenty-three years ago.

"And even so, it is a new concept in loyalty I put before you— loyalty to the nation rather than to the person of a king. I ask you to think long on this idea. You will see as I do that it is necessary, if our so-hard-won freedom is to be lasting. Our allegiance must be to the nation first and then to him who leads that nation. For nations will far outlive our poor years on earth, and we would build a Scotland to last for all time.

"You have witnessed the fealty swearing of these our newly leal subjects to our royal dignity. Let their loyalty and all of yours be to the king of Scots but more so to the nation of Scots. Those who were formerly . . . ah . . . misguided have now joined us to face our common enemy. For we are Scotsmen all, and as such have but one enemy —he who would take our freedom from us!"

It was fortunate that Robert paused here, or his loyal subjects might have been guilty of the discourtesy of interrupting their sovereign, for the cheers that rose would not easily be stifled.

"We have our differences, but they are none so great we cannot settle them peaceably for the greater good. They are none so great that we cannot fight Edward of England together!"

Again he paused for the shouting.

Jamie, shouting with the rest, smiled. Robert Bruce understood the yoking power of exulting together. And that was much of what this parliament was about—exhibiting, declaring, celebrating his kingship. For Bruce would reunite what his ancestor Kenneth mac Alpin united in the first place 450 years before.

In those two days of parliamentary session, all was focused on establishing the kingship of Robert the Bruce and the cementing of Scots unity at home and abroad. The fealty swearing and speech-making were followed by the appointing of important high offices, all confirmed with little debate by the nobles. Then came the matter of replying to a letter from Philip of France, thus renewing the Auld Alliance after a silence of five years. Good news in itself, except that Philip looked for Scots aid for his upcoming crusade.

As the discussion progressed, Jamie shifted restlessly on his bench. There was no doubt as to the importance of the proceedings. But he was man and husband before he was sennachie. And he could not easily keep his thoughts from straying homeward. This was the first time in their many partings that he had left Rhona with an air of anger between them.

No, not anger. It had been confusion on her side and bitterness on his. And now there was distance more dividing than the miles from Dunning Innes to St. Andrews between them. And heaviest of all for Jamie was the feeling that the fault was all his. Guilt washed over him. And with the guilt, the pain increased, and the anger rose again.

This was not a spiral that could go on. It would tear them apart. And yet he did not know how to stop it.

In contrast to his inner turmoil, all around Jamie seemed hopeful. For on every side he heard avowals to defeat the English. Yes. That was it. His anger must be directed toward the enemy of whom Bruce spoke. Not toward Rhona. And when they were finally defeated —when the wrongs of the past were avenged—then he would find peace and former happiness restored. It was really very simple. He could not understand why he had not seen it before.

Jamie returned his attention to the proceedings with renewed vigor.

"When Scotland has recovered her pristine liberty and is at peace, King Philip will find not only the king of Scots but all the natives of his kingdom ready to join the crusade with all their power."

Abbot Bernard, chancellor of Scotland, read the reply letter to be approved by parliament.

Then followed declarations by nobility and clergy that John Balliol should never have been king. That he had been wrongfully imposed on the Scots as a puppet by superior English might. That Robert Bruce, the people's choice, had inherited the best claim to the throne, conquered his enemies, demonstrated the necessary virtues, and was the rightful king.

Early the next morning Jamie rode westward with a lighter heart than he had carried east three days before. The cheers and speeches of unity rang in his head. His fingers on Clarsach's reins itched to be setting it all to paper. And he knew that it was a good thing that the lords were united to the degree they were. For though little had been made of it in parliament, all knew that there was still much to be done before Scotland was truly unified and truly free.

He urged his horse forward. Now that he was headed homeward he wanted to be there. He wanted to tell Rhona, as he had not for far too long, that he loved her. He wanted to take wee Rabbie on his knee and tell him a story that would dazzle his young imagination with the splendid achievements of their brave King Robert the Bruce. He wanted . . .

It was the sight of a newborn lamb barely tottering behind its mother in the garth beside the road that suddenly made Jamie go cold with fear.

How *was* Rhona?

He had known she was near her time, but, blinded as he was by anger, he had not given the matter thought. Now the days he had been gone seemed weeks. Black weeks. Had the babe come? Had the birth been difficult? Had Hannah, the young serving girl, been there to run to the hall house for help? Had Rory's wife, Louise, served as midwife? He remembered anew the cries, the moans, the agony of waiting before Rabbie's birth.

In spite of the rough land, he rode faster. The thirty-mile journey was best accomplished in a day and a half, as the way across the Ochils was no smooth riding, but Jamie was determined not to stop. Even when a drenching rain began to fall, he merely pulled his cloak closer around his shoulders, lowered his head, and pushed onward.

He had always loved the quiet of nighttime. Even on thickly clouded nights such as this one, when no stars shone and no crickets sang, Jamie had liked the sheltered feeling of blanketing dark. But tonight as he approached the Dunning cottage he felt no comfort. Tonight the shivering dark was ominous. The silence like that of a tomb.

Nothing stirred around the house. No cattle lowed, no dog barked. He saw the merest flicker of light in one window as he pulled the saddle from Clarsach and all but shoved him in the byre, barely taking time to lock the door behind him.

Jamie hurled himself across the yard and at the door of his cottage. He stood panting and shaking before the lone figure dozing by the banked fire.

Hannah startled from her sleep. "Oh, it's you. We didn't expect—"

"Where is she? Rhona. How is she?" He swung toward their bedroom.

Hannah grabbed his arm. "She's asleep. She—"

Jamie shook off her hand.

The room was dark. At first he could hear no breathing. Then a thin, wavering cry came from almost under his feet. He had all but tripped over the cradle.

Hannah was behind him with a light. With one hand she scooped up the tiny bundle, with the other she set the candle on the table by the bed.

Rhona stirred. Jamie could not believe how gaunt she looked in the wavering candlelight.

"It's all right, Hannah." Her voice was barely above a whisper. She fumbled at the covers to expose her breast to her hungry bairn. She had not looked up at Jamie.

Once the babe was with its mother, Jamie grasped the servant's shoulder. "Is—is she all right? What is it?"

Hannah indicated that he should follow her out of the room. "I tried to tell you, sir. She's verra weak. The babe—Marion, she calls her—came the day you left. Well, started then—it was the next day before it was accomplished. She has lost much blood . . . continues to bleed . . ."

"O God . . ." Jamie covered his face with his hands. "I should have been here. And I left in anger. O God . . ." It was moments before he could continue. "What has been done? Is anyone attending her? Rory should have gone for help." He made a stumbling start toward the door.

Hannah restrained him. "Aye, Brother Infirmarer from the monastery at Baldinnies has come twice, and he will again. She asked for Brother Simon. Master Rory has gone."

Jamie turned back. All was done, it seemed, that could be done. "A wet nurse? While she is so weak?"

Hannah shook her head. "The mistress won't. And Brother Giles says nursing is helpful to stop the bleeding."

Jamie hesitated. Would Rhona want to see him? Would she blame him for what had happened—as he blamed himself? Would his presence now upset her? But no matter how great his misgivings, he could not hold back. He must see her. Beg her forgiveness.

In his agitation he misjudged the distance around the cradle, caught his crutch on the rocker, and all but fell on the bed. Gathering his courage he raised his eyes to Rhona's, hoping she would see the regret in his. Meeting her eyes was perhaps the hardest thing he had ever had to do.

He blinked. It couldn't be. She smiled at him. A very weak smile. The merest shadow. But she smiled. And lifted her hand as if she would hold it out to him.

"Rhona, can you forgive me? I should have been here. I—"

He stopped as she shook her head. He leaned close to hear her whispered words.

"There's nothing to forgive. You've come sooner than I hoped."

Hannah tugged his arm. "Dona make her talk, sir. You'll tire her. Come, I've made you a pallet by the fire."

Jamie started to rise, but the slightest motion from Rhona stopped him.

"Come. Lie here."

Everything in him wanted to do precisely that. Just to be in the same room. To know he could reach out and touch her. But he had to be sure. "Rhona, will I no' keep you awake?"

Again the passing butterfly of a smile. "With you here, I can sleep now."

Jamie pulled his tunic off. In spite of what she said, he was almost afraid to breathe lest he disturb her—or the bairn. He had given his new daughter little thought. He lay in the warmth of the covers thinking of the slight, fragile form beside him.

Come, she had said. And he so undeserving. He could not comprehend such grace.

Late the next day Brother Simon arrived. It was such comfort just to look again on the beneficence that shone from his kind blue eyes and on the gentle smile above his neat dark beard.

And he had brought a special elixir. He handed it to Brother Giles, who was there at the time checking on his patient. "I have some little experience as herbalist. This I decocted myself—nettles brewed with rusty nails. It is often most felicitious in cases of loss of blood."

Young Brother Giles pulled the cork from the bottle and sniffed. "Ah, vitriol. Excellent."

"And I'm sure you have directed that she be fed thin strips of calf's liver," Simon prodded.

"Aye. And wine thick-mulled with honey."

Simon smiled. "Rhona is in good hands."

"But will she live?" It was agony to Jamie to ask the question, yet he must.

Simon raised his thick dark brows. "That is in God's hands—the best of all." Then he distracted Jamie as best he could from his worries by demanding he be told all about the parliament. "Father Andrew will expect none less than a full report."

Two days later Simon returned to his monastery after saying the churching prayer over Rhona. Normally that would not have been done until mother and child could go to church, but it was obvious that such would be a long time yet, and Simon required none too much urging from Jamie to perform the rite at Rhona's bedside.

"Forasmuch as it has pleased God Almighty out of His goodness to give you safe deliverance and has preserved you in the great danger of childbirth, let us give hearty thanks unto God."

Rhona was still too weak to speak the prayer herself, so Simon read the woman's part as well, but Rhona gave assent to it by moving her lips.

"Lord, you have delivered my soul from death, my eyes from tears, and my feet from falling. I will walk before the Lord in the land of the living . . ."

Jamie prayed with all his heart that the prescribed prayer was not overoptimistic. At least he took comfort that Simon had in no way hinted that last rites would be the more appropriate ceremony.

And although Rhona did not recover much strength, still she did not fail.

The bairn Marion grew fat and rosy, while the summer grew warm. On fine days Luke would carry mother and child to a sheltered lounge between cottage and Jamie's scriptorium. And Jamie would bring his paper and pens and sit with them. More often than not, though, he would push the papers aside as Rabbie would crawl on his lap and demand to be told the story his father was writing.

Jamie did not lose his guilt for the hurt he had caused, but on these soft days he kept it under. Although he worried much about Rhona, it was so good to be together. Yet it was a sore thing to him that if she must be carried, he could not be the one to do it.

But the reports that reached him now from every direction, situated as they were so near the waist of Scotland, were heartening indeed and did much to assuage Jamie's lust for vengeance. For King Robert Bruce made steady headway on his vow to rid the land of English. The king had no mighty chivalry, but he had his band of bold young captains: Douglas, la Hay, Boyd, and Edward Bruce, now joined by Thomas Randolph, a nephew of Bruce's who had after Methven gone to the English until his loyalty was won back by Robert Bruce's honor. These men and a relative handful of common Scots soldiers engaged in brave tactics that made fine, stirring tales.

Jamie, who had spent so much time with these men, had no trouble at all picturing their nighttime raids on English-held castles: stripped to the waist and their bodies rubbed with charcoal so they wouldn't show white, the king himself leading a small band to wade the moat. Jamie could feel the chill of water around his waist, rising chest high, then up to his chin. He could see the stealthy forms moving slowly forward, directly below the castle wall. He could hear the swish of the rope as the grappling hook was thrown upward, the clank and grating as the steel claw scraped the parapet and held—or didn't catch and had to be thrown again.

"And then, hand over hand, the king scaled the rope, pushing his feet against the stones of the wall. Once over the top he overcame the guard and opened the gate to his men, who took the castle in less than an hour."

Rabbie clapped his hands. "And did he wear his crown?"

Jamie laughed. "He didn't even wear his shirt, and I'm none too sure about his breeches. Certainly no crown. It wouldn't do to have the gleam of gold give him away."

Rabbie considered. "Nay. And it might clink against the stones."

Jamie hugged his son, then set him on his feet to go play among the tangle of puppies sunning in the long grass.

And so, steadily, one by one, the English strongholds fell: Forfar, Brechin, Dundee, Dumfries, Caerlaverock.

And just as slowly, but also steadily, Rhona regained her strength. The light came back to her eyes, the color to her cheeks, the laughter to her lips. The day she walked across the room to Jamie unaided was the happiest he had known since the day they had declared their love.

And then a new kind of news reached their quiet dun. Indeed, it was word of victory but a victory hard to write of, because Jamie could feel the agony it cost the king to win such a war.

It was two autumns after the St. Andrew's parliament when at last Edward II mounted his great host to take Scotland. The threat that had lain dormant for three years now materialized. And still King Robert was not strong enough to fight a pitched battle. Someday it would come to that. Even in their fugitive days when the men discussed strategy, Robert had acknowledged the fact. But always he said, not until he was ready. He would choose time and place. Aye, it would come. But not until he could win. And that time was not yet. Still, Edward had to be stopped.

So as Robert always did, and as Wallace before him had done, the king made the land fight for him. But it was a sore fighting. For to make the fertile lowland fight against Edward meant to burn it of its crops. King Robert must burn the land he had sworn to save. He must dispossess the people he had sworn to protect. His land. His people. Robert Bruce cleared and burned all before Edward.

And Edward, finding the land a blackened famine and his soldiers angry and restless, retreated with his vast army to Berwick.

The following year King Robert invaded England, having collected gold from church and town to finance his war.

Then it was back to deal with the final English strongholds on Scottish soil. The Scots had no siege machines. Such engines of war were tools of aggression, designed to take a castle belonging to another. Of these the English were masters. But the Scots had none because they were not an aggressor nation and siege machines were of no use for defense. So now Bruce must devise other means of retaking their own castles that the English had won with their trebuchets, battering rams, and catapults.

Once again the king stripped naked and waded black water to his chin, crossing the moat around Perth. With a mighty heave he set his rope ladder on the wall and was the second man into that English-held town. The garrison abandoned Perth without a fight.

Equally heartening news followed. Sir Thomas Randolph, who had many times proven Bruce's wisdom in taking his once-defector nephew back into his peace, took Edinburgh Castle for King Robert. True to his policy, the Bruce ordered it demolished. Every stone razed. All save Saint Margaret's chapel. He would not have that holy lady's work or memory destroyed.

Of major strengths that left only Stirling. Always it was Stirling—the strongest castle in Scotland. The key to Scotland. Stirling was still in English hands, held by Sir Philip Moubray, a Scots knight pledged to the English. And Stirling was besieged by that fiery knight Edward Bruce.

Rory, who had been fighting with Edward, brought word to Dunning Innes as he had on several other occasions. "So if the English fail to relieve Stirling within a year to the day, Moubray and his garrison will march out, surrendering all to King Robert."

Jamie could not believe it. He hit the table with such force that four-year-old Marion, who had been dozing in her mother's lap, awoke with a start. "What?" he cried. "A year? Edward Bruce gave Moubray a year's truce?"

Rory shrugged. "The king ordered as little bloodshed as possible. And he has done the same himself with many a town south of the Tweed."

"Yes, but *Stirling?* All England will take that as a challenge. Edward will have no choice but to invade. Pray Bruce can be ready."

72

All during the spring of 1314, rumors and counterrumors flew, so that Jamie often burned candles late into the night trying to make some sense of Edward's strength and plans.

There was no doubt that Edward of Caernarvon was on the move. The doubt lay in the vastness of the numbers he brought with him. And again there was no doubt that they were vast, but Jamie strove always for accuracy in his chronicle, and records were kept of each report, tallies adjusted according to various eyewitnesses and evaluated as to reliability.

Edward had crossed Tweed with a host whose baggage train alone extended for twenty miles. Jamie paused. Yes, that could be. But the distance between the carts was not reported. A great difference that could make. Two hundred wagons, half drawn by teams of four horses, half drawn by teams of eight oxen, one scout said. That was probably accurate. Such a train would be necessary to carry the food, spare arms, and equipment for such a huge army—as well as money to pay the men.

And no stranger to English military maneuvers, Jamie knew that many wagons would be filled with furniture and plate carried by nobles who had been promised property in Scotland as a reward for their share in the looked-for victory. Some would even bring their wives—and others—with them.

The infantry was apparently without number, but they mattered little. Jamie shook his head, looking again at the reported numbers of the crucial factors in any contest against the English: archers and heavy cavalry. Was 17,000 archers a reliable report? He hoped not. Bruce could not raise 700. Of armored knights on barded destriers the reports were so wild as to be meaningless. Pray God the messenger who reported 2,000 was nearer the truth than he who reported 40,000. Bruce had 500 light cavalry. None heavy—Scotland did not breed such horses.

And as he bent above his ink-blackened pages, Jamie told himself over and over that his interest in all this was to keep accurate record, to fulfill his long-held task as recorder of Scotland's tales to serve as inspiration to such as young Rabbie and his children and children's children. But when the candle guttered and weariness overcame him, black pictures from the past swirled before his eyes, and he had not the strength to push them back by concentrating on reports of numbers and marching lines.

He knew that his driving motive was still—as it had ever been, although for years kept beneath even his own consciousness—his hatred for the English. And he knew that this, the battle for which both kings had prepared with all the might of their two lands, was to be the ultimate battle. The battle he had dreamed of taking part in ever since he had run, leaping over rocks and crashing around trees, to cry Wallace to the fray.

This would be Stirling, Falkirk, Methven, Loudoun Hill—all the defeats and victories of the past seventeen years rolled into one. And in all those years he had reddened a blade only once since Stirling Bridge. This would be his chance to avenge all that he might have done in those long years.

"Will you stay at your papers all night, Jamie?" Pushing sleep-tangled hair out of her face, Rhona came to him barefoot with only a light shawl over the shoulders of her nightshift.

He turned on his stool and held his hands out to her. She came into his arms and settled on his lap, snuggling as cozily as five-year-old Marion was wont to do, although Rhona's rounded, womanly body filled the space far better. He clasped her to him for many moments, savoring the softness inside the circle of his arms and the sweet scent of her hair. His lips rested on her gently hollowed cheek. He must speak. And yet he couldn't.

Would she understand? Five years ago he had left her. Left in anger and bitterness. And returned to find her almost dead. She was not with child this time. And yet his excuse was much flimsier. Then, he had been invited to the parliament. Now, no summons had come from Robert Bruce calling a crippled sennachie to war. The idea was preposterous. And yet he must go.

He could tell Rhona it was for the chronicle. But in truth it was not. And she would know. Many and many a battle he had recorded in the past years—the whole of Bruce's victories since Loudoun Hill. And he had been present for none of them. Why should this be different, simply because it would be the last—whoever won?

He drew back and held her at arm's length. "Rhona . . ." The words that would not be spoken rose in his throat and choked him.

She brushed his cheek with her hand, tracing the strong line of cheekbone and jaw as she liked to do. "I know, Jamie." She gave a little sighing laugh. "Perhaps I am becoming sennachie too. For I had a dream. There was a great battle—such as all men talk of these days . . ."

She bit her lip and dropped her head so that her forehead rested on his shoulder. "You were there, Jamie. And I woke knowing it was important. I came to tell you." Now it was her arms who held him, clasped him to her as if to stifle the shaking she could not control.

So they would not part with harsh words between them. Only with Jamie's harsh hatred driving him on. And the hope that the reddening of his sword with English blood would at last put the pain behind him.

Robert Bruce had ordered the Scots host to form south of Stirling Castle in the cover of New Park Forest just above the Bannock Burn. Jamie spent the night sharing Brother Simon's small cell at Cambuskenneth. There was not a spare corner to be had at the abbey, for Bruce had commissioned Cambuskenneth as supply depot.

Before sunrise on the morning of June 23, as the monks' chanting of Prime was just beginning, Jamie and Abbot Bernard rode out from the monastery ahead of a large number of the brotherhood the abbot had chosen to assist him in serving mass to the thousands of Scottish soldiers who would face battle that day.

This was the Eve of Saint John the Baptist. The Scots would keep fast that day. If they were to do battle on stomachs filled only with bread and water, it was necessary that their hearts be filled with something more stout. And Abbot Bernard, he who was also chancellor of the realm, had not come to the field empty-handed.

Jamie stood next to the abbot atop Coxet Hill, St. Ninian's Kirk to his left and the ancient Pictish Borestone to his right, as the five or six thousand Scots troops filled the space under all the trees of New Park.

From the portable altar he had directed to be placed behind them, the abbot lifted a golden reliquary containing a long white bone. "You were with King Robert when the Culdee brought this, were you not?" he said to Jamie. "Father Dunchad sent it to the king when his call for troops went out. Hold the arm bone of St. Fillan now as I will hold aloft the Brecbennoch of Saint Columba."

King Robert Bruce knelt in the front line with his most trusted leaders. The first streaking rays of the sun struck the top of the hill and illuminated the identifying surcoats covering the chain mail of Edward Bruce, James Douglas, Thomas Randolph—newly made earl of Moray—Robert Keith, the Marischal, Gilbert la Hay, and Angus Og MacDonald.

Jamie bit back the bitterness that he was not like arrayed, standing strong to do battle with his sword fresh sharpened on the Borestone. Instead, he did the best he could and held Saint Fillan's relic high to catch the morning light so all could be reminded of the blessing that still rested on King Robert. Beside him a light breeze whipped the vestments of Bernard of Linton as he extended the silver house-shaped casket toward the bowed head of the king as if he would crown him.

"On that day there shall be an altar to the Lord in the land of Egypt. My people shall cry out to the Lord against their oppressors, and He will send them a savior to defend and deliver them. The Lord shall smite Egypt severely, but His people He shall heal. They shall turn to the Lord, and He shall heal them.

"The Lord God of Israel says, 'I will put an end to the pride of the arrogant. The insolence of tyrants I will humble. They shall fall by the sword.'

"The oppressor says, 'By my own power I have done it, and by my wisdom, for I am shrewd. I have moved the boundaries of peoples, their treasures I have pillaged, and, like a giant, I have put down the enthroned.'

"But the Lord our God says, 'My people will no more lean upon him who struck them, but they will lean upon the Lord. The oppressor's burden shall be taken from your shoulder, and his yoke shattered from your neck.'"

From his vantage on the crest of the hill, Jamie could just see through the treetops the road from Falkirk to the south. As far as he could see, the sun gleamed off a broad line of colored pennons and shining armor. Thousands strong, proud Edward's army advanced.

When the priests had completed the serving of Communion, Bruce positioned his troops. The English goal was Stirling Castle directly north of them. To reach it, Edward must pass through the wooded park that Bruce occupied or through the marshy, pool-pocked carse, whose ditches often filled from the tidal Bannock Burn. To improve his position even more, King Robert had dug carefully concealed trenches on either side of the narrow road leading into the park and scattered the ground thickly with vicious steel caltrops, which would pierce the hooves of even the heaviest destrier.

Randolph commanded the northern flank by Saint Ninian's, in case Edward should attempt to send a contingent around the park to reach the Roman road leading to the castle. Good Sir James Douglas, the king's staunchest friend, commanded the ground to the west; Edward Bruce, the line to the south. Keith the Marischal commanded the Scots' small cavalry from the slopes of Coxet Hill. The king himself covered the entry to the park along the Roman road where it crossed the Bannock Burn. He took up his position near the Borestone, which came up almost to his thigh, since he was mounted only on a small gray hill pony in order to keep his splendid warhorse fresh for battle.

In addition to Bruce's well-trained and superbly disciplined troops, some two thousand Small Folk—farmers, laborers, craftsmen, even churchmen—all passionately attached to Scottish freedom and loyal supporters of King Robert Bruce, had rallied to the rampant red lion. Bruce ordered Bernard to keep these, armed with clubs, pitchforks, and hunting knives, in reserve, hidden behind Coxet Hill. Jamie knew that was his station as well.

But he would not stay hidden. He set his jaw and gazed southward at the endless flood rolling toward them. He might not be able to kill any English this day, but he would not fail to observe and record. Perhaps vicarious vengeance would serve.

By noon Jamie was sweating in the unseasonable heat. The brilliant-colored sea of English cavalry at the van of their advance pulled up for midday dinner just south of the Bannock Burn. Jamie drew out the dry roll and flagon of water allowed for the Scots' fast day. If he chewed slowly and limited himself to small sips, perhaps the ration would assuage the gnawing in his stomach.

It was not long before he saw stirring in the ranks below, signaling that the advance had begun. The Great Van of the English under the whipping banners of the earls of Hereford and Gloucester pulled off from the main body of the army to approach New Park along the Roman road. They advanced fast, splashing through the ford of the burn, a group of vigorous young knights thrusting forward.

They had detected the Scots among the trees at the entrance to the park—King Robert's own force. Jamie bit his lip and felt his heart thud with the pounding of the charging horses.

Then suddenly the scene changed. The driving band seemed to falter and fall back. All save one rider. The knight in the fore on a red-caparisoned horse bearing a blue shield with six white lions surged ahead. Apparently he had spotted the king, for although no banner flew at the Borestone, Robert Bruce wore a golden circlet around his leather helmet.

Bohun, nephew of the earl of Hereford, had claimed the prize for himself. The English knight couched his twelve-foot lance, bent low over his charger, and spurred forward alone.

Jamie dared not breathe. The Bruce was mounted on only a small garron. He carried no lance. And yet the king of Scots could not run from a challenge to single combat. The situation was impossible. Could it be that the whole battle was to end here before it began?

The great flying hooves of the destrier flung his crimson caparison like splashes of blood. King Robert Bruce stood his ground with only a battle-ax in his hand. Six strides more. Jamie fought against closing his eyes as he felt the imagined collision.

At the last moment King Robert wheeled his mount, missing the lance point by inches. In the same motion he rose on his toes in his stirrups and brought his battle-ax swinging down on the knight's head in a great arc.

Surely Jamie only imagined he heard the clash of impact. He was too far up the hill for the sound actually to have reached him. But he did not imagine the shocked, then jubilant, cries that rose from the Bruce's men.

And it took little imagination to feel the stunning pain in the king's arm from striking such a blow. Sir Henry de Bohun lay beneath his horse, the head of Bruce's ax still in his skull, while the king held only the wooden shaft.

The remainder of the Great Van pushed forward in some confusion, only to run afoul of the Scots' hidden trenches and carefully laid caltrops. In a matter of minutes the advance guard of English chivalry was reeling backward in disorder across the Bannock Burn.

And then Jamie's attention was riveted on his left, just beyond St. Ninian's. Here Thomas Randolph, with a single schiltrom of pike-armed infantry, stood against Clifford's force of eight hundred heavy cavalry, which had circled the park in an attempt to get between the Scots and the castle.

The hedgehog of Scots soldiers stood firm, long spears spiking in every direction as the mass of galloping horses bore down upon it. The horses that could pulled up and shied away in front of the unwavering steel points. But those who could not stop, who were pressed too closely by those behind, were impaled and fell. Soon the English had to ride over their own dead to reach the Scots. It must have been more in frustration than in hope of doing damage that they hurled maces and battle-axes at the Scots before leaving the field.

Jamie spotted Clifford's banner among those bloodied and trampled on the field. He noted only one Scot dead, although several wounded were carried behind Coxet Hill where Abbot Bernard would see to their binding. Most of the injuries had been inflicted by men's spears breaking in their hands rather than by the English.

Earlier in the day Robert Bruce had downplayed reports of the enemy's strength and emphasized, perhaps overemphasized, their disorder and fatigue in an attempt to keep his own men's spirits up. Now there was no need to build morale. Spirits could not have been higher.

The Scots king stood his vantage point until sunset, making as certain as he could of the English movements. Jamie, sitting Clarsach not far from Bruce and three of his captains, watched in amazement as more than two thousand English horse crossed the Bannock Burn and the gorgeously clad knights attempted to bivouac on the boggy, ditch-riddled ground.

"Why would Edward do that?" Gilbert la Hay expressed the astonishment Jamie felt.

King Robert shrugged. "What choice has he? He must have water for his horses and men."

And, indeed, they were making the best of it they could. From all across the field the English foot came carrying doors, timbers, and pieces of roof from nearby farms and the village of Bannockburn, three-quarters of a mile to the east. With these they formed makeshift bridges across the ditches and shored up the soggier parts of the field so the destriers wouldn't sink in it. But it was incredible work for a knight in armor to be performing. Soon it was not the darkness of the sky that covered the brilliant devices on their surcoats so much as the darkness of mud.

Knowing the impossible situation in which their enemy floundered made the Scots' council in Bruce's headquarters—around a fine fire, fitted with camp stools on firm ground behind Coxet Hill—seem even more comfortable than it was.

In spite of the day's victories, however, King Robert hesitated. The seventeen years of guerrilla warfare that had brought the Scots this close to triumph had taught him the deep-seated lesson of avoiding pitched battles against the English, especially when they outnumbered him somewhere between four to eight times his strength.

The council was giving serious consideration to withdrawing westward to the Lennox, a land too rough for the English to follow. From there they could establish new bases to fight another day.

Fully aware that he had no right to speak, Jamie bit his tongue against crying out. Leave their strong position? When they had won two skirmishes? When they had proved that foot soldiers could stand and win against cavalry? When there were so many English yet to kill?

A haze of blood lust swirled before his eyes. He was afraid he had cried aloud. Then he realized the cry had not been his but rather that of a guard approaching the circle, prodding a young knight with the end of his spear.

"Asks to see King Robert, he does," the guard growled. "Shall I run him through for Your Grace?" The man gave three sharp jabs of his spear, making the prisoner jump at each one.

Bruce stood and approached the man. "What is this? You would have word with me, sir knight?" He paused and frowned at the device on the man's breastplate. "I know that emblem. Seton?"

The young man nodded his blond head. "Sir Alexander Seton. I—to my shame I marched with the Scots contingent in Edward's army. But no more." He fell to one knee before the king. "If you will have me, sire, I'll be your leal man. If not, I surrender to your captivity. I'll no more fight with Edward."

"This is what you've come into the Scots camp in the middle of the night to say—that you turn your coat? Why not wait and be taken prisoner in fair battle tomorrow? Or is it fear that drives you?" Bruce did not extend his hand to the kneeling man.

"No, sire. Well, yes—it is. But not as you mean. There is much talk among the Scots in Edward's ranks that you'll no' fight a pitched battle. Some even wager you'll take to the Highlands. I've come to say—to give advice, if I may be so bold . . ."

Bruce held up his hand. "You seem to lack nothing of boldness, young Seton. But to what are we to attribute this sudden change of heart that you would advise your rightful king against the invader you chose to follow?"

Seton hung his head. When he looked up Jamie was certain the blue eyes brimmed. "It was being home, sire. I had lived so long in England—I had forgot. The hills . . ." He choked and lowered his head.

"Aye. I once lived long in England too." Robert Bruce's voice was quiet. "It is such loyalty to the land I seek to build. So speak."

Sir Alexander squared his shoulders and took a deep breath. "Sire, now's the time and now's the hour. Strike now, and Scotland shall be free!"

Silence followed the young man's fervor. Then an outburst of cheers from Bruce's captains. And from Jamie.

One of the captains—perhaps it was Douglas—cried out, "Good king, as soon as it is light tomorrow, order your army for battle. We shall not fail for fear of death nor flinch at any suffering till we have made our country free!"

King Robert accepted Seton's fealty and assigned him to Sir Thomas Randolph's band. Randolph of Moray would know how to deal with this newcomer. No man had ever turned his coat more satisfactorily than Bruce's nephew.

Abbot Bernard held out his hand in a sign of blessing. "The

Lord God Jehovah promised Joshua, 'Tomorrow the Lord will perform wonders among you—and the whole nation completed the passage.' The Bannock Burn will be our River Jordan. And we shall possess our land."

The talk then turned to strategy for tomorrow. But Jamie could sit no longer. All day he had watched and recorded. He who had trained and fought with William Wallace had sat with the small folk and recorded stories to tell to bairns. And somewhere out there were the English dogs that had raped and murdered his family—or others just like them.

And then he thought. A Scots contingent in Edward's army? And wagonloads of gold still lumbering up from Falkirk to pay the soldiery? And spoils aplenty to be gathered after battle? No matter who won?

Jamie had another score to settle, almost as old as that of his family's butchery. And that atrocity had not been committed by a faceless English soldier. He would know Murdo if he saw him again. Murdo, who had betrayed Wallace. All Scotland blamed Mentieth for surrendering William Wallace to the English. But James MacInnes knew who had sold the great patriot to Mentieth. With such promise of treasure ripe for the picking, Murdo would be out there somewhere. Jamie hoped he had chosen the boggiest square foot of the field for bivouac.

Grabbing up his crutches he hurried after Alex Seton.

Later, making his way determinedly through the semidark of New Park, for in June it never got truly black at night, Jamie reviewed what Seton had told him. "Not in the carse with the chivalry. The Scots camp back with the baggage." His laugh had been harsh. "Shows what Edward thinks of northerns, even when they would befriend him. But I avow, they camp drier tonight than their betters."

So. Jamie had clearly seen where the supply train—what of it had arrived before dark—had pulled up. Just to the south of the Bannock Burn, on a loop of land ringed by the curling stream. Yes, that was where Murdo would be.

He rode Clarsach to the western edge of New Park, then tethered him to a tree. He had acted on impulse and given little thought to the guards that would be set around each camp, so it was fortunate indeed that the challenge that halted him soon after dismounting came from a vaguely familiar voice.

"Jamie MacInnes, sennachie." He gave his name and position, such as it was. "But dona I know you?" He drew nearer and peered at the face under the flat steel bacinet. The body inside the thickly padded coat that would hopefully provide protection against arrows on the coming day had filled out considerably, but Jamie was almost sure. "Hugh Danduff, once squire to Sir Kenneth. We long ago fought side by side for Wallace, did we no'?"

Hugh gave him a hearty slap on the shoulder. "Aye. And many a tale we could tell of that time. But what brings you creeping through the woods on such a night?"

"I've an old score to settle for all of us." And he told Hugh of his conviction that Wallace's betrayer was camped not more than a thousand yards from them across the burn.

Even in the dim light Jamie could see Hugh's features tighten. "Aye. If I weren't set to guard duty I'd go with you." He reached to his belt and drew out a long-bladed dirk with a wickedly curved tip. "When you stick it in him, give it a twist for me."

Jamie hesitated. "You'll have need of this tomorrow. I may not find you to return it."

Hugh shook his head. "I've another. It couldn't go for a better cause."

Jamie started to turn, but Hugh stopped him with a hand on his shoulder. "Will you be all right, man? It's dangerous work for even a fleet-footed man."

Jamie jerked a nod. "Aye. I've a mind I can turn it to good."

At the boggy land near the burn he knelt and all but rolled in the mud. If Rhona were to see him now—the tunic she had cut from her finest-woven cloth caked with slime . . . He filled both hands with mud and streaked his hair and face.

Continuing on across the marsh, he found it wasn't necessary to feign the awkward hirple that would make him look like an aged beggar. His crutches sank in the soft ground, and he had never moved with such clumsy slowness in all his years since Stirling.

A challenge by the English guard came just as he reached one of the makeshift bridges put down the night before for the English advance.

"Halt! No beggars. Wait till after tomorrow's battle—there'll be rebel Scots bodies and enough for all you carrion."

Jamie couldn't be sure from the guard's voice whether he was Northumbrian or Lowland Scots, but for either case Jamie thickened his speech. "Nay, nay, now, young laddie." In truth the man was somewhat older than Jamie. "I'm nae a beggar. I've come frae the mill." He jerked his head toward the Mill of Bannock just south of them and fumbled at his belt. He drew out Hugh's dirk and held it by the blade.

"Dinna fash yourself. I've come to bring this to an auld friend. Lang ago, afore he gang south we had a fine time o' it cuttin' purses a twa. Taught him all I knew. That was afore I fell afoul of a Scots sheriff." He gestured toward his damaged leg.

The guard stood straddle-legged across the bridge, his pike held threateningly in both hands. "Oh, aye? And what's the name of your old mate, grampa?"

"Murdo Grant he were then. Mayhap he's changed it since."

The guard let out a shout of laughter that might have wakened sleepers in the encampment behind him—except that there was little sign that any slept in that uneasy camp. "Murdo Grant. I shoulda known. Cutpurse, was he? Well, some things never change." He stepped back to make room for Jamie to pass. "Go on then, but see he doesn't stick that dirk in your own hide. Yellow wagon. Second past the third fire."

Jamie couldn't believe it had been so easy. It took careful control to continue his awkward progress when he wanted to launch out in a jubilant swing. Murdo Grant was within his grasp. He would have his vengeance.

The difference in the two camps was immediately apparent. On the other side of the burn, the Scots slept in well-guarded order, their spirits high from the afternoon's victories. Here all was confusion. Many still tried to make some sort of a camp after a late arrival. Women and camp-followers cooked pots of porridge or fowl that might have been intended for last night's supper or next morning's breakfast. And everywhere men attempted to fortify their spirits and quench the dust of camp with flagons of beer and ale.

Tension and anger simmered beneath the surface—not always kept so far under, for angry shouts jarred the night. To his left someone kicked a dog that sniffed too near a hunk of roast meat. Ahead of him a fistfight broke out. A baby cried. A woman shrieked.

Others, attempting to ignore it all, had rolled in blankets beneath the shelter of supply wagons or sat glumly before small fires. Yet others busied themselves with mending harness or polishing weapons. There was little of the singing Jamie had heard on the far side of Coxet Hill earlier, but here and there he heard a woman croon to a child. Many a soldier brought his family with him on a long campaign. The baggage trains were always burdened with women and bairns—but then, they were not such a burden when it came to providing hot stew and comforts for the night.

In the muddle of the camp, Jamie hoped he was following the guard's directions rightly. Fires were everywhere—which had the man meant as the third? And which yellow wagon? It seemed every fourth or fifth wagontop glowed yellow in the pale night. Slithering in the churned mud, Jamie made his way around a massive wooden cart piled high with sacks—wheat or oats probably.

It was the voice that stopped him—higher-pitched than he had remembered but with the same note of surly insolence. The dark rodent eyes and sharp nose rose in his memory. How could any of them ever have trusted that man?

"Not my right, you say? And who has better right, I'd like to know? I've done my share for Edward's cause—more than the likes of you would know."

"As long as I'm master of the pay wagon there'll be no silver leave without signed order from the treasurer."

Jamie heard the rasp of a blade being drawn.

He stepped around the grain cart.

In front of him was a black-curtained red wagon, its mailed guards leaned drunkenly on their spears. The rear curtain hung loose where its securing rope had been cut. Murdo Grant, thinner, sharper featured, looking more like a ferret than ever, stood with a knife in his right hand. A gleam of silver showed between the fingers of his clenched left hand.

"Guards, do your duty!" the wagon master barked.

One of the mailed men came to unsteady attention.

"Drunken sot, I'll have your head before Gloucester!" The wagon boss advanced on the ineffective guard.

Murdo fled across the open space, straight toward Jamie.

It was more reflex than planning that caused Jamie to thrust his crutch in the path of the escaping man. Murdo Grant fell headlong in the mud with a cursing bark.

Thrown off balance himself by the man's impact, Jamie was slow fumbling for the dirk at his belt. But for that, the prize would have been his. As it was, the spear grabbed from the fumbling guard and hurled by the master pinned Murdo to the ground.

Jamie hesitated. Then Hugh's words rang in his ears, urging on his own enmity. He dropped to his knee with the downward plunge of his hand.

His swing was never completed. The guard's iron grip on his wrist all but pulled Jamie's arm from its socket.

"I can mind my own prisoner well enow on my own."

A groan came from beneath him, and Jamie looked down. He realized then that the spear had only gone through Murdo's tunic, not into his side as he had supposed. The Englishman shoved Jamie aside and hauled Murdo to his feet.

The crowd that had gathered at the sound of the ruckus was more interested in the prisoner and the recovery of the money still locked in his grip than in a crippled beggar, so Jamie simply melted into the shadows between carts.

Robbed of his prize, he had thought to slip back through the lines the way he had come, but finding his way was no easy matter. And suddenly he realized how very tired he was. So tired he could not drag himself one more step. He leaned against a small green wagon and slumped to the ground. Little wonder he was tired—he had not slept for nearly twenty-four hours.

But what of this overwhelming depression he felt? How was it possible? All afternoon he had watched the slaughter of the English he hated. And although he had not accomplished the vengeance he had dreamed of on Wallace's betrayer, he had aided in Murdo's capture. Yet he felt empty, not jubilant. The pain inside him was boiling black, not assuaged as it should be.

"Are you all right?"

Jamie glanced up. A woman in a brown dress and white headrail stood over him, holding out a pewter mug. "It's only ale. I've naething stronger. But you look fair doon."

Jamie took the mug and drank deeply. It was when he raised his eyes to return the cup that he blinked in astonishment. No, it couldn't be. It was his vivid imagination playing tricks again. He had thought he saw this face once, a little less lined, nine years before. In London. But it had disappeared into the crowd then, just as the woman was turning to do now.

"Aline!"

She stopped, then came back slowly. "How do you know my name?"

He rubbed at the dirt he had caked on his face, but it was little use. She would not know him after all these years, for he had changed far more than she. No, she too had changed. It was not Aline's face he recognized but that of their mother.

And for just a moment he was back at Dunning Innes on the autumn morning when he left home to go with Sir Kenneth to Scone. Their mother had stood by the door of the hall house waving a white kerchief as he rode proudly out to the great world of adventure. That had been the last time he saw her alive.

"You do not remember me, Aline. But I've never forgotten you." He grasped a crutch and pushed himself to his feet. "All these years I thought you dead, and yet I hoped." He started toward her.

She took a confused step backward.

"Oh, Aline, can you no' forgive me for not rescuing you sooner? I would have come for you if I'd any idea where you were."

She shook her head. "Rory? Is it possible?"

"Nay. Rory's across the burn. He fights still with Sir Kenneth."

She gasped and gave a strangled sob. "Jamie! You were but a wee lad." Then she clasped both hands to her mouth. "But, Jamie, you—"

He lunged forward and caught her arm. "Aline, we can talk later. I must get you away now. Come, I know the way." He pulled at her urgently. "Leave your things. We've all you'll need at home."

She drew away from him. "Jamie, I *am* home. I've husband here and three weans—although hardly weans anymore."

"Here?" Jamie looked around him. "Here? Among the English and traitor Scots? You make your home among those who butchered your own family and have ravished our land for these many years? My own sister?" He choked on the pain in his throat. At last he ground out, "Better you had been dead as I thought you."

"I would have been if it hadn't been for John."

"John?"

"Aye, my husband. He hid me from ravishment that day at Dunning Innes."

"Oh, aye! So he could have you himself!" Jamie spit out the words with disgust.

She dropped her head. "Yes. It started like that. But then . . . Jamie, he's been a good husband these seventeen years."

"Mother . . ."

They were interrupted by two approaching figures.

Jamie blinked. The young man looked so like himself half a lifetime ago that he thought he must be dreaming.

Aline touched his arm. "This is my son, Jamie."

She had to repeat it twice before he realized she was giving the boy's name, not calling his own. The rage that boiled up in him made speech impossible. She had dared. She had dared to name her illgotten son by a southern soldier after him? It was the final mockery.

"And this is Agnes." She indicated the girl standing beside—beside that boy. "Another—young Johnny—sleeps by the wagon." She looked at Jamie.

He knew she awaited a reply, but he could not.

She turned to her children—his niece and nephew, Jamie realized distantly. "Go you back. I'll come soon."

The boy wore the green and gold checky badge of Preston on his shoulder. Would he fight tomorrow? His own nephew, fight for the English? He fingered the dirk at his belt, but he knew he would not use it. Not now.

Aline turned to him. "Jamie, are you sore wounded?"

He started to answer, then realized she meant his leg. "Aye. It's long ago. A kick from Cressingham's horse at Stirling Bridge. But it's naught to this that you've dealt me, Aline."

"Jamie, will you hear me? John Greene is in service to Ralph Preston—aye, an Englishman who fights Scots. But John is a good man. He took me by force at first, yes. But it's been a good life. I'd not change now, Jamie. Can you never understand? Can you no' forgive?"

Forgive? It was a concept to send him reeling. Forgive? Forgive whom? Aline? John Greene? The English? Edward?

"Forgive? You don't know what you ask, woman."

73

Somehow Jamie passed the guards, regained Clarsach, and stumbled into camp just as the sun was rising fine and bright on June 24, the Feast of Saint John. Already Abbot Bernard, joined today by the abbot of Inchaffray, stood atop the hill, preparing mass.

Bernard of Linton never missed an opportunity for inspiration, whether he served in his capacity of abbot or of chancellor. And on this day, which could prove to be the most vital day in Scotland's history, he spoke as both while King Robert Bruce knelt before him with the courageous Scottish army covering the hillside behind him.

"Listen! The rumble on the mountains; that of an immense throng!" Bernard's voice carried across the hillside.

He extended both arms wide, the sleeves of his robe catching the golden sun. "Listen! The noise of kingdoms, nations assembled! The Lord of hosts is mustering an army for battle. This is the day of the Lord.

"The Lord of hosts says, 'I will put an end to the pride of the arrogant. The insolence of tyrants I will humble. The tyrant shall flee to his own land. They shall fall by the sword.'"

The abbot couldn't have chosen a more heartening passage to quote. But Jamie did not feel heartened. He realized he should be. He had seen Wallace's betrayer fall at his feet. He had found his sister alive and well.

And yet when the priest from Saint Ninian's Kirk passed before him with the elements, he could not partake because of the hatred inside himself. The sacred Host would choke him.

A throng of priests, many themselves armored for battle, served Communion that morning, and the service went quickly. Then King Robert took his place before his troops. While the men broke out the spartan breakfast they had brought with them, their king addressed them, and his message was relayed to the ranks beyond the reach of his words by their captains.

"My lords, my people—accustomed to enjoy that full freedom

671

for which in times gone by the kings of Scotland have fought many a battle!"

Even his greeting was answered with a rousing cheer. And Jamie heard, in the line to the right, Angus Og MacDonald translating to his saffron-and-plaid-clad Highlanders in melodious Gaelic.

"For many years I have struggled with much labor for my right to the kingdom and for honorable liberty. I have lost brothers, friends, and kinsmen. Your own kinsmen have been made captive, and bishops and priests are locked in prison. Our country's nobility has poured forth its blood in war . . ."

Jamie glanced at Abbot Bernard and saw that the careful cleric was doing the job he failed at this morning—recording the king's speech.

Bruce swept the carse beyond the park with his arm as he continued. "Those barons you can see before you, clad in mail, are bent upon destroying me and obliterating my kingdom, nay, our whole nation. They do not believe that we can survive. They glory in their warhorses and equipment."

A rumble of agreement met his words.

"But for us, the name of the Lord must be our hope of victory in battle. This day is a day of rejoicing: the birthday of John the Baptist. With our Lord Jesus Christ as commander, we shall fight today with the saints of Scotland for the honor of their country and their nation. If you heartily repent of your sins you will be victorious, under God's command."

Jamie turned his face away. It was as well he couldn't fight today. For he could not repent of the sins he carried—sins of wrath and of hatred.

The Scottish host formed for battle. The honor of leading went to Edward Bruce. On his left, Randolph of Moray's brigade, then Douglas. Three great schiltroms, the steel tips of their twelve-foot spear quills bristling in the sun. But before all walked two mitred abbots: the abbot of Inchaffray, bearing the relic of Saint Fillan, and the abbot of Arbroath, bearing the Brecbennoch of Columba, he who had first brought the gospel of Christ to this land.

The gleaming host advanced until in full view of the English, who were assembled, albeit in some disorder due to the cramped space and the many ditches crisscrossing the marshy land of the broad, flat carse. At a low signal from Bruce's trumpeter, the Scots stopped. The abbots elevated their relics to the full extent of their reach. The entire army knelt.

As if one man, they proclaimed loudly and fervently, "Our Father which art in heaven, hallowed be Thy name. . ." The prayer echoed across the field. "Deliver us from evil. Amen." At the conclusion of the prayer, the Scots crossed themselves, stood, and couched their spears. They were ready to receive the worst Edward could launch against them.

The first attack was by the English vanguard under the earl of Gloucester. He charged full force at Edward Bruce's schiltrom. The mass of brilliantly clad knights, horses, and banner bearers thundered across the short stretch of intervening ground.

Jamie, today observing astride Clarsach, took a post not far from Robert Bruce's command position. He did not have long to hold his breath. The English charge was a spectacular failure. The mailed knights made no impression on the impenetrable forest of spears. The air filled with the screams of dying horses and the sharp crack of breaking spear shafts.

He groaned as he saw the earl of Gloucester himself fall from his wounded horse and the iron hedgehog close over him. Jamie's regret was not for any pain he would have spared his enemy but for the enormous sum that Scotland could have demanded for the man's ransom.

Now Moray and Douglas brought up their brigades and launched a general attack on the remaining nine English divisions, which were in fact so bunched together they appeared to Jamie to be one vast host. The Scottish schiltroms presented an impenetrable wall.

Even to Jamie's bloodthirsty senses the tumult became appalling. The air grew thick with the clash of spears on helmets, the shrieks of disemboweled horses, the thudding stampede of riderless mounts. The Scots added to the havoc with their shouts. "Press on!" "Press on!" Wherever shifts in the troops left the ground exposed, it was not green underfoot but red.

And then, just when victory was so close, Jamie heard the king shout and looked to the left where he pointed. An English troop, surely thousands strong, advanced with the weapon most dreaded by the Scots, the one armament against which they had no defense. Edward's archers, who had been trapped behind his heavy cavalry, had now broken around and were advancing up Broomridge. From that elevated spot they could rain down devastating terror upon the entire Scots left flank under Douglas's command.

Bruce sounded a desperate signal. The Scots had only five hundred men mounted on light horses, but they were nobly led by the marischal, Sir Robert Keith. Keith spurred forward at a tremendous pace, seemingly oblivious to the damage the English longbows could do to his charge.

Keith did not slow his onrush until every archer was driven

from the field and Broomridge was cleared of its deadly firepower. Now was the crisis. The momentum was the Scots'. The full tide of the battle flowed with them. Victory was within their clasp.

But so also was defeat. The Scots fighting on foot, holding spears against mighty charging destriers, were tiring. There were many hours of battle left. And Edward had thousands of fresh reserves who had not even drawn up to the field yet. If the Scots tired and the English once broke through, all hope of Scottish freedom would be crushed for generations.

Bruce called up his own reserves. Over the noise of battle he shouted to Angus Og MacDonald, commanding the Islesmen and Highlanders, "My hope is constant in thee!"

With an air-splitting skirl of bagpipes and blaze of flying plaid the Islemen and Highlanders surged forward, shouting.

"On them!"

"Press on!"

"They fail!"

And the English fell back.

Then it was that Jamie spotted the green and gold checky banner he had looked for with a knot of hatred in his chest all morning. Aye, there was Preston with his—what? Fifty, maybe a hundred men—impossible to tell in that crush. They had been brought forward just in time to hinder the retreating cavalry. And—Jamie could hope—in time to get trampled by them.

The Scottish spearmen pushed the English cavalry back on their own spears, and the arrows of the archers at the rear now hit not Scottish targets but English backs. Maybe one of them would hit John Greene.

Then his attention moved to the other side of the field. Jamie caught his breath as a small contingent broke off from the English right and spurred toward Stirling Castle. There was no mistaking those gold leopards. King Edward was fleeing the field. Such desertion by their king should signal defeat to the English. Surely now the endless flood of heavy cavalry would pull back. Now the tiring schiltroms would have some respite.

But it was not to be so. Few had seen Edward's cowardly retreat. By the time word spread among the English host, it would be too late. The Scots infantry were the stoutest men in the world—strong of arm and high of heart. But they were only men. No man could stand forever against repeated charges of heavy destriers.

And yet they stood. It was clear that no man among them would turn. But how long could they stand? Would such valor in the end have to submit to Edward's sheer force of numbers?

A ragged but jubilant shout turned Jamie in his saddle. The cheer rose in echoing waves, soaring over the clash of battle. What could it be? Then he saw. Over the crest of the escarpment swept a fresh, unwearied army, several thousand strong.

He squinted into the sun, trying to figure out who they were. Brave banners flapped in the breeze of their coming. They valiantly brandished unbloodied weapons. Their wild battle cries split the air. Where could they have come from?

As they swept past and he could see more clearly, a smile split Jamie's face. It seemed impossible, and yet it was so. The small folk. Those who had waited in patient hiding through long hours. A great mob of yeomen, servants, and laborers with hastily improvised banners and armed with homemade weapons swept toward the ragged English host, yelling as only free men defending their own land can yell.

The English took one look at the new army descending on them, then turned and fled.

With a joyful shout Jamie spurred Clarsach forward, although he kept to the right of the field rather than joining the Small Folk. And his was merely an expression of triumph, not of attack, for in spite of his desire to kill and the fact that he carried two dirks at his belt, the superb balance required to fight from horseback was denied him.

He slowed as he reached the plain, for now the ground was scattered thickly with bodies. A few were Scots, but very few indeed compared to the piles of richly dressed but mangled chivalry. It was a little past noon. The high sun gleamed on golden knights' spurs and gold and silver armament.

And already the scavengers were moving in. As the English fled to the east—the Bannock Burn was filling with the bodies of men and horses until those behind them could pass dry shod—the spoilers spread out on the field, gathering plunder.

With all the swirl of motion and noise around him, it was odd that Jamie should hear the clink of metal being tossed in a bag, even though it came from so close.

He turned—and froze in his saddle. The chaos around him receded. The sound of battle silenced. It was as if Jamie were alone on the field facing Murdo Grant.

Murdo, the first into the field to rob bodies. He should have expected no less. The robber was so intent on the body he was stripping that he had no awareness of the man looming over him on horseback.

Jamie looked around. What he would give to hold one of the weapons littering the field. His knife would be useless on horseback. And he would be useless on foot. Then he saw a spear stuck in the turf, its handle slanting toward him. He backed Clarsach only three steps. His fingers closed around the smooth ash shaft. It was as if God had put the weapon in his hand.

"Murdo Grant! Judas!"

The insolent face turned to him. Recognition dawned. Then fear.

"Don't throw!" Murdo was shaking so that he could hardly fling his hands out. But he did not let loose of the bag of gold. He dropped to his knees. "I yield me. Don't throw that." His eyes flicked to the plunder he held. "Here—I'll give you this. Here—take it all."

Was Murdo seeking to entice him with the sound of gold, or did he shake enough from fright to make it rattle so?

Jamie hefted the spear, testing its balance. Aye, a good weapon, still sharp and true.

This was not an opportune moment for Jamie's pictures to come to him. Yet they did: the reddening of his blade at Stirling Bridge . . . again and again . . . the fury with which he had killed that day . . . and, later, the feel of the knife in his hand as it had gone into the warrior attacking Bruce in the pass above St. Fillan's Chapel. The blood he had shed to avenge blood. As he would avenge again.

And yet he did not throw.

That bloodshed had not satisfied. Would this one more reddened blade be enough? Would one more such help anything? Perhaps just this one last one. Vengeance for Wallace's death. That would be sufficient.

Once before he had had Murdo at his mercy. Then he was prevented by Holy Church from striking his enemy. There were no such restraints today.

He looked Murdo straight in the eye so that the traitor could see his death coming and Jamie could savor the full effect of his vengeance on his enemy.

Then he saw. He saw fear on the weasel face. But he saw something else. Something much worse, more profound than fear.

He saw desolation—the desolation of a life lived for the wrong motives. He saw that killing Murdo Grant would be a kindness.

"Live you. Live with the knowledge of what you've done. Live if you can."

Jamie threw the spear away.

He turned Clarsach to the west. He was immeasurably weary.

He wanted only to get away from the field. There was no revenge here. No triumph. Only great sadness.

He had gone no more than ten yards when he heard a strangled cry from behind. He turned—and did not believe what he saw. Murdo Grant had taken the knife of the knight he had been robbing and plunged it into his own heart. Wallace's betrayer fell across his open loot bag.

Jamie paused. Should he go to him now? Murdo was beyond help and yet . . . He was still undecided when a wounded soldier came reeling toward him. The man's right arm hung limp, his gashed sleeve dripped red. He seemed delirious, sweating in the blazing sun. "Water." He kicked up dirt from the field as he lurched toward Jamie.

Jamie clambered off Clarsach and pulled the leather water bag from his saddle. He had the spout to the man's mouth before he noticed the badge on his ragged sleeve.

Jamie started so that the water sloshed down the man's padded tunic. Surely a hundred men or more served under Preston's green and gold checky banner. There was no need to assume this man was . . . and yet they were just across the burn from where he had met Aline last night. The wounded soldier would have likely been making for his camp.

The water revived the man somewhat.

Jamie seized his shoulder and shook him. "John Greene? Are you John Greene?"

Hugh's dirk was still in his belt. But he would not kill the man without knowing. Pleasurable as it might be to redden his blade with English blood, he would choose to know whether or not it was the blood of . . . He balked at naming this Englishman goodbrother, but he would know whether he was Aline's husband.

Clarsach stood still at Jamie's command as he pushed the half-conscious man across the front of his saddle like a sack of flour. The more miserable the cur was on the ride the better. But Jamie would not have him die. Not yet.

It was nearly a mile and a half to Cambuskenneth Abbey across the rough, marshy carse. Little wonder his prisoner was unconscious when he gave him into the care of Brother Simon, who was well occupied with salving and bandaging.

"My prisoner. Bind his arm, Simon. I'll find some spirits to revive him."

But Jamie did not immediately return to the makeshift infirmary that filled the wide space between abbey and domestic buildings. The smell of stew and warm bannocks reminded him of how hungry he was. And while eating, he spotted Hugh Danduff. He would return Hugh's dirk. Jamie had no need of it now.

It was well after dark when he made his way to the abbey, where Bruce now directed the counting of spoils and disposition of prisoners. He paused at the west end of the transept. Inside, one could hear the jubilant ringing of bells almost as loudly as outside. Irritating as they could be, they were yet a joyous sound.

He thought of the great pealing that would even now be spreading across the land as news of the Scots victory traveled from town to town. He smiled as he thought of Rhona, hearing them from the church at Dunning.

Abbot Bernard and a score of monks occupied one wing of the transept, counting the booty and keeping records of all that the men brought in.

"It will be days before all is counted, sire," Bernard said to King Robert. "But the total will easily go to two hundred thousand pounds."

Robert Bruce nodded. "Aye. That is good. We've an entire nation, long spoiled by war, to rebuild."

Bernard smiled. "And what more fitting than to rebuild it with English gold?"

"And what of our casualties?" Bruce turned to another dark-robed cleric.

"Three Scots knights dead, sire. Many foot, but no definite numbers. Of the English: one earl—Gloucester, who lies in nearby kirk."

"Aye," Bruce said. "He was my cousin. Tomorrow's night I will keep vigil over his body. Who else?"

The monk ducked his tonsured head to check his list. "Clifford, next in rank. Comyn. No less than thirty-four barons and knights. Seven hundred cavalry. Most of their foot and archers."

Bruce nodded curtly and turned away. "Aye. It will do." He shook his head. "Such slaughter. And all because of Edward's overweening lust for power." He turned back to the high seat at the top of the nave where he had sat for most of the time since returning from the field to receive English prisoners.

Gilbert la Hay now ushered forward an elderly knight with a drooping gray mustache. Jamie moved closer with great interest when he saw the yellow and black device on the knight's bloodstained surcoat. Sir Marmaduke Twenge. The one English knight who had acquitted the field with honor at Stirling Bridge.

Nor did King Robert Bruce forget. He refused to hold the old knight for ransom. "You are free to go, Sir Marmaduke. But do not turn your sword against me again."

Jamie clenched his fists. This was not what he wanted to hear. An honored knight would have been worth much gold for ransom, and the king had just acknowledged the nation's need of such. Where was the vengeance he still hoped to find?

Twenge had not yet left the abbey when Thomas Randolph led in another, this no prisoner but voluntarily come. Sir Philip Moubray, keeper of Stirling Castle for the English. He knelt before the king and extended a heavy metal object in both hands.

"Sire, according to the terms of our truce, Stirling Castle has not been relieved. Therefore, I surrender it to His Grace King Robert." He paused. After a momentary ducking of his head, he looked up full into Robert's face. "And myself to his peace. If you will have me, sire."

Robert Bruce regarded the Scots knight who had for so long served Edward. "Aye. If you will serve me as well as you served my enemy, I will have you."

Still on his knees, Philip Moubray clasped King Robert's hand between his and swore his oath of loyalty.

How long is this to go on? Jamie wondered. This forgiving and pardoning, this taking into peace of former enemies. Had they fought for seventeen long, painful years that they might forgive all English and rebel Scots? Were none to be hanged or held for ransom?

Apparently Gilbert la Hay thought the same, for it was in a voice of exasperation that he asked, "My lord, would you forgive all?"

"And where would we, any of us, be if He who is Lord of all refused to forgive us when we have erred?" Silence followed Bruce's reply. For, indeed, there was no answer to that.

But not quite all were to be freed. Next to be brought before the king was the earl of Hereford, commander of Edward's Great Van. Robert Bruce's features tightened. Hereford would not be released. Not yet. The royal decree carried crisply to the farthest corners of the abbey. Hereford was to be held for the highest ransom of all.

The queen, Elizabeth of Robert's heart, his daughter Lady Margery Bruce, his sister Mary, all were to be returned forthwith from the convents where they had been held prisoner for eight long years —returned with the king's sister, the Lady Christian Bruce, and the Lady Isabel MacDuff, who had defied her Comyn husband to fulfill her hereditary privilege and crown the king of Scots. Those ladies, the most shamefully treated of all, had hung in steel cages outside castle walls day and night in heat and cold . . . Jamie shook his head at the thought of what they must have suffered.

Scotland's women would be exchanged for Hereford. Robert Bruce's brothers could not be restored to him, but his womenfolk, who had paid so dearly for Scotland's independence, would be returned. Jamie watched his monarch's face. This great man, whom already many were naming First Knight in Christendom—the title once held by Edward Plantagenet—fought for control. None in the abbey would see King Robert Bruce break down and weep for the return of his queen. But the carefully observing sennachie, who had learned to enter into others' feelings, saw the twitching jaw, the forced swallow, and the whiteness of the knuckles gripping the arms of the chair.

At the shuffling entrance of two further figures, Jamie felt a surge of triumph. The bells overhead began a fresh peal. King Robert had his revenge. Now James MacInnes would have his. Simon led in Jamie's prisoner. His arm was bandaged, and his head drooped with fatigue, but he was clearly conscious and moving of his own strength.

"He has lost much blood, but he'll live," Simon said. "With luck he may have the use of both arms in time."

Jamie approached the king. "My prisoner, sire."

Robert Bruce, now obviously weary, looked at the English soldier. "Name?"

Jamie had known. He had been sure all along. Perhaps it was that his son and daughter had something of the look of him. Even so Jamie felt a new exultation when he heard the answer.

"John Greene."

"And what would you have with him, Jamie?" The king awaited his answer.

Crucify him! Jamie wanted to cry out, then realized that would not be appropriate. Emotion rose in his throat so strong he could not answer for a moment. At last. The revenge he sought for all those years was within his reach. He would pronounce death sentence on John Greene for his family.

And yet a shock followed the thought. Vengeance was not sweet. A sour taste filled his mouth. Emptiness gnawed his stomach. "My lord king, I—" he began.

But he got no further, for at that moment Abbot Bernard in fresh vestments took his place by the high altar, and from the west entrance the monks of Cambuskenneth began to file two-by-two up the aisle. Jamie glanced at the celestory windows. Dawn was breaking. It was the hour for Prime.

King Robert moved quickly from his chair to a bench in the quire, and a servant removed the king's seat from in front of the altar.

The brothers came up the long nave, chanting the words of the prophet: "How the oppressor has reached his end! How the turmoil is stilled! The Lord has broken the rod of the wicked: the staff of the tyrants that struck the peoples relentless blows, that beat down the nations with oppression unchecked. The whole earth rests peacefully. Song breaks forth. The very cypresses rejoice over you, and the cedars of Lebanon."

Bernard led the people in the response: "May we shout for joy at your victory and raise the standards in the name of our God. The Lord grant all your requests."

The king, though still showing weariness, rose to read the canticle from the Holy Book, which an acolyte held open before him. "Now I know that the Lord has given victory to His anointed. That He has answered from His holy heaven with the strength of His victorious right hand. Some are strong in chariots, some in horses, but we are strong in the name of the Lord our God."

The service continued, but Jamie could no longer follow it. He was overcome with fatigue. It was not mere weariness of body, however. It was exhaustion of spirit. The lust for vengeance that had driven him for so long still pushed inside him. But with the sound of bells and prayers all around, he could see the blackness of the pit toward which his hatred drove him.

And as his vision sharpened, so did his understanding. People on every side were moving forward to receive the sacred elements, but in Jamie's mind he was back at Stirling, mounting the bridge in triumph. And now he realized it had been his hatred of Cressingham that had led him onto the bridge to grasp a piece of the English commander's flayed skin. It was his blood lust that had put him in the way of that kicking destrier all those years ago. No English sword, but his own hatred.

And he heard again Wallace's warning, delivered once on a spring morning when all the world had seemed new. *"Your courage and drive are fine things, lad. Scotland has much need of such. But you must remember that it is for love of Scotland that we fight—love of Scotland, love of freedom, love of justice, not for hatred of the English. Don't let your hatred control you, or all will be lost, no matter whose is the battle. Live with peace along our border and peace in our hearts."*

Jamie thought how he had held his anger back for so long. His admiration for Bruce and his love for Rhona had kept all from surfacing for many years. But then it had begun to boil to the surface, driving a wedge between him and those he loved most. It was not the horse kick that had crippled him. It was his own hatred.

He was like King Edward, whose hatred of the Scots had destroyed his greatness. He and Edward were alike.

Abbot Bernard was pronouncing the Prayer over the People when Jamie's consciousness came back to the service. "Let it last, Lord; let this land remain strong; let the realm remain true to You. In You only, O Lord, is our strength. In You only is our glory. Let us keep the victory for this generation and forever through the love and power of the Father, and the Son, and the Holy Spirit."

"Amen," the people responded.

"The mass is ended. Go in peace to love and serve the Lord." The priest made the sign of the cross.

And from every corner of the church the people replied, "Thanks be to God," as the bells continued their peal, ringing joy over all the land.

The monks filed out, and King Robert turned again to the remaining matters of business. He looked at Jamie. "What would you with your prisoner?"

Jamie took a deep breath for fear the words would choke him. But he must speak them. And he must mean them. For he knew now that they had made a great beginning on the field of Bannockburn, a brave and great beginning, but only a beginning. They had won a battle. They had not won the peace. They must not quit the fight too soon, not till all was won. For if they did, all would be lost.

Robert Bruce had understood that, when he forgave the English knights who behaved with honor. That was the forgiveness that must happen between the countries if Scotland was to be true victor.

The king cleared his throat, awaiting answer.

"John Greene is my goodbrother. I would have him forgiven."

74

At last he was free. Now Jamie could return to Rhona, to young Rabbie, and to wee Marion with full room for them in his heart, uncrowded by hatred and desire for revenge. A great sense of lightness bubbled up in him. Now he could tell Scotland's story as it should be told—a tale of courage and valor, determination and faith.

He slept till past noon the next day. He was making his way to the refectory in hope of finding at least a bannock and some cheese to make a meal on when an exhausted Brother Simon, who had apparently not seen his bed yet, came across the garden from the gatehouse.

"Ah, Jamie, the very man. The soldiers have rounded up some stragglers from the English camp. One of the women says she's from Dunning Innes. I don't know, but—"

"*Aline!* Here? Och, that's good news."

It took considerable sorting out, explaining and re-explaining, before brother, sister, and sister's husband were seated at the end of a long table in the refectory sharing roast fowl and a bowl of apricots.

Jamie urged his plan for the third time. "There is much to do before the peace is firm. Already it is said in the Bruce's council hall that Edward will not treat, although we pray God he can be made to change his mind. It is likely there will be more blood shed between our countries before our borders are secure. If you go to Preston you'll likely be called to take arms against your wife's people yet again. Is that what you'd do, John Greene?"

Jamie's blond, blue-eyed goodbrother rubbed his stubbly chin with his uninjured hand. "Nay. I'd be happy for a spell of peace—as we all would."

"Then come back to Dunning Innes, man. There's work enough for all and more." The last time Jamie had seen Rory under Sir Kenneth's banner, his brother had been well. He assumed he lived still. But there were Scots losses aplenty that would make every hand on the plow important in the seasons of rebuilding. "Would you not like to come home, Aline?"

His sister's eyes filled with tears. "Oh, Jamie." She paused to swallow. "Just to see it again—the hall house set in the draw of the hills . . . the apple orchard so sweet and green . . . the duck pond circled with purple flowers . . . to walk the same hills with my children that we walked . . . oh, Jamie, I never thought—"

John Greene covered her hand with his battle-roughened one. "Aye. We'll come."

It was yet another day before Simon was satisfied that his patient was ready to travel. While Aline and John gathered their children, who were sheltering at Saint Ninian's, and what of their belongings they had managed to save from looters, Jamie rode Clarsach slowly across the now quiet field that had been the scene of such tumult only three days before.

Scavengers had plundered everything of value, and men working around the clock had buried as many of the fallen as possible. Jamie wondered briefly where Murdo Grant was buried. And who had claimed his bag of spoils?

For all the attempts at tidying, however, it would be long before the field by the Bannock Burn would be the sweet green place it had once been. In his mind Jamie composed the stirring tale he would recount to Rabbie before he set it all to paper.

He looked forward to bringing the events to life for his son—the brilliant colors, the fervent prayers, the brave deeds. But as always there remained the small doubt at the back of his mind. What would his son, named for Robert Bruce and William Wallace, think of a father who could only sit and watch at Scotland's greatest hour?

He turned his back on the blood-soaked battlefield and rode across the Roman road to the shady slopes of New Park. Here was where it had all begun. He dismounted and tied Clarsach to a tree. He wanted to stand by the Borestone, where Robert Bruce had stood to strike the first blow in the Battle of Bannockburn. He could see it all again: the afternoon sun streaking through the park, Robert the Bruce holding his battle-ax, sitting his horse as unflinching as a statue while the English knight bore down on him.

His mind was so full of the scene that he did not see the figure standing by the ancient stone until she called his name. "Jamie! Oh, Jamie! Simon said I'd likely find you here."

He blinked to focus his vision.

"Rhona! How is this possible?" He came swiftly to her side, and she threw herself into his arms.

"Oh, Jamie, we are hearing such tales. Victory. And slaughter. We can be a nation again—like Wallace saw it. I made Luke bring me—and Rabbie. It will be his Scotland one day. I wanted him to see where it all happened."

She stepped back as the sturdy seven-year-old with springy red gold hair and deep blue eyes so much like his father's came striding through the park as one twice his age.

"Father!" He broke into a run. "Mother said we won a fierce battle—and you were bravest of all, she said."

At a loss, Jamie looked at Rhona, who smiled back at him serenely.

"Because a stout heart is more important than a stout leg, she said. And Scotland has need of many stout hearts. I shall be a stout heart like you, Father."

Jamie bent to hug his son. He had always known Rhona didn't mind—didn't even notice—his hirpling, but that he should be gifted with such a son as well . . .

"It's finer than any tale I've ever told." Jamie shook his head.

Rhona leaned against the stone and wiped at the dampness on her cheek.

* * *

Mary blinked hard and turned toward the ancient standing stone to cover her unfortunate difficulty in stifling her emotions. To think that all that had taken place right beneath her feet almost seven hundred years ago.

At last she looked up. "Oh, Hamish! That's your best tale yet."

"*Och,* do you think it'll do, lassie? I'm right glad to hear that, for I've a mind to tell it at the festival tomorrow night."

"Tomorrow?" She had been living so intensely in the Middle Ages she had a disorienting sense of jet lag as she looked around at the modern tourists wandering across the field from the Heritage Centre. "Yes, that's right, isn't it? We're to go to the Tattoo. I'd forgotten."

But as she came slowly back to the present, she was aware of an aching void. Something was missing. Something vital. Jamie—where had he gone? And then he came limping toward her. "Jamie!" As soon as the exclamation left her mouth, she sensed her cheeks flushing. She felt too stupid for words.

But Gareth didn't seem to notice. His smile soothed all her confused feelings, yet left her more confused than before. "Aye. A fine tale, isn't it? Come have a closer look at the statue."

The three of them walked the short distance to the great bronze equestrian statue of King Robert Bruce, dominating the field. Mary looked up at the flowing lines of his destrier's caparison, the fierce

685

battle-ax he held like a royal scepter, and the strong features of his mail-coifed face.

And although they were so dissimilar, she saw much of the strength she had come to respect and admire in the man beside her. She kept her gaze on the statue, but her mind was on Gareth. She had one week left in Scotland. One week and then she must leave this land, this man, and go back to Michael. Just the thought of the pain of leaving was unimaginable. Like ripping off her own skin.

So she wouldn't think on it. "Amazing, isn't it? The English had the equivalent of a Sherman tank division and the RAF—yet the Scots beat them with infantry."

"Aye, Bruce was a genius. And I can't help thinking he had a wee bit extra help too."

"You believe that business about Saint Fillan?"

Gareth shrugged. "Not exactly."

"Well, whatever," Mary continued. "I loved seeing Edward be defeated. What a thorough-going villain."

Gareth's eyes sparkled with the delight of one playing devil's advocate. "Why? Wasn't he just doing what was right for him?"

"What do you mean?" She frowned.

"Edward was following what he saw as right. Truth as he saw it was that he should rule Scotland."

"But he didn't have any right—" She stopped. He had her. Maybe it *wasn't* all relative. Maybe absolute right and wrong did exist. But she didn't want to think about that now. She turned back to Hamish. "But you can't leave your story there. What about the peace? Did Edward ever sign a treaty?"

Hamish rubbed his firebush beard. "Oh, aye. Fourteen years later. Edward III it was who finally recognized Scots independence and Robert the Bruce as their king. Until then there were battles and skirmishes aplenty, and Edward Bruce got himself crowned king of Ireland—there's many another tale there. But the part you'll be caring about as an American is the Declaration of Arbroath."

"Huh?" Mary pushed back a length of golden hair and wrinkled her upturned nose. She really was interested in what Hamish was saying. It was just that her emotions were so tangled that her attention kept wandering. What was he talking about now? Arbroath? Was that something she was supposed to know about?

"Aye. It was one of the documents your own founding fathers looked to when they wrote your Declaration of Independence."

Mary had always liked history and done well in it. She did recall that a Scotsman, John Witherspoon, was a leader at the Constitutional Convention. But she was certain she hadn't heard of anything called the Declaration of Arbroath.

"Verra similar in purpose—both documents laying out proof that their nations were fighting a just, legitimate war against unjust English aggression."

"Oh. Er . . . what does it say?" She was struggling to recall what the Declaration of Independence itself said. "We the People of the United States, in order to form a more perfect Union . . ." No, no—that was the preamble to the Constitution . . .

Oh, yes. "When in the course of human events, it becomes necessary for one people to dissolve the political bands which have connected them with another, and to assume among the Powers of the earth, the separate and equal station to which the laws of Nature and of Nature's God entitle them . . ."

Yes, that was it. Then suddenly the familiar words took on new meaning. There was a natural law that all were—or should be—subject to. "Nature and Nature's God . . ." Yes, without God, what basis was there for freedom, democracy, justice—for love? And if there was a power, a personal power, behind the order of the universe, then shouldn't she be obeying it? Or Him? Mary shook her head. She wasn't ready to answer that. "Um . . . Arbroath, you said?"

"Aye, because it was written at Arbroath Abbey, probably by Bernard of Linton, who was abbot there as well as being Robert Bruce's chancellor."

Mary nodded. "Yes, I remember." Actually, the story she had just heard was much more alive in her mind than anything else at the moment. If only she could just have stayed in the fourteenth century rather than having to cope with today and today's problems.

"Well, first, the letter, being sent as it was to the pope, set out with extreme tact and skill the work of Saint Peter's brother, Saint Andrew, in evangelizing the Scots: 'Our Lord Jesus Christ, after His passion and resurrection, called the Scots to His most holy faith among the very first, even though they were settled at the outermost ends of the earth . . .'"

Brad joined them just in time to hear the quotation. He laughed. "Well, some things never change. There's many who still think we're at the outermost ends of the earth. Although I don't know how proud Saint Andrew would be of his handiwork today."

Gareth smiled at his friend, but his dark eyes looked thoughtful.

Hamish ignored the interruption. "Then, after a bit of recounting of history, the letter declares the independence of Scotland and states the constitutional relationship between the king and the community: 'At length it pleased God, who alone can heal after wounds,

687

to restore us to liberty from these innumerable calamities, by our most serene prince, king, and lord, Robert . . .' There follows a fine statement of Robert Bruce's right to be king of Scots so long as he kept the people's safety in defense of their liberties. But they declared that even King Robert the Bruce they would not follow if he failed in that defense. 'For so long as there shall but one hundred of us remain alive, we will never consent to subject ouselves to the dominion of the English.'"

Hamish paused for breath, and another, younger, voice with a distinct Glaswegian lilt took up the quotation. "'For it is not glory, it is not riches, neither is it honor, but it is liberty alone that we fight and contend for, which no honest man will lose but with his life.'"

Mary caught her breath at the intensity in Gareth's voice.

That statement so summed him up—an honest man who put his beliefs above glory, riches, honor, even his own life. It took every restraint she could gather not to run into Gareth's arms as Rhona had into Jamie's.

"There aren't really many things worth dying for, are there?" she said softly. "But I suppose freedom is."

"Aye. And truth," Gareth added.

She nodded. "Until I learned about Wallace I didn't realize how alike America and Scotland are. Both were founded on ideas—the ideas of freedom and justice."

Brad grinned at her. "Did I, or did I not, tell you Wallace was our George Washington—five hundred years earlier. That's also why Wallace was a greater hero than Bruce. Bruce fought for a throne, but Wallace fought for the ideas of freedom and justice."

Mary struggled to put into words the ideas forming in her mind. "Yes, and I'm beginning to see that's why faith is so important to a nation founded on those principles. If we lose the belief that anything is objectively true—" she stumbled as she strained after her thoughts "—if we lose that, then we'll lose the belief that there's anything binding from one generation to the next. The loss of the idea of truth is the loss of the rationale for nationhood." The words came haltingly but not quite as a question.

Mary blinked. She couldn't believe she had said that. She had fought so hard against thinking it. Even now it was incredibly hard to put into words—to admit that all she'd argued for for so long might have been wrong. And yet she had to be honest. And as she said the words, the concept became even clearer.

She was starting to say more when she heard the words of a familiar song: "Scots wha hae wi' Wallace bled—Scots, wham Bruce has aften led . . ."

A group of university students approached from the far side of the field, singing lustily.

> "Now's the day, and now's the hour;
> . . . .
> Tyrants fall in every foe!
> Liberty's in every blow!
> Let us do or die!"

Mary dabbed at her eyes. This was crazy. She had to get hold of herself. *Talk about something else,* she thought. "Yes," she said as soon as her voice was steady. "But what about the Stone? That's what we're supposed to be looking for. Remember when Margaret thought Moot Hill *was* the Stone? Do you really think that's where it is?" She looked at Hamish.

"Weel now, it seems like an obvious spot for monks looking for a quick hiding place. Maybe too obvious, but it doesn't seem that the English were overconcerned. They were so sure of their superiority, it probably never occurred to them that anyone would dare defy Edward."

Mary thought back over Hamish's story, recalling the day Jamie ran to Wallace with news of the rape of Scone. "So Edward didn't actually take the Stone with his own hands? He just issued an order and someone rode out with a rock?"

Brad nodded. "It seems he wanted a psychological victory over this renegade lot he was trying to subdue. They wouldn't lie down and be good Englishmen for him. He wanted to crush their ambitions once and for all."

"Yes, I understand that." She sounded just the least bit impatient with her cousin. "But the *Stone*—did he get the real one?"

"Well—" Brad pulled a notebook from his inside vest pocket. "The stone that arrived in London is described by the Royal Commission on Historical Monuments as 'a quarry dressed block of coarse grained old red sandstone . . .'"

Mary, reading over his shoulder, caught the next line and almost shouted, "'These cuttings are probably of the time of Edward I!' So the whole thing *could* have been cut at that time!"

Mary's mind was full of pictures of dark-robed monks hacking furiously at a chunk of the red sandstone that lay in such abundance around Scone, while others, under the cover of darkness, dug a small opening on the side of Moot Hill to bury the real treasure.

"One thing's certain" —Gareth's voice penetrated her thoughts— "if the Stone was kept in a carved wooden casket like a holy relic, the way Hamish tells it, Edward wouldn't have recognized a fake—and neither would anyone else."

Mary blinked at his logic. It was a good thing they were going back to Edinburgh. There in the excitement of the city at Festival time maybe she could recover her senses. And it was a very good thing she was going home in a week. If she didn't get away soon she might never be able to.

75

Moving with the crowd, Mary filed slowly up the steep cobbled lane ascending Castlehill toward the entrance to Edinburgh Castle. Normally she didn't like crowds; she had even been a little put off about going to the Tattoo when she thought of the throng this internationally famous event attracted. But everyone was so friendly, so orderly—there was none of the sense of urgency to get inside and get a seat she would have felt in such a crowd back home.

She smiled at Gareth beside her. "We're lucky. It's warmer than than I'd been warned to expect."

"Ah, but don't be misled. It's a good thing you've a blanket and rain gear. You never know."

They took seats in the center of the temporary bleachers set up on the broad esplanade in front of the castle. To their left the castle made a spectacular backdrop to the wide arena before them. Flags fluttered atop the gatehouse, and behind that the stones of the circular half-moon battery glowed in the floodlights. But Mary was most drawn to the statues on either side of the main gate: Wallace and Bruce, lighted by enormous flaring torches at their feet. Scotland didn't forget her heroes.

They were barely settled when the lights dimmed and the booming of a massive drum announced the entrance of fierce, bearded, horn-helmed Vikings bearing shields and dragon-prowed ships. The invaders filled the esplanade as the story of Royal Scotland began with startling drama. Trumpets sounded, and the dragon ships burst into flames. Mary felt as if she'd been transported back to the time of Kenneth mac Alpin.

The drama shifted to the crowning of MacBeth and the stirring march-on of the massed pipes and drums of the Scottish regiments. The entire esplanade filled with their splendid uniforms and the sound Mary loved so much. As the lively march tunes shifted to the slower "Skye Boat Song," she found it impossible to believe that this time next week she would be back in another world.

Her mind retraced the past month. Had she found any of what she had come for? What would she take home with her? Would the memory of all the beauty she had encountered be enough?

She balked at the idea that it could have all been a waste of time. And yet she had to admit they hadn't found the Stone, she had less peace than she'd come with, and she was less sure than ever about marrying Michael. And yet there didn't seem to be anything to do but follow the inevitability of it all.

The scene before her shifted, and a stained glass projection on the castle wall recalled St. Margaret. Her chapel, the oldest building in the castle, was spotlighted far up on the hill. She thought of Margaret standing on that very spot, seeing her beloved Malcolm off to war for the last time . . . of Margaret receiving word of her husband's and son's deaths, then dying herself, holding her precious Black Rood.

This was like living the past weeks all over again. Mary swallowed. How could she have thought for a moment it might have been a waste? It had been the most marvelous month of her life.

In the midst of the pageantry she stole a sideways look at the charming, unfathomable man beside her. Gareth was so confident, yet so vulnerable. She wished, as she had so often, there were some way she could help him. But if he was right about Alex, what could anyone do?

Now the arena filled with 150 dancers from all over Scotland. Children and adults, in colorful plaids, kilts, and long white dresses, danced intricate strathspeys, reels, and jigs to the fiddling of thirty schoolchildren. Mary felt herself relax, caught up in the freedom of the lighthearted dancing.

But then the massed pipes and drums were back, this time with the bands as well. And she couldn't relax to this music. She had just spent a month listening to these songs, and their words sang in her head. The Scottish soldier dying in the green hills of Tyrol— "These hills are not Highland hills, they're not my land's hills . . ." She couldn't truly claim the Highland hills as her own, and yet could any others ever mean as much to her? She bit her lip to keep from weeping for that soldier.

And then "Scotland the Brave," the first song she'd heard on bagpipes as she stepped off the train in Edinburgh. "High in the misty Highlands, out by the purple islands, brave are the hearts that beat beneath the Scottish skies. Wild are the winds to meet you, staunch are the friends that greet you . . ."

Yes, she did have friends here. Staunch friends. She could think of no better word. But fine as that was, it wasn't enough. She wanted more. She allowed herself another look at the man beside her. Gareth was undoubtedly the staunchest person she'd ever met—faithful, loyal, steadfast. But it wasn't enough that he be merely a friend.

The playing of "Scots Wha Hae" brought her back to the arena. Then the scene shifted again with another projection on the battery wall, and the narrator's voice carried over the crowd. "This castle holds much of the romance and tragedy of Scotland. In a small room here on the nineteenth of June, 1566, Mary Queen of Scots gave birth to a boy. She called him James. Legend has it that as she held the tiny bairn she said, 'This is the prince who I hope will be the first to unite the kingdoms of Scotland and England.' Thirty-seven years later, James VI, King of Scots, became James I of England."

But Mary barely had time to absorb the meaning of the historical scene when a hush fell over the esplanade. The bands, pipers, and drummers all stood at attention. Only the flags circling the bleachers moved as the breeze riffled them. The lights dimmed. A single spotlight shone on the castle ramparts. The strains of a lone piper reached out to her. "Amazing Grace."

"How sweet the sound . . ." Everything Mary had seen and heard and experienced in the past month spread before her: the faith of Columba and Margaret; the courage and love of freedom and justice of Kenneth mac Alpin, of Wallace, of Bruce. Could something so obviously true for their time hold no validity now?

First a solo voice, then a choir joined the piper. "I once was lost, but now am found; was blind, but now I see."

And then the glory of the massed pipes, drums, and bands. "How precious did that faith appear the hour I first believed."

Mary's heart was so full she thought she'd burst. She wanted to grab Gareth. She wanted to laugh and cry. She wanted to tell him everything she was thinking and feeling. The blazing torches and spotlights all blended with her emotions in the fireworks going off from high on the castle.

And yet it wasn't over. "Should auld acquaintance be forgot . . ." All in the bleachers linked hands with arms crossed and sang with the 700 performers on the esplanade the words of Robert Burns that had become the whole world's song of parting.

Mary's right hand gripped Garth's so tightly her fingers felt numb. Her face was wet, but she could do nothing about it because Brad held her other hand.

And then, rather than ending on a high note of ecstasy, a reverent hush fell, and the choir sang Evening Hymn, "O love that will not let me go, I rest my weary soul in thee . . ."

Mary thought she couldn't possibly move. She couldn't imagine going back to everyday life after all that. She wanted to sit there in the glow and absorb it all. She even thought of attempting a prayer. In a way the whole evening had been a prayer. But most of all, she wanted to talk to Gareth.

All around her, however, people were moving. Especially Brad. With one hand he grabbed their blankets and programs, with the other he grabbed her and pulled. "Come on, Sharon's meeting us at the Argyll!"

Sharon? Oh, yes. Brad had mentioned she was getting back from her holiday today. But Mary hadn't realized they had a date to meet her. She forced her feet to move. Her attempt to keep up with Brad was somewhat impeded by the slow-moving crowd. But they darted through spaces and at last arrived at the pub just beyond Greyfriars Kirk.

Sharon was waiting. Mary had seen the picture Brad carried of his intended, but she had no idea the woman who had won her cousin's heart was so delicate, that her cloud of red hair was quite so beautiful, or that she was so lively.

Sharon flung herself first into Brad's arms, then embraced Mary with almost equal fervor. "Mary! Brad's written me all about you. I'm so glad we're to be cousins. I hope it'll be more like sisters, as I've always wanted one."

Mary hoped her reply held the genuine enthusiasm she felt, but the noise of the crowded pub was so disorienting she wasn't sure what she said.

Brad led them to the back room and somehow found a booth for them to squeeze into.

And then Mary realized why it was so much quieter here. At the far end, a storytelling was in progress. This man was small and dark, dressed in tweed jacket and kilt, his style much less flamboyant than that of Hamish, and yet his story appeared to be quite as spellbinding in its own way. She quickly picked up the thread of his tale, following as it did on the scene from the Tattoo. That was probably why the sennachie had chosen to tell this story to the after-the-Tattoo crowd.

"And so, in captivity in the castle amid Loch Leven, Mary Queen of Scots was forced to abdicate in favor of her year-old son, James. But it was thirty-six years later when Elizabeth I of England died childless and her cousin James inherited her throne. And so it was that after all the struggles between the nations, it was nae an English king that ruled Scotland, as sae many had tried, but a Scottish king that took the English throne.

"And so was the prophecy of the Stane fulfilled that 'if Fates go right, where'er this Stane is found, the Scots shall monarchs of that realm be crowned.'"

The sennachie paused for a long drink from his cup while his audience applauded, then seated himself at his clarsach and began to play.

Across the table from Mary, Brad and Sharon were in their own world as Brad told her about his research project and the publisher who had bought his proposal.

"Oh, Brad, that's wonderful!" Sharon paused to give him a quick kiss on the cheek. "I'm so proud."

The light was dim, so Mary wasn't sure, but it looked as if Brad blushed.

"Aye. And he wants pictures too. If I'd thought of that in the first place, it'd have saved me the trouble of going back for them now."

"You're going back to Iona? That's wonderful." Sharon bounced in her seat. "I'll go with you. Can you believe it? I've never been there."

Mary couldn't have been more delighted with her cousin-to-be. Sharon's liveliness was exactly what the studious Brad needed.

Heads together, the two began making plans for the next day.

Their closeness made Mary feel all the more alone. Where was Gareth? She hadn't actually realized until they took their seats that he wasn't with them. At first she wasn't surprised that he hadn't followed at the pace Brad had dragged her through the winding streets, but she had expected him to come on. Surely Brad had told him what the plans were? She craned her neck and looked around.

The friendly figure who waved to her from across the room wasn't the one she was looking for, but it was always good to see Hamish. Muttering, "Excuse me," to Brad and Sharon, which they didn't seem to hear anyway, she made her way to the chair in the corner beside Hamish. She still glanced toward the door occasionally, hoping to see Gareth, but in the meantime she was happy to have Hamish's company.

"I just got in on the end of your friend's story, but it sounds as if Scotland won."

The harper had ended and across the room a group was singing "Flower of Scotland." Mary listened. "Those days are passed now, and in the past they must remain, but we can still rise now and be the nation again."

She turned to Hamish. "It's true, isn't it? Scotland's really a very strong nation—no matter where her parliament sits."

Hamish nodded. "Aye, you've seen the heart of the matter, lassie. Geography's the least of the matter. Nationhood is a matter of common feeling—language, history, beliefs—it's sharing those that make a people one."

Was geography indeed the least of the matter? She wondered. What about the matter of geography when one's family chose to emigrate? And when that made one an outlander? She turned back to her friend with a sigh. "But Hamish, I still don't know the answer. Was—is—the stone James sat on in Westminster the *real* Stone, then?"

Hamish shook his head with the great laugh she found so warming. "*Och,* lassie, who's to say for certain? It's *a* Stane of Scone—for that's where Edward stole it from. And in the end, it's only a symbol. Most believe it to be the Stane of Destiny—so it serves the purpose of a symbol. To people all over the world it calls up all the stories of the great men and women of Scotland's past. You could hardly be asking more of a lump of old sandstone, now could you?"

Mary smiled. "No, you couldn't. But if there *is* another stone somewhere . . ."

"*Och,* then I've nae doubt it'll be found someday. Moot Hill has never been excavated. I've a mind they'll be getting around to it someday. And when they do—who knows?"

Mary didn't answer, so Hamish continued. "But in the meantime the Westminster Stane serves as memorial. And there's many of us fulfilling the charge to Jacob—whether or no' it's his stane." His voice took on the special sennachie ring it held when a story gripped him. "'When your children ask you what it means, you shall tell them—thus the stane shall serve as a perpetual memorial . . . in order that all the peoples of the earth may learn that the hand of the Lord is mighty, and that you may fear the Lord your God forever.'"

76

It was a new experience for Mary two days later to view the Highlands and islands from the backseat. She looked out the side window and noted a group of workers making some minor road repairs. They wore bright yellow helmets with black netting covering their necks and faces, like something beekeepers might wear. She thought of asking Brad about them, but he was busy driving and talking to Sharon, so Mary returned to reliving her conversation with Hamish.

It had been so satisfying—coming as it did so soon after her experience at the Tattoo. She still couldn't believe so much had happened in one evening. And yet for all the fulfillment she felt, there was a gaping void beside her. She had not seen Gareth since Brad had pulled her across the esplanade and off to the Argyll.

She had so wanted him to be the first one she told. But when he didn't come, she had told Hamish—in very halting, confused terms—about her insight.

She hadn't thought to consider his faith or lack of it, but as she talked to him she realized how perfectly he understood what she was trying to say—far better than she understood it herself. And in spite of her desire to save it to tell Gareth, it had all come out so naturally.

"But are you still a wee bit disappointed we no found the Stane, lassie?"

And she didn't really understand how she felt until she put it into words. "I think in a way we did. Finding the meaning of something is really more important than finding the object itself. Besides . . ." She hesitated.

"Aye?" He leaned his head toward her, listening carefully.

"I found something infinitely better. I remember that first night I met you—right here in this pub. I said something about believing in truth beyond mere facts. That's what I found. So I had to be honest with myself. If I believed such existed for literature and history and objects—why not in the matter of faith? If truth—Truth with a captial T—exists in one field, wouldn't it in another? Where would we be if there were no absolute truth in mathematics or science? Would gravity cease to exist just because someone decided he didn't believe in it?"

Hamish just smiled and nodded encouragingly.

"But in the end it wasn't logic. It was that lone piper playing 'Amazing Grace' on the ramparts of Edinburgh Castle."

Hamish was still smiling and nodding when Brad and Sharon came over to tell Mary they were taking her to Iona. And because she didn't have any other plans for her last few days in Scotland, she agreed. And so here she was. Alone.

The sight of a Highland cow flicking its tail at a swarm of tiny black insects made her feel more like crying than laughing. This was not the mood she had wanted to end her holiday on. In disgust at what she could only think of as Gareth's desertion, she made a face at the amethyst thistle on the lapel of her jacket. Why had she worn that?

She made a motion to take it off, then stopped as the click of a tape slipping into the deck distracted her. Sharon had made a selection just as she herself had so often done in Gareth's car.

Not bagpipes, please. I couldn't bear it. And especially not "The Green Hills of Tyrol." It was almost a prayer.

She was infinitely relieved when the soaring, prayerlike voice of a violin wafted above the light arpeggios of a piano in Massenet's "Meditation" from *Thaïs*. Sharon had as good taste in music as she did in everything else.

At first Mary simply followed the sensuous yet reverent music in which the prostitute Thais, in love with a deeply spiritual man, examines her life and thinks about her future.

But then Mary's thoughts turned from Thais to herself. Her life. Her future. Twisting the ring on her finger, she tried to picture Michael as the object of the affections the music conjured up. But all she could think was that if she married Michael she would be as guilty of prostitution as Thais had been.

With a fierceness that all but took a layer of skin off with it, Mary wrenched the ring from her finger and buried it deep in her purse.

At Fionphort they stopped for a late lunch before they caught the last ferry to Iona. Brad had booked rooms for them to stay the night on the holy island. It should have been the perfect ending before she boarded the plane in Glasgow. But as it was, she felt her vacation was already over.

What a shame not to be enjoying this more, Mary chided herself. Here it was, the most beautiful day she'd seen in all her time in Scotland—warm, sunny, not even a ruffle of a breeze. She stepped out of the car and was immediately engulfed in a cloud of tiny black insects.

"Ugh! What is this?" She batted furiously, but they got in her hair, down her neck, in her mouth. In spite of her frantic swatting, they stung her mercilessly.

"Midges," Brad said and made a dash for the ferry.

Mary followed.

And the midges that stung her mind were even worse than those she continued to swat as she took a seat on the boat. Why hadn't Gareth come? Brad said he had rung him, but he was busy. No explanation. Apparently all she had sensed between them had been just good manners on his part and heightened imagination on her part, she tried to argue. But she knew better than that. She had never been surer of anything in her life than she was of the faith and the love she had found in the past month.

As the boat rocked, she closed her eyes against the pain of the very thought of leaving. And yet she must do it. She had dreamed—fantasized . . . Well, at least this way she wouldn't have to face telling Gareth good-bye.

As soon as she stepped onto the white cockleshell beach she knew coming back to Iona had been a mistake. A cloud of midges, from which the motion of the ferry had given her respite, descended again. A moment before, she had thought it would be hard to be more miserable. But being beset by these pests was the last straw. She took a deep breath, then realized that too was a mistake.

Holding her breath and batting furiously, she started up the path to the village. She would find some place to wait inside while Brad took his pictures. He and Sharon wouldn't want her tagging along anyway. Several people seemed to be making their way toward the coffee shop. Some folk singer was probably playing there. That would do to pass the time.

She was still swatting the midges that had managed to get in the door with her when she looked to the far end of the room. She should have been surprised, but she'd seen how these sennachies got around. Somehow it seemed perfectly natural for Hamish to be there. She had taken three steps toward him when a hand on her arm stopped her.

"Mary."

She stood staring. Maybe she was dreaming. "Gareth. I thought—"

"I had to come, Mary. I came over with Hamish this morning. I wasn't going to, but he told me what you told him after the Tattoo. So I had to talk to you once more—to hear it myself."

"To gloat?"

"Mary. To rejoice."

"Sorry. I—I guess it's the shock. I didn't think I'd see you again."

"Mary, I'm such a coward, but I wasn't sure I could stand to tell you good-bye."

They stood there in the middle of the room, just looking at each other.

Mary was the first to turn away. She noticed that the flags that had been hanging limp outside the window suddenly fluttered in a gust of breeze.

The motion caught Gareth's eye too. "Ah, that's fine. We can go out now."

"Out! And get eaten alive by those wee monsters? No, thank you."

He took her arm. "It's all right now—the wind just came up."

"You mean it? As fast as that? They'll all be gone?"

"As fast as that."

They walked westward away from the village toward the back of the island. For all Gareth had said he wanted to talk to her, he was very quiet, and he walked slowly.

Mary stuck her hands in the deep pockets of her khaki skirt and matched her steps to his.

At last he stopped, standing on a rocky ridge. The green machair was to their right, a gleaming white beach framed the bay below them, and the western sea washed into the spouting cave to their left. Mary thought this must be about where Corban had stood to wave to Rom-aln when he heard her singing on the beach on that far-off day.

Gareth stood a little apart, his hands in his pockets also. Except for that brief moment in the coffee shop, he had kept his distance.

"Mary, please tell me. Hamish told me what you said, but I want to hear it from you."

"I don't know, really. It's too complicated. No, it's too simple." She stopped in confusion. "I don't know. I saw the logic of what you'd been saying to me. But then it wasn't logic at all. It was—" how could she say it? "—it was—"

"Love?" Gareth finished for her.

"Yes, that was it. Making room inside myself for love. But not just some vague, feel-good emotion. It was—" She stopped again.

"Personal?"

"Yes, that's it. Like human love—only infinitely better."

"And now you don't think it's a waste?"

She shook her head. "Once you see it—you realize that's the only thing that can't be a waste." She paused to order her thoughts. "I guess that having heard—seen—almost lived so much history in such a short space of time gave me an awesome sense of how short life is. Since it's so short, it only makes sense to make it as meaningful as possible."

"Aye. That's it." He nodded, but his voice sounded wistful.

She couldn't understand it. She had thought he would be so happy. "What's the matter? Isn't that what you wanted? I thought you'd be happy."

He rubbed his hands over his face. "*Och*, I am, Mary. Truly I am. It's the greatest. It's what I want more than anything for all my friends. It's just . . . I . . ." He turned toward the cave. "Let's go down there."

He started down the narrow rocky path, not waiting for her.

Mary stood bewildered. She was so confused by his behavior that she considered turning back to the village. She might have, if she hadn't taken one last glance at him disappearing down the trail.

She leaped forward, unmindful of the tricky footing. She couldn't let him just walk off like that. But her hurry was her undoing. Whether it was a patch of slick grass or a loose rock, suddenly her feet flew out from under her. She tumbled downward, rolling, grasping at the thin vegetation. She landed on the beach in an ungraceful lump, her skirt around her waist. For a moment she was too dazed to move.

Then Gareth was beside her, his face whiter than the cockleshell beach. "Mary, oh, Mary." He gathered her in his arms and buried his face in her hair.

She turned her face to him and met his lips. She made no resistance.

At last he pulled back. "I'm sorry. I had no right. It was seeing you fall. I—I thought—"

She put her hand on his chest and pushed herself upright. "You thought of Alex," she said.

He nodded. A short, jerky nod.

She forced herself to answer brightly. "It's all right. It's really a very gentle slope. I was just awkward."

"You're sure you're all right? Truly?"

She put her left hand over her lips, still savoring the feel of his kiss. "Truly."

Then with a look of amazement, Gareth took her hand. "Mary?" He traced the pale mark on her fourth finger where Michael's diamond band had been.

She smiled. But behind her smile she was so choked she couldn't speak. She dropped her head in an effort for control.

He let go the hand and held her by the shoulders. "Mary, look at me."

She lifted her head, blinking back the tears as she raised her eyes to his. She wanted so desperately to tell him what she felt. But how could she? *Friends,* he had said. Yet his kiss—that hadn't felt like friendship.

At last she found her voice. "I don't want to go, Gareth."

He shook his head. "You must, you know. Ah, Mary. I love you sae much. Far too much to speak now."

She nodded. "Oh, I know I have to go. There's so much to work out. But Gareth Lindsay, it doesn't matter whether or not you ask me. I'm telling you now. I'm coming back to marry you just as soon as I can." What was the good of being an American if you couldn't be pushy once in a while?

"Aye. That's grand. So grand I can't believe it. But are you certain you've thought this through—thought about everything you're giving up—money, comfort, security . . ."

She laughed. "Decent weather, mixer faucets—oh, yes, I've thought."

He started to say something, but she put a finger over his mouth. "I'm not giving up anything—I'm getting everything I ever wanted but didn't know it. All this and heaven too."

He grinned. "Aye, and football."

They sat there for some time, laughing and teasing, then kissing and talking seriously. Clouds on the western horizon were rimmed with the red and gold of sunset when Gareth got up and walked a little out on the beach. After a moment he came back and held out a hand to Mary.

"Ah, Mary, I wanted you sae much. I wanted your soul for God and your dear person for myself. But I thought . . . was afraid . . . I don't really believe God does things this way, and yet I feared it was a punishment for Alex's death."

His arms came around her, and he held her so close she could hardly breathe, but she didn't want to anyway.

Then he continued, "When I see how good God is, I have the faith to hope there was time for Alex too." He paused and flung out his arms. "It's so wonderful! You've given me hope, Mary. For the first time since that awful night I feel truly free. I knew in my head God had forgiven me—but now my heart believes too."

Mary raised her eyes to the sunset that was blazing red gold now. She felt again something of the aliveness she had sensed at

Dunfermline. Only this time the bottom feeling wasn't that of longing but rather of deep happiness. The joy of longing fulfilled.

Arms around each other, they walked to the other side of the
island. The abbey bells were ringing for evening service when they
entered the church on the site where Christ had first been worshiped
in this land more than fourteen hundred years before. The organist
was playing the Mozart "Alleluia" as they took seats. The glow of
sunset tinged the windows, and candles flickered from the iron
holders lining the nave.

Mary thought her spirit could rise no higher than it did with
that glorious music and the pink and gold glow of the ancient
church. Then came Communion. Gareth took the massive goblet of
hand-wrought pottery. He drank, then held it out to her. She put her
hands over his and raised the cup to her lips.

"Rise up in splendor! Your light has come," the white-robed
minister by the altar proclaimed. "The glory of the Lord shines upon
you. See, darkness covers the earth, and thick clouds cover the peoples; but upon you the Lord shines, and over you appears His glory.
Nations shall walk by His light, and kings by His shining radiance."

Sources and Notes

Book 1:

The Celtic prayers are based on those found in: *The Celtic Vision, Selections from The Carmina Cadelica,* edited by Esther de Waal (London: Darton, Longman and Todd, 1988) and *What Is Celtic Christianity?* by Elizabeth Culling (Nottingham: Grove Books, Ltd., 1993).

Readable and recently published lives of the saints, each published separately, have been edited by Iain MacDonald, Floris Books, Edinburgh: *Saint Columba,* from the Life of Saint Columba by Adamnan, written c. 679; *Saint Ninian,* from the Life of St. Ninian by Aelred, abbot of Rievaulx, written in 1165; and particularly pleasing to modern readers, *Saint Mungo,* from The Life of St. Kentigern, by Jocelinus, a monk of Furness, written about 1184.

The Picts and the Scots, by Lloyd and Jenny Laing (Stroud: Alan Sutton, 1993), is the best of the many works I studied on that subject, and I extend a special word of gratitude to Lloyd Laing for his gracious help in corresponding with me.

The Search for the Stone of Destiny, by Pat Gerber (Edinburgh: Canongate Press, 1992), is a useful, if unscholarly, collection of history, legend, and opinion with lots of photographs.

Warlords and Holy Men, Scotland A.D. *80–1000,* by Alfred P. Smyth (Edinburgh: Edinburgh Press, 1984), is the first in a multivolume series on Scottish history—the most complete I've found.

The Celts, by Nora Chadwick (New York: Penguin Books, 1979), is also excellent and highly readable.

Monarchs of Scotland, by Stewart Ross (Moffatt: Lochar Publishing Co., 1990) is especially useful for its charts and photos.

Many miracles were recorded by Columba's hagiographer Adamnan, including defeating the Loch Ness monster, rescuing a maiden from Broichan, opening Brude's barred gate, receiving instruction from an angel bearing a book of glass, and healing Broichan by sending him a white stone.

St. Mungo's mother did, indeed, survive being cast from Traprain Law. And his most famous act is his finding the queen's ring in a fish's mouth.

Book 2:

History is uncertain about whether or not the Scots committed treachery against the Picts and, if so, whether it happened at Forteviot or at Scone, but the rumors persist to this day.

The battle of Strangford Lough and the sinking of 160 Norse and Irish ships is a matter of record—as is the succeeding victory over the Danes.

A daughter of the house of Alpin indeed married Olaf the White of Dublin—after Aud the Deep-minded, who was one of the founders of Iceland.

Einar did harry Charles the Bald. The Danes finally took over the area of France now known as Normandy and in 1066 looked again to the throne of their island neighbors.

Rhodri ap Merfyn did kill Gormr (sometimes called Horm) off the coast of Anglesey some years later.

Einar's sacrifice of Halfdan Highleg to Odin is from the 12th-century Heimskringla and the Orkneyinga Saga.

Book 3:

Saint Margaret, edited by Iain MacDonald (Edinburgh: Floris Books, 1993), based on Turgot's *The Life of St. Margaret, Queen of Scotland.*

Light of the North, St. Margaret of Scotland, by Sandra Marwick, prepared for an exhibition The Life and Legacy of St. Margaret, Edinburgh City Art Centre, 1993.

Father Turgot's Christmas homily based on "Christ the Goldbloom," quoted in Word-Hoard, translated and arranged by Margaret Williams (New York: Sheed & Ward, 1940).

Book 4:

William Wallace Guardian of Scotland, by Sir James Fergusson (London: Alexander Maclehose & Co., 1938). Excellent distillation of Thomas Rhymer, the English chronicler Hemingburgh, the Wallace Papers, and other early sources. Wallace's evaluations before Stirling Bridge are taken almost entirely from this source.

And from the series of Scottish History from the Edinburgh University Press, *Kingship and Unity: Scotland 1000–1306,* by G. W. S. Barrow (1981) and Independence and Nationhood, 1306–1469, by Alexander Grant (1981).

Robert Bruce and the Community of the Realm of Scotland, by G. W. S. Barrow (Berkeley, Calif.: University of California Press, 1965).

All the major events of this section are matters of historical record. It is likely, however, that Wallace dealt with the sheriff of Lanark before he ran Ormesby out of Scone.